RICHES TO RICHES

PART ONE

ABBS VALLEY SERIES

AMES MILLS

Riches to Riches, Part one

First publication: June 2022

Cover design: Maria Christine Pagtalunan (Artscandare Book Cover Design)

Formatting: Ames Mills

Editing: Jenni Gauntt

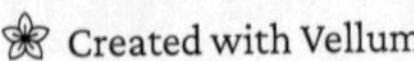

DEDICATION

To everyone who like the guys who are rough around the edges, dirty talkers, control takers, no shit taking, but still treat you like the Queen (or King) you deserve.
Also, to everyone who like sex in the first chapter.

Happy reading!

AUTHORS NOTE

First of all, welcome to Abbs Valley! Abbs Valley is a fictional place in sunny California where Alessa and her guys live while Alessa reigns over the Italian Mafia. Get ready for anything when it comes to these guys. This is part one of a duet.

WARNINGS

Content and trigger warnings include: mentions of sexual assault, kidnapping, murder, thoughts of suicide, explicit sex scenes, group sex scenes, breath play, light bondage, spanking, mm, mmf, mfm, mmfmm, mmmmfm (honestly, whatever way you can add five m's and an f, they do that)

If none of these tickles your fancy or if any of these triggers you, turn back now.

Seriously, you've been warned.

PS: Mom, if you have found this book, please rethink all your choices, and please, for the love of everything.... don't turn the page.

CHAPTER 1
ALESSA

"Ya know, I usually like to play a little longer, but I have a date," I declare, running my blade down my victim's cheek, glorifying in the shiver it causes. "You were a hard one to find, though. So, when I finally found you, I had to snatch you up." I laugh and jump off his lap, where I'm straddling him, my high-heeled boots hitting the concrete floor with a decisive click.

"Who are you?" my victim gasps out.

"You don't know who I am?" I ask with a fake pout. I can tell by the look in his eyes that he knows who I am; he just wants to confirm it. "They call me the Black Demon."

I watch his eyes widen, finally letting it sink in that his life is truly over. "You know why they call me that?" I ask with a tilt of my head. "Because I come in through the shadows, you never see me coming; then you leave the same way. Never to be seen again."

I walk to my row of weapons, running my fingers over each one. Knives of all shapes and sizes. My favorite. But like I told my friend here, I don't have time to play because I do have a date. I have been seeing Leo for about four months, and so far, it's going great, but with everything else in my life, I'm waiting for the other shoe to drop.

Leo isn't my usual type. I usually like them tattooed and rugged. We met at my favorite club, and his blue-green eyes drew me in like a moth to the flame. His eyes change colors with the light or his mood. His dark brown hair is thick on top and has a perfect fade to his neck. He has plump lips that I love to kiss and suck on. He has the perfect amount of stubble, a little thicker around those pretty lips. The gods sculpted his body themselves, lean but cut at all the right angles. Tonight is the night I will see it all in its glory. We've messed around, but we haven't had sex yet because I have been holding back. Not because I don't love sex, I do. But I feel different about him than anyone else, so tonight, I am going to give him what both our bodies have been begging for.

I'm wearing my favorite pair of black high-heeled ankle boots, black ripped skinny jeans that make my legs look long, a light blue baby doll tank that my boobs practically fall out of, and my signature black leather jacket. My long black hair is falling down my back in soft waves, the color of my tank making my light blue eyes stand out.

It's what's underneath that I can't wait to show him; a matching lacy bra and thong, the same color as my tank top.

I hear a whimper from behind me and realize I'm daydreaming. Checking my phone, I see that I'm out of time. I pick up my favorite knife and turn toward my newest victim.

I point my knife at my victim. "Todd Gilroy, you are convicted of rape. Your daddy's money has gotten you acquitted of all charges, but that's where I come in." I walk towards him. "I get justice for all those girls that had to suffer through your rape and see you walk away without even a slap on the wrist."

"I didn't rape anyone!" Todd insists.

I roll my eyes. "That's what they all say. I don't waste my time. I did my research. You're a piece of shit who likes to drug and rape them because you can't get them any other way." I walk behind him and grab his hair, yanking his head back.

"You won't get away with this," he blubbers. "My dad..."

I yank his hair again, making him yelp. "Your dad is next. I see that being a rapist runs in your family." I place my knife against his neck. "*Marciume all'inferno,*" I murmur.

I drag my blade across his throat; it slices like a knife through butter. Always have to keep these babies sharp. I close my eyes and let the calmness of these kills wash over me. I could feel it settle my mind and body like it always does.

I open my eyes and jump back before the blood can ruin my boots, listening to my friend Todd gurgle. "Ugh," I say, walking over to clean my knife and place it back in its spot.

"Aren't you going to be late?" Ryder asks.

I turn around to face him with a smile. He's leaning against the doorway of my little homemade torture chamber, staring at a dead Todd with an eyebrow raised.

Ryder would be more my type if we hadn't known each other since we were in diapers. Six-foot-three, ripped, thighs like tree trunks, and an ass to die for. His ass actually makes me a little jealous. Dark hair and dark brown eyes. Thin hoops in each nostril, tattoos everywhere. The perfect definition of a broody alpha hole. His dad was my dad's right-hand man, so Ryder took the mantle with me when his dad retired after my dad died.

"No. I have a little time," I reply. "What are you doing down here?"

He shoves off the wall, walking towards me. "Your uncle called," I wrinkle my nose, and he chuckles, "He said he needs you to do that charity gala bullshit in two weeks."

I sigh, ruffling the hair around my face. "Micah knows I hate those things. Nothing says let's raise money for needy kids like a bunch of violent crime families."

He chuckles again. "That's what you get for being the leader."

The thorn in my side. Before my dad died of cancer, he handed me the title of Boss, which made me the leader of the Italian Mafia. One of the most prominent Italian Mafia presences in the United States is California, where the Poletti's made a name for themselves. I was twenty-two at the time; now, at twenty-five, I still don't know what the fuck I'm doing.

That's where my uncle Micah comes in. He stepped up to help me out so I didn't drown. Losing my dad was hard enough without trying to keep this family together. Recently, I stepped up, finally deciding to be who my dad trusted me to be. I'm sure that didn't include being a serial killer, however.

No one ever suspected I'm the Black Demon, the female serial killer who goes after all the bad guys or girls that prey on the weak. Since their bodies are never found, no one can pin them on me. Perks of being a part of the Mafia, you can make anything or anyone disappear.

"You want to go with me?" I ask Ryder, batting my eyelashes.

He snorts. "Hell no. Ask Gage. He lives for that shit."

"Come on," I whine. "You're my right-hand man, and you're supposed to do these things for me."

He laughs loudly and pushes off the weapons table he is leaning on. "This is what I do as your right-hand man," he says, pointing to Todd. "I clean up your kills; I don't go to galas." He grimaces at the word gala.

"Fine, be that way," I say and flip my hair over my shoulder. "Gage and I will have all the fun." I check my phone for the time. "Shit. I have to go."

He shoos me away. "Go. I got this"

I blow him a kiss and run for the stairs leading me to the main house. "Thank you!"

When Micah realized what I was doing, he built my torture chamber for me. The door that leads to it inside the house just looks like a wine cellar when you first enter, with a hidden door. That leads to a hallway with several doors with fingerprint locks. The last door leads to the chamber. My dad never knew what I did in my free time; Micah found out by accident. Instead of judgment, he made sure I never got caught.

This is the only way my mind is clear of everything I have ever gone through. I go after the assholes like the ones who raped and tortured me. Some people go to therapy. I murder.

As I round the corner into the house, I run into Gage's chest. "Whoa," he chuckles, grabbing my shoulders to steady me.

"Sorry," I say and take off running again. "I'm late! Gala with me in two weeks, so have a tux ready!"

"Yes, ma'am," he yells back.

Gage is not someone you would expect to be involved in the Mafia. Brown, thick wavy hair over ice blue eyes. Perfectly sculpted face. Two diamond studs in each ear. Lean swimmers' body. Complete pretty boy. But that's why he works as my date for galas. He looks the part of the spoiled rich boy. No one would ever know this fun-loving guy has a mean streak a mile wide if you pissed him off.

I jump into my black BMW M4, one of the more low-key cars I have, and head to the restaurant to meet Leo.

"Damn, Baby, you look gorgeous tonight," Leo greets with a kiss on the cheek.

I sit in the chair he pulls out for me, waiting for him to do the same. "You do too," I reply, looking him up and down. Black button-up over black jeans paired with black boots.

I kept my makeup understated tonight, just black eyeliner in my cat eye and some pink lipstick to make my pouty lips stand out. No foundation for my tan skin, not when I planned to sweat it off.

I slide my black leather jacket off to hang on the back of the chair, and Leo's eyes zero in on my cleavage.

He folds his arms on the table, leaning closer. "Are you trying to make my cock stay hard through dinner?" He looks me over again. "Because it's working."

I chuckle and mirror his pose. "I'll make it all better after dinner," I say as I move my tank to the side to tease the edge of my lacey bra.

"Fuck," he whispers.

I move it back into place when the waiter walks up. "Ms. Poletti," he greets me with a nod since this is one of the places I frequent, and most people know who I am by reputation. They may not know exactly who I am, but they know I'm important. It's funny how that level of respect works. I grew up here, so most people knew me through my dad, but I made a name for myself.

Sure, there are rumors we are Mafia, but no one can prove it. We have legit businesses everywhere. Restaurants, nightclubs, casinos, you name it, we own one. We are right on the beach, so we own sea charter businesses, too, which is how we filter in all the illegal shit.

Leo and I order our food and enjoy some light conversation, but our minds are on what we'll do after dinner. Which hopefully includes being very naked; it's been way too long.

Serial killers don't usually have much time for sex.

Our food arrives, and both of us are lost in the deliciousness. This isn't one of my restaurants, but I love the food here. I've tried to poach the chef multiple times, but he's loyal to the owners, and I can respect that.

"Where's your mind at?" Leo asks with a teasing smile.

"Just thinking about the food," I reply, then look through my lashes. "Then you having me for dessert later."

He unleashes his full megawatt smile, straight white teeth, and a twinkle in his pretty eyes. "Baby, I plan on having you for a full-ass meal later; I'm a hungry man."

I lean forward again. "Why don't we cut the shit and just get out of here?" I suggest.

He signals for the check, and we're on our way to my beach house before too long. I keep it for reasons like this. It's hard to bring a guy home with a bunch of dudes running around, scaring them off.

"Fuck," Leo gasps out, pulling away from my mouth.

He has me against the door with my legs around his waist right after our shoes came off, kissing my lips like he can't get enough. I've kissed Leo plenty of times, but nothing compares to knowing I'll finally give it all to him.

He turns around with me in his arms and follows my directions to the bedroom. It's a simple beach house with a cute kitchen, a small living room, and one bedroom.

I let my feet hit the floor when we get to the bed and look up at him. His eyes are bluer now, showing he's as ready for this as I am. He slides his hands under my tank top, pulling it over my head, causing my hair to tumble around my face. He starts laying open mouth kisses on the swells of my breasts where they're spilling from my bra before moving down my stomach to the top of my jeans. He lowers himself to his knees, undoing my jeans and shimmying them down my hips. I brace my hands on his shoulders so he can pull my jeans over my feet, leaving me in nothing but my lingerie. Leo sits back on his heels, running his eyes all over my body.

"Baby, you are gorgeous." He leans forward, kissing my pussy through my panties, making me gasp his name.

He rises to his feet, jerking his shirt over his head. I can't resist reaching out and running my hands all over his hard body, watching a shudder run through him at my touch. I smooth my hands down his perfectly defined pecs and over his abs which look like they're cut from glass. I notice a tattoo on his left lower ribcage that wasn't there before, so it must be new.

He makes quick work of his jeans, leaving him in nothing but a pair of tight black boxer briefs showing off an impressive bulge. He steps into my space, slanting his mouth over mine again, leading me backward toward the bed. The back of my knees hit the mattress, and he follows me down, stretching his body over mine. He grinds his hard cock against my panties, and I can't stop the moan of anticipation that escapes. He kisses me hard, stroking his tongue in and out of my mouth before pulling back.

"Did you wear this just for me?" he asks in a husky voice, running his finger down my cleavage, down my belly, and stopping right at the top of my panties.

"You like?" I ask breathlessly.

"Fuck yeah," he groans, grinding into me again.

He runs his hand back up my body before popping the front clasp of the bra open, causing my breasts to spill out. He latches onto a nipple with a harsh groan, sucking it hard into his mouth, making my back arch. Lips still on my nipple, he brings his other hand up, rubbing my other nipple with the backs of his fingers. He continues down my ribs, causing goosebumps to pop up on my flesh, then shoves his hand into my panties.

"Fuck," I whisper when he circles my clit.

He lets my nipple go with a pop, sitting up on his knees and yanking my panties off my legs. I sit up, sliding my bra the rest of the way off, exposing me entirely to his gaze. He places a gentle hand on my chest, so I lay back down.

"Goddamn," he rasps. He leans down, running his tongue from the top of my pussy back to my nipple, blowing a gentle breath on the wet skin, causing me to shiver. He hops off the bed and shucks his boxers before climbing back on. I catch a brief glimpse of his cock, but it's enough to know that I will feel it in the morning, which is what I want.

He lays beside me, patting the bed on either side of his head. "Park that pretty pussy right here," he says with a grin.

I laugh and get positioned over his face in sixty-nine. He doesn't give me a chance to settle before he wraps muscular arms around my thighs and yanks my pussy onto his face, sucking my clit into his mouth.

"Oh fuck," I moan, catching myself on his abs with my hands.

He doesn't let up, flicking, licking, and sucking my clit into his mouth. I reach down and wrap my fingers around his impressive cock, licking the precum leaking from the slit, listening to his breath hitch, his cock jerking in my hand. I start with teasing licks around the head and then suck the head of his cock into my mouth while stroking at the base. When his hips start bucking up, I suck him into my mouth as far as I can take him, and his groan reverberates across my clit. His hips lift to push him further, and I relax my throat, taking him as far as I can, my lips meeting my fingers wrapped around the base.

The more I suck, the more he devours my pussy. The man has a talented fucking mouth applying just the right amount of pressure to my clit and knowing when I need his tongue and lips elsewhere.

It doesn't take long before I can feel my orgasm building. I can't stop my hips from moving, grinding down on his face.

"Yes, Baby. Ride my face," he groans out, sucking my clit. Hard.

I let his dick go with a pop. "Oh fuck. Shit," I pant out.

I sit back with my hands on his abs and start rotating my hips, taking all his mouth has to offer, which is a lot. The thought of suffocating him flies from my mind when he anchors his muscular forearms around my thighs so I can't move. He switches his tongue from licking and sucking my clit to pushing into my pussy. When he nips my clit, my release hits me like a freight train. My body goes rigid, and stars explode behind my eyelids. "LEO!" I scream, half collapsing forward on his stomach.

He continues to lick my pussy until I come down from my orgasm. He licks me from my clit to my opening, making me whimper from the sensitivity.

"Fuck, you taste good," he says with a slap on the ass. *Fuck.* Did I dream this man up? "On your back," he demands. "Condoms?"

I pull my wobbly legs from around his head, collapsing on the bed beside him, and point to the bedside table. He rolls over, rummaging through the drawer. He returns with a handful, tossing them on the bed beside my head.

I raise my eyebrow, and he chuckles a deep, delicious sound. "I can already tell once isn't going to be enough, Baby."

He positions himself between my legs on his knees, ripping a condom packet open with his teeth before rolling it on his cock.

Note to self: get bigger condoms.

He gazes down at me spread out below him with a look on his face I can't decipher. It's almost like awe. Leo is gorgeous, and although we never go into details, I know he doesn't lack in the girl department. Leo can get any girl he wants with a wink and soft words in his slight country accent.

He notches himself at my entrance, sliding forward just a little, then places his hands on the back of my thighs, spreading me wider. He slowly slides his cock in, causing both of us to groan at the invasion. He teases me with short strokes before pushing his hips forward, driving every inch of his cock inside me.

"Jesus, you feel good," he breathes when he's finally fully seated.

I can only nod. It feels like he's seated in my throat. He stays still, letting me get used to his size, his eyes never leaving mine. Then he starts to move, slow at first, his eyes tracking down to his cock disappearing where we're connected, slowly dragging his cock back out before slowly pushing back in.

He lets go of my legs, leaning his entire body weight on me, linking our hands together and pulling them over my head. Taking my lips in a searing kiss, he pistons his hips in deeper, harder thrusts.

I rip my mouth away. "Holy fuck," I moan, meeting him thrust for thrust.

"I knew you would take my cock so good, Baby," he whispers against my ear.

Oh my god.

Why in the hell did I wait so long for this? We've come close more than once, but something kept stopping me. And anytime I put the brakes on, he never got mad or annoyed, no matter how hard he was.

He lays his forehead on mine, our hands still linked together. He moves his hips back and forth, rubbing my clit with his pubic bone. I squeeze his hands and spread my legs further apart. He pulls partially out before slamming back in, rotating his hips when he's balls deep, making me gasp.

I can already feel another release building fast. "I need more," I whisper. I'm all for the slow build, but I need this hard and fast. Leo pulls out and flips me to my hands and knees with no real effort, shoving back inside of me.

"Fuck, Leo!" I scream, fisting my hands into the sheet.

He's so deep this way, but *fuck*, it feels good, that bite of pain and pleasure mixed. He latches onto my hips and starts pounding into me, grunting each time his thighs slap against mine.

I have to brace my arms to keep from face planting, the sound of our flesh slapping together and harsh breaths fill the room.

I lay my shoulder on the bed, reaching down to start circling my clit. My hips drop with the contact, and he jerks them back up with strong hands, never stopping his rhythm.

"Are you going to come on my cock?" he rasps.

"Yes. Yes. Yes," I chant, rubbing my clit harder.

My whole body is tight as a bowstring waiting for that one thing to set me off when he slaps the top of my ass cheek, and I shatter. "Fuck! Leo!" I scream.

I clamp down so hard on his cock that his thrusts stutter. He slams into me twice before he stills, buried as deep as he can. He comes with a long groan, his fingers biting into my skin. He collapses against my back, placing kisses down my spine. He gives me one last kiss between the shoulder blades before collapsing beside me, pulling me, so my back is to his front.

"You're fucking perfect, Baby," he says, his hard breaths ruffling my hair.

I giggle. "Not even close, but that was incredible."

He places a kiss between my shoulder blades again before pulling out. He pulls the condom off and ties it before tossing it into the wastebasket beside the bed. He rearranges us so I'm lying on his chest, his fingers making patterns on my back.

We lay there cuddled, getting our breathing under control. He clears his throat. "There's something I want to tell you."

I look up into his beautiful eyes. They're starting to lighten back up to that color where you can't tell if they are blue or green. "What's that?" I ask, unable to decipher the look in his eyes.

"This isn't because of what just happened. I felt it for a while." He rubs his knuckles down my cheek. "I love you."

My whole world stops spinning, and I freeze. *Leo loves me?* I search his eyes for the truth, and it's staring right back at me. The ice around my heart melts completely. Now I know why I feel different about him.

"I love you too," I whisper, and a smile lights up his face.

He kisses me softly, making love to my lips with his, and I feel how right those words are.

He gently kisses my lips before tucking me back onto his chest. "I've wanted to tell you that for weeks," he says quietly like he expected something different, and I smile.

I start running my hand over his chest and that's when his tattoo catches my eyes again.

I run my hand across his tattoo and notice it doesn't look brand new, and I just saw him less than a week ago. It looks like a sniper holding a sniper rifle with a word written over the top in fancy script. I raise my head and look closely, and my heart sinks.

The word reads Perez.

As in the Perez family.

The Poletti's biggest rival and the reason I lost my innocence at thirteen.

CHAPTER 2
LEO

One second, Alessa is excusing herself to the bathroom. The next, she's straddling me with a wickedly sharp knife to my throat, still gloriously naked.

If I make one wrong move, it will slice my throat wide open.

What the fuck?

"Who are you?" she asks in a deadly tone. Gone is the sweet, sexually sated woman from ten seconds ago, whispering she loved me too, and in her place is a woman I don't recognize.

I raise my hands in a placating gesture. "What's going on?"

She presses the knife in further. "Who. Are. You?" she grits out.

"Baby, I don't know what you're talking about." With every word, my throat rubs against the knife, and I feel blood slip down my neck.

"Your tattoo says Perez," she replies. I just look at her, and she scoffs. "Like you don't know who the fuck I am if you're rocking a tattoo for the fucking Perez family." She spits the name Perez like it leaves a bitter taste in her mouth.

I swallow. "Who's the Perez family?"

Her eyes narrow to dangerous slits. "One last chance, Leo. Why do you have the name Perez tattooed on you?"

Everything is running through my head at once. I love this girl; that isn't a lie. I fell for her almost immediately. She has something about her that I want to soak up with a fucking sponge. But falling for her was never a part of the plan.

She grabs her phone from the nightstand when I don't answer, flicking it over to the speakerphone after she dials a number. She lays it on the bed beside me, never taking the pressure from the knife.

A deep male voice answers. "Hello?"

"Ryder, I need you," she replies.

"Where?" Ryder asks, instantly alert.

"Beach house. Bring Gage and Dex."

I hear him shouting in the background. "On our way," he says and hangs up.

"Such a shame," she mutters. "We could have been great."

I feel the sharp sting of a needle in my neck. Her beautiful face wavers in and out, and the last thing I remember is a tear slipping down her cheek.

THE FIRST THING I notice when I wake up is I have a pounding fucking headache, I'm freezing, and I can hear murmurs of voices around me. I keep my head hanging like I'm still knocked out and try to get my sluggish brain to pick up what they're saying.

It all starts coming back piece by piece. Dinner with Alessa, the best sex of my life after, telling her I loved her, then her seeing my tattoo and flipping her shit.

Fucking idiot.

I keep it covered any other time, and in my rush to get to dinner with her, I forgot. I planned to tell her, but it never seemed like the right time.

".... fuck do we do with him now?" a deep male voice filters through the fog. I recognize it from the voice on the phone and risk a peek to see the face. I dig through my drugged brain for everything my brothers told me. Ryder. Ryder Venchelli. Son of Rocco Venchelli. Twenty-five. Alessa's second in command.

"How did you not know who he was?" That voice is like gravel over concrete. Raspy and low. Dexton Barlow. Twenty-six. When Alessa took over, he rose through the ranks quickly. Six-foot-six, easily two hundred and sixty pounds of pure muscle. Covered in tattoos. Thick, dark brown hair that is long enough to cover the scar that runs down the side of his head. Pretty sure he can crush me under his boot. Or with his bare hands.

I finally look up enough to see them standing in front of a table and a wall full of weapons. Weapons you torture someone with.

Fuck.

Alessa shoots the big man a glare, causing the one with the wavy brown hair to chuckle. Gage Lawson. Twenty-four. He came into this life when his dad, Connor Lawson, was recruited when Gage was a kid. Now he stood side by side with Alessa in pictures, hiding behind the pretense that they are just spoiled, rich kids.

"He doesn't look like either of the Perez brothers, asshole," she spits out, causing the big guy to put his hands up. "I'm not a fucking idiot."

"He didn't say you were," Ryder says gently. "We just need to figure out what to do now."

Sensing I'm awake, her head slowly turns toward me, and she smiles. It's not that sweet smile I got earlier. This one is full of malice and slightly unhinged. My brothers warned me going into this that all of them wouldn't hesitate to shoot first and ask questions later. I figured I wouldn't ever fall in love with her. It was supposed to be an easily executed plan, and we could all get what we wanted. I was wrong.

And I'm fucked.

"Look who decided to join us," she purrs, twirling the knife she had pressed to my neck earlier. "You ready to fess up?"

I have two options.

Lie and die for it.

Tell the truth and die for it.

Either way, I'm dead.

I take a deep breath and decide on the truth. "My name is Leonardo Janelle Perez. Half-brother to Evander and Mateo Perez.

Son of Frankie Perez," I tell her while looking her straight in the eye. I see the hurt flash through those pretty eyes before she can cover it up. "That's all I lied about," I insist.

"That's enough to lie about," she barks. "You knew who I was, didn't you?"

I shake my head. "Not the first night, and I didn't find out until I showed Mateo a picture of you."

That's the truth, and that's how we ended up with this half-cocked fucking plan. Bag the Poletti princess and call for a truce. I didn't know who she was the first night I met her. All I saw was this gorgeous woman with a smile that lit up a room, blue eyes I wanted to get lost in, and hair black as night. My brothers wanted the truce after our father died but didn't know how to do it. We didn't want his lifelong blood feud to last any longer. The blood feud that scarred up Dexton's face.

I didn't expect to start having feelings for her. Just after four fucking months, she already had me wrapped around that tiny finger before we ever slept together. Now I'm gone for this girl, and she is, without a doubt, going to kill me. I don't think now is a good time to mention that she lied to me too.

"How the hell did you not know who she is?" Gage scoffs, spinning a chair around to sit in it backward, two feet from where I'm currently tied up.

I look down at him and know why I'm cold. I'm in my boxer briefs, tied with my arms over my head, toes barely touching the ground. I'm in a concrete room, which they all seem familiar with.

"I'm new to the family," I tell them honestly. "I didn't even know who I was until a year ago. Dear old Dad paid my mom off to disappear when he knocked her up so his wife wouldn't find out. Evander and Mateo found me and welcomed me into the family."

"Why did you keep seeing me, then? I know your brothers told you about the family rivalry," Alessa points out.

"We don't want to be rivals anymore, and we wanted to find a way to end it when I ran into you."

"You don't believe this shit, do you?" Ryder asks, then looks at her face. "You're fucking believing him right now!"

"Shut up," she hisses at Ryder, then walks toward me, stopping to look up at me. "So, if I call for a meeting with the families, Evander and Mateo will confirm what you just said?" she asks, and I nod. "Keep in mind that if you're lying, I won't hesitate to start a war by killing all of you," she warns.

I believe with one-hundred percent certainty that she will. Me getting caught wasn't a part of the plan, but here we are.

I nod. "I get it."

"Everyone out," she orders.

Ryder bristles. "Les, I don't..."

"Out!" she cuts him off; that one word rings through the room with authority.

They all make their way through the door to the right. Ryder gives her one last meaningful look before shutting the door.

She looks at me without the mask she's been wearing while they were in here. "Was any of it real?" she asks softly.

"It was."

"I can't believe I fell for your shit," she says with a humorless laugh. "Apparently, I still am because I want to believe you so bad."

"You can believe me, Baby. I swear." I'm pleading at this point, and I don't even care. It isn't even that I'm begging for my life, which I am. I'm pleading with her to believe me because I don't want to lose her. I could feel my heart breaking just thinking about it. These past four months have been the happiest I've ever been.

"How?!" she asks, throwing her arms in the air, knife still in hand. "You have lied to me for *months*, Leo. You told me you lov..." She shakes her head hard once, shaking out what she was about to say. "You made a plan to set me up."

"To unite the families," I insist. "We wanted to show you that we aren't like Frankie."

She rolls her eyes heavenward. "That is not how you do that. All you showed me is that you're all liars. Just like him and the rest of the Perez family." She looks at me again, and her eyes look haunted like some old memory is creeping up. She blinks, and it's gone.

What the fuck was that?

"Do you know why the feud started?" she asks, sitting in the chair Gage vacated, crossing one leg over the other, tapping her knife on her thigh. I shake my head. "Evander and Mateo didn't tell you?"

I shake my head again. "They said they didn't know why or when it started. They were young and raised to hate the Poletti's. They formed their own opinion when they realized Frankie was a fucking monster."

"Do you know how Frankie died?" she asks with that weird tilt of her head.

"He was tortured. They always figured it was one of his many enemies and never investigated it."

She nods. "It was," she confirms, then looks me dead in the eye. "It was me."

I know my face shows my shock. This beautiful girl tortured Frankie Perez? Did I know her at all? Apparently not. The only real thing I know about her is what my brothers told me.

"Why?" I ask and she immediately shuts down.

She stands up. "That's not important. What is important is that you expect me to believe your brothers would want peace with us. I can't just let you go, and I'm not ready to stick my neck out for a meeting yet." She turns to look at me. "Don't make me regret not killing you." She walks to the table, laying her knife down before walking to the door; she turns one last time. "Even though that's not completely off the table."

The door clicks behind her, and I let my breath out in a whoosh. Everything I told her is true. Evander and Mateo are nothing like Frankie, and I don't even know the man personally. I only regret the hurt in her eyes when she found out who I really am. If I get out of this alive, I'm killing Evander and Mateo for talking me into this shit.

I don't know how long I stay like that before I hear the door click back open, and Ryder steps through the door. My shoulders are screaming from being stretched out so far, and my fingers are numb from how tightly my hands are wrapped together.

He walks over, stopping right in front of me, crossing his arms over his chest. His eyes are narrowed, and he looks fucking terrifying. He's about two inches taller than my six-foot-one, but he's twice my size. My brothers showed me everything they know about fighting styles and guns, but I wasn't raised for this. Ryder was.

"I wanted to kill you on the spot," he says, a muscle ticking in his jaw. "She didn't." I don't need him to clarify who 'she' is. I don't say anything because I can tell he has more to say. He steps closer, and I see murder in his dark eyes. Reaching over, he releases the chain holding me up; the sudden release has me hitting my knees on the concrete floor. I grit my teeth so I don't make a noise, which is what he wanted.

He squats down in front of me so I look into his eyes. "You better not be lying to her or your brothers," he spits the word, "are as good as dead. Along with you."

He unhooks the longest chain, jerks me up by my still tied arms, and drags me through a long hallway, going through several doors. I don't fight him because there is no point. He would put a bullet through my brain with one of the Glocks hanging in the holster over his shoulders and deal with her wrath later.

What the hell is this place?

We finally come out in a room that looks like a wine cellar before stepping into a huge kitchen. He continues through the kitchen before taking a left into another hallway, shoving me into a room under the stairs with the door open. I stumble and then right myself. Now I'm starting to get pissed off.

He laughs. "There's that backbone, pussy boy." He points to the chair in the corner, where Alessa is waiting. "One hair on her head gets harmed, and I'll cut you into little pieces." He laughs again and shuts the door.

She motions to the bed. "Sit." I sit down, and she comes over to unlock the chain around my arms. I rub them to get the feeling back. "You're going to call your brothers. You'll tell them you're staying with me at my beach house for a couple of days. Keep it on speakerphone. If you try to tell them what's going on or I even sniff out a code word," she pulls a Glock from the back of her jeans, "I will end you."

She hands me my phone with her other hand before sitting back down in the chair, the gun lying on her thigh aimed casually at me.

I pull up Evander's number, dial it, and flip it to speakerphone. He's my best option not to say something stupid like Mateo would. Evander is the oldest and, mostly, the more mature of the two.

"Hello?" he answers on the second ring.

"What's up, bro?" I ask in my most 'I haven't just been kidnapped' voice.

"Just got back in. Where are you?"

"I'm staying with Alessa for the next couple of days," I tell him and close my eyes.

Please don't say something to get me killed. Please don't say something to get me killed.

He chuckles. "Are you now?" I hear him relay the message, knowing he just told Mateo.

Mateo's voice filters through the line. "Damn. Pussy that good?"

Fuck. I look over at Alessa, and she raises an eyebrow.

"Shut up," Evander growls to Mateo, and I could fucking kiss him. "Keep in touch, brother."

"Will do," I tell him and hang up, laying the phone in Alessa's outstretched hand.

"That's all it took?" she asks skeptically.

"I'm not a prisoner there. I told you they aren't like Frankie."

"That remains to be seen," she retorts, jamming the gun into the back of her jeans. "You have a bathroom, and I brought you some of Gage's clothes because they're the closest to your size." She walks to the door and opens it.

"Alessa," I say softly before she can step through. "I'm not lying to you. I do love you."

She turns back with sadness in her eyes. "I wish I could believe you."

She walks out, shutting the door behind her. I can hear the lock click into place from the outside.

I flop back onto the bed in my newly found jail cell. It's a standard room, except there are no windows or way of escape. It could be worse. They could have left me in the cold basement.

Small favors.

Now I just need to find a way to make her believe me. I already decided I'm not letting this girl get away from me, even if she just had me tied up in a basement.

Of all the scenarios we ran through when we made this plan, this wasn't one of them. Evander talked to someone and got some makeup to keep my tattoo covered until we were ready to tell her. I got the tattoo almost a month before I met her; we all three had them now. It was our way of embracing the change in the Perez family. I had been helping out at one of the restaurants today and lost track of time, leaving just enough time to shower, get dressed, and run out of the house.

I have never seen so much hurt and betrayal in someone's eyes before. I wasn't the type of person who went around purposely hurting someone. Seeing that in Alessa's eyes with whatever haunted look came along with it broke me. I've been begging my brothers for a month to let me tell her the truth, and they kept saying it wasn't time.

It looks like it was time, after all.

It also looks like it might be my time to leave this world.

Violently.

CHAPTER 3
ALESSA

What a clusterfuck.

I showered as soon as I got into my room to get Leo's scent off me. His cologne and something just him was clogging my nose and hurting my heart. After I shower, I lay in bed, staring at the ceiling.

How could I have been so fucking stupid?

Someone knocks softly on the door. "Come in," I call out, and Gage sticks his head through the door with a smile. He walks in and lies on the bed beside me, one arm behind his head, staring at the ceiling like I am.

"This isn't your fault," he tells me. "We're running checks on him now that we know his real last name and everything by the last name he gave you before checks out. He was with his mom." He looks at me. "You like him, don't you?"

"Yeah," I answer honestly. "But it doesn't matter now, Gage," I reply.

"Les, look at me," he says gently, and I look over into his blue eyes. "He's a fucking idiot," he declares, causing me to laugh. "No, seriously. He got to see you naked, and he fucked it up."

"Shut up," I tell him teasingly. Gage is always saying stuff like that, trying to get a reaction out of me. We've known each other since his dad came to work for my dad when Gage was ten. He became instant friends with Ryder and me, and we've been inseparable ever since.

He sobers. "I get it, but what if we can make peace with the Perez's? Can you do that?"

Gage knows what I went through with them. "No one from that time is alive anymore," I muse. "It's what needs to be done, and ending a feud like that will shake the foundation of the families."

Gage nods. "In a good way," he points out. "Your office dweller is working through everything now. We'll have answers by morning."

My 'office dweller' means Holden, my hacker.

"Stop calling him that," I tell Gage.

"Why? He never comes out unless it's to eat or work out with one of us. Then he drags his ass back in there like a zombie."

"That's where he's comfortable."

Gage leaps up from the bed and starts shuffling around like a zombie, arms stretched in front of him. "Must have food. Must hack shit. Must please Master."

I throw a pillow at him. "Stop," I say, starting to laugh.

Gage turns his grin on me, dimples on full display, leaping on the bed on his knees, making me bounce. "So, what are we doing with your prisoner downstairs?" he leans in. "Maybe we can play with him. Did you see his abs? Damn.

Yes, I saw them. Up close. Also, everything else about him.

"There will be no playing with the prisoner," Ryder announces, entering my room. Gage and I both turn to him with a pout, causing us to crack up.

"But why?" I whine. "He's fun to play with," I say, waggling my eyebrows, knowing it will get a rise out of Ryder.

He points at me. "No, Queen Stabby. But I want to know the answer to your equally psychotic sidekick's first question. What are we doing with him?"

Ryder lays down on my other side, propping his head on his hand."I told him to tell his brothers that he's staying with me for a few days. By that time, Holden should have some information on this situation."

"They bought it?" he asks with a little frown line between his eyebrows.

I reach up and smooth it out. "They sounded like they did. He called Evander."

"You know what it means if he's lying, right?" Ryder asks.

I sigh. "Yep. All out fucking war between the Poletti's and Perez's. Fucking wonderful. I need to call Micah."

Gage pops back onto his knees. "Look at it this way. His story could be completely true. Micah isn't your real uncle; he's your half-uncle," he points out.

He is. Granddad Poletti stepped out on my grandma late in life, which is how Micah came to be, and only seven years older than me. But unlike Leo's dad, if his story is true, my granddad owned up to his mistake and raised Micah as his own. My grandma was a freaking saint to deal with that.

"Even if this never happened," I start and stare back at the ceiling. "It would have been over the minute he found out what I do."

Ryder shrugs. "You take out the bad fuckers that the courts can't. If he can't stomach that, he doesn't deserve you anyway." He reaches over a gently nudges my chin to look at him. "Let's find out what the hell is going on and go from there." He kisses my forehead before standing up. "My vote is still to kill him, though." He gives me that grin that is all Ryder and strolls out of the room.

"I just want to touch his ass once," Gage declares, watching Ryder walk out of the room, making us both laugh.

Gage is good at breaking the tension in a room, so I ensure he's by my side. I knew who I wanted there from the very beginning, and we just worked together too well not to.

I reach over for my phone to look at the time, and then dial Micah's number. It's after midnight, but I know that he's still awake.

"What's wrong?" he says when he picks up.

"What makes you think something is wrong?"

"Because it's after midnight," he replies, and I hear a female voice murmur something in the background and the sheets rustling as Micah gets up.

"Ew," I say with a wrinkle of my nose. "Please tell me you didn't answer the phone while having sex."

He chuckles, and I hear a door shut. "No, Shithead, I didn't." He pauses. "We just got done."

"Micah!" I exclaim.

"What's going on, Les?" He knows me well enough to know I don't randomly call because I see him daily.

"We have a situation at the house. It's under control now, but you need to know." I pause to gather my courage. "The guy I've been seeing. Leo?"

"Yeah. What about him?" He's fully alert now.

"His real name is Leonardo Perez. Half-brother to Evander and Mateo."

"What the fuck?" Micah explodes, and I wince. "Shit, Les. How the hell?"

"It's a long story, but he says he's only been a part of the family for a year. Frankie paid off his mom to disappear. Evander and Mateo found him."

"What does this have to do with you?" He asks in that voice that reminds me so much of my father. The one that sounds concerned and that he wants to murder someone at the same time.

"He says he didn't know who I was the night we met. Mateo told him after Leo showed him a picture. Then they planned to unite the families."

"Unite the fucking families? How the fuck do they plan on doing that after what his father..." He takes a deep breath. "Is he alive?"

"Yeah. He's in the holding room and told them he's staying with me for a couple of days. I need to call a meeting when we get the info we need from Holden."

"And if he's lying?" he asks with an edge to his voice.

"He's a dead man," I say without hesitation, even though I feel my heart breaking. But I can't let this go and make the Poletti family look weak. My father raised me to run this family, being the only heir. I've seen many families fall because their sole heir was a girl, and it is almost unheard of to hand the reins to a daughter, but my dad never cared.

"Fuck," Micah says harshly. "Okay. We can deal with this. I'll see you tomorrow."

"Okay. Love you," I tell him.

"Love you too, Shithead," he replies and hangs up. He's called me shithead for as long as I can remember, and it's not like we have a normal uncle/niece relationship with a seven-year age gap.

I sigh and look at Gage, who is scrolling through his phone. I look closer. "Are you on my social media?" I ask with a laugh.

"Yeah," he shrugs. "I'm leaving dirty comments under your pics."

I look at my notifications, and sure enough, he is. "Stop," I laugh, trying to grab his phone. He rolls off the bed, landing smoothly on his feet.

"The tabloids already think we're dating," he points out.

"Exactly. You're adding fuel to the fire."

He gives me a look that says that's precisely what he's doing. "No shit. Night, Wifey."

He walks out with a laugh, leaving my door wide open. "Shut my damn door!" I yell.

"Fuck off!" he yells back.

With a sigh, I roll out of bed, slamming the door. I can hear Gage's manic laugh down the hallway.

And they call me fucking crazy.

THE FOLLOWING day when I woke up, I almost forgot about the predicament I found myself in. Every morning I would wake up and wait for Leo to message me good morning and he always did without fail. This morning would be the first time I wouldn't get that text in four months.

I roll out of bed, twisting my hair into a bun. I make my way to the shower, making the water as hot as I could stand it. While I wash off, I let my mind wander to last night and the look in his eyes when he said he loved me. It seemed so real; his eyes were wide open and honest, with no hint of deception. Then I think about how he made a plan with his brothers to make me fall for him just for a fucking truce between the families. He lied to me for months, and I never picked up on it. Was I so blinded by him that I couldn't see it?

I didn't like that at all. I was usually a good read on people and their intentions, but I never caught a whiff of anything wrong coming from Leo. He was almost squeaky clean compared to what I usually went after. The first night I met him, we talked for hours, and he never seemed to get bored. At the end of the night, I usually propositioned the guy for a night of sex with no strings because I didn't do relationships. At the end of the night with Leo, though, I found myself handing him my number and leaving it in his hands to message me the next day; he did. It was the first morning I got that good morning baby text, and I was hooked.

I know I'm stalling in the shower, so I turn the water off and step out, wrapping a fluffy towel around my body. Wiping the steam off the mirror, I stare at my reflection and almost don't recognize the girl staring back at me. Her eyes are sad, but there is also hope hiding behind them. If he's telling the truth, can I forgive him? He didn't know what his father did to me, that I knew for a fact, but did Evander and Mateo? Leo said they were nothing like Frankie. So, could they set a plan in action to have their brother pursue me, knowing Frankie set me on a crash course of having to grow up too fast?

Shaking those thoughts from my head, I brush my teeth and put on minimal makeup, jeans, and a t-shirt, not even close to ready to take on this day. It was just after seven in the morning, and I had barely slept. All the thoughts of Leo ran through my head.

I walk into the kitchen to find Micah fixing breakfast. Walking up, I snag a piece of bacon, and he swats at my hand with the spatula. "Back off."

"What are you, Betty freaking Crocker?" I ask with a laugh.

He has his usual three-piece suit on, without the jacket at the moment. At thirty-two, he looks so much like my dad that it hurt to looks at him sometimes. He has the same black hair and blue eyes as my father and me. He is tall, broad, and doesn't look a day older than me.

"For your information, shithead, I like to cook. I don't have the staff do it all for me." He points at me with the spatula before resuming to his eggs.

"I don't have the staff do it all for me," I defend.

He scoffs. "You can't cook for shit, Les."

I laugh. "Fair point, but we order out. We don't always keep staff here."

He looks around. "No kidding. This place is a mess."

"Shut up, asshole," I say, throwing a kitchen towel at him.

He chuckles. "I'm just fucking with you. You never were the princess people made you out to be."

"Like mom would have ever let me," I say sadly. Mom died when I was twelve, but she never let me use our lifestyle as an excuse to be lazy; Dad was the one who spoiled me to no end.

He wraps me in a one-arm hug. "I know.." He squeezes me once before ushering me to the other side of the island to sit down. "Where are the guys?"

I shrug. "I don't know; it's not my day to keep up with them."

He blows air out through his nose. "Yes. It is. They are your team."

Getting under his skin is my favorite pastime, so I keep pushing buttons. "Who was the girl last night? Am I going to have an auntie?"

He glares at me. "Not a chance in hell."

"Come on, Micah," I beg. "I need a woman figure in my life." I grimace. "Unless she's younger than me."

Micah shrugs. "She had big tits. That's all I know. I don't even remember her name."

My mouth drops open. "You're disgusting."

"You started this game."

Fuck, I did. "Truce," I declare. I do not need to hear about Micah's little flings. He grins and turns back to his eggs. I might fuck with him to get a reaction out of him, but he does the same to me. I didn't have siblings growing up, so Micah was the closest thing I had to a brother, and I didn't know what I would have done without him after my dad died.

Gage walks in, laying a noisy, sloppy kiss on my cheek. "Morning, wifey."

"Stop calling me that," I say, wiping his kiss off my cheek.

Micah turns around, jabbing a finger at Gage. "And stop putting that shit on her pictures."

"What?" Gage asks innocently.

"Don't play stupid, dickhead. You get the gossip mags fired up every time," Micah points out.

Being in a high population area like Abbs Valley, the paparazzi and gossip magazines follow you around like vultures if you have any type of status. I have seen so many laughable stories that it was crazy. We didn't play into their shit, so we never sat for interviews. They ended up making up their own stories.

"I'm just playing my part as arm candy," he says with a wink at Micah.

"If anyone is the arm candy, it's her," Dex rumbles as he walks in, covered in sweat.

"Ha!" I laugh and point at Gage, who's scowling.

"You're a bunch of fucking children," Micah sighs. "What about your locked-up friend?"

"Haven't been in there. I'll take him some food, though," I tell him.

"Do you think you should? Maybe one of the guys could do it." I narrow my eyes at Micah, and he backpedals. "Fine. Do it yourself."

We all sit down around the island after Ryder and Holden come in from their workout. I dig in, plating eggs, bacon, and biscuits, savoring each bite. Micah doesn't just like to cook; he loves it and is damn good at it, too. It's the only time we get home-cooked meals, so I usually beg him to cook for us.

I look over at Holden; his long dark blonde curly hair and brown eyes make him look boyish. But I knew the time he was putting into the gym with the other guys. Just because he sat behind a desk all day didn't mean he was letting himself go.

"Anything new?" I ask him.

He glances up with a small smile before looking back down. "Yeah. I'll bring it out after breakfast."

Progress. Holden looked me in the eye for a second.

Holden is the newest addition to the team. He has been with me for over a year, and when he first started working for me, he was the office dweller Gage picked on him about. I found him when a lower family of the Mexican cartel was trying to make a rise, using him against us. It didn't take long to track him down, and how we found him was awful. So, instead of killing him for hacking my systems, we offered him a better life. They kept him locked in a room since he was sixteen; we got him out at twenty. Now at twenty-one, the guys have given him the confidence he needs to work out and stay healthy. He's the best hacker I have ever encountered; he could find *anything* you needed.

"Thanks," I tell him before plating up more food. "I'm taking this to Leo. I'll meet you back out here."

He nods, so I walk in that direction. I knock on the door to announce myself before unlocking it.

Leo is standing in the middle of the room, a towel around his waist, water dripping down his body from his wet hair.

"I brought you food," I say lamely, sitting the plate on the metal desk, trying to tear my eyes from the water running down his abs.

"Good morning, baby," he smiles. "Thanks."

I shake my head and shut the door back. I'm so confused. This man is part of one of the most powerful crime families. He was locked in a room and just took it without a fight. I can't help but think he is up to something; there is no way he's ok with all this.

When I get back to the kitchen, everyone is gone except Holden, sitting at the kitchen island with papers in front of him.

I slide onto the stool beside him. "Hit me."

"He's telling the truth," he says, sliding some papers towards me.

My heart leaps in my chest, and I try to push it back down, trying not to get my hopes up.

I peer down at a birth certificate, bank statements with a large amount of money deposited, and a few pictures of him and his mom; he looks almost identical to her. She was tall for a woman, thin, and beautiful.

"Fucking hell," I say, running my fingers over his baby picture.

"I'm going to have to sit down with Evander and Mateo, aren't I?"

Holden shrugs. "Looks that way," he mumbles. "I have more proof if you need it."

I shake my head. "No. I believe you," I say with a smile, making him blush. "Where is everyone else?"

He chuckles. "Gage swatted Ryder on the ass with a towel, and they took off. Dex and Micah are in your office."

I squeeze his shoulder. "Thanks, Holden," I say and scoop up the papers.

I hear Gage's crazy laugh from the living room and head that way. He and Ryder are standing at opposite ends of the couch, with Ryder throwing out threats. I'm not even surprised because this type of thing happens way too often.

"Serious time," I say, walking towards the office, knowing they will get the hint that it's time to stop playing around.

I push into the office, everyone sprawling out where there is a chair; I sit in the chair that used to be my dad's. Micah refused to sit here, saying it was disrespectful to me since he was just filling in. I didn't know how to tell him; he was better at this than I would ever be.

I fold my arms on the desk. "Leo's telling the truth." I spread everything on the desk so they could see.

"Son of a bitch," Micah says, surprised, and looks up at me. "So, that means...."

I shrug. "He lives for now. But I have to call a meeting with his brothers."

Micah's eyes soften. "Are you sure? I can if you need me to."

"They were too young to be involved, but I need to find out what they know." I swallow. "I have to do this."

I could kill a man in cold blood but couldn't face two men attached to my past. Even though they are way too young to have been involved, the last name Perez still gives me fucking nightmares.

Get your shit together.

I pick up the phone and dial the number I stole from Leo's phone.

Evander Perez.

CHAPTER 4
LEO

I've paced this room so often since Alessa brought me breakfast that I'm surprised I haven't worn a hole in the floor.

She came in a little while ago and announced my brothers were on the way, then tossed me some jeans and a button-up shirt. She said I can't meet them in Gage's basketball shorts and a t-shirt. I didn't miss the look of trepidation on her face. She has no idea what's going to happen at this meeting, either.

What did Frankie do to her?

Evander and Mateo have stayed mostly low key since Frankie died, trying to fix everything he messed up. Frankie was a horrible leader, so he didn't leave them *any* allies, hence the reason for going after Alessa. What better way to get allies than becoming allies with the strongest ally in the world?

On what felt like my five-hundredth pass around the room, the door opens, and Ryder steps in. "Let's go," he barks, his face giving nothing away. I know if he gets the chance, he will be the one to kill me. I can see the hate simmering in his eyes, just waiting to be unleashed.

I reluctantly follow behind him, and I don't know if I'm walking into a massacre or not. I know I'm telling the truth, but did Les want to believe me, or does she want me dead for lying to her?

He leads me into a conference room where everyone is already seated with Alessa at the head of the table, and Evander at the other end, so they face each other. I take a closer look at Alessa and notice how pale she is. Ryder points me to a seat on her right before leaning against the table behind her with Dexton, both with arms crossed over their chests. Everything about it screams protective, but something tells me it's all for show because she doesn't need it. Her scary as fuck uncle Micah is sitting to her left, casually leaning back in his chair. Evander and Mateo told me some gruesome stories about Micah growing up, and the look he's throwing me right now is worse than the death glares I keep getting from Ryder. Gage is sprawled out on the couch against the wall. His legs are spread wide, arms on the back of the couch, staring at me with a tilt to his head. Mateo is sitting to Evander's left. He looks at me with a raised brow, and I subtly shake my head, trying to convey for him to keep his big mouth shut.

Evander and Mateo are two years apart but look almost identical, except Mateo has green eyes instead of dark brown like Evander's. They both have the same shade of dark brown hair. Mateo's hair is just a little wilder than Evander's perfectly styled hair. They both look like Frankie, which seems to piss them off.

Evander clears his throat. "What's this about, Ms. Poletti?"

Alessa stares him down for a full minute, and you can see her trying to collect herself. I wish I could reach out to her in comfort, but I figure that's a bad idea since you could cut the tension in this room with a fucking knife.

Kind of like the one she held to my throat last night.

"There is no easy way to put this, gentleman, so I'm just going to lay it out there," she says finally, looking every bit like a Mafia queen sitting in a black pantsuit, her hair braided and twisted at the base of her skull. She looks gorgeous. "I know about your plan." She lets that bomb drop, and you could hear a pin drop. To their credit, Evander and Mateo don't react. "But as you can see, it didn't quite work out."

"I'm not sure I know..."

"Cut the shit, Evander," she barks. Everyone straightens their spines, and it almost makes me laugh. This little woman has this whole room on pins and needles just from reputation. "This meeting will go much smoother if you tell me the truth. Why did you send your brother to me?"

I told her they didn't. She's trying to catch me in a lie. It's fucking smart.

Evander and Mateo share a look before Evander sighs. "We didn't send him to you. He was showing you off the next day because we didn't believe him. We told him to get closer to you when we realized who you were."

"Why?" she says between clenched teeth.

"We don't want this feud anymore, Ms. Poletti. We want to run this family differently," Mateo finally speaks up, giving me the evil eye. I shrug. Yes, I got busted, but that's what you get for sending a novice against the rival family.

Micah sits up in his chair, leveling Evander with the same look he's been giving me. "Are you aware of why these families feud?"

I'd like to know that myself.

"No, we don't. Father told us it was from years of fighting for the same land, but he never elaborated."

Micah looks at Alessa, and she shrugs with a resigned look on her face. Something needs to be said here, or this will end bloody. One wrong word and Ryder and Dexton are going to level us. I noticed we don't have any guards inside this room; they are stationed outside, not enough time to react before we are dead.

"Your father," Micah spits the word, "had Alessa kidnapped when she was thirteen ordering his men to," he pauses visibly, collecting himself, "keep her. All because my brother Luca outbid him on a casino they were fighting for. So, you can see why the fuck this seems a little like bullshit."

My head whips to Alessa, but she won't look at me, so I look at Evander and Mateo. They both look pale, but they don't look like they knew. Did they?

"Mr. Poletti, I assure you we had no idea," Evander says, then looks at Alessa. "I swear we didn't know."

"You're around my age?" she asks Evander, and he nods. "I want to believe you didn't know then, of course, but you could have been told about it later."

"Our father never told us anything. We figured it out on our own," Mateo adds. "We discovered a lot after he died, but that was never mentioned. Anywhere."

"I remember a bunch of his men dying, but I always assumed it was some bad job my father sent them on," Evander says, and I look between them, seeing the truth all over their faces.

I can tell Alessa is doing the same thing, trying to find even a hint of dishonesty. She glances over her shoulder at Ryder. He and Dex stand up taller, ready for anything.

Alessa's face is carefully blank when she looks back at Evander and Mateo. "I killed your father," she announces, just as she did to me. There is no emotion or warning, just throwing it out for the reaction. Evander and Mateo exchange surprised looks before looking back at her.

"Good," Mateo spits. "He deserved everything he got."

My brother filled me in on the type of person Frankie was, even with his family. He was verbally and physically abusive to both of them until they were old enough to fight back. That's what kind of coward Frankie was. I could never quite figure out what the hell my mom saw in him, and she never really talked about that time in her life.

Ryder steps forward, rubbing his chin thoughtfully. "You're telling me that you're all good with the fact she just told you that she killed your father?"

Evander shrugs. "We aren't like him, and the world was a better place when we found out he was dead."

Alessa rubs her temples. "Okay. Say we agree to this cease-fire. What does that mean, exactly?"

"You can't be serious," Ryder starts. Alessa flicks her hand up, and he steps back, shutting his mouth. It's funny to me that she can handle them with a slight gesture or word. It shows the level of respect they have for her.

"No more fighting over businesses. No more fighting amongst our men. We coexist peacefully side by side," Evander tells her exactly as he told me. "Truth be told, the Perez's can use all the allies we can get. Father didn't leave many of those."

Alessa waves a hand towards Dex's scarred face. "You do realize that your men did that to him? I see one of them standing in the hallway out there."

"He's as good as dead," Evander assures her.

"Just like that?" She asks with that tilt to her head that makes her look a little crazy and a lot sexy.

"Yes. We thought we weeded out our father's loyalists, but I see we missed one. We don't want those kinds of people."

"What happens if we bid on the same business?" Micah asks.

"We fight for it fair and square. The highest bidder wins. I hope for a bright future between the families, Mr. Poletti," Evander answers.

Alessa turns to me. "Anything to say?"

"No. I told you everything last night," I reassure her.

She looks back to Evander. "I can't let him go." He goes to open his mouth, and she holds up a hand. "Not until I know I can trust you. This trust will go both ways with you leaving your brother in my hands."

"I see he's been treated with the most care," Evander says dryly, motioning towards the marks on my neck from her knife.

She shrugs. "You're lucky he's alive if you want to throw stones, Evander."

He acknowledges that with a nod, but I can see he wants to argue. He's not used to taking the backseat to people telling him what to do, but he knows he doesn't have the upper hand here.

"He will be treated fine from here on out. I won't apologize for what happened after I found out, but I assure you it won't happen again. Unless any of you fuck up," Alessa warns. "If everything goes to plan, he will accompany me to the charity gala in two weeks as a Perez heir. That will show the other families that the Poletti's and Perez's have formed an alliance. That should cause them to follow suit."

"Thank you, Ms. Poletti," Evander says politely.

"Don't thank me," she says harshly. "I don't think you realize how close I came last night to slitting your brother's throat."

"I apologize for how this came about, Ms. Poletti," Evander says, his eyes flicking over me again.

"Call me Alessa," she tells him. "If we are going to start on the right foot. We're of equal power, Evander."

"Let's agree to disagree on that, Alessa," Evander says with a smile. He stands up and buttons his suit jacket. "If there is nothing else, we have some things to take care of."

Throughout this exchange, I notice that he never called her by her first name, whereas she never said his last name. It's a power balance, and Evander is letting her know he acknowledges her as the leader.

She nods, and we follow them outside. Evander turns to Dex when we step through the front door. "Which one?" he asks, and Dex points to the taller, beefier guard standing to Evander's right.

Everything else happens in slow motion. Evander grabs a Glock from the other guard's holster, chambers a round, and places the barrel against the guard's head that Dex pointed to, pulling the trigger before the guy's eyes even widen.

He hits the ground with a thud, and Evander hands the gun back to the other guard. "Clean that up," he says to the two guards standing at the car, mouths hanging open. I keep my eyes carefully averted from the body because it's not something I'm used to seeing. My brothers took care of business whenever needed, but I usually wasn't present.

He turns to Alessa. "I told you. No one on my team will be left who caused harm to anyone in your family."

He strides up to me, locking me in a bear hug. "You good?" he whispers.

"I'm good," I assure him.

He pats me on the back, nods at Alessa, then climbs into the car. I can hear Mateo laughing his ass off, the sound cut off by the remaining guard shutting the door.

I was an only child growing up, so imagine the shock when I

found out I have two brothers who welcomed me into their family with open arms.

Alessa looks at me and then at the fading taillights of their SUV. "Did he just kill a man in my front yard?"

Micah chokes on a laugh. "I think so."

"It was his way of keeping his word," Dex says.

"Thank you, Captain Obvious," Ryder snarks.

"Fuck you," Dex replies with a shake of his head.

You can tell they're all close, so it makes me wonder about their relationship with Alessa. It all looks platonic, but looks could be deceiving. I would have laughed in your face if you asked me a few months ago if I thought Alessa was the queen of a crime family. All five-foot-four of her is every bit of a fucking queen, though.

After Evander and Mateo left, Alessa left me out of the room. I always have one of her guys at my back, but at least I'm not locked up. I have only been in my jail cell, the kitchen, and the living room, but this house is gigantic. The kitchen is all stainless steel with black marble countertops, a huge island in the middle, and enough seats to fit everyone. The living room is massive but cozy, with a huge TV on the wall over a fireplace. There's a couch with an oversized chaise lounge, a love seat across from it, two chairs facing the TV, and several more chairs placed throughout the room. I can see all their personalities everywhere, and it's more like a family than a team. I'm not sure how I feel about that, coming in as an outsider.

Dex doesn't say much, and Gage mostly just jokes around, but Ryder makes shitty comments whenever she's out of earshot, and I'm getting fucking sick of it.

"Dude, just get it off your chest and shut the fuck up," I finally tell him.

He raises an eyebrow. "You find your balls after your brothers left?"

"No. I'm getting sick of hearing your voice."

He chuckles, but there is no humor in it. "You think you're big and bad now?" He steps into my space, and I refuse to step back. "I can kill you, and no one will ever find your body, motherfucker."

"Ryder," Alessa snaps, walking into the room. "Back off." She's changed into the clothes she was in earlier, her hair hanging down her back again.

He gives me one last look before spinning on his heel and leaving the living room.After he's out of the room, I flop down on the couch, all of my bravado fading the minute he leaves. I'm a pushover, but I know when I'm outmatched.

Gage walks in behind her. "Don't mind him. It's the steroids," he announces, flopping down on the couch beside me. He doesn't seem to care that I'm here. He doesn't seem to care about much at all.

"Don't start that shit again," Alessa says, sitting on the love seat in front of us, tucking her legs underneath her and doing everything she can to avoid eye contact with me.

A guy I haven't seen before with shoulder-length curly hair walks into the room, head down. He hands her a folder and then sits in a chair beside her, typing furiously on a laptop that was in his other hand. I raise my eyebrow at her in question.

"Holden," she answers and shrugs. "He's quite talkative." I remember my brothers mentioning him, but they didn't know much about him, just that he was newer to her team.

Gage snorts, turning the tv on. "Yeah. You can never get him to shut the fuck up."

Holden never even looks up, but I can see his lips twitch.

I shake my head at Gage. He's done nothing but joke around with me, but I can see the watchful way he observes around him. Evander and Mateo warned me about him. He seems easygoing, but he hid a wealth of crazy.

Alessa opens the folder, flipping through what looks like pictures and separating them into piles.

I want to ask, but it's none of my business, and I'm sure she won't tell me anyway.

"Anyone interesting?" Gage asks.

"A few," she replies.

"Tonight?" he asks.

She looks at me and then back to Gage. "Sure. Why not?"

Gage whoops. "Yes!"

"Holden," she says gently. He finally looks up, but I can tell he won't look her directly in the face. "Get me more on these two." She hands him two pictures and shoves the others back into the folder. He nods and disappears from the room.

"I guess you aren't going to tell me what that was about," I ask her.

"Um. No," Alessa answers. I can't tell if she's still pissed or not. Her face is devoid of all emotion, and it's starting to wear on my nerves.

"Fair enough." I nod. "But I had to ask."

"You want to know what she does?" Gage sits up on the couch, animated. "She's a superhero. She flies around with her megabat wings and saves the city."

Alessa rolls her eyes. "Shut up, and stop reading my smutty books."

"Hey. I learn a lot from those books," Gage defends.

I shrug. "He's not wrong."

Her mouth pops open. "You read them too?" *Finally, a reaction.*

I grin. "I've learned a thing or two from them."

Her face looks suspiciously like she's blushing, remembering our night together like I am, but she hides it with her hair. I pulled a few things out of those books.

"Dude," Gage exclaims. "That's fucking awesome. I have something you need to read," he says, jumping from the couch and jogging from the room.

Alessa watches him go. "You don't know what you just got yourself into."

Before she can elaborate, he rushes back into the room and thrusts a book into my hands with a hot, curvy redhead on the cover. "Read it. There are five books, and I stole them from Les. They're about these six dudes banging the same witch."

Alessa giggles. "Gage, they're about so much more than that."

"Oh, for sure," he nods. "The dudes bang each other too."

That causes her to laugh, and I can't get over the sweet sound. "They love each other is what I meant, you dumbass," she says between laughs.

He shrugs. "That too, but it's hot as fuck."

"I'll read it," I tell him with a chuckle.

It's not like I have anything better to do with my time.

Gage sits back on the couch, flipping through Netflix for something to watch. I wonder what exactly he does for her. Ryder and Dex are her muscle, Holden is her hacker, and Gage is...what? My brothers couldn't pinpoint what he does; they just said to watch my back around him.

Holden walks back into the room, handing her another folder. "They all check out," he informs her and disappears again.

What the hell is his deal?

She flips through the folder before pulling one out and handing it across the table to Gage.

"Bingo," he grins, handing it back.

She stands up. "I hate to tell you, but you are stuck with Ryder and Dex tonight for a while."

"I'll be fine," I assure her. I don't know whether that's a lie or not. I don't worry about Dex, no matter how big the man is, because he seems to respect whatever Alessa says. Ryder, on the other hand, I'm not so sure.

Gage jumps up and tosses her over his shoulder, running from the room with her laughing the whole way. Stuff like that is what makes me wonder about their relationship. They all seem to watch her in their own way. True, it's their job, but their eyes linger too long. It's killing me that she makes sure we aren't alone together. We dated for four months, and now she's avoiding me like the plague. Not that I blame her. I fucked up. When I realized I fell for her, I planned on telling her everything, but there was never a right time. Nothing like the right time being right after you shared your first time.

Dumbass.

Truthfully, I stalked the hell out of her on the internet after I met her that first night. Pictures of her and Gage are plastered everywhere, always looking like they are a couple but never confirming or denying it. I understand it's a cover, but some things you can't fake, like how he looks at her when he thinks no one is watching.

I'm not the jealous type, but she's mine. At least she was. I wish it didn't start the way it did, but there's no changing it now.

I will have to be patient and accept anything thrown my way.

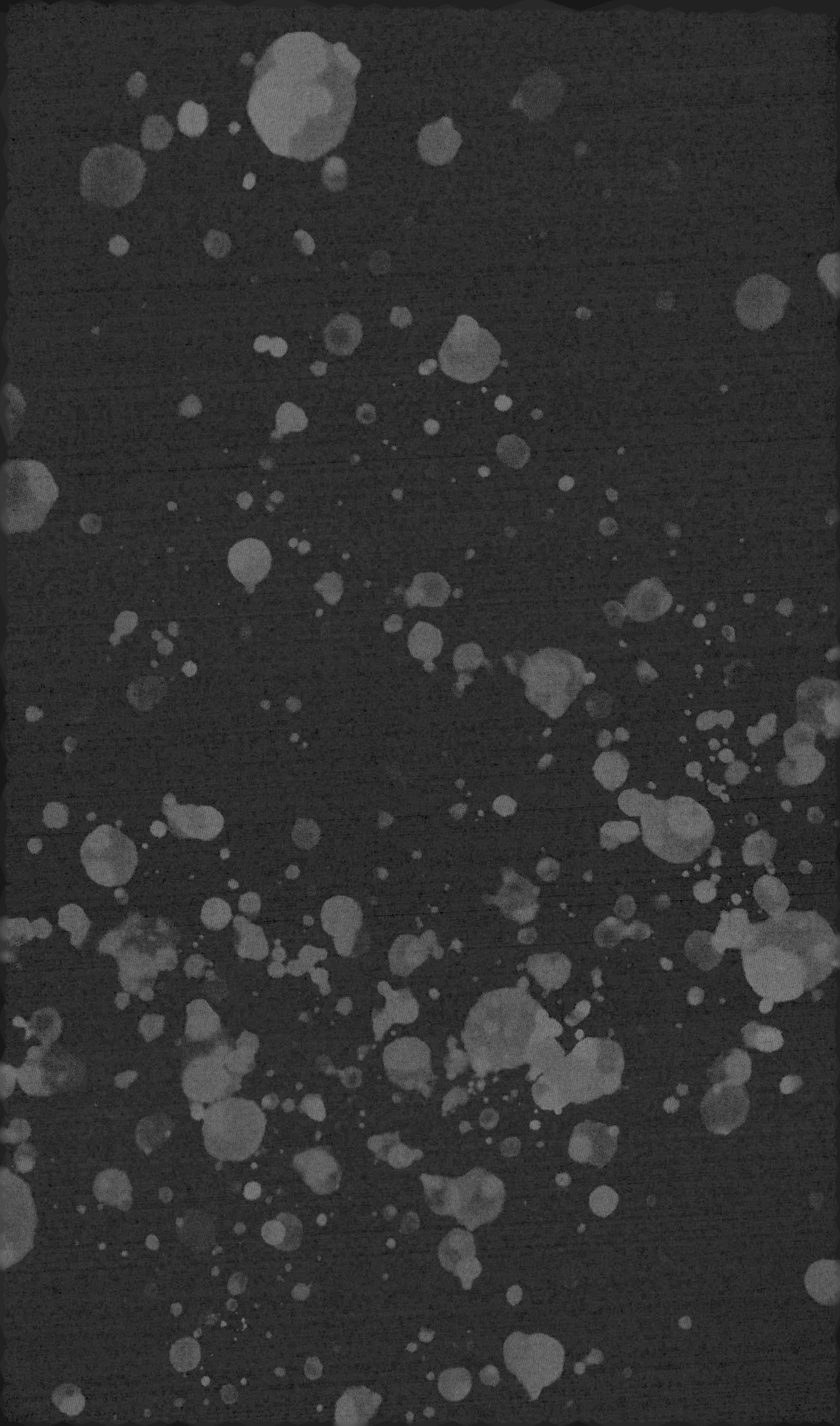

CHAPTER 5
GAGE

"Right there," Les announces, handing me binoculars. I look through them, and sure enough, it's her latest victim.

None of us let her go on these alone, even though she doesn't need us. It's her way of dealing with what happened to her, and who are we to judge? We aren't fucking saints.

"Let's go," she whispers from her perch on the roof across the street from Chadwick Wentworth's office. *What a douche name.* I read his profile in the car on the way over. Six counts of rape, including minors, acquitted of all of them, all because of his fucking name. If it wasn't such a risk, we would start going after these judges and lawyers who get these dirtbags off.

We scale down the building and disappear into the alley across the street, right where he has to walk by. We wait a few minutes before I hear him loudly talking on the phone, telling his wife that he loves her and would be home soon.

Piece of shit. I wonder if his wife knows he's a fucking liar.

I reach out and snag him, clamping my gloved hand over his mouth and jerk him into the alley. Les sticks his neck with the needle before he can react. "Nighty night," I whisper.

"Come on," she says as she heaves his legs. We carry him down the alley and unceremoniously dump him in the hatch of the stolen SUV.

We climb in, and Les pulls back onto the main road, ripping her mask off. Even though there's no chance they can catch us, we always stay covered, and Holden is at the house hacking the cameras, making any sign of us disappear.

Our masks are plain black with nothing painted on it, and it's creepy as hell. With our hoods up, it looks like we have no face in the dark.

Micah had the masks specially made for all of us. You can see and breathe out of them, and the eyeholes have night vision. They are cool as shit.

"Take your mask off," she laughs.

"No. I like it," I say, striking a pose before pulling it off.

"You're seriously more deranged than I am."

I scoff. "I'm not the one about to torture someone."

She shrugs. "Fair point, but you helped me grab him."

We pull into the garage at the house twenty minutes later. We go through the second hidden entrance so we don't have to drag this guy past Leo. No one else in the house asks questions; they know better. Mani, the head of Les' guards, will dispose of the car we stole to grab him.

We drag his unconscious ass into the basement and chain him to the chair. We only tie people who are a threat to the ceiling, and this guy isn't. We thought Leo was we grabbed him, but something about him screams innocent. He's lucky she has feelings for him, or he would have been dead without a second thought. I've seen her kill people for less.

Alessa strips her gloves off and peels off her black hoodie. Her shirt rides up, showing off her stomach's tanned, toned skin. I unglue my eyes before her head pops back out, so she doesn't see me staring.

There's no mistaking Alessa is gorgeous. She is thick in all the right places. Thick ass, thighs, and hips, but she still has serious muscle tone from lugging these assholes around and working out with us. Thanks to her dad and Micah, she can kill with her bare hands, and she never lets her size stop her from being the badass she is. I never have a chance in hell with her, though. She knows too much about who I am. I can charm the pants off any other girl or guy, literally. But not Alessa. Not that I've tried. Now she has Leo, even if that is up in the air. I've always looked at Alessa as more than a friend, but she never looked at me that way, keeping me firmly friend-zoned. I feel more of a pull toward her lately, urging me to try. I can't put my finger on it, but things are changing around here.

What would it hurt if I took my chance?

She waves an ammonia capsule under his nose. "Wakey wakey," she sing-songs. His eyes flutter open, and he immediately jerks his arms only to realize he's tied up.

"Who the fuck are you?" he demands. "Do you know who I am?!"

"I know exactly who you are," she answers, and I hand her his profile. "Chadwick Wentworth. Twenty-nine years old. Top prosecutor in Los Angeles. Married. Two kids." She snaps it shut. "Too bad you didn't prosecute yourself. Six counts of rape on minors. You walked away a free man."

"Because I didn't do it!"

She waves that away. "That's what they all say. DNA doesn't lie."

"That was dismissed in court!" he fumes. "Who the hell are you?" he asks again.

"Oh. How rude of me?!" Les exclaims, making me laugh. "I'm Alessa Poletti. That over there is Gage Lawson." I give him a little wave when he looks my way.

He narrows his eyes, then they widen. "You're that rich girl that flashes her tits for the paparazzi."

She leans close to his ear. "Better known as the Black Demon." I love when she lets that drop. They go from real brave to pissing their pants in seconds. "Stupid name, really," she continues. "They got one glimpse of me in my gear and ran with it." She walks over to her torture table, gliding her fingers over all the shiny knives before she snatches one up, pointing at Chadwick. "You know why you're here?"

He gulps, "But I have a wife and kids!"

"Exactly," she snaps, her whole playful demeanor changing. She is indeed a goddess.

Of death.

"I'm giving those kids peace of mind that you will *never* fucking touch them."

"I would never touch my kids!" he yells.

"So, you just like other people's kids, you fucking scumbag?" I ask.

I hear the door open, and Ryder steps in, leaning with his back against the closed door. I walk over and lean beside him.

Les slams her knife down on the table before picking up a wicked-looking dagger. She turns and launches it right into Chad's shoulder, causing him to scream so loud it echoes around the concrete walls.

"I will never get over her like this," Ryder says lowly. "It's like a different person when she comes down here."

"I know," I say happily. "It's great."

Ryder grunts, and I take that as an agreement.

Les walks over and runs her fingers over the blade's hilt before ripping it back out. He screams again, tears running down his face.

"I never know what goes through someone's mind when they decide to take another person's innocence," she says, trailing her hand over his shoulder as she walks behind him. She leans down beside his ear. "I've asked myself that question countless times since I was raped repeatedly for days." She rounds in front of him again. "At thirteen." She stabs him in the exact spot again. "The same age as the girls you took advantage of!" she yells over his screams. She twists, and his cry is cut short when he passes out.

"Well, that was fast," she comments, walking back to her table, picking up the ammonia capsule to wake him back up.

She walks back over, snapping the capsule under his nose; he wakes with a jolt. You can tell by the look in his eyes that he's hoping it was all a nightmare.

"Sorry to disappoint," I comment. "You are still here. About to die. Painfully."

"We have a winner. Ryder, tell him what he's won!" she announces into her knife like a microphone.

"A one-way ticket to Hell. With the rest of us," Ryder says dryly.

"I like to think us taking care of the real criminals atones for some of the other stuff," I defend.

"Real criminals?" Les laughs. "We *are* real criminals."

"We don't do that, though." I flap a hand at Chad, indicating what I meant.

"I hate to admit it, but he has a point," Ryder points out begrudgingly.

"Wait." Les' black eyebrows hit her equally black hairline. "Did you just agree with Gage?" She looks at me. "Hell has officially frozen over."

"Can we get back to the point here?" Ryder asks, pointing his finger at a blubbering Chad.

She shrugs. "Sure," she says before jamming the knife into his thigh, always missing the major arteries so he doesn't bleed out too fast.

I cringe at the scream. I wish she would gag these assholes, but she says she wants to relish in their misery. Good thing this room is soundproof. I have to give Micah points for creativity when he built this place for her.

"Where's Leo?" she asks, jerking the knife back out.

It always amazes me that she can have a normal conversation while she's torturing the fuck out of someone.

"Please stop," Chad begs, snot rolling down his face.

"Shut up," she barks, then looks back at Ryder, waiting for an answer.

"His room. Still alive." He looks away. "For now," he mutters under his breath.

"I heard that," she announces, and his head whips back to her. "If he dies, you start a war. Remember that."

"Why do we need this fucking alliance, anyway? The Perez's aren't worth a shit," he spits out.

"I won't deny that they used to be. But I'm willing to see how they are under new reign," Les says before walking back to her table, picking up her slicing knife, signaling this is almost over.

"Because of Leo," Ryder barks.

She turns to him with narrowed eyes. "I'm not one of these girls being led by my pussy. I can make adult decisions."

"You could have fooled me," He spits out, and I know it's the wrong thing to say.

Her eyes turn hard. "You have one more time, Ryder," she warns.

"Or what?" he bristles, standing up from the wall. "You going to kill your lifelong best friend for that asshole upstairs?"

"You have done nothing but question me since all this went down. I'm still your superior, whether you like it or not." Les walks over, jerking Chad's head back. "*Marciume all'inferno*," she says her signature line before slicing clean through his throat. She lets his head drop, and it hangs at an odd angle.

"I don't have a problem with you being my superior when you're making the right fucking decisions, Alessa. This isn't the right one."

I wish these two would fuck and get it all out of their systems. So much sexual tension pours from them in waves that it chokes you. Maybe they just need a push.

I am the man for the job.

She whirls around from the table she just laid her knife down on, her black hair fanning out behind her before stalking right into Ryder's space. "I can't wait for you to eat those fucking words. Until then. Back. The. Fuck. Off." She shoves him in the chest, and it catches him off guard making him smack the door behind him.

He jumps back up, towering over her. In her flat boots, he's almost a foot taller than her but she never even flinches, mostly because he would never lay a hand on her in anger. He would be dead before the hit even landed, anyway.

"Is this how it's going to be from now on?" he seethes.

"Like what?" she asks, frustrated.

"We are a team!" he bellows. "You made this decision on your own!"

"What would you have me do?" she yells back. My head is flipping back and forth between them like I'm watching a ping-pong match. *I wish I had some popcorn.* They've always had arguments, but it's gotten worse she started dating Leo."Kill him and start a fucking *war*!"

"If you weren't fucking him, he would have been dead already!"

She takes a step back like he punched her in the gut. I inwardly wince at the look she's giving him. "You're a fucking asshole, Ryder." She pushes by him, leaving the basement.

"That was an asshole move," I say, agreeing with her.

"Fuck!" he yells. "I know," he says softer.

"Go kiss and make up. I'll clean this up."

He jerks a nod and exits the basement.

When those two finally hook up, they will tear this house down. I chuckle to myself, cutting the ties holding Chad to the chair, letting him hit the floor, and his neck snaps almost clean off.

"It's me and you, Chad-O," I tell his corpse before setting out to dismember him to dispose of his body.

What a fucking life.

CHAPTER 6
ALESSA

What a fucking egotistical asshole.

I'm still fuming when I make it to my room. I scrub the blood from my hands and strip my jeans off. Killing Chadwick didn't even curb my anger. Who in the fuck does he think he is insinuating I'm being soft on Leo? I just don't want to start a fucking war.

Someone knocks at the door, and I jerk it open in nothing but my shirt and red panties. *Oops.*

Ryder's eyes snap down and snap back to my face. "Can we talk?" he asks with that muscle ticking in his jaw.

I motion for him to enter, shutting the door behind him. It's not the first time we've had a yelling match, and I'm sure it won't be the last.

He starts pacing, and I lean against the door, waiting for him to talk.

"I was out of line downstairs."

"You don't say," I remark sarcastically.

He whirls around. "Goddamnit, Les. I'm trying to apologize."

"If you weren't an asshole, you would have nothing to apologize for."

He runs both hands through his hair. "I'm fucking sorry. I shouldn't have said that."

"No, you shouldn't have," I remark.

"What is it about him?" Ryder asks, and I narrow my eyes. "I'm just trying to understand."

I walk over and go into my closet, pulling a pair of shorts off the shelf. I refuse to have this conversation with Ryder in my underwear. I pull them on before walking back into the room, getting comfortable on the bed, and leaning against my headboard. "I like him, Ryder," I tell him, even though it's more than that. I can't tell him I love Leo, or he will continue to accuse me of going easy on him. Honestly, I probably am. Anyone else would have been more than dead by now, but here he is, still alive and still in my house.

"Why? He just screams fragile as fuck."

I roll my eyes. "He doesn't."

"Why him? He's been lying to you for months, Les." Ryder slides onto the bed beside me, kicking his boots off.

"I'm well fucking aware of that, Ryder."

"I'm not saying it to rub salt in the wound," he sighs. "You could have any man you want."

I snort. "Who?"

"You're so dense sometimes," he says with a chuckle, but it sounds off. "All I'm saying is you don't need him."

One second, I'm looking at Ryder with a glare for calling me dense, and the next, his lips are sealing over mine. He uses my surprise to his advantage, pushing his tongue into my mouth. I place my hands on his chest to push him away but end up yanking him closer with fists in his shirt. The first touch of his lips is like electricity running through my body. He hooks an arm around my waist, pulling us both to a laying position on the bed, his body half over mine. I run my hands up his chest and around his neck, running my hands through his hair, pulling him closer. His mouth is magic against mine, pulling me into his kiss. Stroking my tongue with his, he braces a hand on the back of my head, holding me against his mouth just as hard as I'm holding him to mine. He shifts his body, settling between my thighs, rubbing his hard cock against my shorts covered pussy. He groans into my mouth when I push my hips up to meet his, and it's like a bucket of ice-cold water being dumped over my head. I finally gather myself and shove at his chest. He releases my mouth immediately and rolls over to the other side of the bed, staring at the ceiling.

I touch my lips, wondering what the hell just happened. This is *Ryder.* My best friend of twenty-five years. Hell, our birthdays are a month apart, his in February, mine in March. We never crossed that line. Until now.

"You can't tell me you didn't feel that," he says.

I shake my head in denial because I did feel that, but I also feel guilty. I just told Leo I loved him, and he's lying in the room below us while I'm making out with someone else.

"We can't, Ryder," I whisper.

"Because of him?" he retorts.

"Because I won't ruin our friendship."

He jumps off the bed, scooping his boots out of the floor. "One of these days, you will open those pretty blue eyes to the truth." He strides out of the room, leaving me to figure out his cryptic remark.

The truth? What truth? With that rolling through my head, I jerk my shorts off, slide my bra off through my shirt, slinging it across the room. I settle into bed, and all I can smell is Ryder, his cologne, and that woodsy scent that follows him around. *Ugh!* Why the hell did he have to kiss me? What the hell even was that?

I punch the pillow, trying to get comfortable.I can still feel how his lips move over mine, and how his body felt pressed against me.

"Oh my god," I groan into the pillow, not wanting to admit how much that little bit of contact made me want more.

When I finally fall asleep, it's full of dreams of Ryder and Leo.

"You look like shit," Gage remarks from the passenger side of my BMW.

"Fuck off," I grumble.

I woke up in a shitty mood because of Ryder kissing me, and I didn't sleep for crap. We won't even talk about the dreams that would wake me from a dead sleep, moaning. I took care of myself twice throughout the night because of those damn dreams. Each time I woke up, I almost found one of them to take care of it for me. I made it to the door once ready to find Ryder and demand he finish what he started. Luckily, I talked myself out of it before I went to find him. Now it's eight in the morning, on a Monday at that. It's mid-June here, and it is too hot for this shit. Fucking hell, my mood is turning dark, fast.

We are on our way to one of our clubs, Club Maximus, to do some administrative work. I hate every second of it, but it's how these places run as well as they do. It's one of the biggest clubs I own. It's in an old warehouse, so we have a lot of space for two bars, two dance floors, lots of seating, a DJ, and my newest addition soon is going to be dancers. People line up for miles to get in any day of the week.

He chuckles. "What's your problem?"

"Ryder. Ryder is my fucking problem," I snap and then take a deep breath. It wasn't Gage's fault. "He's an asshole."

"I thought he came up to apologize last night," he says with a frown over his mirrored sunglasses.

"He apologized, all right," I reply. *With his tongue down my throat.*

"Okay," Gage says slowly. "Then what's wrong?"

I whip into the club's back parking lot and push my oversized sunglasses up on my head, shoving the car into park. "He kissed me."

Gage's mouth drops open, and he pulls his sunglasses off. "Fucking finally."

"What do you mean, finally?" I ask, shocked.

"Come on. There is so much sexual tension around you two, and it's not even fucking funny." I narrow my eyes at him and push my door open. I stride to the building, Gage right on my heels, laughing. "You don't see it, do you?"

"See what, Gage?" I ask without turning around. I key in the code for the backdoor, and when the lock pops, I swing it open. "There's nothing to see."

I keep walking down the long hallway that leads to the offices. The only door on the other wall is the back entrance to the club. This part is for employees only. I unlock the door to my office, shutting it behind Gage. I take my place behind the desk, and he drops into a chair in front of me.

"You're a smart woman, Les." He sits forward in his chair. "You can't tell me you've never thought about kissing him."

I throw my hands in the air. "Of course I have. When we were both hormonal teenagers around each other twenty-four seven. We aren't teenagers anymore."

"No, you're two consenting adults fighting your attraction to each other like toddlers," he retorts.

"Do you want to get shot in the face today?" I threaten. That's the second time he's said something smartass in the past five minutes.

He snorts, "You wouldn't shoot me. What's holding you back?"

I sit back in my chair with a sigh. He isn't going to let this go. "Twenty-five years of friendship." I swallow. "Leo."

He waves his hand in the air. "If anyone can make a relationship work and keep the friendship intact, it's you and Ryder." He sinks back in his chair with a thoughtful look, and I'm immediately suspicious. "As for Leo, do you still want to be with him?"

"I don't know," I say miserably. "I love him, Gage," I whisper.

He shrugs. "Duh, or he would be dead." Sometimes, I do want to shoot him. "What if you didn't have to choose?"

"This isn't a book, Gage, and it doesn't work that way in real life."

"Why?" he asks, looking genuinely confused.

Is he fucking with me?

"For one, there is no way in hell Ryder is the sharing type." I open my laptop. "This conversation is done. I'm not doing this with you."

He gets up from his chair, striding to the door. He pulls it open. "I never took you for a coward, Les." With that parting shot, he shuts the door behind him, leaving me gaping at the door.

A coward? How does wanting to save my friendship with Ryder make me a coward?

Pushing everything out of my head, I get to work. I don't want to be here all day. No matter how hard I try, my mind keeps returning to what Gage said. We can't have that type of relationship. Can we? Do I even want a relationship with Ryder? Do I even want to stay in one with Leo?

"Fuck you, Gage Murphy Lawson," I mutter. "Fuck you for putting this shit in my head."

He just has to add to it like I don't have enough going on. I've have three guys I thought I could be serious with in my life. It started with Dex until all that went up in smoke, then there was Zane until I found out he was a traitor, and now Leo, who I just found out had been lying to me for months. I didn't have a stellar track record with relationships. It would eventually blow up in my face, and I would lose my best friend. Right?

It isn't unknown in the Mafia world for a family of mostly men to share a woman; it happens more than you think. Polyamorous relationships are common for made families, like the one I have with the guys. None of us are related by blood, but they are still my family.

Two hours fly by before Gage cautiously sticks his head back in. "Do you have weapons?"

"Step into the room and find out."

He walks in with a grin, popping them damn dimples out. "You wouldn't hurt me." He falls into the chair with a sigh. "I'm bored."

"Go flirt with one of the girls," I tell him, gesturing towards where my bar manager, Gia, and one of my bartenders, Katie, are taking stock.

He wrinkles his nose. "Not feeling it."

I clutch my chest. "Gage, isn't feeling flirty?" I lean up on the desk. "Are you okay? Did they turn you down?"

"I don't get turned down."

"You did, didn't you?" I laugh.

"No." He stands up and rounds the desk behind me, leaning down beside my ear. "I said I don't get turned down. I just don't want to flirt with them. I have someone else in mind."

I roll my eyes, even though he can't see me. "Okay. Go find them, then."

He places his hands on the arms of my chair, bringing him even closer. "I did," he whispers in my ear.

I jerk my head over my shoulder to look at him. *Wrong move.* It puts my lips within kissing distance of his. They're so close that if I lick my lips, I will touch his. His eyes shoot to my lips and then back to my face.

"What are you doing?" I ask huskily. *Why does my voice sound like that?*

He spins my chair to face him, bracing his hands back on the arms of the chair. Mine are locked in my lap. "You told me to go find someone I want to flirt with, and that's what I'm doing." He leans down and runs his nose up my neck, under my hair.

Gage flirts shamelessly with everyone, me included, but never like this.

"You smell so good," he groans.

"Why are you fucking with me?" I whisper. It's just cruel after what he put in my head and then doing this, *knowing* what happened with Ryder.

"I'm not fucking with you, Pretty girl," he murmurs against my neck, kissing where my pulse is beating wildly out of control. *Pretty girl?* "When I said you didn't have to choose, I meant me too." I know I should push him away, but something holds me still.

Okay, he has to be fucking with me now.

"You feel that?" he kisses my pulse point again. "Your heart hammering out of control? Mine's doing the same thing." He jerks my hand from my lap and presses it against his fast-beating heart. "That's what it does when you walk into a room."

"Stop," I whisper, closing my eyes, blocking out his hypnotizing ice-blue eyes.

"Why?" he whispers in my ear, making me shiver. "I've wanted this for years. I want to know how those lips feel against mine, how soft your naked skin is sliding against me, how good you smell this close." He inhales into my hair, still whispering into my ear. "How good that pussy tastes."

My breath hitches, and I can't gather a train of thought. It's like he has me under a spell with his husky voice whispering into my ear. What is wrong with me?

"Why now?" I ask. Why would he tell me this after he knows about Leo and when he knows about Ryder?

"Because you're finally ready. You opened yourself up for Leo. Let me show you what else you can have now." He kisses my neck again. "You can have it all, Pretty girl. Leo, Ryder, me, Dex, Holden."

I jerk back. "What?"

He chuckles, and it comes out deep and husky. "We're already family, Les, and you can't tell me you've never seen one of us looking just a little too long." He runs his nose up my neck again. "Or maybe you looking at us a little too long."

I shake my head because I haven't. Am I that oblivious to what is going on in my house?

"Hm," he hums, running his nose up and down my neck, causing goosebumps to pop up on my skin. "Well, we do. Let us give you the world, Pretty girl."

"It will never work," I whisper, still under his spell.

"Yes. It will," he answers adamantly, then groans. "Please let me kiss you now. I've dreamed about this."

Too caught up in the moment to deny him, I pull back and kiss him instead. He doesn't hesitate to accept the kiss. He jerks me to my feet, burying his hands in my hair. I'm just in my pink Converse today, so he has to bend his six-two frame over me, but he presses it to his advantage, bending my neck back and taking over my mouth.

I run my hands up his sides, under his arms, and down his back, causing his whole body to shudder from my touch. He slides his hands down to my ass, running his fingertips across the bottom of my ass cheeks poking out from my jean shorts. He grips it, lifting me smoothly off my feet. He kicks the office chair out of the way and sits me on the desk, stepping between my thighs, never breaking the kiss. He sinks his hands back into my hair, holding the sides of my head. His tongue glides smoothly over mine, and if I thought that his voice is hypnotizing, it has nothing on his lips on mine. I can feel how wet I'm getting just from a kiss, my clit pulsing in time with my heart. What is going on?

He pulls back and lays his forehead on mine. "Fuck," he whispers, pecking my lips again.

"You guys have to stop kissing me," I say breathlessly, and he laughs in my face.

"I don't think we do." He pecks my lips like he can't get enough. "Because your mind might be saying one thing." He pecks my lips again. "But your body is saying another." He deepens the kiss, and my body responds instantly, craving his touch.

Can what he's saying be true? Do they see me as more than their friend and boss? Do I see them as more?

Gage jerks my hips to the edge of the desk, rubbing his hard cock against my pussy through my shorts. "Shit," I moan, rocking my hips.

"See? Your body wants it," Gage says huskily, just as affected as me. He sinks into the kiss, rocking his hips. I want to rip his clothes off and see what Gage is made of.

"Alessa, we need...oh. Shit. Sorry," Gia, my bar manager, stutters out before slamming the door behind her. I didn't even hear her come in.

Fuck.

I groan. "Please tell me that did not just happen."

"It did," Gage chuckles and takes a step back. I want to jerk him to me to finish this, but I also know I need a minute to process. He rubs his knuckles down my cheek. "When your mind gets on board with your body, just know we can make this work."

He kisses me on the forehead before leaving the office, softly shutting the door behind him. I lay back on the desk with a groan, letting my mind run wild. He left the decision in my hands now that he also threw his hat into the ring.

Why now? Why would he bring this up once I was involved with Leo? He's had *years* to say something, and so has Ryder. But they both waited until I'm...whatever I am with Leo.

Just the thought of his name brings so much guilt I can barely swallow, but then comes anger because he lied to me. There's no denying I love him, but if I truly love him, would I be able to kiss Ryder and Gage? Is Gage right about Dex and Holden too? I need to think about this rationally.

Ryder is my best friend. We know each other inside and out. He is my go-to for advice or someone to talk to. We *never* crossed that line until last night. I can't deny how my body responded to him, begging him to take it further. Truthfully, the only thing that stopped me was Leo.

Gage came into my life when he was ten, and I was eleven. He had an instant connection with Ryder and me. Gage is my person when I need to laugh or just do something stupid to let go. People underestimate Gage because he's cracking jokes or goofing off, but I see the real him. The guy that will do anything for anyone he cares about without a second thought.

Dex was one of my dad's lower guys when he first appeared. When I met him, I was seventeen, and something about his grey eyes drew me in. He was open, easy to laugh, and quick to smile. After Perez's guys grabbed him the night he got the scars, he changed. He barely talks and can't stand to be touched. He's my voice of reason, the one I can go to, and we can have a rational discussion to figure out pretty much anything. He's also the one who pushed me away all those years ago.

Holden can't even look me in the eye for more than two seconds. I don't know what happened to him for the four years he was locked in that room, but I know it's not good. He was emaciated, bruised, and scared of every sound. Until four months ago, he didn't even leave his office unless he was going to bed. We took all his meals in there until Ryder put his foot down one day and made him eat with us. He's done it ever since. I can count on him for any information I need, and he never asks questions. He will just go to his office, and I have what I need within hours.

And Leo, I don't even know where to start. I couldn't get him off my mind. What we shared these past four months went up in smoke when I found out he was a Perez, and I'm still not sure if I can trust him. Why hasn't he tried to get away? Can I trust Evander and

Mateo? Leo is the epitome of the perfect boyfriend. He is understanding, affectionate, a good listener, and he spoils me to no end.

"Fuck," I groan, sitting back up on the desk. I wasn't getting anything else done today.

I am going to find Gage and kick his ass for filling my head with this shit.

Then I'll find Ryder.

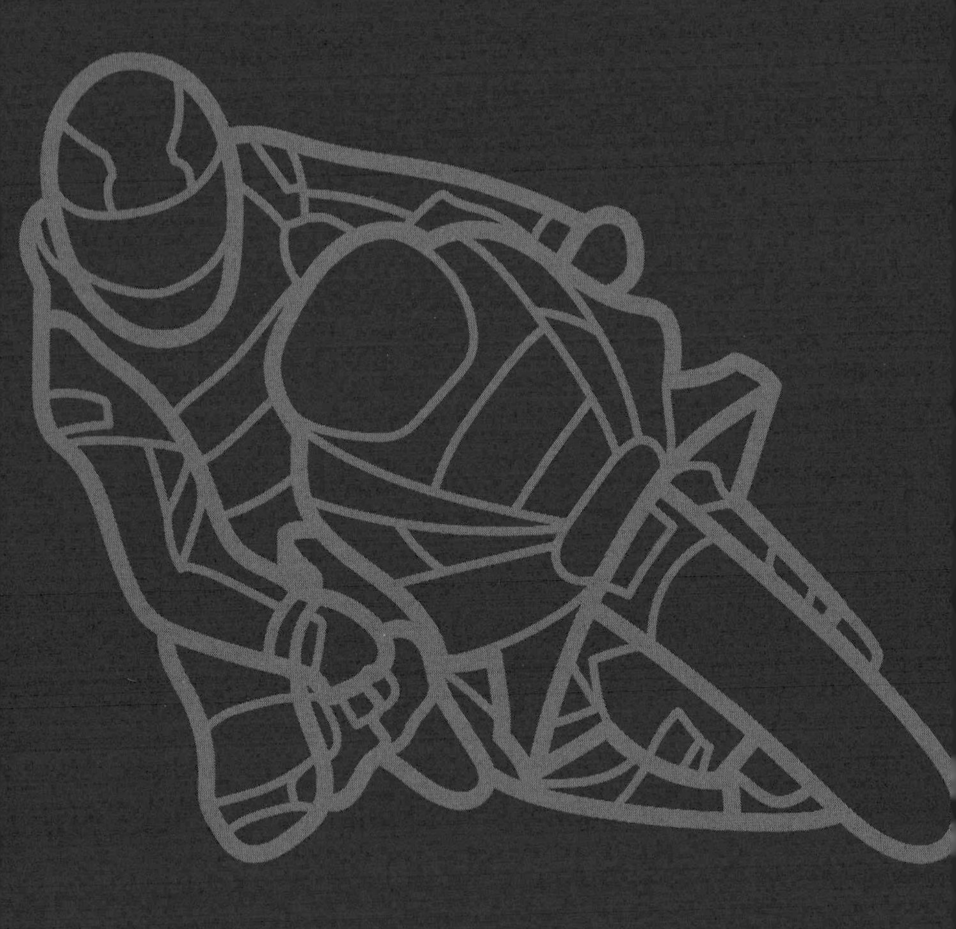

CHAPTER 7
RYDER

I finally kissed Les. She was responding beautifully, and then I felt the moment she froze. Bad timing on my part? Probably. I've harbored a crush on her since we were young, but I never wanted to step over that line and lose years of friendship. I've sat back and watched her run through every guy for random hookups, finding my own to pass the time, listened to her talking about it in *detail* to Gage, watched her back, made sure she never got outed as The Black Demon, and the list goes on. Always the best friend, Ryder.

The Ryder, who's been in love with his best friend and couldn't tell her.

I thought Leo would be the same. She would hook up with him once and be done. But then she saw him again, and I knew something was different. I've sat back for four fucking months watching her get closer and closer to him, and then this motherfucker betrays her. I would have put a bullet between his goddamn eyes at the beach house if it wasn't for her. Instead, this prick is locked up in this house. The only peace I have is that she hasn't been near him. I see the sad as fuck looks she gives him, but she won't be alone with him.

I wanted to talk to her, but she was gone by the time I got done in the gym, taking off with Gage, leaving me with babysitting duty again. At least he stayed out of my fucking hair by staying in his room.

I hear the door open from the garage behind me from my seat at the kitchen island and can't help looking over my shoulder.

"You're clinically insane. You know that, right?" she asks Gage, kicking her shoes off.

"You still haven't given me a good reason why it wouldn't work," he says, kicking his own off. "Think of the possibilities."

"Yeah, the possibility of one of you killing..." she stops mid-sentence, stopping in her tracks when she rounds the corner and sees me sitting there.

Gage plows right into her. "Damn, Les, if you want me to feel your ass, all you have to do is ask," he says, running his hands down her thick hips.

She elbows him in the stomach, making him grunt. "Go away. I'm done dealing with you today."

I can feel my blood boil just from seeing his hands all over her. He finally looks up, gives me one of those signature Gage grins, and strolls out of the room, but not before he slaps her right on the ass.

She walks over to the fridge and yanks the door open. She grabs a bottle of water and drains half of it before finally looking me in the eye. "We need to talk," she declares before walking out of the room toward the back of the house.

I pinch the bridge of my nose. I know that look. She's about to tear me a new asshole. I slide off my stool and follow the way she went like the whipped fucking lap dog everyone thinks I am. I find her sitting on the back patio beside the pool, her feet swinging back and forth in the water.

I sit down beside her and slide my feet in. She doesn't look at me when I sit down, and I hate that I might have fucked this up with her.

"Why now?" she asks finally.

"Why not now?"

She finally looks at me. "Don't do that. Don't give me some flippant response instead of the truth."

I scrub a hand down my face. This is where I need to be careful about what I say. I don't want to lie to her, but I can't come out and tell her I fucking love her. "I thought I lost my chance when you started seeing Leo. I felt the pull, so I fucking went with it."

"Twenty-five years, Ryder. Twenty-five fucking years, you've had your chance, and you choose the moment after someone I care about hurts me to take it."

"You didn't seem to mind it," I remind her, which is the wrong thing to say.

"Are you kidding me?" She jabs a finger at me. "You surprised me."

"Come on, Les. You didn't feel anything?" I say, looking her in the eyes, trying to get a read on her emotions, but she has that infamous mask in place, her face carefully blank.

She throws her hands up. "I don't know what I felt, okay? One minute I'm talking to my best friend, and the next, he has his tongue down my throat."

God, I want to kiss her, kiss that confusion off her face, until she can't think about anything but me. But I feel if I try this time, she will kick my ass.

I lean back on my hands. "It was bad timing, but I won't apologize for doing it. I've wanted to kiss you for far too long to take it back now."

"Why is everyone suddenly going crazy?" she asks, but it's more like she's talking to herself.

"What do you mean?"

She shakes her head. "Nothing. Just something Gage said."

"What did he say?" I ask.

"Doesn't matter," she snorts.

She's up and walking toward the door before I even register she's moved, too lost trying to figure out what she's talking about.

I jump up, and two long strides has me grabbing her arm and spinning her toward me. She launches herself at me, and at first, I think I will have to defend myself, but then her lips are on mine.

Holy fuck.

My surprise lasts less than a second before I hook my hands under her thighs, wrapping them around my waist. I wrap my arm around her waist and use the other to find the side of the house. The moment I feel it, I press her against it, molding our bodies together. I use the wall to steady her so I can have my hands. I run one up into her hair, tangling the strands around my fingers. I pull slightly to tilt her head the way I want it so I can control the kiss. She moans into my mouth, and I almost fucking lose it. I run my other hand under the back of her shirt at her waist to feel her soft skin.

Finally.

I could yell it from the rooftops. Finally, Les is mine. I can feel it in this kiss, her hands roaming all over my back, her hips rocking on my cock. She. Is. *Mine.*

I don't know how long we kiss before we both pull back breathless. I lay my forehead against hers, untangling my hand from her black hair. I run my knuckles down her cheek, getting lost in those blue eyes.

"You felt it," I whisper, afraid to talk louder and break the moment.

She grips my cheeks, legs still wrapped around my waist. "Yes," she whispers back. "But it's not that simple."

How is it not simple?

"We can make it work, Les. Trust me."

"I do trust you, Ryder. With my life," she sighs. "It has nothing to do with trust."

I pull my head back. "What does it have to do with then?"

"There's Leo." She swallows. "And Gage. I feel it with them, too."

I step back and let her feet touch the ground. "You kissed Gage?" I growl. What the fuck? Did I imagine everything I just felt between us? Why the fuck would she kiss me like that?

She reaches out to me, but I jerk back. She drops her hand with hurt in her eyes. I yank the patio door open and slam it shut behind me. Where is that motherfucker?

The motherfucker in question is at the kitchen island. He turns when he hears me storming toward him and jumps up. He smoothly slides across the island, landing on his feet on the other side, putting it between us. I go to round it.

"Wait!" he yells, but I swear the little asshole is trying not to laugh. "Why do you look like you're going to kill me?"

"You kissed Alessa," I hiss.

He rolls his eyes. "So did you."

I round to one side, and he moves the other way, keeping the island between us. "This isn't a game, Gage."

All teasing drops from his face. "This isn't a fucking game to me, asshole, and if you opened your eyes, you would see what's happening."

"All I see is you pushing in on Les now that Leo is about to be out of the picture."

He laughs loudly. "Bro, are you blind? He's not going anywhere."

I narrow my eyes. "Then why the fuck would you kiss her? I know why I did."

"Because I fucking can." He braces his hands on the island. "Just like you can, or Leo. As long as she wants it."

I fake going one way but move the other; he anticipates it and is still firmly across the island from me. *Fucker is fast.* "She doesn't know what she wants." Why else would she be kissing all of us?

"Yes, she does. She just has to admit it to herself."

"Would you stop talking in riddles?" I grit out. Sometimes he's the most complicated person to talk to, his mind always going fifty different directions.

"Would you stop being a fucking idiot?" he retorts. I bare my teeth, and he just grins. "You'll figure it out. I'm not spelling it out for you."

He steps out to walk away, and I take my chance. I hook my arm around his neck in a chokehold. "Watch it, big boy. I like it rough," he wheezes out.

"What the hell are you two doing?" Dex asks, walking into the kitchen.

"He's trying to kill me," Gage laughs weakly.

"You want to tell him why?" I ask, then squeeze harder.

He moves so fast I don't see him before he slams an elbow into my gut, using my pain to spin out of the chokehold. *Asshole.*

He takes a step backward, away from me. "I kissed Les," Gage answers, causing Dex to raise both brows. Gage points at me. "So did he."

Dex frowns and crosses his arms across his chest. "Let me get this straight. You kissed her too, but he is going to die for it?"

"It's not the same thing," I argue.

"Why?" Dex asks, genuinely confused. "I've kissed her before. You going to kill me?"

"That was a long time ago." I wave that away. I remember their brief fling; it was eight years ago.

"Whoa," Gage throws in. "When did you kiss her?"

Dex shrugs. "Years ago."

Gage grins, and it looks purely evil. "Fantastic." I could practically see the wheels running in his head. What the hell is he up to?

"How the hell is that fantastic?!" I yell. I can't help it; he's pushing every button I have.

"You'll find out." He gives me another toothy grin before disappearing from the kitchen.

Dex ambles over to the island before leaning against it. "What's going on?"

I run my hand through my hair. "I don't know."

He shakes his head. "Don't you think you should figure that out before you bring this onto Les?"

"Fuck." I throw my arms in the air. "I want her, man."

"So does Gage, apparently. How is that going to play out?" He tilts his head to the side. "Then there's Leo."

"Fuck him," I say harshly. "He'll be gone soon."

Dex chuckles. "Looks like to me he's right down the hallway where Les wants him." He pushes off the island. "Because if she wanted him gone, he would be."

I watch him walk out of the kitchen, leaving me more confused than before Les said we needed to talk.

Why did I have to choose now to come to terms with my fucking feelings? And why the fuck is she kissing Gage? He flirts with her all the time. It's just how he is, but he's never shown any interest in her other than that. Or did he, and was I just too blind to see it?

I can't even pinpoint when I fell in love with her because I'm pretty sure I always have been. I was just too young to understand the feelings; then, one day, I woke up realizing Les was the only girl for me. I found girls to pass the time until Les was ready, but they were always just placeholders if I kept them around for more than a night. It was like an unspoken rule between us that we never brought anyone into the main house since we all had our hideaways for when we just needed time to ourselves.

I wander through the house until I end up in my room. I lay back on my bed, put my arms behind my head, and stare at the ceiling. I have a ton of shit to do today, but I can't find it in me to leave, knowing Leo is right down the hallway.

Les might be the boss, but we all have certain things we do to help her out, so she isn't doing it alone.

I find my mind wandering back to both of those kisses and can't shake the feeling that she is fighting what she's feeling for me. She was honest with me downstairs and told me she felt what I felt, but she also said the same about Leo and Gage. I think about the moment Gage ran his hands over her hips, trying to imagine what it would be like if we did share, and immediately throw that idea away. I could feel my blood boiling from just the fucking thought. There is no fucking way I can stand by and watch her being touched by someone else or being brought to pleasure by someone else's hands.

I have never had any complaints when I took a girl to bed, so I *know* I could be enough for her. I just have to convince her of that. I just need one time with her, and she would be mine. I can feel it in my very soul that I'm meant to be with Les.

Good people don't come around often in this life, so you hold onto them for dear life when they do. That's how we ended up with the team we have. I was convinced she would kill Leo after talking to his brothers, but all that seemed to do was harden her resolve to keep him alive.

I hated Evander and Mateo on principle for what their father did to her, but even I can admit that they didn't know shit. They were as shocked as Leo that Frankie had Les kidnapped at fucking thirteen years old to teach Luca a lesson. I didn't get a vibe from them that they were being dishonest, so it was even harder for me to get rid of Leo.

I could kill him and deal with her anger. She would eventually get over it. Right? Even as that idea pops up, I dismiss it. She would make my life a living hell if I stepped out of line. I might not always agree with her on some things, like this shit with Leo, but I truly trust Les to lead us in the right direction. I know she doubts herself sometimes, but I wish she could see what I see.

She may be the leader of one of the most ruthless crime families, but she never lost her heart. Her dad was the same way. He ruled with an iron fist when you got out of line; he also tried to save as many innocent people as he could. Luca was like a second father to me. When he died, it was like losing my own. I have a close relationship with my dad, and I can't imagine life without him. I didn't want him to retire, but it gave me peace knowing he was no longer in danger all the fucking time.

Sighing, I finally roll off my bed and head toward the stairs. Lying around isn't getting shit done.

CHAPTER 8
HOLDEN

I'm just putting some finishing touches on Alessa's new security when I hear a knock at the door.

"Come in," I call out.

I hear the door open and don't look up, thinking it's probably Ryder. He's the only one who comes in here to hang out. Then her sweet vanilla scent hits me, and my head whips up and I drop my eyes just as fast. It's fucking sad that I still can't even look her in the eyes.

"What are you up to?" she asks, sitting in the chair beside mine. She puts her bare feet on the edge of the desk, and I have to force myself to stop looking at her legs.

"I'm working on your security," I mumble and mentally slap myself. A whole year and she still intimidates the shit out of me. Not because I'm scared of her, she's been nothing but nice to me; it's because she's gorgeous.

"Oh," she replies, laying her head back on the chair. "Can I hang out in here while you work? Everyone else out there is fucking nuts."

"Sure." There's no way I can work with her this close. Her arm is so close that if I move, my arm rubs hers.

"Can I see your file on Leo?"

I reach over and hand it to her. She flips it open, giving me the chance to look at her profile. Her long black hair is hanging down her back, and I want to reach out and see if it's as soft as it looks. It's so black that it looks almost blue when the light hits it. Her cute button nose is scrunched while she's reading, and she's biting her bottom lip in concentration. I want to sink my teeth into it to see what it tastes like.

Whoa.

I jerk my head back to my computer and pretend to be working.

I worked hard on that file for her, just like I do everything, but that folder holds a lot more important information. I don't know Leo, but I hear them talking around the house since she's been seeing him. Who would ever lie to a girl like her? I can't figure it out. If you have a girl like that, you don't lie to her or do *anything* to hurt her.

She sighs and closes the folder. I want to ask her what's wrong, but that part of my brain doesn't function anymore. I can't form many words in her presence unless it's work-related.

A year ago, I was locked in a corner bedroom, fed one meal daily, and given energy drinks and beef sticks any other time. I worked nonstop for a piece of shit. Then this black-haired angel busts into the room and tells everyone with her not to touch me. She got me out, got me medical attention, and gave me food, clothes, and a place to stay. In return, she asks very little of me.

She knows I was hacking her by his command. But she doesn't know that I was laying a trail right back to me so she would finally find me and kill me. I knew who she was from conversations around that shithole of a house, so I made the plan hoping she would put me out of my misery, but she gave me my life back—sort of.

I'm free to go whenever I want, but I want to stay and help her. I wish I could offer her more than the broken man I've become. I can hold an entire conversation with the guys with no problem, but one look from those blue eyes and I lose all train of thought.

"You really didn't find anything on him?" she asks, breaking me from my thoughts. Does she want me to find something wrong?

"No. He was with his mom. She's an elementary school teacher, and he worked for a company that helped save restaurants from failing. Then about a year ago, Evander contacted him after discovering they had a brother. You know what happened from there."

"Why would an elementary school teacher get involved with someone like Frankie Perez?" I don't miss how her voice breaks when she says his name. I know there's history.I just don't know the full story.

I shrug. "People hide their true colors all the time."

"Don't I know it," she mutters cryptically, then sighs. "Have you found anything on Evander or Mateo?"

I hand her another folder. "They check out too. They dispatched or killed almost all of Frankie's men before finding their own. They closed his seedy businesses and focused more on the bigger ones. They've been mostly quiet."

"Where's their mom? What was her name?"

"Rhonda," I answer. "Dead."

"Good riddance. She was as bad as Frankie."

She lapses back in silence, slightly spinning the computer chair. Every time she turns my way, her leg brushes my arm.. I swallow back the panic to stop myself from jerking my arm away. I don't want to hurt her feelings, thinking I'm disgusted by her touch; it's the exact opposite.

"Do you want to go on a drive with me?"

I whip my head to her. "What?"

She smiles softly. "I have a place I've been wanting to show you. Come with me?" I nod on autopilot because I've never been able to tell her no. "Meet me in the garage in ten minutes." I nod again, and she leaves the room, leaving her smell lingering behind her.

What the hell? She doesn't ask me to go anywhere with her because she knows I prefer to stay home. Ryder makes me go out. Not that I mind going anywhere with him; he's become one of my closest friends. But her?

I can feel my anxiety creeping to an all-time high.

Get your shit together, Holden.

I find every bit of courage I can to gather myself enough to leave this room. It might sound weird after being locked up all that time, but it's my safe place. I have my bedroom upstairs and my office; both places are where I feel the best.

When I first moved into this house, the size scared the shit out of me. I was always waiting for something to jump out of the corner, but the longer I stayed, the more at ease I became. Ryder took care of me physically the first night we got here, sensing I would feel more comfortable around a man than Alessa. Gage was the first to start joking around with me instead of tiptoeing around, and I've never felt more grateful for his crazy ass. Dex always made me feel safe because nothing was getting past that man.

Alessa was like the sun after a bad storm. I knew she carried her demons. They all did, but she kept mine at bay. The nightmares would still creep up when I least expected them, but they got further and farther between until I could finally sleep all night long without waking up in cold sweats and screaming. I tried not to think about what happened when I was with those guys, but sometimes my mind would conjure up a memory that almost made me run for the fucking hills.

These guys took me in like it wasn't even a question. They accepted that I needed help and did just that. I would never be able to repay them for what they've done for me, so I work my ass off on whatever they need.

Les' security measures were outdated whenever I moved in, so I spent the first few months making sure they were locked up tighter than Fort Knox. Nothing was getting by them without me knowing. After that, she started giving me jobs, but nothing to overwhelm me or make me uncomfortable.

Knowing I'm stalling, I make my way slowly to the garage. I can't help the fear that settles into my stomach that I have done something wrong, and she is about to take me out of this world.

CHAPTER 9
ALESSA

I don't know what possessed me to ask Holden to go with me today, but it just felt right after what Gage said to me. I need something to break him out of his shell and make him more comfortable around me. Not the guy who is currently as close to the passenger side door of my BMW as he can get.

I'm taking him to one of my favorite places with a motive.

Pulling out of the garage, I take the back exit from the estate we use so paparazzi don't spot us. Micah talked my dad into installing it when people started noticing us and would sit at the end of the driveway waiting for us to leave.

It's about a forty-five-minute drive to where we're going and on a rural road on the outskirts of Abbs Valley, where we live, so it gives me time to think. Holden doesn't require constant conversation; he doesn't require any at all. He is content to stare out the window.

My conversation with Gage is a constant buzz in my head. He made me admit what I wanted, even if it was just to myself. Now that Ryder and I have swerved past the line of friendship, he acts differently. Jealous. I feel like our friendship is crumbling at its very foundation. I knew he had girls throughout his life, and he knew I had guys, but he never acted jealous of them until Leo.

Leo is a different problem within itself. I still haven't worked up the nerve to talk to him, just a few words in passing. I know I need to clear the air, at least for my own sake, but I've never been in this situation before. I sleep with guys. I don't date them. Now I have Leo, Ryder, and Gage vying for my attention, although Gage is the easiest of the three. It was easy as breathing when he kissed me in my office. I didn't feel like we were risking our friendship as I did with Ryder. Not because I'm not as close to Gage but because Gage is easier to read than Ryder. Ryder hides his emotions the same way I do, with a carefully placed mask. I'm finding it harder and harder to hide mine. I feel like I'm losing control.

Growing up with Ryder, he was everything to me, and I was everything to him. He was my protector, my date for dances, my shoulder to cry on, my video game buddy, and the one who used to scare the guys away in school. I was his cheerleader at football games, his voice of reason, the one who didn't take his shit, and the one girls were intimidated by because of my relationship with him. Now I feel like we are losing everything we built. People end up dating their best friends all the time. Could Ryder and I pull that off? I don't think we can when I'm still entertaining the idea of dating the other guys. Am I thinking about dating them? At this point, I have no fucking idea.

I take a right off the main road onto a long dirt road, and Holden finally looks up, staring out of the windshield. We travel the two miles before the wrought-iron gate finally comes into view, with my name hanging from the top. I enter the code, and the gate swings open, allowing us to enter. No sooner than I pull up in front of the cute ranch house, the woman who runs the ranch walks out, a huge smile on her weathered face.

"Alessa!" she crows as I step out of the car in her thick Italian accent, clasping my cheeks in her hands and kissing both sides.

"Hey, Marcella," I greet with a smile. It's been too long since I came out here.

Dad bought this farm from Marcella when her husband died, and she was about to lose it. Then he told her she could stay there and run it. When he died, I never changed much; this one was one of them.

"It's been too long," she chastises and then casts a glance at Holden, standing beside the car. "Who is this lovely young man?"

"Marcella, this is Holden." She raises an eyebrow as if asking if he is my boyfriend, and I shake my head.

"Nice to meet you, ma'am," Holden mumbles with a polite nod.

She prances over to him. "None of this ma'am nonsense. Call me Marcella." She kisses him the same way she kissed me. He returns the gesture with a shy smile, making my heart melt.

"I'll get Vincenzo to take you up," she offers, referring to my secret place.

"That's fine. We can walk it."

"It is such a lovely day. Come in when you get back. I made cupcakes." She spins on her heel, her loose colorful skirt swishing behind her, and heads back into the house.

Marcella is sixty years old and still looks like she's in her forties. The only things that give her away are the laugh lines that line her eyes and around her mouth, and her long black hair is streaked in grey. She lives here with her two sons, Vincenzo and Giovanni, with other ranch hands milling around. Marcella knows who we are but treats us like long-lost family.

"Come on," I beckon Holden with a smile and head to the back of the house.

We head through the back gate and down the little trail leading to where I want to go. We are silent on the walk, with it only being about a two-mile hike, and it still takes my breath away when we finally break through the trees.

It's a meadow that overlooks the field below, where you can watch the horses, goats, and cows graze. The bench my dad had built still stands in the little gazebo. The meadow is in full bloom with flowers I can't name, some wild, some Marcella planted and tended to.

"This reminds me of home," Holden says with wonder.

I lead him over to the bench, both of us breathing in the fresh air. "Texas?" I ask.

I know some of Holden's history, but a lot of it is still a mystery. He doesn't talk about his past.

"Yeah," his smile is sad, "before things went bad." He lapses into silence, and I know I need to tell him my story, hoping it might prompt him to talk to me.

I pull my feet onto the bench, hugging my knees to my chest. "I want to tell you my story." He whips his head towards me. "I know you've heard bits and pieces, but I want you to have a better understanding of me. I need you to know I understand what you're going through." I turn to face him. "I need you to know I would never hurt you like they did."

"I know," he says softly.

I look back at the field, trying to figure out where to start. This isn't easy for me to talk about, but I feel like Holden deserves to know. "As you know, I was born into the Poletti life. Generations after generations have run Abbs Valley and Los Angeles's underbelly, among other places. My mom and dad were good people, as good as you can be in the Mafia." I smile at that. No matter how good we are, we're still criminals. "My mom died in a car accident when I was young. I was old enough to remember her but still too young to have gotten a good life with her. She was beautiful. Long blond hair, tall, the prettiest green eyes, and one of the gentlest souls, and my dad was madly in love with her."

I still remember the stolen kisses and the dances around the house when they thought I wasn't watching. I knew if Mom could have had more kids, there would have been a horde of us. But complications from her pregnancy with me took that away from them. They loved me just as fiercely as they did each other, and I missed that so damn much. That was the type of love I had always dreamed of for myself. But I feel like that was robbed from me. Frankie took more than just my innocence that night.

"It broke him when she died, but he still did his best to raise me and run an empire. When I was old enough, he trained me in combat, knives, guns, anything so I could protect myself, along with Micah. With our age difference, he always felt more like a brother than an uncle."

I take a deep breath. This is where the story turned ugly. I don't want to gloss over it, but I also can't drag the story out. "When I was thirteen, I was out with my guards to meet Ryder and Gage, and someone ran a red light, smashing into the side of our SUV. That someone worked for Frankie Perez."

Holden's whole body is turned towards me, taking in every word. "They killed both guards and took me. I was locked up in a smelly old house for days where his men would rape, sodomize, and torture me for hours. All at the order of Frankie because my dad outbid him at a casino he wanted."

My voice cracks on the last word, and I can feel tears leaking down my cheeks without any recollection of when I started to cry. Holden places his hand on my knee without a word. It's the first time he's ever initiated contact. I lay my cheek on his hand, staring into his soulful brown eyes, seeing the pain on the surface. Pain for me and pain for whatever he went through.

"When my dad found me, I was covered in blood and completely shut down. I ran into a place in my mind and hid, trying to block out what was happening. It took a while for me to return from that place, and my mind wasn't right when I did. No matter how much therapy he put me through, it didn't help. I felt every man was looking at me like those men did. I jumped at every sound. I cried over everything. I didn't trust anyone." I look back at the field, watching a colt run around his mom.

"When I was seventeen, I made my first kill. This guy's face was plastered all over the TV. Some rich asshole had gotten away with raping a ten-year-old girl. I planned, hunted him down, and murdered him. It was the first time my mind felt clear, and I knew what I needed to do. I started researching every court case where the person got away and took them out. After my fourth kill, Micah busted me." I laugh at that. He wasn't even shocked. "He's the one who built the underground torture chamber, helped dispose of the bodies, and got my gear. All under my dad's nose." I hated hiding that from him, but it wasn't something I ever wanted him to see me as. A murderer. A serial killer. "My dad was diagnosed with cancer soon after, went into remission, then got sick again right after my twenty-first birthday. He died thirteen months later. He had already put everything into place for me to continue to run his empire, even though I wasn't ready and probably still not."

I look back at Holden, and he has tears on his cheeks. I reach up and wipe them away with my thumb. "I'm telling you this because I need you to know I trust you. I trust you with the information you find, I trust you with the innermost secrets of this family, and I trust you with my truth. You *are* a part of this family, Holden." He closes his eyes, more tears leaking out. "I'll be here when you're ready to talk to me. I'll never push you."

He nods and crushes me to his chest. It's awkward how I'm sitting, so I drop my knees and bury my face in his chest.

It is the first time he's ever hugged me, and it's like a balm to my soul.

He rubs his hands up and down my back, lending me his strength, even though I can feel the rigid set of his body. I'm serious about not pushing him, even though I want to know so I can understand him better. I want to know if there is something I can do so he will look me in the eye.

He pulls back from the hug all too soon. He turns and looks out at the view. "I'm not ready," he whispers.

I hook my arm through his and lay my head on his shoulder. "That's okay."

This is why I think Gage's plan will never work, and I'm kind of pissed he put it into my head, anyway. I'm not fucking blind. All these guys are sexier than sin. I can appreciate them from a distance when they walk around the house shirtless, in ball shorts or grey sweatpants. But one wrong move and this will blow up in my face, and I'll lose all of them. I also can't afford any distractions; that's how people in my position died.

But would they be a distraction?

Fucking hell. I'm going to think myself into an early grave. I'm Alessa Fucking Poletti. I am not a coward like Gage accused me of earlier today.

"The day you got me out, I laid that trail on purpose," Holden says after some time. I don't look up at him, too afraid to scare him back into silence. "I was hoping you would kill me."

I close my eyes, my heart sinking. "I figured you wanted to get caught. You're too good, and the trail was too easy." I finally look at him and nudge his chin to look at me. "But I would never have hurt you. There was something so *pure* about you."

"When I heard the gunshots," he swallows. "I smiled for the first time in four years because I knew I would finally be free."

"Oh, Holden," I choke out, laying my forehead against his. "This place would be so much darker without you in it." I gently place my lips against his before I realize what I'm doing. I pull back from him before muttering, "Sorry."

"No," he croaks. "Please don't move."

I lean my forehead against his again. When he looks up and locks those beautiful brown eyes with mine, I almost weep with joy. There is no fear, hesitation, or uncertainty in his gaze, just an openness I've never seen in him. This close to him, I notice the light smattering of freckles across his proud nose and a tiny scar below his left eyebrow.

"Beautiful," he whispers, taking the words from my mouth of what I was thinking about him. "Will you kiss me again?"

I gently lay my lips on his as I did before with a little more pressure. There is a naivety surrounding him I can't quite put my finger on. He finally slides one hand onto my cheek, laying several pecks on my lips but never deepening it. I follow his lead, not wanting to rush him, and I'm perfectly content to feel his lips on mine.

He lays his forehead back on mine with a sigh. "Thank you for bringing me here."

I smile and run my hand through his curly hair. "This is your place now too, and someone will bring you whenever you want to come out here."

I would make it happen because this place brought me so much peace at a very dark time in my life. I need to work on teaching him how to drive, but he never seemed confident enough to try. I notice that the more I push, he comes out of his shell, so my plan now is to nudge him little by little until I see the real Holden. Looking into his eyes, I can see him lurking in there. I just needed to coax him out.

We get settled onto the bench with his arm wrapped around my shoulders and my head on his. We watch the colts playing in the field and the cows grazing. There is just something about getting out of the city. Holden by my side makes it even more special today.

I know now more than ever that I need to straighten things out with Leo. He needs to know the truth about how I feel, and he can take that how he wants. I'm already up to my eyeballs in guilt because of him and Ryder, and I'm sick of it. I'm a person that goes after what I want and am damn sure going to do just that.

Fuck what anyone else says.

CHAPTER 10
LEO

Three times.

That's how many times I've seen Alessa since the meeting with my brothers. I've had the pleasure of hanging out with Ryder, but at least Gage is here. Ryder no longer talks shit, he just glares, and it isn't always aimed at me.

"Will you stop before you burn a hole through my fucking head?" Gage says, not looking away from the TV. He's kicked back on the chaise at the end of the couch with me at the other end, Ryder sitting on the love seat across from us.

"Fuck off," Ryder replies, a muscle ticking in his jaw.

"You're being ridiculous," Gage laughs.

Ryder glares harder. "Nothing about this is funny."

Gage shrugs. "Sure it is." He finally looks at him. "I'm not the one who can't pull my head out of my ass and figure out what needs to be done. The *right* thing."

My eyes are swinging between them in confusion.

"Maybe you should just tell me what you're talking about," Ryder points out, and it's the first time I've been on his side. I'm curious as hell.

"Where's the fun in that?" Gage asks with a grin. Gage swings his head toward the kitchen, listening. That's when I hear Alessa's sweet voice filter through. Gage told me that she left with Holden earlier. "And let the fun begin," he mutters, and I think I'm the only one who hears him.

"Hey," she greets Gage, flopping on the chaise beside him and kicking her feet up.

"Hello, Pretty girl," he replies, kissing her on the cheek.

Ryder growls and storms out of the room, causing Gage to crack up. I love that he can get under Ryder's skin. I see her roll her eyes.

She finally looks at me. "Hi."

"Hey, Baby," I greet back with a smile even though it's a little forced with how she's cuddled up to Gage.

"What are you watching?" She looks closer. "Are you watching Supernatural again?"

"You're just mad because I didn't wait for you for this rewatch," Gage answers.

"Fair point," she laughs. "Is this all you've done today?"

"Not all of us had dates," he teases, but I turn her way anyway.

"It wasn't a date." She elbows him in the ribs.

Could I even be mad if it was?

He cuddles her into his side with his arm around her shoulders. "We going to The Games tonight?"

She shrugs. "If you want to, yeah."

"What are The Games?" I ask with a frown.

Gage grins and sits up on the chaise, animated as hell. "Illegal Street races. Bikes. Cars. It's badass. Wait until you see it."

How the hell did I live here for a year and never know about this? I can probably add that to the list of shit Evander and Mateo kept me away from. "I'm going?" I ask. They haven't even let me step outside, much less leave the house.

"Well, you can't stay here alone," Alessa answers, and it pisses me off. She's only taking me because she has to, not because she wants me to go. "We will leave at eleven, so we can be ready by midnight." She gets up from the chaise, stretching her arms over her head. Her shirt rides up, and I have to shift my gaze so she doesn't see me staring. I look at Gage, and he has no qualms about it. "You can ride with Dex," she tells me and walks away. Gage watches her ass in those short shorts until she disappears.

He looks at me with a sly grin, and I don't know whether I want to laugh or punch him in the face.

Riding with Dex was quiet as hell. He never said a word the entire thirty-minute drive, and I gave up trying to make conversation after the grunts as answers. He drives us down an old road that eventually turns onto a dirt road. When it opens up, it looks like an old airstrip and is huge. Bikes and cars of every variety line the strip we drive down. We brought Dex's black, jacked-up Ford Raptor; the rest were on the way on bikes. It bothers me to know she's wrapped around one of them on the bike; my only hope is it's Gage and not fucking Ryder.

Dex pulls in and parks beside a group of guys leaning against their fast cars. One of the guys grins when we pull up, walking up to Dex's window.

"Hey, man," he greets Dex with a slight Russian accent, his strange dark eyes sliding over me.

"What's up, Alexey?" Dex rumbles. At least he talks to someone.

"Where's the boss?"

Dex chuckles. "On her way." Dex pushes his door open and looks at me. "Don't do anything stupid," he says before he jumps out.

I roll my eyes and climb out behind him. I'm not an idiot. I don't miss the Glocks he has hidden beneath his leather jacket.

"Who's your friend?" Alexey asks when we walk into the group.

"Leo," Dex answers with no last name. Interesting.

Alexey leans against a dark blue Lamborghini. His stance might seem casual, but I don't miss the hard glint in his eyes. "I'm Alexey. That's my brother, Dmitri." He gestures to a guy with the same black hair and equally black eyes. Dmitri nods but doesn't say anything. Alexey's head snaps up with a grin. "There she is."

I look in that direction with confusion until I hear the screaming of the bikes. Three crotch rockets stop beside us, and to my surprise, the one on a dark purple Kawasaki Ninja ZX-6R jerks the helmet off to reveal Alessa in matching riding leathers. Holy shit, that's fucking hot. She swings her leg over the bike, and I see how molded those leathers are to her ass. She unzips the jacket, peeling it off to reveal a tight as fuck black shirt, dipped low in the front, showing off ample cleavage. I want to bend her over that damn bike, like right now.

Gage hops off a white matching bike, Ryder getting off a black one. Both dressed in leather to match the bikes.

"Well, look who it is." She smiles and gives Alexey a big hug, then his brother Dmitri. Each of them linger a little too long.

Dmitri pulls back from his hug, slinging an arm around her shoulders, guiding her toward their group. I look back at Ryder and notice I'm not the only one who wants to rip his fucking arm off. Ryder looks like he could spit nails.

Same man, same.

"Isn't this awesome?" Gage asks, propping himself on the front of Dex's truck.

"Who are they?" I ask instead of answering his question. I'm sure it would be awesome if I weren't here just because she had to bring me.

He looks at me like I'm crazy, then laughs. "I forgot you don't know shit about this world." He points to where Alexey is whispering in Alessa's ear, making her throw her head back and laugh. "That's Alexey and Dmitri Orlov." He looks at me again. "Russian Mafia."

What the fuck did I step into?

I thought about messaging Evander and Mateo with the phone Alessa gave me because I couldn't keep my own; she couldn't track that one. I've stayed in contact with my brothers, but this doesn't seem like something they would be interested in or maybe not invited to. Frankie didn't leave much room for them to have friends with how he was.

"This won't kick off for another thirty minutes or so. Want to take a lap with me?" Gage asks, pointing to all the cars and bikes. "Check out the competition."

I jerk my head to him. "You're racing?"

"Uh yeah," he grins. "I didn't get all dressed up for nothing," he says, gesturing to all the leather.

I shrug. "Sure."

He throws his jacket on his bike, telling Ryder what we're doing. He's leaned back against his bike, glaring at a laughing Dmitri, Alexey, and Alessa. Gage shakes his head and gestures for me to follow.

We pass rows and rows of every vehicle and bike you can imagine, most greeting Gage with a smile or wave, primarily out of respect. You can tell they know who he is. We walk a little further, where I can see them setting up the actual track for a quarter-mile run.

"Is that all they do here?" I ask, pointing to the track.

"Nah." Gage shakes his head. "They do contests and shit, too. Burnouts. Stunts."

I look around and wonder how the hell they set this up without getting caught. They have huge lights shining everywhere, so bright it almost looks like noon and not midnight.

"How do they pull this off?"

Gage chuckles. "Cops know who's here, and they aren't busting it up."

That made sense. No cop in their right mind would come here against these guys.

We loop back around the other side, looking at everything there, and I start getting excited, listening to cars and bikes rev their engines. I didn't get to do this in North Carolina because I didn't hang out with people that did. Now I'm here with the Italian Mafia leader, who is talking to the Russian Mafia.

It sounds like the start of a good movie.

We walk back toward the group while Gage describes everything that goes down here, and I find myself interested in what he's talking about. I don't know much about cars and such, but I know enough to follow most of his conversation. Gage is easy to talk to, and I feel myself being pulled into the conversation, listening to everything he has to say.

"Hey, Gage," a sultry voice purrs in front of us.I look from Gage toward the voice, and it's a busty blonde girl in a bikini top that barely covers her boobs.

Gage barely spares her a glance. "Hey, Victoria."

She runs her long red fingernail down my t-shirt. "Who's your friend?"

"Leo," I answer.

"Leo," she lets the name roll off her tongue with a purr. "I like that."

"Fuck off, Vickie," Gage says, surprising me.

"Oh," she pouts her red painted lips, "Why the grump face, Gage?" she asks, running her fingernail over his arm.

"I think he said fuck off," Alessa says, walking up behind Victoria. Alessa puts this barely dressed girl to shame while she's still fully clothed. I might be biased, though. Is Alessa jealous?

Alessa walks by her and puts herself right in front of Gage and me. The girl sneers at Alessa, looking her up and down like she's shit on the bottom of her shoes. "If it isn't the Italian whore."

Alessa raises an eyebrow. "And you are?" she asks, and I can tell she legitimately doesn't know who this girl is.

Victoria throws her blonde hair over her shoulder. "I used to date Gage. Like you didn't know that"

Alessa slowly looks at Gage, and his mouth hangs open. "We fucked one time."

Alessa shakes her head and turns back to look at Victoria. "You can go now."

Victoria huffs. "You can't tell me what to do." She reaches for Gage again, and he takes a step back. "You know I can make you feel good, Baby."

Gage laughs. "Right." He slings an arm over Alessa's shoulder, letting her know she doesn't stand a chance. "Now. Fuck. Off."

Victoria's eyes zero in on his arm. "You guys are a thing now? Is that why you never called?"

"Oh, honey," Alessa says and shakes her head. I can almost guess why Gage never called the next day, and Alessa picked up on it, too.

Victoria bristles, and her eyes land on me. Does she think she has a chance with me? I follow Gage's lead and slide my arm around Alessa's waist.

Victoria laughs a little too loudly. "Both of them? So, you really are a whore?"

"Call her a whore again, and I'll slit your fucking throat," Dex threatens, walking up behind us. Victoria shrinks about two sizes, causing Gage to laugh. I find myself chuckling with him.

"Let me tell you something, Victoria," Alessa sneers the name, taking a step forward. "The next time you want to start shit for no reason, just know you won't have to worry about Dex." Alessa pulls a knife from the sheath on the back of her pants, the same one she threatened me with, twirling it around her fingers. "You will have to worry about me."

Victoria's eyes widen, and she hustles back to where she was standing, half hiding behind a tall bald guy.

"Well, that was fun," Gage chuckles. "But it's almost time." He slings his arm back around her shoulders, looking over his shoulder. "Meet us at the track." He leads Alessa away and back to their bikes.

"Come on." Dex jerks his head for me to follow him. He leads me to where the riders are starting to line up, and I see Gage's white bike pull up with the purple one right in front of him.

"She's racing?" I ask in concern. What the fuck?

Dex looks at me like I'm a complete fucking idiot. "Yes. She does every time."

"They underestimate her," Ryder says, stepping up on my other side. He gives me a look. "A lot of people do."

"I never underestimated her," I argue, knowing he meant me.

"You still are. You think just because you fucked her, she won't kill your ass at the drop of a hat," he replies, and I'm fucking done with this shit.

I turn towards him, and I don't give a fuck if he kills me. "You think that's all this is?" I scoff. "I love her, you fucking asshole."

Ryder's face goes blood red, and I see him reach for his Glock. *Shit.* "Enough," Dex barks. "She's up."

Ryder gives me a stern look. "Fuck this," Ryder says and storms off.

"Do you have a death wish? Close your fucking mouth," Dex warns, and I jerk a nod. That was stupid, and I know it, but he doesn't know what he's talking about. I'm not after her for a piece of ass. I *love* her. My feelings for her were never a lie, and I don't know if she will ever give me a chance to explain myself.

I take a breath and focus on the track right as Alessa is doing a burnout, warming up the back tire.

"Two thousand says he wipes the track with her," a guy says to my right.

"Four thousand says your pussy friend goes home crying," Alexey replies, holding his hand out for the bet. They shake hands, and I don't miss the twitch of Dex's lips.

The light on the side of the track blinks red, then yellow, and finally green. Alessa takes off; the guy never even stood a chance. She handled the bike like she was born to, and I start cheering with everyone else.

Dex chuckles and leans forward. "Pay up, asshole."

Large amounts of money start switching hands everywhere, including cash getting slapped into Dex's hand, and he grins, the massive scar on his face twisting his lip evilly. It runs from his hairline through his eyebrow, down through his top lip on the right side, and sits so close to his eye that it's a wonder he didn't lose it.

Gage pulls up to the line after his burnout and flips the other guy off with a white-gloved hand, making me shake my head with a smile. I really can't help but like him. He's all over the place, loud, and sometimes he can't carry a conversation to save his life, but he's fun to be around. And he doesn't treat me like shit.

Gage dusts his opponent, too, and more money gets passed around. When someone hands more to Dex, Dmitri laughs. "That's fucked up. You know what they can do on those bikes."

Dex shrugs. "It's not my fault they choose to bet with me against them."

I laugh. "He has a point."

Me, Dex, Alexey, and Dmitri make our way to Gage and Alessa coming off the track. They pull their helmets off, laughing like crazy, and I get lost in the sound of Alessa's carefree laugh, the one she used to use around me. They hop off the bikes. Dex hands them the wad of cash he collected, and Alessa fans her face with a smile before they hand it back to him. I love her like this.

One of the guys from their race roars beside us, ripping his helmet off. "What the fuck was that?"

"Uh. A race?" Alessa answers like the guy is stupid.

His buddy pulls up on the other side. "There is no way those bikes beat these." I don't even know what kind of bikes they're on; my knowledge only goes so far. The only reason I know Alessa's bike is because it's my dream bike if I ever get a chance to learn how to ride.

Alessa laughs. "It's not just the bike. You have to know how to ride."

"Dude, she had you out the gate." Gage throws his arm around her shoulders. "You ride like shit."

"No one's talking to you," the one guy sneers. "We are talking to this cheating cunt."

Everyone's demeanor changes. Alessa and Gage's faces drop all teasing simultaneously; it's fucking eerie.

"Shit," Dex mutters when he sees more people coming up behind them, backing them up.

"Who are you calling a cunt?" Alessa says in that deadly voice she used on me.

"You, you cheating bitch." The guy puts his kickstand down, hopping off the bike.

Does he have any idea who he's talking to? Who the hell talks to a woman like that? I look at Dex, and he doesn't seem like he's going to step in.

Alessa tilts her head to the side. "You really want to be that stupid?"

"We have you outnumbered. I'd say we aren't the stupid ones," the other guy says, getting off his bike. He isn't wrong; there are at least twenty of them and seven of us.

"If you fight like you ride. I'm not fucking worried," Gage laughs, but it has a weird edge. "Let's fucking go!" Gage yells, bouncing on the balls of his feet.

"Goddamnit," Dex mutters under his breath, then all hell breaks loose.

Alessa jerks her leg up and back before kicking it forward, smashing the one who called her a cunt right in the face, blood spurting everywhere. Fists and feet start flying around, Alessa right in the middle. What the fuck? Why doesn't someone grab her? I go to step forward, and a hand hooks into my shirt and jerks me back.

"Stay back," Ryder barks and disappears into the madness. More people are gathering around and pushing me back, some joining either side and some to watch.

I hear someone howl like a fucking wolf, Gage's manic laughter following it.

Crazy fucker.

Between the two sides, they finally get everyone separated, and I'm relieved to see Alessa standing right in the middle in one piece and even have to admit I'm relieved to see Gage too.

Alessa spits blood from her split lip. "You have anything else to say?"

The one she kicked in the face glares, but it's ruined by his hand against his bleeding nose. "This isn't over." They all start leaving the way they came in, and I walk back over to Alessa and Gage. Ryder jerks Alessa's face up, looking at her lip.

She swats his hands away. "I'm fine."

"What the fuck were you thinking?" Ryder grinds out.

Her mouth pops open. "Me? What the fuck was I thinking?"

"Yes," he says between clenched teeth. "Starting a fucking fight."

She spits more blood, and it lands right beside his boot. "Fuck you," she says sweetly before swaying her ass back to her bike, Gage following. "Come on," he says to me, so I go to follow, and Ryder grabs my arm.

"You stay here."

"Let him go," Alessa barks, and he squeezes my arm harder than necessary before he drops it.

Gage nods to the back of his bike. "Get on." I raise my eyebrow, and he rolls his eyes. "Your weight on the back of her bike will throw her off balance."

Alessa shrugs. "He's not wrong. We're just riding over there." She points to the other side of the lot, where I see bikes lining up.

Gage waggles his eyebrows. "Come cuddle me, Leo."

I shrug because why the fuck not. He climbs on and I get on behind him. Dex thrusts a helmet into my hands. "If you are going to be stupid, at least be smart." I put it on when he gives me a hard look.

Alessa swings her leg over hers, shoving her helmet on; she lifts the face mask with a grin. "Go the long way." She slams it closed, and they fire the bikes up.

I have never been on a bike, much less a crotch rocket. Gage grabs my arms and jerks them around his waist, so I have to lean against his back. "Lean when I lean. You will get used to it," he says, and I realize they can talk to each other through the helmets, so the one I'm wearing is either Dex's or Ryder's. My money is on Dex. Ryder is probably hoping my brains will splat everywhere if we go down.

"You guys look hot as fuck right now," Alessa laughs, her voice filtering through the helmet.

"I'm not usually a bottom, but I could get used to this," Gage quips, and I pause. Does he mean what I think he means?

Alessa's laugh filters through again; they kick their kickstands up and pull away from the group.

"Hold on," Gage instructs, and I tighten my arms around his waist. I might look weird as fuck snuggled up to another guy on the back of his bike, but I don't feel it. I don't know him well, and he is undoubtedly off his rocker, but I feel safe with him, as weird as that is. But it also makes me want to examine some things I'm not ready to examine yet, like how I like my body pressed against his or how his hips are lodged between my legs.

We do several laps around the airstrip, and I feel myself getting lost in the ride. All too soon, we are pulling up to the group again and climbing off the bike. Gage pulls his helmet off with a weird look on his face before shaking his head like he's shaking away a thought. What the hell is that?

Alessa pulls away from us on her bike and pulls up beside the Lambo Alexey is leaning against. She pulls her face mask up and says something to the passenger, who I assume is Dmitri, and I could have sworn she asked how much they trusted her. She slams her mask down, and they ride side by side until they are away from the crowd. Alessa keeps riding ahead, and I frown. What is she doing? She drives about twenty feet in front of his car before I see her headlight swing around to face him.

"You think the race was hot? Watch this shit." Gage bumps my shoulder while pointing at Alessa. She starts moving forward before putting one knee in the seat and hooking her other foot behind her into a foothold I just noticed before pulling it up on the back wheel, riding a wheelie forward straight toward Alexey's car. She drops it right in front of the car, and I can imagine he is shitting his pants right about now.

"Damn," I mutter because he isn't wrong. It is hot as fuck.

She does several more wheelie tricks, and the crowd is eating it up. But I don't think she did it for that. She just seems to love the bike, and I didn't even know she rode. Did I know Alessa, as I thought?

She takes off in the opposite direction before spinning the bike around, flying back towards Alexey's car. Gage pulls me around until we can see the front of the car. She stops suddenly, putting the bike up on the front tire, stopping just when the tire kisses the front bumper. When the back tire drops, Alexey jumps from the car.

"What the fuck?!" he exclaims, running to the front of the car. She pulls her helmet off, grinning from ear to ear. He slides his hand between his bumper and her bike tire. It barely fits, and that's when I see how close she came to it.

"You look a little pale, Alexey," Alessa purrs, and he jerks his head up from staring at his car.

"Fuck you," he laughs. "I thought you were done for."

"What a shame," she tsks. "No faith."

Dmitri calmly steps out. "You didn't see that from the inside. This dude pissed himself."

"Fuck you too," Alexey says, flipping Dmitri the bird.

Alessa hollers her goodbyes to them and rides the bike back to us.

"Done?" she asks, and Gage nods. "Let's go. Dex, we'll see you back at the house."

My heart sinks again; they are all going to ride off and leave me with Dex.

Gage thrusts the helmet back into my hands. "Want to ride some more?"

"Really?" Does he want to carry me around when he can ride freely with her?

"Yeah," he replies, throwing his leg over his bike and firing it up. "We know this awesome place."

No way I'm saying no. I put my helmet on and swing my leg over, wrapping my arms around him.

Who knows what the night will bring now?

CHAPTER 11
GAGE

I have never had a guy on the back of my bike but riding through Los Angeles's back roads, staring at Les' ass perched up in front of us with Leo felt right, which complicated an already complicated situation. Ryder is going to be a lot harder to convince than I thought. Dex doesn't seem to care that we both kissed her. We just have to pop his anti-touch bubble. Holden is another matter, but I see how he looks at her, and I'm sure something happened on their little date today. Leo may take some convincing, but I have an idea of how and think it will push Alessa to accept this idea. Before we left for The Games, she seemed to have something on her mind, and she was looking at me differently. Like she's finally noticing me after all this time. So maybe it won't be so hard to convince her after all.

I wasn't lying when I said I have wanted her for years and wasn't just running game on her like she thinks I am. I was lying back and biding my time. So, when all this went down with Leo, I knew I had found my opening, and I'll be damned if I sit back anymore. I had already convinced myself she would never want me until she kissed me back in her office. I don't know what came over me when I initiated that kiss, but I'm glad I did.

I know she feels the spark between us. Fuck that. It isn't a spark; it's a fucking inferno. If Gina hadn't interrupted, I would have had her right there. But I need her mind to accept what her body already knows; she wants us all. I'm going to help her figure out how to get it.

I don't just want sex with her, either. My dad hated my ADHD because it drove my brain in forty different directions, and I couldn't control it. Les not only accepts it, but she also understands it. What she doesn't know is that when I am around her, it quiets the constant flow and lets me just fucking breathe.

Leo tightens his arms around my waist, going around a curve, pulling me from my thoughts. That's another confusing thing, the way he just leans into me with no questions. We practically kidnapped him, and he feels at complete ease leaning onto my back, taking curves faster than I should with a passenger. I don't like that he isn't protected with leathers like Les and me, so we ride a lot slower than we usually would. I'll look into getting him some.

What? I shake that thought from my head, one step at a time.

Alessa's voice filters through the helmet, low at first, and then I realize she's singing. I listen closer, and she's singing *Sure Thing* by Miguel, one of her favorite songs, no matter how old it is. She starts singing louder and way off-key, but it's the cutest thing. I hear Leo chuckle quietly, and we just listen to her soft voice.

Yeah, even when the sky comes fallin'

Even when the sun don't shine

I got faith in you and I

Just put your pretty little hand in mine

Even when we're down to the wire, babe, even when it's do or die.

We can do it, baby, simple and plain

Cause this love is a sure thing

She listens to this song all the time, but I can't help to think it has more meaning right now. Is she talking about Leo? Me? Us?

I join her on the next chorus, her music filtering through the helmets, and she laughs when the song ends.

"That was beautiful," she says.

"You're beautiful, Pretty girl."

I feel Leo tense up behind me and choose to ignore it. Once he sees what this has to offer, he'll be game. I just have to convince him of it. Which I plan to do when we get to mine and Les' secret hideout.

"You're not so bad yourself, Gage Lawson," she purrs, and I swear my dick jumps.

"What about my passenger?" I ask, hoping to break the ice by including him.

"Hm," she hums. "He's pretty cute, too. Killer abs." She goes quiet. "Big dick," she mutters, and I lose it. I hear Leo laugh, too, and almost whoop with joy.

"You know you're gorgeous, Baby," Leo says. *Fuck. Yes.* My ideas aren't always crazy; this might work.

"Keep talking. I'm getting all hot under these leathers," she replies, keeping the game going.

"Fuck," Leo whispers, and I grin.

"What else do you have going on under those leathers, Pretty girl?" I ask, following her turn signal to the right, down the last road before our hideaway.

"I'll give you three guesses to guess the color."

"And if we get it right?" Leo asks, and I want to high-five him.

"You can see for yourself," she breathes, and I realize this is turning her on, talking dirty to both of us. Is she about to make this decision for herself? I'm fucking game.

"You had that baby blue on the other night that looked hot as fuck against your skin, so not that one," Leo says, then shifts on the seat behind me. Les and I aren't the only ones getting off on this.

She chuckles, and it's a low husky sound.

"You were fire tonight, so red," I throw out there because I know Les has plenty of matching sets of panties and bras. Don't ask me how I know.

"Nope. That's one."

"Yellow," Leo guesses.

"Nope. That's two. Come on, boys," she says.

"What about a hint?" I beg.

"It matches...everything else right now," she says finally, and I roll my eyes. All of her silky stuff matches.

"Purple," Leo throws out huskily.

"Ding ding. We have a winner."

Holy fucking shit. I could kiss him.

She takes a left, and we pull down a long dirt driveway in front of our oasis, looking over Los Angeles. We found this place when we were out riding one day. It was just a little cabin sitting in the middle of nowhere, and Alessa and I paid triple for what it was worth to get the owners out. It has a wide porch surrounding it to see the view. It's perfect. We have people taking care of it daily, so it's always clean and fully stocked.

She shuts off her bike and pulls her helmet off. I steady the motorcycle so Leo can slide off, his hand sliding across my waist slowly. Am I imagining shit now?

She hops off her bike and turns toward me with the same look she had in her office. Lust. I pull my helmet off and don't hide what I'm thinking, not that I could when I got off the bike, anyway. My dick is going to rip through my leathers. I step off, and her eyes zero in on my crotch, causing me to grin.

We walk into the cabin, and she turns to Leo and me. "Here's the deal." She unzips her jacket, slides it off, and tosses it on the couch. "We still have a lot to discuss." She aims that at Leo, and he nods. "I want one night." She aims that at me. "No jealousy. No talking. No promises. Whatever happens, happens." She hooks her hands on the hem of her shirt. "We'll talk about it tomorrow. Can you do that?"

Leo and I share a look before turning to her. "What are you saying?" Leo asks.

"I want to fuck." She enunciates every word slowly.

"Both of us?" I clarify.

"Yes." Her voice has gone breathy, and I will strangle Leo if he says no.

We share another look, and then both nod. She whips her shirt over her head, revealing a dark purple lacy bra that has her ample tits pushed to her fucking chin.

"Damn," I mutter, walking behind her. I push her hair to the side, kissing her neck. "Are you sure?" I whisper just for her.

"Yes," she whispers. "Show me what it will feel like, Gage."

I step back, take my jacket off, and toss it with hers before stepping back behind her. "Come kiss her, man," I tell Leo, breaking him out of his trance and pulling him from his mind. I know they still have things to work out, but I have my hands on his girl. His head jerks up from my hands on her hips, and I give a look that I hope portrays that I will kill him if he fucks this up, and he steps forward.

"You want this?" Leo asks.

"No talking. Kiss me or get out. That's your only option."

He instantly crushes his lips to hers, sinking his tongue into her mouth with a groan. She responds immediately, meeting him kiss for kiss. They look hot as fuck right now. I start laying kisses down her neck to her collarbone. She has one arm around his neck, so she reaches back, placing her other hand on my thigh so she's touching both of us. I run my hand across her stomach, right above her leather pants. She arches into my touch, and I know we're going to do this.

We move in on her simultaneously, pressing her between us. He jerks his mouth away from hers. "Kiss him," he says breathlessly, gauging his own reaction to see if he can handle this. He has Alessa in his grasp; it can't be easy to give that up.

I spin her in my arms without hesitation, sinking my hands into her silky hair before devouring her mouth. She moans low, and I hear Leo cuss under his breath. Feeling her lips moving against mine freely again is almost more than I can take. I've imagined this moment for far too long to fuck it up now.

I kiss her harder, pressing her tighter between us. Her hands roam over my chest and stomach before sliding under my shirt, and I pull back long enough to jerk it over my head before sinking back into the kiss. Her soft hands land on my abs' , and I can feel my muscles bunching from her touch.

I pull away from the kiss, laying a peck on her lips. I look into Leo's eyes over her head, and he subtly nods, letting me know he's okay with me touching his girl. His pupils are blown, color high in his cheekbones.

Thank fuck.

"Time to pay up," I tell her. She laughs breathlessly before pulling off her motorcycle boots and socks. She shrinks another inch once the boots are gone, and Leo and I tower over her. It's hard to believe this little woman is the leader of the biggest crime organization in the world.

She jerks the five snaps loose. "Wait," Leo says, and I jerk my eyes up to his. He better be fucking joking. "I've wanted to peel these off your ass since I saw them."

I internally breathe a sigh of relief. I would hate to kill him for messing this up. I kind of like him.

She moves one hand to my shoulder when he drops to his knees behind her. Leo hooks his hands on the top of her pants before shimmying them down her thick hips while she holds her panties up with her other hand so we can see her in the matching set. He lifts each leg, helping her step out of them.

"Fuck," he groans, massaging her ass in his hands, and I notice they're thongs, her gorgeous globes on full display. He kisses each cheek before popping back to his feet. We step back in unison to see her completely, and I step to his side behind her.

She doesn't shy away from us, letting us look our fill. "Turn around," I tell her, and she turns slowly to face us with a sexy smile.

"Damn, Pretty girl. You take my breath away."

"Gage, you already have me almost naked. No need for flattery."

I jerk my eyes from her tits to her face. "I'm just telling you the truth."

She takes the two steps that put her in front of me and runs her hands up my abs to my pecs, taking her time to scrape her fingernails over my nipples. She runs her hand over my shoulders while walking behind me, causing my body to shudder again. My cock is so hard just from her touch and kiss that I can't imagine what it will be like to sink my cock between those lips. Or when I finally get to feel that pussy, I just know will ruin me for anyone else.

She runs her hands down my back, sliding them around my waist from behind. She reaches down and runs her hand over my hard cock through my pants, making me hiss. "What are you hiding in here, Gage?"

I look down at her small hand, massaging my cock. "Find out," I challenge, and she jerks the snaps of my leathers open. Fuck, she's bold, and I love every second of it.

She giggles and moves to Leo, not letting either of us turn around. She steps in front of him and runs her hands under his shirt. "This has to go." She pushes his shirt over his head. She isn't wrong about his killer abs; the dude is ripped. I'm not a slouch in the gym, but damn, Leo is built for sex.

She runs her hands up his abs, her hands bumping over each one. She takes the same path around him that she did me, rubbing his cock through his jeans before unbuttoning and unzipping them.

She walks back in front of us, unhooking her bra from the back before letting it slowly drop from her arms and revealing her perfect breasts with dark pink, perky nipples. They're pointed in stiff peaks andI want them in my mouth. Now.

I reach my hand out and hook it around her hip, pulling her to me. I seal my lips over her nipple, and her back arches, pushing it into my mouth. Leo leans forward, doing the same with her other nipple. Now we're finally on the same page.

"Oh, shit," she whispers, sinking her fingers into our hair.

I know Les is built for this, more than capable of handling more than one guy in more ways than one. Her responses to us just proves that. I look up at her and her head is thrown back, her mouth slightly parted in ecstasy.

Leo and I work together to get her panties down, watching them hit the floor. She steps out of them, completely naked in front of us. I run my hand down her bare pussy before sliding between her pussy lips, groaning. "Fuck, Pretty girl, you're soaking wet." I nip at her nipple, and she arches into my touch again.

Leo starts kissing down her body, dropping to his knees. He runs a hand up the inside of her thigh, causing her to shiver, her nipples hardening further. He sinks two fingers into her pussy while I work her clit in tight circles, watching the emotions play across her face. Her eyes are closed, her head thrown back, grinding her pussy down on his fingers.

"Open your eyes," I tell her. "I want to see them when we make you come."

Her eyes flutter open, locking on to mine. We start working her faster while I suck and lick her nipple; Leo is laying open-mouth kisses on her hips.

I step in closer, adding more pressure on her clit. "Fuckkk," she moans.

"You going to come for us, Baby?" Leo asks, and I think he's over whatever initial jealousy he had. He's all in right now. I just hope he doesn't regret it tomorrow.

"Yes," she pants and then moans again when he shifts his hand. She reaches for my pants, jerking them off my hips. I kick my boots off, pulling my pants off with my socks, now fully naked. She wraps her hand around my cock, stroking it hard from base to tip, while I start rubbing her clit again.

"Fuck, your cock is pretty," she whispers, stroking me again. I've never had any complaints about my cock. It's longer than average, thicker than most, with a little curve in the middle, but hearing her say it makes my chest puff out. She starts stroking me in time with our fingers, and my cock jerks hard in her hand. Her back bows and she explodes with a scream. "Leo! Gage!"

My name on her lips like that almost has me coming in her hand like a fucking teenager.

Leo kisses back up her body, his eyes lingering on her hand, stroking my cock. "We should move this to the bedroom," he suggests, and we both agree. He throws Alessa over his shoulder; her laugh turns into a moan when he slaps her hard on the ass.

Filing that information away for later.

We enter the bedroom, and he lets her slide down his body onto her feet, sinking into a kiss that could burn the place down. I walk behind her. "How do you want this to go? You want us to take turns?" I kiss the pulse point on her neck. "Or at the same time"?

She jerks her mouth away from his. "Same time," she moans, grinding her ass back on my naked dick. I rub my hand down her ass, squeezing one cheek. "Has anyone ever had this ass?" She nods. "Do we have lube and condoms here?"

She giggles. "No. But I brought them. They're in my jacket pocket."

Leo's mouth drops open. "You planned this?"

She looks over her shoulder at me and grins. "Yes."

"You dirty girl," I laugh, laying a kiss on her grinning lips. I smack her ass. "I'll be back."

I jog to the living room and dig through her jacket pockets. I pull out several condoms and a small bottle of lube. Grinning, I walk back to the bedroom.

When I walk into the room, I run my eyes from Leo's head thrown back, down his toned back, and over his tight ass.

Eyes on the prize, Gage.

Shaking my head, I find the prize on her knees, his cock down her throat. I step beside him, and she wraps her hand around my cock, shuffling over on her knees between us. She starts switching between sucking him and sucking me. The first feel of her lips on my cock almost has me coming on the spot. I look down at her on her knees in front of us with lust-filled eyes. I could die a happy fucking man watching her take what she wants, and right now, she wants Leo and me. I never thought I would see Les on her knees in front of me in a million years with my cock in her talented mouth.

She switches back to mine and sinks as far as she can go. I place my hand on the back of her head, pushing her further. She moans around the head of my cock. "Fuck," I grunt. She likes it rough, huh? Pushing harder, I feel her throat relax, letting me slide down easily. Her nose brushes my pubic bone, and her eyes flash to mine. Les' pupils are huge, the blue in her eyes darker than usual, showing she's turned the hell on. I fist my hand in the hair on the back of her head, pulling her back. She lets go of my cock with a wet pop. "Him," I instruct and lead her to his cock and get my first real look at him. *Damn.* I wouldn't mind having that in my mouth. She puts his cock in her mouth, and I push her head down on him, guiding her. She braces her hands on his thighs, and I can watch her visibly prepare herself. It takes three tries before he slides almost all the way.

"Fuck, Gage," he breathes. "Do that again." I pull her head back and push her down again. "Damn." His eyes are latched onto hers. He rubs his knuckles down her cheek. "Damn," he says again, like he's at a loss for words.

I feel that. Seeing Les on her knees for us makes me want to make this the best experience for her, not just because I want to do this again. She deserves her body to be worshipped like the fucking queen she is.

She sinks her mouth back onto my cock. "I need to be inside you." She looks up at me, and I swear I can see the smile in her eyes.

She lets my cock fall from her lips. "Do it then."

I pull her to her feet, crashing my lips against hers.

Fucking finally. I've wanted this for years, so there's no way I'm passing up my chance now.

I walk her backward until the back of her knees hits the bed. I wrap my hands around her thick thighs, putting her legs around my waist. I walk us up onto the bed on my knees, stretching my body against her longways on the queen size bed. I pull my lips from her pouty ones. "I want to taste you." I kiss her neck, her nipple, and down her ribcage. "Then I want to feel this pussy wrapped around my cock." I kiss right above her pussy. "Then I'm going to fuck your ass while Leo fucks your pussy."

I don't give her a chance to answer before I dive between her legs, sucking her clit into my mouth. Her back bows, her fingers sink into my hair, and her thighs close around my head. I place both hands on her thighs and spread her wide open. I need all the room in the world to explore this pussy.

"Fuck, Gage," she moans when I spear her with my tongue. Her taste explodes in my mouth. Sweet, a little tangy, and all Alessa. She's delicious.

Leo stretches out beside us, massaging her breast, rolling her nipple between his fingers. "She tastes good, doesn't she?"

"She tastes like my new favorite meal," I agree before diving back in. I couldn't get enough. I could live down here.

"Is he making you feel good, Baby?"

"Yes," she moans, raising her hips to meet my mouth.

"Good," he replies, leaning down and sucking her nipple into his mouth.

"Shit," she pants, her breasts rising and falling with each breath, her body on stimulation overload. I sink two fingers into her pussy, twisting them to hit her magic spot before alternating between flicking her clit with my tongue and sucking it into my mouth. "Yes," she moans, lifting her hips with each suck of her clit. I stroke her g-spot with my fingers, and her moans start getting out of control. I look up at her face and can't believe I'm buried between Les' legs, with my mouth all over her pussy. I watch her body tighten, the walls of her pussy clamping down on my fingers. I gently nip her clit, and she explodes on my tongue. I lick everything that leaks out of her, savoring the flavor.

"Fuck," Leo groans, fisting his cock and watching her come apart for me. I kiss back up her body, and he hands me a condom. *Teamwork makes the dream work.* I rip it open with my teeth and roll it down onto my cock.

I knock her legs apart with my knees, notch my cock at her entrance, both of us gasping at the contact, and sink balls deep into the sweetest pussy I've ever felt. I lean down, bracing my hands on either side of her head while she wraps her arms around my neck. I gently peck her lips a few times before I slowly start to move.

"You feel so good," she moans, running her hands down my back.

"So do you, Pretty girl," I breathe. Her pussy is so hot and sweet that it takes my breath away. I slowly slide out, loving the feeling of her pussy tightening around me, trying to hold me hostage inside her.

No wet dream that I've ever had involving her will ever compare to the real thing. Her body is perfect, from the roots of her black hair to the tips of her little pink toenails.

"Roll over and turn her ass towards me. I'll get it ready."

I roll us suddenly, making her giggle, causing her to clamp down on my cock. I pull her leg over my hip. "You're the best teammate, Leo," I groan.

"Fuck's sake, Gage," he laughs, smoothing his hand down her ass. He uncaps the bottle, squirting a generous amount of lube onto his fingers. "You aren't so bad yourself."

Alessa giggles breathlessly. "Better watch. That's what I said to him, and now his cock is inside me."

He pauses, then barks a laugh. "Fair point." That's what started the little flirting game on the bikes and thank fuck for that. He slides a slick finger inside her, working it a couple of times before adding a second finger.

"Oh shit," she moans, and it's low, throaty, and makes me want to fuck her so hard she sees stars.

I start rocking my hips back and forth, working her ass onto his fingers. "Just think how good it will feel with both our cocks," Leo whispers against her neck, his fingers still working inside her.

"Have you done this before?" she asks us.

"Nope," we both say at the same time.

"Me either," she moans again. "You guys will be my first."

Somehow, that just feels right.

Leo works his fingers in and out of her ass, ensuring she's ready, while I slowly slide my cock in and out of her pussy. "You ready, Pretty girl?" I ask. I'm going to self-combust before we get any further at this point.

"Please," she begs, and I'm never one to say no to her. I kiss her hard and deep one more time before rolling her onto her back, and slowly pulling out of her. Her pussy tightens around me, trying to pull me back in.

"Suit up," I tell Leo with a grin, and he just rolls his eyes but rips a condom open, sliding it down his long cock. I watch for a little too long before I look up into his eyes. He raises a brow but doesn't look offended.

He gets positioned on his back, helping her straddle his hips, her ass facing me. He places his cock at her entrance, and I watch every delicious inch disappear into her delicious pussy. She braces her hands on his chest when he's fully seated. I hear them both sigh when they're fully connected. They might have a lot of shit to work out, but this isn't one of them. Their bodies call out to each other like I can feel hers calling to mine.

She leans down, kissing his lips before dragging her pussy up his cock and then sinking slowly onto him. "Fuck," he grunts, gripping her ass in his hands.

I flip open the lube and squirt some onto my hand, rubbing it all over my condom-covered cock. I hate condoms but *always* wear them, no matter who I'm with. But I catch myself wishing Les will let me take her bare.

Another time. I tell myself. We hopefully have plenty of other opportunities.

I scoot in between Leo's spread thighs, the hairs on his legs rubbing mine, causing goosebumps to pop up all over my body. He stiffens, and I realize I'm not the only one affected. *What the fuck is that about?*

I smooth my hand up her spine, pressing her between the shoulder blades so she leans further onto Leo, pushing her ass up for me. I rub my hand over her pert ass cheek, feeling the soft skin in amazement. I rub the excessive lube around her back hole before sliding a finger into her. Fuck, she's tight. I test her a few times before pulling it back out. I notch my cock at her asshole. "Get ready, Pretty girl." I keep a tight grip on the base of my cock and push my hips forward.

When the head of my dick pops past the resistance, her back bows. "Fuck," she grits out, and I immediately pause.

"Are you okay?" I ask. *Please say yes. Please say yes. Please say yes.*

"Yes," she breathes. "Go."

I wrap my hands on her hips, pushing slowly into her ass. I grit my teeth to keep from slamming into her like I want, but then I feel her push back on me, letting me slide the last inch. I settle my thighs against her ass. "Fuck, this is tight," I groan, kissing the middle of her spine. Between Leo and me, we aren't small, and she's stretched around both of us, making it almost unbearably tight.

I am fucking Les' ass right now. I still can't believe it.

Her breathing is ragged, and her fingernails are dug into Leo's chest; he smooths the hair out of her face. "This okay?"

She nods. "Move, please," she begs, rocking her hips between us. Leo's hands fly to her hips, right on top of mine.

I thrust slowly inside of her a few times. "I can feel your cock rubbing mine inside her," I grit out.

"It feels good," Leo groans.

Filing that away for later, too.

It takes a minute, but we finally get a rhythm with him pushing in when I pull out and vice versa. It doesn't take long before she's grinding between us, begging us to fuck her harder.

"Your body was built for this, Pretty girl," I pant.

She lets go of one of those sultry moans, and I feel Leo's fingers tighten on mine on her hips.

"It is," Leo agrees.

"Harder, please," she groans, moving between us.

I lift one leg over Leo's, placing my foot flat on the bed, giving me better leverage. I put my hand between her shoulder blades and increase the pressure until her chest is flat against his. I slowly pull out before slamming back into her.

"Yessss," she hisses, pushing back against me again.

We set a faster pace, sawing in and out of her, her hips moving to meet us stroke for stroke. The feel of Leo's cock rubbing against mine inside of her is about to send me over the edge. She feels so damn good.

She starts bucking between us harder, and Leo digs his fingers into my hands on her hips. "Yes, Baby," he groans. His voice has taken on a deeper tone, and between the two of them, their noises are driving me insane.

I slide her hair to one side, kissing my way down her neck and spine, still snapping my hips forward, fucking her ass with hard, deep strokes. I look down to where we are all connected and want to remember this moment forever.

She moans long and loud, throwing her head back. I turn her head towards me and kiss her deeply, stroking my tongue in and out. When she sucks my tongue into her mouth, it sets something off inside me. I pull my hips back and slam forward so hard I grunt at the impact. Her body starts shaking, and I know she's close. I pull out and slam forward again, and she shatters with a scream. It's music to my fucking ears, the sound bouncing around the walls.

"Gage! Leo! Fuck!"

It starts a chain reaction with her orgasm. Her pussy grips us so hard that I can feel Leo swell inside her, emptying himself. "Alessa," he groans low in his throat, and the effects of both of them set me off.

I slam into her two more times, feeling my balls draw up. "Pretty girl," I groan out my release, holding myself as far inside her as I can get.

She collapses on his chest, nearly making me fall on top of her. I stop myself last second with one hand braced beside Leo's head. I look up into his eyes, and they flash with heat when he sees me looking. Is Leo bisexual, or is it just in the moment? I pull out of her tight ass and fall to the bed beside her. Leo rolls, so she's in between us and slides his cock free.

He pinches the condom to pull it off, knots it, and tosses it in the wastebasket beside the bed. I do the same and throw it in the general direction. "I'll pick it up later," I say, refusing to move from beside her right now.

She giggles, and I'm glad to hear the sound.

Leo and I take turns kissing her slowly before tucking her between us. She cuddles into Leo's chest while I spoon behind her, loving the feel of her sated body against mine. She lets out a sleepy sigh before I hear her breathing even out, signaling she passed the fuck out.

I chuckle under my breath, and Leo looks over her head at me. I raise an eyebrow, and he smiles, shutting his eyes.

I mentally fist-bump myself. One down. Three more to go.

I snuggle closer to Les' back, loving that her naked skin is against mine.

I knew I would never get enough when I kissed her in her office.

She is mine now too.

I let Les and Leo's soft breathing lull me into sleep, happier than I've ever been in my life.

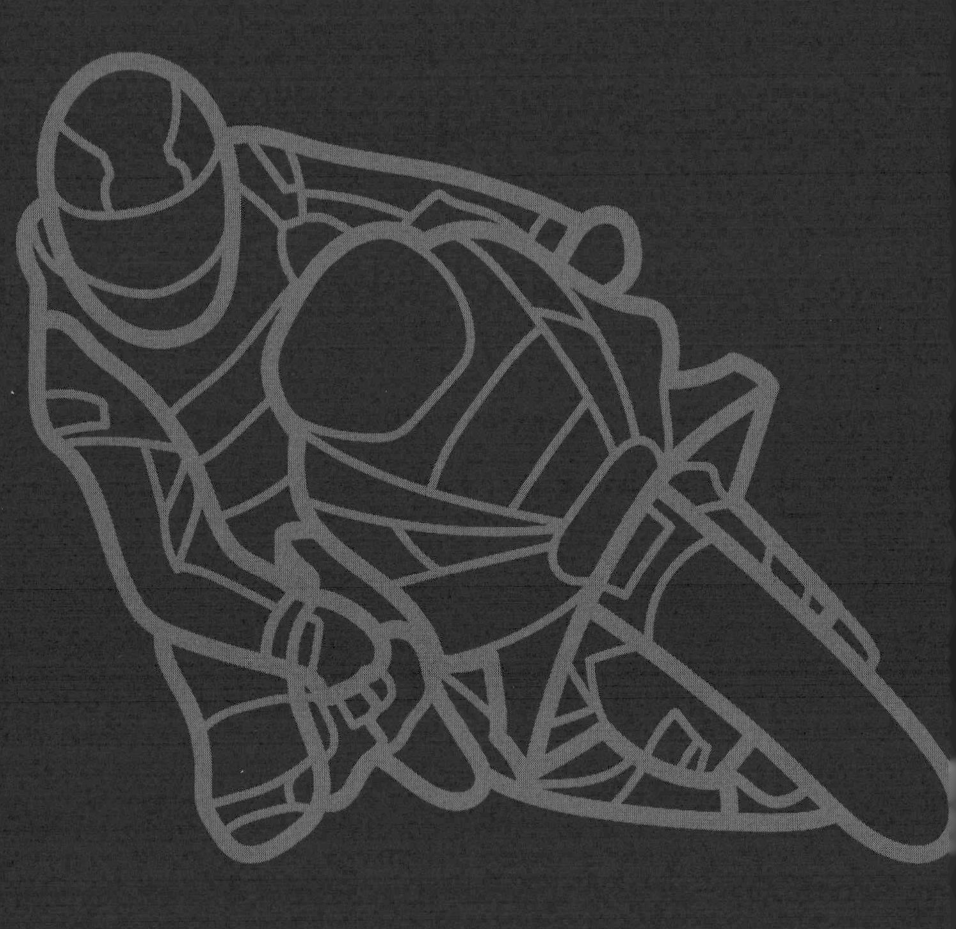

CHAPTER 12
RYDER

"I'm calling one more fucking time. If they don't answer, we go," I tell Dex, and he jerks a nod.

We haven't heard from Les and Gage since they took off with Leo last night after The Games. Between Dex and me, we have called them a hundred times with no answer. I even tried calling the phone Les gave Leo when we took his, but nothing. I finally broke down and had Holden check the tracking on their phones that all of us have. All three red dots are blinking in the same spot. I wouldn't be so damn worried if they weren't with Leo, and I didn't get an anonymous message this morning with a picture of us from The Games. It looked like it was taken at pretty close range, so someone was watching us last night, and they wanted me to know it. I don't like it, and now they aren't answering.

I pull up Gage's number and redial it.

"Hello?" he finally answers on the third ring, sounding half asleep.

"Where the fuck are you?" I bark, pissed and relieved all at the same time.

"What?" he asks sleepily, and I grit my teeth. I hear a familiar feminine voice in the background, making me grind my teeth even harder. Are they in the same bed?

"Where. Are. You?"

"The cabin," he yawns. The cabin only Les and Gage are allowed to go to. We all have secret places we go to when we hang out one-on-one with her, which doesn't happen often, and it sure as fuck doesn't happen overnight. I hear Les giggle and another male voice murmurs in the background. What the fuck?

"You could have fucking let someone know," I grind out.

"Chill out," Les' voice filters through the phone. "We're grown-ass adults."

"I can't protect you if I don't know where you are," I point out. It's my number one job.

"I'm with Gage and Leo." I can practically hear her rolling her eyes. "Is something wrong?"

Is she serious? "No. Just that you guys disappeared last night and went ghost."

She sighs. "I'm sorry. We should have let you guys know," her voice softens. "We just fell asleep."

I drop my head forward, hanging my head. Fell asleep after doing what? My stomach rolls and acid burns my throat. Did she fuck them? Every vision I have for her and me evaporates before my very eyes.

"I'll see you later." I end the call before I say something stupid and lean back in the chair in the living room, staring up at the ceiling.

"Everything good?" Dex asks from his spot in the other chair.

"Yeah. They fell asleep," I tell him, and even to my ears, I sound bitter as hell. Dex grunts in answer, and I want to punch him in the damn face. "Spit it out." I know he has something to say.

"They? As in all three of them? Together?" He asks, and I look at his face. He doesn't look pissed. He just looks thoughtful. I'm definitely going to punch him.

"Yes, asshole. All three of them together." I swear I'm going to throw up. Visions of Les pressed between them flash through my mind, and I want to stab my fucking eyeballs out.

"Maybe that's not a bad thing," he says, and I sit up so fast I make myself half dizzy.

"What the fuck?"

He shrugs. "She deserves to feel good, man."

"I can make her feel good," I say harshly. She doesn't need them to make her feel good. She has me. She's always had me.

He lifts a scarred brow. "So could I." He raises a hand when he sees my face change. "Don't get pissy. Just because you've known her the longest doesn't give you some kind of claim to her." He stands up. "If you want to get down to it, I was the first one to grow balls and go after her."

I snort. "You lost those balls, so it's a moot point." As soon as it's out of my mouth, I immediately feel like shit. I know why Dex didn't continue to go after her, and like an asshole, I just threw it in his face.

He gets that haunted look in his eyes. "Yeah. I did," he says before walking out of the room.

"Dex," I say, but he's already gone then a door slams further into the house.

I sit back in the chair, running my fingers roughly through my hair. This shit with Alessa has me fucked up, making me act out against the wrong people. It isn't even her fault. It's mine for burying my feelings for so long and then letting them be known at the wrong time.

"Ryder," Holden says softly from behind me, and I turn to look at him. "Is she okay?"

I sigh. "Yeah, man. She's fine."

"Good," he says, all the air leaving him in a rush, like knowing that one thing hit a pressure release. I know about his little crush on her. It's obvious, but is it more?

"They fell asleep at the cabin," I tell him, testing him to see how he'll react.

"Oh," he frowns. "All three of them?" I can feel my eyes starting to cross from that fucking question.

"Yes," I say gently. I already hurt Dex. The last thing I need to do is hurt Holden. Alessa would shoot me on sight.

"Oh," he says again, then shrugs. "That's cool."

He walks away, leaving me staring at his stooped shoulders. I don't even have it in me to yell at him to stand up straight like I usually do.

Does anyone else in this fucking house care besides me that they all spent the night together?

Two hours.

Two fucking hours later, I finally hear the bikes coming up the driveway, then hear all three of them laughing while walking into the house. I don't look up from my spot in the living room where I've been since Holden walked out. I don't need to see them to *know* what happened. I've gone through every emotion sitting here alone.

Jealousy.

Anger.

Sadness.

And the one I don't want to admit? Curiosity.

They all stumble into the living room about thirty minutes later, freshly showered. I just sit and glare at the tv.

"Your face is going to get stuck like that," Les quips, jerking the remote from my hand and flopping on the chaise, stealing Gage's spot. He squeezes himself beside her and the arm of the couch, making himself comfortable. Leo sits on her other side, just as fucking close. I grind my teeth so hard I can hear it.

"He's not going to have any teeth either," Gage says, taking the remote from her and flipping to Netflix. "He's going to be an ugly motherfucker." Leo covers a laugh with a cough when I turn my glare on him. Smart guy.

"Ryder could never be ugly," Les throws in. "Now give me that back." She reaches for the remote, and Gage moves it out of her reach. She reaches further, placing her face right in front of his. As if in slow motion, he kisses her, not wasting time sinking his tongue into her mouth. She moans, kissing him back, and it's like they realize at the same time that they have an audience. They jerk apart and look over at me.

I storm out of the room without a word. Fuck this. I don't need them to tell me what happened because they just told me without words. I don't need it shoved in my face, though. I jerk the door to the garage open, heading straight toward my vintage black Ford Mustang Shelby in the back that I'm rebuilding. I work on it when I need to think or am pissed off. Right now, it's both.

I jerk my shirt off, toss it onto the workbench, and then start getting the tools I need. I lay them on the table I have beside the car before getting to work. I work for about fifteen minutes before I hear the garage door open and then shut. Les' vanilla scent hits me before I see her, and I steel myself.

"Ryder," she says softly. I can't even look at her. Them fucking her keeps plaguing my mind, and Gage kissing her inside burnt into my brain. "Ryder," she says louder, "Talk to me."

I jerk upright, slamming my wrench down. "Sure, Les. Let's fucking talk."

To her credit, she doesn't even flinch. "It doesn't have to be like this."

"Doesn't it?" I say, throwing my hands in the air. "How else is it supposed to be?"

"You're my best friend, Ryder," she says softly, looking more vulnerable than I've ever seen her.

"Yeah. I am. That's all I'll ever fucking be, right?" I scoff at the look on her face. It says everything I need to know. "Right," I answer myself before grabbing my wrench and bending back under the hood.

"Please don't do this."

I come back up so fast that I almost crack my head on the hood. "Don't do what?!" I yell. "Be fucking hurt?! Fine, Les. I don't fucking care."

This time she does flinch, but not out of fear. I hurt the one person with my own fucking feelings that I swore I never would. Her face falls, and she storms back into the house.

"Les!" I call out after her, and she slams the door in my

face. *Fuck!* I take several calming breaths before I follow her, knowing where she's going since I pissed her off.

When I walk into the gym, she's taping up her hands, shoving them into boxing gloves. She starts pounding into the punching bag. "Les." No answer; she just starts hitting harder. "Alessa." No response. I walk up to her and touch her shoulder, then have to jump back, narrowly missing one of her mean right hooks. "Fuck, Les."

"No fuck you, Ryder Jett Venchelli." She socks me right in the chest hard, knocking the wind out of me. "Fuck you." Each sentence is ended with a sharp punch to the chest, pushing me toward the grappling mat. She starts advancing on me, fire burning in her blue eyes. "Fuck you for making me feel like shit for liking Leo." Left punch to the chest. "Fuck you for spilling how you feel right after shit blows up in my face." Right punch to the chest. "Fuck you for treating me like shit because I told you how I felt." Both fists punch me in the chest. "And fuck you for taking what was the best night of my life and turning it to shit with your fucking attitude." She jerks the ties on her gloves loose before slinging them to the ground. I don't have time to react before she jumps up, grabbing me around the neck in a rear naked chokehold and slamming both of us to the mat, letting go before we hit so she doesn't break my damn neck. She doesn't want me dead, at least.

We grapple for control for a good five minutes, something we have done a thousand times, and I can never pin her. So, when I straddle her hips, squeezing them together with my thighs, grabbing her wrists, and pin them above her head, I know she let me. We stare at each other, both breathing hard, then in a flash, meet in the middle with a crash of lips. It's all tongue, teeth, sloppy, and fucking desperate, both of us trying to get closer. I take one leg and push her legs apart, sliding my body down hers. When my hard cock grinds against her, she moans into my mouth, responding exactly how she did upstairs and outside on the patio. Her hands are sliding all over my sweaty, naked back. Everything about why we shouldn't do this leaves my head as I push her harder into the mat, grinding my dick against her pussy. Tucking my hands under the hem of her shirt, I jerk it off before our lips crash together again. Les wraps her legs around my waist, pushing her hips up, seeking friction from my hard cock through her thin cotton shorts. I kiss down her neck, and she turns her head to the side, giving me better access. I kiss the top of her breast, where it's about to spill out of her red bra. I bet twenty bucks that her panties match. I couldn't wait to find out.

She sinks her hand into my hair and tugs, trying to get me back up to her lips. I growl, latch my mouth back on her breast, and suck hard. She moans, grinding her hips up again, loving the feeling of my mouth on her, so I suck and bite, marking her. I look at my handiwork and groan, licking over the spot. I kiss between her breasts, down her sternum, and run my tongue around her belly button. I kiss above her shorts, hooking my hands in the top of them.

"Wait," she says breathlessly, sitting up on her elbows. "Not like this," she says when I look up at her.

"What?" I ask lamely. All the blood has rushed from my brain straight to my cock so I can't think straight.

"Not while we're pissed and not until you understand what this is," she explains. I sit up on my knees, separating our bodies.

"What is this, then?"

She swallows and flops back on the mat. "I fucked Leo and Gage last night." Even though I already know what happened, it's like a punch to the gut hearing the words straight from her mouth. "I won't stop just because you and I sleep together."

"You still want that fucking dick?" I ask, and I already know the answer. I was seconds away from blowing his brains out last night when he told me he loved her.

"I love him, Ryder," she whispers and rolls smoothly to her feet, reaching down and pulling her shirt back on.

I feel my heart shatter into a million pieces. If she loves him, there is no place in her heart for me, not like that. There is no way I can fuck her for fun while she loves him.

She walks out of the gym when I don't respond, and I let her walk away. What else am I supposed to do? Follow her and beg her to love me instead? I always thought that when she was finally ready to settle down, I would tell her how I felt, and we would have the life she always dreamed about, the one her mom and dad had. But I kept my head buried in my own shit and missed when she fell in love with him. Looking back, I can see the moment it went from simply dating to her gushing about all the shit he did with her, all the stuff he did *for* her. All the shit I never did, all the shit I didn't do because I thought I had it on lockdown as her best friend. I let her walk right into his arms and out of mine.

I fucked up, and there isn't a damn thing I can do about it.

CHAPTER 13
ALESSA

One minute I was ready to kill Ryder, and then his hard body was sliding against mine. We are like two magnets being drawn together without the hope of fighting it. I'm so pissed at myself for the look on his face when I told him I loved Leo. The look in his eyes ripped my heart out. I don't want to hurt Ryder, but he needs to know the truth.

I hear the patio door open and hastily wipe away the tears rolling down my face without looking to see who it is.

Watching from the corner of my eye, I see Dex fold his large frame onto the lounge chair by the pool beside mine. My eyes meet his, and he frowns, his face becoming thunderous.

"Who the fuck made you cry?"

I laugh without humor. "Myself." I angrily wipe the tears that won't stop falling. "What's wrong with me?"

"You're human, Les. Talk to me." I shake my head, and the tears start falling harder. I can feel a sob trying to bubble out, causing Dex to look at me in panic and go to stand. "I'll go get one of the other guys."

My hand shoots out and grabs his arm. "No. Please don't." He sits back down, and I move my hand when I see him tense up. "Stay."

"I can't give you what you need right now," he says so softly I barely hear him with his already raspy voice.

"Just sit with me?" I ask. "Then we can talk."

He looks at me skeptically but nods his head, leaning back in the chair and kicking his legs up. I bought the biggest ones I could find so he could fit with his giant stature, but his feet still almost hung off the end.

I try to gather my thoughts so I could talk to Dex. I know he'll listen without judgment because he always has. Would he about this, though? I've made so many wrong choices over the last couple of months. Am I still making them by hooking up with Leo *and* Gage? Leo and I still haven't worked through everything. But I won't even try to deny how good it felt or how freeing it was to let myself feel what my body has been begging for. The more I get involved in this, I realize Gage is right. I want them all, and things are already falling apart with Ryder. There is no way he can share me. He's made that clear without even having to say it. His face earlier said it all. What about Holden? He seems so innocent. How would it be fair to bring him into some unconventional relationship? He deserves a woman that spends every minute doting on him. How can I do that when I'm trying to entertain four other guys?

And Dex. He doesn't like to be touched by anyone at all. I can't even get by with it most of the time. Every time I slip up and do, this haunted look crosses his eyes like he is being sucked back to that place where Frankie's guys tortured him for weeks before dumping him in front of the gate, beaten to shit, and bleeding out. The light went out in his eyes and never turned back on after that night.

I always wondered why he stuck by my side after that. Dad would have let him leave, no questions asked, but Dex wouldn't budge. He healed physically but never did mentally. He functions fine, his mind sharp, his body stronger than ever, but with one wrong touch, he withdraws in on himself unless he's causing someone pain. It hurts to watch because he used to be so open with affection. I would know. I would sneak around with him, falling more and more in love with him as the days went by. He would kiss you without care and hug you like he was holding you together. That Dex seems to be gone, and I don't know if I can get him back. I've tried for years, and there's no sign of him. The night he disappeared, I thought I was going to fall apart. It was the first mission my dad let me go on because I wouldn't stop begging. We turned this city upside down looking for him. Dad issued threats to anyone we thought was involved, even going as far as burning down one of Frankie's bars.

Frankie sent his final message when he dumped Dex off with a bleeding knife wound straight down his face. Dex said Frankie did it himself in the car before they pushed him out. I helped him heal as I was the only one he would let change his bandages, then he pushed me away, and nothing I could do would bring him back. That's when I fell into a wild, inappropriate affair with Zane. *Nope, not going there.*

Then there's the unresolved stuff with Leo. But can I be mad? I omitted truths too. He may have known who I was going in, but I never told him myself. He sure as hell don't know I'm the Black Demon. How would he even react to that? He has to know that in this life, we kill people for the family, but snatching someone off the street to murder is different. Isn't it?

Shaking my head to rid myself of those thoughts, I look over at Dex's profile, running my eyes down the massive scar. It doesn't take an ounce away from how attractive Dex is. He has a mess of thick brown hair, these weirdly beautiful gray eyes that used to tell me everything he was thinking, pouty lips that would make any woman jealous that felt so good against mine, and a beautiful smile, when he uses it, which is rare these days. He has tattoos covering every inch of his skin, from his neck to his knuckles.

"What are you looking at?" he asks without ever looking my way, just staring at the water in the pool.

"You," I tell him honestly, and he turns his eyes on me.

"Why?" he asks with a frown.

I shrug. "You're hot, Dex. Get over it," I reply, trying to keep my tone joking so he doesn't spook.

He shakes his head, and I know he doesn't see what I see. The night he pushed me away was the first and last time he ever raised his voice at me. He yelled at me that there was no way I would want a scarred, fucked up freak like him and to get out of his face. No matter how much I cried and told him that wasn't true, he just pushed harder. Shutting me out so much, I finally took the hint and left him alone.

"You never did believe me after that night," I say softly.

"No," he says but doesn't comment further, and I sigh, laying my head back on the lounge chair. "You ready to tell me what's going on with you?"

"I feel like I'm losing control, Dex."

"What do you mean?" I hear him shift and know he sat up.

"Stupid decision after stupid decision."

"Are you talking about Leo, or did something else happen?" I see him swing his legs over the lounge chair to face me fully, leaning his elbows on his knees.

"Everything happened."

"Ok. Let's start with Leo. The only reason you're mad at him is that you were on the receiving end of what happened. Yeah, he lied, and that's fucked up, but we've done worse to make alliances with people. Don't pretend we haven't. Work your shit out with him or let him go," Dex says in a rush, like he was just waiting to say it.

"Wow, Dexton. Tell me how you really feel," I say sarcastically. I can feel his glare on the side of my head.

"You didn't come to me for coddling. You came to me for the truth. What else happened?" I don't point out he came to me; I know what he means.

"Leo. Gage. Ryder." *Holden.* I leave that one out because I haven't completely crossed the line with him. Yet. "You name it."

"Rewind. What happened since yesterday?"

I turn my head to look at him. I need to see his expression to know I'm beating myself up for the right reasons. "I slept with Gage and Leo last night." His face doesn't change, just raises a brow. "Together," I add, just in case he didn't get it.

"Okay," he says slowly, making me frown. What does that mean?

"I was just dry-humped and half naked with Ryder in the gym." He still doesn't change his expression. Just keeps looking at me I'm crazy. "Then I told him he had to stop because I loved Leo, and he couldn't have me all to himself." That gets his attention, causing both his brows to shoot up.

"Ah," he nods. "I get it now."

I throw my hands up when he doesn't elaborate. "I'm glad someone does because I sure as fuck don't."

"You aren't upset you slept with Leo and Gage. You are upset because you hurt Ryder."

"I hurt Ryder because I slept with Leo and Gage," I say with exasperation. Are we not having the same conversation?

"Ryder knows where you stand?" he asks, and I nod. "Then that's on him. It's not like you weren't upfront about it." How the hell is he making this seem so simple? Now I'm getting pissed again.

"I want Gage and Leo." Dex just looks at me. "And Ryder." He shrugs. *Grrrr.* "And Holden." He looks at me harder then just shrugs again. *All right, asshole.* "And you." He sits up ramrod straight and freezes like that. Not the way I wanted to tell him, but there it is. It serves him right for his nonverbal reactions.

"What?" he croaks, and I roll my eyes so hard I see the back of my skull.

"Come on, Dexton. We had something once. Don't act like you forgot what it was like." We never slept together. There were too many obstacles with him living at the house at that point. But it was going there fast; then he was taken. "I want you all as mine."

He stands up and paces two steps away before swinging back around. "That's not possible."

"Why not?"

He rubs the back of his neck, the first sign he's two seconds away from freaking out. "You have all of them. You don't need," he gestures towards his face, "me."

I stand up and walk until I'm standing right in front of him, careful not to touch him. "I do need you. All of you. I don't care about the scars, Dex. I only care about what happened for you to get them. The scars don't make you the man you are." I stab my finger into his chest over his heart fast before I move it. "That does. "

I see so many emotions cross his face that it's not even funny. "Les, I..."

"Save it," I cut him off. "I already know what you're going to say. I didn't forget what you said to me that night, but that doesn't change how I feel or what I want." I shake my head, watching him shut me out again. "And what I want is all of you." I start to walk away and hear him suck in a breath. I slow, hoping I finally broke that wall of his.

"You don't get what it was like," he says hoarsely, and I whirl around.

"I don't?" I say through gritted teeth. "I don't get what it's like to be touched without my permission?"

"That's not what I meant!" He runs his hand through his hair. "You recovered, Les."

I have no idea what my face looks like, but his eyes widen. "Recovered? Do you mean sleeping with anything with a dick? Oh, or do you mean murdering rapists? Or do you mean the current predicament of wanting five different guys?" My voice is rising with each word, so I take a deep breath and quote my therapist. I didn't see her after she said this either. "Sometimes young girls who are raped or molested at a young age turn to sex with multiple partners to deal with the trauma." I laugh without humor. "I guess the old bitch was right. Look at me fucking *thriving*."

I take one step away, and his hand latches onto my arm. It shocks me so badly that all the anger drains out of me. His fingers squeeze my arm gently before he drops it like it burned him.

"She was wrong," he says softly. "You dealt with it the way you needed to, and we all deal with shit in fucked up ways. You shouldn't live your life because of what that bitch said or what Ryder thinks. Live your life for you, Baby girl."

My heart leaps into my throat. He hasn't called me baby girl since our last good time together. It used to make me melt into a puddle at his feet like it is now, but this time I know I'm getting my hopes up for nothing. "That includes a very different version of all of us. That life includes you, Dex." I finally reach the door, and Dex still hasn't moved. "Tell them I'm going out and not to follow me." I slam the door shut behind me, done with this day. I woke up this morning happy, fulfilled, and hopeful. Now I feel like the walls are closing in on me, and I'm kicking myself for even thinking this could work.

It's time to take things back to how they used to be.

Friends.

CHAPTER 14
LEO

Gage and I are watching tv when my phone rings, Mateo's name flashing across the screen.

I slide to answer. "What's up, man?"

"You know where your girl is?" he asks cryptically.

I frown. I knew she and Ryder got into it. I could hear them yelling from the garage. And I have no idea what happened between her and Dex. All I know is he came inside like the weight of forty worlds was on his shoulders and relayed Alessa's message not to follow her.

"She said she was going out."

I could hear the thumping bass in the background. "She's at Skyline. Drunk as fuck."

I sit up on the couch, and Gage gives me a concerned look. "Is she okay?"

Mateo sighs. "No. She's not. That's the only reason I'm calling. I promised her I wouldn't, but that's before she put away enough liquor to drown a fucking elephant."

"I'm on my way," I tell him before hanging up and turning to Gage. "Alessa's at Skyline drunk as hell."

His brows knit together. "Why is she at your brother's club?"

I shrug while standing up. "I don't know. But are you taking me, or am I stealing a car?"

"I'll take you. Let me go put some jeans on." He jogs up the stairs, and I realize we're both in ball shorts. I walk quickly to my jail cell and jerk a pair of jeans on, sliding my feet into my boots. When I step back toward the garage door, Gage is sliding his on, nodding his head for me to follow.

I still can't help staring at the garage in amazement. It's huge and wrap-around style, so they can park anywhere and still be able to get the cars out. There are cars everywhere, of various kinds, along with the bikes and the vintage Mustang Alessa said Ryder is restoring. When we returned this morning, I commented on the cars, and she joked about them being children with grown-up money.

Gage hits the fob on a black Range Rover. We both slide in, and before he can shut his door, Ryder appears from the back of the garage, covered in grease. He must have been working on the car, and we didn't see him.

"Where are you going?" Ryder asks Gage.

Gage's face changes to that level of crazy I saw right before the fight last night. "Out." He slams the door before stabbing the button for the garage door. He backs out of the garage when it slides open, but not before flipping Ryder off through the windshield. He also heard them yelling at each other and said this happened sometimes. I didn't like it, and from how his demeanor changed from joking to silent, he didn't either.

He breaks every traffic law driving there, and I don't even say anything; he is just as worried as I am. Alessa doesn't seem the type to drown her worries with booze, so something major went down. He swings into the lot, and we get out, making our way inside. The bouncer just waves us through when we walk in, probably expecting us. We find Alessa tucked into a corner booth with Evander and Mateo. Evander is beside her like he's blocking her from exiting the booth, but they are laughing and joking with her. I can see the worry in Evander's eyes when we walk up.

"Leo!" she crows. "And Gage! The only two people who like me in the house right now." She downs a shot, and I shoot a glare at Evander, and he subtly nods his head for me to follow him.

When he gets up, Gage slides into his spot. "Hey, Pretty girl," he greets softly, throwing his arm around her shoulders.

"What the fuck, man? Why is she still drinking?" I ask when we round the corner toward the offices.

He raises an eyebrow, looking at me over his shoulder. "You want me to tell the woman who could kill me with a look that she can't drink in my bar?" I glare harder. He pushes the door open to the back office before shutting us in. "It's watered down, and she's too drunk to notice. What the fuck happened?"

I run my fingers through my hair. "I don't know, bro. Things were fine this morning, and they went to shit quick with Ryder and Dex."

"Because of what happened?" he asks.

I told him and Mateo what happened between Gage, Alessa, and me because I needed someone to talk to. They didn't judge me; they helped me make up my mind. If this is how I can be with her, then that's what I'm going to do. I'm not turning my back on her, not now, not ever.

"I'm sure that was Ryder's fucking problem," I grit out. "I don't know about Dex. He never talks."

"I'm going to say something, and I need you to listen without getting pissed off," Evander says, and I immediately know it's going to piss me off. "Ryder's been in her life for twenty-five years. Maybe you need to step back and see it from his point of view."

"What the hell, Van?" Did he just take that asshole's side? "He's why she's here drunk on a Tuesday night before ten."

He shakes his head. "I don't think it's just that. I don't know her well, but I know this isn't her. She burns shit to the ground when she's pissed, not drown in tequila. That girl out there," he points in the club's direction, "is hurting."

"Because of me?"

"I think it's been building, and whatever happened today tipped it over the edge. You guys still haven't talked?"

I give him a sheepish look. "No."

He punches me hard in the shoulder. "Talk to her before you

put your dick in her again." He jerks the office door open, muttering "dumbass" under his breath. I can't even be mad. I don't regret last night—quite the opposite. I realized a few things about myself that I probably need to look closer at after I take care of my girl.

We walk back to where Alessa is sitting, and she's staring at Mateo, head tilted to the side. It's cute in her drunken state instead of scary like that move typically is. "You know," she starts, pointing at him. "You're kind of pretty." She leans her elbows up on the table. "But your brother is hotter," she whispers loudly, jerking a thumb at Evander. Mateo's face goes from smug to shocked in a second flat. Gage loses it, laughing so hard he almost slides out of the booth. I take another look at Mateo's wounded expression and join in his laughter.

"Thanks," Evander says with a chuckle.

"Don't get a big head." She points at me. "That brother, though? Hm," she hums, and it sounds distinctly sexual, almost like a moan. "Is the hottest."

I feel my chest puff out, giving Evander and Mateo a smug grin, causing them to roll their eyes.

"What about me, Pretty girl?" Gage asks teasingly.

She snorts, then hiccups. "You know you're hot. Dark hair, blue eyes, dimples. You're a walking wet dream."

Gage gives her a smacking kiss on the cheek. "That's you."

He's not wrong. Even inebriated with a plain band t-shirt over ripped jeans, hair in a messy bun with no makeup on, she is easily the prettiest girl in the room.

"And here I thought we were making friends," Mateo comments with a pout.

"Oh. Yeah. Sure," she giggles. "Friends." She waves a hand between Gage and me. "My friends get lots of perks. I have lots of friends, friends I like to fuc...."

"Okay," Gage interrupts, trying to fight a laugh. "I think it's time to go."

"Aw," she pouts, and it's the cutest damn thing I've ever seen. "But I'm making new friends."

"Pretty girl." Gage rubs his knuckles down her cheek. "Let's make friends with them when you're sober."

"Why?"

"Because I'm pretty sure you just propositioned Mateo and Evander for sex in a roundabout way." Gage loses his battle and laughs but covers it up with a cough.

"Did I?" she asks, her brow creasing in confusion. She isn't even following her own conversations anymore.

"I agree, Baby. Let us take you home."

"Fine," she grumbles. "Thanks for hanging out with me," she says to Mateo.

"Anytime, Alessa." He grins, but it's strained around the corners. I need to find out what exactly she said to make Evander *and* Mateo's protective instincts kick in.

Gage slides out of the booth holding his hand out to help her. She slides out and almost goes right back down. His arms flash out, locking around her waist, pulling her against him. She giggles. "Whoa." She tilts her head back to look up at him. He's almost a foot taller than her when she has flat shoes on. "Hot and chivalrous. Rest in peace to my panties."

I hear Evander and Mateo snort a laugh behind me and have to struggle to control my face. She might be cracking jokes and seem one hundred percent fine, but I didn't forget what Evander said.

Gage locks his arm around her waist and leads her to the door. "Thanks, guys," he calls over his shoulder. "We owe you one."

"No, you don't," Evander says with a nod. "This is what allies do." Gage acknowledges that with his own nod.

"Bye, fellas!" Alessa yells, waving over her head. They call out their goodbyes, and I push the main door open so they can step through. Gage bundles her into the front seat while I climb into the back.

"We will come to get your car tomorrow," he tells her, and she nods. He closes the door, and she's passes out against it before he even gets in.

He looks at her for a second with so much softness that it makes my heart clench. I had my suspicions that this was more than just sex for Gage, but I didn't see it until now. What does that mean for the future? I shake my head and tell myself one thing at a time.

I sit up between the seats when he pulls from the lot, heading home. "I'm going out on a limb here and guessing this isn't normal."

Gage glances at her, then back to the road, shaking his head. "She drinks, but never to this extent, and sure as fuck never alone."

I would assume going out alone drinking with her status is dangerous as hell, and that scares the shit out of me. Anything can happen to her while she's out. I'm glad Les came to Skyline; maybe she did it on purpose. Les knows she shouldn't be out alone, and if anyone is going to protect her, it will be Evander and Mateo to prove she can trust them, and that's just who they are. They are nothing like the Frankie I've heard about.

"We need to find out what the hell happened from last night to when she left," I say.

Gage's hand tightens on the steering wheel. "I have a pretty good fucking idea."

He seems to have come to the same conclusion as me. Ryder. I keep running through my head what Evander said about seeing it from Ryder's point of view. What the hell does he even mean by that? Not that anyone talks in front of me, but I can piece together enough on my own that when I came barreling into Alessa's life, I shook the foundation of everything they knew. It also made buried feelings rise to the surface. Gage was honest about what he wanted, and I didn't even question him for a second. But Ryder? Why the hell would he wait until she felt betrayed to show his feelings?

Gage glides into the garage. "You get her, and I'll handle Ryder."

I jump out and carefully open her door, so she doesn't fall out. I slide one arm around her back and the other under her knees; she doesn't even stir when I lift her out. She just snuggles into my chest with a content sigh. I use my hip to shut the door and carry her into the house through the door Gage is holding open.

"What the fuck happened to her?" Ryder explodes as soon as he sees her.

Gage steps in front of him, blocking him from grabbing her from me. "Back off." He looks over his shoulder. "Take her upstairs. Last door on the left."

I nod and carry her up the stairs, following Gage's direction. As soon as I open the door, her sweet vanilla scent hits me square in the face. I love that smell; I probably could have found the room by smell alone. I lay her gently on the bed, pulling her shoes off and wiggling her ass out of her tight jeans. I plug her phone in beside the bed and flip the sheet over her. She snuggles into the pillow, her breathing evening out again, completely passing out. As much as I want to climb into bed with her, I'm not going to leave Gage to deal with Ryder alone. I know he can, but I didn't want to.

I follow the voices and find them in a faceoff in the kitchen when I round the corner. Ryder's fists are clenched at his sides, and Gage looks seconds away from throwing a punch. Dex is sitting on a stool at the kitchen island, hopefully, ready to intervene, and I even see Holden standing to the side. All of them worried about Alessa.

"You can't tell me that motherfucker," Ryder points at me, "didn't play a part in all this."

Gage looks over his shoulder at me, and his emotions are hidden from his face for the first time. Does he think I have a part in this?

Gage looks back at Ryder. "He probably did," he answers, and my heart sinks, thinking I lost my only ally in the house. "But so did you. We all fucking did."

"How come this didn't start until he came along?" Ryder comments, and I want to yell, I'm right here, but I keep my mouth closed and lean against the doorframe leading into the kitchen.

"You aren't this stupid, Ryder," Gage says harshly, causing Ryder's eyes to narrow. "This has been going on for a while, and we just ignored it. Let her do whatever she needed to do to deal." Deal with what? "True. What he did probably set everything off, but it's been a long time coming." He looks back over his shoulder. "Sorry," he says, apologizing for agreeing with Ryder, but I wasn't going to argue. He was probably right.

"All good," I answer.

Ryder turns those dark eyes on me. "You can fucking go." He points his finger, indicating my room.

"No. He stays," Gage argues. "Whatever happened between you two today needs to be fucking fixed. *His* brother is the one that tipped us off to where she was."

Ryder barks a laugh, but it's humorless. "You mean the shit Perez brothers that came up with this asinine plan?"

That's enough. "Talk shit about me all you want, Ryder, but leave them out of it," I say and stand up from the wall. I don't have a chance in hell against Ryder, but I'll fucking die trying. He already pisses me off with how he talks to Alessa, and now he's talking about my brothers? Not happening.

"They kept her safe while she was there, which they didn't have to fucking do. Quit throwing blame everywhere and own up to your shit!" Gage yells the last word, making Holden flinch from his position in the corner.

Ryder steps into Gage's space, and Gage stands his ground. There isn't much height difference, but Ryder has a good thirty pounds on Gage. Something tells me Gage can hold his own, though.

"All right, that's enough," Dex says, sliding his massive bulk off the stool and walking over, separating them with hands on their chests before dropping his hands just as quickly. "This isn't fixing anything." He looks at Ryder. "Gage is right. We've let it go for too long, and we've all added to it."

Holden's eyes widen. "If I did, I didn't mean to."

Gage smiles, but it's forced. "You didn't, and you're probably the only one."

From what I've seen, they all treat Holden with kid gloves, speaking softly around him, and I can't help but wonder why. He seems scared of his own shadow.

"What the hell happened earlier?" Gage demands, swinging his eyes between Ryder and Dex. "Because Leo and I left her sated and fucking happy."

"You motherfucker," Ryder growls, stepping back up and pushing Dex's hand away.

"Please do it, Ryder," Gage begs between clenched teeth. "I've been dying to fucking deck you for how you talked to her."

"What goes on between her and me is between her and me," Ryder argues back.

"Not when it ends with us having to pick her up drunk from a bar," Dex says quietly. "I fucked up too. Now we fix it." What the hell did Dex do? He gestures to me. "Him too, whether you like it or not. She wants him here. Get over it."

"I don't have to get over shit." Ryder takes a step back and swings his eyes around the room. "I'm out," he says, storming toward the garage, slamming the door behind him, and making Holden jump out of his skin. We listen to his bike fire up and scream down the driveway.

"Fucking hell," Dex mutters, scrubbing a tattooed hand down his face.

Gage's eyes narrow. "What did you do?"

Dex shakes his head. "Later," he offers and strides out of the room.

Gage watches him leave before turning to me with a sigh. "I'm going to bed," he says, walking around me. I nod and head toward my room downstairs. "Leo," he calls out, and I turn around. "Come on," he jerks his head towards the stairs.

"Where are we going?" I ask, following behind him.

"To cuddle our girl," he replies. Our girl? Is that what she is? I search for the jealousy of Gage calling her his girl, but it never comes. Not with him, anyway.

We let ourselves into her room, and she's exactly like I left her. We both strip down to boxer briefs and slide into bed with her. She snuggles into Gage's chest, immediately searching for me with her other arm. I slide in closer behind her, molding my body against hers. It doesn't take long for sleep to come full of dreams of her.

And Gage.

When I wake up the following day, Alessa is gone, but Gage is still fast asleep. He's sprawled on his stomach with both arms tucked under the pillow. I take a minute while he's sleeping to examine something I've been running from.

His long black eyelashes are fanned across his cheeks, and he looks so much younger with his wavy hair sleep tousled. I let my eyes roam down his muscled back to his muscled ass. Gage is attractive. I have no problem admitting that about any man. What makes me question it about Gage is the fact that I feel...*things* I've never felt before. Curiosity is the top one. I know Gage is bisexual just by the comments he's made; he doesn't hide it. Being pressed against him on his motorcycle was one thing; feeling his cock slide against mine inside Alessa was another.

I let my eyes slide back up his body and look into Gage's very blue and amused eyes.

"See something you like?" he asks in a sleepy voice.

My first instinct is to deny it, but something is telling me to tell him the truth. "I think so."

He raises the brow over his visible eye. "Really now?"

"I don't know," I say defensively before sitting up. I'm so fucking confused about my feelings for him, and I don't know him at all. But something keeps pulling me toward him.

He rolls to his side facing me, and the sheet slides down, revealing his toned abs. I saw them while we were with Alessa, but my eyes find them anyway. Gage clears his throat, and I jerk my eyes back to his. I thought I would find a smug look or even amusement, but what I find is understanding.

"There is nothing wrong with being curious, Leo." He sits up, leaning on one elbow.

I don't know how to respond to that, so I ask the one thing I've been dying to know. "Why have you been so accepting of me?"

He shrugs lazily. "Because Les was. I don't feel like you're a bad person. I would know if you were."

"I lied to her," I argue. I don't know why I am arguing against myself. Maybe I'm trying to get the subject off my attraction to Gage.

"She lied to you too," he points out and shrugs again. "You just need to figure out if you want it to work from here. Just know that if you do, I'm not backing down. I'll still be involved with her as long as she wants me to be."

I think about that a minute before I answer. He just laid it out there that she's no longer just mine, that the girl I've been seeing for the past four months is his now too. Do I want that? I look back into Gage's eyes, and he's staring at me with an open and honest expression.

"I want it to work. I'll do anything to make that possible, and I don't have a problem with you being involved. I'm just confused about how I feel about," I gesture to his naked torso on display, "this."

He leans closer. "There is only one way to find out how you feel about this," He suggests, letting his own eyes roam down my body. "Because I know exactly how I feel about that."

When his eyes connect with mine, I can see the truth there. He's attracted to me, but he's not afraid to admit it. I feel the pull to touch my lips to his just to see what it's like. He's leaning toward me too, eyes zeroed in on my lips. He gets so close I can feel his breath on my lips, then he stops, letting me close the last bit of distance.

"Oh," Alessa's voice cuts in. "Uh. Wow." We jerk apart like we've been shocked. "Don't let me interrupt," she laughs and disappears into her massive walk-in closet.

Guilt slams into my chest, and I look at Gage, and he's grinning from ear to ear.

"How is this funny?" I hiss, ashamed we got caught by the woman I love.

Gage snorts. "She's fine. If she wasn't, we would both be dead."

I hear rustling in the closet before she walks out dressed in a tailored dark blue pantsuit that hugs her curves, the jacket folded over her arm. I look closer and realize she has a little makeup on, and her hair is in soft waves down her back.

"Hey, Pretty girl," Gage greets, sliding off the end of the bed and kissing her cheek. "What's with the suit?"

She kisses his cheek back, seemingly unaffected that she almost caught us kissing. "I have that meeting with Helena for the restaurant."

"You want me to go?" he asks.

She looks at the clock. "If you can be ready in fifteen minutes."

"Done." He slaps her on the ass and jogs out of the room.

She shakes her head with a laugh before crawling up the bed towards me. She climbs up, so I have to lie back against the pillows with her straddling my waist. Even though she seems fine now, I still worry about last night and the fact that I was about to kiss a man in her bed.

"Hello there," she purrs, pecking me on the lips. She sits back and looks at me closer. "What's with the face?" she asks, smoothing her thumb between my eyebrows to smooth out my frown line.

"Last night," I say in the way of the answer, and I don't know how to bring up the other thing.

She sighs. "We can talk about that later, okay? We can talk about everything."

I place my hands on her thighs. "Even what you just saw?"

She smiles. "I saw how you looked at him at the cabin, Leo."

I frown again. "That doesn't bother you?"

"No." She pecks my lips. "If you want to explore things with him, then I'm okay with that."

"I'm not gay or bi or whatever."

She cutely tilts her head. "Are you sure you aren't bi? I mean, Gage is smoking hot, but I don't know if he's hot enough to turn a straight man bisexual." She crosses her arms on my chest before putting her chin on them. "I can't think of someone better than Gage to explore with."

I tuck her hair behind her ears. "I'm not sure yet."

She shrugs. "I won't push. I just need you to know I don't care as long as it stays between us. In this house."

"I don't see anyone else but you, Baby."

"And Gage," she teases.

I smack the side of her ass. "Stop."

"Fine, but I want to watch when you do." She swings her leg over me and slides off the bed, leaving me gaping at her.

"You are a dirty girl, aren't you?"

"The dirtiest." She bats her eyelashes at me, and I laugh. "You want to go too?"

I raise my eyebrows. "You want me to go?"

"Yes." She motions towards her bathroom. I jump off the bed, kissing her cheek on the way by. "Clocks ticking, though! There are spare toothbrushes under the sink!" she yells when I shut the door.

I climb into her massive shower and grin when I realize I'll smell like her all day. Ten minutes and I'm ready. I tuck the towel around my waist to search for clothes when I walk into her empty bedroom, and everything is laid out on the bed for me. I smile at her thoughtfulness and start dressing. She laid out a pair of black slacks that aren't mine, so probably Gage's, and a light-yellow button-up that Evander brought me when he brought some of my stuff over.

When I make it downstairs, Gage and Alessa are waiting for me. Gage has on black dress slacks and a blue button-up, making his eyes stand out even more, and she's slid her jacket on with high-heeled boots.

I am a lucky fucker. By two counts.

We load up in Gage's Range Rover with her up front, and she slides on a pair of oversized sunglasses when he backs out of the garage. "We can order food on the way and deliver it there."

Gage groans. "Dolly's. Please."

"You're obsessed," she laughs. She pulls out her phone and asks what we want before placing an order. "It should be there when we get there."

"Good." He grabs her hand and kisses her knuckles before laying their locked hands on her leg.

I can see her smile when she looks away. When I first met her, I didn't think she would be openly affectionate, but she surprised the shit out of me by loving the constant touch. Which I'm okay with because I'm the same way. Gage seems to be following that same path.

"Ryder's at his dad's," she says softly, looking at her phone.

"We can fix this, Pretty girl."

She smiles sadly. "Maybe."

I don't like Ryder, but I know it hurt her that he isn't home. I don't want her to hurt, so I need to try with Ryder. If she wants him in her life and I want her in mine, I can be the bigger person to a certain extent.

Her phone rings, and she picks up, answering in something I assume is Italian. She has an animated conversation with someone until we pull up in front of a huge building downtown with a large sold sign in the window. We sit out front while she finishes her call.

She hangs up and turns to Gage. "That was Aldo." He nods and slides out of the car. He strides to her side, pops her door open, and helps her out. I slide out behind them, not asking who that was because they won't tell me.

"Aldo is our New York man," she explains, surprising me. "And even though the old fart can speak perfect English, he only talks to me in Italian. Says it keeps me fresh," she finishes that with a fond smile.

Gage pulls open the front door, holding it so we can enter. The air conditioning hits me in the face, and I breathe a sigh of relief. It's much hotter in California than in North Carolina, and they don't seem to be affected by it because they grew up here.

"I don't understand a word you say, but it's hot as fuck," Gage says.

"Same," I agree, and Gage fist bumps me.

She rolls her eyes with a laugh.

We see our breakfast order sitting there waiting for us and dive in. Alessa said Helena could wait while we ate. As soon as I bit into my breakfast sandwich, I know why Gage is obsessed with the place. She fires off a text when we're done eating to let her know we're ready.

A robust lady with greying red hair greets Alessa with a kiss on both cheeks. "You look ravishing," she says, holding her at arm's length.

"You look beautiful too," Alessa says. The lady wears a loud green dress that clashes with her red hair. "Helena, this is Leo," Alessa introduces, and Helena pulls my face, smacking her lips right on my cheeks, not just the air kiss she gave Alessa.

"Nice to meet you," I greet.

"Oh, manners." She claps her hands and turns to Gage.

He swoops in, bending her at the waist, smacking a kiss on her cheeks before sitting her back on her feet. She fans her red face. "He always was my favorite." Gage grins at her, letting the full force of his dimples pop out. She fans herself harder, visibly collecting herself. "Come, come," she gestures for us to follow. I see I'm not the only one Gage effects like that.

Alessa giggles quietly, wiping her thumb over my cheeks to get rid of the bright red lipstick. "I said keep it in the house, Leo."

"Ha. Ha," I gesture at Gage. "I didn't maul her, at least."

Gage snorts. "At least she didn't grab my ass this time."

Alessa laughs and follows Helena.

She sits us at a table with Gage and me on either side of Alessa before sitting across from us. "These are what I have so far," she says, sliding design plans across the table. Alessa looks through them carefully, one at a time.

"These are excellent," Alessa comments. "Can we expand this, though?" she slides a drawn-out picture of a bar back to Helena. "Maybe curve it around both sides, so we have more room."

"Certainly," Helena jumps up. "I almost forgot some samples came in." She bustles out of the room with a swish of the green dress. I can't help but like the woman.

"Is this your restaurant?" I ask. I knew she owned several, but I never put the connection together when she said she had a meeting.

"Yeah," she smiles. "It's the first one I've bought and designed. The other ones were Dad's."

"Can I look?" I ask, gesturing towards the plans. This is what I did in North Carolina. I helped the designers get everything up and running to make it successful and helped restaurants out of the red to survive.

She shrugs. "Sure." She pushes them in front of me, and I look through them, impressed as hell.

"Is it themed?" I ask, looking at different looks that looked digitally made.

"Each Friday and Saturday, the staff will pick a different country, and we will make the dishes from that country, and also dress code for that night will be in the theme they picked."

"Damn, baby. You came up with that?"

"Of course she did," Gage answers, kicking back in his chair with an arm slung over the back of her chair. "Our girl is smart."

"Our girl, huh?" she asks, looking at him.

"You're damn right," he answers without hesitation. She turns to me with a raised brow.

I shrug. "I have to agree with Gage."

"Was I going to be consulted on this?" she asks.

Gage leans in close. "You were consulted the night we had our cocks inside you at the same time."

She shrugs"Fair point."

"Real classy, Gage," I laugh.

"What can I say? I'm a real classy guy," he replies, making me and Alessa snort with laughter. Gage is many things, but I don't think classy was one of them. He just grins, not at all offended.

Helena busts back into the room with fabric laid over her arm. She lays them out in front of Alessa before saying she would give her time to look before disappearing again.

While thinking, she runs her hands over a shimmery gold and then a shimmery silver.

"Where do you want this to go?" I ask, trying to help. Gage is just content to watch her work.

"Over here." She points to a picture of tables that sit to the side of the bar. "It's VIP. It gives a sense of privacy but doesn't close you off from the rest of the bar if you don't want to be." She points to a deep burgundy. "This one could be there too if you wanted the extra privacy. There are seven VIP booths and one large one in the middle for groups."

I lay the gold with the burgundy before switching it to silver so she could see them together. "Silver," we both say at the same time and then smile at each other.

"I can use the same burgundy for the tablecloths," she says, mostly talking to herself.

Helena bustles back in. "Thoughts?"

"Silver and burgundy for the VIP drapes and burgundy for the tablecloths. Will you see about getting different ones for the themed nights? The burgundy can be used on weekdays."

"Of course, dear," she answers as we stand. "I'll text you when I have them."

She gives us all the smooching cheek kisses before we exit the restaurant. I wipe the lipstick off as Gage does, making Alessa laugh. We slide into the car, and head back to the house. Alessa's phone constantly rings the whole trip, and Gage rolls his eyes, indicating this is the norm for her. No wonder she was stressed enough to drink last night. She's running a criminal empire and dealing with all our bullshit. I need to talk to Gage. Somehow, we need to make this easier for her. First, I'm going to start by talking to her.

When we get back to the house, I take my chance. "Can we talk now?" I ask.

We're both putting this conversation off. Gage kisses her cheek, gives me the thumbs up behind her back, and disappears into the back of the house.

She nods, motioning for me to follow her up the stairs. She climbs onto her bed with her legs crisscrossed underneath her getting comfortable. I slide up the bed so my back is against the headboard.

"I'm so fucking sorry for lying to you, Baby," I start. "I never thought I would fall for you the way I did, but I knew by the second date that you were mine."

"I lied to you too, Leo," she says softly, looking at her hands in her lap. "I knew when I accepted the first date that there was something about you. I was drawn to the light in you." She looks into my eyes. "No more lies. I can't handle anymore."

"You didn't lie to me for gain like I did, and for that, I feel like shit." I lean up and grab her hand. "I never want you to feel from this point on that I'm being anything other than honest with you. I love you, Alessa."

She pulls her hand away, and I frown. "You know how I feel about you. I just feel like we should table that for now." She holds up a hand when I open my mouth, a soft smile on her lips. "We need to get to know each other. The real us. You also need to accept that it won't just be us in this relationship anymore." She stretches her legs out and lies on her back on the bed. "I don't know where things stand with anyone but you and Gage," she turns her head to look at me, "but I need you to know I'm not giving up on any of them."

"I need you to know I'm not giving up on you. On us." I lay beside her, turning my head to see her eyes. "I don't care what that involves. I'm in this for the long haul, Baby."

"Are you sure you're okay with this, Leo?" she asks.

"I wasn't," I tell her honestly. "Until I saw how you responded between Gage and me." Watching her come undone for Gage was the sexiest thing I've ever seen. I saw her body's reactions and the emotions slide over her face. I'm addicted to that sight now. "Everything else will work itself out."

"Even with Ryder?"

"Ryder and I have a long way to go," I say with a chuckle. "But if he wants you as much as he says, he will do whatever it is to make you happy."

Her eyes turn sad, and I hate it. "Ryder has never left before. No matter how mad we've gotten at each other, we always work it out."

"That's before feelings were involved, Baby," I sigh. "You guys will work it out." I grab her hand and lace our fingers, kissing the back of her hand, and lay them down on the bed. She leaves it this time, even squeezing it.

"I figured you were hoping we wouldn't."

"I'd never want anything that would make you unhappy." I reach up with my other hand, running my knuckles down her cheek. "I'll do everything in this world to make sure you stay happy. Even if that includes Ryder." I rub my thumb on the back of her hand. "What happened last night?"

She sighs. "I don't know," she answers. "I told Ryder I had feelings for you, and the look in his eyes broke my heart." That made sense why he was pissed off enough to leave. How does she not see how much Ryder is in love with her? I'm not going to be the one to tell her; he needed to man up and tell her himself. "I just needed out of the house and ended up at Skyline. When I started drinking, I knew my places would call Ryder."

I chuckle. "You know Mateo called me, right?"

"That traitor," she gasps, clutching her chest in mock outrage.

"He was worried about you. They both were."

"I know." She turns her head to me again. "I gained a lot of respect for your brothers last night. They entertained me for hours and never left my side." She rubs her hand down my face. "I still have some shit to work through when it comes to them, but I'm trying. For you."

"I get it, Baby. I appreciate that you're trying with my brothers, but do it for you. Not me." I still didn't know what happened with Frankie completely, but now didn't seem like a good time to ask. This is the most we've talked about since all of this went down, and I wasn't messing it up now. Something told me she would shut down if I did; she could tell me on her own time.

She rolls over onto her side, kissing my lips before wrapping her arms around my neck, holding me tight. I could feel relief flood my system. Is everything perfect between us? No. But I'm going to make damn sure that they are.

Between Gage and me, we could get this woman anything she ever wanted.

Starting with getting Ryder back home.

CHAPTER 15
HOLDEN

I waited fifteen minutes after I heard Les and Leo walk downstairs before I searched for her to make sure she was okay. I watched them bring her in last night, and I've never seen any of them have to carry her into the house. I find her on the back patio by the pool, but she isn't alone. Gage is kissing her deeply, with Leo sitting on the other side. She turns from Gage, and Leo kisses her the same way. I know I should walk away, but I find myself frozen to the spot one step outside the door. I should be upset that she just kissed me, but I wasn't. I heard a lot more around the house than they thought, and I've listened to Les and Gage talking. I heard him tell her she could have whoever she wanted, including all of us. I'm just happy that I even have a chance with someone like Les. I don't care who else is involved.

Gage says something, causing Leo and Les to break apart laughing. Her eyes catch my movement stepping back into the house, and her smile freezes me to the spot again. She says something to the guys, and they get up, walking toward the house.

"You don't have to go," I tell them. I don't want to interrupt their time with her.

Gage slaps me on the back. "She just wants you out here, man. No biggie."

They disappear into the house, and Les beckons me over. She's wearing a bright pink bikini that has her body on display.

She is stunning.

I try to avert my eyes from her cleavage when I sit down on the lounger facing her, unsuccessfully if the smile on her face is any indication. I look down at my lap; I don't want her to feel weird about me staring.

She tilts my chin up with her fingers. "Don't hide your face," she reminds me. She and Ryder often remind me to look up and not slouch or try to hide, and I'm trying.

"Okay," I say softly.

"Did you need something?" she asks with a tilt of her head. She knows I don't seek her out often. Too scared to talk to her. It's a little easier since our trip to the ranch.

"I wanted to make sure you're okay."

"I am," she sighs. "It was just a bad day, and I let it get to me."

"Is Ryder home?" I ask and immediately regret it when sadness enters her eyes.

"No, but he's okay at his dad's. He will come home." I wonder if she's convincing herself as much as me.

I nod when I can't think of anything else to say. I'm about to run for the house when she pulls my chin back to her eyes. "Was there anything else?"

I swallow and shake my head. It's a lie, especially after I saw her kiss Leo and Gage. I want that too, but I'm too big a coward to go for it.

She sits up and swings her legs toward me. Her knees brush mine, and I swallow again, kicking myself for not being bolder. "Are you sure?" she asks, tilting her head in the way I love. All the other guys except Dex would go for it. They would just kiss her, but I can't get myself to move. I'm gripping the sides of the lounger so hard my fingers are hurting. I shake my head again.

She reaches down and pries my fingers loose. She moves my arms to the side before standing and sliding both of her knees beside my hips, straddling my lap. I have the most gorgeous woman in the world on my lap, and I can't fucking think or move. My hands itch to touch her, but I can't move them from their position on the lounger.

She leans in beside my ear. "What do you want, Holden?" Her breath blows over my ear, making me shiver. My cock is paying attention too, and I'm embarrassed because I know she can feel it through my shorts. She rubs her hands down my hot cheeks, leaving them there, holding my face. "Don't be embarrassed. If you didn't react, I would worry more." She leans in and presses her lips against mine like she did at the ranch. This time, she licks the seam of my lips. I open my mouth and feel her tongue slide against mine, freezing on the first stroke. She pulls back with a slight frown. "Do you not want this?"

"No," I say too fast. "I mean, yes. I want this." I pull her face back to mine, crashing my lips against hers. It's sloppy and uncoordinated. Embarrassment floods me again when she pulls away, and she stares at me for so long that I start to get uncomfortable.

"Are you a virgin, Holden?" she finally asks softly. I try to look away, but she holds my face in her hands. Too mortified to answer out loud, I just nod. No way she wants a bumbling fucking virgin when she has guys who know what they're doing.

"I should have told you before."

She smiles again. "It's not a problem. We will just go slower. If that's what you want." I nod because I do. I want this so bad. "You know I'm with Gage and Leo, right?" I nod again. "That doesn't bother you?"

"No," I croak out. "I want you happy."

She loops her arms around my neck. "They do make me happy." She runs her fingers through the hair. "But you make me happy too." Her smile turns sad again. "Dex and Ryder too."

"He will come home," I say with more confidence than I feel. I heard them arguing. What if he doesn't come back? I'm not sure I want to admit how much that thought hurts me.

"Hm," she says, running her fingers through my hair again. It feels so good. "Dex is another matter. But we will work that out later. For now--" She lets her total weight down on my cock, and I grunt. *Fuck.* She takes my hands and puts them on the sides of her hips. Her tanned skin is soft and hot from being in the sun. "We will start with this."

She presses her lips to mine, teasing them open with her tongue. When it slides in this time, I'm more prepared. Sure, I've kissed girls before, but I was sixteen when my uncle sold me off after my parents died. Even in school, I was a computer nerd, and that didn't bring many girls banging on my door.

She strokes my tongue several times before I feel bolder, following her tongue into her mouth. She pushes in, deepening the kiss. I finally find my courage and start kissing her back harder. I slide my hands up her hips and ribcage, marveling at how soft she is before sliding them around her back, pulling her, so her breasts are pressed against my chest. Les moans into my mouth, grinding her hips down on my cock. A shocked gasp escapes me at the sensation, and I end up breaking our kiss. I stare into her blue eyes, seeing lust there—lust for me. I hear someone layout on the lounger behind her and don't even care. I don't want to look away from her.

"This looks cozy," Gage remarks, and I finally look at him, making sure he isn't mad. He's wearing a sly smile but doesn't look to be upset. "Don't stop on my account." He puts his hands behind his head, closing his eyes.

She giggles softly before leaning in and kissing me again. I know what I'm doing this time, so I take over, and she melts against me. I start sliding my hands over her skin, content to feel her against me. Like I've dreamed about. She's so much softer than I imagined.

She jerks away from the kiss. "Gage!" She laughs, grabbing the front of her top, holding it against her breasts where he jerked the ties of her top loose.

"Oops," he chuckles.

She turns to him. "Be good," she warns.

"Why? What's the fun in that?"

She looks at me with the question in her eyes, and I nod. They would find out sooner or later that I'm a virgin. She pecks my lips before turning back to Gage. "We're going slow," she explains, then huffs when he looks at her in confusion. "He's a virgin."

I can feel my cheeks flame again when he jerks his eyes to mine, then grins. "You lucky bastard. You get that sweet pussy for your first time?" I feel my face get hotter, but not from embarrassment, from the thought of her naked with my cock inside her. I groan at that thought before I can stop it, and his grin widens. "Trust me, whatever just went through your head will never compare to the real thing."

"Shut up or go in the house," she tells him sternly.

"Not a chance in hell, Pretty girl." He mimes zipping his lips shut and throwing away the key, making me chuckle, breaking some of the tension in my body.

She shakes her head and looks back at me. "You want me to let this go?" She nods her head to where her hands are holding her top. I nod so fast that I almost make myself dizzy. She lets her hands drop and lays the top beside us. I was too focused on my nerves earlier to notice the bruise on one of her breasts, and my brows furrow in concern.

"It's okay. It was Ryder," she tells me, and Gage leans up and looks around her.

"He marked you?" he asks, and I can't tell whether he's mad or not.

She shrugs. "I liked it. Let's move on."

She takes my hands and places them on her naked breasts, moving her hands with mine, so I'm gently massaging them. They are perfect, more than my hands can hold, and her nipples are a dusky pink color and in hard points. She drops her hands, looping them around my neck, letting me feel her.

"Play with her nipples," Gage says hoarsely, and I look to see he's focused on my hands.

"Do you want him to go?" she whispers just so I can hear, and I shake my head because he's helping me feel more confident.

I hear him sit up and scoot his lounger closer. He reaches around to her breast and rolls her nipple between his fingers. "Like that," he instructs, and I follow his direction on the other side.

"Oh, shit," she whispers, arching into our touch.

"Is this okay?" I ask. I wasn't good at reading cues yet.

"Yes," she breathes.

"You like Holden's hands on you, don't you, Pretty girl?" Gage drops his hand, so I place my fingers on that nipple, rolling them between my fingers, watching her face.

"I do," she answers, grinding her hips down on me again. If she doesn't stop I'm going to come in my pants, but I don't want to stop her; it feels too good.

"Suck one into your mouth," Gage says, and my eyes jerk to his face. He laughs. "Trust me." I just look at him, hoping, without me saying, he'll show me. How do you ask another guy to teach you to please a girl? Gage is the easiest going, and I always feel comfortable around him. He's the first one that made me laugh again with his antics, and I feel at ease like this with him. He gets up and sits beside me, much to my relief. He leans in and sucks the stiff peak between his lips, tugging slightly. Her hips buck, and she sinks her fingers into his hair.

I lean in and copy his movement, making her hand go to my head. I can't see her face anymore, so I go with how her hips move. They move more when I put more pressure on her nipple. "You're a fast learner," she moans, rocking her hips.

Sliding my hands down her ass, I jerk her harder onto my dick. I don't care anymore; I need to feel her.

Gage lets her nipple go with a wet pop. "Atta boy," he encourages when he sees me moving her hips against me.

I move her against my cock through my shorts, so turned on that I know I'm about to come. I can't even be embarrassed. My breathing starts to speed up, and my grip on her hips tightens, grinding my hips up while I pull her down. She leans in. "It's okay," she says, crashing her lips against mine. I feel my balls tighten up and groan into her mouth, letting myself go. She continues rolling her hips through my release until I get too sensitive. She pulls back, pecking my lips. I couldn't stop the blush I can feel coming on.

Gage laughs. "You lasted longer than I did the first time I had a girl dry hump me, and she didn't even have her tits in my face."

I can't help it; I laugh. He knew just what to say to save me from embarrassment, and she seems fine with it, sweetly rubbing her hands down my stubbly cheeks.

"What about you?" I whisper. I have no idea what to do, but I know she didn't get off.

"I'm fine," she smiles.

"Bullshit," Gage exclaims and then looks at me. "You ready for your next learning experience?"

"Gage," Les groans in exasperation. He didn't take his vow of silence very seriously.

"No. I want to," I tell her, and she takes a shuddering breath. "If you want me to," I say uncertainly.

"I want you to," she laughs breathlessly. "Knowing Gage will show you has me so turned on."

Gage moves back to his lounger, his knees bracketing mine. He stands her up from my lap and slowly unties the ties on the side of her bottoms. He lets them drop, and all the breath leaves my body in a whoosh. Her whole body is perfect. I can see the various scars she's acquired; it doesn't take away from how gorgeous she is. He sits her down on his lap, throwing her legs over his. He spreads his legs wider, opening her legs; my eyes are glued to her bare pussy.

He pulls her back against his chest, kissing her neck right below her ear. "How wet are you knowing anyone could walk through that door and see you all spread out for Holden?"

"Find out," she challenges, and I can see the heat flare in his eyes. He slides his hand down until it's between her thighs, dipping them inside of her. He pulls them out, and they're glistening.

Holy fuck, this is happening.

"Fuck, Pretty girl," he groans. "I love this dripping pussy." I wish I was as bold as he is with his words. "Give me your hand," Gage says to me, so I reach out. He grips my wrist and places the pad of my fingers at the top of her pussy. He rubs my fingers in a circle, pushing down on the top of my fingers, causing her hips to buck. "You feel that?" I nod. "Rub that in slow circles. Watch her body and listen to her. It will tell you all you need to know."

He moves his hand from mine to her nipples, rolling them between his fingers. I follow his instructions and rub her clit in small circles. I know the basic anatomy of a girl. I watched porn as a teenager but seeing it firsthand is something else. Her eyes are getting darker, her breasts rising and falling with each breath, her hips rolling with my fingers.

"Take your other hand and slide two fingers inside of her." He shows me with his hand, flipping his hand so his knuckles are down. I do it and almost lose my shit. It's so tight, wet, and hot. How am I ever going to survive with my cock inside of her? "Now do this." He crooks his finger in a beckoning motion. "You will feel skin a little different." I search a few times before I find it, and she responds instantly. "There ya go," Gage encourages. "Rub that and her clit. She'll explode for you, man."

I do as he says, changing speed and pressure depending on her body. When her hips start rolling with me, I know I have the right tempo.

"You're right, Pretty girl." He kisses her neck again, still idly rolling her nipples. "He is a fast learner."

"Fuck," she moans, pushing her hips down on my fingers. Her whole body is tight as a bowstring.

"Suck her clit into your mouth like you did her nipple. She tastes so fucking sweet."

I don't need to be shown what to do. He spreads her wider to encompass my shoulders, and I dive between her legs, ready to taste her. I suck her clit into my mouth while still moving my fingers.

I can feel my cock hardening again and have to chastise it.

Not your turn.

I focus all my attention on her, sucking harder on her clit, and she moans low and throaty, almost making me bust in my pants again.

"Holden!" she screams, sinking her hand into my hair. I feel her walls tighten on my fingers; then I feel wetness gush out of her soaking my hand. I slide my tongue over her clit until I feel her body tense and pull away. I gently slide my fingers out of her and suck them into my mouth. The taste is just too good to pass up.

"Oh my," she breathes and then giggles. "That's hot."

I let my fingers go with a wet pop, savoring the flavor. "Holy shit," I say, causing them both to laugh.

Gage slides her back up on his lap. "Holy shit, is right." He nods to my lap. "Already?"

I look down at my hard cock and shrug. "Yeah, I guess so."

He kisses down her neck. "Lay back on the lounger."

I raise an eyebrow but do as he says. To my shock, she climbs over to me, straddling my thighs, and hooks her hands in the top of my shorts. "I want to taste you too."

Words fail me again, so I nod, swallowing my nerves. If I didn't last with her touching me through my clothes, I won't last with her mouth on me. She pulls my shorts down enough for my cock to pop free.

Her eyes widen. "Of course, you were hiding an anaconda in your pants."

"It's always the quiet ones," Gage comments with a laugh, and I frown. Is there something wrong with it?

She smooths out the frown line. "Your cock is huge, Holden," she explains, so I know what they meant. She wraps her tiny hand around the base; her fingers don't even meet. I've seen other cocks in porn, but I didn't have anything else to compare mine to. My cock jerks in her hand, and I have to grip the side of the lounger to keep from grabbing her.

She leans down, and her tongue licks up the slit at the head. "Fuck," I grunt. She smiles up at me and does it again.

She sucks my cock into her mouth; as far as it will go, it's less than half, but it feels so fucking good. She gets my cock wet with her saliva before sucking the head into her mouth while twisting her hand around the base.

"Goddamn," Gage mutters from his lounger, watching everything she's doing. I'm vaguely aware it should be weird to have another man watch you get your cock sucked for the first time, but I couldn't care less.

She slides her mouth down again, twisting her hand to meet her lips, milking my cock. My hips jerk by themselves, pushing me further into her mouth. She moves her hand and then slides both under my cut-off shirt, scraping her nails down my abs.

"Put one of your hands on her head," Gage instructs, so I do. "Now tighten your fist." I almost question him until I feel her moaning around my cock at the suggestion. I tighten my hand, wrapping my fingers in her hair. "Now push gently down on her head. She will tell you if you need to stop."

Her eyes flick up to mine, letting me know it's okay. I push down on her head, sending my cock into her mouth, bumping her throat, and her eyes roll back in her head with a moan. Encouraged, I push again, and I feel myself slide further when she swallows around the head of my cock. "Fuck!" I shout before groaning. "Fuck Fuck Fuck," I chant when she starts sucking my cock faster. When one of her hands slides down, gripping and rolling my balls between her fingers, I know I'm fucking done. "Alessa," I try to warn. "I'm going to come." I wanted to give her time to move, but she sucks harder. Gage puts his hand on top of mine and shoves her head down. I feel the first jet pump into her throat, and she just continues to swallow. I groan louder, emptying everything into her throat and running my fingers through her hair after Gage moves his hand.

She lets my cock go with a pop, wiping her mouth with the back of her hand, and smiles. "I'd say this was a good learning experience."

I laugh and crush her to my chest. I kiss her with more confidence than I've ever felt, not caring that I could taste my salty cum in her mouth. She pecks my lips, pulling back. "Was that okay?"

"Yeah," I breathe. "It was perfect."

"The best is yet to come," Gage says, waggling his eyebrows.

I laugh again, feeling lighter than I have in a very long time.

CHAPTER 16
ALESSA

After I cuddled with Holden on the lounger for a while longer, he said he needed to get cleaned up, but I suspected he needed to decompress. I didn't mean for all that to happen, but with Gage encouraging us, I couldn't help it. Holden was a surprise, and he learned fast. And his cock? *Holy shit.* I was going to feel that the next day after we slept together for the first time. It. Was. *Huge.*

Even though I know Holden needed a minute to collect himself, he walked into the house with his head held high. As soon as he disappeared, Gage pulled me to him, flipping us in sixty-nine. He made me come three more times with his mouth before he finally let himself come down my throat.

After my talk with Leo, I felt more myself than I have in a while. I know I told him no more lies, but I can't tell him about the Black Demon. At least not yet. I'm just glad we could work the other stuff out.

I'm completely blissed out, Gage and I still lying naked together on the lounger, but thoughts of Ryder are still plaguing me. I hate that he feels he had to leave, but I messaged and called all day, and the only thing I got from him was a text saying, "I'm fine."

"Go get him, Pretty girl," Gage says, breaking into my thoughts.

"Who?" I ask, confused, looking up at his face.

He looks at me softly. "Ryder."

"How did you know?"

"You were here, but your mind was a million miles away," he answers.

"I'm sorry," I apologize, feeling like shit for making him feel like I wasn't here with him.

"Don't apologize." He rubs his hand down my cheek. "Go get him."

He helps me get back into my bikini and then slides his shorts back on. He walks me to the bottom of the stairs, kisses me, then pats my ass to move me up the steps.

I throw my hair in a bun and hop in the shower. Nerves start attacking me, and I chastise myself. This was Ryder, my best friend, and he needs to come home. After my shower, I dress in jean shorts and a tank top, then go downstairs.

I turn the corner toward the garage, and that's when I see Dex coming in. I don't know what to say to him, either.

Everything blew up in my head last night with Leo, my many fights with Ryder, the discussion with Dex, trying to run businesses, opening a new one, and running this family. I just...broke. I drove to Skyline because I know their security is good, not expecting to see Evander or Mateo, and I suspected someone there called to tell them I was there. They hung out with me all night, letting me get drunk and keeping me company. It's a point in their favor.

"Hey, Les," Dex says when he sees me. "I'm sorry about yesterday."

I shake my head. "Don't be. I pushed, and I should be the one apologizing."

"No, Baby girl," he says, stepping closer to me without touching. "I need you to push."

I knit my brows in confusion. "What?"

"Push me," he swallows. "Please."

I search his eyes before I answer. "I'll try, but Dex, I don't like the place your eyes go." It's like he's sucked back in time and not seeing what is right in front of him.

He looks away before looking back at me. "I need you to push," he repeats, and I nod. He runs his hand over my arm when he walks away, barely a touch, but it's something.

That's one less thing off my plate from yesterday, and meeting Helena this morning helped get a lot of stuff off my mind. I climb into my Ferrari, ready to fix the next thing.

"BELLISSIMA!" Ryder's dad, Rocco, greets me when he sees me standing in the foyer and jerks me into a bear hug. "It's so good to see you."

I hug him back tightly. "It's been too long." He was like my second dad growing up.

"Don't stay away like that," he says, pulling me back to look at him.

Ryder is his spitting image, except Rocco has streaks of grey in his hair. Even in his mid-fifties, the man is still handsome and well-built. I know what I would look at in thirty years with Ryder, and I'm not complaining.

"Dad, who's here?" Ryder asks, rounding the corner. His eyes land on me, and that muscle in his jaw starts ticking. "Why are you here?"

Rocco levels his son with a glare that could kill. "Don't you talk to her like that, boy."

Ryder nods politely. "Yes, sir."

Rocco is easygoing, but Ryder still respects him. Rocco demands respect with how he holds himself. Ryder also has that in spades. It broke my heart when he retired, but he couldn't stay in second without my dad, and I understood.

"Can we talk?" I ask Ryder.

"I'm a little busy," he says, jerking his head into the other room.

"Nonsense." Rocco waves that away. "Quit being a pussy," he says and walks out of the room.

A shocked laugh leaves me before I can stop it. Ryder turns his glare back on me, and I return it. "Is this how you want to do this?" I ask.

"Do what?" he asks, crossing his arms over his chest.

"Cut the shit. Can we talk, or do you want me to leave?"

"I don't feel like talking."

I swallow the hurt and nod. "Fine." I jerk the door open, and he grabs my arm.

"Stop. Shit," he mutters, dropping my arm. I turn toward him as he runs his fingers through his hair. "Come on," he nods, and I follow him to the back of his dad's house. He leads me up the steps to his old bedroom. The motorcycle and car posters still hang everywhere, along with pictures of me, him, Micah, and Gage. I can't tell you how much time we spent in this room watching tv, playing video games, or just hanging out. When we weren't at my house, we were here. I run my fingers over the picture of Rocco and Elaina on their wedding day. Ryder was born a year later. She died of complications when Ryder was six giving birth to his brother. They lost him too. Rocco grieved his beloved wife while trying to raise a confused six-year-old. I was six then too, but I know my mom stepped up a lot to help.

Ryder shuts the door, sits on the bed, and scoots up, so his back is propped against the wall. "Nothing has changed," I say in amazement. The only reason anything changed at my house, which used to be dad's, was that I needed to do it. I needed to make it my own.

Ryder snorts. "Nah. The old man is too sentimental."

I run my fingers over a picture of Ryder and me, arms slung over each other's shoulders, laughing at something. Probably Gage, if I had to guess. We were about twelve or thirteen, and from the light in my eyes, I would think it was before Frankie's men took me. Our dads finally brought us to The Games for the first time, and we had a blast.

"What happened to us, Ryder?" I ask, emotion clogging my voice, getting sucked into the past from looking at us through the years.

"We grew up."

"Grew up or grew apart?" I can't hide the hurt in my voice. Why is he so flippant? Did I do this to him?

"You know I don't want us to grow apart," he says harshly, sitting up on the bed, his feet hitting the floor with a thud. "You decided that when you brought Leo into your life."

I whirl around to face him. "That's not fair, and you fucking know it. Did you expect me to die alone? Never meet anyone?"

"You could have had me!" he shouts.

"I didn't know!" I yell back.

"That's because all you've ever seen me as is your fucking lap dog." He stands up. "You knew I would always be there, no matter what. Guess what, Les? I'm not that guy anymore. You can have Leo and Gage and whoever the fuck else you want in your life. Because I'm done."

"So, that's it? Twenty-five years, and you're throwing it away?" My words come out in a whisper-yell, trying to keep my voice down because I don't want his dad to hear us yelling at each other. Does he not realize he is one of the most important people in my life?

"I can't do it, Les," he says hoarsely. "I can't watch you with them."

"I want you too," I beg. "I want you in my life too!"

He's already shaking his head. "I want you in my life too, but I want to be the only guy in yours."

My heart sinks to my stomach. I'm either giving up Ryder or the other guys. How the hell am I supposed to make that decision? Despite our differences, I love Leo, but that's four months versus twenty-five years. Gage is also working his way further into my heart. Holden is finally opening up to me, and Dex trusts me enough to push him out of his head. Can I give that up to save my friendship with Ryder?

"I can tell by your silence that this isn't what you want. And that's fine." He runs his fingers through his hair. "Go be with them, Les."

"What about us?" I ask, tears gathering in my eyes. I can't stop them from forming.

"There. Is. No. Us," he says through clenched teeth.

I stare at him, and it's like I don't even know who he is right now. I can feel my heart breaking into pieces, but I can also tell by the stubborn set of his jaw that we aren't getting anywhere. I jerk the door open before tears start streaming down my face, running down the stairs and past a worried-looking Rocco. I can't stop to say anything; I need to get out. Now.

I jump into my car, slamming the door shut and stabbing the button to start it. I shove my sunglasses on and peel out of the driveway, apologizing to Rocco in my head as I make the turn in the circle driveway, heading back towards the gate. I barely give it time to open before flying through them.

I know I'm going way too fast, but I can't stop slamming through gears, pressing the gas harder and harder. I need to slow down because I can't see through the tears, but I can't bring myself to stop.

I hit the main highway, swerving in and out of cars, mentally flipping off whoever beeps their horn. I can't go home like this, not when my world is crumbling beneath my feet. My phone starts ringing, and I see Rocco's number pop up. I hit ignore, nearly taking out the back of a minivan. I swerve at the last second, and it scares me more that it doesn't scare me.

My phone rings again and again; I keep hitting ignore. I don't want to talk to anyone. When Ryder's number pops up, I stab the window button and toss the phone out of the window before rolling it back up.

Fuck him. Fuck this. Fuck everything.

I drive aimlessly for fifteen minutes, just weaving through traffic, and that's when I hear the sirens wailing behind me, only catching up because I'm hitting a stall in traffic. I can run; there is no way they could catch this car, but what good would that do?

I jerk over to the shoulder, killing the engine. I wipe my eyes the best I can, but the tears just won't stop. I look in my side-view mirror and narrow my eyes.

Mid-thirties. Tall. Built. Dirty blonde hair. Whiskey-colored eyes. Sexy as sin.

And wearing a goddamn detective's badge.

I stab the window button for the passenger side when he walks around the back of the car so he's not in traffic.

He leans his elbows on the window frame, mirrored sunglasses hiding those sinfully hot eyes. The eyes that used to look at me with lust now look at me with disdain. I'm the enemy now, not the teenage girl he used to spend hours inside of.

"What can I do for you, Detective?" I ask. At least the tears stopped.

"You were going a little fast, don't ya think, Ms. Poletti?" he replies, looking around inside the car.

I have to suppress a snort at the formal name. This man used to groan my fucking name. "Didn't notice."

"Have you been drinking?" he asks, and I roll my eyes even though he can't see me.

"No. I haven't." I'm done with the pleasantries. "What do you want, Zane?"

Of all the luck after what happened, it's none other than Zane Ayers, son of the late Zeus Ayers, one of my dad's most trusted men before Zeus died. The same Zane I had an on-again-off-again relationship with for over a year. We had no business messing around, but that didn't stop us from sneaking away when we could.

"You almost took out a fucking car back there," he says, his voice sliding over me like honey. It ended for good because he decided his life was on the other side of the law, and he lied to me while going to the police academy. To say I was pissed was an understatement.

I jerk my sunglasses off, leveling him with a glare. "Last time I checked, detectives don't pull people over, so what the fuck do you want?"

"What's wrong?" he asks harshly, and I'm confused for a second until I realize my sunglasses hide bloodshot, puffy eyes from crying.

"Nothing," I reply, shoving them back on. "Are we done?"

"Who made you cry, Alessa?"

"Oh, we're on a first-name basis again? Good to know. Step away from the car," I warn, stabbing the button and firing the car up. He just leans both arms on the window frame. "Don't test me, Zane."

He finally pushes up his mirrored sunglasses, revealing those strange eyes that burn you up with one look. "Tell me who the fuck made you cry, and I'll move."

"Why do you even care?" I ask, shoving the car into first gear and revving it in a warning. "Move."

He gives me a long look. "I'll see you around, Les," he says before stepping back.

I take off like a shot with nowhere to go.

CHAPTER 17
RYDER

"Fuck!" I yell, slinging my phone onto the bed before roughly jamming both hands through my hair. I've called Les several times after she left, but it goes straight to voicemail, so she either blocked me or turned her phone off. Not that I fucking blame her; I'm an idiot.

My door opens, and Dad steps in. "What the hell is wrong with you?" he asks in that voice that still makes me want to shit myself.

"What do you mean?" I contain the wince. He hates when you answer a question with a question.

"Don't play that shit, boy," he barks. "Why did that girl just run out of here crying?"

I jerk my head up. "What?" I knew she was upset, but crying? Les?

"Are you trying to piss me off?"

"No," I sigh. "I didn't know."

"That girl has been in your life since birth. What did you do?" He walks further into the room, pulling out the rolling computer chair before lowering himself into it.

I flop back on the bed, staring at the ceiling. "I'm a fucking dumbass."

"No shit," he grumbles, and I raise my head a little to look at him. "Tell me what's going on."

How the hell do I explain to my dad that I want her, but she also wants four other guys? Yes, I'm included in that, but I can't imagine watching another man touch the girl I've pined for ever since I can remember. It was never the right time to tell her. First, we were too young, then she got kidnapped and had to heal, then she wasn't ready, then her dad died, then she met fucking Leo. The list goes on and on.

"I told her how I felt after shit went bad with Leo." I stop and try to gather my thoughts.

"She didn't return those feelings?" Dad asks softly. No matter how intimidating he is, he's still the best father I've ever known. He and Alessa's dad did whatever they could to give us a normal life.

I laugh humorlessly. "Oh, she does, but she also has the same feelings for four other guys."

He doesn't say anything for so long that I finally sit up on my elbows to look at him, and he's staring off into space with a contemplative look. He turns his eyes back on me, eyes that match mine perfectly. "Let me get this right. You finally tell her what we've all seen for years and then fuck it up because you still haven't learned how to share?"

My mouth pops open. "We aren't talking about sharing a toy, Dad. This is *Alessa*."

"I know who we are talking about." He narrows his eyes in warning at my tone, then softens again. "Ryder, don't let her get away from you because of jealousy."

"That's not the life I want with her," I say miserably, sitting up on the side of the bed.

"Life doesn't always turn out how we want it." His gaze lands on the picture of him and Mom. "Trust me when I say if you love someone, you will do whatever you can for them." He turns back to me, and his eyes are sad. "Go find that girl and beg her to forgive you. Then man up and do what you have to do to keep her."

"I don't know if I can, Dad." I drop my head into my hands and hear him stand up.

He sits beside me on the bed. "Do you love her?"

I swallow the lump in my throat. "Yes."

"Good," he says, and I can hear the smile in his voice. He always was the biggest supporter of Les and me, mainly because he was the only one I ever told how I felt. "Girls like Alessa are rare." He reaches over and squeezes my shoulder. "I won't tell you what to do, but I hope you make the right choice."

He squeezes my shoulder again and walks silently out of the room, shutting the door softly behind him.

I lay back on the bed, throwing an arm over my eyes. I'm pissed at myself for spilling all that hateful bullshit, but I'm also pissed at her and have no right to be, which just pisses me off even more.

Can I do what dad said? Can I do what I need to keep her, or would I fuck it up even more when it all comes crashing down because I'm a jealous bastard? I remember how I felt when she kissed Gage in front of me, and I hated that feeling. I wanted to beat the shit out of him for even *thinking* about touching her, and that was just a kiss. What about when he was inside of her, and I was there? If it wasn't Gage, what about Dex? Holden? Leo?

My anger immediately flares when I think about Leo. I wish Les would have just let me fucking shoot him like I wanted. But that wouldn't have mattered. I still have three other guys as competition.

Did it have to be competition, though? There is no doubt Les deserves the world laid at her feet. Would there be any harm in having other guys help with that? Help me worship at her feet like the queen she is? I could probably handle the other guys; the real issue is Leo. Could I watch Leo touch her, or would I put a bullet between his eyes?

I reach for my phone and try Les again, but it goes straight to voicemail. I suck it up and dial Gage.

"What?" he answers on the third ring.

"Where's Les?"

"I don't know," he answers shortly, probably still pissed about the other day.

"What the fuck do you mean you don't know?" I say, standing up from the bed. Didn't she go home?

"What I fucking mean is, I sent her to come to get you, but instead, I get a call from Zane saying he saw her hauling ass down the highway, nearly killing herself. What the fuck happened?" He sent her to me? Zane called him? I grind my teeth over that name.

"I fucked up, Gage," I tell him honestly.

"You're damn right you did because now I'm standing on the side of the highway with a smashed cell phone and a missing Les."

He must have tried to call her and had Holden find it when it went to voicemail. Even turned off, he could still track it to the last place it was when it was powered on. Then it hits me what he said. "What do you mean missing?"

"Missing as in, we can't fucking find her now!" he yells. I hear him slam his car door and then hear several blowing horns. "You better pray to everything that we fucking find her in one piece, Ryder."

I ignore that because I believe he will follow up with whatever threat he was about to throw out. "Her car has tracking," I point out.

"No shit," he says harshly. "Holden is trying to pin it down now."

"Where are you? I'll come to you," I say, already heading down the steps.

"No. I don't want to see your fucking face. You've done enough."

The line goes dead, but I'm already jamming my feet in my boots. I grab the key to my bike and run back to the garage door. As soon as I swing my leg over my motorcycle, my phone rings, the display reading Micah.

"Hello?"

"You want to tell me why my niece is here crying her fucking eyes out, and the only word she can say is Ryder?" he grinds out. *Shit.*

"We fought earlier." *Understatement of the fucking century, Ryder.* He is going to fucking kill me. "I'm on my way," I tell him, firing my bike up.

"You better be coming here to fix her because if not, I'll rip your intestines out through your throat and strangle you with them."

I wince when the line goes dead, then dial Gage.

"She's at Micah's," I tell him when he answers, and the fucker just hangs up. If they're up on the highway, I'll get there faster, especially with the bike.

With that thought, I shove my phone into my pocket and cram my helmet on my head. I back out and hit the gas.

It takes ten minutes to get to Micah's house, but it feels like fucking years. It doesn't help that I'm racing the clock trying to beat Gage here.

I run up and bust in because I never knock coming here, anyway. A hand wraps around my throat and slams me back against the front door.

"What did you do?" Micah grits out, getting in my face and squeezing my throat hard.

I don't even fight back because I deserve it if he kicks my ass. "I'm coming to fix it," I force out.

He squeezes harder before slamming my head back against the door. He lets go and steps back. "I don't know what the hell is going on in that house, but if I ever see her like this again, I'll burn that motherfucker to the ground with all of you in it." He jerks his thumb over his shoulder. "Go."

I step around him and head toward her favorite room in this house, the music room. She doesn't play, but Micah does. He used to play the guitar for us, but I haven't seen him pick it up in years.

I twist the knob only to find it locked. I knock lightly. "Les?" She doesn't answer, but I can hear her crying softly through the door. "Please open the door, Les," I beg. It's killing me knowing I did this to her because of my jealousy over Leo. "Please."

I slide down to the floor with my back against the door. "I'm so fucking sorry, Les. I was an asshole. You didn't deserve what I said." I scrub a hand down my face and make a decision. "I'll do whatever it takes to have you in my life. Please let me prove it to you."

She jerks the door open, and I roll to my feet so I don't fall back into the room. Tears are still leaking down her face, and I can't remember the last time I've seen Les cry like this. "Les," I say softly. She goes to open her mouth and then looks past me. That's when I see Gage barreling down the hallway with Leo behind him.

Gage elbows me back and jerks her into his arms. "Pretty girl," he breathes while she clings to him. Leo steps around me and up behind her, squashing her between them.

I swallow everything I'm feeling, all the hurt and jealousy threatening to bubble over. I used to be her person to come to, but now she has to go to other people because of me. Gage gives me a hard look over his shoulder before ushering her back in the room, shutting the door in my face, and sliding the lock home again.

Fuck fuck fuck!

I raise my hand to pound on the door, then drop it. I'll give Les the time she needs with him; it would be the first test of my self-control. I head down the hallway toward the front door when Micah steps in front of me from the living room, making me eye him warily.

"Get in here and tell me what's going on."

I sigh and follow him like a chastised toddler. I flop down on the couch and wait for him to sit in his favorite chair across from me. I watch him for a second and decide just to spill it. "I told Les how I feel; she feels the same and wants to be with Leo, Dex, Gage, and Holden."

Micah raises a brow. "I know."

"What do you mean, you know?"

"We do talk, dickhead. Why did she show up here like that?" He points to the room she's currently in.

"I told her I couldn't be in her life if she didn't choose me." Well, that's the condensed version, anyway.

His eyes narrow. "Then why are you here?"

"Because I changed my fucking mind."

He reaches under the table beside his chair and pulls out a Glock. He lays it on his thigh and casually aims it at me, laying it on his thigh. "You sure?"

"Yes," I answer, then look at the gun. "You going to shoot me, Micah?"

He slides the safety off. "You aren't going to make her feel like shit for wanting what she wants ever again?"

"No."

He chambers a round, the click echoing through the room. "You better hope so, Ryder, because I don't give a fuck who you are when it comes to my niece. I will fucking end you." He unchambers the round, and the bullet hits the ground, clanking ominously.

I nod because I have no idea what to say to that. Micah puts the gun back and stands up, striding out of the room.

Holy shit.

Only three people in this world scare me: my dad, Alessa, and Micah. Anyone else I would have put down for talking to me like that without a second thought.

I sit there and stare at nothing, trying to figure out how to fix this because I am going to.

No matter what it takes.

CHAPTER 18
GAGE

I'm going to kill Ryder in the most horrific way I can think of for making Les cry. She doesn't cry, ever. We've been in this room for thirty minutes, and even though she's stopped crying, her face is red and splotchy, her eyes puffy, and her occasional little sniffle is killing me. She hasn't said a word, just stared out of the window on the seat she's sitting on, her knees tucked to her chest. Leo and I tried to talk to her, but we finally just sat back and let her do what she needed to, letting her know we were there for her.

"He said he didn't want to be in my life anymore," she says, finally breaking the silence. I lock eyes with Leo, and he looks torn apart too. "Twenty-five years, and he just throws me away." I can hear her tear up again. I want to rip his heart out and stomp on it, just like he did her.

"I don't think he meant it, Baby," Leo says, and my head jerks to him in surprise. "He's here for a reason."

She turns slowly towards him. "You're taking up for him?"

He moves to sit at her feet. "I'm not saying what he did was right, and he deserves his ass kicked for that. All I'm saying is, I think you should talk to him."

I raise my eyebrow at him when he looks at me and shrugs. *What the hell?*

"I can't right now," she says, turning back to the window.

"That's fine, Pretty girl," I assure her. "Eventually, though, right?"

"What's the point? What's the point in any of this?" she asks.

"What's the point in what, Baby?" Leo asks, and dread sinks into my chest.

"Anything!" she explodes. "You live, you die. What's the fucking point of all the hurt in between?" She stands from the seat. "There is no point."

She goes to leave the room, and I jump over the back of the little couch, sliding in front of the door, blocking it so she can't leave. Her eyes narrow to those tiny, scary little slits.

I hope she isn't armed.

"Move," she warns, her tiny fists balled up. I know what she can do with those fists.

"I can't do that, Pretty girl," I tell her, and her whole body stiffens.

"What?" she asks in a deadly voice.

"We need to work all this out," Leo says, standing up from his seat.

She whirls on him. "Okay. Let's do that."

"Not like this, Baby," he begs. "I don't want you to say something you don't mean."

"Let's go back to the house," I suggest. "Get some wine. Hang by the pool. Then we can talk when you're ready."

"I don't need to talk," she argues.

"Sorry, Pretty girl. I call bullshit." I hold my hands up when she glares again. "Let us take care of you."

"I also don't need someone to take care of me," she says, and I watch as her eyes harden. What happened to make her shut down? I hate it.

"There is nothing wrong with needing someone," Leo comments, walking up behind her. I warn him with my eyes that her punches hurt like a motherfucker. "Let me and Gage take you home. We will talk, and we can take care of you. Let us do that for you." He's talking to her like she's a wounded animal, taking slow, measured steps toward her like she might attack at any minute. Maybe he read the sign in my eyes after all.

"Fine," she says fast--too fast. "Let's go." She goes to grab the door handle, but I block her again. I grimace, waiting for her to punch me right in the balls. "What is your deal?! I said I'll go. Now let's fucking go!" Her voice rises with each word, betraying what her eyes try to hide...pain.

I don't trust her not to make a break for it, and there is no way I can catch her in that car. "Leo is going to drive my car home, and I'll drive yours." I stick my hand out for her key fob, and it surprises the shit out of me when she slaps it into my hand.

Point one for Gage, bitches.

"You trust me in your car?" Leo asks with a raised eyebrow.

I shrug and grin. "Make a break for it, and I'll send Dex after you."

Leo visibly shudders. "I'm good. Thanks."

"Scared of Dex?" Les snorts.

"He's the size of a fucking building!" Leo argues, stretching his arms, trying to encompass how big Dex is.

Les giggles, and it's such a relieving sound. "Fair point. I would say he's harmless." She shrugs. "But he's not"

"That's really reassuring, Baby," Leo remarks, but I can see the relief in his eyes.

Something is going on, and I don't think it has everything to do with us. I'm sure this is playing a part, but there's something bigger.

I pull the door open, ushering her with my arm around her shoulders. She stops dead in her tracks when she sees Ryder sitting in Micah's living room, head buried in his hands. He looks up, and I can see the pain in his eyes from hurting her. I want to be mad at him, and I am for making her cry, but I know what it feels like to want her and not have her. The only difference is I figured it out sooner that Les isn't a one-guy kind of girl; she needs all of us, whether she wants to admit to that or not. But we need her too. She's the glue holding us all together, keeping us from losing our shit and falling over the edge.

She shrugs my arm off and marches over to him. He stares her dead in the eyes, showing her everything written on his face without the mask he usually wears. He opens his mouth, and she holds her hand up, halting whatever he's going to say; he snaps it closed. That always makes me want to laugh.

Not the right time.

"I'll talk; you're going to listen," she says, and he nods. "Never in my life have I felt like I did when I left your dad's house, and I will *not* feel like that again." She stops, and he nods again. "You want to be a part of my life? You do not get to judge how I choose to live it. If you want to be with me, you need to accept I'm with them too. You need to decide, Ryder, because I can't mentally handle thinking you don't want to be in my life." She wipes angrily at the tears sliding down her face again.

He stands up and takes her face in his hands. "I want to be with you, and I'm willing to accept that in whatever way I can." He looks over at Leo, and I see his resolve harden, making some mental decision. Then he looks back to Les. "In *whatever* way I can, *Il mio sole,*" he says again. Something about what he just said causes her to start crying again, and he crushes her to his chest. She wraps her arms around him, burying her face in his shirt.

"What does *il mio sole* mean?" Leo whispers, and I shrug. I was shit when Les tried to teach me Italian.

"It means my sun," Micah answers quietly, walking up behind us. He sees the scene in the living room and grins. "Good. I really didn't want to kill him," he remarks before turning on his heel and disappearing up the stairs.

Scary bastard.

Ryder places a gentle kiss on Les' lips before deepening it, and I look at Leo out of the corner of my eye, gauging his reaction. Ryder has been a dick to Leo, so this would have been the hardest to accept. He's watching them intently but not in a turned-on way; it's like he's testing his reaction. I'll have to ask him about it later.

Ryder pulls back from the kiss before whispering something in her ear, and she nods. She pecks his lips again before walking toward Leo and me. I sling my arm around her shoulders and lead her outside. She shrugs off my arm again and walks over to my Range Rover. What the hell?

She turns back. "No way in hell I'm riding with you in that car."

My mouth pops open. "Why not?"

"Because you're a maniac, that's why." She shudders, probably remembering the last time I was behind the wheel of this car and almost ran us over a cliff. In my defense, the cliff jumped out in front of me, and I stopped in time.

I huff. "Fine." I toss my key fob to Leo, and he catches it one-handed. "Precious cargo," I remind him before sliding the seat back and getting comfortable behind the wheel. God, I love this car.

I look in the rear-view mirror as Leo opens Les' door for her before jogging around the other side. He flips me off with a grin before getting in and shutting the door.

I grin to myself and fire the car up. I glide the car around the circle in Micah's driveway and hit dial on my phone. I have someone to thank, even though I'd rather eat dog shit than talk to him. But he did me a solid by giving me the heads up.

"Yeah?" Zane answers.

"Thanks," I say curtly.

"She good?"

"Yep," I say and hang up. That's all he needs to know because I don't trust him. Not only is he on the same task force as the one who's been trying for *years* to bring the Poletti's down, but I also see how he looks at Les whenever they have any run-ins with each other. I hated their little fling as much as Ryder did. He had no fucking business with her when she was only eighteen.

I hit the main road and floor the gas, knowing Les will kick my ass when we return to the house, but it's worth it.

After Les told us everything Ryder said, so much made sense. We plied her with wine to get her to talk, and now Leo, Les, and I are piled on the chaise on the couch watching Supernatural. I still need to get to the bottom of what's wrong, but that can wait until another day. She's finally relaxed, and I'm not messing that up.

"Hey, assbutt," Les and I say at the same time as the character Castiel from the show does. Les drops her voice as much as she can to match the characters, and we dissolve into laughter.

"How many times have you seen this?" Leo asks from her other side. He's got his arm over her legs, and his fingers brush my leg every so often. I'm not sure if it's intentional, but it's driving me crazy.

"Too many to count," Les laughs. "The things I would let Dean Winchester do to me," she groans sexually and starts laughing again.

I tighten my arm where it's wrapped around her shoulders. "I could do those things for real."

"Aw," she pouts. "Are you jealous, Gage?"

"No," I scoff, but it's a lie. I don't know why, but the thought of her with anyone but us makes my blood boil.

Leo laughs. "Holy shit, he is."

I smack him on the back of the head. "Shut up."

"Who's jealous of who?" Dex asks, walking into the room and flopping down in a chair facing the tv. "Jesus Christ. This again?"

"Dean makes my panties wet; what can I say," she remarks offhandedly, and I swear I can feel my teeth grind to dust.

"That answers the jealous question," Dex chuckles, looking at my face.

"Shut up," I repeat, making them laugh harder.

Dex looks at Les. "Everything okay, Baby girl?"

She smiles. "It is now"

"We have that Moretto thing tomorrow," he reminds her.

The Moretto thing is Joey Moretto and his slimeball brother Jerry. They're a smaller Italian family. Les busted up their shit bar a week ago for having kids selling their dope; it was glorious. Now she needs to make sure they got the message.

"I haven't heard anything, so it will probably just be a reminder," she answers.

Dex nods, his eyes lingering on her when she turns back to the tv. Les said he told her to push him, but I'm not sure what that means. I saw what he did when he was pushed by accidentally hugging him one day. Dex hit me so hard that he almost knocked my teeth out. He felt like shit immediately afterward, but he just reacted. I'm sure Les isn't going to rub her body all over his, though that would probably do the trick.

Les cuddles more into my side like she's cold, so I reach over and toss the throw blanket over her bare legs. She smiles at me and lays her head on my shoulder, and it feels good to hold her like this without hiding it.

I sit there for about five minutes before I get an idea and grin in my head. What better way to push Dex than a little sneak preview?

I angle my body more and arrange her so she's lying back on my chest. She throws her legs over Leo's, her eyes still glued to the tv. *Perfect.* I slide my free hand under the blanket, running my fingers under the waistband of her shorts, and her eyes snap up to mine. I raise an eyebrow in question, bending down to her ear. "Ready to give Dex a push?" I whisper. She looks at me for a second before nodding and turning back to the tv.

Game on, Dexy boy.

I knock one of her legs further down Leo's outstretched legs and slide my hand into her shorts under her panties. I don't give her a chance to back out before I circle my fingers around her clit. Her body jolts and I can see her bite into that lush bottom lip to keep the sounds in. Leo turns his head to her in question, and I just grin, circling her clit, making her hips jerk again. His eyes widen in understanding, and his head snaps to Dex, who still seems oblivious. He won't be oblivious for long; Les is *loud.*

"Take them off," I whisper in her ear. She slides her hands under the blanket and shimmies out of her shorts and panties, keeping her eyes glued to the side of Dex's head. She dangles them in front of Leo's face when they're free, and he snatches them, shoving them back under the cover. She lets out a breathless giggle. I feel like we're hiding from our parents by doing something we shouldn't be doing.

It's hot as fuck, knowing he's sitting less than a foot away and has no clue what's going on.

She props a bent leg up on Leo's chest, widening herself for me. I slide my fingers to her entrance, gathering her wetness before returning to her clit. I see Leo's hand disappear under the blanket, then the back of his hand brushes my fingertips, and I know what he's about to do.

"Shit," Les breathes when he shoves his fingers inside her, working them in and out while I start making faster circles on her clit. Her breathing is starting to get erratic. You can hear the suction of his fingers in her pussy, and I know we're about to be busted.

"Why the hell do you like this show so much?" Dex asks, turning towards us.

There's no hiding what's going on. Mine and Leo's hands are under the blanket, moving, and Les' face is flushed, her body starting to bow.

"What are you doing?" Dex asks hoarsely, even though he already knows.

"I'll give you one guess," I tell him, working harder on her clit. "Get it right, and I'll move this blanket." His eyes snap to mine, and I raise my brow. "You want the blanket moved?"

"You want him to see what we're doing, Baby?" Leo asks in that sexy voice that drops an octave when he's turned on.

"Yes," she breathes.

I look back at Dex. "What's the call?" This is his chance to beat a hasty retreat or man up.

"You're playing with her pussy," Dex answers, gripping the arms of the chair.

Leo jerks the blanket off with his free hand, and Dex has the perfect view of us fingering her. Her hips are moving freely now, fucking our hands, seeking her release since she doesn't have to hide.

"Fuck," Dex whispers, sitting up in the chair so he can angle his body more toward us to see better.

"Isn't that pussy pretty?" I ask. I know they had fooled around before, but that was years ago. She moans low in her throat, signaling that she's close. "You going to come for us? Remind Dex what it's like to watch you come apart?"

"Gage. Leo. Yes," she moans again. "Yes. Yes. Yes," she chants, rotating her hips. I pinch her clit between my fingers, and she comes apart with a scream. It echoes off the fucking walls; that shit will never get old. Leo pulls his fingers out of her pussy and sucks them clean with a grin. It surprises me that he's this comfortable around Dex or a damn good actor.

"That was embarrassingly fast." She laughs and moans when I circle her sensitive clit.

"Goddamn," Dex mutters, scrubbing a hand down his face.

Les looks up, locks eyes with him, and something passes between them. She sits up and whips her shirt over her head, and I unhook the back of her bra so she can slide it off her arms. She's now sitting gloriously naked in front of us. I look at Dex and see the war he's fighting with himself; it will take more than a slight push.

Dex stands up so fast that the chair almost tips over. "Baby girl, I...."

"It's okay, Dex," she says softly. He jerks a nod and walks out of the room.

Did I fuck up? "I'm sorry, Pretty girl."

She looks up at me. "It's not your fault," she sighs. "I need to figure out what to do." I can already see the wheels turning in her head. Leo and I help her back into her clothes before settling back in to watch tv.

"I'm sorry," she says quietly.

I jerk my head towards her. "For what?"

"For ruining the mood."

"Baby," Leo says, picking up her hand and kissing her palm. "I'm perfectly happy just being here with you."

"Me too," I agree, kissing the top of her head on my shoulder.

"I don't deserve you guys," she says, and I can hear her voice get emotional again.

"You deserve the world, Pretty girl, and we will find a way to give it to you."

I'm going to make damn sure I make good on that promise.

No matter what it takes.

CHAPTER 19
ALESSA

I woke up sandwiched between Gage and Leo, which is becoming the norm lately, but I woke up with a clearer head, like my cry yesterday cleared up the fog. I know I'm pushing myself too hard with everything, but it's what I have to do.

My talk with Leo settled so much unease that I can finally breathe to figure out the rest.

Ryder hurt me yesterday; there was no denying that, but I've been hurting him too, without even knowing it. He seems sincere that he's willing to work this out, and we can figure the rest out along the way.

I slide out of bed and sneak to the bathroom; it isn't even six A.M. yet. I take care of business and jump in the shower. Before Dex and I go to this meeting, I have something to do. I shampoo and condition my hair, shave, wash, and exfoliate, doing everything to make my body as smooth as possible. When I get out, I slather myself in my favorite body lotion and then blow dry my hair in soft waves down my back. I don't worry about makeup when nerves are attacking me for what I'm about to do. I wrap a towel around my body and open the bathroom door, looking at the bed. They are both still sound asleep, sleeping the same way with both arms tucked under the pillows on their stomachs. I shake my head with a smile and tiptoe to my walk-in closet. I'm sneaking around, not because I'm doing something I'm not supposed to. I just need to do this alone.

I slide on my dark blue bra and thong set. It's satiny, and the bra pushes my boobs to new dimensions. I put on my favorite light stone-washed cut-off shorts that show the bottom of the pockets in the front and a dark blue baby doll tank.

I walk out of the closet and meet Gage's sleepy blue eyes. I hold a finger to my lips to signal him to be quiet. He smiles and snuggles back into the pillow, passing back out in seconds.

I quietly open and close my bedroom door before creeping down the steps. I feel like I'm sneaking out of my own house, which, in a way, I am. I make a beeline for the garage door when I don't hear anyone else awake in the house, slamming my feet into my flip-flops.

I slide into my car with a smile and a plan.

Today is going to be a good day.

"He's upstairs, Ms. Poletti."

"Thank you," I say politely before heading that way.

I find the room I'm looking for easily since I've been here thousands of times and slip in, shutting the door behind me. I hear the shower running in the attached bathroom and slide onto the bed to wait.

It doesn't take long before Ryder exits the bathroom in a cloud of steam with a towel wrapped around his waist. Ryder's body is built to perfection with broad shoulders, barrel chest, trimmer waist, an ass girls pay top dollar for, and huge thighs. Tattoos line his body like Dex's, except they stop at his collarbone and wrists. Water is still rolling down his body, sliding down his deep v-line before disappearing under the towel.

His eyes finally lock with mine. "Les?" he asks in confusion.

I smile and slide off the bed. "In the flesh." I walk up to him and run my hands up those defined pecs before going up on my tip toes to slip them around his neck. "I want this to work. I want *us* to work. All of us." I run my fingers through the wet hair at the back of his neck. "You're either in or out. You can't just meet me halfway."

"I'm in," he answers, slamming his lips on mine and sinking his tongue into my mouth. I kiss him back, desperately ready to take this next step with him. There is no stopping it this time.

He slides his hands under my tank top, breaking the kiss to pull it over my head. When his eyes darken to black, taking a look at my bra, I know I made the right decision. He runs his pointer finger over my breasts, where they are heaving over the top of the bra. "Did you wear this for me?" he asks hoarsely.

"I did." I planned it because this is Ryder's favorite color.

He groans. "Please tell me they match."

I grin and undo my shorts, letting them slide down my legs. He tracks the movement with his eyes before slowly letting his gaze trail over my body, lighting me up from the inside.

He finally meets my eyes, and his eyes are glittering with appreciation. The tented towel is also giving away how turned on he is. "I don't want to take them off, but I need to see you naked. Now." He reaches out and unclips the front clasp of my bra, letting my breasts spill out. I shrug the material off my shoulders. "Fuck," he whispers, reaching up and rubbing a thumb across the mark he left behind; the look in his eyes seeing his mark is almost primal.

He takes my breasts in his hands, pushing them together before leaning in and sucking a stiff peak into his mouth. He switches his attention back and forth until they are tight and throbbing before dropping to his knees in front of me. He kisses my stomach before hooking his hands in my panties, slowly peeling them down my legs. He helps me step out of them before running both big hands up my thighs until he reaches my hips. He jerks me forward until his nose is buried between my thighs. He inhales deeply and lets out an almost pained groan. "You know how often I laid in that bed and jacked off thinking about how you felt? How you smelled. How you taste." He inhales again, then licks through the slit in my pussy. "My mind didn't do this pussy justice, *Il mio sole*."

"Me too. I used to imagine what it would be like to kiss you. Touch you," I admit with a smile. "Right here in this very room."

He stands up so fast that his towel parts before falling off his hips. His cock springs free, and I have to bite my lip to keep from moaning.

Thick. Veiny. And pierced. The underside of his cock has five barbells lining it in a Jacob's ladder. "Holy shit," I whisper, wrapping my hand around it, letting it slide up his piercings.

"Fuck," he grunts, his cock jerking in my hand.

I can't believe I have finally taken this step and am about to have sex with my best friend.

I stroke his cock up and down several times before he knocks my hand away. He jerks me closer, molding his lips against mine in a bruising kiss before reaching down, hooking his hands around my thighs, and lifting me to wrap my legs around his waist with his cock nestled against my ass. Without breaking the kiss, he walks us blindly to the bed. When his knees hit the mattress, he climbs up the bed with me still hanging from him, then stretches his big body over mine.

I could have waited until he got home today, but it feels right for our first time to be in his dad's house because I imagined this very thing too many times growing up.

He kisses down my neck, stopping to torture my nipples into hard points again, then kisses down my stomach. He settles between my thighs, spreading them wide to accommodate his shoulders. He parts my pussy with his fingertips, then leans down and circles his tongue around my clit.

"Oh," I breathe, my hips leaving the bed.

He licks from my entrance to my clit, circling his tongue again. "You taste so fucking good," he groans against my clit before diving in.

He licks, sucks, and nips at my clit, flicking his tongue back and forth. He spears me with two thick fingers, finding my magic spot with scary precision, moving his fingers roughly while attacking my clit. Holy shit, this man can eat pussy. Why did I wait so long again?

Dimly aware we are in his dad's house, I clamp a hand over my mouth to hide the noises, and Ryder chuckles before devouring my pussy. He doesn't let up, fucking me with his fingers and circling my clit with his tongue. I look down, and he's staring at my face. Our eyes lock together, and I can't look away. He starts moving his fingers faster, and I can feel the pressure start to build, signaling my release. He teases my clit a few times before sucking it into his mouth hard.

When I come, it's harsh, my back bowing, clamping down on Ryder's fingers. I scream into my hand, seeing stars burst behind my eyes. Ryder kisses my thighs, gently bringing me down before kissing up my body and slanting his mouth over mine.

I run my hand down his body, and he clamps a hand around my wrist to stop me before I reach his cock. "If you touch me now, I will come before we start." He pulls my hand up, kissing my fingertips. "I need inside you, *Il mio sole*. Please tell me you brought condoms."

This is where my nerves start again. "I'm clean." I didn't want anything between us; I didn't have to explain the rest.

"I'm clean, too, and I'd never do anything to put you in danger." I nod because I know. He groans low in his throat. "You're going to let me take this pussy bare?"

"Yes," I whisper. I don't know why I thought he would say no, but I had a lump in my throat thinking he would because I've been with Gage and Leo, but we always used them, and I didn't want to with them either.

He reaches down and lines his cock up at my entrance, locking eyes with me as he slides in. I feel him stretching me with his girth, and his piercings are rubbing every nerve ending. When he's fully seated inside me, we both sigh because the connection is finally complete after all this time.

"You feel so good," he says softly. "So wet and perfect." He slides back out, and I moan loudly, but it's cut off by his hand clamping over my mouth. We both laugh breathlessly, which makes him groan when I squeeze him. "Maybe doing this here wasn't a good idea."

"You want to stop?" I tease.

"Fuck no." He kisses up my neck until he's at my ear. "I've waited too long for this," he whispers.

"Me too," I whisper back.

He braces his hands on either side of my head, laying his forehead on mine, then he begins to move slowly, dragging his cock in and out of me, so I feel everything. I wrap my legs around his waist and my arms around his neck, holding him tight. I want to see every emotion cross his face, and I want him to see mine too. I don't want anything left to wonder between us; I am completely open to him in more ways than one.

The only thing you can hear is our labored breathing and the wet slide of his cock in and out of my pussy. I can feel my orgasm slowly building from the tips of my toes to the top of my head. Every time he bottoms out, he grinds down on my clit.

"Ryder," I moan.

"God, *Il mio sole*," he groans. "I've wanted to hear my name being moaned out of those sweet lips for years."

He sits up and locks his arm under my knee before leaning back on his hand, changing the angle. My back bows, pushing my breasts in his face; he latches onto one of my nipples, sucking it into his mouth.

His pace quickens, and I can feel my toes curl. "Ryder," I moan again, moving my hips with his.

"I know, *Il mio sole*," he replies. He slants his mouth over mine and starts fucking me harder with short, deep thrusts. It feels like we are made for each other; he fits perfectly inside me.

I scream into his mouth when I finally let go, my whole body tight like a bowstring.

He slows his strokes, kissing me through it. I can feel sweat slicking our bodies and see sweat gathering at his temples. I run my fingers through his hair, kissing him slowly, marveling that this is Ryder.

He starts to move again, rolling his hips. "You're amazing, Alessa," he whispers, saying my name like a prayer.

I start moving my hips with his again, trying to tell him without words that I feel the same way, but the words are locked in my throat.

"What do you need, *Il mio sole*?"

"Fuck me, Ryder. Take what you need," I beg. I can tell from his body that he's holding back. "I can take it."

"Fuck," he groans, sinking into my pussy and holding himself there. He drops my leg before rolling onto his back so I'm straddling him, making me squeal.

He pushes my hair out of my face with a smile. "We're going to get busted."

I laugh. "You did it."

He wraps big hands around my waist. "Can you stay quiet?" I give him a doubtful look, and he chuckles. "Ride my cock. I want to see those titties bounce."

I brace my hands on his chest, rocking my hips back and forth before lifting and slamming my pussy down on his cock. His grip on my hips tightens, and he makes a noise between a groan and a growl.

I start lifting my hips up and down, riding his cock, letting his piercings inside me drive me insane. He holds my hips and starts fucking me from the bottom hard enough to make my titties bounce like he wanted.

"Fuck, Ryder." I start meeting him thrust for thrust, the sound of our skin slapping filling the room, but neither one of us care anymore. He sits up, wrapping his arms around me, pulling me down to grind my clit on his pubic bone. "Oh god," I breathe, "That feels so good."

"Come on my cock again, *Il mio sole*."

I tighten my arms around his neck and kiss him like my life depends on it. My orgasm is teetering on the edge, so my hips start moving erratically with his. "I'm going to come," I moan, jerking my mouth away from his. He places his mouth over the mark he left behind the other day and sucks hard. "Ryder!"

He kisses me again, but it's too late to hide that one. "Hands and knees, *Il mio sole*," he slaps my ass, making me moan again. "Fuck. Now."

I flip over to my hands and knees, and he's inside me before I even get my hands planted on the bed. He grips my hips and starts slamming into me, his hands gripping my hips so tight I know he's going to leave bruises, his thighs slapping against mine. "Fuck me, Ryder," I encourage.

"Shit," he hisses and ups his speed. "Rub your clit. Give me one more."

I reach down between my legs and start rubbing my clit in tight circles. With the way he's fucking me, it won't take me long to come, especially since this position makes him even deeper. Noises are coming out of me that I've never made before, whimpers and moans, and it just seems to spur him on. "There you go, *Il mio sole*," he says when he feels me tighten. "Give it to me." He slaps my ass, and I explode, burying my face in the bed and screaming his name.

I feel his thrusts start stuttering before feeling him swell inside me. He empties into my pussy with a long groan, holding himself as deep inside me as he can.

"Fuck, Alessa," he groans, and it almost sounds pained.

His fingers flex on my hips before he slowly pulls out with a gush of his come. I can feel it running down the inside of my thighs. "Fuck, that's hot," he breathes. He takes his fingers and gathers up his come before shoving his fingers back inside of me.

It is the most caveman thing ever, but hot as fuck.

My legs collapse from under me. He lies beside me, gathers me to his chest, and lets me use his arm as a pillow. He laces our hands together and lays them on his stomach. We lay there for a few minutes, allowing our breathing to even out, with him kissing my head every so often. He tilts my face up, kissing me so slow and sweet that I just melt into him. He pecks my lips and nose before pulling me tighter to his side.

"So, your cock is pierced," I say, breaking the silence.

He barks a laugh. "Yeah. I got it done about four years ago."

"Why in the hell would you let someone shove a needle through your cock five times?"

He gets quiet, so I look up at his face, and he has a faraway look in his eyes. "I think I did it to punish myself."

I frown. "Why?"

He clears his throat. "For not getting to Dex in time."

I roll over to lay both arms on his chest with my chin on them.

"That wasn't your fault, Ryder. No one could find him."

I remember that day like it happened yesterday. Dex had been at Club Maximus like he was on most weekends for my dad; Frankie's men grabbed him from the parking lot, getting into his car. I watched with my heart being ripped out as Dad and his men got ready to go find him; they looked for weeks and ultimately determined he was dead when there was no sign of him.

"I was the one who started the fight with them the weekend before. It was supposed to be me they grabbed."

"What?" I ask, shocked. I didn't know that part, and I know they fought with Frankie's men the weekend before because I was there. It was one of the biggest brawls I had ever witnessed.

"I was supposed to be at Maximus that weekend, but your dad sent me somewhere else last minute and sent Dex instead. It was supposed to be me," he says harshly, blaming himself for what happened to Dex.

I smooth my hand over his cheek until he looks at me; his dark eyes are pained. "Nothing could have changed what happened that night."

Or any night, for that matter. The night Dex was grabbed, the night Frankie's men took me, Holden being sold to the highest bidder by his uncle, the list goes on and on. We just learned to deal with it, usually in the unhealthiest ways, but we did it anyway. There are plenty of times I just wanted to end it. Bite the bullet, literally. But the man I'm currently looking into the eyes of stopped me every time, even though he doesn't know it.

He pulls my face up, giving me a long, slow kiss; he pulls back and looks into my eyes again. "I'm so fucking happy you forgave me, *Il mio sole*, and I'm so fucking sorry I hurt you."

"We used to be able to talk to each other about anything without fighting; we need to find that again."

He nods. "I know."

I'm still not sure Ryder can handle seeing me with the other guys, but he promised he would try.

I just hope this doesn't blow up in my face, and I lose Ryder for good.

CHAPTER 20
DEX

This morning, I had a text from Les telling me she had to take care of something before we paid a visit to Moretto. That something has to do with the sappy way she and Ryder are staring at each other.

I'm glad to see it because I was starting to worry they wouldn't be able to fix whatever's between them. I was also afraid I would have to fucking kill him after the state Gage found her in at Micah's. After they brought her back to the house, they took her outside by the pool with wine and got her to talk to them. They were out there for hours, but when she came back inside, she seemed to be back to herself. I wanted to go out there, but I couldn't comfort her the way they do, and it pissed me off. It's not for lack of trying because I want to move past the mental block that told me all touch is terrible, but I can't, so that's why I told her she needs to push me.

Last night watching Gage and Leo make her come, I was *almost* there. She looked at me with those blue eyes, begging me to touch her by taking off her shirt and revealing those gorgeous tits. I made up my mind and then fucking froze. I had a moment of such intense panic that I thought I was going to puke. Then I ran like a coward.

How much longer is she going to be so understanding? She has four other guys who can make her happy. Hell, even Holden. They don't know it, but I saw what went down by the pool, heard Gage coaching Holden on how to pleasure Les, and my feet stayed frozen to the ground. We never had sex, but I know what it's like to watch her come apart for you. Her body is still so fucking responsive.

"Earth to Dex," Les says, waving her hand in front of my face.

"What?" I ask lamely. I was so far inside my head that I didn't even see her standing beside me.

"I've said your name like four times. You okay?" she asks, concerned. Concerned because I ran out of the living room like my ass was on fire.

"I'm good," I assure her.

"Okay," she says doubtfully, not that I blame her. "How are we doing this? Just us or full crew?"

"I think we go full out on this asshole," Gage says, walking into the kitchen. Gage spots Ryder leaning on the counter and squeals like a fucking girl before running and jumping into Ryder's arms. Ryder stands up to catch him just in time before Gage knocks him over. "You're home!"

"Damn it, Gage," Ryder grunts, peeling Gage off him. "Yes. I'm home."

Gage whips his head between Ryder and Les, then grins like a fool when his gaze lands on Les. "That's where you snuck off to this morning."

She shrugs nonchalantly. "I have no idea what you're talking about."

Gage advances on her. "Snuck out of here with those fucking shorts on that I love." He walks her backward, then cages her against the counter in between his arms. He runs his nose up her neck, making her shiver. "Smelling good enough to eat."

I watch Ryder for a reaction and see the tightening of his eyes. I still wonder if he can do this.

"Oh, trust me," she purrs. "He did."

Ryder chokes on a laugh, all uneasiness disappearing from his body. "More than once," Ryder says, his eyes heating up.

Gage groans. "Tell me more."

She wraps her arms around Gage's neck. "He fucked me so good, Gage," she tips her head back with an exaggerated moan, "In his bed. On his desk. In the shower."

Gage steps back and looks down before looking up at her. "Now look what you did," indicating what I assume is his hard cock, because mine is just as hard. I see Ryder subtly adjust his through his jeans.

"You asked." She pecks him on the lips before ducking under his arm. "Where's Leo?"

"Shower," Gage replies, jerking his head towards the stairs.

"I think he should go with us," Les says, surprising all of us. "One, I agree we need a full force against Moretto for breaking the rules, and two, Leo needs to know what he's getting into."

I acknowledge that with a nod. "I agree. I say we ride into Moretto's territory and see who he has on the streets."

"You want to take someone untrained with us to go against another family?" Ryder asks with a muscle ticking in his jaw.

Les raises an eyebrow. "I thought we moved past this. "

He slices his hand through the air. "It has nothing to do with this being Leo."

Les saunters over to him, wrapping her arms around his neck; he slides his hands down her back until they are braced on her hips. "If he's going to be a part of us, he needs to go. Evander and Mateo didn't leave him untrained." She pecks his lips. "This is just a reminder to Moretto. If it gets bloody, we can handle it and protect Leo."

Ryder jerks a nod. "Got it."

She pecks his lips again before stepping back. "I need to change." She looks to Gage. "Fit Leo with a holster and weapons. Let him know not going is not an option."

"You got it, Pretty girl."

She walks out of the room, and when she's out of earshot, Gage looks at Ryder. "Everything good?"

"Yeah. We worked it out this morning."

"Good, because the next time you make her cry like that, I will drown you in your own blood," Gage says, then grins like the crazy person we all know is there, but he hides so well. He leaves the kitchen without a reply from Ryder, searching for Leo.

"Crazy fucker," Ryder mutters under his breath.

"Are you sure you can do this?" I ask Ryder. I know he would tell me the truth, and the last thing we need is for Les to get hurt because of this.

He sighs. "I'm trying. It's still hard to see her with someone else, but I have to remember how fucking happy she looks with Gage."

"And Leo," I point out, "And Holden."

His head jerks towards me. "Holden? When did that happen?"

"The day you left for your dad's. Les, Gage, and Holden had a...teaching lesson by the pool."

His eyebrow shoots up. "Teaching lesson?"

I chuckle. "Holden's apparently a virgin."

Both brows shoot up. "No shit? And he gets Les as his first? Damn."

That's exactly what I'm thinking. Holden doesn't have to deal with the awkward first time with a girl just as inexperienced as you. He gets a girl who is a fucking goddess in bed and four guys to help him not fuck up. I don't think he realizes how lucky he is.

I've watched Holden over the past year come out of his shell, but this last week he's been out of his office more than I've ever seen. I know he and Ryder are close, so he'll be happy to know Ryder is back. I don't know how close, though. I've witnessed Holden staring at a shirtless Ryder a little too long, sometimes in the gym, but that could be admiration for the work Ryder puts in. I feel it has to do with a little more than that. Not that I'm going to mention that to Ryder.

"We roll out in ten," I tell Ryder, sliding off the stool.

Time to show this Moretto motherfucker Les is not to be fucked with.

We all pile into Ryder's Explorer because he doesn't care if this car gets shot up. He doesn't get into the cars like Les and Gage; he's like me. He likes fast bikes and vintage cars. He doesn't care what he drives daily. I prefer my truck to the fast-ass cars Les and Gage like.

Les sits in the back between Gage and Leo, so I won't have to be squished between them, for which I'm grateful. But she also doesn't seem to mind them rubbing up against her. She came downstairs in black ripped skinny jeans, a tight blue shirt, a black leather jacket that hid her holster, and her high-heeled boots with spikes on the heels she always wears. I asked her why once, and she said it's to remind these assholes they're dealing with a woman of power that can still kick your ass in heels. And she can. I've seen her fuck up more shit in those heels than I ever have with her wearing anything else. Her dad taught her everything she needed to know. He also made sure she could run in any footwear because you never know when your enemy could attack; it was fucking brilliant. Plus, it gave height to her five-foot-four frame.

"Pull over right here," Les tells Ryder, pointing to the curb across from two teenagers hanging out by the corner. "I guess Joe didn't listen."

I shake my head. "Doesn't look like it, Boss."

"This should be fun," Gage says, practically bouncing in his seat' This is his favorite thing to do.

She turns to Leo. "I don't know who else is here, so stay behind us."

"I got it, Baby," he assures her.

"It's Boss or Les out here. Okay?" she tells him, squeezing his hand to soften the blow. He jerks a nod in understanding.

We sit and watch several cars pull up, money and drugs exchanging hands. Les snaps a picture that I'm sure she will shove in Moretto's face if needed. "Come on."

We all climb out of the car, Ryder to her right and me to her left, Gage and Leo behind us. It's the formation we always walk in, with Les in the position of power. Ryder and I are there to step in front of her if needed for protection.

"Hello, boys," Les greets, getting their attention. These aren't the same ones we found the last time. "What do you have there?" she asks. She won't hurt them, but she will scare them until they told her where the product came from.

"None of your fucking business," one of them sneers, oblivious to who she is. I cross my arms over my chest, dragging their attention to me. A closer look tells me they are twins and no more than sixteen or seventeen.

Ryder walks up behind them. "You see, that's where you're wrong." He throws his arms around their shoulders like they're old friends. "It is her business."

The shorter of the two swallows and I know they haven't been doing this long, so they will be easy to fold without the threats. "Tell her what she needs to know," I tell them.

"We can't," the taller one says, trying to step away from Ryder. He clamps a big hand on his shoulder, jerking him back.

"You can, and you fucking will. Answer her question," Ryder growls, making the kid go pale.

"Blow," he answers, looking at all of us, knowing he doesn't stand a chance.

"Fucking cocaine," Les hisses. "From who?"

Cocaine is one of the Poletti's businesses. It is shitty, but money has to come in somehow. It also gives her the power to control who gets ahold of it.

The boys shake their heads at the same time, making their floppy blond hair fall over their eyes. Jesus, these kids are young, too damn young to be out here in the worst part of town slinging dope.

Gage steps up. "Answer her."

I truly hate this part because they are, for the most part, innocent. Kids from bad homes or down on their luck. Moretto uses that to his advantage because they are expendable, most not having a family or one that doesn't care what happens to them.

Les shrugs. "Fine. Tie them up and throw them in the back." She turns on her heel, heading towards the car. It's a bluff, but they don't know that. I look at Leo out of the corner of my eye to see how he's handling this, and he just seems to be soaking it all in.

"Wait!" the taller one calls out, and I have to hide a smile. Works like a charm every time. This is how you weed out the little fish from the big fish. Big fish won't fold that fast.

She turns back around. "From who?" she repeats.

"Jerry Moretto," he answers, looking around like he's going to jump out.

She just shakes her head and pulls out her phone. "Gerald, we have two more. Corner of 96th and Mikee."

"We told you what you wanted to know!" the smaller one calls out when she hangs up.

The other two kids Les sent home with a warning that she better not see them again. Gerald used to be one of her dad's guards, but as he got older, Les put him and his partner, Boone, on easier jobs, like transporting teenagers back home.

"Calm down," she says softly. "He's just going to take you home. My beef isn't with you."

"We don't have a home," he says gruffly.

Les looks at Ryder and me. "What do you mean?" she asks with concern.

"We live in a shit foster home. Trust us; it's safer out here."

I see her soften immediately. "What's your name?"

"Lucas," the taller one says, then jerks his thumb at his twin brother. "That's Landon."

"How old are you?" Leo asks, speaking up for the first time.

"Seventeen," Lucas answers, and I hear Les sigh.

"How much longer before you age out?" she asks, wondering when they're old enough to be kicked out of foster care.

"Six months," Landon says with a frown.

I can see the wheels turning in Les' head. She might run one of the most ruthless empires in the world, but she has a soft spot for kids of all ages.

When Gerald and Boone pull up ten minutes later, I follow Les to their car, not trusting this neighborhood to let her walk alone. Those boys might not know who she is, but other people will. If you are on this side of crime, you know who she is. It's everyone else she hides it from.

"Hey, G. Hey, Boone," she greets with a smile when they climb out of the car.

"Hey, Boss," Gerald grins. He is just shy of sixty and watched Les grow up, but he still respects her in public by calling her Boss. He's still built like a solid brick wall. He's almost bigger than me, with a slick bald head and watchful green eyes. Boone is on the smaller side, not even six feet, with grey-streaked black hair and blue eyes, but the man can fight like a maniac.

"I need you and Boone to take them somewhere until I figure out what to do with them."

"What's their story?" Boone asks, leaning against the side of the car.

"Foster care. Seventeen. Hired by Jerry Moretto to sling blow," she highlights, still sounding pissed.

Gerald raises both brows. "He knows that's Poletti's territory."

"We are on our way there next," I answer.

"He has a lot to answer for," Les says, then gestures toward the boys. "You good with taking them?"

Boone nods. "Yeah. They can stay with us."

No one knew for the longest time that not only were Gerald and Boone partners, but they were also a couple because they hid it. It shocked us, but Les told them never to hide who they are in front of her.

"I'm going to have Holden look into their foster home, so get me some info," Les informs them. I know whoever these foster parents are, they're going to wish she never stumbled on them.

"Give them hell," Gerald grins, and it's not a nice one. "And fuck up some of Moretto's shit for me."

"If you weren't such an old man, you could go," Les quips.

Boone bares his teeth at her jokingly. "Watch it, Lessie."

She laughs. "I haven't heard that in forever." She waves at the other guys to bring the boys over. "This is Gerald and Boone," she says, pointing them out. "That's Lucas," she says, pointing to the taller one. "That's Landon." She gestures back to Gerald and Boone. "You will stay with them until I figure something out for the next six months."

"Who are you?" Lucas asks with a perplexed look on his face.

Gage snorts. "You can tell they aren't a part of this life."

Gerald gestures towards the car. "I'll explain on the way. See you later." He gives us a mock salute before sliding into the car, Boone, Lucas, and Landon following him.

We get back into Ryder's car, and Les sighs. "This is going to get worse, isn't it?" she asks everyone.

"Fuck yeah," Gage says excitedly, making her shake her head with a smile.

"What happens now?" Leo asks.

Les sighs again. "It gets bloody."

"Joe!" Les calls out like they are old friends when we walk into his dive bar, Danny's. Leo was given the option to stay in the car this time, but he refused, saying he could handle it. We are about to find out because Les is done with warnings.

Joe's eyes widen a fraction, but he keeps his composure. "What can I do for you, Ms. Poletti?"

It looks like it's only their people in the bar this time of day, which consisted of four guards, no innocent bystanders. Good. I can tell by the set of Les' shoulders that she isn't playing anymore.

"I warned you, Joe," Les shakes her head sadly like she cares about this slimy piece of shit. "You didn't listen."

"Because we don't take orders from women," Jerry growls to our left.

"Hello, Jerry," she smiles sweetly, and it's anything but sweet. I know exactly what's lurking just behind that smile. "A little birdie told me you had more kids selling for you. Imagine my surprise when I find them slinging none other than coke."

"I guess you need a reminder that coke is Poletti's business, and she didn't fund that," Gage says and taps his lips thoughtfully. "Which begs the question; who did?"

"I can assure you, Ms. Poletti, we would never step on your business. I heeded your warning last time. Your informant is wrong," Joe answers, standing up from his stool at the bar, jerking his jacket over his gut that's hanging over his pants. His thinning brown hair is slicked back, his beady eyes running over Les. I have to grit my teeth to keep my mouth shut.

"I wouldn't take another fucking step," Ryder warns menacingly, not bothering to stay quiet.

"Let's talk about this like adults, shall we?" Joe offers like he's talking to a bunch of children.

"This happens when you let a woman run a man's empire!" Jerry explodes from his seat. Not everyone accepted Les in her role, but they don't have a fucking choice, and she runs it better than most men.

"Shit," I hear Leo mutter, already figuring out that this is going to shit. Fast.

Gage snorts. "Like you run yours? You weak fuckers couldn't even control the little piece Alessa allowed you to have without messing it up."

"This is how this is going to go." Les steps up closer to Joe. "We," she gestures between us, "will burn this place to the fucking ground with you in it if you don't shut your limp dick, brother up."

I love seeing her like this. Shoulders pushed back, head held high, dishing out threats I know she will follow through with.

"We didn't break your rules," Joe insists.

"No," Les says, "But he did." She points at Jerry.

"Bullshit!" Jerry says, but I can see sweat gathering at his temples. He looks just like his older brother and just as slimy.

"Cut the shit," Les barks at Jerry, running out of patience. "You have a decision to make. Give me your supplier, or I will ruin you." Jerry stares at her, his jaw locked. "Have it your way." She turns to Gage and jerks her head toward the door; he jogs outside with a grin.

"Wait a damn minute," Joe says, hiding behind his guards like a coward. "You got the wrong information. He wouldn't do anything without my knowledge."

"Oh, but he would." Ryder smiles wide. "And he did."

Gage jogs back in with two full gas cans, handing one to Ryder. "Burn, baby, burn," Gage says before he and Ryder start shaking gas around the floor.

"Wait!" Joe yells. Les holds up a hand, and they stop pouring. "You can't just come in here and burn down my fucking bar without proof!"

"I have proof, but I don't have to prove anything to *you.* Poletti's word is the law, whether I have a pussy or not." She aims that last bit at Jerry. He jumps from his seat, and she has a Glock out of her holster, a round in the chamber, and pressed to his forehead before he even touches her. "Sit. Down," she says between clenched teeth.

Fuck, she's glorious.

"You heard her," I tell him, jerking him back down in his seat.

"Why are you blindly following her?!" Jerry asks, shooting daggers at Les with his eyes. Some men can't handle a woman in power, but women like Les in control are what this old-world mafia life needs.

She tilts her head to the side in that creepy way. "They don't blindly follow me, you misogynist piece of shit."

"We respect her and choose to follow her," Gage says. "Can you say that about your men?"

None of the guards reacted to Les pulling a gun on Jerry; they stayed more protective around Joe. *Interesting.*

She presses the gun harder, never taking her eyes off Jerry. "What's it going to be, Joe?"

"Tell her what she needs to know. Now!" Joe demands Jerry. There doesn't seem to be any love lost between the brothers. Jerry doesn't say a word, just glaring at his brother past Les' gun. "NOW!" he yells again.

"I will find out one way or the other," Les warns. "So, save me the trouble."

"I'm not telling you shit, you stupid cunt." Jerry insults.

Goddamnit. If anything will trigger Les, it's that word. It's what Frankie's men called her the whole time they had her. You can call her any other name in the book and not get a reaction.

She pushes the gun harder into his head, her finger hovering over the trigger. "What did you just call me?" she asks in that deadly tone.

"You heard me," Jerry says, calling her bluff. "You stupid cu..."

I pull Leo back just in time before she pulls the trigger, blowing Jerry's brains all over the wall behind him. He slumps in the seat, surprised, dead eyes looking up at her.

She swings the gun toward Joe, and his guards tighten ranks around him, blocking him from view. "Is this how it's going to be, Joe?"

He pushes past his guards, sliding unaffected eyes over Jerry. "You did me a favor."

"That's your brother," Leo says incredulously. I look back at him, and he's staring at Jerry, his face pale. *Please don't fucking puke.* I know he saw his brother kill that guard at the house, but he wasn't as close as he is now. He was almost sprayed with blood and brains.

"He's been trouble for years." He waves his hand like he is nothing more than a stray dog. "You won't have any more trouble from me, Ms. Poletti."

She holsters her gun. "This is your last fucking warning. You won't get another one." She jerks her head for us to follow her out. Gage and Ryder put the gas cans in the hatch before climbing into the car.

"Are you okay?" Les asks Leo when we're headed back to the house.

"Yeah," he answers, but he still looks like he's going to hurl. If he does in Ryder's car, he will die before the first drop hits the floorboard.

She slides her hand into his. "It's okay not to be okay."

Gage chuckles. "For real. My first dead body, I couldn't stop puking."

"Your first one?" Ryder lifts his eyes to the rearview mirror to see Gage. "Try the first ten."

"That's bullshit!" Gage says, sitting up in the seat.

"No, it's not," Les laughs. "You gagged every time anyone mentioned dead bodies."

I turn around in the seat. "You had to clean out the backseat of Luca's car more than once."

"Whatever," Gage grumps, pouting, crossing his arms over his chest.

Les runs her hand down Leo's face. "That's better," she says, noting his color coming back.

"I've never seen this before," Leo says, embarrassed.

Ryder shrugs. "We all have our firsts, and it's never easy."

Leo frowns at the back of Ryder's head, probably confused that he's not tearing him down. It could be because Les is in the car, or Ryder is actually trying.

Leo handled that pretty well, considering it was his second time seeing someone's brains being blown out, and the one that blew their brains out is the girl he loves.

CHAPTER 21
ALESSA

There's a reason I made Leo go with us today. I needed to know how he would react to who we really are. He was told, I'm sure, but nothing like seeing it firsthand hammers it home. It was a gamble. But if he wants to run, he needed to do it now before I got into it deeper with him. But the truth is, I'm already all the way in.

When we got back to the house, he disappeared, and I gave him space, letting him make up his mind. He could return to his brothers anytime since I told him he was free and gave him a room upstairs, but he chose to stay here.

"Quit worrying," Gage says from my office door.

"You saw his face," I say miserably. I shut my laptop because it's not like I'm getting any work done, anyway. I gave all the information that I had to Holden so he can track down Moretto's supplier, and Gerald's working on figuring out who Lucas and Landon's foster parents are, so now it's a waiting game.

Gage sits in the chair in front of the desk. "It was his first one seeing you take someone out, Pretty girl. Leo is stronger than we give him credit for."

I tilt my head to the side. "What's going on with you two?" I ask because I haven't heard anything else about their almost kiss the other morning.

Gage shrugs. "Nothing." I raise an eyebrow, and he sighs. "I don't want to push him. He wants it; he just hasn't accepted it yet."

I smile. "Thank you for not pushing him."

Gage will eventually charm him into knowing it is okay, but he will never push him into anything Gage thought he might regret. I know they spend a lot of time together when I'm busy, and I'm glad Leo has Gage.

"You know that's not my style. I have other ways." Gage grins, and his dimples pop out, his blue eyes glittering.

I snort. "Trust me. I know those ways."

"Not even the great Alessa Poletti can resist me."

"Shut up." I laugh because he's not wrong. Gage flirted all the time, but when he turned the full force of his charms on me, I was putty in his hands.

"So, you and Ryder are good?"

"We are." I sigh in contentment, remembering spending the morning with his cock buried in me, bringing me pleasure over and over again.

"Damn, I hope you get that look when you think about me."

"What look?" I ask, confused.

"The 'I just had the best sex of my life' look."

I stand up and make my way to Gage, straddling his lap in the chair and wrapping my arms around his neck. His hands go straight to my ass. "You have nothing to worry about, Gage," I assure him, and he doesn't. None of them do; they make damn sure I'm taken care of.

He buries his nose in my hair, rubbing it down my neck. It never fails to make me shiver. "You were fucking hot today, Pretty girl, and my dick was hard as a rock watching you take care of business."

I laugh, but it comes out husky. "You would be turned on by that."

"I get turned on with you just breathing," he replies, then kisses me. It starts slow and then starts burning hotter. Gage and I are like fire and gasoline in the best way. Just when he's sliding his hands under my shirt, there is a knock at the door. He pulls back from the kiss with a sigh and smooths my shirt back down.

"Come in," I call out, not bothering to move.

"Hey. Holden gave me some info...shit. Sorry," Dex rumbles, walking into the room, taking in the position Gage and I are in.

Gage slaps my ass before lifting me to a standing position. "All good." He stands up, pecking my lips. "You take care of that. I'll find Leo." He looks at me pointedly, reminding me of what we talked about, and I nod.

"Thank you."

"Anytime, Pretty girl." He strolls out of the room, adjusting his cock in his pants.

"I didn't mean to interrupt," Dex says, rubbing the back of his neck.

"It's okay." I suck in a breath nervously. "Come upstairs with me."

He frowns but nods. It's time to put mine and Gage's plan into the works.

I lead him to my room, opening the door and motioning him inside. I shut the door behind us and ask the one question I need to know.

"Do you trust me?"

CHAPTER 22
DEX

"Of course."

The answer comes automatically, without a thought. I trust her with everything in me, even though I have no idea what she has planned. She looked nervous when we first walked in here, but now, she is standing there with her shoulders back, set on whatever she's going to do.

God. She's gorgeous.

I wish I could hold her like I saw Gage doing downstairs.

She nods and pulls the chair that sits in front of her makeup table into the middle of the floor. "Sit," she orders, pointing to the chair.

"Les, what's this about?" I ask, getting comfortable.

"You said you trusted me. I'm going to prove to you that you can. Even with this," she walks in front of me, holding up a satin blindfold. "You still trust me?"

"Les," I say roughly. "I don't know if that's a good idea. I go to a dark place and can't control how I react."

She lets it drop so it's hanging from her fingers. "The goal is to replace that dark place. I want to replace it with pleasure, not pain." She lets the tail of the blindfold trail across my legs, covered by my jeans, and I can feel my muscles tense. She walks around me, letting the material trail across my clothes, never touching my skin. "I want you to accept my touch and be able to touch me," she says from behind me, close to my ear but not touching. I shiver and don't know if it's from fear or feeling her breath rush across my neck. She steps back in front of me, holding the blindfold in front of her again. "I won't force you to do this, Dex," she says softly.

I look into those blue eyes I've dreamed about for years and decide. I take it from her and tie it around my eyes. I let my hands drop and grip the edges of the chair. I refuse to do anything to hurt her.

"We're going to start slow. I want you to listen to my voice." She is behind me again, and I didn't even hear her move. "Are you ready?" I nod, afraid to open my mouth. "I need your words, Dex."

Shit. "Yes," I croak out.

"Good," she replies, and I can hear the smile in her voice. "The point of vision deprivation is that you have to focus on your other senses. Touch, smell, hearing." I focus on her voice; she's on my right side, the side with the scars. "What do you smell?"

"You."

"Be specific. This is what I want you to remember when you go to that place," she murmurs, moving while she's talking.

"Your vanilla scent mixed with a man's cologne." Gage's cologne, I figure out when I focus on it.

"Good," she says, moving again. "What do you hear?"

"Your sweet voice, fabric moving."

I feel her touch me before she ever does; it's just a brush of her hand on my shirt, nothing I can't handle. "What do you feel?"

"Your hand on my left shoulder."

"Is it a bad touch?" she asks from my right side, running her hand across that shoulder; my skin bunches under her hand, but it's bearable.

"No."

"When you put all those things together, what do you get?"

"You. Your smell, your voice, your touch."

"So, think of this moment when you sink into your mind."

Her voice has taken on a hypnotic state. Soft, slow, seductive. I wish she would touch me again, something I haven't wanted. But I know she won't when I expect it. The point of this is that spontaneous touch isn't always bad.

I exhale and nod.

She trails her hand from one shoulder to the other, just a light brush of her fingers. Her smell washes over me like an aphrodisiac, calming my pounding heart.

"Dex," she whispers in my ear, her lips barely touching the lobe. I shiver again, and I know it's not because I'm afraid. I can feel my cock start to harden. Amazed, I shift my hips. "Are you okay?" she whispers again.

"Yes," I say, nodding, letting my fingers loose from their death grip on the chair.

She runs her fingers over my back again, firmer this time. She squeezes my shoulder, and my whole body turns to stone. "Dex," she whispers in the other ear. "It's just me."

Alessa. It's just Alessa.

I force myself to relax, and she squeezes my shoulder again. This time, I don't tense up as bad. I think of her smell, her touch.

Every time I tense up, she reminds me of where I am.

She squeezes both shoulders before she slides her hands to my biceps, down my pecs, and my abs, still never touching my skin. She does this until I only react in a good way, leaning into her touch. I find myself trying to follow her hands wherever they go.

"Are you ready for the next step?" she whispers again, and it's starting to fucking kill me. My dick is painfully hard, straining against my zipper, begging her to touch me.

"Yes."

I hear her take a breath. "Take your shirt off."

I freeze. Touching me through my clothes is one thing; this is different. I would be able to feel her skin on mine, the heat from her touch. Can I do it?

"I won't push, Dex, but I think we're in a good place right now." Her voice still has that soft cadence, reminding me she won't harm me.

I jerk my shirt over my head before I can rethink it, careful not to dislodge the blindfold.

"I need to push a little harder," she warns. "You need a safe word. You say the word, and I stop. No questions asked."

"A safe word?" I croak, alarmed.

"This isn't about pain, Dex. Just pleasure. I would never do that to you."

I slow my breathing and think of a safe word. "Peaches."

"Why peaches?" she asks curiously, and I can hear her moving again.

"Because that's what you were eating the first time I saw you."

"Peaches, it is." I can hear her softly laugh under her breath. "You remember what I was eating?"

"I remember everything about that day. You were wearing a yellow sundress, sitting on that huge swing behind the house, eating peaches straight from a can."

I was still a street thug for her dad, too young to be in the big boy business but strong enough to fight on the streets. Why she ever paid me any attention at all blew my mind. But once I had her full attention, I knew I could never let this woman go.

"Hm," she hums. I know she doesn't remember. I was following a group of other guys in the backyard and stopped dead in my tracks when I saw her. She was lost in her little world, staring out over the city. "Are you ready?" she asks.

"Yes," I rush out. I need her to do something before I run from the room.

"Just breathe, Dex," she says, pulling me back under her spell.

What the hell is she doing to me?

She starts with light touches again, but the moment her skin touches mine, I tense up so tight my muscles scream in protest, and her hand drops instantly.

"Dex," she whispers. "Who's in this room with you?"

"Alessa." My breathing is harsh, and I feel like a fucking pussy.

"Would I ever hurt you?" she asks, and I can tell she's close to me, almost touching because that vanilla scent got stronger.

"No," I answer honestly. I *know* that. I just need my mind to accept it.

She touches me again, lightly, with just the tips of her fingers. She sweeps them slowly across my back. I can feel her fingers bump over my scars, and I want to hang my head in shame. They should have never gotten the jump on me, but there were five of them and one of me.

"These scars don't make you weak," she says, like she's reading my mind. "I have scars too. Some are visible, and some of them aren't." She flattens her palm between my shoulder blades. I focus on the softness of her skin. "Most of them are in my mind."

"How did you get past that?" I ask hoarsely. She went through something way worse, something I could never imagine, and she functions on mostly normal levels, killing perverts aside.

"I had to push past the walls in my mind." She runs her hand to my left shoulder. "I had you, Ryder, and Gage to help me through it. I had you guys to remind me that not all guys were bad." She runs her hand to my right shoulder. "I never truly let my guard down until Leo." She runs her hand up my neck, fingers combing through my hair. "I only ever trusted you guys, then I found Holden. Then Leo." She runs her fingers softly through my hair from my forehead back when she moved in front of me. I can reach out right now and crush her body to mine, but it's like I'm frozen in place. "It was almost like it was meant to be."

I know she slept with other guys before Leo. She would go for it if they caught her eye, and I always hated it. Hated that it could have been me giving her what she needed. But she never went back for seconds, always one-night stands. Then there was Leo. I knew she was gone the second she said she was letting him take her on a date. I would never get a chance to push past my bullshit and touch her. Kiss her. Hold her. *Fuck her.* Then Gage told me what she wanted, and everything opened up in front of me again.

And now she's taking her time, so I can be a part of this because she *wants* me to be.

She places both hands on my shoulders from behind, waiting for me to relax. When I do, she runs them down my pecs and abs—

moving her hands apart when she hits the tops of my jeans, lightly scraping her nails up my sides over my ribs.

"Fuck," I grit out.

"How does that feel?" she whispers in my ear, and I want to crush my lips against hers.

"It feels good," I rasp. I forgot what a feminine hand felt like.

She rubs all over me above my waist, and all I can feel is her. No bad thoughts creeping up to take this from me.

I feel her soft lips press against mine, and it's like a dam burst. I crush her mouth to mine like I've wanted since the last night I kissed her, the night she came out of the fucking water naked like a siren, drawing me to my death. I can't bring myself to reach out and touch her, but her mouth moving against mine is all I need right now. I need it like I need air. I gently massage her tongue with mine, making her moan into my mouth. She places her hands on my shoulders, and I don't feel the panic, the overwhelming urge to bolt.

The kiss goes on, and neither of us gets tired of it. I feel her straddle my legs, sitting her ass on my knees, not pressing too much touch onto me. She runs her hands around my neck, running her fingers through the short strands of hair at the base of my skull. I finally reach out and place my hand flush against the skin on her thigh, thankful she changed into shorts, reveling in the feel of her soft skin.

"You're a dead motherfucker," he says as he slashes my back again.

NO! I'm not there. Vanilla. Alessa. She's kissing me. I'm okay.

I move my hand higher up her thigh. Her lips still fused with mine.

"You aren't such a fucking badass without your buddies," he laughs cruelly as he cuts my back.

Shit!

"I want you to give a message to daddy Poletti."

Vanilla.

"That fine piece of ass he calls a daughter," he groans in a vulgar way. "What I would have given to be there when they nabbed that girl."

Alessa.

"You bleed pretty, bitch boy," he laughs cruelly again, another one landing a solid punch to my gut.

Fuck!

"Tell Poletti this isn't over."

I can feel my mind start to take me back there. I keep repeating over and over in my head what she told me, but it's getting harder. I can feel the panic clawing up my throat, cutting off my air supply.

Shit! Fuck!

"Peaches!" I say as I jerk my mouth away.

Her touch instantly disappears, and she rips the blindfold from my eyes. It takes me a minute to get my breathing under control, my heart pounding out of my chest. When my eyes finally focus on the present, she's standing in front of me with a soft smile.

"I'm sorry," I whisper, pissed at myself. I had her *right* there in my arms and fucked it up.

She smiles again. "You have nothing to be sorry for. This isn't over."

I stand up, knocking the chair to the floor. "Why do you want me?! I'm a fucking wreck, Baby girl."

She shakes her head. "No. You went through some horrible shit. We all have."

"But you guys fucking deal with it, not hide from it."

Her face never changes, she never loses that softness in her eyes, and I want to kick my ass. "I kill people to deal with mine. Ryder fights anything that gets in his way. Holden hides in an office all day. Gage covers his up with humor." She bends down and hands me my shirt. "We just hide it in different ways."

I take it from her and pull it back on. "I know." I run my fingers through my hair. "I just don't know if I can do this," I whisper hoarsely.

"Dex," she waits until I look into her eyes, "You just did." She walks closer but doesn't touch me. "You just trusted me enough to let me take your sight. That means the world to me."

"How slow are you willing to go, Les? Because eventually, you'll get bored."

She shakes her head again. "No, I won't. I want you, Dex, and that kiss was just a reminder of how you make me feel. We have already established the boundaries and can move further next time."

I touch my lips, amazed they were touching hers. "That kiss was everything good I needed."

Her smile is radiant. "It was for me, too. You'll get there, Dex."

She pecks my cheek, leaving the room and giving me a chance to get my shit together. And just like that, the moment is over. I had her hands on me, her lips on mine, and I turned into a fucking coward.

CHAPTER 23
LEO

I just saw Alessa blow someone's brains out right in front of me. I don't know how to deal with that. The body itself doesn't bother me, I notice. It's the fact I saw her pull the trigger with no remorse on her face. He called her the same name that triggered her the night of the fight, so I know that word means something to her, and it isn't good.

Can I really do this after seeing the real her?

Someone knocks on the door to my room, and then Gage sticks his head through. "Can I come in?"

I motion him in, and he walks in, shutting the door. It's like all the air has been sucked out of the room. I haven't been alone with him since our near kiss, and I don't know how to act around him anymore.

He sits on the bed beside me. "How ya doing, man?"

I look over at him and give him the truth. "I don't know."

"Talk to me about it, then. Work it out." Can I really talk to him? Attraction and sharing Alessa aside, we don't know each other. Will he listen without judgment? "Whatever you say stays between us," he promises like he can read my mind.

"That was hard to watch," I start. "Not that asshole dying,

although that should bother me too, but watching her kill like that without a second thought. That's not the girl I know."

"It's always been the girl you know," he says gently. "You just didn't know all of her. Les does what she has to do to protect this family and anyone else she can. Jerry Moretto is a low-life piece of shit who was having kids sell dope for him to other kids."

"I get that," I say, standing up from the bed to pace. "I just have to wrap my head around the fact that she's a killer."

"A killer who does what she has to do," Gage says harshly, and I look at him. He's sitting on the bed with his arms braced on his knees, watching me pace. "This is the life, Leo. Take it or leave it."

"So that's it? Accept it, or fuck off?"

He stands up. "That's exactly how it is. You can't come in here and expect to change something we've known our whole lives."

"I thought you guys are supposed to protect her," I scoff. "All I see is you guys standing on the fucking sidelines while she handles everything." I know the moment that leaves my mouth, I fucked up. Gage's whole expression changes, and he's pissed. *Fuck.*

"She's the leader of the Italian Mafia. Do you know what that fucking means?" he asks, taking a step forward. He continues, not waiting for an answer. "It means that if people see us doing what she does, it makes her look weak, and more people will come after her. Is that what you want? You want every fucking family coming for her blood just because you can't handle that your girl is a badass?" By the time he's done talking, he's standing in front of me, and I can see that crazy look in his eyes. "You don't think we would rather tuck her away somewhere safe and do it for her? We would in a fucking heartbeat, but that's not who Les is. She doesn't need to be put in an ivory tower; she needs someone to respect and accept her for who she is. If that isn't you, you need to get the fuck out. Now."

He walks around me to leave my room, and I reach out, grabbing his arm. "I'm not going anywhere," I tell him, knowing I will have to suck it up and accept who Alessa is, no matter what.

He grabs where my hand is holding his arm and spins us, so my back is to the door. He pushes in until his chest is pressed against mine, his face inches away. I know it's meant to be threatening, but I can't help my reaction. My breath quickens, and my cock jerks to attention in my jeans.

What the fuck is wrong with me?

Gage catches my reaction and steps in closer until our entire bodies are touching, not even a breath separating us. "You like this, don't you?" he asks. "You like my body pressing into yours." How did we go from arguing about Alessa to him pressing me against the door? He shifts his hips, and I feel his hard cock rub against mine. My head falls back onto the door with a thud, all the fight leaving my body. "Tell me," he demands.

"Yes."

"Yes, what?" he demands again, moving his hips and rubbing against me.

"Yes, I like this," I grit out. He has my dick so hard in my jeans that I think I'll bust.

"Then why are you fighting it so bad? You know I want it," he muses, pressing his face closer to mine, his breath fanning across my lips. Just when I think he's going to kiss me, he takes a step back, breaking the connection. "I won't force you. This decision has to be yours."I know he'll wait for me to make the first move. Can I do that?

He runs his teeth across his bottom lip, and my control snaps. I take one step forward to press my body back against his and slant my mouth over his. He instantly sinks his tongue into my mouth and walks us backward until my back hits the door again. He hooks his hand around my neck, holding me closer, and I slide my hands around his back because I need to touch him.

He kisses me harder, and a half groan, a half moan escapes my mouth before I can stop it. It's like an electric shock to my system when my lips met his. My heart is hammering so hard I think it'll pound out of my chest, and I can feel his beating in time with mine the way he is pressed against me.

Gage breaks the kiss, and my immediate reaction is to jerk him back. He kisses my lips once. "I got you, Pretty boy," he says before jerking my shirt over my head and then doing the same with his. He steps back in so his skin is on mine, and it's so much different from being pressed against Alessa. Instead of the softness of her breasts pressed against me, it's all hard planes from his pecs. And I can't get enough. "You want more?" he asks, moving his hips again. "Or do you want to stop here?"

"Fuck," I rasp when he grinds his cock into mine; I respond, pushing my hips into him.

"Goddamn," Gage breathes, placing his hands on either side of my head on the door, looking down to where our dicks are rubbing together. "Take what you want," he encourages.

Right now, I want Gage.

I swallow and slide my hand between us, sliding it over his cock, massaging him through his jeans.

His eyes snap to mine; they are the darkest blue I've ever seen. "You want my cock, Pretty boy?" He pushes into my hand. "Because I want yours."

He reaches between us, undoing my jeans. He pulls them down enough for my throbbing cock to spring free and then wraps a hand around it.

"Shit," I choke out. His hold is tighter than Alessa's and rougher. His hand isn't soft like hers; it's calloused from working with his hands. I push my hips forward, fucking his fist, seeking more. I undo his jeans and shove them roughly down so I can feel him in my hand. I stroke him just like he's stroking me, staring him right in the eye.

There is no turning back now; I'm addicted. There is no doubt in my mind if I want Gage anymore, I will take whatever he's willing to give me.

"Fuck Leo," he groans. He swings us back around before stumbling to the bed with our pants still around our ankles.

We fall onto the bed in a tangle of limbs, his lips crashing down on mine. We rid ourselves of the rest of our clothes, and he slides his naked body against mine.

He straddles my waist, so his cock is directly on top of mine and starts moving his hips like he's fucking me.

"Holy shit," I whisper, breaking the kiss, my head dropping back onto the mattress. My eyes find his again, and he's focused intently on my face.

"You feel this?" he asks, grinding his hips forward, and then groans, "because I do."

I know what he's talking about. He feels the absolute pleasure of our cocks rubbing together, jerking against each other.

He sits back on his heels, wrapping both hands around our cocks and pushing them together. He's still moving his hips, and I feel so close to coming that it isn't funny.

"Gage," I groan, my hips moving with his.

His grip tightens, and he starts moving his hands in time with his thrusts. We start moving faster, and I know he's close too. Our breath is sawing out of our lungs. I look down to where we are rubbing together but get drawn back to his eyes.

"You feel that?" he asks again, and I know he's no longer talking about the physical part; he's talking about the pull to stare each other in the eyes and not look away. I feel my release blazing up my spine with no hope of stopping it.

Stream after stream of cum hits my stomach and chest. "Gage," I groan when it won't stop. He drops our cocks and wraps a hand around his own, jerking himself roughly. He locks his eyes with mine and groans out his release, mixing it with mine.

Fuck, that shouldn't be so hot.

He finally releases his hold on my eyes, letting them travel down to the mess we made on me. His eyes take on a primal look before he runs his finger through it, swirling it around, mixing it together.

When he leans his head down and licks a path up my chest, gathering it on his tongue, I'm more than ready to go again. He moves up my body again and sinks his tongue into my mouth, with our combined cum still on his tongue. The flavor explodes in my mouth, and I jerk him closer. He relaxes against me, not caring that he's a sticky mess like I am.

Someone bangs on the door with their fist, scaring the shit out of us and causing us to jerk apart. "Les wants you downstairs!" Ryder yells through the door.

"Fuck," Gage breathes out with a chuckle. "Okay!" he yells back and then looks at me when he realizes he just got us busted for answering for me.

I can't help but laugh at the look on his face. "It's fine," I assure him.

"Hm," he hums, leaning down to kiss me again. "We better go," he murmurs, deepening the kiss. We start getting lost in each other. Ryder bangs on the door again, and we spring apart.

"Come on!" Ryder yells.

"We're coming!" Gage yells back, then looks at me again, waggling his eyebrows. "Well, we already did."

I shove him off me with a laugh. "Let's get cleaned up." I go to slide off the bed, and Gage grabs my arm.

"You okay with what just happened?" he asks with so much worry that I can't help but kiss him again.

"More than okay," I tell him and feel that tug on my heart again.

There's something about Gage that's drawing me to him, and it has from the first time I saw him, even tied in Alessa's basement.

Now I just need to figure out what it is.

Les sits across from Gage and me at the table on the patio. Her elbow is on the table, and her chin is propped in her hand, just staring. Her brow is furrowed, and her eyes are swinging between us. It's unnerving, and I feel myself fidgeting in my chair. Gage is relaxed and leaning back in his chair, staring her down the same way she's staring at us. I wish for his level of calmness.

"Something happened," she finally says, and I can't make out the expression on her face.

"It did?" Gage asks, sitting up and leaning his arms on the table.

She props her chin in both hands and looks cuter than hell. "Uh-huh. First of all, Ryder said he went to get Leo, and you answered," she says, talking to Gage. "Second, Leo is looking forty shades of guilty. Third, you look like you just won the fucking lottery."

Gage grins. "I did when I got you, Pretty girl."

She rolls her eyes. "Cut the shit. What happened?"

He leans back in his chair and throws an arm on the back of mine. "Wouldn't you like to know?" he says.

She drops her hands. "I would."

"How bad?" Gage asks with a smile.

"Please," she begs, realizing she was messing with me a minute ago. She turns her pleading eyes to me when Gage doesn't answer. "Please," she says again, poking her bottom lip out.

I exchange a look with Gage, and he shrugs, letting me know he doesn't care what I tell her. I look back at her; she has the cutest, most hopeful look. "We got...acquainted with each other."

"How acquainted?" she asks, crossing her arms on the table, all ears.

"We messed around," I say, unsure how much I should tell her.

Gage snorts. "If you call coming all over pretty boy, then yeah, we messed around."

Her mouth pops open, and her eyes go wide. "You did?"

I can feel my face flush with heat, but it isn't from embarrassment. I'm remembering everything that happened upstairs. If Ryder wouldn't have interrupted us, what would have happened? That thought has my dick rock hard again.

"I should not be this turned on by that," she laughs.

"You like that idea, don't you? You dirty girl," Gage replies with his own laugh.

"Duh," she deadpans. "Two hot as fuck dudes sweaty and giving in to their desires? Holy shit," she says, fanning her face with her hand.

I adjust myself discreetly as I can. "Shut up," I tell them with a laugh. I look at her harder when she glares at me. "Are you mad?" I ask with worry. She said she didn't care. Did she change her mind?

"Yeah. Actually, I am." She flips her hair over her shoulder, and my heart sinks. "I'm pissed because I didn't get to watch."

A relieved laugh bursts out of me. "Fuck, you scared me for a minute."

"I told you I don't care as long as it stays in this group." She shrugs. "I wasn't lying when I said it's hot as fuck."

"Why did you need him downstairs, anyway?" Gage asks with his arm still on my chair.

"Oh," she laughs. "I forgot I actually had a reason. Tell your brothers to come over for dinner." I raise an eyebrow. "That okay?" she asks.

"Yeah. I'll message them. But why?"

She shrugs. "It's time to put a real test to this alliance. They're your brothers, Leo. I'd like to get to know them."

I pull out my phone and send a group message to Evander and Mateo. She returned my actual phone but told me it's fitted with the same tracking as theirs. There's an underlying warning that if I fuck up, they'll be able to find me. She also said they use it in emergencies when someone isn't picking up or thinks something might be wrong. I let that fill me with the warmth that she'll be worried about me instead of dwelling on the fact that if I skip out, they can find me.

Alessa wants you guys to come over tonight for dinner.

EVANDER

Why?

MATEO

She probably plans on stabbing us. 'insert knife emoji'

No, dumbass. She wants to accept this alliance and get to know you guys.

EVANDER

What time?

"What time?" I ask Alessa.

"Six is fine."

Six.

EVANDER

We will be there.

MATEO

Speak for yourself, bro. I don't want to die today.

I roll my eyes before answering. He reminds me so much of Gage that it isn't even funny.

She's not going to kill you.

MATEO

How do I know this isn't her and Leo is already dead?

EVANDER

You're an idiot.

See you at six.

I lay the phone down. "They'll be here."

"Okay," she says with a smile. "You looked like you were struggling there."

"Mateo's an idiot," I laugh. "He said you were the one talking and luring them here to kill them."

She grins. "If I were to kill them, I wouldn't get blood in my house."

"That's reassuring," I say with an eye roll.

Gage laughs. "You're too easy to fuck with."

"Who said I'm fucking with him?" Alessa asks with a perfectly straight face. The longer I stare at her, the more she struggles to keep her composure. She finally laughs, and I breathe out. Today made me nervous as hell of her, but not enough to back down. My small fight with Gage opened my eyes to the fact that no matter what she does, I'm not going anywhere. Whether that makes me fucked up, I don't care anymore. Now I have Gage too. No way in hell I'm walking away from the feelings they both give me.

I hear the patio door slide open, and Ryder steps out and walks over to the table. He pulls out the chair beside Les, sits down, and lays a kiss on her lips. She just smiles at him, and I don't feel as much hate toward him anymore. If these guys can make her as happy as she deserves, I can suck it up. Dex ambles out behind him and takes the seat on her other side.

"Holden already knows about this, and he's already looking into it," Ryder says, pulling his phone from his pocket.

Les turns towards him. "Knows about what?"

"I got a picture of us from The Games and didn't think much of it." He slides his phone to the middle of the table, and we all lean in to look. It's the perfect shot of us standing around with Alexey and Dmitri.

"Who's it from?" I ask with a frown.

"It was sent anonymously," Ryder answers before scrolling again. "These came in today."

He scrolls through several pictures. One is Gage and Les on the bikes with me on the back, us walking out of Moretto's bar, talking to Lucas and Landon, and one shot from Les and me walking into her beach house.

"Someone is following us?" I ask, looking around the table.

Ryder shakes his head. "I thought that at first. They aren't following *us*. They're following *her*. "

"How do you get that?" Gage asks, scrolling back through the pictures.

"What's the common theme of those pictures?" Ryder asks, looking at Gage.

I frown, confused until it hits me. "She's the only one in every one of them."

Ryder snaps his fingers, pointing at me. "Bingo."

"Come on," Alessa snorts. "You really think I have a stalker?"

"I found this when I ran to Maximus earlier," Dex rumbles, laying a folder on the table. He slides it to her. "It was under my windshield wiper."

She frowns but opens it. When the pictures come into view, all color drains from her face. "How the hell did they get these?"

She hands them to me, and I flip through them with a queasy feeling. They are shots taken through the window of us the night at her beach house and then ones of me, her, and Gage at the cabin. Both show us in the throes of passion.

"That proves you have a stalker, Baby girl," Dex says, and I realize he saw these pictures already.

I pass the pictures to Gage. "What does this mean?" I ask the table.

"Holden has my original phone, and he transferred everything to a new one so he can track it back to who sent them." Ryder shrugs. "If anyone can find them, it's Holden."

"What does this mean for her?" I clarify. Who the fuck stalks the leader of the Mafia?

"She doesn't go anywhere alone," Dex says, looking at Alessa, waiting for her to argue.

"I don't need someone to hold my hand, Dex. If I want to go alone, I will," she replies, the frown on her face deepening.

"This isn't something to mess with, Pretty girl," Gage says, slapping the pictures in front of her. "Those are personal fucking pictures, so that means this is very personal. Stalkers are unpredictable."

"Why are you explaining that to me like I'm fucking stupid? I can handle myself," she says defensively.

"No one said you couldn't, *Il mio sole*," Ryder says, picking her hand up and kissing the back of it. "It would just make us feel better."

She shrugs, but I know that's far from an agreement. Alessa is going to do what she wants when she wanted. No matter what any of us have to say.

"Someone has to be fucking crazy as hell to stalk you, Baby," I add. "That means they are capable of anything."

"Exactly," Ryder says, shocking me by agreeing.

She rolls her eyes. "It's just some pictures," she says dismissively.

It would take more than us to convince her she needs someone with her more than ever. I just hope she didn't get hurt in the process.

We stay out on the patio until it's almost time for Evander and Mateo to show up. After we moved past the possible stalker situation, it felt nice just to hang out with them. Even Ryder. I know he didn't just fully accept me overnight, but I can breathe around him now, at least.

We walk into the house, and it's the first time I've seen kitchen staff bustling around. The whole time I've been here, I've only seen the cleaning staff. I look at Alessa in question.

She shrugs. "I can't cook."

"You could have just ordered something, Baby," I tell her, kissing her head and wrapping my arm around her.

"Now, what impression would that make?" Gage remarks, throwing his arm around my shoulders. I can't stop the reaction, my whole body shudders thinking of earlier, and he just grins, walking away.

"Okay," Alessa says. "I need to be around next time."

I exhale a breath. "I don't know if I'll survive with both of you there."

"Ohhhhh," Alessa says, running her hands up my chest. "You don't want Gage and me touching you at the same time?" she purrs.

"Stop," I warn.

She laughs. "Why?"

I go to open my mouth to answer, but it's cut off by someone from her staff.

"Evander and Mateo Perez are here, ma'am."

"It's Alessa, Shawna. Thank you."

"Yes, ma'am," Shawna replies with a smile and leads my brothers into the living room.

Alessa treats all her staff with the utmost respect, never talking down to them. Hell, she barely keeps staff here except for the guards surrounding the place twenty-four-seven.

"Gentlemen," Alessa greets politely. "Let's sit until the food's ready."

She leads us into the living room, gesturing to the loveseat in front of the couch for Evander and Mateo. They at least listened to me when I said this is a very casual dinner and are in jeans and t-shirts.. Alessa doesn't make big deals out of stuff like that, and Gage told me it's because her dad never did. He said Luca didn't see the point in getting dressed up in your own house for dinner. On the other hand, Frankie made it a formal affair every night.

I sit on the couch, and she surprises me by sitting right beside me, lacing our hands together, and laying them on her lap.

"Thanks for having us, Alessa," Evander says politely.

Alessa lets out an inelegant snort. "Cut the shit, Evander. I'm not your superior."

"Ah, but you are," Evander says with a grin, not bothered by that fact.

She waves her hand. "Schematics of the family lines. I invited you here for two reasons. I want to move further with this alliance, putting us on equal footing."

"The second reason?" Mateo asks, kicking back in his seat.

"For Leo," she says softly, looking over at me.

"You did this for me?"

She shrugs. "I unfairly kept you here, away from them. You're a part of my life, and you're a part of theirs."

"How would you like to move forward?" Evander asks, relaxing a little more.

She smiles. "I want you three to attend the gala with Gage and me."

Mateo raises his eyebrows. "To announce the alliance?"

"Exactly." She tucks her legs under her crisscross style and leans forward, still holding my hand. "Leo needs to be announced as the new Perez heir." She shrugs. "It will make other families follow suit if they see I can put what happened behind me."

Evander looks at me. "Are you okay with that? Being announced as an heir?"

I've been waiting to be introduced as a Perez. It'll change the whole trajectory of my life. Until I met Alessa, I didn't plan on staying in California long-term. I was going to get to know my brothers and then visit occasionally. If they tell everyone I am now an heir to Frankie, there is no way I can go back home around Mom; too much danger followed these names. I don't question what I'm doing now that I have Alessa.

"I'm good with that," I answer honestly, surprising Evander and

Mateo. We've already talked about me going back home, but my home is now wherever Alessa is. And Gage, if I have to admit it.

"This is an invitation-only, and we don't have one," Evander informs Alessa. "My father made sure we aren't welcome."

"Consider this your invitation as a thank you for taking care of me at your bar," she answers with a smile.

"There's no thanks needed. You were fun," Mateo laughs.

She groans. "I don't even remember what I said."

"Don't worry. You didn't share any trade secrets," Evander says with a chuckle.

"Thank fuck," she mumbles, then shakes her head with a laugh.

I love how she handles things with the most confidence in the world. She took on five uniquely different guys at the same time without batting an eye.

"Food's ready, ma'am," Gage says with an exaggerated flourish, stepping into the room.

"Fuck off, *sir*," Alessa replies with a glare.

"Oh, Pretty girl, you can call me sir any time you want," Gage says, waggling his eyebrows. "You too, Pretty boy," he adds, blowing a kiss at me before walking out of the room.

Alessa loses it and starts laughing. Evander and Mateo's eyebrows hit their hairline at the same time. it's almost comical if I wasn't dying of embarrassment.

Evander looks at me, and I shake my head. "Later," I tell him.

"You better count on it," Mateo adds.

I told them about the whole thing with Alessa, but I didn't say anything about Gage. I didn't know how to bring it up, and my reaction just now showed everything they needed to know.

After a surprisingly laid-back dinner, Alessa told me to spend some time with Evander and Mateo, so I led them to my new favorite spot in this house, the patio by the pool.

"Things seem to be going good," Mateo comments, sipping the beer Alessa brought out for us.

"Yeah," I agree.

"What about with Ryder?" Evander asks, kicking back in the chair.

"He doesn't say much, but he stopped glaring at me." That's all I can really ask for right now. For a while, if he could kill me with his fucking eyes, he would have. "I went on a job with them today." Evander raises his eyebrow. "We paid a visit to the Moretto's." I left out the part where Alessa shot one of them at point-blank range. I'm not sure what I'm allowed to tell them.

"You know there's a rumor Jerry Moretto is dead," Evander says, tilting his head to the side. Well, I guess I won't have to hide too much. "There's also a rumor your black-haired beauty in there took care of him."

I stare blankly at them and let them draw their own conclusions. Mateo laughs. "Good. He was a fucking worm."

"I know you have to keep some things to yourself, Leo, because not even a week ago, we were the enemies, but you have to talk to someone," Evander says, squeezing my shoulder.

I scrub a hand down my face. "I get that. I just don't want to say something I'm not supposed to."

He nods and looks off at the view from the patio. There's so much land in between that you can barely see the big ass gate surrounding the house in the distance. There's a giant swing on the side where you can see the entire city below. I can't imagine growing up in a situation where you have to be surrounded by a massive fence and guards. The same way my brothers grew up.

"What's the deal with Gage?" Evander finally asks. He can sense my reluctance to talk about it. "We won't judge you."

"We might give you shit, but we won't judge." Mateo grins, putting me at ease.

"I can't explain it," I say, thinking about all the times he's barely touched me on accident or vice versa and my immediate reaction to it. And now I've had a small taste of what he has to offer. "I'm attracted to him."

"On a sexual level?" Evander asks curiously.

"Yeah," I sigh. "Gage is happily bisexual with experience."

"So, you're intimidated by that," Mateo says, and it's not a question because he's right.

"Well, yeah. He knows what the fuck he's doing, and I don't even know why I'm attracted to him."

"Sometimes people catch our eye, and we can't explain it," Evander remarks with a faraway look. Is he talking about himself?

"Do you think I'm crazy for considering it?"

"Does Alessa care?" Evander asks, and it's a fair question; I shake my head. "Then no. Do what makes you happy, brother."

"Have either of you...?" I let the question hang in the air.

Mateo shrugs. "I have."

Just like that, open and honest. I've never had siblings, but finding Evander and Mateo was one of the highlights of my life. They might try to protect me from most things, but they never hide anything.

I look at Evander, and he shakes his head. He still has that look in his eyes, a look I've never seen before. It's like he's thinking of someone, one that hurt him. I don't want to ask and ruin the night, so I file it away to ask later.

"Things...progressed today," I say and then sigh. "It more than progressed."

"Are you fine with that?" Mateo asks, leaning his arm on the table.

"Yeah. I didn't think I would be, but Gage somehow makes it easy."

"That's how it should be," Evander says.

I feel a little better getting it off my chest. My brothers are the only ones I have to talk to, and I'm glad they're open with me.

We lapse into silence then the patio door busts open. "Pretty girl," Gage says, holding his hands up like he's warding off a dangerous animal, and from the look on Alessa's face, he is. This should be good.

"Don't pretty girl me," she says and shoves him in the chest hard enough to make him stumble. What the hell did he do?

Gage laughs and then tries to cover it up. "I'm sorry."

"I thought we were done with the stupid pranks after you dyed Ryder's hair pink," she says, pushing him again.

Mateo barks a laugh. "He did what now?"

"Oh, he almost fucking killed me," Gage says, oblivious to the fact he's two wrong moves from going in the pool fully clothed.

"He taped a fucking air horn to the bottom of my office chair, so when I sat down, I almost shit myself."

Gage finally loses his battle and doubles over in laughter. Alessa takes two precise steps forward and shoves his shoulders, causing him to stand up. She plants a foot in the middle of his chest, giving him a firm shove. He hits the pool with a splash causing everyone else to laugh.

He comes back up, spluttering, swiping water out of his face. "You think that bothered me?"

"Not you, but maybe the shit in your pockets," she laughs.

"Fuck!" he exclaims, pulling himself out of the pool. I can't help but admire the clothes plastered on his body. He drops his wallet, keys, and phone in front of me on the table. "Something funny, Pretty boy?" he asks, ripping his shirt over his head and dropping his shorts. I'm lucky he has on a snug pair of boxer briefs, or his cock would have been right in my face. He advances on me, and I narrowly miss his grab by jumping up from my chair.

"Gage," I warn, laughing. He keeps advancing, and I take a step back, running right into Alessa. I turn pleading eyes on her. "Baby?" She grins and starts advancing from the other side. I sidestep Gage, and they both have me cornered, and I know I can't outrun either of them. *Shit.*

"Throw him in the pool!" Mateo yells, and I shoot him a look of betrayal.

Gage rushes me, dropping his shoulder, and hits me in the midsection with a tackle that rivals a professional football player, and we both go into the pool. Luckily, all I have on is ball shorts with a shirt, and my phone is sitting on the table. We both break the surface at the same time to see Alessa execute a perfect dive in a bright orange bra and panties set. I don't even worry about Evander and Mateo seeing; it covers more than her bikini.

"What the fuck?" Ryder asks, walking outside with beers and looking into the pool. He sets two of them in front of Evander and Mateo.

Alessa pops up behind me, wrapping her arms and legs around me. "The water's warm," she says, patting the water with a laugh.

"I'm good, *Il mio sole*," he says with a chuckle, sitting down where I was sitting. He picks up Gage's dripping phone with a raised eyebrow.

Gage shrugs. "She pushed me in."

She punches him in the arm. "Because you are an overgrown man-child that won't stop with the stupid pranks."

"Don't start that shit again," Ryder warns, pointing at Gage.

"Does anyone have a picture of the pink hair?" I ask.

"I do," Alessa and Gage say at the same time, dissolving into laughter.

He narrows his eyes at me. "Don't turn your back. Gage is a dirty fucker with pranks."

Gage's mouth pops open. "Me? You super glued my fucking shoes to the floor."

"That was high school," Ryder defends himself, but I can see his lips twitch.

"He had to call my dad to bring him shoes!" Alessa says, now wheezing from laughter.

"And you," Gage says, rounding on Alessa. "You put icy hot in my lotion. Set my fucking ass on fire."

"Literally," she says, now howling with laughter again.

I wince. "The lotion you...?"

"Yeah, the fucking lotion I jacked off with," Gage says, unashamed.

"I remember that shit," Ryder says with a laugh, and I think it's the first I've heard the sound. "We all got a forty-five-minute lecture from my dad and Luca about how our pranks were getting out of control."

"While Gage was blubbering, thinking his dick was going to fall off," Alessa says, wading back through the water.

Gage moves faster than a blink, grabs her, hefts her up, and tosses her into the water. She comes back up laughing. "Is my dick going to fall off?" she fake cries mocking Gage. She lets out a shriek when he dives for her.

I hate that I missed that part of them, the time in their lives when they seemed more carefree even than they are now. I missed out on a whole lifetime with her that Gage and Ryder got to have. I can't help but feel a little out of place.

"You're telling our secrets to the enemy," Ryder says, jerking a thumb at Evander and Mateo, but I can tell he's joking.

"Put icy hot in lotion to torture enemies. Got it," Mateo jokes.

"It works!" Alessa yells, shrieking again, still dodging a grabbing Gage.

"You will surrender," Gage declares.

"Not a chance in hell." She sticks her tongue out and dives beneath the water, swimming right through his legs. I feel her brush mine, so I widen my stance, and she surfaces right between me and the side of the pool where I'm holding on. "Hello there," she says, waggling her eyebrows.

"Hello yourself, Baby." I peck her lips and try to catch Ryder's reaction without being obvious. I still don't believe he is all about this. He looks...fine. What the hell? Did someone body snatch Ryder?

Gage makes a grab for her around me, and I cage her against the side of the pool, protecting her, which is fucking laughable.

"That's not fucking fair," Gage pouts. "Two against one."

"Aw, poor baby," Alessa pouts back.

He jumps up and pushes us both under. We spend the next fifteen minutes wrestling in the pool until Evander and Mateo start saying their goodbyes.

It feels so normal that I can't help but wonder when the other shoe will drop.

CHAPTER 24
HOLDEN

I'm watching TV in my room when the door opens slowly. I look up expecting Ryder, but Alessa walks in. Her hair looks damp, and she's wearing an oversized shirt that looks like Gage's. She softly pads over to the bed. "Can I watch with you?"

I nod, and she slides onto the bed beside me. I haven't seen her since all that happened by the pool, but I know she's busy, and I'm deliriously happy she's in here with me now. I've never jacked off so much at the thought of anything, but I couldn't stop after getting a small taste of Les.

She snuggles into my side, and I wrap my arm around her shoulders. "What are you watching?"

"Peaky blinders."

"Oh. Good one. Nothing like old-school English gangsters," she laughs, and the sound goes straight to my heart. She seems so happy today, even after everything that went down with the Morettos and her finding out about a potential stalker. I'm running everything on Ryder's phone I can think of, and I *will* find this asshole.

"I have that file for you." I go to move from the bed to grab it, and she pulls me back down.

"I'm not here for that," she says softly, rubbing her hand down my bare chest. "I just wanted to be with you."

"Oh," I say lamely. I'm so used to people coming to me for work-related stuff that it's hard to separate the two, and Ryder's the only one who will hang out with me in my room or office. Thinking about Ryder with Alessa makes me feel guilty. I think I see Ryder as more than my best friend, but I also think I'm confusing myself because Ryder helped me out so much when I first got here.

"What's on your mind?" she asks, and I look down, noticing she's staring at me.

"Nothing," I say too fast, then remember what she said about honesty. "Ryder."

"Ryder?" she asks in confusion. "Is everything okay?"

"Uh," I clear my throat, "Yeah."

"You can tell me anything, Holden." I look into her blue eyes and know she's telling the truth.

"I look at Ryder...differently than the other guys."

She nods. "I could see why. He took you under his wing when you got here." I can feel my face heat, and her mouth forms an 'O'. "You mean you don't see him as just a friend?" I nod, unable to speak. "Does Ryder know?"

"No," I whisper. "He's my best friend."

She giggles. "He's mine too, and you see where that went."

I chuckle. "Yeah, but you're you."

"And you, Holden Jones, are you." She runs her thumb over my bottom lip. "I've never known Ryder to be attracted to other guys, but that doesn't mean anything. Look at Leo."

"What about Leo?"

"Leo and Gage have developed certain feelings for each other. Up until now, Leo has been straight."

"I've liked a guy before, but I was so confused by it that I never got a chance to figure it out." Then I got kidnapped but didn't need to say that out loud. I look into her eyes. "You don't care? About Gage and Leo, I mean?"

"Or you and Ryder? No. Like I told them, as long as it stays within our group, I don't care."

"You're kind of perfect." She's more than perfect. I was confused about my feelings, afraid she would get mad at me for looking at Ryder, but she just accepts it. Just like she has with me.

She laughs. "Not even close."

She goes back to watching TV, and I kick myself for even worrying she would be mad. I watch with her as long as I can before I become hyper-aware of her lying with me. Her head on my arm, the smell of her hair, her breasts pressed to my side, her bare leg touching mine. I shift in the bed, trying to hide that her touch gives me a hard-on.

"Holden?" she says softly.

"Yeah?" I ask, my voice hoarse.

"Are you okay with this?"

Does she think I'm uncomfortable with her lying on me?

"I am," I answer. Just my cock is painfully uncomfortable.

She looks up at me, and I don't think. I just act. I kiss her just like she showed me outside. She opens immediately for me, and I groan into her mouth. Her lips fit perfectly against mine and are pouty and soft.

I roll so she's on her back so I can deepen the kiss. She runs her soft hands down my back, meeting me kiss for kiss. Her body feels amazing against mine. Ever since I got to touch her outside, it's all I can think of.

"Touch me," she whispers against my lips before deepening the kiss again.

I swallow the nerves since I don't have Gage coaching me. Would I be a complete ass if I ask him to come here?

I run my hand up her thigh and realize she doesn't have shorts on, just panties. The shirt fits her like a dress, so she doesn't need them. I slip my hand under the shirt, up her toned stomach, until I touch her bare breast. I don't know why that turns me on even more, knowing she was almost completely bare for me before she walked in.

As Gage showed me, I roll her nipple between my fingers, and she arches into my touch. "Can I take your shirt off?"

She smiles. "Yes."

I sit up on my knees and pull her with me. I lift her shirt over her head, then lay her back down, rubbing my chest across her hard nipples on my way back to her mouth. Her beautiful breasts are pressed against my chest while I devour her mouth. I'm not shy about kissing her anymore, so I take whatever she gives me.

"Mine," I say when I pull my mouth away from hers, looking her in the eyes. I know she isn't just mine; she has them too, but right now. She. Is. Mine.

"I'm yours, Holden," she whispers, and I feel my heart expand.

I kiss her lips once before kissing down her neck, stopping to pay attention to her sensitive nipples. She opens her legs wider, grinding her pussy against my hard cock through my shorts.

I have to close my eyes and breathe through my nose to stop myself from coming in my shorts again. I kiss down her stomach, right above her panties, then her pussy through her panties.

"Oh," she breathes, raising her hips. I hook my hands in them and pull them slowly down her legs. I toss them behind me before placing my hands on the inside of her thighs and spreading her legs wide. I try to run through everything Gage told me while I'm getting situated between her legs. I lick her from the opening of her pussy to her clit. I circle my tongue around it, hoping I make this enjoyable for her. Her hips jerk closer to my face, making me feel like a fucking superhero. I circle her clit with my tongue until her hips rotate with me, then suck it into my mouth. "Fuck," she moans, grinding into my face.

She could smother me with her pussy, and I wouldn't care.

I slowly slide two fingers inside her, marveling at how wet I make her. I move my fingers around, searching for that magic spot. I get frustrated until her hips jerk up and her back bows.

I found it.

I start thrusting my fingers in and out while sucking and licking her clit, watching her face the whole time. She makes the most beautiful face when you make her feel good. Her eyes darken, her cheeks bloom with color, and her lips part slightly. Her chest is heaving harder with each thrust of my fingers or each time I suck on her clit. I feel her start to get tighter and tighter on my fingers. I reach up with my free hand, rolling her nipple with my fingers. I thrust two more times with my fingers and then suck her clit into my mouth.

"Holden!" she screams. I have to grind my cock into the mattress to keep from coming, just from hearing my name leave her lips. I did that to her. I made her scream my name.

I slide up her body, and she jerks my lips to hers, licking her taste off my tongue. Her hand slides down into my shorts; I have to grab her wrist to stop her. "I'll come, Les."

She giggles softly. "That's the point."

How do I tell her I want to come, but I want to be inside her when I do? I'm not brave with my words like the other guys; they tell her exactly what they want. I suck in a deep breath and gather all the courage I can.

"I want to..." I take a breath. "I want to be inside of you."

She runs her hands down my cheeks, searching my eyes. She pecks my lips before she whispers, "Please."

I push my shorts and boxers down, then kick them off. I'm so fucking lost on what to do. I know the basics, like where to put my cock, but I'm afraid of hurting her. I look at her tiny body and down at my cock, apprehension setting in. She looks so damn small lying there.

"Holden," she rubs my cheeks again, "Where did your head go?"

"I don't want to hurt you," I admit.

"You won't," she promises. I have her naked in my bed, her legs wide open for me, my cock hanging free, and I'm going to fucking choke. "We don't have to yet."

"I want to, Bright eyes," I say, then my eyes snap to hers. I've never called her that to her face, only in my head. Her face softens even more.

"Bright eyes?" she asks, gently rubbing her hands up my arms where they are braced beside her hips.

"The first good thing I saw was your bright blue eyes."

Tears gather in her eyes. "Oh."

I lean down and kiss them away. I don't know why, but I know I'm ready at this moment. "Do you have a condom?"

She shakes her head. "If you trust me, you don't need one."

"I trust you with everything," I tell her honestly. There has never been a doubt in my mind that I can't trust her.

I move my hand between us and place my cock at her entrance. She looks so fucking small. I look up at her, worried again.

"Just go slow," she says, rubbing my arms again. I move one hand beside her head and use my other hand to guide my cock.

The head of my cock barely enters before I have to breathe again. She is so tight and wet, and it's so fucking hot. I don't know if I will get all the way in before I come.

I slowly push forward and only get halfway before her body tenses up."Holy shit." She reaches down and starts rubbing her clit. "Pull out and push in again." I watch my cock slide out, covered in her arousal, then watch it slide back in. Holy fuck, I'm really doing this with her.

I do what she says, and on the fourth try, I slide all the way in, with her rubbing her clit the whole time. A full-body shiver wracks me when I feel my balls up against her ass, her pussy pulsing against me. My other hand lands beside her head with a groan.

"You're fucking huge," she moans, her hips lifting against me. "But you feel so good." She moves her hand from between us, placing her hand on the side of my face.

All I can do is stare into those eyes, afraid that if I look away, this whole thing will have been another dream, and she'll disappear.

"Tell me how to make you feel good, Bright eyes." Now that I'm inside her, I can feel my control fraying. I want to make her feel good, so she won't regret this.

She moans again at the nickname. "Pull out a little and thrust back in slowly." She guides her hands to just above my hips, moving them how she wants them—pushing when I should pull out and pulling when she wants me to move back in. Once I get it, she moves her hands up my back, scraping it with her nails. "Faster," she moans, moving her hips with mine. I pick up the tempo, and she moans deep and throaty; I almost lose it right there.

I keep the same tempo moving in and out of her with long, deep strokes; she is so damn wet.

"Fuck," I groan. I can already feel sweat gathering at my temples, but I refuse to let go before her. I need to feel what it feels like when she comes on my cock.

"Pretty girl. I have a ques...." Gage says, walking in without knocking. "Oh." I freeze, and my head snaps to him, and he's grinning from ear to ear. "Don't mind me." He obviously didn't expect to walk in on this. "Let me see that horse cock disappear inside of you one time, and I'll leave."

We both laugh and then dissolve into groans when it causes her to tighten on me.

"I don't care if you stay," I tell him breathlessly. Nothing is going to stop me from making love to this girl.

Gage shuts the door and dives onto the bed from the foot, causing the mattress to jostle. It sinks me even deeper, and she gasps.

Afraid I hurt her, I go to pull back, and she stops me. "Don't." I push back in, and her head tilts back with her mouth open. "Oh god."

"Does he feel good, Pretty girl?" Gage asks. He's stretched out on the bed on his side, his head propped up on his hand.

"God, yes."

"Pull out, man. I've got to see her take that cock." I pull all the way out until the head of my cock is the only thing inside of her and push back in slowly; she takes it the first time. Gage groans and adjusts his cock. "Fuck."

"Holden," Alessa moans. "You have to move."

I start moving at the same tempo we were in before. "Harder," she begs, and I freeze again.

"You won't hurt her. Our girl loves it rough," Gage says, rolling over onto his back, and pulling his cock free. Why is that hot knowing we turn him on enough that he has to take matters into his own hands? I've looked at Gage in appreciation before, but not like I do Ryder. But with Gage lying here with his cock in his hand, I don't know what to think. "Watch her face like I told you."

I pull out halfway before thrusting my hips forward, burying myself like I was when Gage jostled the bed. Her hands fly to my hips, encouraging me to move, so I do it again.

"Hook your arm in the bend of her leg and lean forward," Gage instructs, lazily stroking his cock. I would never have done this without him. She helps me get her leg on my arm when I lean forward and brace my hand on the bed. I see why he suggested it; it makes me sink deeper. "Now fuck her."

Alessa nods her head wildly. "Please."

I start moving again, faster and harder this time. "Harder. Make your skin slap against hers," Gage instructs. I shuffle my knees almost under her ass and slam my hips harder. Her fingernails bite into my skin, but she has the same face she did earlier, letting me know she likes it. I don't know what snaps inside of me, but I start fucking her so hard her breasts are bouncing, and she's making all kinds of noises, pushing me harder. The headboard is smacking the wall in time with my thrusts.

"OH FUCK!" she screams. I feel her tighten so hard against me that it takes my breath away. The pressure gets so intense that it starts to push me out. I slide out, and liquid gushes out of her pussy. Gage reaches between us and starts rubbing her clit back and forth, causing it to spray all over my abs and cock. Her whole body is bowed, her eyes squeezed shut like she's in pain. When her back drops to the bed, she's struggling for breath.

"Goddamn, Pretty girl," Gage says hoarsely. He looks at me. "Don't stop." I hesitantly line back up and slide inside her, still concerned. "You made her squirt, you big fucker," Gage explains with a chuckle after he sees the concerned look on my face.

"That's a good thing," Alessa pants out. "Please don't stop."

I breathe in again and start to move. I don't know how often I can stop myself from coming, but there is no way I'm passing up doing that again.

I start slamming into her again, sweat glistening off both of us. She starts making those moan-mewling noises that are driving me insane. I can see Gage from the corner of my eye stroking his cock harder and faster, and I know he's affected by the noises too. When I feel her tighten again with that pressure against the head of my cock, her fingernails scratch down my back, and I know they'll leave marks.

I'll wear those fuckers proudly.

I pull out when it gets too tight and reach down, rubbing her clit like Gage did. "HOLDEN!" she screams, soaking the bed and us when she comes. When she's done, I shove my cock back inside her. Her back bows and she wraps her legs around my waist. There is no way I'm holding off this time. I slam into her three more times before emptying everything inside her with a long groan; I can feel my release in my toes up to my scalp. It's the most intense release I've ever had in my life. I can hear Gage groan and can't resist looking over at him when he comes all over his hand.

I collapse on the bed on her other side, both of our chests heaving; she's as limp as a rag doll. "I think you killed her," Gage chuckles, rolling off the bed and walking to the attached bathroom. I hear the water running in the sink and then the bathtub.

Her legs are still sprawled out, and I can see the mess we made on the bed below her. My bed is soaked, and my come is leaking out of her.

"Are you okay, Bright eyes?" I ask, kissing her lips.

She giggles. "Yeah. More than okay." She turns to me. "Are you?"

"Fuck yeah."

She giggles again. "Damn, that was amazing. Are you sure that was your first time?"

I jerk up to look at her but can see she's teasing. "Yes." I kiss her smiling lips.

"That thing should be registered as a lethal weapon," Gage says, walking out of the bathroom and pointing at my softening cock lying on my thigh.

Alessa laughs, then groans. "I can't move. Holden broke my vagina."

"Pretty girl, that was the hottest fucking thing I've ever seen." Gage kisses her lips, then looks at me. "You take her to the bathtub, and I'll take care of your bed."

I slide off the bed and pull her into my arms with my hand under her back and legs. She snuggles into my chest, and I'm still reeling from having a naked Les in my arms.

I climb into the bathtub with her and clean her up by gently running a washcloth over her. Her soft little sighs are making my heart swell ten times its size. She is so open and honest with me all the time that I know it's time to tell her what happened to me. She trusted me with her story; it's time to tell her mine. I told Ryder one night when he came into my room to comfort me after a nightmare. The whole story just sobbed out of me before I could stop it. Now it's time for Les to know. I quickly wash off and rinse us both before sliding in behind her, laying her against my chest.

"I was raised in a good family in Dallas, Texas, as an only child." She stiffens slightly, and I know she's figured out what I'm about to tell her. "They died in a car accident when I was fifteen, and my only living relative was my uncle, Winston. He got my mom and dad's farm when he moved in to take care of me." She pulls my arms tighter around her but doesn't turn around. I don't know if I can tell her this while looking her in the face.

"Everything was fine at first. He took care of me the best way he knew because he didn't have any kids. He sure as hell didn't know how to take care of a grieving, pissed off fifteen-year-old." I take a breath and push through. "He started getting really interested in what I was doing, and it didn't take him long to figure out that I taught myself how to hack."

At twelve, my love for computers took a turn, and I started coding websites. Shortly after, I figured out I could hack my way into anything. When I was thirteen, I hacked into the school's computers to change a bunch of grades just because I could. It spiraled from there, and I could get into anything I put my mind to.

"He would push me harder and harder. I thought it was him encouraging me, but he had other plans." Les' hands latch onto my arms in support. I lean down, placing my chin on the top of her head for comfort. That vanilla scent swirling around my nose reminds me I'm safe. "He woke me up in the middle of the night two days after my sixteenth birthday by dragging me from the bed. He ignored my questions and pushed me into the living room, where a guy I didn't know was sitting." That guy was Hector Castillo, a small-time arms dealer trying to make it big. "My uncle laughed in my face as he threw me at Hector's feet, telling me I was sold to the highest fucking bidder."

"Oh, Holden," Les whispers, and I can hear the emotion clogging her voice for me. I tighten my hold on her. My own fucking uncle sold me for his own gain, and to this day, I still don't know how much I went for. All I know is that I lived a life of hell while he lived happily on my parents' farm.

"They threw me into a trunk of a car blindfolded in nothing but the boxers I was sleeping in. After that, we got onto a plane, and that's how I ended up in that hellhole you found me in. They gave me one meal a day in that room, and I could bathe once a week and only sleep for four hours a night. The rest of the time, I was hacking various people, filtering money into Hector's pocket, or stealing whatever information I could." That isn't even the worst part; what I have to tell her next is. I swallow past the lump in my throat, determined to tell her everything. "The house was always busy with people, but there was this guy they called Major who paid particular attention to me."

He was big and always smelled like body odor and weed. I shudder at the thought of him. "He would sneak into my room at night when he was there, which was a lot, and with a gun to my head, he would make me do things with him."

"Did he rape you?" Les whispers, but she already knows the answer. She can sense it; that's why she said she knows what I'm going through because she went through it too.

"Yes," I answer honestly. I can feel her body start shaking and know she's trying to cover up the fact that she's crying. "One day, Hector came to me with my biggest job yet. You. I didn't know who you were, but I heard them talking about you around the house and knew this was my chance. You know what happened next."

I laid a trail so easy a toddler could follow it, so I knew if Les were as good as they said she was, she would find it.

She spins around in my arms, wrapping her arms around my neck; I don't even cover up the fact that I have tears sliding down my face. I squeeze her to me with my arms around her waist and breathe her in.

"I'm so sorry that happened to you," she whispers into my neck. "If I could take it away, I would."

"I would take yours away too," I whisper back, wishing like hell I could take away the feeling I know she felt while those men took advantage of her. No one should have to live with those memories. The only thing keeping me together were Ryder and Les and the family they gave me after I lost mine.

We stayed wrapped around each other until the water starts getting cold. I help dry her off before drying myself. Taking her hand, I lead her back to my bed.

The sheets are freshly changed, and Gage is missing. I send a silent thank you to him and tuck us both into bed. She lays her head on my chest, drawing patterns on my pec with her finger. I run my hands over her soft hair and down her back before pulling her closer to me. I reach down and flip the sheet over us. I don't know if bringing this up will bring back the nightmares, but I'm not passing up sleeping with her in my arms.

That's the last thing I remember before falling asleep with my favorite girl in my arms.

CHAPTER 25
RYDER

"Les isn't going to like this," Holden says for the third time, and I suppress an eye roll.

"It's just a simple trip," I point out, helping him unwrap his hands from sparring with me. He's getting damn good, and I'm not as worried about him getting into a fight if I can ever get him out of the house.

He gives me a doubtful look before sitting on the weight bench and lying back. He hooks his hands on the bar and lifts the weights off. I've gotten him lifting two-seventy-five, and he barely breaks a sweat anymore. I still spot him closely, though. I watch his biceps ripple and tear my eyes away.

I've never found a guy attractive, but working out with Holden all these months has made me pay attention to him in ways that I shouldn't. Especially knowing what I know about him.

"Yeah," he grunts, lifting the bar back up. "What if something happens?"

"Nothing is going to happen, Holden."

"You don't know that."

"She's busy. It'll be fine."

Les runs several smaller gangs all over Abbs Valley and Los Angeles. I got a call from a guy named Squid that runs the Disciples. He says they're having problems with their rival gang, and it's starting to heat up. I'm just going down there to remind everyone who they're really fucking with, and that's it. It doesn't matter who I take with me.

He finishes his sets with the weights and racks the bar. "It's your funeral."

I chuckle. "She wouldn't kill me."

"She would in a fucking heartbeat."

"Whatever, you little shit."

Holden and I have become close over his time here. He's more open around me than he is around the other guys, but I see him starting to open up with everyone, including Les, and I couldn't be prouder.

"I'm not so little anymore," he says with a grin, whipping his shirt over his head with confidence.

I started calling him little shit when he first came here because he was skinny as hell. Now he has defined pecs and abs of steel. Nope. Definitely not little anymore.

Stop looking at him like you want to fucking eat him.

I shove his shoulder playfully. "You're still smaller than me."

He snorts. "Not everyone can be built like a linebacker." He turns around to head toward the door, and I see angry red marks all down his back.

"What the fuck happened to your back?" I growl. A flash of white-hot anger runs through me at the thought of someone hurting him.

He spins around with guilt all over his face."Les," he finally answers, staring at something over my shoulder.

I frown in confusion. I spin him back around to take a closer look. Holy shit. "Are those from her fingernails?"

"Uh," he replies, rubbing the back of his neck. "Yeah." I run a finger down one, and his whole body shudders, and I jerk my hand away.

"Sorry," I mutter. I didn't mean to hurt him, but holy shit. She did that to him?

"It's fine," he says hoarsely, without turning around. "Are you mad?"

I search around for anger or even jealousy. But all I can find is a curiosity about what he did that caused her to claw his back up. "No. What did you do to get those?"

He slowly turns around. "Do you really need a lesson in the birds and the bees, Ryder?" he says sarcastically.

"No, smartass." I shove his shoulder again with a laugh.

"Well, I mean. You know when a guy and girl are," he says, waggling his eyebrows suggestively, "Things sometimes happen."

I advance on him with a step forward, and he grins. "You and Les, huh?" I wait for some type of jealousy, but I don't find it with Holden. I only feel it with Leo and sometimes Gage. I'm trying my hardest not to fuck this up with my stubborn feelings.

He looks guilty again, and I feel like shit. "Yeah."

"Hey," I say, gently laying my hand on his shoulder. "It's fine. I'm not mad."

"I know how you feel about her," he says quietly, dropping his head.

"Look me in the eye," I remind him, and his head slowly comes up. "I know you feel the same. It's all good, man."

"I told her what happened to me," Holden says, dropping to the floor to sit.

I sit down beside him, knowing this is a big deal. "You good?"

"Yeah," he shrugs. "She deserved to know. I feel better now that she does."

"Nightmares?" I ask. I know how bad they used to be because I was always the one that ran to him in the middle of the night. I know he felt more comfortable with me, and Les never wanted to make him feel any other way. He used to wake up screaming, covered in sweat with tears rolling down his face. The longer he's here, the better they are, but I know bringing it up has the potential to bring them back in full force.

He shakes his head. "No. I slept like a baby."

I give him a dry look. "Sleeping next to a certain someone probably helped with that."

"You jealous because it wasn't you?" he jokes.

"You little fucker," I growl, lunging for him.

We playfully wrestle on the floor like we've done a thousand times. Something changes, though. It's like an electric storm is lighting up the room, firing up every nerve ending I have that is touching him. That's everything since I have him pinned to the floor, my hips between his legs and his hands above his head.

I look down at Holden; his eyes are wide, pupils huge, but it isn't out of fear. I know what he went through during his time in hell, but he isn't afraid of this; he is feeling it too.

I let his arms go, but before I can move, he latches onto my arms and jerks me, so we are chest to chest. He slants his mouth over mine, surprising me, and making me freeze. Does he feel this attraction too? He pulls back just as fast. "Sorry," he mutters, "I just...never mind." He shoves at my chest, but I lean in further so he can't move.

"You what, Holden?" I ask, placing my hands beside his head.

"I read this wrong. I'm sorry. I won't do it again," he says quietly and shoves at my chest again. I let the bottom half of my body rest between his thighs.

"Does that feel like you read it wrong?" I ask, indicating my hard cock I was trying to hide while we were wrestling. He's just as hard as I am.

His brow furrows. "But when I kissed you..."

"You surprised me. That's it," I interrupt. "Do it again," I challenge, leaving this in his hands. I will never do anything that might scare him.

I lower my head, so my lips are hovering over his. His eyes flash down to my lips, and he licks his. If he doesn't do something soon, I'm going to self-combust. He presses his lips against mine, and I'm ready for him this time. With the first stroke of his tongue against mine, every bit of willpower I have not to push him flies out the window. I sink my tongue into his mouth, taking over the kiss. He groans and flattens his hands on the base of my spine, holding me closer. Bracing myself on one hand, I lower most of my weight on him, running my other hand down his stubbly cheek.

I never thought in a million years I would kiss a dude, but kissing

Holden feels right and fucking good. Our naked chests rubbing together is sending me into overload. I know we need to stop this before it goes any further because I want to take my time with him and ensure this is what he wants.

I pull back from the kiss reluctantly. "To be continued," I tell him when I take in his confused face.

"You liked that?" he asks shyly.

My cock is hard as fucking steel, my heart is hammering out of my chest, and everywhere he touches lights me up. "Yes, I did," I tell him simply. Unable to resist, I kiss his lips once more before jumping to my feet. I reach down for his hand and jerk him to his when he puts his hand in mine.

"Then why did you stop?" he asks, looking uncertain.

"Because, *Bello*, I can't spend the time that I want to explore this with you." His eyes widen with my honesty, and his mouth forms an 'O'. "I want to take my time."

"Me too," Holden replies with a slight smile.

I grapple for every bit of self-control I have with that innocent smile. "Come on," I say and jerk my head towards the door.

Before I rip your clothes off.

"You're coming with me today," I tell Leo, walking into the living room an hour later after a freezing shower. I can't get that kiss with Holden out of my head.

He turns from the TV with a frown. "What?"

"You wanted in. You're fucking in. Now get dressed," I tell him and spin on my heel before he can reply.

It's just a trip to check on Squid, and that's it. Les wants him to be involved, so I'm about to involve him, whether she means it or not. It's time for us to find out what he's made of. I don't blame him for the look he just gave me; I wouldn't trust me, either. But I refuse to treat him with kid gloves because he grew up with an apple pie fucking life. If you want to date the leader of the Italian Mafia, you have to fucking work for it.

"Les is going to kill you," Dex says with a chuckle when I walk into the kitchen. He must have heard me when I told Leo to get dressed. I see Leo pass by the kitchen on his way to the stairs, and I have to admit, I'm impressed. He could tell me to fuck off, and there isn't anything I could do about it because Les would likely take his side, but something told me he wouldn't refuse to go. Leo has something to prove, and I'm going to let him.

"She wanted him to be a part of us."

Dex gives me a doubtful look. The same one Holden gave me. "Why are you really taking him?"

"Because it's time he showed what he's fucking made of. Les will coddle him forever, and he needs to man up."

"So, taking him into gang territory *without* telling Les is your plan?" Dex asks with a shake of his head. "You really are a fucking idiot."

I shrug. "Call me what you want. I'm still taking him."

Leo rounds the corner, having changed into jeans and a button-up. He moves, and I see the flash of his holster and the Glocks Gage gave him.

Impressive. Maybe he isn't as soft as I thought.

I jerk my head for him to follow, and he does reluctantly. We slide into my Explorer, and we're on the main road before he finally breaks the silence.

"What's this about? I know it's not just because you enjoy my company," he asks, and I can feel his eyes boring into the side of my head.

"I told you. You wanted in, so I'm giving you your in." I glance over at him and then back to the road. "You know Les would never let you fucking do this."

He barks a laugh. "Les doesn't know, does she?"

"Nope," I reply honestly. Okay. Maybe she'll kick my ass. But he needs this freedom to see what he's made of.

He nods and looks out the window. "What are we doing?"

"Small-time gang rivals. It's not a big deal, but we need to make our presence known, so they back the fuck off."

"Why do we care about a small-time gang rivalry?"

"Les owns them. She tells them to jump, and they ask how fucking high. We don't usually get involved, but she's fond of this gang. I'm helping out before shit gets too far out of control."

Squid is one she pulled back from the brink of addiction when she found him at one of the clubs we raided last year. She cleaned him up, and he took over the Disciples a few months ago at twenty when she realized he's made for that shit.

"The more this shit goes down, the more I realize I don't know," Leo says angrily.

"Ask dumbass," I say back just as angrily. "Half the time, we fucking forget that you don't know. So quit being a bitch and ask."

"You're a fucking dick."

I shrug. "Yeah. Most of the time. But you know I'm right."

"Whatever. Just fucking drive," Leo says, staring out of his window.

In silence, I drive into Concrete Row, gang territory, letting Leo stew in his bullshit. I don't have it in me to be easy on him. I barely tolerate him being around Les.

I pull in front of Squid's pool hall and throw the car into park. "Stay with me," I order Leo before sliding out of the car.

To his credit, he falls into step with me when I round to his side. He may hate me, but he isn't stupid.

"Yo!" Squid yells from the back of the place. He walks over and pulls me into a one-armed hug, slapping me on the back. "Long time, man." He looks good and healthy. He put most of his weight back on, and his face doesn't have that sunken look anymore. His hair is cut neat, even if it is dyed blue, and his brown eyes are clear. Les would be happy to see him like this.

I return the hug before stepping back. "You got somewhere we can talk?" I ask, eyeing the innocents in here shooting pool.

"Yeah." He motions for us to follow him. We walk through a door labeled employees only, and most of his guys are sitting around the backroom. "Have a seat," he says, nodding his head at a table.

We all get situated around the table, and I get the first thing out of the way. "This is Leo," I introduce, so he will stop giving me curious looks. "What's going on?"

"Like I said on the phone, man. I've got problems with Tink." Tink is the leader of the rival gang, The Hellraisers. The irony doesn't escape me that the Disciples and the Hellraisers are rivals. "He started pushing in on my territory, and I warned him. He retaliated by shooting up my fucking pool hall." I noticed the wood covering the windows and didn't figure they were just redecorating.

"Was anyone here?" I ask, sitting back in my chair.

Squid shakes his head. "Nah. It was after hours; it was a warning."

"Where's his spot at?"

"About two blocks north. We have a long-standing agreement that we don't cross paths. He broke it." Squid runs his fingers through his hair. "I didn't want to call, bro, but I don't have a good feeling about this."

"You did the right thing," I assure him. "We'll pay him a visit."

"I appreciate it, man."

We talk about business for a little while before Squid asks us to shoot a couple of games of pool. We make our way to the main pool hall; I stay back at the bar while Leo goes off to shoot pool with a bunch of Squid's guys.

Squid leans back on the bar beside me. "What's his deal?"

I stroke my chin and watch Leo laughing and talking shit with the other guys. "He's with Les."

Squid frowns. "I thought you were." That's a common misconception even when we were younger; we usually just let people think what they want. But now I can answer that question differently.

"I am."

His frown deepens, and I almost laugh at the look on his face. "You just said he was."

"He is."

"Are you fucking with me, asshole?" Squid asks, turning to face me.

I shake my head. "Nope."

"So, you're both dating her? How the fuck does that work?"

I sigh. "We're all dating her. Together." Squid's eyes widen comically, and I bust out laughing.

"You are fucking with me!"

"No. I'm not. She's dating me, Leo, Gage, Dex, and Holden. We are all in it together."

Squid finally picks his mouth up off the bar. "So, you're telling me I still have a chance?"

I turn narrowed eyes on him. "A chance to fucking die if you say some dumb shit like that again."

"Come on, man. What's one more?" he asks with a grin.

"Do you want to choke on your fucking tongue today, Squid?" I ask, standing up straight.

He holds his hands up. "I'm good," he laughs. "Let me kick your ass in pool."

We all play several rounds before I decide it's time to go. Squid walks us outside, and we are just standing on the sidewalk bullshitting when Leo knocks my arm to get my attention. "What are they doing?" he asks.

I squint at a black SUV rolling slowly toward us. Before I can react, the SUV speeds toward us with a squeal of tires, and a guy with a ski mask hangs out of the passenger side with a semi-automatic.

"Get down!" I yell, jerking Leo beside my Explorer, Squid diving with us.

The bullets spray against the side of the car, littering us with glass from my windows.

"Motherfuckers," I growl, jerking my Glocks from my holster. I wait until the gunfire stops before jumping up from beside the car. I walk forward, emptying both clips at the SUV before they speed away.

"Get your guys, and let's fucking go," I bark at Squid, walking to the back of my SUV. I jerk the hatch open and get the spare clips I keep out from under the spare tire, grabbing two more for Leo.

Squid comes running out with six of his guys loading into their cars while Leo and I slide into mine. I pull out with a bark of tires with Squid right on my tail. I glance at Leo; he looks like he's trying not to laugh. What the fuck?

"We just got fucking shot at. What's so damn funny?"

"Alessa's going to kill you!" he says and then starts dying laughing.

He isn't wrong. *Fuck.* So much for a simple trip. Not only did we get shot at, but I'm also taking him deeper into gang territory to find these assholes. It's not like I can hide it, either. Both driver's side windows are gone, and so is the front passenger side, and I have bullet holes all down the side of my Explorer.

We go to where Squid told us and drive around aimlessly with no sign of them. We check a few more places before I tell Squid they are probably lying low and we would come back to help him take care of them.

I turn around to head back to the house when I see the SUV that the guy shot out of parked down an alley. I signal for Squid to pull over. We all stop and unload with weapons already in hand. I go to tell Leo to stay in the car, and he's already getting out, pulling his Glocks from his holster. Alright then.

We all converge on the car and open fire. It doesn't matter if they are in there or not. This is a warning that we will find you no matter where you hide. I signal for everyone to stop firing and creep to the door with my gun raised, jerking the door open. The driver slides out of the car, blood running from his mouth, his body littered with bullets.

"You know him?" I ask Squid.

Squid walks over and crouches down, getting a closer look. "Yeah. He's one of Tink's."

"Where's the passenger?" Leo asks, walking toward the SUV to stand beside me.

I shrug. "No clue"

Leo's eyes swing up behind me as his gun does. I jerk my head, following his line of sight. Leo pulls the trigger on the guy getting ready to shoot my ass right in the head, hitting him neatly in the middle of the forehead. The guy's head snaps back before slowly folding to the ground.

I jerk my head back to Leo, and he's staring at the guy he just shot.

He just saved my ass without a second thought. I can't tell by his expression if he is okay with that.

"Holy shit," Squid breathes, slapping Leo on the back. "Nice fucking shot!"

Leo looks up, and I see a look in his eyes that I've seen before. He's just taken his first life, and I know you never return from that. I need to get him home before he loses his shit.

Now I have to go home and face Alessa with a freaked-out Leo.

Fuck.

CHAPTER 26
ALESSA

I'm fucking pissed.

When I found out Ryder took off with Leo, I panicked. Ryder barely speaks to Leo. Now he's taking him on jobs? Not that I think Ryder will do anything to hurt Leo, but he might try to scare him off, and I can't handle that.

I pinch the bridge of my nose, trying to reign in my temper. Ryder and Leo are sitting on the couch in the living room while I relentlessly pace.

"Baby?" Leo says gently, and I hold up a hand to stop him. I just need to get my tongue under control before I kill Ryder.

I swing my eyes to Ryder, and he's leaning back on the couch with his arms over the top, looking way too relaxed, but I can see how he's warily staring at me.

"Did I miss it?" Gage says, running into the living room. He takes in the scene before him and flops down in the chair, ready for the show. He was just as worried that Ryder took Leo with him, and now he's ready for me to chew Ryder out.

"Let me get this right," I start, still pacing. "You woke up this morning, got a call from Squid that I didn't know about." I stop and move my eyes back to Ryder. "Then you decide to take Leo into Concrete Row *without* telling me. Then you get him involved in a fucking drive-by!" My voice starts rising by the end. I'm so keyed up with anxiety over Leo or Ryder getting hurt that I'm about to fall right off the edge. "And if that's not enough, you go looking for the guys who already fucking shot at you, and Leo has to save your sorry ass."

"Wait. What?" Gage asks, sitting up in his chair. I forgot he missed that part.

"Leo saved my ass," Ryder repeats, looking at Gage. "Some dude was trying to get the drop on me, and Leo took them out." He turns dark eyes on me. "*Il mio sole...*"

"No," I say, shaking my head, "Don't *il mio sole* me and try to sweet talk your way out of this, Ryder. You took him without telling me where you were going. Do you know how fucking worried I've been since neither of you answered your damn phone?"

"Baby, they were in the car. I'm fine. Ryder's fine," Leo says, sitting up on the couch. What? Are they blood bonded now, taking up for each other?

"You just fucking killed someone, Leo!" I yell and watch Leo wince. I take a breath to pull myself back together. "I need a minute."

I hold a hand up when Ryder and Leo open their mouths before walking out of the room. I'm on the verge of a full-blown panic attack. I want Ryder and Leo to bond, and I knew there would come a time when Leo has to defend himself. But I was in meltdown mode when they wouldn't answer the phone. I couldn't get my heart rate to return to normal, I knew I was overreacting, but I was so damn scared.

I walk out onto the patio and take several calming breaths. Why the hell couldn't he have just told me? Would I have been okay with it, then?

Probably not.

I hear the door open behind me and whirl around, expecting Ryder, but Dex walks out, shutting the door softly behind him. He nods his head to the table, and I follow him, sitting in front of him.

"I know this is hard, Baby girl, and I'm not excusing what Ryder did." He crosses his arms on the table. "But you wanted Leo to fit in and be a part of us."

"I know," I say miserably. "He killed someone today, Dex."

"We all have," he says simply. "Leo is a big boy. I think he can handle it."

"I never wanted this for him," I whisper.

"No one wanted this for any of us. This life sucks sometimes, Les, but he doesn't need you to protect him. You need to start letting him make up his mind." He squeezes my hand quickly, surprising me. "He saved Ryder today, and that's got to give him some credit."

I bark a laugh. "I'm actually surprised he did."

"Leo is just like the rest of us, Baby girl," he says softly. "We will never do anything that will hurt you, even if that means saving the one we hate the most."

I understand what he's saying and need to figure out how to handle this. If I yell at Ryder for taking off with him, it will cause him to freeze Leo out again. I just need to figure out *why* Ryder took him. Sure, it seemed like a simple job, but Ryder knows how quickly those jobs can turn into shit. Just like today.

"I need to talk to Ryder," I say with a sigh.

Dex nods and stands up. "I'll get him."

He disappears into the house, and I lean back in the chair, trying to get my thoughts together. The door opens, and I hear the chair scrape against the patio. I lift my head and watch Ryder sit down, still giving me that wary look he was giving me inside.

"You undermined me today. One, for not telling me about Squid, and two, for taking Leo without telling me," I say as calmly as I can. "Why did you take him today?"

"You said you wanted him involved, Les. So I fucking involved him."

I sit up and cross my arms on the table, mirroring his pose. "Is that all, or did you have another reason?"

He raises an eyebrow. "What are you asking?"

"Did you take him to scare him off?"

He shrugs. "No. I took him because I knew you wouldn't."

"I've taken him on jobs."

"Yeah. The ones you went on so you could watch him. You can't protect him forever, and he needs to man the fuck up."

"You realize he's been involved in this life for a year, and up until a couple of days ago, he's never even been on a fucking job?" I say, getting pissed again. "He took a life for you today, and I say that makes him pretty fucking manly." I push back from the table and storm back into the house with Ryder right on my heels.

I hit the doorway to the living room before he grabs my arm, spinning me to face him. "You don't get to just walk away in the middle of a conversation."

I raise both brows. "Excuse me?"

"You heard me," Ryder says, stepping into my space and still holding my arm. "You said we need to work shit out from now on. So, let's work it out."

I jerk my arm away, aware of Leo and Gage sitting behind us. "Fine. You were careless today. You went into a job blind and took someone to go down with you."

"I go on jobs alone all the time. The only reason you're fucking mad is that I had Leo with me. What about me, Les? Were you worried about me?"

"You can handle yourself!" I yell. Did he just insinuate that I don't care about his safety?

"So can Leo. Look at him, *Il mio sole*. Does he look like someone that's worried about what fucking happened today?"

I huff and turn around. Leo is sitting there beside Gage, looking cool as a cucumber.

"I'm fine, Baby," Leo says, standing up and walking toward me. "It was a shock at first, and I might have freaked out in the car a little," he says with a chuckle. "But Ryder talked me down."

I throw my hands in the air. "So, you guys are just best friends now?"

They both snort at the same time. "No. But we can work together," Ryder answers, and I turn back to him. "You just have to let that happen."

"You can't go off without telling me," I say, looking between them. "I thought something bad had happened to both of you, and I can't handle that."

"We're sorry for worrying you. We will let you know from now on, but you have to let me make up my own mind. You can't control everything I do." Leo walks up in front of me, wrapping his arms around my waist and kissing my forehead. "I want to be a part of your life, and that's what I'm going to do." I wrap my arms around his waist, hugging him to me.

I feel Ryder step up behind me, moving my hair to the side and kissing my neck. "You can't do everything yourself. That's what you have us for. Let us help you, *Il mio sole.*"

"I'll try," I whisper into Leo's chest. I really will, but I'm not used to giving up control, and that's what they're asking me to do.

"That's all we can ask," Leo says, and I look up into his blue-green eyes. He lays his lips on mine, giving me a tender kiss before spinning me toward Ryder. Ryder kisses me the same way, and I know they are showing me they can work together in more ways than one.

"You guys!" Gage exclaims, running over and wrapping his arms around all of us.

We all laugh, and just like that, the tension breaks. Am I still upset Ryder left without telling me? Yes. But I know they're right.I need to give up some control, or I'll spread myself too thin.

I need to learn to lean on my guys.

"THE FOSTER's names are Ginger and Markus Wright. They don't live far from where you found the boys," Gerald tells me. I came to my office after fixing things with Ryder and Leo, and Gerald called shortly after. "What's the play, Lessie?"

I smile at their old nickname; only Gerald and Boone call me Lessie. "I don't know. I need to see how many kids they have in the house." Holden sticks his head through my office door, and I wave him in to sit in the empty chair, memories of last night slamming into me. If his red face is any indication, he's thinking about it too. My heart broke in two when he told me what happened to him, but he somehow seems better today after telling me. "How are Lucas and Landon?"

Gerald chuckles. "They settled in just fine."

Coming from a rundown foster home and the streets to a house like Gerald and Boone's is probably a dream come true. Even though they don't do much for me anymore, I still ensure they are well taken care of for everything they did for my dad. "Are you sure you don't mind them there?"

"Honestly, Lessie, if you wanted, they could stay here until they turn eighteen, and they can decide what they want to do. They're good kids in a bad situation."

My heart melts. "Thank you."

"No thanks needed. Take care of your other business. Come see us soon."

I promise I will and then end the call.

"Hey," I say with a smile toward Holden.

"Hey, Bright eyes," he greets with a smile that seems bigger and brighter today.

When he called me bright eyes and then told me why I almost started blubbering like a baby. I knew sex with Holden would be memorable, but it did not prepare me for the waterfall it would cause. The length and girth of his cock rubbed everything in me at the same time. No one has made me come like that before.

He slides two folders toward me. "One is Moretto's supplier, and the other is the foster home."

I raise my eyebrow. "Already? Gerald just told me who they are."

"I can't take all the credit. While we were busy, Ryder and Dex went to shake down some of Moretto's people. They gave them a name, and I started running it this morning. I had the stuff for the foster home last night. I just dug up what foster home the boys were at."

I vaguely remember him mentioning a file, but I only went in there to be with him, not to see if he finished his work or seduce him.

"That is why you are the best," I point at him, "Among other things."

He blushes a deep red, and it's always endearing to know someone in this house can still blush. He smiles again, and I can't get over how much it changes his face. "How's your broken pussy?"

My mouth pops open shocked. I can't believe that just came out of my sweet, timid Holden's mouth, then I laugh. "It's purring just fine."

He laughs, and I soak in the sound. "Good."

I'm not going to tell him I'm sore this morning, in a good way. He was worried enough last night about hurting me. I'm not going to add to that.

I open my mouth, getting ready to ask him about what he told me, when Micah walks into the office. "Will you tell your dipshit boyfriend that he can't wear lime green to the fucking gala?"

I know he's talking about Gage, but I need to rile him up. "Which one?" I deadpan.

Micah's lip curls back in disgust, and Holden chuckles. Micah whirls on him. "Not you too?"

Holden shrugs. "Guilty."

"What is going on in this fucking house?" Micah mutters, leaving the office.

Gage loves getting a rise out of Micah as much as I do, and I know Gage's pretty boy ass wouldn't be caught dead in lime green.

I open the folder Holden gave me about the foster parents and curse under my breath. "Six fucking kids in that house. Four of them under six."

Holden nods. "Yeah. That part sucks. No way you can hide kids that small."

I shake my head. "No," I say, sliding that folder to the side that would have to come later, mostly because I need to call in a favor I don't want to do.

I open the next one, and my blood starts boiling. "This name belongs to the fucking Russians."

Russians as in Viktor Orlov, Alexey, and Dmitri's dad. They are nothing like their shit dad and friends of mine, not that Viktor knows that. He *hates* women in any position; his mindset is a woman should be there to serve her husband.

Fuck that. I don't have anything against a woman with that mindset, but that isn't me.

"I tracked it back as far as possible without hacking Viktor's server. I'm ninety-nine percent sure the orders are coming from him."

That's fucking great.

I text Micah to come back to the office. When he enters, Holden excuses himself, and I can't get over how proud he looks walking through the door.

"Did you have something to tell me, shithead, or are you just going to drool all day?" Micah asks dryly, flopping down in Holden's chair.

"I don't know, probably drool. Have you seen the man candy in this house?"

"Alright, I'm done." Micah goes to get up.

"I'm kidding," I laugh before sobering to slide the file to Micah. I stab my finger at the sheet. "That name look familiar?"

"Is that one of Orlov's?" Micah growls. No love is lost between the Russians and Italians, but Micah still holds a grudge over how Viktor talked to me at the last gala.

"Sure is," I reply, then run my fingers through my hair. "This isn't like taking out some small time like Jerry. This is Viktor Orlov, and he just declared war."

Italians might be the most powerful, but the Russians run a close third, right behind Evander and Mateo for Mexico.

"We can't let this go," Micah points out, and it pisses me off.

"No shit," I bark, and he raises an eyebrow.

"I didn't say that because I didn't think you would."

I sigh. "I know. Fuck. I'm used to everyone thinking I can't do this because I have boobs."

Micah chuckles. "I assure you no one in this house, including me, doubts you." He shudders. "Just don't mention your boobs again."

"Oh my God. And you call me a child," I say with a roll of my eyes.

He tilts his head to the side, the same weird thing I do, and my dad did. "You seem better," he states, referring to me being a hot mess when I showed up at his house.

"I am."

He leans forward in his chair. "Les, if you ever need someone to talk to, you know you can come to me, right?"

I smile softly. "I know. I just got overwhelmed, but everything is falling into place," I say and hope I didn't just jinx myself. "You can go now," I tell him, knowing it will crawl under his skin at being dismissed. I try to hide my smile when his eyes narrow.

"I'm going to let that one go." He gets up and storms from the room, my laughter following him.

I shoot off a text to Evander, letting him know I might need some help with the Russians, and his response is immediate.

EVANDER

Anything you need.

I tell him that I will fill him in later and then make the phone call I've been dreading to make, but I need help, and this is the only person I know who can get it done.

"Hello?"

"Can we meet?" I ask.

"Where?"

"Loading docks on 64th."

"Done."

I PULL my Ferrari into the loading dock parking lot twenty minutes later and pull beside a white Dodge Challenger. Zane is casually leaning against the side of it, one leg crossed over the other, arms crossed over his chest, his usual mirrored sunglasses covering his eyes. I climb out of the car, and he peeks into the car before I shut the door.

"You came alone?" he asks.

I raise an eyebrow over my own oversized sunglasses. "Yes. I'm more than capable of taking care of myself." I peek into his car and see a guy on the passenger side. "You didn't?"

"We were working when you called." He slides his sunglasses down his nose, letting his eyes run slowly down my body. "You look good," he says, pushing them back over his eyes.

I roll my eyes. I'm in jeans, a t-shirt, and my boots. I'm not dressed to impress. I choose to ignore that comment. "Since you were working, I'll get to it." I hand him the folder on the foster home. "Proof that they're dealing out of that house with four kids all under the age of six." I can't tell him about Lucas and Landon because he will make me turn them over since they are technically still underage.

Zane opens the folder, flipping through it. I hear the passenger door open, and his partner steps out. He is tall, a trim body, but you can see his muscles moving under his shirt, light brown hair, and sunglasses like Zane's. He looks more like a model that just stepped out of GQ than a detective. He leans against the car beside Zane, taking a slow stroll with his gaze looking me over and I instantly dislike him. That's a power move to put someone ill at ease. I hate to tell him, but he has the wrong bitch.

"You must be the infamous Alessa Poletti," he drawls.

"And you are?" I ask and tilt my head to the side, letting him know his little tactic didn't work.

"Jay Hoover." He holds out his hand for me to shake, and I look down at it, then look back to Zane, dismissing him. Asshole move, but something about this guy gives me the wrong vibes.

Zane is trying to cover a smile by rubbing his top lip. "We good?" I ask. I need to get out of here. I don't like that his partner got out of the car.

"How am I supposed to explain where the tip came from?"

I shrug and jerk the folder from his hand. "I'll find someone else."

I pull my door open, and Zane reaches out, grabbing my arm. I look at him and then look pointedly at his hand until he drops it.

"Wait a minute. I didn't say I wouldn't."

His partner snorts. "You going to do dirty work for the Poletti princess?"

I push my sunglasses up on my head. "If you call getting kids out of a fucking foster home that sells drugs, and pushes the older ones into gangs to make them money dirty work, then yeah, that's what I asked him to do."

He raises an eyebrow. "Anything for the Poletti's is dirty."

"Get back in the car, Jay," Zane barks, standing up from his relaxed position.

"Are you fucking kidding me?"

"Now," Zane growls, and I have to hide a grin.

Jay stomps off, slamming the door when he gets back in the car. I look back to Zane. "Temper tantrum much?"

"He's not your biggest fan. I'll see what I can do." He holds his hand out for the folder. I hand it back to him, and he brushes my fingers when he takes it, even though he had plenty of room to grab the end. He crosses his arms back over his chest, the folder tucked under his arm. "What happened the other day?"

Time to leave. "Nothing." I pull my sunglasses back down. "Bad day."

"The Les I know doesn't let bad days get to her."

"The Les you *knew*," I emphasize because he doesn't know me anymore, "is gone. You don't know me, Zane."

"I know you pretty good." He lets his eyes slide over me again. "Damn good."

"Was that before or after you betrayed me? Don't pretend we had anything more than what it was."

"If you want to pretend all we had was sex," he shrugs, "that's on you. I know better."

"Keep lying to yourself. Whatever helps you sleep at night." I jerk my door back open and slide into the car, getting the hell out of there.

The truth is, what we had *was* more than sex, even though we broke it off several times within that year. Mostly because I wasn't ready, too young to give him what he wanted, what he needed. When I found out that he was becoming a cop, I was crushed. That same day, I had decided that I was going to give in and tell my dad about us like he had been wanting me to do, fully committing myself to Zane.

Then I realized he was a lying piece of shit.

CHAPTER 27
ZANE

I stand there and watch the taillights of Alessa's black Ferrari disappear before I get back in the car with a fuming Jay. I knew dismissing him would piss him off, but I can't let him stand there and talk to Les like that. He's been my partner ever since I became a detective two years ago, and he's the closest thing I have to a friend, as sad as that is.

I fire the car up without saying a word. "You still bend over backward for that bitch, and she doesn't even give you a second glance."

Now is when I thoroughly regret getting drunk and spilling the whole tale of Les and me. The truth is, I had no damn business pursuing her at eighteen when I was twenty-eight fucking years old, but damn, I couldn't help myself. She was drop-dead gorgeous at eighteen and just kept getting better with age.

"Call her a bitch again, and I'll put a fucking bullet through your brain," I warn, jerking the car into drive and tearing out of the parking lot.

He scoffs. "Why are you still hung up on her? She's a criminal; *you're* a detective investigating her."

I grimace at that. It's true my department is investigating Les and her merry band of men, among others.We have been for as long as I can remember but they've never gotten enough to bring them down. What Jay doesn't know is all I do is feed them little information to keep suspicions off me and the heat off her. I also couldn't tell Les any of that because she would shoot me on principle.

"I'm not hung up on her," I argue.

He pulls the folder from my lap, waving it in the air. "What's this then?"

"That's a damn good tip, no matter who it came from."

I know Les has a soft spot for kids, mostly because she can't have any, so it didn't surprise me when she handed me the folder. I found out the hard way about her being unable to have kids. I spilled my heart to her one night and told her I wanted her to tell her dad so we could quit hiding, maybe get married, and have kids.

She shut down immediately, and it took her *weeks* to tell me Frankie Perez's men fucked her up so bad she had to have all her reproductive organs removed, rendering her infertile. That was also the downfall of our relationship. We would break up and get back together repeatedly until the fateful night when she found out I was in the police academy. I didn't care that she couldn't have kids; I just cared that it hurt her so bad.

She wouldn't listen to me when I told her I was doing it for us, so I could get her away from all the danger she was always in. She never talked to me again after that night. The first time I spoke to her in the years after was when she took over for her dad. She had an altercation at one of the clubs, and I was the beat cop that showed up to investigate. I waited late in life to pursue law enforcement because I didn't want to disappoint my dad, but he died thinking I hated him for still following Luca Poletti.

Jay sighs, and I know he looked over the information in that folder. "How do we play this?"

I do work for Les most of the time when she can't put herself in the middle, but she never hands me anything illegal. I think it's her way of making sure I don't become a dirty cop, or I'm just telling myself that. I'm already a dirty cop for not turning over what I know, stuff that could put her and her crew in prison for life.

"We?" I ask. He seemed less inclined to help in front of her.

"You going to sideline me?" he smirks.

"No," I sigh, "I have an informant down there. I can convince him to sign that he gave the tip."

I take the exit to head downtown toward the address of the foster home. I park two buildings down, shoving the car in park, just watching the building. Who the hell would put kids in danger like that? I'll never understand why people become foster parents if they don't give a shit about the kids besides the check they bring in. My dad may have raised me while working for one of the most lethal crime bosses in the world, but he loved me unconditionally and protected me the same way.

"So, what's the deal with you and her?"

"You already know the story," I reply without looking at him.

"I mean now. Why does she still have you by the balls?"

Because I'm still in love with her. Because I never got over her. Because I hate myself for fucking it up. Because she was the only girl ever to captivate my heart and soul. "She doesn't have me by the balls. You know it's better to keep them in your pocket than your enemy."

"You have that wrong. She has you in her pocket. You know damn well you don't keep people like her in check."

I finally look at him. "People like her?"

He looks at me like he's talking to someone that's slow. "Violent. Murderers. Criminals. Do I need to keep going?"

I shake my head. I refuse to keep having this same argument with him. I know what they are because I used to be one of them. I'm not going to lie and say I haven't thought about turning over what I have on Ryder fucking Venchelli to put him under the prison and away from Alessa for the things Jay just described, but it wouldn't do any good. I hate Ryder with every fiber of my being, and every cross word that comes out of his mouth toward me pushes me that much closer to getting rid of him for good. I tolerate the rest of her guys, Gage, more than others because I witnessed what his dad did to him more than once when he couldn't deal with Gage's ADHD and mood swings. He isn't my friend, but he isn't my enemy either.

"Ignore me all you want, Zane, but one day, these little jobs you do for her will bite you right in the fucking ass, and the only one who will go down for anything is you."

Deep down, I knw that she'll throw me right under that bus if I ever get busted for running her jobs. "I won't get caught."

"Come on," he says harshly, "Get your head out of her ass. You need to move on. Find you another girl. A good girl."

I shrug. "I don't want a good girl. I don't want a girl, period." *I just want her.*

"Man," he throws his head back against the seat in exasperation, "wasn't she just seen getting close to the new Perez brother?"

I used to be able to follow her all over social media and watch her every move like a fucking stalker, but she's been missing from any paparazzi pictures for over a week. The last picture I saw of her was the night she was seen leaving her favorite restaurant, Catch 35, with a guy no one knew. I found out who he was in minutes, except he came back as Leonardo Janelle, not Leonardo Perez. That shock came later when he was pictured with Evander and Mateo Perez, except no one had put the connection together until now. What she was doing with them after what their father did is beyond me. They are also on the list for investigation, and I have no ties to them, so it's easier to give over information. One wrong move and the Perez brothers are going down.

"It was just dinner," I point out. "And she can do what she wants." I look closer out the window. Tall, slim, pants hanging off his skinny ass, pale white face, greased back blonde hair. "There he is," I say, nodding toward my informant. He walks to the driver's side window, leaning in like he's doing a drug deal.

"What's up, Jeffrey?" I greet him with his real name with a grin.

His eyebrows turn down over his watery blue eyes. "It's Playboy."

"I need information," I tell him, ignoring that stupid ass name.

"On what?" he asks, casting a nervous glance around.

"6567 Mikee. In that white building."

"The apartment with all the kids?"

I nod. "What do you know?"

"They sell for Xander out of there." Xander is the leader of the

Vipers, the gang who runs this part of town, and a thorn in my fucking side. "They had twins that slang out here, but they disappeared, man."

I frown. "Disappeared?"

"Disappeared, bro. Like they ain't here no more."

"When?"

"Yesterday. They were at their corner, and this dime in a black Explorer talked to them, and they got into a car with a big bald dude."

Jay raises an eyebrow thinking the same thing as me. "What did this dime look like?"

"Yo, man, she had black hair and a fat ass." He bites his lip and groans. "Fuckin' dime."

"Did she have anyone with her?" Les isn't the only girl with black hair running around, but Ryder drives a blacked-out Ford Explorer. Coincidence?

"Four dudes. One of them was the crazy one who busted up Xander's garage a month ago for not following the rules." That would be Gage Lawson, so it was Alessa. But where are the missing twins?

Playboy here was so high that he didn't even put the connection together that the "dime" he saw was Alessa. She rules all the criminals, so everyone usually knows who she is.

"Will you sign that you gave me the tip on the foster house?"

"Yeah, man. I get paid, right?" His eyes light up, knowing I'm going to pay him for his next hit.

"Yeah," I sigh, "I thought you were done with the shit?"

"What shit? I'm clean, man," he says defensively.

"Your eyes say otherwise," Jay throws in, not even looking over at him.

"This tip pays off; I'll find you."

He signs the informant statement, grins, and jogs off. I can fill in everything later to turn in to my boss.

"Looks like we are going on a raid tonight," I say with a grin.

CHAPTER 28
GAGE

"We are going where?" Leo asks from the backseat. Les looks over at me with a grin.

"To get pedicures," I answer with a shrug. Our girl wants to get her nails and toes done, so that's where I'm going to take her.

"Why are we," he motions between him and me like I don't know who he's talking about, "getting pedicures?"

"Because it feels amazing," Les answers, pushing her sunglasses up on her head and turning in the seat to look at him.

Leo gives her a doubtful look. "I'll pass."

She shrugs, turning back around and covering her eyes again. "Suit yourself." I squeeze her thigh where my hand has been sitting since we got in the car.

I'm still replaying what happened with Leo in his room then watching her squirt for Holden last night, and can't get the images out of my head. It was hot as fuck.

"I met with Zane today," she says, staring out her window.

I jerk my head toward her before looking back at the road. "Why?"

"I gave him the tip on the foster house because we can't be near a bunch of kids going missing."

"You went alone?" I don't know why that crawls under my skin, but I hate when he comes sniffing around her. Plus, she has a fucking stalker.

"Yes," she answers, finally looking at me, "I can take care of myself."

"Wait. Who's Zane?" Leo asks, confused.

I look at Les and raise my eyebrow; no way am I telling him. "He was a friend of the family," she lies, and I snort before I can stop myself.

"He's a detective that Les used to fuck," I tell Leo, looking at him in the rearview mirror. I see his eyebrows drop down in a frown.

"Seven years ago," Les adds, shooting daggers at my head; I can feel them even through her sunglasses.

"You used to fuck a cop?" Leo sits up between the seats, putting his arms on the console.

"He wasn't a cop then. Can we drop this? It's ancient history."

"Then why did you go alone?" I wonder.

"Because I can get him to do more for me when you guys aren't fucking glaring at each other," she answers, pushing my hand off her leg. Shit. "You seemed to have forgotten I don't need your permission to take care of business, and I don't need your protection."

"I'm not saying you need my permission or anyone else's. But you shouldn't go alone because, Pretty girl, you might not fucking need our protection, but you're going to get it," I say hotly. I'd never tell her what she could or couldn't do, but it's our job to protect her. It's even more imperative now that she worked her way into my heart even further.

"In case you've forgotten, I'm the Boss, and I say when I need you and when I don't," she says, just as pissed off as me. "And I didn't need you today."

I grit my teeth so hard it hurts before I slam on the brakes, jerk the car to the curb, and throw it into park. I turn in the seat to face her and jerk my sunglasses off. "We're here to fucking protect you and take care of you. Why can't you just let us do that? Instead of being fucking stubborn. You have a fucking stalker, Les. Did you forget about that?"

She pushes her sunglasses on her head again, and I wish she didn't. Her eyes are narrowed, and she's fucking pissed. "Who the hell do you think you are talking to, Gage? You get a little taste of my pussy, and you think you own me?"

Leo's eyes are ping-ponging between us, but he's smart and keeps his damn mouth shut.

"That's not what I meant, Les, and you know it. You know you shouldn't go alone to those meetings. That's how it was before I got a taste of your pussy."

"I make the decision whether you go or not. That's how it's always been, and it was just Zane."

"It doesn't have to do with Zane!" I yell and then take several calming breaths when her eyes turn hard. "It has to do with going anywhere without backup. You aren't invincible."

"I never said I was," she grits out before jerking the door open, climbing out, and slamming it behind her. She struts her ass down the street four doors down from where I'm parked, jerks the door open to the nail salon, and disappears inside.

"Fuck!" I explode, slamming my hand down on the steering wheel.

"What the hell was that?" Leo asks, staring at me with concern.

"That was me being a fucking idiot," I answer honestly. I overreacted. Big time.

"I'm guessing this has to do with the fact you are with her now?"

I nod. "She used to go alone all the time before, no questions asked, and she can take care of herself."

"But you don't want her to have to?" I shake my head. "Then why didn't you just tell her that?"

"Because I'm a jealous bastard, apparently." I know it sounds stupid, given she is sleeping with or almost sleeping with four other guys, but this is different. Those guys I trust, Zane, on the other hand, is the literal enemy and got a taste of Les way before we did. He knows what he's missing out on, and he's not above trying to steal her back.

"You have to trust her, Gage," Leo says gently.

"I do trust her. I don't trust him."

"Then you need to tell her like that, man. Just because there are feelings involved doesn't mean she's automatically going to know. You need to tell her that you know she doesn't need protection, but you want to protect her."

I run my hand through my hair. "I will. I just got pissed."

He shrugs. "I get it." He slaps me on the shoulder. "Let's go make our girl happy."

We climb out and make our way into the nail salon. Les is already in the back of the shop, waiting for her pedicure. She looks up when we walk in and looks right back at her phone.

Damn it.

"Gage!" Staci, the shop owner, greets. "You must be Leo?"

I nod, answering her question. "We're here for the appointment with Alessa."

"Follow me. Pick any chair. We'll be with you shortly." She bustles away. We each take a chair on either side of Les, kicking our shoes and socks off.

"Pretty girl, I'm sorry." She won't even look at me. Leo gives me a look to get me talking. "I know you don't need my protection, but I want to. I can't stand the thought of something happening to you."

"I get that," she says quietly, still sounding pissed. "But you can't suddenly dictate how I run my life."

"I don't want to dictate it. I just want peace of mind knowing you have someone at your back. All of us do. Can you give us that?"

She finally turns her eyes on me. "Maybe start like that next time," she grumps, then softens, grabbing my hand. "Gage, I've done this on my own for a long time. You have to be patient with me." She leans over and gives me a sweet kiss.

"Oh my God. It's about time," Staci says, sitting in front of Les' station; two other girls sit in front of Leo and me. Leo gives his girl a dubious look before letting her put his feet in the water.

Les smiles at me. "Yeah, it is."

Staci's eyes land on Les' other hand holding Leo's, and her mouth forms an 'O,' her eyes huge. "Him too," I confirm with a shrug.

"What?" The blonde girl in front of me jerks her head up, looking between the three of us. "Sorry," she apologizes when she realizes she just butted into our conversation.

"It's fine, Amanda," Les tells her softly when the girl looks seconds from running out the door.

"So, you guys are like in a relationship together?" Candy, the redhead fussing with Leo, asks.

"Yeah," Leo answers.

"That's so cool," Candy breathes, staring at Les like she hung the moon.

"Ryder, Dex, and Holden too," I add, watching all their eyes widen as big as saucers in amusement.

"Gage!" Les laughs, smacking my chest.

"Wait. Wait. Wait," Staci says, waving her hand around before picking up Les' other foot and massaging it. This is my favorite part. I look at Leo, and I can tell he's already sold. "Ryder? Tall, dark, hot as fuck, Ryder?" Les nods. "And Mr. Tattooed sex god on two legs?" Les nods again and laughs at the descriptions. "Who's Holden?"

"You've never met him," Les tells her before pulling out her phone and pulling up a picture of her and Holden that looks like it was taken this morning. She turns it around to the girls, and I swear they all fucking sigh at the innocent-looking little fucker. If they only knew what I know.

"So, you have five walking wet dreams for boyfriends?" Candy asks, and Les throws her head back and laughs.

Les looks between Leo and me. "I sure as fuck do."

I breathe a sigh of relief that the disaster of earlier is averted. I've always had trouble controlling myself, or more like controlling my words. They tumble out before I can stop them, but I know how to control it with Les. She doesn't need me going all caveman on her.

She has Ryder for that.

"THAT WAS FANFUCKINGTASTIC," Leo says when we get back in the car.

I pull away from the curb. "I told you."

"So, does that mean you're going with us next time?" Les asks with a smile.

"Uh, fuck yeah, and every time after that." He leans up between the seats. "I'm digging that gold, Baby." She picks up her hand and lets the glitter in the gold polish sparkle when the sun hits it. "Where are we going?" he asks, noticing I missed our exit to take us home.

Where it all began. "The cabin." I look at Les. "Do you have anything else to do today?"

She shrugs. "Nothing that can't wait"

"Good." I have another plan in mind, and I think all we need is the place that brought us all together.

"Aren't you going to ask me?" Leo jokes, acting offended.

"Sure, Pretty boy," I laugh. "Do you have anything to do today?"

His face flushes at the nickname. "I've just been set free from a kidnapping. Maybe my plans are booked."

"Unbook them," I tell him, looking at him in the rearview mirror, letting my intentions broadcast all over my face.

He takes a shuddering breath, then nods. "Done."

Les looks over at me with a raised brow, and I nod. She'll know what I'm planning without me saying a word. She wraps her hand around mine on her thigh and squeezes, her silent way of letting me know she understands.

The drive to the cabin feels like it takes forever when it's only thirty minutes. We all walk in, and you can feel the sexual tension fill the room immediately.

"Oh wow," Les breathes, feeling it too. She leads us to the couch on either side of her. Leo looks nervous as hell, and Les looks at him. "Do you want this?" she asks him, and I could kiss her. She's getting everything out in the open when all I want to do is bend him over the closest surface and see how tight his ass is.

He swallows and then looks at me, reading whatever is written on my face. He must like what he sees. "Yeah."

Thank fuck.

Les kisses him, and he takes the kiss over, slanting his mouth over hers. She pulls from his kiss and turns to me, doing the same thing. She switches back to Leo, but I feel her slide her hand into my hair at the back of my head, pulling me closer, then I'm kissing them both. It's sloppy but still hot, all of our tongues sliding together. Les pulls back, and I take my chance sinking my tongue into Leo's mouth. Les giggles softly and slides out from in between us, giving us space.

Leo freezes, and I think he's going to pull away. Then he hooks his hand in my shirt, pulling me closer, so I place my hand on the nape of his neck, deepening the kiss.

Fuck he can kiss. It's as hot as it was yesterday.

"Fuck," Leo breathes, pulling away from the kiss.

I want more, but I don't want to push him. Les climbs back onto the couch on her knees behind him; she rubs her hands down his chest. "That was fucking hot." She keeps running her hands down, and my greedy eyes take it in. She rubs her hand across his hard cock through his shorts. "Wasn't it?"

"Yes," he hisses when her hand makes contact again.

She gives me a seductive smile over his shoulder. "Let us make you feel good, Leo."

I think I just fell in love with her. She's helping me seduce him because she can tell he's still nervous. We might have fooled around yesterday, but that was nothing compared to what I have planned.

She hooks her hands on the hem of his shirt. "Say no, and this stops without question. Say yes, and we can blow your mind."

He stares at me for so long that I almost cut my losses. Then he utters that one word that will change us forever. "Yes."

"Hell yeah," I say, letting him know how much I want him. Les whips his shirt over his head, and I still can't get over how fucking cut he is. "Let's go to the bedroom."

She gets up and leads Leo through the house while I send a quick text to Ryder so he doesn't track our asses down again and wait for his reply, so I know he got it.

I kidnapped Les and Leo. 'grinning emoji'

RYDER

'middle finger emoji'

Fucker.

'laughing crying emoji' Catch ya later, asshole.

I toss my phone on the couch, chuckling to myself, and make my way to the bedroom.

They are both laid out on the bed blissfully naked; she's on her side with her leg over his thigh. He's lying on his back, showing off everything, including his hard cock against his stomach. She looks up from kissing his neck. "This is a clothes-free zone."

You don't have to tell me twice. I kick my shoes off and strip in record time. I slide onto the bed on the other side of him. He chuckles under his breath. "Now I know how Alessa feels when we do this to her."

"We haven't gotten to the good stuff yet." She looks at me, then places her hand on his chest. I scoot closer, letting him feel my naked body against his. I mirror her hand with mine. Together we stroke down each side of his chest, ribs, and abs, letting him get used to me touching him like this. We rub up and down his body until he's arching into our touch. She grabs my hand and pushes it right over his cock, and goes back to kissing his neck. I wrap my hand around him and stroke him hard, his cock jumps in my hand, and he groans.

"Shit," he groans again.

"You like the feel of my hand, Pretty boy?"

"Fuck, Gage," he breathes when I start working his cock faster.

Les leans over his chest, kissing me hard and fast. She pulls back with a mischievous look in her eyes. She starts kissing down his body, running her tongue over his nipple, nipping at his pec, kissing down his ribs, running her tongue over his abs, and I follow right behind her. When we get to his cock, she smiles, her blue eyes darker than usual, pupils blown, letting me know she's turned the fuck on too. If I reach over right now, her pussy will be dripping wet.

We both lean down at the same time, licking up the side of his cock, our tongues meeting and tangling at the head. His hips jerk. "Goddamn," he grits out, eyes latched onto Les and me.

I look right into his blue-green eyes before I suck the head of his cock into my mouth. His eyes darken, and a long groan escapes him. She wiggles down the bed and starts licking and sucking on his balls. "Fuck, you guys are going to kill me."

"We haven't even started yet," Les says, licking up the underside of his cock before meeting my lips. "Suck him, Gage."

That's all the invitation I needed; I suck him into my throat in one long stroke, swallowing around the head.

"Come here," he groans out to Les, pulling her over to sit on his face. I move between his thighs to watch him eat her pussy like his life depends on it.

He jerks her thighs down so hard to smother him with her pussy that she loses her balance and catches herself on his abs with a smack, putting her right in my face.

I let him go with a wet pop "Hey, Pretty girl."

"Hey," she moans, grinding back on his face.

"You like watching me suck his cock don't you, naughty girl?" I ask, licking the head of his cock.

"God, yes," she kisses me so fast and hard that her hands slip down his stomach. "You taste like him."

We take turns sucking his cock, sometimes letting our mouths run over him at the same time. I suck him into my mouth again, and he lifts his hips, bumping the back of my throat.

I will never get tired of his taste on my tongue. When I went to talk to him yesterday, I had no intention of seducing him in any way. I just wanted to make sure he was okay. But something in me snapped what little control I had about him. Before I knew what was happening, I was licking our come off his stomach.

I move off his cock, and Les slides her mouth down, swallowing his dick whole.

Her mouth pops off, causing his cock to bounce right in my face. Her hips start grinding down, her thighs wrapped tight against his head. His arms are anchored over her thighs, and I know if he died right now, he wouldn't even be mad. How could you when Les is smothering you with her sweet pussy?

Her whole body tightens to where it almost looks painful, then explodes with a scream, "Leo!" He doesn't let up, and she's squirming all over his face. I can hear the wet slurping noises of him drinking in everything she's giving him. It's the hottest fucking sound in the world. "It's too much!" She stiffens her arms on his stomach with her whole back bowing. Her whole body starts to quiver, and her breath is coming in short little pants. "Oh god," she moans, her fingers curving into his abs. She lets one of those low throaty moans loose, and I have to pinch the head of my cock to keep from coming. *Holy shit.* He loosens his grip on her thighs, and she slides to the side, her chest heaving with each breath. His face glistens with her wetness, and he looks pretty pleased with himself. I don't blame him.

"You okay, baby?" he chuckles, then groans when I remind him we aren't done by stroking his cock.

She holds up one finger to signal us to give her a minute, making us both chuckle. "I think it's his turn," she says, nodding her head toward me, still out of breath.

Leo's eyes widen a fraction, and I almost let him off the hook until he looks at her spread out beside him. The top of her head is near me, so he gets the perfect few of her wet pussy. "Come up here," he says, so I slide up his body, letting my cock rub against his. He jerks my mouth to his without hesitation, sinking his tongue into my mouth. Tasting her on his lips is more than I bargained for, and I groan into his mouth. I move my hips back and forth, rubbing our cocks together because I can't stop myself. He twists us until he has me on my back, stretching his body out over mine. I'm not usually the bottom because I like the control, but with Leo, I'll be whatever the fuck he wants me to be.

Fuck, this feels good.

Les and Leo start the same torment on me that we did to Leo, except he's more timid than I am, and that shouldn't turn me on.

He reaches down and wraps a fist around my cock, stroking hard from base to tip like he did yesterday. My cock jerks in his hand, begging for more, and he doesn't disappoint.

Les leans in, sucking the head of my cock into her mouth. Knowing it's her mouth and his hand on me is enough to drive me crazy. She slides her mouth down to meet his hand, then sucks her way back up my cock with his hand following her mouth. They continue until my breath is sawing out of my lungs, and I'm two seconds away from taking control back.

She lets my cock pop free. "Suck him, Leo," she whispers, and I can feel it in my fucking bones.

Few women would be into this. I've found out the hard way. But Les is not only into it, but she's also encouraging it.

Leo leans down and mimics her by sucking the head of my cock into his mouth. Watching it disappear between his lips makes my hips jerk. I grab a handful of the blanket to keep from grabbing the back of his head, forcing his mouth on me. They take turns on my cock; everything she does, he mimics, her showing him what to do until he completely takes over, sliding his mouth up and down on my cock, taking me as far as he can. During the first few passes, he gags. Les runs her hand up his back. "Relax your throat," she coaches, and I almost die. She's teaching her boyfriend how to suck her other boyfriend's cock. Did I die and go to heaven? He slides his mouth back up and then meets my eyes before sliding back down, doing what she told him to. My cock disappears into his mouth, and I can't take it anymore; my hand flies to the back of his head. She slides up beside me, kissing me wildly.

"Fuck," I groan against her lips when Leo takes me deeper. "How far do you want to take this, Leo?"

I need to know if he wants to go all the way or not. I need to ensure he's okay with what I want to do to him. I know he's turned on by sucking my cock; I can feel it pressing up against the side of my thigh.

"I want you to fuck me," he says after releasing my cock from his mouth. He says it in such a rush like he's trying to push it before he loses his nerve.

I reach down and pull him up to me. "You need to understand that you don't have to. We can stop this now, no hard feelings."

"I want to. Fuck, I want to." He kisses me, and it's all teeth and tongue. It's so fucking hot knowing I turn him on as much as he turns me on. When we fuck, it changes everything between us. I'm not going to hit it and quit it with Leo like I usually do. Am I ready for that?

I hear Les moan, and we both look at her. Her hand is between her thighs, rubbing her clit, watching us. That's it. It's time.

"Fuck our girl while I get you ready." I kiss him one last time before sliding off the bed. He doesn't waste time sinking into her sweet pussy, fucking her hard.

I walk over to the bedside table, pulling out the lube we left here the last time.

"Fuck, Leo," Les moans, gripping his arms. He's relentless with his thrusts, his ass flexing each time, his thighs slapping against hers.

I climb onto the bed behind them and smooth a hand up Leo's back, making him shudder. I grin and push between his shoulder blades to push him further onto Les.

I squirt a generous amount of lube onto my fingers because I want to make sure he loves this as much as I do. The first contact of my hand between his ass cheeks, his strokes slow, and Les grabs his hips to stop his movement. "Let him make you feel good," she encourages.

Yep, definitely love this girl.

I slide my finger around his virgin hole until I can feel him relax; as soon as he does, I slide my middle finger inside and push until my other knuckles press against his tight ass. "Oh fuck," he breathes, laying his forehead against Les'. I work my finger in and out a few times before slowly adding a second finger. Goddamn, he's tight.

His body goes rigid; Les smooths her hands down his back. "Relax," she tells him. "His cock feels so good, Leo. Just wait." He takes a shuddering breath and then lets out a long groan that has me almost coming everywhere. I know he's feeling the pressure and the pleasure that ripples through you after that.

I spend five minutes working my fingers in and out, scissoring them apart. I know he's ready when his hips start moving with my fingers.

"You ready for my cock, Pretty boy?"

Les moans. "Wait until you feel his cock, Leo."

"Goddamn, Les," he groans. "You're squeezing me so tight," he breathes and looks over his shoulder. "I'm ready," he says before leaning his forehead back on hers.

"Do you want me to wear a condom? I've never gone without one, but something about this ass makes me want to break all the rules," I ask, hoping he'll say no but will if he wants me to. "I'm clean."

His head jerks up. "Shit, Les. I didn't put one on."

"I'm clean." She smiles. "It's okay."

"I'm clean too, Baby." He looks at me. "I trust you."

Something about that makes my heart flip and makes my cock pay attention.

I reach down and grab the lube, uncap the bottle, and squirt it on my cock. Still working my fingers in and out of his ass, I slick my dick with my free hand.

He lays his head back down, so I gently slide my fingers free and line my cock up. I smooth one hand up his back, using my other hand to guide myself into his tight hole. I push until I feel the resistance and stop to let him adjust. Les smooths her hands down his back again. "Breathe, Leo, and push back on him when he pushes in."

He gives her a jerky nod and takes several breaths. When I push forward, he pushes back, letting me slide past the muscle and straight into his tight hot ass. "Fuck," I grit out. His ass is squeezing me so fucking tight.

"Oh shit," Leo groans, and it's half in pain.

"Breathe," Les says softly. "It will feel so good."

I feel him relax at her words, and I push forward slowly until I'm fully seated in his ass, my thighs touching his. I breathe out through my nose to keep control. I refuse to hurt him no matter how much I want to slam into him. I stay still so he can get used to me stretching him, then slowly drag my way back out, rubbing over his prostate. I slide in and out slowly until I feel him start to relax.

"Fuck," he groans. "Fuck, that feels good."

I stroke slowly in and out a few more times. "Your ass is amazing, Baby," I groan, moving a little faster. He starts pulling out of Les when I pull out of him, pushing his ass back onto my cock. "Hell yeah. Fuck us, Leo," I encourage, massaging the globes of his ass in my hands, watching my cock disappear.

He reaches down and hooks Les' legs over his arms, bracing his hands back on the bed. The move makes him sink deeper into her and me deeper inside of him, causing all kinds of noises to tear from all three of us.

I pull out until I'm halfway inside, giving him room to move. When he starts to move, he jerks his hips back and forth, fucking her pussy and fucking his ass back on my cock.

I know what he's feeling. The fullness of my cock in his ass, the drag against his prostate that feels amazing, a man's hands on his hips.

"Goddamn," he groans, moving faster. My control snaps, pushing forward when he pushes back, slamming me into him. His back bows, his head falling back on his shoulders. "Fuck yes."

"Oh my God," Les moans.

"How are you doing, Pretty girl?" I ask, rubbing my hands down her legs over his arms.

"Perfect," she breathes.

I squeeze her legs before moving my hands back to his hips, squeezing, then I start to move faster, deeper, fucking him into her. The sound of our skin slapping, mine and Leo's groans mixing with her moans, is music to my fucking ears. If there's a heaven for a guy like me, this is it.

"Fuck, Gage," Leo says, slamming his hips back onto me, taking me in one stroke. "Les, your pussy feels amazing."

I can't imagine the overload he's in right now. I can't wait to try this the other way with Leo fucking my ass like he is her pussy.

His hips start moving faster, his thrusts getting uneven, and I know he's about to come.

"Fuck. Fuck. Fuck," Les chants, digging her fingers into his biceps.

"Come on his cock, Pretty girl," I groan.

Les' scream echoes off the walls when she comes, starting a chain reaction.

"Oh shit," he gasps, his ass tightening up on my cock. His groan vibrates through him when he empties inside of her.

I let his body relax before I slam into him three more times before I let myself go. Pushing as far as I can go, I come right in his ass. I've always worn a condom, so I didn't know how good it felt raw with anyone, and there is no going back now.

I just marked him, and he's mine just as much as Les is.

I rub my hands up and down his back before slowly pulling out, watching my cum leak down his balls.

He leans down and kisses Les before pulling out of her. Leo and I lay down on our sides, with her in the middle facing me. I kiss those pouty lips, thankful that she's mine. I look over at Leo. "You good, Pretty boy?"

He chuckles. "So now I'm Pretty boy, but when you're in my ass, I'm Baby?"

Les giggles. "You caught that too, huh?"

"You want me to call you Baby?" I ask. I was in the moment, and it just felt right.

He links his hand with mine that's lying over Les' hip, making my heart do that little flip again. "You can call me whatever you want."

"Mine," I mumble. "You're both mine."

Les' head pops up off my shoulder. "He's mine," she laughs.

"We can share him," I offer.

"I can work with that as long as you make sure he makes that face he made when you were in his ass."

"I'll have to make sure I see his face next time so I know what face he made."

"He's right fucking here," Leo laughs. "Do I get a say?"

"No," Les and I say at the same time, dissolving into laughter.

"Now I know why Ryder hates when you two do that," Leo grumbles.

Les shoots up in the bed. "Ryder!" She goes to crawl out of bed, but I pull her back down.

"I messaged him, Pretty girl."

She breathes a sigh of relief. "That's all we need is him and Dex busting in here trying to find us," she says, then laughs. "No, it would be kind of funny."

"Wait!" I exclaim, jumping out of bed and running towards the living room, Les and Leo's laughter following me. I scoop my phone off the couch and run back to the bedroom. I dive over them and back onto the bed. "Selfie," I grin.

"Really?" Les says, but with a roll of her eyes, she looks up at the phone. We all smile at the camera, Les' tits on full display. I laugh to myself, pushing buttons on my phone. I count down in my head when her phone chimes from the living room; Leo's right behind it.

"What did you do?" Leo asks, looking over her at me.

"You'll see," I grin.

CHAPTER 29
RYDER

I scrub a hand down my face after looking at the picture Gage sent to a fucking group chat. "Fuck," I mutter.

Les is snuggled between him and Leo, smiling from ear to ear, those perfect tits squashed against Gage's side.

Holden chuckles. "You got it too?" he asks, looking at his phone, color creeping into his cheeks. It's hard to believe this innocent fucker is walking around with Les' fingernail scratches down his back and the same one who kissed me in the gym.

I still can't get that kiss out of my head.

"Fuck you, Gage," I gripe and toss my phone on the coffee table where Holden and I are watching TV. I knew Gage was up to something when he volunteered to take her to the nail salon, dragging Leo with him. Plus, his ass loves going too.

"Are you mad?" Holden asks, concerned.

"Nah, man. Jealous," I laugh. I'm still not sure how I feel about this, but I need to figure it out. And soon.

My phone chimes again, and I scoop it up; Holden is already chuckling.

GAGE

'image sent.'

It's a picture of Les in the shower, water cascading down that hot tan body.

Fuck you.

GAGE

Bring it on, big boy. 'kissy face emoji'

LES

'laughing crying emoji'

HOLDEN

When are you coming back?

LES

Holden 'heart eyes emoji' we are leaving in like ten minutes.

What the fuck? I don't even get a hi, and he gets heart eyes?

GAGE

It's because he has a monster cock.

Holden makes a choking noise, and my eyes snap to him. His face is blood red all the way to his ears.

LES

Ryder's is pierced. 'drooling emoji'

LEO

What?

GAGE

What?!?!? Let me see!

DEX

You guys are distracting as fuck.

Hey, Baby girl.

Hey to you other assholes.

LES

Hello, Dexton. 'smirking emoji'

GAGE

Shut up, all of you!

Ryder!

Send a pic of your dick!

LES

Les changed the name of the group to: Les' coop of cocks

GAGE

'laughing crying emoji'

I'm not sending a pic of my cock.

GAGE

I'll just see it in person. 'eyes emoji'

I roll my eyes with a chuckle and lay my phone down. Leo saved my ass today; there's no doubt about that. If the guy he took out had gotten a shot off, it would have been lights out for me. He didn't even hesitate to save my ass, either. He proved himself to me today even after he spazzed the fuck out in the car, just like I figured he would.

He kept staring at his hands, and they were visibly shaking. I couldn't even fault him because I felt the same way he did the first time I took a life.

My dad had just started letting me go on jobs with him and Luca, saying I was old enough. I was just shy of eighteen at that point. We went on a job to take out some assholes that were trafficking women through the ports, and this guy came out of nowhere. Just like Leo, I pulled the trigger without a second thought, and it didn't hit me what I did until we were back in the car on our way home. My hands were shaking, and I didn't even realize I was crying until my dad pulled me in for a hug. He told me that if it were easy, everyone would do it and that we were in a place to protect people, so we had a job. It stuck with me through every person I dropped after that, even to this day.

I told Leo that, and it seemed to calm him down. By the time we got back to the house, he seemed to have accepted what happened for the most part.

Like we told Les, we're by no means best friends now, but I'm willing to give him a chance.

"Do you think she's happy?" Holden asks quietly, breaking me from my thoughts.

I think about it for a minute and answer honestly, "Yeah, man. She is."

"Are you happy?" he asks with a tilt of his head that he's picked up from Les.

"I am," I answer. What is he getting at? "Are you?"

He smiles. "For sure."

"You're okay with all of this?" I worry about him getting involved in a relationship like this, but I know Les wouldn't involve him if she didn't think he could handle it, and neither would I. He's a lot stronger than we give him credit for. Not even a week ago, he couldn't even look Les in the eyes.

He nods, then shrugs. "Yeah."

"Would you tell me if you weren't?"

"You know I would," he answers but then lets his eyes drift from mine.

"Holden," I warn, reminding him to look me in the eye.

He sighs. "Are we going to talk about what happened?"

"We can talk about it whenever you want."I've been waiting on him to bring it up mainly because I didn't know how, and I don't want him to regret it, and that thought has been eating at me.

"I need to tell you something," he says, rubbing his hands together, showing his nervousness. "I'm bisexual." He looks up and locks eyes with me. "Is that a problem?"

Just like that, I see Holden's spine straighten and challenge me if it's a problem. My cock should not be getting hard because of that but fuck if it isn't.

I sit up in my chair, bracing my arms on my knees. "It's not a problem with me. Where do you want this to go, Holden?" I need to know what he expects out of this. I can't risk taking things too far and scaring him off.

Before he can answer, Micah struts into the living room, wearing a three-piece suit. I suppress an eye roll. "What's up, fuckface?" he greets, flopping down on the couch. "Where's Les?"

I raise an eyebrow at the name he hasn't called me since I outgrew him. "With Gage and Leo."

"When will she be back?"

"You know, Micah, there's this cool invention called a fucking cell phone. Message her," I say, then flip him the middle finger. Holden laughs but tries to smother it when Micah narrows his eyes at him.

"Don't encourage him," Micah says, pointing at Holden. "You could just answer the fucking question, dickhead."

I shrug. "What's the fun in that?" I didn't suddenly forget he threatened to murder my ass.

He stands up with a huff, jerking his suit jacket to button it. "Tell her to call me."

"Fuck off," I yell when he strides back out of the room, and I swear I hear him growl from the other room until the front door slams.

Holden beats a hasty retreat in the other direction before finishing our conversation. I don't want to push him, but he needs to tell me what he wants. Because after that kiss, I know what I want. I aimlessly flip through channels until I hear Les and them coming through the garage door into the house. I jump out of my chair, heading toward her, and have her pressed against the wall with my lips on hers before she can take more than two steps inside.

Those pictures have me all kinds of fucked up.

"Hello to you too," Gage mutters, slapping my ass before laughing and walking away.

I ignore him and get lost, stroking my tongue against hers. It is so damn freeing to finally be able to do this when I want.

I pull back and peck her lips one last time. "Hey, *Il mio sole.*"

She strokes her hand down my face. "Hey," she says breathlessly. "I missed you."

I close my eyes, soaking in those words before opening them. "I missed you too." I sling my arm over her shoulders, leading her into the living room. "What's this family meeting about?"

She sighs. "I found some stuff out, and I need you all here."

"Dex said he would be home for dinner, so he should be here soon." I take in her face. "Is everything okay?"

She shakes her head. "No. We've got trouble."

Shit.

Dex gets home about the time Les is passing out the food we ordered. We all pile in around the dining room table and dig in. I'm dying to know what she wants to talk to us about because if Les says there's trouble, you can bet on it. Gage and I clean up the table and settle back, passing out beers.

"What's up, Baby girl?" Dex asks, breaking the silence.

"I know who Moretto's supplier is from the name you gave, Holden," she says, giving a small smile to her hacker. "It's Viktor Orlov."

"What?" I explode, "That Russian motherfucker knows better."

She acknowledges that with a nod. "He does, which poses the question. Why would he make a move like that against me?"

"He thinks you're weak," Dex mutters apologetically. He doesn't mean anything by it, and Viktor isn't shy about his displeasure with Les being in the position of power to make rules for him too.

"What's the play, Pretty girl?" Gage asks, casting a look at Leo. It doesn't escape my notice she's talking freely in front of him or the eyes he and Gage keep giving each other.

"This is the tricky part," she says, taking a sip of her beer. "I can issue a warning that he's not going to listen to. You know what I say about second chances?"

"They don't get one," I say proudly. She handles this family just like her dad did, with an iron fist and a soft spot when she needs it.

"So, you know what that means?" She runs her fingers through her hair, her only nervous gesture.

"War," Dex rumbles, looking at her. "It means we go to war with the Russians."

"War?" Leo asks with a frown.

"Viktor Orlov is the leader of the Russian mafia," Gage explains. "He doesn't like Les ruling over him too."

"I know this is a stupid question, but how does she rule over him too?" Leo asks.

"Nah, man, it's not stupid," I say. I feel bad for him; I can't imagine what's going through his mind. "Les runs the most powerful crime organization in the world. Whoever lives where she rules follows her, and she does it to keep as much peace as possible."

"I thought it was just California," Leo remarks, confused.

She shakes her head. "I'm just based in Cali; I have people everywhere. They run their own syndicates but still answer to Micah or me."

"Oh," Leo says, impressed. Damn right. He should be. "Even North Carolina?"

She smiles. "Even North Carolina, although that's a small group and more towards Charlotte instead of Spindale, where you're from." She turns back to me. "I have more news."

I already don't like it from the way she's looking at me. "Hit me."

"Can we keep the commentary to a minimum until I'm done? Gage already tore my ass up over it," she says dryly, shooting a glare at a smug Gage. "I met with Zane today." I bite my tongue so hard it hurts. Not only did she meet him, but she also met him alone. "I gave him the info on the foster home because we can't be near that shit. He said he would take care of it."

"It's about fucking time he makes himself useful," I grit out. Just the mention of his name makes my skin crawl and the fact he was alone with Les? I want to rip his fucking head off.

"That's not it. Zane had his partner with him, Jay Hoover, and he gave me an uneasy feeling."

"What do you mean, Baby girl?"

"He didn't give me that begrudging respect that I usually get. He didn't even try to hide his hate."

Jay Hoover. Why does that name sound familiar? It hits me like a ton of bricks.

"Hoover. As in Hoover enterprises?" I ask, picking up my phone and shooting off a quick Google search pulling up his dad's picture, Gregory Hoover. I slide it to Les, and it takes her two seconds for it to register.

"We went to school with his younger brother Trevor." She buries her face in her hands. "Fuck."

"Someone want to explain?" Leo asks, spreading his hands out.

"We went to a private school with Trevor Hoover. He got initiated into the Poletti family his senior year," Les answers, looking at me. "He was killed a year later."

"What would Poletti's need with a high school senior?" Leo wonders, completely confused. It's going to take him forever to catch up to everything.

"Les runs smaller factions, kind of like gangs in the smaller parts of the city to handle the street shit," Dex comments. "That's where I started."

Leo's eyes widen. "I'm never going to figure all this shit out."

"You will," Gage says with confidence, squeezing his shoulder. "It's a lot to take in."

"So, do you think Jay is pissed about Trevor?" Holden asks Les, speaking up for the first time. I'm surprised he's still sitting here when he usually bolts during these meetings.

"That would be my guess. It was more than me being a criminal that crawled under his skin."

"What do we do about him?" I'm not against killing a fucking cop if he is coming for her.

"We watch him. Holden will get all he can on him. I'll talk to Zane." She holds a hand up when Gage opens his mouth. "I won't go alone again. Save it."

"You lit into her for going alone?" I ask Gage, and he nods. "Good."

Her eyes narrow. "I get it, okay. Save the lecture and the back-patting."

I hold my hands up. "We just want you safe, *Il mio sole*."

Her eyes soften. "I know, and I'm trying to make better decisions about running off alone. Like I told Gage, you have to be patient with me."

"We can do that, Baby girl," Dex says, looking around the table. "I have news too. I went to the casino on the boulevard for a security issue and found something else." He pulls his phone out, scrolling through until he finds what he's looking for, then slides the phone to Les.

She squints at it. "Was he the security issue?"

"No, we took care of that. When I was looking at the cameras, I spotted him."

She grunts and slides the phone to me. "What the fuck is Xander doing there?" I ask. Xander is the leader of the Vipers, who has no business in her casino.

"I don't know, but I say we go find out." Her smile is feral, and I love it.

We all get dressed and head toward Xander's garage. Holden is back at the house, watching through the street cameras to ensure he stays there.

We load into Gage's Range Rover since mine is shot to shit. He lets me drive so he can squeeze between Les and Leo. Leo was warned about what would happen but insisted he that he can handle it, and I had to give it to him; he has so far. We pull directly in front, pulling on gloves and doing a weapons check before we pile out. The guys he has watching the garage start scurrying inside to warn him. We fall into formation around Les, and she walks straight into the garage like she owns the place.

"Xander," she calls out in a sing-song voice, making Gage chuckle. "Come out, come out, wherever you are."

He walks out from the back of the garage, his black hair in its usual fauxhawk. His green eyes light on Les, lingering a little too long. Looking from the tips of her high-heeled boots, up her black ripped skinny jeans, and her black leather jacket finally to her eyes. Whatever he sees there makes him snap out of his fantasy. I grind my molars to dust, so I don't shoot him on site.

"There you are," she greets like she's happy to see him. "You want to tell your boys to stand down before I clean house?"

"Back off," Xander barks at the seven guys on edge, hands hovering over weapons. "What brings you to my side of town, Alessa?"

"Can't I just come to visit?" she asks, tilting her head to the side.

Gage finally steps to the side so he's visible, and Xander's eyes widen at Gage's crazy grin. Xander remembers the mess Gage made the last time he delivered a warning for Les.

"This isn't a social call," Xander points out like we're idiots. Gage starts wandering around the front of the garage, looking under random tarps to get under Xander's skin. "What do you want?"

Les taps her chin thoughtfully. "A giant birdie told me that you were at Racks today. You were banned from there months ago because you didn't know how to handle yourself accordingly. So, Xan, why were you there?" Racks is the casino Xander was spotted at, it used to be a stripper joint before Les bought it hence the name, but it made her laugh, so she left it.

Gage laughs at Les, calling Dex a giant birdie. "Good one."

She curtseys. "Thank you."

I shake my head at the antics. These two can play up their crazy so much that people think they are actually insane, which makes people wary of them, and it's a fun game to watch.

"I thought maybe it was cool for me to come back," Xander explains, knowing there is no way she would let him back after the fight he started the last time.

"See, I would have believed that," she says, walking over to where Gage waved her over, peaking under the tarp across a car. "Except you avoided all the cameras like you *knew* they were there. There is only one reason you avoid cameras, Xander. You missed one, though." She peeks under the tarp and whistles. "What do we have here?" She whips the tarp back with the help of Gage. They pull it off to reveal a car almost identical to my Mustang Shelby, except this one is silver instead of black like mine.

"Damn," I comment, walking over. "What did this set you back? Two hundred grand?"

"Nah, bro. That ain't mine." Xander waves that away like I'm crazy. "We've been working on it."

Gage pops the passenger side door open, digging through the glove box. He pulls out a bunch of papers, tossing the ones he doesn't need over his shoulder until he finds what he's looking for. "Xander King." He looks up from the paper, fake shocked. "There is someone else with your same name, and you're working on it." He looks at Les. "How fucking cool is that?"

I hear Leo snort a laugh and swallow down one of my own.

"So cool," Les gushes. "What are the chances?"

"I'd say pretty fucking slim," Dex rumbles, tossing me a crowbar lying beside him. I catch it one-handed and spin it around.

"What were you doing at Racks?" I ask, pointing at him with the crowbar.

"I told you, man! I thought she wouldn't care."

"Wrong answer," she says, waving her hand at me. I finally let my crazy out to play and swing the crowbar, smashing into the driver's side headlight.

"Oof," Gage mutters, "That hurt me."

Les walks around the front of the car toward Leo who's standing beside Dex, her heels making an ominous click against the garage floor. "Okay. Next question. I know what you deal in, and I know there is no way you could afford that car. Where did you get the money?"

"My boy Andre boosted it."

"Wrong answer," she says again, and I swing at the other headlight.

"Come on!" Xander yells. "What do you want from me?"

"I just want the truth, Xan. You know how much I hate when you lie to me." She pokes her bottom lip out in a pout.

"Oh shit. You made her sad, Xander," Gage says. "You know what that means?" Gage grins that crazy grin again.

She takes a step back toward us, and before I can blink, Leo has his Glock pressed against a guy's forehead that stood up fast behind them. "Sit. Down," he grits out, and I raise both my eyebrows. *Well fuck.*

"That was hot," Gage and Les say at the same time, making me roll my eyes. I *hate* that.

Dex turns slowly toward the guy. "What the fuck was that?" he asks the kid with greased back blonde hair and completely wasted blue eyes.

He gulps and shrinks back into the couch. "I don't know."

"Playboy is just jumpy," Xander smooths over.

"Playboy?" Leo asks, holstering his gun. "What the hell kind of name is that?"

"A stupid one," Les laughs, then spins back to Xander. "We're two for two. Should he move to the taillights, or will you start talking?"

"You know," I say, spinning the crowbar around. "I think if we find out how some low-level street creeper can afford this car, we can figure out the rest." I pop open the driver's side door and scoop up the keys I spotted lying in the seat. I have a sneaking feeling, so I unlock the trunk; when I pull it open, my blood boils. "Les," I call out. She walks over and looks inside, all playfulness sliding off her, and in its place is the ice queen we joke about.

"You want to tell me why your trunk is full of fucking cocaine? When I know good, and goddamn well I didn't give it to you?" she barks, and I swear she grows a foot when she's pissed off.

Xander immediately starts sweating. "I didn't know that was there," he stutters.

"Seriously. That's the best you got?" Gage deadpans. "I expected better from you."

She pulls both Glocks from her holster. *Shit.* "This is how this is going to go. You start talking, or I start fucking shooting." She points her Glocks at Xander and a random guy. We all follow suit leveling weapons on the rest of the guys, the crowbar hitting the floor with a clang when I drop it.

"What's it going to be?" she asks again.

"Fuck!" Xander runs his hand through his hair. "You'll fucking kill me."

She gestures with her Glock. "Who did you get it from?" She knows who it came from but needs him to say it. Xander clams up, and she pulls the trigger on the other guy. His body slams into the far wall, a perfect circle in the middle of his forehead. "Who. Did. You. Get. It. From?"

"Fuck! Spinner! I got it from Spinner Sade!"

"Jacob "Spinner" Sade?" Les asks, and Xander nods. "YOU ARE SELLING COKE FOR THE FUCKING RUSSIANS?!"

Everyone winces at the volume of her voice, and even I eye her warily; she doesn't raise her voice like that.

"I needed the cash! You kept me on a tight lea...." Xander argues, but he doesn't finish before Les is on him and smashes a high-heeled booted foot in the middle of his chest, knocking him to the floor.

She presses her Glock to his forehead. "You couldn't be fucking trusted," she grinds out. "You were never meant to be more than a fucking street thug." She presses harder when he looks like he might move. "Tie them up and take their phones," she tells us without looking away from Xander.

Gage digs through a toolbox and pulls out zip ties. We get them tied up like she asked, and I approach her. "What's the play here, Les?"

"Get the coke out of that car but take one with us so it can be tested so I can see where it's coming from." Her finger tightens on the trigger. "Kill them all. Set it up to look like the Russians."

"Boss," Leo says quietly, and I look at him harshly. He holds up a phone. "You might want to see this."

I nod my head toward him and take her spot, gladly shoving my gun into this motherfucker's forehead. She walks over and jerks the phone out of his hand; to his credit, he doesn't react. You just have to roll with it when she is like this; she doesn't mean anything by it.

"The dime is here. I repeat, the dime is here," she reads from his phone; she turns to the kid with greasy blonde hair and bloodshot blue eyes. "Who is Z-Mack, and what does the dime is here mean?"

The kid shakes his head, shrinking away from her.

She presses her Glock into his temple. "I'm getting real tired of you assholes thinking you don't have to answer me." She pushes harder. "Answer me!"

He folds like wet paper. "You," he says with a shaky voice. "You're the dime."

"Who's Z-Mack?" Leo asks.

The kid whimpers. "He's my contact officer."

"You're a rat?" Dex growls, making the kid shrink in on himself even more. "For who?"

"Detective Ayers," he answers.

Motherfucker.

CHAPTER 30
ALESSA

"Did he say what I think he just fucking said?" Ryder barks from his position, holding Xander to the floor. It speaks about what kind of person Xander is when not one of the guys in this garage will speak up on his behalf.

"Yes," I sigh. "Fuck!" I dig my phone from my back pocket and dial Holden.

"What's wrong?" he answers on the first ring, and I smile despite myself.

"Any activity outside of the garage since we got here?" I ask, and hear him tapping away on his computer.

"No. The last car to pull up was you guys. Nothing since then. Why?"

"If you see a white Dodge Challenger pull up, call me asap. Or any car. Okay?"

"Yes, Boss," he answers immediately.

"Thank you." I disconnect the call and stare at Playboy's phone like Zane is going to pop through the screen.

"What are we doing, Boss?" Dex asks.

I run through my options as fast as I can. We can kill Xander, but we don't have enough time to frame the Russians if Zane is on his way. The message was sent fifteen minutes ago, which could mean he's here, or he could be busy and hasn't read it yet; the chances for that are close to zero. Why the hell did he call me a dime, and why would Zane care I'm here? I turn to the kid, and he looks close to pissing himself.

"Why did you tell him I was here?" I ask as softly as I can. I'm teetering on the edge of burning this garage down with their bodies inside.

"He was here today," the kid whispers.

"For what?" I ask impatiently. "Don't make me drag the shit out of you."

"He was asking about the fosters up the road. Told him that the twins that used to slang for them disappeared, and you were here right before that."

"Do you know who she is?" Dex asks, and the kid shrinks again. Dex's voice is rough all the time, but when he is pissed, it's raspy and deeper.

"N...n...no."

"Do you know who the Poletti's are?" I ask, and he nods. "I'm Alessa Poletti."

I give that a minute to sink in before his drug-addled brain catches up, and his eyes widen. "I didn't kn...kn...kno...know."

"Clearly," Gage says dryly.

I need to figure out what to do with the other guys in here besides Playboy and the one I shot. He was a good choice because he's been on my list for the Black Demon hit for molesting a fourteen-year-old boy. Of course, Xander has to die to send a message to Viktor. I also need to call Alexey and Dmitri to warn them about what's going to go down. Their dad is such a pompous ass he never lets them know anything; they are pushed out to the sidelines, which suits them just fine for the time being. They're content with cash and cars being thrown at them to stay out of the way. They hate Viktor on the best of days and are good friends, but how will they handle me starting a war with their dad?

"Les. We need a decision," Ryder remarks. I have no clue what to do. Zane will turn a blind eye to stuff he doesn't see me do but cold-blooded murder? He would bury me, the guys, and a very innocent

Leo. "Les." We can take Xander with us, but what about the six witnesses staring at me? Xander was going to die whether we found the coke or not; I didn't issue second chances. The coke just let me know Viktor is coming for my income, taking over my street factions; none of this is good. "Les!" Ryder yells, jerking me from my thoughts.

I whirl around, pissed off. "What?!"

"We need a decision," Dex repeats for him, trying to use that soothing voice that never fails but to piss me off more.

I look at Playboy's phone; there are messages back from Zane. *Fuck.*

Z-MACK

Still there?

Playboy? Fucking answer me.

"If you let us go, I swear to God, dude, we won't say anything." One of the other guys is pleading with Gage.

"Do I look stupid to you?" Gage asks with a laugh. "No fucking way."

"We didn't know whose coke that was!" another one speaks up.

"Everyone shut up!" I yell and make one of the many decisions I'll make tonight; I dial Zane from Playboy's phone.

"What the fuck, Playboy?" Zane growls when he answers.

"I'm sorry. Playboy can't come to the phone right now. He's a little...tied up."

Silence. "Les?" Zane says like he doesn't want to believe I'm here. "Where's Playboy?"

"You see, we came to see Xander, but we stumbled upon this little fucking rat. And you know who he was texting, Zane?" I pause for the dramatic effect. "You."

"I have informants everywhere," Zane says casually. Ryder and I exchange a look. This isn't good.

"Are you investigating me, Zaney baby?" I purr, and that muscle in Ryder's jaw immediately starts ticking. The silence on the other end of the phone is telling. "Let me put it this way, Zane. When I catch a whiff of you in my business, I will take away anything you have left."

"Are you threatening me, Beautiful?"

"It's not a threat. It's a promise. You know who I am and what I'm about." I hear a bunch of commotion on the other end of the phone before I hear a door click shut.

"Les, I need you to listen to me," Zane rushes out. "You need to get the fuck out of there. Now. We're about to raid that address you gave us."

My heart sinks; we're only two buildings down. "When?"

"Five minutes. Tops."

I hang up and drop the phone to the floor. Dex smashes it under his big boot. "We have to go. Now."

"What about them?" Leo asks, gesturing around the garage.

"Let them go." I push my Glock in the face of the first guy who was pleading with Gage. "You say a word, and I will be back. You won't leave here alive the next time." He nods like a bobblehead. "Grab Xander and the rat."

Playboy whimpers when Gage jerks him to stand, Dex cuts the zip ties off the others, and they scatter out the back door. Ryder knocks Xander in the temple with the butt of his gun, knocking him out cold, then zip-ties his hands.

"What about the coke?" Ryder asks, heaving an unconscious Xander over his shoulder.

"Looks like you just got a new car," I tell him. "Take it to the docks."

Ryder grins like crazy, dumping Xander in the backseat. "Be careful," he says, kissing my lips firmly.

"You too." I turn to Dex. "Go with him."

He jerks a nod, and folds his large frame into the too-small car. It fires up with a roar, echoing through the garage. Damn. I should have chosen that car.

Ryder slowly backs it out while Gage and Leo close the garage doors. I jump into the driver's seat of Gage's Range Rover; Leo and Gage cram Playboy in between them. No sooner than I hit the button to start the car, I hear sirens wailing in the distance.

"Shit," I mutter, shoving it in drive and tearing off behind Ryder.

Five minutes my ass.

Ten minutes later, we're sitting at the docks where my shipments come in. The shipping containers are mostly for show, but I have legit stuff shipped out of here. We pull in behind them for cover.

I look at Leo. "You good?"

"I'm good, Baby," he says with a smile.

I look at Playboy. "Don't try anything stupid." He's shaking his head before I even finish my sentence. I honestly don't think he'll try anything; he looks seconds from shitting himself.

"Take him to Gerald and meet us back at the house," I tell Gage and slide out of the car.

"On it, Boss," he replies, jumping out of the backseat. He gives me a quick kiss before climbing into the driver's seat and taking off.

I walk over to Ryder and Dex, who dumped Xander on the asphalt unceremoniously. I send a quick text to Gerald to tell him I'll explain later and just keep an eye on Playboy.

"Morning, Xan," I greet when Xander groans. Ryder roughly pulls him into a sitting position by his shirt. "You know I've given you more than one chance which I don't do. Call it whatever you want, but the only reason you're still alive is that you worked under my dad." I pull my Glock out and aim it at him. "That ends now."

"Wait. Wait! I can be your inside man with Viktor!" Xander begs.

"You think we can trust you now?" Ryder asks in disbelief.

Xander swallows, turning pleading eyes on me. "I fucked up, but I need the money."

Don't ask. Don't ask. Don't ask. I beg myself.

"Why?" I ask anyway. *Dumbass.*

"My mom is sick, and I needed the money for medical bills and her medicine."

My heart drops to my feet. Why did I have to ask?! I know I can't trust him for shit, but what if he's telling the truth, and I sign his mom's death warrant when I take him out?

My phone starts buzzing in my pocket, so I pull it out to see Holden's name flashing across the display.

"Hello?"

"Oh, thank fuck," he breathes out. "No one was answering, and I saw blue lights flashing all over the cameras."

I wince. "Sorry. It's been crazy. We're okay, though. I promise." *I'm a horrible girlfriend.* "I need you to run something for me. Xander King's living relatives and if they're being treated for anything."

"It's okay, Bright eyes; I'm just glad to hear your voice. I'm running it now."

I smile. "We will see you in a bit."

"I lov..." he pauses. "I'll see you later," he says, disconnecting the call. I stare at the screen, confused. Was Holden getting ready to say I love you? What would I have said if he did? I shake my head, deciding to cross that bridge when the time comes.

Two minutes later, I get the text I need.

HOLDEN

No living relatives.

I laugh, but it's not one full of humor. "You lying motherfucker," I growl, shoving my gun back in his face. "You think I wouldn't check that?"

I see the moment Xander knows he's done. I would kill him, or Viktor would for ratting him out. He bows his head. "Please take care of my son."

"You don't have any kids. No living relatives," I repeat what Holden told me.

He shakes his head. "I'm not listed as his father. He's in foster care."

"Which one?" I ask.

"The one up the street from the garage," he answers.

Ryder jerks Xander's head back by his hair to snarl in his face. "You left your son in that shit hole?"

"I didn't have a choice," he says hoarsely. "His mom kept him from me. She told me after she went to jail."

"How old is he?" I don't know why I'm asking questions, except kids always pull at my heartstrings. Heartstrings I can't afford to have right now with a brewing war.

"Nine months."

"I knew you were a piece of shit, Xander, but I didn't realize how much until just now." I chamber a round and pull the trigger.

"Damn it, Les," Ryder says, looking down at the blood on his jeans, which splattered from the hole in the back of Xander's head.

"Oops," I laugh, holstering my gun. "Call Mani and tell him we need a cleanup crew." He fake glares, jerking his phone out of his pocket. He dials the number and walks away.

"You could have warned him," Dex says with a chuckle.

"That's no fun," I laugh, walking over to the Mustang. Dex unlocks the trunk, and we both just stand there and stare at all the product. "What the hell do we do with this?"

"That depends on what kind of message you want to send to Viktor," he answers.

That I don't know yet. "We can stash it in one of the shipping containers until we figure it out."

Dex follows me into the trailer we use as an office to get a key for one of the shipping containers. I'm digging through the keys when Ryder walks in. He stalks straight to me and slants his mouth over mine, taking my breath away when he sinks his hand into my hair. He walks me backward until my ass hits the desk; I scoot up, so my ass is perched on the side. Stepping between my thighs, he deepens the kiss. He jerks away, out of breath, when I moan into his mouth.

"What was that for?" I ask breathlessly.

He jerks my hand to his hard cock, rubbing my hand over it through his jeans. "Those fucking pictures and seeing you tonight made me so fucking hard." He jerks my head back with his hand in my hair, laying open mouth kisses on my neck.

"I can make it feel better," I whisper, and his whole body shudders. He steps back, and I slide off the desk. I take my jacket and holster off, tossing them onto the desk. I cast a look at Dex, who's standing against the door with his arms crossed over his chest, but I can see his obvious erection through his jeans. I wish he would let me take care of his too. I drop to my knees in front of Ryder, making him groan. I look into his eyes, and he doesn't seem fussed with Dex still standing there; neither am I.

I pop the button on his jeans, then slowly slide the zipper down, staring into his eyes the whole time, watching them darken to black. Being on my knees for Ryder has me soaking through my panties. I've always known he's gorgeous, but the fact that I can touch him whenever I want makes him even sexier. I jerk his jeans and boxers over his hips. His pierced cock pops free, so I wrap my hand around the base causing Ryder to hiss. I run my tongue over the underside of his cock, letting the five barbells bump across it.

"Fuck," he grunts when I close my mouth over the head of his cock, swirling my tongue around it. I suck him into my mouth, and place both hands on his thighs, letting him know he has control. He doesn't hesitate to put a hand on the back of my head, thrusting into my mouth. I breathe through my nose and open my mouth wider to accommodate his size so he can slide into my throat. He places both hands on the side of my head and starts ruthlessly fucking my mouth, just the way I love it. "Goddamn this mouth, *Il mio sole*," he groans, sliding in until my nose brushes his pubic bone, stealing my breath; I lock eyes with him again. He slides all the way out until just the head of his cock sits on my tongue, letting me take a breath before sliding back in again. He does this several times before jerking me to my feet. He slants his mouth over mine, only breaking away to rip my shirt over my head. He has me naked in record time.

"Shit," Dex groans.I look over at him, and he's massaging his cock through his jeans.

Ryder turns me in his arms, my back to his front, exposing me entirely to Dex. He runs a hand down my stomach before it disappears between my legs; he rubs my clit in lazy circles, causing my hips to jerk. "You're so wet. Did sucking my cock make you like that?"

"Yes," I moan, rocking my hips with his fingers.

"You want her mouth, Dex?" Ryder asks, and time stands still, waiting for Dex to make up his mind. I can see it all running across his face before it all clears. He reaches down roughly, undoing his jeans and shoving them down enough for his cock to pop free. He wraps a fist around it, stroking it hard.

Holy shit. I forgot how gorgeous Dex's cock is. It's thicker than Ryder's but not as long; it's also tattooed like the rest of him. It has a snake wrapped around it, its tongue flicking out right at the head of his cock.

"Just your mouth," he rasps. I don't have to ask to know what he means.

I walk over and drop to my knees in front of him. I place my hands behind my back, and he guides his cock into my mouth. He holds it while I circle my tongue around the head, getting the drop of precum leaking from the slit. I slide further down, and his head hits the door with a thud, his grey eyes glittering and glued to my mouth. "Fuck, Baby girl," he groans.

I hear clothes rustle behind me, then Ryder drops to his knees, sliding his hands between my legs. "Let me take care of you while you take care of him," he whispers, and my heart soars. This is his way of accepting this. I widen my legs, and the first contact of his fingers on my clit causes me to moan against the head of Dex's cock. Dex's hands are fisted at his sides, pressed against the door.

Ryder sinks two fingers into my pussy, and his other hand runs to the back of my head. He applies pressure, pushing me further down Dex's cock until my nose is brushing Dex's pubic bone, just like I did to Ryder.

"Goddamn," Dex grunts, flexing his hips forward. "Good girl."

"Someone likes being called a good girl," Ryder chuckles. "She tightened up on my fingers."

Ryder lets my mouth slide back up Dex's cock. "I don't like it," I say when my mouth is free. "I love it."

Dex makes a choked sound and then feeds his cock back into my mouth. Ryder continues to thrust his fingers into my pussy, using the heel of his palm to grind against my clit, using his other hand to push me up and down Dex's cock.

"Fuck," Dex grits out. "Fuck." I can see the decision running across his face again. Then he knocks Ryder's hand away before sinking his own into my hair. He tightens his fist and starts fucking my mouth so hard his balls slap against my chin.

I can't believe he's actually touching me.

Ryder starts finger fucking my pussy harder with one hand and roughly pulling at my nipples. I can feel my orgasm build fast, and when it crests, it's sharp, almost painful. I scream, but no sound comes out, with Dex's cock buried in my throat. Dex pulls my mouth off his cock with my hair wrapped in his fist, letting me suck in air, saliva dripping down my chin.

"Fuck, you're beautiful," Dex says gruffly. He tips my head back with his hold on my hair and stares into my eyes.

"Yes, she is," Ryder agrees, sliding his fingers out of my pussy. I can feel my pussy tightening, trying to hold him inside. "Someone's being greedy," he chuckles.

"Someone, please fuck me," I beg, not ashamed of it.

"I want to watch you fuck her," Dex says harshly; the words sound like they are being pushed out of his throat.

Ryder helps me to my feet, and Dex leans in, sealing his lips over mine, sinking his tongue into my mouth. I moan and go to step forward, but Ryder locks his hands around my wrists, warning me not to touch Dex before stepping back.

I got so carried away with the kiss that I forgot the no touching rule.

Dex pulls back with the same wonder in his eyes that I'm sure I have. "Baby girl," he says softly before nodding his head to Ryder.

Ryder is sitting on the little couch in the office, legs spread wide, stroking his cock, just watching Dex and me. "Come here, *Il mio sole,*" he says, patting his thigh with a grin.

He turns me so that I'm facing the desk in front of the couch in reverse cowgirl with my feet braced beside his big thighs. He braces his hands on my hips while I reach between us, notching his cock at my entrance. I watch Dex step around to the front of the desk, leaning against the edge, stroking his cock. I brace my hands on Ryder's arms and sink onto his cock, letting his piercings drag slowly, savoring the feeling it causes.

"Shit," Ryder grits out, "You feel so good." I use my hold on

Ryder's arms as leverage to lift my hips. Dex's eyes are glued to where Ryder and I are connected, still slowly stroking his tattooed cock. "Show him what he's missing, *Il mio sole*," Ryder whispers. "Make him so fucking crazy he can't stand it."

His words make me start riding him faster. His hips start lifting, fucking me from the bottom every time I sink down. "Just like that, Les," Ryder groans. "Fuck." His fingers dig harder into my hips, and I can feel his muscles flex in his forearms from my grip.

My eyes are glued to Dex stroking his cock, his breathing harsh. I slide my hand between my spread thighs and start rubbing my clit, wishing it was Dex with Ryder pounding my pussy. "Dex," I moan, letting him know what I'm thinking. Ryder's grip gets tighter, taking over, thrusting so hard my tits are bouncing out of control, his thighs slapping mine. His thrusts are hitting that magic spot, and I can feel that pressure building like when I was with Holden, and I already know what's about to happen. "Please don't stop," I beg. "Oh fuck," I moan, and my whole body tenses up.

"Fuck, *Il mio sole*. Squeeze my cock," Ryder groans.

I lift up until his cock slips free, squirting all over the floor in front of us with a scream. "Ryder!"

Dex's eyes widen as his hand tightens on his cock; he groans deep in his throat, taking one step toward us.

Ryder runs his hand down my stomach and over my sensitive clit, making my hips jerk. "Do that shit again."

He starts hammering into me again while rubbing my clit. When I squirt this time, I can't even scream.

Dex takes another decisive step forward. "Stand up," he rasps. Ryder helps me to a standing position, steadying me on my jelly legs. "Turn around and put your hands on his thighs." I clench my thighs together at his order and turn around to do what he says. Ryder grins when I slide my hands up his thick thighs. I feel Dex step up behind me and tense in anticipation. He notches his thick cock at my entrance and thrusts in with one firm stroke, causing fire to rip through me at the invasion. "God, I missed this pussy."

Ryder reaches up, rolling my nipples between his fingers. "You like his cock, *Il mio sole*?"

"Yes," I moan, pushing back onto Dex.

"Fuck my cock, Baby girl," Dex groans. "Take what you need." I can feel his hands hovering around my hips, but he still won't touch me. Using Ryder's thighs as leverage, I slam my hips back, taking all of Dex's cock into my pussy again. "Good girl."

Fuck, I love that.

Sliding my hands off Ryder's thighs and onto the couch, I take Ryder's cock into my mouth, all the way to the back of my throat. "Fuck!" he shouts, running his fingers through my hair and moving it to one side. "You like both our cocks in you?"

I moan in answer, vibrating on Ryder's cock and tightening on Dex. "Fuck yeah, she does," Dex grits out, fucking me harder. The harder Dex slams into my pussy, the faster I suck Ryder's cock.

Ryder braces one hand on my hip, holding me in place for Dex to pound into me, and that just sends me up even higher. "I need to see her face," Dex grits out before pulling out.

Ryder flips me around to sit on his lap before hooking his hands behind my knees and spreading me wide for Dex. Dex leans down, braces one hand on the couch beside Ryder's head, and slams back into my pussy.

"Oh fuck," I moan, latching my hands onto Ryder's arms so that I don't accidentally touch Dex. Dex leans in to kiss me again, and it's like all my dreams have finally come true, as stupid as that sounds. But kissing Dex and being this close to him makes my heart swell. I want to run my hands all over his huge chest, so I dig my fingernails into Ryder's arm to stop the temptation.

"Fuck," Dex breathes. I could feel my release building again from just looking into his beautiful grey eyes. "Come on my cock like a good girl."

His words set me off, and my back bows against Ryder's chest. "Dex!"

"Squeeze my cock, Baby girl," he groans, slamming into me harder. I can feel him swell inside of me then he comes with a shout. He strokes in and out a few times before pulling out with a rush of cum; he pecks my lips before taking a step back.

Ryder lets my legs drop, slapping the side of my ass. "Hands and knees on the couch."

He helps me get positioned with my knees on the cushions, and my hands braced on the back before slamming into me; Dex's cum makes him slide in easily. He grabs my hips in a bruising grip, sets a relentless pace, and all I can do is hold on. "That was fucking hot, *Il mio sole,*" he pants out. "Watching you take his cock while he called you a good girl." He reaches down and rubs my clit. "Come with me."

My moans mixing with his groans make for a dirty soundtrack I would love to listen to on repeat. I love that all my guys are vocal during sex. It makes me feel good that I make them feel good too. He pinches my clit, and I shatter, taking him with me.

"*Il mio sole,*" he groans, holding himself still, emptying himself inside me. He smooths his hands up my back before kissing my spine. "You're amazing." He pulls out, and I can feel their cum leaking down my thighs, mixing together. "Let me take a picture of this beautiful pussy dripping our cum for Gage."

I giggle. "Go for it."

I hear Dex laugh, and I'm so relieved because that means he's okay with what just happened. Ryder digs his phone out of his jeans, snaps the picture, then turns it around where I can see. He has his middle finger against my ass in the picture just for Gage, making me laugh. "You dirty, dirty boys."

"You like us dirty," Ryder says, planting a firm kiss on my ass cheek. "Let's get you cleaned up." He rummages around until he finds some paper towels in the little kitchenette. He gently wipes between my thighs. "Sorry, *Il mio sole,*" he apologizes, kissing my ass cheeks. "I'll run you a bath when we get home."

I don't know how I ended up with five amazingly sweet men, but I'm not going to take it for granted anymore.

CHAPTER 31
LEO

I asked Gage where Alessa and the guys were, and the answer came in picture format ten minutes later. It's a perfect view of the backside of Alessa with her legs spread open, her swollen pussy dripping cum.

Fuck, that shouldn't be so hot.

"Well, I'll be damned," Gage chuckles from his position on the couch beside me. "That asshole is flipping us off," he laughs.

I snort. "Probably just you since you started this."

I look at Holden, who's out of his office, sitting on the loveseat in front of us with his eyes glued to his phone.

"You good, Holden?" I ask with a laugh.

"Huh?" He jerks his head up. "Yeah."

Gage and I exchange a look but don't comment, too afraid to run him off. It surprised us when he came out and asked where they were, and when we told him they were still gone, he stayed out here. Gage holds my eyes longer than necessary, rolling his teeth across his bottom lip, grinning when heat rushes my cheeks.

What happened at the cabin has run on repeat in my head. I was so fucking nervous at first, but Gage and Les made sure I enjoyed it, and I did. I never really thought about what it would be like to be with a man, so I didn't know what to expect. Once Gage kissed me the first time, I was done for. I couldn't wait for him to touch me again after what happened in my room. He and Les working together at the cabin almost made my head explode, and I wanted more.

Les is cool with it, even encouraging me to explore with Gage because that's what I want. It makes me fall in love with her even more. There isn't anything that girl can do wrong in my eyes anymore. I'm not even shocked she pulled the trigger in Xander's garage, and I'm sure Xander is now dead also, but I now understand she has to do it to survive.

Ryder and I are finally on our way to working things out, and I will make the same decision again. I didn't hesitate to save him because he was important to Alessa. The fact that Ryder talked to me in the car on the way home instead of fucking with me about my freak-out gave him points in his favor. He's still a dick, but I'm coming to terms with the fact that it's just his personality.

I won't lie and say I don't miss having Alessa all to myself, but she's so fucking *happy* that I would never dream of taking that from her.

The garage door to the house opens, and their voices filter through the house. Ryder and Dex stroll into the living room, sitting in the chairs.

"Where's Les?" Holden asks with a hopeful look on his face.

Ryder smiles softly at him, the same look he gives Les. "Taking a shower."

Gage snorts. "I wonder why?"

Ryder shrugs. "It wasn't only my fault."

"You?" Gage asks, his head swinging to Dex. Dex raises an eyebrow but doesn't answer. "Holy shit! It's about fucking time."

Dex shrugs his massive shoulders, refusing to answer, but I don't miss that look on his face, the look you get when you finally sink into Alessa.

"Where's the kid from the garage?" Ryder asks, stretching his legs out in front of him.

"Gerald's. The kid was fucked out of his mind. He's going to come down hard," Gage answers. "Where's Xander?"

"Dead," Ryder says simply. "I'll call Doc and see if he can help clean the kid up."

"He's Zane's fucking rat. You think that's a good idea?" Gage asks, sitting up on the couch.

"What are we going to do? Kill him?" Ryder points out. "Les smashed his phone, and he doesn't have contact with that motherfucker right now."

"Didn't Zane warn us to get out of there?" I ask, looking between them.

Ryder's eyes harden. "Yeah. Seemed a little suspicious they were a lot closer than what he said, though."

"Zane wouldn't throw Les under a bus," Gage says. "No matter how much I hate that asshole, you know I'm right."

"Les? No. Us?" Dex adds, "In a fucking heartbeat."

I still don't know the whole story and feel like now isn't the time to ask.

"When I get Playboy's real name, I'll run some checks on him," Holden says quietly. "Maybe if we pay him more than Zane for information, we can flip him."

"Hm," Ryder grunts. "That's a good idea."

Holden smiles and blushes. "Les would have thought of it too."

"Give yourself some credit, man," Ryder says gently. "The shit you do is badass."

"Fuck yeah," Gage says excitedly. "Les asks for information, and it's there before we can blink."

"I definitely couldn't do it," I add, sensing that Holden doesn't think highly of himself. "I don't know how you do it."

Holden chuckles. "It's not that cool."

"Yes," Ryder says, a little more determined. "It is."

Holden looks at Ryder, and it's like his eyes get captured by something. I look at Ryder, and he's giving him the same look. I look at Gage at the same time he looks at me, then we both look between them and back at each other.

"What the fuck?" Gage mouths. Relieved I'm not the only one that sees, I just shrug because I'm just as confused. Do Ryder and Holden have a thing? Or the beginning of one?

Alessa walks into the living room in an oversized shirt that I'm sure she stole from one of us because that's her new thing. Not that any of us mind seeing her in our clothes. She has her phone in her hand on speakerphone while it rings. She sits on the loveseat beside Holden, snuggling into his side with her legs tucked under her. I swear I see all the tension leave his shoulders when he wraps an arm around her.

"Hello, *Moye sokrovishche,*" the person on the other end answers in a faint Russian accent, one I remember from the games. I swear I hear Ryder and Dex both growl at the greeting.

"Hey, Alexey," she says with a roll of her eyes. "This is a business call. Where's Dmitri?"

Do they have phone calls that aren't business related? They both seem familiar with her in the way they hang on her.

"Yeah. You're on speaker."

"There is no easy way to say this," Alessa sighs. "But your dad is making a move against me."

"What?!" they both shout at the same time.

"What do you mean?" I'm guessing this voice is Dmitri. They sound very similar, but his voice isn't as deep as Alexey's.

"He's gained a new interest in blow and the Vipers."

"What does he want with street vermin like Xander's crew?" Alexey asks.

"It's not Xander's crew anymore," Alessa says casually. "They were doing the selling."

"Father knows blow is your business. Are you sure?" Dmitri asks. I don't think he's asking because he doesn't believe her. This is their friendship on the line, one I think they aren't supposed to have.

"I'm sure. Spinner is the middleman." She runs her fingers through her wet hair. "You know what this means."

"Fuck," Alexey mutters. "I don't want this, *Moye sokrovishche.*"

Whatever he just called her again makes her eyes sad. "I don't either, but I can't let this slide." She pinches the bridge of her nose. "I won't ask you to go against your father, and I also don't want to see you guys hurt."

"Don't worry about us," Dmitri says, whispering something in the background. "We actually would like to speak with you about something else."

Ryder and Alessa exchange a look. "About?" she asks.

"Not on the phone. Meet us at the gala?" Alexey answers.

"I can do that," Alessa replies then they say their goodbyes.

"What could they possibly need to talk to you about?" Ryder asks, sitting forward in the chair.

Alessa shrugs. "I don't know. I guess we'll find out at the gala."

"Anyone else get the feeling they already knew?" Gage asks.

Alessa laughs. "No. That's your jealousy talking."

"I'm not jealous of them," Gage snorts. "Much."

"What did he call you?" I ask because I need to know.

"My treasure," Ryder growls, answering my question. "He's going to lose his tongue for that shit."

"Are you jealous, Ryder?" Alessa purrs.

"I don't fucking like it," Holden speaks up, and every head turns to him.

"What?" Alessa squeaks, shocked.

"I don't like anyone but us calling you names," Holden answers, pulling her closer.

She grins and kisses his cheek. "I will let him know to cut it out, okay?" He nods and kisses the top of her head.

I see Ryder trying to fight a grin, but he loses the battle and starts laughing. "That's my boy."

Holden turns a deep shade of red. "It's not funny."

"I'm not making fun of you." Ryder tries to smother the laugh but fails. "I never pegged you for the possessive type."

"Les is ours," Holden says hotly, surprising us even more. "You shouldn't like it either."

"Trust me, we don't," Gage agrees.

Alessa turns to face him. "I'm yours, huh?"

"Yes," he says without a moment's hesitation.

I shrug. "I'm with Holden on this one."

"Face it, Baby girl. You're stuck with us."

"I kind of like the sound of that," she answers. She pecks Holden on the lips. "You're mine too."

"Damn right, Bright eyes."

"Leo," a sweet voice sing-songs the next morning. I would know that voice anywhere. I snuggle further into the pillow so the dream won't go away. The sweet voice giggles. "Leo."

Soft hands run up my back, and I realize it's not a dream. I crack one eye open, and Alessa is sitting beside me in my bed on her knees. "Hey, Baby," I greet, my voice still rough with sleep.

"You want to go with me to Gerald and Boone's this morning?" she asks, still running her hands up and down my back and then kneading my shoulders.

I shake my head. "You keep doing that," I joke.

She throws her leg over my waist and sits on my ass. She starts working the stiff muscles in my back, and I can't stop the groan. It feels so damn good.

"Ya like?" she asks, working deeper into a stubborn kink in my shoulder.

"Fuck yes."

She runs her hands all over my back and shoulders, massaging and kneading the sore muscles. It doesn't take long until I sink further into the mattress, limp as a noodle. She stretches out on my back, crossing her arms under her chin on my shoulder blades. "How are you doing, Leo?" she asks, and I know she doesn't mean from the massage.

"I'm fine, Baby."

"A lot has happened. It's okay if you aren't."

"Baby," I say and roll so she slides off my back and I can look into her eyes. "I'm fine. I promise."

"Okay," she says softly, pecking my lips. "Did you want to go with me?"

"Of course." I would take any chance to spend time with her.

Her smile lights up her face. "Good. I'll let you get ready, and I'll be downstairs." She pecks my lips again before sliding off the bed and slipping from the room.

As much as I want to lay around with her for a while, I know she's busy. With that thought in mind, I finally drag my ass out of bed and head to the shower.

I step under the spray and process everything that's been going on. I've come to terms with the person she is; to be honest, she's still the woman I met that first night, just a little rougher around the edges.

I took my first life and handled it okay; I don't know if that's a good thing. My only consolation is that I did it to save Ryder, but something tells me there would be many more if I continue on this path with them.

Things have changed between Gage and me but in a good way. I don't know what exactly he wants from this, and I don't want to ask him because I'm not sure either. What if something happens between him and me, like we just don't work out, and I'm still with Alessa or vice versa? What kind of disaster would that cause? I like Gage, and I know it went way beyond simple attraction after yesterday. I don't want to think about anything going wrong between Alessa and me. The thought sends a sense of despair through me so deep that I can feel my lungs seize up. There's no doubt that I'll never let that girl go. Gage, either.

Another thing plaguing my mind is that I'm not sure what my job is here. I worked hard for what I had in North Carolina, and my brothers consulted me with their businesses, but I need *something* that's mine. I refuse to make my brothers or Alessa think I'm living off of them. It's something I need to bring up with both of them. I can't stay cooped up in the house all day, waiting for one of them to take me somewhere. Maybe I can talk to her about it today.

I quickly finish my shower, brush my teeth, and dry myself off. Wrapping the towel around my waist, I walk back into my bedroom to find something to wear, but I'm not alone.

Gage looks up from his position sitting on the side of my bed, letting his eyes slowly follow a water drop sliding down my chest and disappearing into my towel. I clear my throat, and his head jerks up. Instead of being ashamed for getting caught staring, he just grins.

Fuck, he's sexy. He shows off straight white teeth and deep dimples when he grins, giving him an almost boyish appearance with his mess of wavy hair. Gage is all man, though.

He stands up from the bed and slowly walks toward me. "I wanted to talk to you about yesterday."

Something about the way he says that makes dread settle in my chest. "What about it?"

He looks over my shoulder, refusing to look me in the eye. Does he already regret it? He seemed fine last night. What changed? Determination is written all over his features when he looks back at me. "That wasn't a one-time thing," he says finally.

"Okay," I say slowly, hoping he will elaborate.

He runs his fingers through his hair, making it stick up even more. "Yesterday and the cabin between you and me. That wasn't a one-time thing." He steps closer until he's standing right in front of me. "Truth be told, Baby, I'm fucking addicted."

His admission sucks all the air from my lungs. I know this is what I wanted to know, but I don't know how to process it now that it's out there. When he calls me baby, it does something to my insides, and I don't think he uses that term loosely. He advances, walking me backward until my back hits the closed bathroom door. It's what he did the first time we kissed, but it isn't meant to be threatening this time.

"I'm not just talking about the sex either." He swallows, and I realize he's actually uncomfortable admitting this. Something I didn't think Gage could get. "I want to be all in with you if that's what you want too."

I search his eyes for the truth, and it's staring right back at me. Gage wants a relationship with me beyond what we already have.

"I want that too," I surprise myself by saying, but it feels right. "I've never dated a guy before, though." I don't know why I'm explaining that to him; he already knows.

He laughs. "That makes two of us."

One of my eyebrows shoots up. "Never?"

He shakes his head and runs his knuckles down my cheek. "I've never wanted a relationship until Les and you."

"You've never been in a relationship with anyone?"

He shakes his head again. "Nope. I was fine on my own, just playing around until Les was ready, and then you came along."

"You've waited on Alessa?"

He shrugs and actually looks embarrassed. "Yeah. Nothing mattered but her. Now I have you."

Holy shit. This changes a lot, but it doesn't change how I feel. "I want you too. I'm all in too."

He gives me that smile that's all Gage again and hooks his hand on the nape of my neck, jerking me to him. There is only about an inch in height difference, but he feels way bigger when he takes control of me like this. I don't want to admit how much I like that. He gives me a kiss that is so tender that I'm not sure what to do with the torrent of emotions running through me. He pulls back all too soon, laying a peck on my lips and stepping back.

"Les is waiting for you. I just needed you to know that."

I nod because I can't get my voice past the lump in my throat. He smiles again and walks from the room, leaving me staring after him.

Shaking my head from my stupor, I slide on a pair of jeans and a regular t-shirt. I don't think a trip to Gerald and Boone's calls for anything else.

Jogging down the stairs, I follow the sound of Alessa laughing into the living room. Ryder has her pinned down on the couch, lying between her thighs, and her hands pinned above her head; it looks like they are in some kind of stand-off. Weird that not even a day ago, that sight would have pissed me off, but it just makes me shake my head with a laugh.

"Apologize," he growls into her face, making her laugh even harder.

"Not a chance in hell," she replies.

"What did you do, Baby?" I ask, leaning against the doorway leading into the living room.

She bites her lip to stop laughing but loses the battle, laughing right in Ryder's face.

"She thought it was a good idea to stick the handle of a spoon right up my fucking ass," Ryder answers, not looking at me.

I choke on a laugh. "I guess you didn't like it?"

Ryder whips his head around. "Not from a wooden fucking spoon." Does that mean Ryder likes things up his ass? No way in hell am I asking that, though.

"Aw. Poor baby," Alessa says with a fake pout. "Can't even take a little spoon. Wait until you get a look at Holden's cock," she says, waggling her eyebrows.

He slowly looks back at her. "What do you know about that?"

She snorts. "Like I don't see what's going on between you guys."

He sits back on his heels, pulling her into a sitting position. "Nothing's going on," he says, and I can sense the but coming. "Not yet, anyway."

She wraps her arms around his neck, sensing his discomfort. "It's okay if it does, Ryder." She pecks his lips and then slides off the couch. "Just ask Leo how good it feels."

With that parting shot, she takes off from the living room laughing the whole way.

I know my face is beet red when Ryder looks up at me, and he barks a laugh. "You don't have to say shit. Your face says it all."

I flip him the middle finger, backing out of the living room. "Fuck you." I turn on my heel and go in search of Alessa.

"That's Gage's job!" Ryder yells, roaring with laughter.

Asshole.

I find her putting on her shoes and pin her with a stare. "What the fuck was that?"

She giggles and gives me the most innocent look she can muster. It's not much since I know Alessa is anything but innocent. "I have no idea what you're talking about." She smiles sweetly and jerks the garage door open.

I jam my feet in my tennis shoes and follow her. "You're full of shit today," I say with a laugh.

"I'm happy; what can I say," she says, and when she smiles this time, it's a genuine smile making her blue eyes twinkle.

I wrap my arms around her waist, kissing her upturned lips. "I'm glad, Baby."

She slides her arms around my neck. "Are you happy?"

"The happiest I've ever been," I tell her truthfully. No matter what happens, I am truly happy.

"Good." She pecks my lips. "Which car do you want to take?"

I look around the garage and immediately spot which one. "That one," I say, pointing to her black Ferrari.

"How did I know you would pick that one?" She laughs, stepping back and pulling the key fob from the line of keys on the wall.

We climb into the car, and I sigh when my butt hits the soft leather seats. "This car makes my dick hard."

She snorts a laugh, smoothly backing out of the garage. "It doesn't have anything to do with the driver?" she quips, shifting into first and heading toward the back gate.

I slide my hand over her bare thigh right below the fringe on her short shorts. "Everything to do with the driver," I say, squeezing her thigh. I can't get enough of touching her, feeling her soft skin.

She pulls out onto the main road before glancing over at me. "Are you flirting with me, Leo?"

"What if I am?" I ask, sliding my fingers up until they brush under her shorts. I'm not joking about my dick being hard. Something about her behind the wheel of this car has me hard as steel.

"Leo," she warns, but it comes out as a moan when I slide my fingers higher, brushing against her panties.

"I want to bend you over the hood of this car and fuck you so hard you forget your name."

This time she does moan, and I can feel her thigh flex when she shifts gears and sets her foot on the gas. The road that connects to the back gate is a deserted back road that you can take into the more rural areas or go towards the highway. I have no idea where we're going, but she seems content to drive this way since it's a straight stretch, and she can push the car how she wants. I get an idea and can't shake it, no matter how dangerous it is.

"How well can you handle this car?"

She shoots me a look. "Damn good. Why?"

I slide my hand out from under her shorts and reach up, flicking the button open, letting her know precisely what I'm doing. Her hand tightens on the wheel, but she doesn't stop me. I'm feeling bold, and she's looking good enough to eat. I jerk the zipper down and get a peek at the light-yellow lace at the top of her panties. *Damn.* They look sexy as hell pressed against her tan skin. I reach over and undo my own jeans, pulling them and my boxers down until my cock springs free.

"What are you doing?"

I don't answer. I reach over, slide my left hand into her panties, circling her clit, wrap my other hand around my cock, and start stroking slowly. She's looking between the road and my hand stroking. I start circling her clit at the same tempo that I'm stroking my cock.

"Fuck, Leo," she whispers while changing gears. I look at the speedometer, and she's going almost eighty miles per hour. I've never been much of an adrenaline junky, but being around all of them has made me one.

I circle her clit faster, and I can tell she's trying to control the rhythm of her hips.

Ninety miles per hour.

I dip my fingers down into her pussy at the same time she changes gears again, laying her foot harder on the gas.

One hundred and ten miles per hour.

"Fuck you're wet, Baby," I groan, stroking my cock harder. I slide my fingers back up to her clit and add more pressure.

"Leo," she moans, both hands on the steering wheel, her knuckles white from her death grip.

One hundred and thirty miles per hour.

I start circling and stroking faster, our breaths harsh inside the car. She slams on the brake and the clutch so hard I have to stop myself from slamming forward with my hand on the dashboard. She jerks the car to a wide spot beside the road and sets the emergency brake. "Out," she says before she slides out of the car.

Hell fucking yeah.

I push my door open and meet her at the car's hood with a crash of lips. "Fuck me like you said," she begs against my lips.

"Hands on the hood," I demand, my voice rough. I'm so turned on that it's almost painful.

She shimmies her shorts until they land around her ankles and turns around, bracing her hands on the hood. I don't want to expose her entirely just in case a car drives by, so I slide those pretty panties to the side and line my cock up with her pussy.

I brace my hands on the hood beside hers and slam my hips forward, sinking inside her.

"Shit," she moans, pushing back against me. "Fuck me, Leo," she encourages.

I leave one hand on the hood and wrap the other around her waist. I pull out, then slam back again, holding tight to her so she feels every inch going in.

She pushes against me again, begging for me, and something inside me snaps. I lock my arm tighter and start hammering into her so hard I grunt with each thrust.

"Yes," she moans, throwing her head back.

I move my hand from the hood and wrap it around her slim throat, pulling until her back is bowed, and feel her pussy clamp down on me. Using the anchor I have on her waist, I unleash on her. Fucking her ruthlessly, my thighs slapping against hers, sweat already beading on my temples, making mewling noises leave her mouth. I know this will end fast because of how hard I'm fucking her and how keyed up I am.

"You like when I fuck you like this?" I ask, never slowing my pounding.

"God, yes," she moans, pushing back against each thrust.

I can feel how much wetter she's getting and realize she likes how I'm manhandling her.

"Tell me how much you like my cock, Baby," I demand, and have no idea where this is coming from. I just *need* to hear her say it.

"I love your cock," she moans again, and I can feel it vibrate against my hand on her throat. "So fucking much."

"Who's fucking you?"

"Leo," she gasps when I slam into her harder, making her hands slide up the hood. I feel her pussy clench around me and know she's close.

"Come on my cock, Baby," I groan when she tightens up even more. "Let me feel it."

Alessa's pussy is one of the sweetest things I've ever felt. She's tight, wet, and so fucking responsive. Her body takes what it wants, and right now, it wants me.

Her body tightens up, and then she explodes with a scream, "Leo!"

I pull out her pulsating pussy, stroking my cock hard and fast. I grab her hair, pulling her to stand. "On your knees," I grit out.

She spins and drops to her knees, mouth open, ready for my cock. I don't waste any time sinking into her mouth straight to the back. She locks eyes with me, and I let go with a long groan coming down her throat. She greedily swallows around the head, causing more to rush out of me, making my whole body shudder. "Goddamn, Baby," I groan, still looking into those crystal blue eyes. She milks my cock of everything before pulling back, letting my dick pop free, a wide smile on her face.

I pull her to her feet, sealing my lips over hers. Tasting my cum on her tongue makes me ready to go again. I kiss her until we're both breathless before pulling back and laying my forehead on hers. "I love you."

Her eyes snap to mine, and I realize what I just said. I'm about to take it back when she rubs her hands down my cheeks. "I love you too," she whispers, and I could weep with joy.

I slant my mouth over hers, floating on fucking nine. I pull back before I really want to, but I can feel my cock getting hard again, and I know she has stuff to do. I tuck myself into my pants before bending down, helping her back into her shorts.

I peck her lips once more before giving her a sound slap on that delicious ass. "Let's go, Baby."

CHAPTER 32
ALESSA

I pull through Gerald and Boone's gate and park in front of the house. Lucas and Landon come bounding out, already eyeballing the car.

"Holy shit," Lucas says when Leo and I step out. His eyes are glued to the car, and I can't help but laugh. "Can I look inside?"

I shrug and sweep my arm out. "Be my guest."

They both whoop before sliding into the car. I shake my head with a smile and look up at Gerald coming out of the house. He loops down the steps and jerks me into a bear hug. "Hey, Lessie."

"Hey, G," I reply, returning his hug.

He pulls back and looks over my shoulder. "I don't think I was properly introduced last night," he says, talking to Leo.

I step back and turn to the side. "G, this is Leo."

"Nice to meet you," Leo says, sticking his hand out for him to shake.

Gerald gives it a hearty shake. "You too." He drops Leo's hand and slings an arm around my shoulders, leading us into the house. "Mind your manners in that car!" he yells at Lucas and Landon.

"Yes, sir!" they yell back in unison, and I can't suppress the smile. They look so much happier since they've been with these guys.

"How's that going?" I ask when we step into the door, kicking our shoes off.

"Like I told you, they're good kids," he replies, leading us to the living room, where Boone gives me the same bear hug before ushering us to sit on the loveseat.

"What about Playboy?" I ask, tucking myself under Leo's arm on the back of the couch; he lets it drop and pulls me closer. G and Boone exchange a quick look over the action.

"He's doing better now. Doc came over and gave him something to help with withdrawals," Boone answers leaning back on the couch. "You going to tell us who he is?"

"All I know is his street name is Playboy, and he's a confidential informant," I tell them and brace myself for what I have to say next. "For Zane."

Boone sits up again, fast. "Zeus's boy Zane?"

Leo tightens his arm in support. "Yeah. I couldn't let him go back to Zane and tell him what he saw at Xander's garage last night."

"Gage told us what happened. He just failed to mention how the fuck he came across Playboy," Gerald says, leveling me with a look that says he isn't happy.

I shrug. "I did what I had to do, G."

He sighs and sits back. "I know, Lessie, but fucking Zane?"

I nod. "I know it's not ideal, but I was hoping to talk to him, maybe flip him to our side."

"You can try," Boone says, "But he's not really with it. Why don't we chat outside until he wakes up?" he finishes, and I don't miss his hidden meaning. He wants to talk to me alone, and I feel like I'm in trouble with my dad.

I look at Leo, and he smiles. "I'll be fine."

I squeeze his thigh before standing up and following Boone through the back of the house. He pulls open the backdoor, holding it for me to walk outside. I love this part of the house. It's surrounded by flowers and has a man-made pond in the middle that Gerald did himself. I sit on the bench beside the pond and watch the coy fish swim around.

Boone slides onto the bench beside me. "Please don't tell me you're thinking about getting back with Zane."

Gerald and Boone found out about my secret relationship with Zane when it was almost over. My dad sent them to find me one night when I didn't answer my phone, and they caught me leaving Zane's apartment. They said they had their suspicions anyway, so they took a shot looking for me there.

"I'm not," I tell him. "I have enough guys in my life."

"That young man in there?" he asks, putting the connection together before I have to say anything.

I breathe a laugh. "One of them."

I can see his head jerk toward me from the corner of my eye. "Come again?"

"He's one of them," I answer and turn toward him, unashamed of where my love life has taken me. "With Ryder, Gage, Dex, and Holden"

His eyes widen. "Damn. I saw you and Ryder happening a mile away, maybe even Gage. But I didn't see this coming."

"I didn't either," I tell him honestly, "but I'm glad it did."

"You deserve to be happy, Lessie. It's what your dad would have wanted," Boone says, causing tears to spring into my eyes at the mention of my dad. He wraps his arm around my shoulders, pulling me into his side.

"I miss him," I whisper.

"I do too. He would be proud of you."

I let out a watery laugh. "Even after I cause a war with Viktor Orlov?"

I filled Gerald and Boone in on what's happening so they're alert for anything.

"Especially then. Your dad would be proud of you no matter what."

Even if he found out I'm a serial killer? "I know."

"You make sure those boys know that if they treat you with anything less than the respect you deserve, I will castrate every single one of them."

I let out a laugh, the tension leaving my body at that threat. "You might have to beat Micah to it, but I'll let them know."

He chuckles, pulling me closer. Gerald and Boone were like surrogate fathers to me when my dad passed away, and there's nothing in this world they wouldn't do for me or I wouldn't do for them. They have been in a relationship longer than I've been alive, and it is indeed one of the greatest love stories I've ever heard. It still breaks my heart that they had to hide it for so long because of how judgmental the Mafia world actually is, and they didn't want to do anything to embarrass my dad. Which it wouldn't have, ever.

We sit there and watch the fish swim around until Gerald pokes his head out of the door, telling us Playboy is awake. I follow him into the house to the back bedroom downstairs. Gerald pushes the door open, and as soon as Playboy's eyes land on me, he shrinks back into the bed.

"I'm not here to hurt you," I tell him softly and sit down on the edge of the bed.

"Wh...why are you here?" he asks.

"I need to ask you a few questions."

Gerald shuts the door and leans back against it with his arms crossed over his chest. "And you will answer them," he warns. Playboy nods like a bobble head making his hair flop over his eyes.

"What's your real name?" I need to get his real information so Holden can look him up.

"Jeffrey," he swallows, "Jeffrey Barnes."

"How old are you?"

"Nineteen."

I finally look him hard in the eye, letting him know I'm not playing games. "What do you do for Zane?" He swallows again, and I can see him shutting down. "You have to know what would happen to you if anyone from that strip found out you were a rat. Right?" He nods. "Then tell me what I want to know."

"I just give him tips on big movements."

"And he pays you?" I know how that works, but does Zane know he's paying for this kid's drug addiction?

"Yeah."

"What do you do for Xander?"

"I just deal for him."

"Are your tips to Zane just about Xander, or do you just run around snitching on everyone?"

"I'm not a fucking snitch!" he yells, jumping up from the bed and rounding behind me. I stand up to keep him in my line of sight. Not that I'm scared of him, but he's unpredictable if he's withdrawing from drugs.

"I suggest you keep your fucking voice down," Gerald growls, stepping away from the door.

I raise my hand, so he doesn't come closer and scare Playboy anymore. "Does Zane know you're using?"

He deflates, all the fight leaving him at once. He shakes his head. "He's suspected. He sent me to rehab, and I promised to stay clean so he would still pay me. This last tip was the first one he's asked for since he figured out I slipped."

I frown. "Zane sent you to rehab?"

He nods. "Z-Mack is my boy. I fucked up."

Why the hell does Zane care enough about some street kid to send him to rehab? I guess the same reason I do. My heart is bigger than my fucking brain.

I straighten my spine and rid myself of thoughts of Zane being a decent human. "You have two options here, Playboy. You work for me, feeding me information, or I turn you out and tell everyone on Concrete Row that you're an informant."

I threaten it, but I'll never do it. This kid would be shot on the spot and doesn't deserve that.

His eyes widen. "What about Z-Mack?"

I roll my eyes at the nickname. "I'll handle Z-Mack. What's your choice?"

"I'll work for you. I don't want to die."

I nod, walking to the door. "I'll get you into rehab first."

"No!" he yells, making me turn back around. "Please don't send me back there."

"You can't work for me while you're doping," I tell him. It's my number one rule. Several of my guys have been killed because they were high and didn't react to a bad situation fast enough.

"I'll get clean by myself. Please! Don't send me back."

I look at Gerald and see him softening toward the kid. "He can stay here," he tells me with a shrug.

I turn back to Playboy. "I want you clean. I want you to treat G and Boone with respect. If I catch even a hint you're using again, I'll come back as the person you saw yesterday." He nods comically again, remembering what I did in Xander's garage. I pat Gerald on the chest. "Congratulations, it's a boy."

He laughs, leading me back out of the room. "We went from no kids to three in a short time, Lessie."

"You sure you don't care, G? I can find somewhere else for them to go."

He shakes his head. "Nah. Boone likes having the twins around, and Playboy will come around."

"Just Boone likes having them around?" I tease. I saw the respect they gave Gerald.

"Okay. So, it's nice having them here."

"Yo! That car is sick!" Landon says as soon as I walk into the living room. Leo is sitting on the loveseat where I left him, giving me a soft smile when I walk in. Heat flashes through me before I can stop it, remembering him fucking me on the hood of my car. I don't know what came over him, but I'll take it over and over again as long as he offered.

"Thanks," I tell Landon with a laugh, sitting beside Leo. He pulls me right back under his arm.

"Those cars are hella fast. Like no fucking joke," Lucas says, fist-bumping his twin.

"Language," Boone warns, walking into the living room, and I can't stop the giggle that escapes. Boone has the mouth of a sailor, and he's fussing at the twins for cussing? He gives me a fake glare. "Something funny, Lessie?"

"Nope," I answer, popping the 'P'. "Nothing fucking funny at all," I say because I can't help myself.

Lucas and Landon crack up while Boone narrows his eyes at me. "Still a smartass, I see."

"I learned from the best," I say with a grin. I was raised primarily around men, and every single one of them was smart-asses.

"What did you do to get that car? Because I need to know *all* the secrets to have one of those bad motherfuc..." Lucas trails off, shooting a look at Boone. "Mofos in my driveway." It spoke to the level of respect they already have for G and Boone that he would listen to the language warning.

"I can't give my secrets away," I say and nudge Leo with my elbow. "Can I?"

Leo shakes his head. "If she told you, she would have to kill you."

Landon's mouth drops open. "For real?" I shrug as an answer, enjoying messing with them. "Damn."

"Are you Mafia or something?" Lucas asks with a laugh, fist-bumping his twin again.

Leo hides a laugh with a cough, and I hear Boone and G chuckle. If they only knew how right they are.

"You are, aren't you?" Landon says, taking in the faces in the room. "That's so freaking cool!"

"Did you see the guys she had with her? Man, they screamed Mafia," Lucas says, agreeing with Landon.

"What exactly screams Mafia?" Leo asks with a laugh.

"The guys she had with her. Duh," Lucas laughs and then focuses on Leo. "Wait! You were there!"

Landon starts bouncing on the couch, animated. It's like looking at Gage. "I bet the big dude's the leader. Did you see his freaking arms?"

"Nah!" Lucas disagrees. "It's the one who walked up behind us."

Leo and I exchange a look; I have to try so hard not to start laughing.

"You don't know how wrong you are," Gerald says with a chuckle.

"Alright, G," I say, standing up and pulling Leo to his feet. "We have to head out. If you need anything, call."

"Oh, come on," Lucas whines. "You can't leave us hanging like that."

I shake my head and walk toward the front door with them hot on my heels. I slide my feet into my shoes and then give my hugs to Gerald and Boone.

"See ya, Boss," Boone says with a grin, shutting the door behind us.

"No way!" I hear one of the boys exclaim. "She's the boss! That's so fucking cool."

"You hear that, Baby?" Leo says with a laugh, slinging his arm around my shoulder. "You're cool."

WHEN LEO and I return to the house, Gage, Holden, Dex, and Ryder are sitting in the living room with grim faces.

"What's going on?" I ask, sitting beside Gage on the couch, Leo on my other side. He pulls me to his side, kissing me on the forehead.

"We have problems," Ryder says, slamming a folder down on the coffee table.

I pick up the folder and flip it open, and a feeling of doom settles over me.

It's pictures of everything we've done over the past few days. Every shot of the guys has their faces scratched out. I flip through them, and that doom feeling intensifies. There's a picture of Leo pulling the trigger on that guy yesterday, me meeting Zane at the docks, a shot of us walking into Xander's garage and us leaving in Xander's car, one of me pulling the trigger ending Xander's life, and then Leo, Gage, and I at the cabin. Leo's forehead is against mine, Gage's head is thrown back in pure ecstasy, and you can see the bliss all over my face. If it weren't so creepy someone else took these without my permission, they would be hot.

The last one is of just me, and it looks like I am looking directly at the camera, the word 'mine' scrawled across it in red.

"How the fuck did they get these, and how did you get them?" I ask, handing it to Leo. Some of the pictures look like they're close-ups, and others looked like they were taken with a long-distance lens. The one of Leo pulling the trigger looks like it's taken off a street camera.

"I ran to the store to grab a few things," Gage says. "They were plastered all over my car when I came outside."

"I ran every camera I could find from where Dex found his and now Gage. Everything's been wiped. I'm trying to track it now, but I can't find anything," Holden says, running his hand through his curly hair nervously. Holden will take this personally if he can't find out who is doing this.

A pale-looking Leo lays the folder down, and Ryder picks it back up. Ryder pulls out the last picture and lays it on the table. "This is serious now. Do you get it? Whoever this is, is claiming you." He stabs his finger at the picture with 'mine' written on it. "They think you're theirs."

"I never said it wasn't serious," I reply. Maybe I didn't take it as seriously as I should have, but I understood. "My life can't stop because of this, though."

"Goddamnit, Les," Dex says hotly. "Two of those pictures implicate you and Leo in two different murders."

"I'm aware," I say evenly. "What do you expect me to do?"

"How about not going alone to meet fucking Zane?" Ryder says through gritted teeth, tossing the picture of Zane and me on the table. I notice that Zane's face isn't scratched out; it's just my guys.

"I already got shit for that, Ryder," I tell him, sitting up on the couch. "I promised I wouldn't."

"No more going out without at least two of us," Ryder orders, and I can feel my blood boil. "No more little fucking trips to your cabin or anywhere else this freak knows about."

I raise an eyebrow. "You remember who you're talking to right now?"

"Yes. A stubborn ass woman who thinks she's untouchable," Ryder says, standing up from the loveseat so fast it causes Holden's eyes to widen. "*My* woman that I won't let someone get their fucking hands on because she doesn't want to listen to us."

"I'm not *yours* to tell what to do, Ryder," I reply, standing up. No way I'll sit here and let him tower over me, even if he's on the other side of the coffee table. "I can take care of my damn self."

"You don't even know when you're being followed!" Ryder yells.

I snatch the pictures from the table and toss them at his chest. "Neither do you," I hiss. They hit his chest and flutter to the floor; when they settle, the one on top is the one with one word. Mine. Ryder and I stand there in a staring stand-off, both breathing heavily.

"Okay," Dex says, standing up from his chair. "Let's talk about this calmly."

"Fuck that," I tell Dex, pissed the hell off. I jab my finger at Ryder. "We might be involved now, but I'm still the fucking boss."

"You might be my boss on the streets, *Il mio sole*, but in here, you aren't," Ryder grits out. "My number one job is to fucking protect you. Let me do that. Let *us* do that."

"He's right, Pretty girl," Gage says quietly.

"It's just some pictures!" I say and throw my hands in the air. Do they think this freak will jump out of them and grab me?

"Very personal pictures, Baby," Leo adds, and I whirl on him. He gives an apologetic shrug. "I agree with Ryder." I look around the room, and all the guys are nodding, agreeing with him also.

Fuck this. I don't need them dictating what I do.

I storm from the room and make it just past the kitchen when one of them grabs my arm, spinning me around. I come face to chest with Ryder. I look up, and his eyes are entirely black, showing how pissed off he is. Good. Because I'm fucking pissed too. I jerk my arm away, and his lips peel back from his teeth.

"You don't get to walk away this time," he snarls, stepping into my space. "I let you after your little tantrum about Leo, but this is bigger. This is about your fucking safety."

"My little tantrum?" I ask, my voice calm. I'm anything but calm. "You could have gotten him killed."

"I didn't. Any one of us could die the moment we step out those doors."

"Exactly! I'm not hiding in this house like some precious princess!" My voice is rising again, and I can't seem to keep a lid on my temper.

"No one said you had to hide," Ryder says, stepping up close. I take a step back. He advances until my back hits the wall beside the stairs. He presses closer until his body is pressed against mine, and I have to look up at him. "You would know if you shut your damn mouth and open your ears."

That's it.

I let my body deflate like I'm giving up the fight. As soon as I see him relax, pushing me further into the wall, I make my move.

I run my hands up his chest and shove him away, using the wall as a support. He stumbles back, and I sweep my leg behind him, knocking him off his feet. He hits the floor hard, and I'm on him. I wrap my hand around his throat, applying pressure while sitting on his stomach. I see the guys running from the living room after hearing Ryder hit the floor but don't even spare them a glance.

"You don't talk to me like that," I grit out.

His eyes glitter with defiance, and I know he's fighting a war within himself. He can buck me off at any time, and he hasn't made a move. He narrows his eyes. "I wouldn't have to if you let us do our fucking job."

I apply more pressure to his throat as a warning. "I tell you when to do your job, and I don't need a babysitter."

"Baby girl," Dex says quietly. "You need to let go." My head snaps up, and Dex raises his hands in a placating way, and I frown. It's a typical tussle between Ryder and me. It happens all the time, so why the hell is he talking to me like I have a knife to Ryder's throat and not my hand?

"*Il mio sole*," Ryder says, and I look down at him. He grabs my hips and shoves me down over his obvious erection. He grinds his hips up, and I realize this exchange turned Ryder on. I move my hand from crushing his windpipe to squeezing just below his jawbone, cutting off his air supply, testing a theory. His eyes roll back in his head, and I swear he just bit off a moan.

I tilt my head to the side, temporarily distracted from my anger.

"You like this, don't you?" I squeeze tighter when he doesn't answer, and this time he doesn't try to bite back the moan. It comes from deep in his chest, and he grinds his hips up again while holding me over top of him.

"Well, I'll be damned," I hear Gage chuckle.

I lean down until my lips are hovering over his, my hand still on his throat, loose enough so he can get air. "Answer me," I demand.

"Fuck," he grits out. "Yes. Okay? Yes, I fucking like it."

I lick across his top lip and pull back before he can kiss me. I have to admit I like this too. Something about taking control of Ryder like this has my panties soaked. Now isn't the time, though. Ryder and I have some things to discuss, which don't include him sinking his cock inside me. "Bad boys don't get fucked," I tell him, grinding over his hard dick and then jumping to my feet, leaving him panting on the floor. "They get to walk around with a hard cock while listening to me fuck someone else."

With that parting shot, I march my ass to my room and slam the door.

CHAPTER 33
LEO

"You nervous about the gala?" Gage asks. We came back to the living room after the display between Alessa and Ryder. She's now in her office, still pissed, and I'm not sure where Ryder has disappeared to.

"Yeah, a little bit," I admit. "Not about going but about being presented as a freaking heir."

Gage shrugs. "The name comes with respect, but it also comes with enemies. But you have us now too."

"Do I?" I ask the question that's been plaguing me without thinking. Gage's brows furrow. "I just mean you and Ryder have a lot of memories with her, Dex too. Holden might be new, but he's been here too. I haven't."

"That doesn't make us see you any different. Les accepted you into this family, so you *are* family."

"He's right," Dex rumbles, walking into the living room.

He plops down in his favorite chair. "Once you're in, you're in. No matter how long you've been here."

"You guys don't know me," I argue. I'm not sure why I'm arguing, but I haven't been here long.

Dex shrugs. "Les does."

"So, she says so, and you agree?" I ask.

Dex chuckles. "She's the Boss."

It still amazes me that these guys never bat an eye about taking orders from her. Ryder may question it, but he still respects her decisions most of the time. I thought for sure she was going to kill his ass today, though.

"Her and Micah still in the office?" Gage asks.

"Yeah," Dex nods. "They're putting everyone on high alert."

"Is this going to happen?" Gage asks Dex, and it's the first time he's looked uneasy about all of this, which doesn't sit well with me.

"It has to. Viktor has been trying to make her look weak since she took over, and she has to prove that she isn't."

"This is the Russians, bro," Gage argues. "This isn't some small-time family like the Moretto's."

"That's why she's calling in all favors," Ryder answers, striding into the living room and sitting on the loveseat. "See where the alliances really lie."

"Viktor forgot Les' army reaches worldwide," Dex soothes.

"She's made sure to keep old alliances and made new ones. We've got this."

"You know that includes your brothers, right?" Ryder asks, cracking open a bottle of water.

I frown. "Includes my brothers? How?"

He drains the entire bottle before answering. "They're now an ally."

Does that mean Evander and Mateo will go to war with her? What will happen if they don't? I don't understand any of this shit, and it's not like anyone took the time to explain it; they shouldn't have to. I'm the outside man; I don't know how a war with another family goes besides people can die. It's never said, but it's implied.

"Our main priority is protecting Les," Dex shrugs. "We took an oath when we became her inner circle."

"What the hell are we going to do about this stalker problem?" Ryder asks since it's on the subject of protecting her.

"What are we supposed to do?" Gage asks with a snort. "The more we fight to protect her, the harder she'll push back against us."

"Then we don't fight her. We just do it," Ryder argues.

"She almost choked your ass out in the hallway," Gage chuckles, "Even though you fucking liked it."

"Leo." I look up at the sound of my name and see Micah standing just inside the living room; he jerks his head and disappears back toward her office.

I stand up from the couch and follow him. Evander and Mateo are both sitting there when I push open the office door, much to my surprise. I didn't even hear them come in. Alessa smiles softly and gestures to a chair in front of the desk; I sit beside Evander with Mateo at his other side. She's handling all this in stride, but I can see the stress in her tight shoulders. I hate that she even has to deal with this. She has a war breathing down her neck and a stalker.

"What's up?" I ask, looking at everyone's grim faces.

"We want to give you a chance to bow out of being a Perez heir," Evander says quietly.

"You don't want me to be?"

Alessa shakes her head. "That's not what he means." She leans her arms on the desk. "What happens next puts everyone's ass on the line."

"So, you're going to war with her?" I ask Evander.

He nods. "We are."

I look at Alessa. "You're pulling out all cards, huh?" I ask angrily. "Using this newfound alliance to get them killed too?"

"She gave us a choice," Mateo answers, leaning forward. "It's the least we can do after what Father did to her."

"That I still don't know about." I swipe my hand through my hair, pissed. "I don't know about any of this because no one will fucking tell me."

"We don't either, Leo," Evander says evenly, leveling me with a look to shut up. "This is what alliances do. We don't need to know everything."

"So, you just trust her at her word? This is a death sentence." I don't know why I'm getting so worked up. I guess everything from the past week is just to a boiling point. I'm scared to death for my brothers and my newfound family that I can't process this. I also can't help but be pissed at Alessa for involving them.

"I called them here to protect you, Leo, not to go to war with me," Alessa says in a deadly tone that I know too well."This was their decision. You can either sit there and blame me or shut up and listen."

I take a long look at her after she delivers that ultimatum, knowing I have to make a decision that could make or break what I'm building with her. The decision she's telling me to make means either in or out; there's no in-between. It's either stay and potentially watch them all die or run back to North Carolina. I look into her blue eyes and make my decision. "I'm listening."

She rolls her shoulders back, trying to relieve some tension. I can't tell if that was the answer she wanted or not. "I'm not going to bore you with all the history, so I'll give you as much as I can." I nod. "The Italians and the Russians have a long-standing feud that goes back for generations ever since Italians took over their power here. My dad kept the peace by allowing them certain avenues for illegal cash; theirs was heroin. He even allowed them to use our port to bring the product in." She rubs her temples, and that's when I realize how exhausted she looks. "Viktor's mindset is a woman should never hold any power, so when I was named Dad's successor instead of Micah, he made it his mission to make me look weak in front of the other families at every opportunity."

"By stepping in to take over the cocaine game from you was his way of saying he was done following you," I summarize for her. I might not know everything, but I'm not stupid.

"Exactly," Micah breaks in, leaning against the table behind Alessa. "He knew what he was doing."

"If I don't do something, he will work to tear down everything my father and many generations before him worked so hard to build here. I can't allow that." She crosses her arms back on the desk. "I would never put your brothers in danger on purpose, Leo. Or you," she finishes softly, and I can see how much it's wearing on her that I'll be in the middle. "I'm not going anywhere, Alessa," I assure her.

"I don't want you to, but Leo, you need to understand people *will* die, and there's no way to avoid it." And there it is. The implication that people will die is finally said out loud. I look at her and realize one of those people could be her, Gage, or one of my brothers.

"We're giving you an option." Evander finally looks at me, and I can see this is tearing him up too. "Stay with us or go back home to your mom without a mention of you to put a target on your back."

"You want me to run?" I ask, looking between Evander, Mateo, and Alessa. "Just forget everything that I've found here?"

"We want you to make it out of this alive," Alessa says vehemently. "We grew up knowing this was the direction our lives were going to take. Your life can take a different direction, where you stay alive."

I can't imagine a life where you knew at a young age you would probably die bloody in a war that started long before you were born. Even though it was just mom and me, I had a damn good childhood filled with love and laughter. Evander and Mateo grew up with a tyrant as a father and a spineless mother that wouldn't stand up for them. Alessa's dad seemed to do everything he could for her, but he still raised her as a criminal. A criminal that is now

pleading with me to save my ass. No way in hell I'm leaving.

"I'm not fucking running," I say, looking around the room at all their faces. Everyone holds the same sadness in Alessa's eyes except Micah. I can never get a read on him, and I'm not even sure he's happy I'm around.

Alessa straightens up, and I can see the mask slamming into place. "Okay," she nods, "then you need to be prepared. I know you know how to shoot, but Gage will show you how to use all the weapons at our disposal. Over the next several days, this place will be crawling with more guards." She turns to Micah. "Can you bring the other guys in?"

Micah squeezes her shoulder before doing as she asks. She doesn't even look at me when we're waiting for them to pile in. Ryder and Dex take up their spots at her back; Gage, Holden, and Micah sit on the couch she has set to the side of the desk. She's squared her shoulders, and all trace of sadness in her eyes is gone, and I realize this is the ice queen they joke about. One where she has to hide her emotions, so she doesn't look weak, even in front of us. Something tells me I'll see her more than ever instead of the soft Alessa I've gotten used to.

"Tell us the plan, Boss," Ryder says, crossing his arms over his chest. I realize every single one of them has that same mask in place.

This isn't the girl they're in a relationship with anymore; this is their boss. I envy them the ability to shut everything down.

"We need Spinner." She looks at Holden. "Find him. We grab him and get him to talk. That's how I get the proof I need to wage war against Viktor." Holden nods, and I see he can't hide behind a mask, either. She smiles, but it's strained. "I've called Aldo in New York and Romeo in Chicago. They're on standby for my word."

"What about Carlo?" Micah asks.

Alessa shakes her head. "We don't need the Italy family. Yet."

"What about the gala?" Mateo asks, and it's the most serious I've ever seen him.

"We go as planned, but we're all going now. Dex and Ryder will be the security of sorts. I need all the eyes I can get because Viktor will be there," she answers. "I need to find out what Alexey and Dmitri need to talk to me about."

"I don't like that, Boss," Gage speaks up. "Viktor makes a move, and suddenly, his sons need a meeting that can't be done over the phone?"

"I would be worried if they asked to meet in private. They're aware I won't be alone," she sighs. "They've never liked the way their father runs things."

"Potential allies?" Evander asks.

"Possibly." She shrugs. "I won't ask them to go against him, but I won't turn down an offer to have people on the inside."

"Viktor doesn't share much with them," Ryder points out.

I can't wrap my head around how they're all casually sitting around talking about a war, a nuclear bomb getting ready to explode within these families.

"We will cross that bridge when we come to it. Until then, we find Spinner and someone else to lead the Vipers. Who was his second in command?" Alessa turns and asks Ryder.

"Ghost," he answers. "We need a meeting?"

"Yeah. We need to find out if he knew what his leader was doing. Something tells me he doesn't." She turns back to Evander and Mateo. "How deep are you guys willing to go?"

"Tell us what you need." Evander shrugs. "We'll be there."

She tilts her head to the side. "Forgive me for being suspicious, but why? You haven't been an ally long enough to throw in everything already."

Evander clears his throat. "We may not know what Frankie did, but we know it isn't good. We need you to know that we aren't him."

"I do know that, though, and as far as I'm concerned, you weren't involved either since you were around the same age as me." She swallows, and her mask slips a little. "What he did was worse than bad, but I can't hold that against you."

"Doesn't matter." Mateo shrugs. "We're in."

"Alright." She nods. "Our first order of business is Ghost."

CHAPTER 34
ALESSA

I'm in my room changing clothes when my phone rings for the tenth time, Zane's name flashing across the screen. He's been trying to get ahold of me all day, and I don't have the time to deal with his shit. I scoop it up from the bed.

"What?" I bark.

"It's about time," he drawls, and I ignore my body's reaction to his voice. "I have news."

"Okay?"

"We got the kids out and arrested the horrible excuse for foster parents."

"Is that it?" I ask. He blew my phone up for something I could have seen on the news?

"No," he chuckles. "You want to tell me why you were at Xander's garage?"

I bark a laugh. "Are you fucking joking? You want to tell me why you said I had five minutes, and you guys rolled in two minutes later?"

"We moved faster than I thought."

I roll my eyes. "I don't have the time or patience for your shit, Zane."

"Where's Playboy?"

"How the hell should I know? He's your informant," I say, playing dumb. I know exactly where he is. He's currently going through withdrawals from whatever shit he was on with Gerald and Boone. They helped many of our guys when they started sampling products when they shouldn't.

"You're the last one to see him," Zane sighs. "Look, he's a good kid. Shit life. You know the story."

The same story every gangbanger usually has. Shitty home life and turned to a life of crime. "He's fine, and that's all you need to know."

"You can't blame me for asking. I paid a visit to Xander's garage, which was locked up tight, which is weird, don't you think?"

"Okay. What's your point?"

"I let myself in through a side door; it was suspiciously clean for a garage."

That's because Mani cleaned it up after he took care of Xander's body for me at the docks. "Are you going somewhere with this or?" I let the question hang in the air; he would eventually get to the fucking point.

"You were there, Alessa," he says. "Where's Xander?"

I snort. "Come on, Zane. What do you want me to say here?"

"The truth."

I can't help but laugh. "That's rich coming from you. I have important shit to take care of now." I hang up, and before I can toss it back on the bed, it pings with a message. I swipe it open.

ZANE

I'm not your enemy.

You still a cop?

Then yes, you are.

I toss it on the bed and ignore the pings coming from it. I know I shouldn't entertain Zane, but I need to keep him on my side as much as possible, even if I have to ignore that his voice still slides over me like honey.

My door opens, and Dex steps in, stopping dead in his tracks, when he notices I'm standing in nothing but a white lacy bra and matching thong. My mind goes back to his control, finally snapping and taking what he's been wanting. I know we haven't completely cured him, but it's close. I can't explain what it feels like to finally have this part of Dex back, even if he's still fighting his demons.

"Can I help you?" I tease because he's still staring.

"Fuck," he rasps. "I came up here to check on you."

"As you can see, I'm fine."

"Fuck yeah, you are." He takes a step toward me, and I hold myself perfectly still. Bending down, he slants his mouth over mine, and I have to clench my hands into fists to keep from reaching out to jerk him closer. I want nothing more than to mold myself to his big body, to feel those muscles slide against my naked skin. He jerks his mouth away. "Bend over the side of the bed."

My breath hitching, I do what he says, laying the top half of my body on the bed, and tilting my ass toward him. I feel his hands at my hips, peeling my panties down my legs, careful not to touch me anywhere else. I want nothing more than to feel that thin string he has on his control snap. I want to feel that dominant side I can feel lurking just below the surface. I want him to take me, own me like I know he wants but can't push past his fear of touch. "Spread your legs wider." I widen my stance, and he groans, "Good girl."

I moan at his words and arch my hips toward him, begging him to touch me. "Please, Dex."

"What do you want, Baby girl? You want me to fuck this needy pussy?" I hear his clothes rustling and the sound of him unzipping his jeans. "You want me to bury my cock so far in you that you forget everything else?"

"Yes," I groan. "Please."

"Put your knees on the bed," he commands, and I know I'm not the only one who needs this. I do as he says, leaving my ass hanging over the edge. He's tall enough that the bed is the perfect height for him to fuck me like he wants. "Touch your pussy. Show me how wet you are." I slide my hand between my thighs, my hips jerking when I brush my clit. I'm still keyed up from my tussle with Ryder and everything else. I sink my fingers inside my pussy, pull them out then hold them over my shoulder, showing him that I'm dripping for him. He sucks them into his mouth to taste me, and we both groan. "Your pussy was always my favorite taste. One of these days, I'm going to eat that pussy like it's my last fucking meal."

We got that far before, but something always happened before we could take it further. He would get a call for him to do something for my dad, or we were interrupted. Dex had a talented mouth which he would use to make me come so many times I would almost pass out.

I feel him line his cock up with my pussy, so I brace my hands on the bed. He slams his hips forward, burying himself to the hilt in one firm push. My back arches with a moan while I push my hips back.

"Fuck, you feel good," he groans. I feel his hands brush my hips and shiver at the contact. He does that a few times, testing his reaction before he latches on tight in a bruising grip. He groans again. "Hold on and take my cock like a good girl."

I lock my arms and know that this isn't going to be a sweet coming together. Dex is going to fuck me stupid, and I'm more than ready.

"Fuck me," I encourage, and that's all he needs.

His fingers flex on my hips before tightening. He pulls out and slams back in, causing the whole bed to jerk. He starts pounding into me, his thick cock stretching me every time he slams back in. It's almost painful, but I want it like that, need it like that. When he takes control, it allows me to just exist. The bedroom is the one place I don't *need* to be in control.

I start pushing back against him just as hard as he's pushing into me, our thighs slapping together. I can feel my release building fast. I'm so keyed up from everything today that I know it won't take long. "Scream my name, Baby girl. Let them know who's fucking you."

I reach between my legs and start rubbing my clit fast, thankful Micah, Evander, and Mateo left right before I came upstairs, not that I would have stopped this anyway. I need this release more than I need air. I can feel myself tighten around him. I pinch my clit between my fingers, and shatter. "DEX!" I scream, giving him what he wants.

"Fuck," he grunts, pounding into me harder. He grabs a handful of my hair, jerks me off the bed, and pushes me to my knees. I moan again at the pain, little aftershocks from my orgasm rolling through my body. "Open," he says between clenched teeth. I open my mouth for him to slide his cock between my lips, and I suck him into my mouth when he does. He uses his hold on my hair to stroke in and out of my mouth before he buries himself in my throat, groaning when my nose brushes his pubic bone. His hold on my hair tightens and tilts until he can see my eyes, then explodes down my throat. I swallow greedily around him, taking everything he has. He groans again, and it comes from deep in his throat, causing a quick sharp orgasm to rip through me, much to my surprise. I've never come from no stimulation. It was all Dex with his cock buried in my throat, his possessive hold on my hair, and the look in his grey eyes. The thought that I did that to him makes me what to fuck him all over again.

He slides his cock free when he's done. I suck in several breaths licking his taste off of my lips. His hold on my hair loosens, and he tenderly runs his fingers through my hair. "You're perfect," he motions for me to stand, "and mine," he growls when I'm standing in front of him.

"Yours," I whisper. I'm equally all of theirs, but right here in this room, I'm his.

He hooks his hand on my neck and slants his mouth over mine again with a groan, not caring he can taste his cum on my tongue. He pulls back, gently pecking my lips. "I'm almost there. Please don't give up on me."

I know he means letting go of everything that happened and finally allowing me full access to him. "Never," I reply without hesitation. "You're mine too, Dex."

He sighs. "I need you, Baby girl."

"I need you too." I kiss his scarred cheek. "More than you know."

"We need to work out this stalker problem," he says and then raises a hand when I open my mouth. "Not right now. But I need you to keep a level head. We just want you safe. We aren't saying you can't handle this yourself." I jerk a nod, and he gives me a quick peck on the lips, then chuckles, "I was supposed to be coming to get you so we can leave."

I smile. "So, they're waiting downstairs while you were fucking me?"

He grins, and it transforms his whole face. "That wasn't the intention, but walking in here and seeing you in that sexy as sin outfit changed the plans a little."

I laugh. "A little? There's nothing little about you, Dexton."

He growls in his throat. "Don't push me. I'll have my cock buried in you again before you can blink." He strokes his knuckles down my cheek, just barely a graze. "Now, get dressed like a good girl."

"You keep calling me a good girl, and we won't ever make it out of here," I warn, but it isn't much of a threat.

"You *are* my good girl. Giving your body to me willingly, and you take my cock so good." His eyes darken again, taking a step toward me. He stops, shakes his head, and takes a step back. "Fuck, you're dangerous."

I laugh. "You are too."

He pecks my lips again from a safe distance before tucking himself back into his jeans. "I'll see you downstairs," he says with a grin, sauntering out of the room.

I wash myself up quickly before getting dressed in ripped denim skinny jeans with holes down the thighs. I throw on a grey tank top that coincidently matches Dex's eyes. I grab my high-heeled boots and head downstairs.

It's back to business whether I want to or not.

This quick session with Dex did wonders for the tension in my shoulders, though.

I PUSH open the doors to the pool hall down from Xander's garage, the place Ghost told Ryder for us to meet him. I gaze around and notice two guys from last night avert their eyes. I make the decision to bring Evander and Mateo with me too. I need to let it be known they are with me to protect Leo more than anything. I didn't like his decision to stay when we were giving him the option to leave, to stay safe. The thought of Leo leaving breaks my heart, but I want him safe more. I could tell by the stubborn set of his jaw that I wasn't going to be able to convince him to go, though. He doesn't know that I will push him away if shit gets too deep. I can't stand the thought of something happening to him.

"Alessa," Ghost greets, standing up from one of the corner tables in the small pool hall. I never understood why Xander was the leader of the Vipers and not Ghost. He has an air of authority surrounding him, and he earns respect, unlike Xander.

Ghost stands about an inch shorter than Dex's six foot six with shaggy blonde hair and blue eyes that almost make him look innocent, but I know what's lurking behind those blue eyes, and it's anything but innocent. He's lean too, but I've watched him fight in the underground fights I run. The man is a powerhouse, and people underestimate him much like they do Gage when he fights.

"Ghost," I nod. "Can we talk somewhere?"

He nods his head toward the back of the pool hall. "This way."

He leads us back through a set of double doors labeled employees only into a room with a large table in the middle. He takes the seat at the head of the table, and I take the seat at the other end with Leo and Gage on either side of me. The rest of the guys are lining the wall behind me,

watching.

"What can I do for you?" Ghost asks, leaning back in his chair, looking relaxed. He's anything but if the set of his shoulders gives me any clue. He's ready for me to make a move because he isn't stupid, unlike Xander.

"Xander's dead," I say without preamble. Might as well get it out in the open.

His eyebrows raise. "I knew something was up when he didn't open the garage this morning." He looks at the guys with me. "What's with the muscle?"

I wave my hand. "Let's just say Xander chose the wrong side and met an untimely end. Did you know he was selling for the Russians?" I watch his face closely for any sign that he knows, and except for the slight furrowing of his brows, his face doesn't change.

"He was doing what now?" Ghost asks, sounding genuinely confused. "Why the fuck would he do that?"

"I wasn't giving him enough freedom, according to him."

Ghost snorts. "Rightfully so. He was a fucking idiot."

I raise a brow. "Then why follow him?"

"I didn't have much choice, did I?" Ghost leans forward, bracing his arms on the table and lacing his hands together. "He was your dad's chosen man."

That I still can't figure out. Why the hell would my dad put an idiot like Xander at the helm of one of his bigger street gangs? I shrug. "That's in the past now. Did you know?" I repeat.

Ghost shakes his head. "No. I'm loyal to the Italians, always have been."

Ryder steps up on my right side. "That's good to hear because the Vipers are now yours," he says, and Ghost's eyebrows shoot to his hairline. He knew that in the case of Xander's death, he would step up unless I chose otherwise. "It doesn't come without stipulations, though."

Ghost nods. "I figured that."

Gage slides him a folder. "Have you seen him before?"

Ghost opens it and looks at a picture of Spinner. "I've seen him at the garage several times, and Xander said he was restoring that old Mustang for him."

Gage chuckles. "Nah. Spinner was the plug from Viktor Orlov to Xander, and that Mustang was loaded to the gills with coke."

I got a call today from Joey, one of the guys that I sent to clean up the car and stash the coke until I had a plan. He tore the car apart, and there was coke not only in the trunk but lining the car's floorboard and under the seats. If you name a hiding spot in a car, there was product. That shipment would have been too large to come in through our dock, so I need to find who is covering for Viktor.

"I'm now in possession of that car and the product. I need you to find a way to reach out to Spinner and tell him Xander is requesting a meeting," I say, pulling Xander's phone from the inside pocket of my leather jacket and sliding it to Ghost. "Everything should be in there. I need you to tear that garage apart because something tells me that car wasn't the only hiding spot."

I need to get to it before Viktor finds out Xander is dead. I need to hit him where it hurts, and nothing would hurt more than taking one way of him making money; the next is shutting down his shipments coming into my fucking port.

Ghost leans back in his chair again, spinning the phone around in circles on the table. "I never talked to the man. What makes you think he will agree?"

"Get creative," Ryder says. "Just get the meeting."

"You also need to make sure some of your guys keep their mouths shut," I warn him. "There were some guys there last night that heard everything. Two are sitting at the bar right now."

"Hm," Ghost hums, rubbing the stubble on his chin. "Funny they never said a word that they saw anything."

I shrug. "That's how you weed out the ones you want under you, Ghost. Anything else will be your downfall."

"Which ones?" Ghost asks, standing from his chair. I'm impressed by the initiative to take care of it and not bristle under my orders like Xander did.

Gage walks out with him, and as luck would have it, all five of them walk back in with them. I have the sixth one stashed away. Their eyes widen when they walk in seeing me sitting there.

"Sit," Ghost barks, pointing to the couch and chairs lining the wall. They all sink into their seats, warily eyeing their new leader. "Which one of you motherfuckers was going to tell me what happened last night?"

"Man, she killed Tony," one of them answers. "And she said not to tell anyone!"

"You dumbass," Gage laughs. "She meant the Russians, not your second in command."

"How the fuck were we supposed to know that?" another one asks, leveling a glare at Gage. I look at Gage and see his eyes take on that crazy look, and the guy looks away quickly.

I get up and walk over to where Ghost is standing. "Meet your new leader, boys." I tilt my head to the side. "Xander's taking a long vacation." I motion for the guys that it's time to leave. "Just know that if I find out you have anything to do with the Russians, you will join him. I'll be in touch, Ghost."

Ghost nods. "I got this."

Ryder slaps him on the back on the way by. "I hope so."

We make our way outside, and I climb into the passenger side of Ryder's new Explorer with Gage and Dex in the back. Leo rode with Evander and Mateo in Evander's black BMW Alpina XB7. We always joked that driving a black car is your way of initiating into the Mafia.

Ryder pulls from the curb. "You believe he didn't know?"

"For now. I just need to keep an eye on him. Closer than I did Xander."

"You mean we, Pretty girl," Gage says, leaning between the seats. "We."

Ryder slides his hand into one of the rips in my jeans, squeezing my thigh. "He's right. You have yourself stretched thin enough as it is. Let us handle the Vipers."

This is a massive test for me. I'm used to just doing it myself, not because I don't trust them. I do, without question. Ryder and I still haven't fixed anything after our showdown, but I can give them this. I take a deep breath. "Okay," I agree.

Ryder looks at me, then back at the road. "Thank you, *Il mio sole*."

I can feel some responsibility slide off my shoulders, and it feels good. I can trust the guys to handle the Vipers until I need to step in. "You and Dex need a tux for the gala."

Ryder groans. "I'm not wearing a fucking tux."

I laugh. "You can't wear jeans and boots, Ryder."

"I have something to wear, but it won't be a damn tux."

I roll my eyes and turn to Dex. "Are you fighting me on the tux too?"

He chuckles. "Yes, Baby girl, I am."

I cross my arms over my chest, fake pouting, "Fine."

"I got a tux," Gage throws in, and I look over my shoulder at his grin. "So does Leo."

"See, they're wearing tuxes," I plead to Ryder.

Ryder gives me a dry look before looking back at the road. "No tux for me, *Il mio sole*."

"And that's why Leo and Gage are my favorites," I joke and laugh when Ryder's grip on my thigh tightens.

"It sounded like Dex was your favorite before we left the house," Ryder says, cocking an eyebrow at me.

I grin unashamed. "He was," I exaggerate a moan. "He fucked me so good."

"Damn right, I did," Dex replies.

"Goddamn it, Les," Ryder says, adjusting his hips in the seat. "That should not turn me on."

Gage chuckles. "It does, though. Knowing at any point in time you can walk into a room and she's getting railed is a fucking turn-on." Gage leans between the seats again. "Wait until you're buried inside of her with someone else." Gage groans and flops back in the seat. "It's like fucking paradise."

"Shut the fuck up," Ryder grinds, adjusting his hips again.

I turn in my seat to see Ryder better, wanting to join in on the fun. "Let's talk about what happened in the hallway."

Gage's head pops between the seats again. "Oh fuck yeah. Let's talk about that."

"Let's fucking don't and say we did," Ryder replies.

"No. I think we should," Dex agrees.

"He was all," Gage throws his head back and moans, copying Ryder, "It was kind of hot."

"Him getting choked out or the fact he liked it?" I ask with a chuckle. Ryder's hand keeps getting tighter on my thigh while slowing down for a red light.

"Both. Pretty girl, you were gorgeous, all perched up on him, squeezing the life right out of him." Gage reaches around the seat and locks his hand on Ryder's throat, squeezing it like I did with a crazy grin on his face. Ryder's grip tightens on the steering wheel, and he sinks his teeth into his bottom lip, stopping his reaction. "Fuck," Gage breathes, watching Ryder's reaction in the mirror. Gage lets go when the car starts moving again. "Damn it. Now my cock is hard."

I can't help it; I laugh. Ryder shoots me a look, promising retribution.

Bring it on.

CHAPTER 35
ALESSA

Time passes in a blur, and before I know it, it's the day of the gala. I did listen to the guys and let them stay as close to me as they wanted, but I'm only going to deal with that for so long. Holden couldn't pull the footage from those cameras or track the number from the first message to Ryder. He took it personally, no matter how much we told him it wasn't his fault. Pictures still appear on vehicles when we're out, but they're just of me now. It looks like I'm posing for the camera in them, and the word 'mine' is scrawled on them. We've all been so busy trying to get ready for whatever Viktor decides to do that we don't have time to dwell on it. Ryder and I had another heated argument over me going to the gala tonight, which resulted in him bending me over my bed and fucking me so hard that I saw stars. In the end, he knows I need to go, and I won't hide from Viktor or whoever my creepy stalker is.

"Done," Bridget, my stylist, exclaims, clapping her hands and turning me toward the mirror.

She put my hair up in a loose twist with curls hanging around my face. My makeup is thicker than usual with foundation I don't usually use, blush, bronzer, and highlighter. My eyes are smokey with gold glitter on the lids to match my dress, and my lips are a light pink color that makes my lips look extra pouty.

"You're a genius," I tell her, looking in the mirror.

She snorts. "You always give me a good canvas."

Bridget is the daughter of my house staff, Shawna. They have the same fiery red hair and green eyes. I hired Bridget as my stylist when Shawna started bragging about how good she is, and she wasn't lying. I've had her on my payroll for years now. Bridget is the closest I have to a female friend, but I keep her at arm's length because I can't let any more people get close to me.

"Time for the dress." She claps again, and I laugh at her enthusiasm. I wish I still had that, but I know how boring these things are. It always made it more fun with Gage there, though. All this is an excuse to get the crime families together and flaunt their money. I have to admit I'm excited all my guys are going; I just wish I could have talked Holden into it.

I get up from the chair, take the garment bag out of the closet, and walk back to the bedroom. I slide my robe off, revealing a gold, strapless, bodice style one piece that is lacy, and push my boobs up for the dress. Bridget helps me step into it and zips it up in the back. I step in front of the floor-length mirror, and I smile to myself. The guys are going to love this dress.

The dress itself is cream-colored with glittery gold accents all over it. Wide straps on the shoulders then dipped down in a deep v neckline showing off a healthy amount of cleavage. The waist is cinched, then flares out at the hips with two slits up the thighs that stop right before my panty line.

"Damn, girl," Bridget whistles, "You might not make it out of this house."

I laugh. "They better not ruin your hard work."

While doing my hair and makeup, she peppered me with questions that I gladly answered, just happy to have someone to talk to that wasn't the guys or Micah.

She bends down, helping me step into the gold stilettos that give me another four inches of added height and a strap that winds up my calf.

She fusses with my hair for a minute, then steps back, admiring her handiwork. "Oh, I can't wait to see their faces," she laughs, hooking her arm with mine. She walks like that with me down the stairs, so I don't fall in these heels and leads me to the voices I hear in the living room. She steps back when I walk into the room, and all eyes turn toward me.

"Fuck," Leo chokes. "Baby, you look incredible."

I take him in and have to remember how to breathe. He's dressed in a tailored tux, complete with a gold vest and bow tie that matches me. His hair is messy but pushed to the side to reveal his beautiful eyes. "You too," I finally breathe out.

I look around the room and second-guess, going to this thing in favor of dragging them all upstairs. Gage is dressed identically to Leo, his wild wavy hair still wild, just like I love.

Ryder has a black button-up shirt with black slacks tailored to fit his ass to perfection; he even has on shiny black shoes. His hair is slicked back from his handsome face.

Dex has on a grey button-up that makes his eyes stand out with tailored black slacks; he has on boots which, for Dex, it's to be expected. Someone has fixed his hair where it's fluffy in the front and tamed in the back. I'd say that someone is Gage because Dex never fusses with his hair.

Ryder steps up, gently kissing my cheek, so he doesn't ruin my makeup. He takes my hand and spins me in a circle, so my dress spins at the bottom, revealing my thighs through the splits. "You look beautiful, *Il mio sole*."

I kiss his cheek back, thankful for the smudge-proof lipstick. "You look good too."

Dex steps up, taking Ryder's place, gently pecking my lips. "Baby girl," he rumbles, "You look like a fucking queen."

"You look good enough to eat." He grins and steps back.

Gage slides his hand around my waist when he steps up. "Please let me fuck you in this dress."

I hear Bridget bark out a shocked laugh. "My work here is done," she says, color blooming in her cheeks. I feel bad that I forgot she was there.

"Thank you," I tell her softly. "You always come through."

"Anything for you," she says and gives a little wave, heading to the door.

Gage's hand tightens on my hip, bringing my attention back to him. "You do look like a queen." He kisses my cheek. "Our queen."

Holden stands up from his place on the couch, taking both my hands in his. "I...you...wow," he says, mesmerized.

I kiss his lips. "Thank you," I tell him, so he doesn't have to form words.

"Ma'am, the Perez..." Shawna stops mid-sentence placing a hand over her mouth. "Alessa, you look gorgeous."

"Thank you, Shawna," I reply, getting misty-eyed because she never calls me Alessa.

Shawna clears her throat. "The Perez brothers have arrived outside."

Leo steps up, holding his arm out for me; I link mine through his. "You look...wow. I can't even put it into words."

"You guys are good for my ego," I quip, then look at Leo. "You look...damn."

He laughs. "I guess we're both at a loss for words."

He leads me to the waiting limo, Evander and Mateo's idling in front of ours. We want to arrive at this as a united front because these things are filled with paparazzi. They may not know who we are, but they treat us like celebrities.

Leo helps me in before the rest of the guys pile in behind me. Holden is standing at the door with his hands tucked into his pockets; he's the only one I'm missing in this limo. I hoped he would start going with us more since I was dragging him out of his shell.

I end up between Gage and Leo, with Ryder and Dex facing us. Gage runs his hand from my calf up to my thigh, running his finger across where my body suit meets my leg. "I'm dying to know what you have hidden under here," he murmurs in my ear.

"That's a surprise for later," I say, hiding a smile with a glass of champagne Ryder hands me.

"Just a peek?" Gage asks, grinning that full dimpled grin, running his hand higher.

I grab his wrist before he can see anything. "No. Hands to yourself."

Ryder laughs when Gage pulls his hand back. "Serves you right, you little asshole."

"Tell me you don't want to know what's under this dress?" He gestures toward me. I cross my leg over the other so the split falls open further, exposing my whole leg but still not showing him what he wants to see. All their eyes track the movement, and Gage's head falls back against the seat. "This is going to be the longest fucking night ever."

Leo chuckles and runs his hand down my leg, leaving his hand beside my knee. "You torturing us, Baby?"

"I would never," I tease.

We pull in front of the hotel where they're holding the gala. It's massive with a huge ballroom, perfect for this. The outside is equipped with a red carpet, with cameras lining each side. I roll my eyes that these people have no idea they're worshipping criminals.

"Gage and Leo are going to lead me in with Evander and Mateo," I repeat, ensuring they follow what I say, no matter how badly they don't want to. "Ryder and Dex, you take up the rear with the Perez security."

"Take it up the rear," Gage laughs under his breath.

"I said take up the...You know what. Never mind." I just shake my head at his antics.

Gage pulls himself together when the door opens. He steps out and sticks his hand in to help me out of the car, his eyes lingering on my legs. "I want to fall at your feet, my queen," he jokes, bowing when I get out.

"Stop," I laugh, hooking my arm with his and Leo's when he steps up. Evander and Mateo take up the ends, dressed sharply in classic tuxes with white dress shirts. "Gentlemen, you clean up nicely."

"You look ravishing as always," Mateo comments leaning around Leo, who elbows him in the stomach.

"Eyes off our girl, brother," he warns Mateo.

I hear Ryder chuckle. "That's more like it."

Mentally shaking my head, we walk into the hotel lobby before being led to the ballroom. The usher pushes the doors open to extravagant decorations. Way too many fairy lights line the room. Ice sculptures, a huge bar, a dance floor, and tables are set up.

"This is awful," Gage mutters under his breath, making Evander choke on a laugh.

"You know the drill," I say to Gage and then turn to Leo.

"We dance a few times. Make our rounds. Donate and get the fuck out of here." I highlight mine and Gage's usual MO. "After I talk to Alexey and Dmitri."

"We," Ryder reminds me.

"Yes, dear," I say sarcastically. "Fan out."

Ryder, Dex, and the Perez security fan out around the room like the rest of the security detail. I hate that they can't be right here with me, but I need eyes everywhere.

Gage leads me to the table with Poletti and Perez written on the place cards, thankful the people throwing the gala rearranged the tables so we can sit together. I sit in the chair Gage pulls out for me; he and Leo sit on either side of me, with Evander and Mateo in front of us.

I look around the room and lock eyes with none other than Viktor Orlov, his dark eyes matching his sons. His beautiful wife, Nina, sits at his side along with Alexey and Dmitri. I give Viktor a tight smile before looking away.

"Viktor to our left," I say under my breath. They all nod but don't look. "I need to make my presence known. Then you two owe me a dance." I look between Leo and Gage.

"I don't get a dance?" Mateo pouts.

Gage snorts. "Sure. If you want your fucking arms ripped off."

Leo laughs, then shrugs at Mateo. "I warned you outside."

Leo pulls my chair out, taking my hand when I stand. "M'lady," he says with a grin.

"You guys are the worst," I laugh, then make my way through the crowd.

Several people greet me on my way through or politely nod their heads in respect. It's still surreal that people show me the type of respect they showed my dad.

I walk to the bar and order a glass of wine. I turn around while taking a sip, scanning the room. My eyes land on Ryder leaning against the wall with his line of sight on me and look to his left, pinpointing Dex doing the same, knowing when I move, they mirror me. They both look sexy as hell leaned back, eyes locked onto me. I give them a flirty smile before turning back to the bar.

"You look beautiful, Les." *What the actual fuck?*

"What are you doing here, Zane?" I ask without looking in his direction, ignoring his compliment.

"I was invited." I finally look at him, and he nods toward a blonde at the end of the bar. I raise an eyebrow. "The person I wanted to take me wasn't interested."

I look harder at him. "Do you mean me?"

He grins, flashing his perfect white teeth. "I do, Beautiful."

I roll my eyes. "Keep dreaming, Zane. I'm spoken for."

I can't help but glance over him in his perfectly tailored tux. Zane is fucking hot, and he knows it.

"By who? Leo Perez?" He snorts.

I turn my body to face him and lift a hand when I see Ryder getting ready to move, stopping him in his tracks. I look Zane directly in the eyes, leaning closer to his ear. "You think you have what it takes to take me away from him?" I whisper, letting my breath brush against his ear.

"Yes. I do," he says confidently. I smile, making him think he has me.

"What about from four other guys?"

He jerks his face back. "What?"

I smile bigger, but it's not friendly. "You can figure it out, Zaney baby." I pat him on his chest and step around him.

He grabs my arm to stop me. "What does that mean?" he growls.

I look pointedly at his hand and then back to him. "Unless you want to lose that hand, I suggest you remove it. I held Ryder off once; I won't do it again."

"You need Ryder to protect you now?" he sneers.

"No, but I'd love to watch him take out seven years of aggression on you."

He drops my arm, giving me a long lingering look. "You do look beautiful," he repeats softly before returning to his glaring date. I give her a smug smile before turning away.

"Dance with me?" Gage asks, coming up beside me and sliding an arm around my waist; no doubt he was on his way when Zane was talking to me.

I lay my glass of wine on the bar and hold out my hand. "Gladly." He slides his hand into mine and leads me to the dance floor.

We may hate these things, but dancing around the floor to classical music is always fun. Dad beat dance lessons into me growing up because these types of events are common. I taught Gage later when Dad realized he was the perfect type to fit my date. When we were younger, and my dad was still alive, Gage and I would make an appearance, then disappear to get drunk somewhere when dad wasn't watching.

Gage slides one arm around my waist when I slide my arms around his neck, gliding around the floor. We are much closer this time than we were at previous ones.

"What did Zane want?" he finally asks.

"Same old shit," I shrug. "It doesn't matter."

"He's glaring a hole through my head," Gage grins and leans in to kiss me. That would answer one of the questions Zane is probably asking himself. He pulls back. "God, you look amazing."

We dance two more songs; just when I'm about to find Leo, Alexey walks up behind Gage. "May I cut in?"

Gage gives him a stern look. "Watch your fucking hands." With that warning, he pecks my lips, but he doesn't go far. He leans against the bar, his eyes locked on me.

I slide my arms around Alexey's neck, and to his credit, he is cautious about where he puts his hands. Alexey and Dmitri are walking wet dreams even without the tuxes, then you slap a tailored one on them, and they look like they stepped out of a magazine cover.

"You look radiant, *Moye sokrovishche.*"

Remembering what Holden said, I lift an eyebrow. "Cool it with the pet names."

He chuckles. "Your men don't like it?"

"You know they don't." I tilt my head to the side. "What did you need, Alexey?"

He casts a glance over my shoulder. "You know the boardroom in the back?"

"Yes."

"Meet us there in five minutes."

"You know I won't be alone," I remind him. The guys will kill me if I disappear without them.

He nods. "I know."

I take a longer look at him and notice he looks worried. Alexey and Dmitri don't have a care in the world, or so I thought. "Five minutes," he reminds me and turns me around to face Leo, who walked up.

We take the same stance and start swaying to the music. Leo probably never learned the fancy dances, but I'm happy to just be in his arms.

"What's the deal?" he asks, watching Alexey disappear into the crowd.

"We have to meet them in five minutes in the boardroom."

"I see you finally learned the word *we*," he quips.

"Ha. Ha," I joke back.

"Who was the guy at the bar?"

I brace myself. "Zane."

"The cop Zane?" he hisses. "Why is he here?"

I shrug. "He said he was invited."

"That doesn't worry you?"

"Not really. He can't start shit here. He's surrounded by criminals," I point out. The cops could raid this place right now and have nothing to go on.

He looks over my shoulder and narrows his eyes. "I don't like the way he watches you."

"Leo," I say softly, waiting for him to look at me; I kiss his lips when he does. "I don't give a fuck about Zane Ayers. He's a means to an end." Part of that is true anyway. "I need him on my side until he's no longer of use to me." He nods his understanding. "We need to go talk to Ryder. I want that boardroom checked before we go in."

"You don't trust them?" he asks, grabbing my hand and leading me to where Ryder is standing.

"I don't trust Viktor hasn't pulled them into his games with his usual threats."

Leo frowns. "Those are his sons, and he would hurt them?"

"In a heartbeat," I answer.

"What's up, *Il mio sole*?" Ryder asks when we're standing in front of him. I relay what Alexey said and that I want the boardroom searched. He nods. "I'll be back to get you." He squeezes my hand on the way by to talk to Dex and Evander's guys.

I tell Gage everything when he walks up, and Ryder walks back up to us within minutes. "It's clear."

I look at Leo. "I need your eyes out here," I tell him. He frowns, and I rub my hand down his face. "I'm not cutting you out. I need eyes on Viktor."

He gives me a doubtful look. "Okay, Baby," he agrees before walking back to the table.

"That man's ass was made for a tux," Gage remarks, watching Leo walk away.

"For fucks sake, Gage," Ryder laughs, leading us back to the boardroom.

"It is," I agree, making Dex chuckle.

"Such a greedy girl," Dex says, pulling open the boardroom door.

I grin at him when I pass to let him know I am and wasn't ashamed of that.

We take our seats and don't have to wait long for Alexey and Dmitri. They sit across from us, and I see they are both wearing resigned expressions.

This can't be good.

"I'll cut to the point, Alessa," Alexey says, enunciating my name after what I told him about pet names. "We need your help."

I raise an eyebrow. "You kind of picked a bad time, guys. I'm a bit busy."

Dmitri nods his head. "We understand. We wanted to talk to you before, but there was never a good time." He sighs, running his hand through his hair. "It's Mama."

My ears perk up. Nina, their mom, is such a sweet lady. Why she's with the likes of Viktor, I will never know. She's no taller than five feet even, long black hair barely streaked with grey and the prettiest, kindest brown eyes I've ever seen.

"What's wrong with your mom?" Ryder asks, sitting up in his chair. He feels the pull toward Nina too, since we both grew up without moms. She always doted on us whenever she was around, and Viktor's back was turned.

"Father," Alexey grits out. "He laid hands on her."

Gage sits up too. "Excuse me?" he asks, feeling the same way as Ryder and me.

"He's always been a monster. But we didn't realize how much of one until we saw it first fucking hand," Alexey says, his jaw flexing, showing his emotion. "We aren't around much because we don't want to be, and we missed the signs."

"This isn't your fault," I soothe, looking at Gage, Dex, and Ryder. They all nod in agreement. "What can we do?"

"We need your help getting her out. She's in full agreement but knows she can't just leave. He will kill us all," Dmitri answers with the same emotion as Alexey. How in the fuck could you raise a hand in anger to a woman as sweet as Nina?

"You will have to give me some time, but I'll come up with something. Meet me at the games on Tuesday."

"Thank you," Alexey says with sincerity and relief.

I shake my head. "Don't thank me yet. Thank me when we get her out."

"I have no doubt you will," Dmitri says, standing up and buttoning his tux jacket. "Thank you for even considering it."

Alexey follows suit with Dmitri, leaving us in the boardroom. I sigh and lay my head on the table. "How the hell did I just add more to my plate?"

Ryder rubs a hand down my back. "Our plate, *Il mio sole*. You aren't alone in this."

"This might work to our advantage, Baby girl," Dex says, and I turn my head toward him. "We can storm the place like a kidnapping. If Viktor just so happens to get killed in the process," he shrugs, "Two birds, one stone."

I sit back in my chair. "You're a fucking genius."

He chuckles. "No."

Gage's phone starts pinging like crazy before I can reply. He pulls it out with a frown. He flashes me the screen; they're all from Leo.

He swipes it open, then curses. "Shit. Viktor is looking all over the place for Alexey and Dmitri, and Leo said he looks pissed."

If he saw where they came from, he can't see us come from the same door. I nod toward the other door. "We go the long way. Back through the lobby."

We get up and make our way back through the lobby, entering the ballroom the same way we first came in. Viktor spots us immediately and storms toward me. I feel Ryder and Dex bristle behind me; Gage slips his arm around my waist, closing ranks.

He towers over me when he's closer; it's such a dick move. "Stay the fuck away from my son!" Viktor growls in my face with his thick Russian accent, looking me up and down with disdain.

"Um," I tap my chin thoughtfully, "What?"

"He doesn't need to be seen with the likes of you...Italians." He spits the word Italians like it left a bad taste in his mouth.

"Forgive me, Viktor," I start politely. "But what the actual fuck are you talking about?" His face immediately turns beet red for me using that type of language in his presence. It's laughable, as I've heard how he talks to Alexey and Dmitri.

He steps closer, and Ryder plants a hand in the center of his chest. "I suggest you back the fuck up."

He drops back a step. "You and Alexey on the dancefloor are a disgrace to *my* family."

I can't help it; I laugh right in his face. "You're serious? That's what has your panties in a bunch?"

"Where did you go with them?" he grits out.

I run a gold fingernail down his chest, knowing it's eating him up inside that I dare to touch him, and there isn't a damn thing he can do about it with all these people around. "I wasn't with them." I lean closer. "Gage here just couldn't wait to see what's under this dress. Ryder and Dex gave him a helping hand."

Viktor turns an unhealthy shade of purple before storming off in a slew of Russian. I don't know what he said, but I'm sure he called me every name in the book.

Gage laughs. "That was fun. Pretty sure he blew a fucking blood vessel." Gage places a hand on the small of my back, leading me back to the table. Gage and I sit while Dex and Ryder return to their post with security. Viktor's back at his table, glaring daggers into the side of my head; Alexey and Dmitri are still nowhere to be seen.

"What the fuck?" Leo hisses. "I don't understand Russian, but he just came back to the table pissed the fuck off." He darts a glance at Viktor. "He's fucking scary."

Gage kicks back in the chair, giving Viktor a cheery wave. "He hasn't seen scary yet."

"You're one crazy dude," Mateo laughs. "I love it."

Evander snorts. "Of course, you would. I would think you two are related if I didn't know better."

"What happened back there?" Leo whispers.

I shake my head. "Later." No way I can tell them anything here with Viktor less than five feet from our table. "I'm going to go make our donation, and we can get the hell out of here."

"Thank fuck," Gage breathes.

I peck him on the cheek and stand up, making my way to the donation table. I scribble down the enormous pledge for my donation that I always give because the money does go to the cause they are raising money for, surprisingly. It's my way of trying to atone for all the bad shit I do, even though I know nothing can make up for anything I do.

"Hey, Baby. Can I get your number?"

I smile, playing along. "I'm sorry, I already have someone that calls me baby."

"What about *il mio sole*?" Ryder purrs right beside my ear.

"Oh, that one's new." I turn around and run my hands up his chest. "That one can get you more than my number."

"What about a dance?" He takes my hand and leads me to the dance floor. Surprised, I wrap my arms around his neck. He slides his hands around my waist, jerking me closer. "I wanted one dance with the most beautiful woman in the room."

I smile. "You might be a little biased."

"No," he pulls my arms from his neck, takes my hands, and spins me in a circle, making my dress flair out before jerking me back to his chest, keeping my hands tucked in his over his thumping heart. "I've seen every guy in this room watch you wishing it was them. That gets to kiss you, touch you, fuck you, or get a little taste of having your attention for one second." He leans closer to my ear, our hips still swaying to the music. "You know what the best part of that is?" I shake my head, lost in whatever trance he's pulling me into. "I get that with you, *Il mio sole*. You're *mine*." He growls the word mine in my ear, making goosebumps pop up on my skin.

I pull back and look at his dark eyes, the obscene amount of fairy lights making them gleam like a feral animal. I slant my mouth over his in a kiss not meant for the public, letting this room know I'm finally *his*, and I don't give a fuck who knows it. I don't care that this room saw me kiss Leo and Gage before. They are mine just as much as I am theirs. He lets go of my hands to grip the side of my face and deepens the kiss. I slide my hands around his waist, sliding them up his back. He pulls back with his grip still on my face.

"I love you, *Il mio sole*," he says gruffly, emotion making his voice rougher. He's told me he's loved me before, but I can tell by the look in his eyes he doesn't mean it in the same way. My breath hitches and all I can do is stare into his eyes. "I'm in love with you. I have been for years but didn't know how to tell you. You *are* my life, Alessa."

I can feel tears gather in my eyes, but happy ones. "I love you too, Ryder. I don't know what I'd do without you."

He takes his thumbs and brushes the tears away that fell. "You won't ever have to find out. I'm in this for the long haul with you." He takes a breath. "And with them."

I don't think he will ever know how much I mean I can't live without him. If it weren't for him, I would have said a long goodbye to this world the day after my dad found me and many more times after that. When I thought about ending my life, his smiling face would pop into my mind, and I would change my mind. He doesn't realize how many times he's saved my life, not just from the dangerous situations we put ourselves into, but he saved me from myself.

"I love you," I tell him again, and his face transforms with the most beautiful smile.

He lays his forehead on mine. "Say it again."

I giggle, but it's watery. "I love you so much, Ryder Jett Venchelli."

"I love you too, Alessa Jade Poletti," he says and kisses me again. "Let's get out of here."

I couldn't agree more.

CHAPTER 36
ZANE

Watching Les make out with Ryder on the dance floor made everything she said fall into place. She's in a relationship. With all of them. How the fuck do I compete with that? The truth is, after watching how Les and Ryder were staring at each other, I know I can't. She had the same look with Gage and Leo, the same look she used to give me, but I was too fucking stupid to see it until now. When I can't stand it anymore, I storm out to get some fresh air, praying to everything that my date don't follow me. The only reason I came with her is that I knew Les would be here; I just needed to see her, as sad as that is.

Les has consumed my thoughts for seven years, making it impossible for me to find someone else. I hooked up with women, but they all had one very similar quality. Long black hair. Their eyes didn't matter because I didn't look at their face anyway. That worked until I had Les back in sight, and none of that mattered. I was determined to get Les back no matter what it took; now, I have at least three guys to compete with. If I'm honest with myself, she's probably with her whole crew, which makes that a grand total of *five* guys.

"Fuck," I mutter, scrubbing a hand down my face.

I hear a familiar laugh, and like a siren's call, I follow the sound until Les rounds the corner, surrounded by those assholes. Ryder slides his hand down her back, cups her ass, and pats it when she climbs into the limo behind Gage. I grind my teeth to dust. Ryder's the bane of my fucking existence. He always followed Les around like a little lost puppy, but that's not what always pissed me off. What pissed me off was Les *wanted* him there even when she was with me. I knew that Ryder would be a problem if we ever took our relationship public.

The valet finally pulls around in my jacked-up black Chevy Silverado, looking way out of place between the limos and fancy cars. My dad left me money when he died, a lot of fucking money, but I never touched it. It sits in a savings account, drawing interest because I convinced myself it's blood money.

I pull out onto the main road, one car behind the limo Les got into. I should be the bigger man and just be happy that *she* looks happy, but fuck that. She's the only woman ever to capture my attention and keep it, even at eighteen. Now she's a woman and grew into the leader her dad knew she could be when he handed the torch over to her, the leader I knew she could be. I never doubted that she would become the most powerful woman in the world, but she was convinced he would hand everything over to Micah and seemed okay with that fact.

Slowing down at the red light behind the car in front of me and Les' limo, I'm so lost in my thoughts that I almost miss the SUVs roaring up to block the limo. The one I have been following pulls closer to the back of the limo, and four guys pile out, holding fucking assault rifles. I jerk my truck to the side of the road last minute, and they start opening fire, littering the limo with a hail of gunfire. I jump out without hesitation, unsure of what I'm going to do; all I have with me is my service weapon. I had enough sense to grab it when I jumped out of the truck but was obviously not smart enough to avoid jumping into an ambush to save the one woman who loathes my very existence.

Fuck! My heart is pounding out of my chest, knowing they killed everyone in that limo, including Les. There is no way they didn't with that much firepower. I swallow the panic and duck behind the row of cars lining the side of the street. The limo rolls forward into the SUV in front of it, and I know the driver's been hit.

Fuck fuck fuck!!!

I don't think; I just act. I pull my weapon and aim at the passenger side window, pulling the trigger to shatter it. Cars this new locked when in drive, and I need in that car *now.* I jerk open the door, and the driver is lying on the steering wheel, blood pouring from his mouth. I send up an apology when I lean into the car, open the driver's side door, then shove him out; all the while, bullets are whizzing past my head. I can feel one slice right through the arm of my tux jacket and hiss at the pain, but there isn't any time to check. It's completely silent behind the partition, and I have to swallow bile, the image of Les' body littered with bullets running through my head at Mach speed. I slam the driver's door and cram the car into reverse, slamming my foot on the gas and jerking the wheel to the right. It hits the SUV behind us with a lurch; shifting into drive, I smash into the SUV in front of us. One more time in reverse, I can swing the huge limo onto the road so I can make a getaway, almost taking out a small sedan. I floor it and don't stop until I know we aren't being followed. There's no way I can outrun SUVs in a limo that is swaying like crazy just with a slight turn of the wheel. After five minutes of no headlights, I finally jerk the car into a parking lot. I take several steadying breaths before I lower the partition, waiting for the worst. I finally steel myself and turn around in the seat.

They have all managed to fit in the floorboard, Ryder and Dex laying over Les. Gage and who I assume is Leo are further to the back, Gage's body protectively over his. I can see blood on the little piece of Les' dress I can see.

Ryder's head finally lifts, and his eyes instantly harden when they meet mine. "What the fuck?" he growls.

I don't spare him a second when Les lifts her blue eyes to mine. "Zane?" she whispers, and all the air whooshes out of me at once.

"Hey, Beautiful," I greet through the panic that I'm still trying to squash down, thinking she was dead. "Is everyone okay?"

"What the fuck are you doing?" Ryder explodes, helping Les to sit up. He sees the blood, and all focus goes to her. "*Il mio sole,*" he says, his hands fluttering around her in panic.

"I'm fine, Ryder," she says softly, grabbing one of his hands. "It's from the glass." Her eyes dart between the rest of them, lighting on a very pale-looking Leo. The rest of them look fine. "Leo?"

He groans in pain, and Gage is instantly on his knees. "Are you hit?" he asks, looking Leo over. When Gage jerks Leo's jacket open, blood is soaking through his white shirt at an alarming rate. I jerk the car into drive and swing back onto the road.

"Where are you going?" Dex rumbles, sticking his head through the partition, looking just as pissed as Ryder.

"The hospital," I answer like he's a fucking idiot. His guy is bleeding out; where does he think I'm going?

"No hospitals. Take us to the house," Les answers, worry evident in her voice. "Leo?" she says softly.

"Hey, Baby," he says but groans in pain again.

"Zane's not going to the fucking house," Ryder interjects.

"We don't have a choice," she barks, then looks into the rearview mirror at me, her eyes begging. "The house, Zane. We have a doctor on standby."

I jerk a nod and swing the car in the other direction, racing against the clock. I know the Poletti's have a doctor on standby and a fully stocked room in the back of that house that will have anything they need. Hospitals ask questions they can't answer, and now they have a detective driving a getaway car. If Leo needs surgery, though, that will be a different story.

I drive as fast as the car can go, listening to Les and Gage whisper to Leo, begging him to stay awake. I can hear Ryder and Dex relaying everything that happened on their phones.

I swipe a hand down my face. I'm about to be in a house full of criminals as a detective, and if the look in Ryder's eyes says anything, a dead detective. It looks suspicious as hell even to me that I'm the one who rolled down that window. No way in hell they'll believe I just saved their asses.

I pull the car up to the gate, and it swings open at the sight of the bullet-ridden limo, and I can see all of the guards jerking to attention, running toward the house. I put the car in park in front of the house. "I will deal with you later," Ryder warns before shoving open the door. "He doesn't leave," he says to Dex, who jerks a nod, leveling me with those creepy grey eyes.

I step out of the car and stay out of the way. Gage helps Les out of the other side, keeping an arm tight around her waist with Dex standing protectively behind her.

Ryder leans back into the car. "I'm sorry, man. This is going to hurt like a motherfucker," he says to Leo.

"I can help you," I say dryly.

"You can fuck off," he growls back.

I watch through the window as he puts Leo's arm around his neck and, as gently as possible, wiggles Leo to the open door with his arm around his back and under his knees. "Hold your breath," he warns before lifting Leo out of the car. The scream that rips out of Leo makes me sick to my stomach, and my eyes lurch to the pained sound Les makes hearing it. Tears are pouring down her face, and Gage doesn't look much better.

"Fuck," Ryder breathes. "Fuck, I'm sorry."

I'm just shocked that Ryder has a soft bone in his body, especially helping a guy dating the girl he's been in love with forever.

Leo's head lolls on Ryder's shoulder as he strides into the front door, everyone filing in behind them. "Just don't drop me, asshole."

Ryder barks a laugh. "Should have let your ungrateful ass bleed out in the car."

Leo chuckles, then groans in pain again, causing Ryder to pick up the pace, Les hot on his heels. He rushes him to the back of the house through a door held open by a very concerned-looking redhead. He gently lays him on a hospital-type gurney and steps back. Les rummages around, pulls out a pair of scissors, and walks back over to him.

"Docs on the way," she assures him. "I need to get your clothes off."

She cuts through the arms of his jacket, letting it fall open underneath him, then does the same to the center and arms of his dress shirt with the precision of a doctor. She lays the sharp shears beside him and then gently peels his shirt off the wound, all the blood soaking through, causing it to stick to his skin. She chokes back a sob when she sees the huge wound and the look on his face.

A tall guy with salt and pepper hair bustles in still in his flannel pajamas, a shorter blonde woman following behind him. He doesn't waste any time snapping gloves on and looking closely at the wound, palpitating around it, causing Leo to groan in pain again. "It looks like it ripped straight through." He looks up at me, and I notice it's Doc Sorenson. The same doctor who took care of this family for years and his wife. "Detective Ayers," he greets politely before looking back at Les; I don't miss the what the fuck look. "I need to scrub up, and I need the room. Loretta will get an IV started for fluids, and he'll need blood." Loretta hands him several thick gauze pads that he shoves against the wound. "Do you know your blood type, son?" he asks Leo.

"B-positive," he whispers well on his way to passing out.

Evander and Mateo bust into the room, looking like they ran to get here. They rush to Leo's side. "Hey, brother," Evander says, gripping his hand tight.

Loretta bustles to the refrigerator I know is stocked frequently with blood bags. She digs relentlessly, then looks at her husband. "There is none." I can tell by the tone of her voice that Leo doesn't have much time. "Any of you guys a match?" They all shake their heads looking more and more worried by the second.

Internally kicking myself again, I step forward. "I am." Leo doesn't mean shit to me. I can let him die, and one less person will be standing in my way, but the relief on Les' face is worth it.

"What's your play here, Zane?" Ryder growls, taking a step toward me, Les steps in front of him.

"Not now," she begs, then looks at me. "Thank you."

I shrug out of my tux jacket, remembering the graze from those assholes. I test my arm, and it seems fine. I've had worse.

"Zane, you're bleeding," Les says, actually sounding worried. *In my fucking dreams.* She's probably just concerned I won't have enough blood to save her little boyfriend.

"It's just a graze," I tell her. Her eyes still look worried for me, giving me the slightest hope that she might still care.

"Sit, sit." Loretta bustles over, leading me to a chair. "Doc needs everyone else out." She shoos her hands.

Les kisses Leo's sweaty forehead. "I'll be right outside."

He weakly nods, and she leans down, whispering something in his ear that relaxes his face. They all lead her out of the room, glaring at me on the way by. *You're welcome.* The door shuts behind them, and Loretta walks up, holding a wicked-looking needle. I lay my head back on the wall so I don't have to watch. I fucking hate needles.

Why am I doing this again?

CHAPTER 37
ALESSA

I can't stop pacing outside the door, waiting to see what they say about Leo.

I angrily tore off my heels on the third pass and kept pacing. All the guys keep eyeing me warily after I bit off Ryder's head for trying to lead me away. Now they're all lined up against the wall, just watching me. I didn't mean to snap at him, but this is *Leo.* The one who should have never been involved in this is lying in a room with a gaping bullet wound because of me. I know, I fucking know this is Viktor. They weren't aiming to kill; it was a warning of his capability. He doesn't understand that he just pissed off the one woman more powerful than him by hurting one of her guys. I don't give a fuck I was in that car, but my guys were; my whole life was in that fucking car.

"Les," Ryder says gently from his position sitting on the floor. "Please let me take care of your leg."

I frown. "What?"

"Your leg. It got cut," he reminds me, slowly standing up. My eyes light on all the blood on his arms where he rolled up his shirtsleeves in the car, all of it from Leo, and it all slams into me again.

"I'm fine." I wave my hand and start pacing again.

What the fuck was Zane doing there? He saved our asses, no

doubt, but why? Now he's saving Leo by giving him blood? I've never been more confused and pissed off in my life.

"Pretty girl," Gage says, stepping in front of me, holding up his hands when I glare. "There isn't anything we can do right now. Let Ryder take care of you."

I finally let my eyes focus on his face, which is lined with worry. "This is Leo," I whisper, knowing he'll know what I'm trying to say without saying it.

"I know," he whispers back, leaning his forehead on mine. "I'll be right here. Take care of the leg, and you can come right back."

I nod and can hear everyone in the room take a breath of relief. Ryder gently places his hand on the small of my back and leads me toward the stairs, where he swoops me up in his arms.

"I can walk," I say much harsher than I mean to.

He closes his eyes, and when he opens them, I can see how fucked up he is over this. "Please let me have this, *Il mio sole*. I could have lost you." He swallows. "Give me this."

I nod because I don't know what else to say. What can I say? That I don't care that I almost died? That I only care that *they* almost died?

He shoulders his way into my room, goes straight to the bathroom, and sits me on the vanity beside the sink. I look at his arms again and have to swallow back bile. I'm not squeamish about blood; I've seen it more times than I should have, but it's Leo's blood.

"Please get rid of that." I gesture weakly to his arms. He looks down like he forgot it was there.

He unbuttons and shrugs off his shirt, then starts scrubbing his arms of the dried blood. I watch it wash down the drain, remembering him being so gentle and apologetic to Leo when he was getting him out of the car. The same guy he hated a week ago; he just dropped all of that and helped him. He takes a washcloth, wets it, and starts scrubbing at his stomach, where the blood soaked through to his skin. He dries himself off and digs underneath the vanity for the first aid kit that's in all rooms. He stands up and lays it in front of him, taking out what he needs. Gently propping my foot onto his leg, he looks over the cuts. They don't look bad on closer inspection, not that I care anyway.

He cleans the dried blood off, and gently pushes around the cuts to ensure there isn't any glass stuck there. I watch the top of his head the whole time he's working, overwhelmed with emotion.

"Thank you," I whisper.

"For what?" he asks without looking up from spreading alcohol over the cuts; I don't even feel it.

"For being so good with Leo." I can hear tears clogging my voice again.

He looks up finally, and I see the worry in his eyes too. "As much as I didn't want it, *Il mio sole*," he sighs and looks back down, continuing his cleaning. "He's a part of this family now. He saved my ass. This means he's mine to protect, just like all the others." He slathers antibiotic ointment on my leg, then covers it with a big gauze, taping it on. "Get changed, and you can go back to wait for Leo." He places his hands on my waist, helping me down from the vanity. He kisses my forehead. "I'll be downstairs."

I wrap my arms around his neck, hugging him tightly. "I love you," I whisper. The same thing I whispered to Leo downstairs. It seems so stupid now to hide our love. If anything, it makes me want to announce to them that I love them.

"I love you too, *Il mio sole*." He pecks my lips, disappearing from the room.

I go to my walk-in closet in search of clean clothes. I reach every way, trying to unzip my dress, but I can't reach the zipper. On the fourth try, that's when I lose it. Busting into tears, all emotion slamming into me like a freight train just because I can't get my fucking dress unzipped. I collapse to the floor on my knees, big sobs racking my body and no way to stop them, crying so hard I can't catch my breath.

"Les!" Gage busts into the closet, dropping to his knees beside me. "Les," he says, worried, pulling my face up to him.

"I can't get my dress off," I sob.

"Pretty girl," he murmurs, tears gathering in his eyes. He sits on the floor, gathering me on his lap, rocking me back and forth against his chest. "He will be okay." I know he's saying that for his sake too. Gage might not want to admit it yet, but he has more than sexual feelings for Leo. I knew it when I saw him protecting Leo with his own body.

"He has to be," I sob, tears soaking Gage's shirt.

"He will," he says adamantly. He pulls my face up with a finger under my chin. "He will," he says again, tears spilling down his cheeks.

We stay like that until my sobs are just hiccups. "Let me help you out of your dress," he offers, and I nod.

He helps me to my feet before jumping to his. He gently turns me around, unzipping the dress. "You know this is not how I wanted to see what was underneath this."

I laugh despite myself. "I'll wear it again," I promise. This isn't how I wanted him to see it, either. I had plans for tonight that involved all of them in my bed.

He lets the dress slide off my shoulders and puddle at my feet on the floor; he takes my hand, helping me step out of it. His eyes take in the lingerie. "Definitely wear that again." He shakes his head, jerking his eyes away. "See you downstairs?"

I lean up on tiptoes, kissing his soft lips. "I'll be down in a few."

He takes one last look before leaving the closet. I unlace the lingerie and grab for whatever is in the panty drawer, not caring if it matches. I slide some panties and bra on and shove my legs into a random pair of cotton shorts with one of the guy's shirts I've been collecting every time they leave them in my room after a night with me. I don't even know who's belongs to who anymore.

I rush back down the stairs to the room Leo is in. All the guys are still sitting vigil, having also changed into more comfortable clothes, except Evander and Mateo, who stayed behind at the gala when we left.

"I'm sure one of the guys has some clothes you can change into," I offer, walking into the hallway.

Evander smiles sadly. "We're fine." He looks around. "What happened?"

"Viktor," I answer angrily, ripping out the bobby pins that are holding my hair up. Ryder knocks my hand away and more gently starts plucking them free.

"You think this was Viktor?" Mateo asks, unbuttoning the top button of his dress shirt. The jacket and bow ties on both of them are long gone.

Ryder runs his fingers through my now-loose hair, and I have to take a minute to appreciate the relief. "Without a doubt."

Zane pops the door open, looking deathly pale. "Doc said he'll be fine and that you can see him later," he says, shutting the door behind him.

All the air whooshes from my lungs so fast that I feel like I might pass out. "Let's go to the living room," Ryder suggests, rubbing my back.

I go to argue, but we'll be close just in case Leo needs us, so I nod and let him take my hand, leading me to the living room. He tucks me into his side on the loveseat, and Gage tucks into my other side. Dex sits in one of the chairs while Evander and Mateo take up the couch. Zane looks two seconds from making a break for it. "Sit," I say, pointing to the chair beside Dex. I need answers. He looks resigned but sits down. Holden pops around the corner, looking around the room.

"Is he okay?" he asks quietly. I didn't even know he knew what was going on.

"He will be," I assure him and myself. He looks relieved, walks over, and sits in front of the loveseat next to my legs. I run my hands through his curly hair, relieved we couldn't talk him into going.

"I heard what happened, but I didn't want to get in the way," he answers my unspoken question.

Ryder reaches down and squeezes Holden's shoulder. "You're never in the way, Holden."

I look at Zane. "Explain."

He looks relaxed in his seat; I know he's anything but. His shoulders are rigid, and his eyes are taking in everyone in the room. He's in the room with criminals who will kill him without a second thought. "I was behind the SUV at the red light."

"You were following us?" Ryder grits out.

Zane turns cold whiskey-colored eyes on him. "No, asshole. My apartment is the same way."

I hold a hand up before they can start arguing. "Okay. Keep going."

He shrugs. "There isn't much to tell. I saw the SUVs rush in and open fire. I shoved the driver out and got you guys out of there."

Mani walks in, tosses keys to Zane, and Zane catches them out of the air with a confused look. "We got his truck out of there right before the cops rolled in."

Ryder had sent Mani and his crew down there to check the scene. I messaged him immediately to look for Zane's truck or department-issued car. I knew he didn't fucking walk to us, and I was just hoping the keys were in it.

"Thanks, man," Zane says with a nod.

Mani grunts. "Don't thank me. Thank her," he says before striding back out of the room.

The whole place outside is crawling with guards making rounds, on high alert. I don't think Viktor will try to attack my home, but I didn't think he would order an open hit, either.

"Why?" Gage asks the one question I can't figure out.

He looks at me and doesn't need to answer that question. "Her," he answers honestly.

Does he think this is his way back into my life? He's still a cop; it doesn't matter that he just saved our asses.

Gage laughs without humor. "You think that will win her over? You're still a fucking traitor."

"Why save my brother?" Evander asks, sitting forward on the couch, eyeing Zane like everyone else. With hatred.

"I couldn't just let him fucking die, okay?" Zane stands up from the chair. "Can I go?"

"I don't have to remind you to keep your mouth shut?" I say out of habit. Something tells me Zane won't be mentioning this to anyone.

He scoffs, "No. You don't."

"Thank you," I tell him honestly. It's hard to tell what would have happened if he didn't get us out of there. Or if he didn't volunteer to donate his blood. "For everything."

He jerks a nod and hastily leaves the room, slamming the front door on his way out.

"You're just going to let him leave?" Ryder asks me incredulously.

"What do you want me to do? Shoot him?" I rub my temples against a building headache. "We have bigger things to worry about."

"He saved us out there," Dex points out. "Whether you want to accept that or not."

"That piece of shit is up to something," Ryder argues.

"He might be. But I don't care," I cut in. "We need to figure this Viktor shit out. We will deal with Zane if that time comes." I sit up on the couch. "They weren't shooting to kill."

Mateo nods. "I saw the limo on the way in, and those bullets were strategically placed."

"I'm so sorry about Leo," I say, my eyes searching theirs for any animosity.

"No need, Alessa," Evander says, waving that away. "We knew bringing him into our lives that this could happen."

Mateo smiles. "He knew what he was getting into, and something tells me he won't leave you even now."

I acknowledge that with a nod, and my throat constricts with emotion again. I clear my throat. "This was his warning."

"What's your answer going to be?" Dex asks.

"That he just fucked with the wrong Poletti." I look around the room. "Viktor just brought a war to his doorstep."

I see everyone's resolve hardening, especially Evander and Mateo. Viktor just pissed off the woman who loves their brother and, in turn, pissed them off for shooting their brother.

If you believe in a God, Viktor, you better start praying to him.

Because we're coming for you.

CHAPTER 38
GAGE

"He's heavily medicated with pain meds. I have fluids running along with the blood Zane donated," Doc explains, finally walking into the room after Les' declaration of war. "I cleaned the wound, packed it, and covered it up. Loretta and I will hang out for the night, and I'll stitch him up in the morning."

Les rushes him, wrapping her arms around the big guy's neck. "Thank you, Doc."

He hugs her back. "Anytime, dear. He's lucky. It didn't hit anything vital but sliced him up enough to cause all the bleeding. He'll make a full recovery."

"When can we see him?" Les asks, wiping tears from her cheeks again.

"You can go see him now. After he rests some more, you can move him somewhere more comfortable, and the rest can visit," Doc tells her.

She shakes her head. "His brothers need to go."

"Nonsense," Evander interrupts. "He would much rather see you than us."

I shrug. "She is prettier," I joke, trying to lighten the mood, and it's my defense against what I'm really feeling.

Mateo chuckles. "He's not wrong. Go on, Alessa."

She smiles gratefully, following Doc out of the room. I need to see Leo for myself; I need to see his face to believe he's okay. The moment I saw all the blood on his shirt, I knew he would die, and the overwhelming sadness that came with that surprised me. I can't picture life now without Leo. I don't know how to deal with those feelings. I came to terms with being in love with Les long ago, but I don't know when I can tell her. Growing up, my only love was from Luca, Les, Ryder, and even Micah. My dad hated the very thought of me and told me every chance he got. I don't know what love is, but I know I love Les. Do I love Leo? Or is it just because of what we did? I told him that I'm all in with him, but does that mean love? I shake my head, knowing now isn't the time to examine those feelings.

Ryder stretches his legs out in front of him, his leg rubbing Holden's arm. Holden stiffens but shifts closer. I clamp my lips shut, so I don't blurt out anything. I know I can make shit awkward with my comments. It isn't in my nature to know when to shut the fuck up.

Ryder lays his arm on the back of the loveseat, laying his head back. "We're going to war with the fucking Russians," he says, coming to terms with it.

"Any way we can hide Leo and Holden *with* Les somewhere?" I ask jokingly, knowing the answer to that question. No way in hell Les will hide and let us take the heat.

Dex chuckles. "Keep dreaming. Did you see the look on her face earlier? She is more than pissed off. Viktor doesn't know what he just did."

He unlocked the killer that lurks just beneath the surface. The one that commands that she kill all the rapists, molesters, and woman beaters she can find, which she hasn't done since we all started this weird relationship. It's bound to come out now, ten-fold. I look at Dex, Ryder, and Holden and know they're thinking the same thing.

"In short...he fucked up," Ryder replies, lifting his head. "Queen Poletti just took her throne."

Les might have been running things for a few years, but she tends to fly under the radar unless she needs to remind someone that she's the Boss. That's what makes people think she's weak. It doesn't make her weak; it makes her fair to let people know the rules and let them live their lives. She doesn't put people under her thumb; it's what makes her the fucking Queen. The guys and I have already discussed that it will take something like this before she comes to terms with who she is now, and watching her declare war on Viktor, that time has come.

"We already agreed to back you no matter what," Evander says. "Viktor fucking Orlov dies."

"I'm already running a virus through his systems to let me in," Holden says quietly.

Ryder looks down at him. "That's my boy."

Holdens face goes beet red. That's what Ryder said to him the other day with the same reaction that made me start questioning everything. Does Ryder know that means more to Holden than just praise?

"He's asleep, but he's going to be fine," Les announces, walking into the room, collapsing on the couch between Ryder and me, giggling. "He's loopy as hell. He asked if I was an angel."

"You are an angel," Ryder says, running his fingers lovingly through her hair.

"Of death," Les and I say at the same time, making everyone laugh but Ryder.

He flops his head back on the couch again. "I hate that shit."

"Don't worry. Leo hates it too," I joke.

I was going to my room earlier when I heard a thump coming from Les' room. Going in there, I never expected to find her in a heap on the floor, tears flowing down her face. I didn't need to ask what she whispered to Leo downstairs; the relief on his face said it all. It doesn't bother me, but it does make me question if she feels the same way about me or if she ever will.

"Are you sure we can't get you something to wear?" Les asks Evander and Mateo. "You are more than welcome to stay here."

Evander looks relieved. "Yeah. That's fine." He looks at Mateo and back to her. "You sure you don't mind us staying?"

"Of course not," she smiles softly. "He's your brother."

"Come on," Ryder says, heaving himself off the couch like the night has aged him ten years. I think it's aged us all. "I'll find you something."

He steps over Holden on the floor, and I can't resist slapping his ass on the way by. I might not be sexually attracted to Ryder, but he has one of the nicest asses I've seen on a dude besides Leo. I narrowly miss his arm swinging back, trying to clock me in the face.

Les laughs at Ryder grumbling, walking out of the room, Evander and Mateo chuckling behind him. "One of these days, his fist is going to connect."

I shrug. "It won't be the first time he's punched me in the face."

Holden slides onto the couch, stealing Ryder's spot. "He almost knocked you out last time."

"He broke your nose once," Les adds.

"Split your eyebrow," Holden continues.

"Broke your ribs," Les remarks.

"Okay. I get it," I grump. "Ryder can kick my ass."

Les laughs again, and I'm just relieved to hear the sound. She kisses me noisily on the cheek. "You fought a good fight, though."

"No." I jokingly push her face away. "Keep your mean lips away from me."

She shrugs, turning to Holden and laying a kiss on his lips. "Holden doesn't mind," she says, and the little asshole grins.

"You fucker," I mutter, which makes his grin widen.

Evander and Mateo walk back in dressed in more comfortable clothes. Mateo is in a pair of what looks like my ball shorts and a faded shirt, and Evander is in an equally faded shirt and grey sweatpants. I avert my eyes away from his cock, perfectly outlined, showing what Evander is packing. I look at Les, and she's trying not to look either. It looks huge. We lock eyes and dissolve into laughter, giggling like fucking schoolgirls.

"What the hell?" Evander asks, sitting on the couch, which causes us to laugh harder.

Holden clears his throat, drawing our attention. When we look, he raises an eyebrow and then waggles them, letting us know he saw it too. Holden is a whole different person lately, thanks to Les.

Ryder steps in front of the loveseat looking between Les and me. "I'm not even going to ask." He looks at Holden. "I leave for two seconds, and you steal my seat."

Holden shrugs, plucks Les from her seat, flops her down in his lap, then scoots over.

Ryder drops down beside him with a laugh. "Well played." Ryder stretches his arm across the loveseat, letting his fingers lay on Holden's shoulder.

Les and I notice and give each other the eyes again, silently talking and then laughing again.

"What the fuck is wrong with you guys?" Dex asks.

"It must run in the family," Les says, wiping tears from her cheeks, this time from laughter.

Dex frowns, then shakes his head, looking back at his phone.

"It was fucking huge," Holden whispers.

"This coming from the guy with a monster cock," I whisper back, making Les choke.

"Don't make me separate you three," Ryder says, shoving his hand in my face and pushing me back from Holden before laying his hand back on his shoulder.

Les widens her eyes comically, darting a glance at Ryder's hand. "Did he just piss on Holden?" she whispers.

Holden makes a choking, laughing noise before turning blood red. "NO," he says too loud, causing all eyes to snap to him. "No," he whispers.

I snort. "A little late for subtly, bro."

"I feel like you two talk without actually talking," Mateo says, gesturing between Les and me.

"I feel like they're a bad influence on Holden," Ryder adds, pushing my face away again.

"Motherfucker, I will bite you," I warn.

He leans around Les. "Really? Bite me?" I snap my teeth and then grin. "You're fucking crazy," Ryder says, shaking his head.

"Wait. Did you just call me a bad influence?" Les asks, catching up to the conversation just a bit too late.

"Wow, *Il mio sole*," Ryder laughs. "Where was your head?"

"In Evander's sweatpants," I mutter quietly. Ryder's head snaps to me with narrowed eyes. *Oops.* Maybe not quiet enough.

He wraps a hand around her throat and pulls her head back to look at him upside down. "Is that true?"

"I would never," she says, clutching her chest like she's clutching pearls.

He lays a smacking kiss on her lips. "Uh-huh," he comments, letting her go.

She sits up and winks, making me laugh again.

"So, this whole thing really works?" Evander asks, looking between us. He seems genuinely curious.

"It's not easy," Les says. "You have to want it to work."

"You guys make it look easy," Mateo says, cocking his head to the side.

Ryder laughs. "We're still working it out." He looks at Les. "She's the one who makes it work."

Doc walks back into the room. "You can see him now." He looks at Ryder. "You want to move him somewhere else?"

Ryder nods and follows Doc out of the room. Almost losing Leo showed Ryder how much he really means to Les. The only person I've ever seen him soft with was us; now, he is accepting Leo. Ryder is protective of us all, and so is Dex. I saw the worry in the big guy's eyes too. Leo is family; Les and I will do everything we can to make sure he stays around.

After Ryder gets him situated in his room upstairs, Evander and Mateo go to check on him. When they return, Les stands up from the couch and gives Ryder and Holden a kiss before reaching her hand out to me and pulling me to my feet. She also stops at Dex, kissing him before leading me up the stairs.

She gently pushes open Leo's door, and I almost don't walk all the way in. She tugs my hand. "He's fine," she reminds me.

He's lying in the middle of the bed, pale as a ghost, a white bandage lying in stark contrast to his tan skin over the wound. Someone slid a pair of loose ball shorts on him, and I smile, knowing it was Ryder. We go to each side and gently slide onto the bed with him. He doesn't even stir, his breathing staying even.

We each grab one of his hands and lock our other hands together over his head, forming a protective bubble around him.

We almost lost him, and there's one thing I know for sure.

Viktor Orlov fucked with the wrong person when he fucked with Leo.

CHAPTER 39
LEO

I slowly peel my eyes open, confused as to why it's so hard. Then it hits me like a ton of bricks. The shooting. The searing hot pain slicing through my stomach. The yelling and screaming. The rush back to the house. Ryder carrying me into the house. It got really blurry after that. The last thing I remember is Alessa's ex-boyfriend saying he was my blood type.

I turn my head to the side, and I'm met with Gage's sleeping face, his arm awkwardly over his head, his other hand tucked securely into mine. When I look the other way, Les is lying the exact same way.

They both stayed with me.

I remember Les whispering she loved me last night and the instant relief it brought from the pain for a split second.

"You're awake," Gage says sleepily, pulling my eyes back to him.

"Yeah," I croak and then wince. What the fuck did they give me? I feel like I can fall back asleep, but other things are screaming urgently at me. "I have to piss."

Alessa giggles, and I realize she's awake too. I look over and take in her beautiful face. "You can't get up, so it's Gage or me helping. Take your pick."

Gage rolls smoothly off the side of the bed onto his feet and snatches a urinal bottle off the dresser, wiggling it in his hand. "Gage," I say without hesitation. No way she's holding my dick while I take a piss. I don't want Gage to do it, but I'll take him over her. "No offense," I tell Alessa.

She kisses my cheek. "None taken." She rubs her hand down my face. "It's so good to see your eyes," she says softly before gently sliding off the bed and padding out of the room.

Gage professionally helps me take care of business while I'm dying of embarrassment. He walks to the bathroom; I hear the toilet flush a minute later, then the water running. He walks back empty-handed and stretches out on the bed beside me with his head propped up in his hand. I can see the worry lining his eyes, something I've never seen on him.

"I'm fine," I assure him. "How bad is it?" Thankfully I was knocked out the whole time; Doc pumped some serious pain meds into my veins.

"Man," he sighs, "It was bad. There was all this blood." He swallows like he's seeing it all over again. "We thought you were going to die," he whispers.

On instinct, I reach over from the good side and grab his hand. "I didn't, though."

"Doc still has to stitch you up. That's why you can't move yet. After that, he said you could; you just have to take it easy." He kisses me gently, surprising me. "You can't leave me."

"I'm not going anywhere," I promise, knowing with all my soul that I will never leave him or Les.

"You want pain meds before or after I carry your ass back down the stairs?" Ryder asks, striding into the room. His usual gruffness with me is back, but his eyes aren't hard anymore.

"Thank you," I tell him, remembering him apologizing for hurting me and getting me out of the car.

He nods. "Yep," he answers, and I realize that's as good as I'm going to get.

"If I say before, does that make me a pussy?" I ask because it's already hurting.

Ryder snorts, "Fuck no." He pulls a syringe from his pocket with a grin. "Your leg or your ass?"

I look at Gage, alarmed, and he's struggling not to laugh. He gestures to my hand where the IV still is. "It goes in there."

I look back to Ryder. "How do I know you aren't trying to kill me?"

He rolls his eyes. "If I wanted you dead, I would have let the bullet wound take you out." He walks over to the bed. "I've done this before. Doc loaded it downstairs," he says, softening his voice a little.

"When?" I ask, giving him my hand.

He swipes an alcohol pad over the top of the IV and then uncaps the syringe, screwing it on the top with a twist. *Huh.* I guess he wasn't lying. "Too many to count," he finally answers, slowly pushing the plunger. "Hospitals ask too many questions, so we were taught to take care of ourselves and each other."

That makes sense. I heard Les tell Zane to take us back to the house and was confused at the time, but now I realize why.

"The time that fucker broke Les' arm," Gage answers the unanswered question, ticking them off on his fingers. "The last gunshot wound that I got, the stab wound to Les, the gunshot wound to Dex's leg. I can keep going," he says, looking at my stunned face.

I look at Ryder. "You took care of them?"

He shrugs uncomfortably. "It's my job. They take care of me in turn. Doc can't stay here twenty-four seven."

"What the hell was in that?" I ask when he unscrews it again; my head is already fuzzy, making the pain sink into the background.

"No clue," Ryder laughs. "It's Doc's special concoction."

I don't even have it in me to be worried anymore. I hear Gage chuckle, but it sounds too far away. "He's ready."

"Hold your breath," Ryder repeats the same thing he said to me last night. I suck in a breath, and he slides his arms under me, lifting me up.

"Fuck," I groan.

Ryder winces but doesn't comment. He goes as slowly down the stairs as he can, and I try to keep the expletives from falling out of my mouth. He goes straight to the room I was in last night, the one I didn't even know was here, laying me on the table.

"Next time you fucking walk," Ryder quips, walking out of the room. Gage laughs, following him out.

Doc walks over, snapping a pair of gloves on. "I need to unpack the wound and stitch you up."

"Great," I mutter.

His sweet blonde wife Loretta walks over, grabbing my hand. "He's going to numb it. That hurts the worst." She frowns. "You're still too pale."

"We'll get blood levels," Doc says, all business. He peels back the tape holding the gauze on, and I have to grit my teeth to keep from screaming. She squeezes my hand tighter to distract my attention from the sick feeling of him pulling gauze out of the wound. I take a quick glance and wish I hadn't. It's huge and ripped right through the Perez part of my tattoo; I don't miss the irony.

"A few sticks, and then you won't feel a thing," Doc says, pulling something up into a syringe. I close my eyes when he starts coming near me. "First one," he warns.

"Motherfucker," I grit out when he sticks again. With each one, the pain fades away until I don't feel anything. I still don't open my damn eyes.

"You might feel a tug but no pain," Doc says, and I nod. I don't trust my voice. The pain meds are still swirling through my head but only dulling the pain.

"Leo," Loretta says softly, and I crack one eye open. She gently smiles. "I'm going to draw some blood; we need to check your blood levels just in case you need another transfusion."

"Something tells me my donor from last night won't be up to donating today," I joke, but I'm still grateful as hell that he was here. I'm sure Les found out why he was in that limo.

She laughs softly. "They made a supply run last night, and we have plenty."

"What did they do? Boost a blood bank?" I ask.

Doc snorts. "You probably don't want the answer to that."

Fair enough.

She gets to drawing my blood, and I don't even feel the stick. She puts a tiny band-aid over the stick and drops the tubes into a bag with ice.

Thankfully, Doc finally puts a fresh gauze over my stitches, taping it up. "Keep them dry and clean. Alessa knows the drill, and I've left plenty of pain meds. If you need anything, she has my number. Move freely but carefully."

"We'll put a rush on the blood and give her a call with the results," Loretta finishes for him. "If you need another transfusion, we'll be back."

"Thank you," I tell them both.

Doc finally smiles. "Alessa is like a daughter, and we worked for Luca. My dad did too."

"How does one get into being a doctor for the Mafia?" I wonder.

Doc chuckles. "That is something else you probably don't want the answer to." He bustles out of the room and comes back with Gage in tow.

"Come on, Pretty boy." He helps me from the table, steadying me when I sway on my feet, causing him to frown. "Do you want me to get Ryder?"

I put my arm around his neck and shake my head. "It's just the pain meds."

We make our slow trek to the living room, where he gets me set up on the chaise, his usual seat. He tucks a throw pillow under the wounded side, and I sigh in relief from the pressure it takes off. "Micah's fixing breakfast. I'll be back when it's done." He squeezes my hand and goes in search of food.

I hear Mateo laugh in the kitchen and smile that they stayed here last night. I vaguely remember seeing their faces last night, and it shouldn't surprise me that they're still here, but I'm not used to having people by my side besides my mom. Although a little dysfunctional, I'm glad I found Evander and Mateo and my found family with Alessa.

I must have dozed off because the next thing I feel is Alessa's soft hand on my forehead. "Leo," she says softly.

I open my eyes and stare into her blue ones, so much love washing over me for this woman. "I love you," I tell her sternly.

"And I love you." She kisses my lips. "Do you want to eat in the dining room or here?"

"I need to move," I tell her honestly.

"I'll be right back," she tells me, holding her hand out for me not to move. She comes back with a grinning Mateo.

"At your service, bro," he quips, helping me from the couch and wrapping my arm around his neck. "Don't ever fucking get shot again."

I laugh weakly. "Not a problem."

He starts walking forward. "Seriously though, man. You scared the shit out of me."

"I'm fine," I say for what feels like the hundredth time today.

"No chance of me talking you into going back to your mom?"

I roll my eyes. "No. I'm not leaving them. Or you guys."

"Stubborn ass," he mutters, leading me into the dining room. I feel like such a fucking invalid, but I know they're just helping because of whatever strong shit Ryder pushed into my IV.

I ease myself into a chair beside Gage, and it doesn't hurt as bad now that it's stitched up, just a weird tug. Or it's because I'm still numb.

They pass bowls and plates around with biscuits, sausage, bacon, eggs, hashbrowns, and pancakes. Gage loads my plate up and his with everything that passes by, causing my stomach to rumble loudly.

He raises an eyebrow and looks down at my stomach. "Down, boy," he jokes, pouring me coffee and a glass of orange juice.

"My hands work," I remind him.

He shrugs. "I want to do it. Now shut up and eat."

Everyone chuckles around the table, and I just shake my head. Flirty Gage, I can handle; attentive Gage, I'm not so sure about. It makes me want to examine everything I'm feeling, and being on pain meds probably isn't the best time for that.

We all eat, safe conversation flowing around the table. I want to know what the hell happened last night, but I'm content with eating and listening to them talk and laugh.

Les sits back in her chair at the head of the table after she's done eating, looking at Micah at the other end. She looks at me and fills me in on their theories about what happened, convinced it was Viktor. I nod because there isn't any doubt after his little tantrum over her dancing with Alexey and the fact he's trying to steal her business. She looks back at Micah when she's finished. "This ends now."

He nods. "Agreed. What's your plan?"

"I need to get Nina out of that house." He opens his mouth, and she holds up a hand. "Non-negotiable, Micah. I already told you that." He grits his teeth but nods. Something tells me they've already had it out over this. "We're going to rush it and take her like a kidnapping. After his show last night, his place will be swarming with guards." She shrugs. "They die, and that's less we have to worry about." It should scare me that it doesn't bother me how she casually talks about killing people without batting an eye. "I cut off his use of my port this morning. Holden is doing his thing getting into his system to find out where else he's using, and I can cut that off too unless I can get my hands on Spinner first."

"So, you want to piss him off enough that he comes to you?" Evander asks, looking between Micah and Alessa.

"That's the plan," Micah answers. "It's easier to fight someone on your own turf."

"And if that doesn't work?" I ask.

"We take it to him," Ryder says with a scary grin. "Full force."

"Les has people all over coming in; he doesn't stand a fucking chance," Gage adds.

"For now, it's life as usual, but no one leaves this house alone," Alessa says, looking between everyone, waiting for the agreement. Everyone nods, and she seems relieved.

"Wouldn't it be safer to stay here?" Holden asks quietly.

"It would," Ryder says, squeezing his shoulder. "But then it makes us look weak for hiding. We can't have that."

Alessa sits up, folding her arms on the table, looking at Evander and Mateo. "Our show of alliance last night makes you guys a huge target."

Evander nods. "We've talked about that."

Alessa looks at me and back to them. "I want to offer you to stay here. Closer to Leo and under my protection."

Mateo's eyebrows hit his hairline. "You want us...to stay...here?"

Alessa raises an eyebrow. "I think that's what I said." She looks to Dex on her left. "That's what I said, right?" she asks sarcastically.

Dex chuckles. "That's what I heard, Baby girl."

"I heard you, smartass," Mateo laughs. "I just wanted to clarify."

I know this whole thing started out rocky, and she only initially agreed to this alliance, so she didn't have to kill me. Still, I'm happy they can sit in the same room and joke around.

Evander frowns. "That wouldn't be an imposition?" He looks around the table, his eyes landing on Micah and lingering before looking back at her. "You seem to have a full house." What is that look he gave Micah? I look at Gage to get his reaction, and for once, the nosey fucker isn't watching. *Of course.* Maybe the pain meds are making me crazier than I thought.

She shrugs. "You can stay in the main house or the pool house. It's four bedrooms and is fully stocked. Micah stays in there when he's here."

"That's because he isn't allowed in the main house," Ryder jokes, earning a glare from Micah.

Micah flips him the middle finger. "Very funny, dickhead." He looks at my brothers. "You're more than welcome to the pool house with me."

"You're staying?" Alessa asks Micah, then groans when he nods. "Fuck my life."

"You don't care about my safety, shithead?" Micah asks, looking wounded.

"No," Alessa and Gage say at the same time.

"Fuck, I hate that shit," I grumble.

"Me too, bro. Me fucking too," Ryder agrees.

"Well," Micah says, pushing back from the table and standing up, "Since no one gives a fuck about me, I'll be in the pool house."

"Love you!" Alessa yells at his retreating back.

"Love you too, shithead!" he yells back further into the house.

Alessa laughs before turning her attention back to Evander. "The offer stands."

"We'll talk about it," Evander promises. I'm not sure how he feels about moving out of their house, even if it's temporary. I don't think Mateo cares either way. I know she's mainly offering for my benefit, knowing I'll be worried about them.

Alessa stands up from the table, kissing me as she walks by. "We have some stuff to do. Spend time with your brothers and rest."

Gage lays a sound kiss on my lips before throwing Alessa over his shoulder and running out of the room, her laugh carrying all the way down the hallway. The same thing made me wonder about their relationship when I first came here. Now I know.

I look back at Evander and Mateo, shock written all over their faces. I shrug. "Things have progressed."

Ryder snorts, standing up. "You could say that."

Dex and Holden follow him out of the dining room, leaving me to answer questions I'm damn sure my brothers have. "Spill it," I finally say when I can't take them staring at me anymore.

Evander rubs his chin, thinking. "I'm not surprised, but you never said anything."

"It was recent. I told you my feelings about Gage."

"No judgment, remember," Mateo reminds me. "We want you happy."

I look at where Alessa and Gage left. Bullet wound aside; I couldn't be happier.

CHAPTER 40
DEX

This day has been busy as hell for Les, with constant phone calls trying to make sure everything is in place for when Viktor makes his move or forces us to make ours. I'm more than ready to end that Russian bastard for stepping on Les' toes. Now he ordered people to shoot at her. Leo getting hit was a blow to the gut. I'm just now getting used to him being around, and then he was almost gone in a flash. I don't know if Les can handle that or Gage.

After dinner, Gage and Les took Leo upstairs with pain meds and strict orders that he needed to sleep. I see Les sneak out the backdoor about twenty minutes later, so I decide to make sure she's okay, leaving everyone else to their conversation in the living room.

It's dark, but I can see her silhouette on the massive swing in the backyard that gives you an unrestricted view of the city below. The swing is about the size of a day bed her dad had built for her when she was younger. This is where you could usually find her when she needs to think.

I walk around the side of the swing, and that's when I hear her crying.

"Baby girl?"

"I can't do this," she sobs out, and it's the worst sound I've ever heard. "I can't fucking do this!"

The sobs wracking her body are hard, her whole body shaking. I sit down on the swing at a loss of what to do; I can message any of the others inside to come to help her. The sounds she's making are ripping my heart into shreds.

Alessa. Vanilla. Safe.

I don't give myself time to second guess it; I jerk her into my chest, wrapping my arms around her. The sensation is weird and uncomfortable, but I'll be damned if those motherfuckers keep me from comforting my girl ever again.

She buries her face in my shirt, and I can feel the wetness from her tears. She cries like that for so long I start to get worried.

"Baby girl," I say, rubbing my hand up and down her back, my head laying on hers. "You're scaring me."

"I don't think I can do this, Dex." She sniffs. "We're getting ready to fight the Russians. We almost lost Leo. I feel like I'm losing control of myself and everything around me." She looks at me with such sad eyes I wish I can take it all away. "I miss Dad," she whispers. "He wouldn't fall apart like this."

I pull her up, wiping her tears off with my thumbs. "You can do this. You're strong. There's nothing wrong with taking a minute to get your emotions together. You have us to lean on when you need, Baby girl."

She wraps her arms around my neck, squeezing tight. I wrap my arms around her back, squeezing just as tight, sinking into the feeling of her pressed against my body with no panic. I don't even feel it creeping up in the background. I just feel her finally wrapped in my arms again.

"I missed this, Dexton," she whispers against my neck.

"Me too," I whisper back.

She pulls back, and I want to jerk her back, but I need to give her space. She lets out a watery laugh, wiping her face off with her shirt. "I'm a mess."

"Maybe, but we all are; that's why we work." I wipe more tears away with my thumbs. "We will get through this. Together."

She looks back up at me, her eyes searching mine. I tuck her hair behind her ear, rubbing my hand down her cheek, marveling at the softness and the fact that I'm fine with it.

I want to kiss her so damn bad. I lean toward her, leaving a breath between our lips, letting her take that last step. She closes the distance pressing her lips onto mine, tentatively putting her hands on the sides of my neck. I sink further into the kiss, letting her know I'm okay. With a sigh, she wraps her arms around my neck, pressing her body against mine.

I pull her over so she's straddling my lap without breaking our lips apart, running my hands up and down her back because I can't get enough. I massage my tongue against hers; before long, her hips are grinding, and mine are pushing up to get closer and closer.

"Make me forget, Dex," she whispers against my lips.

"Are you sure?" I need to ask. No way in hell do I want her to think I'm taking advantage of her.

"Please. I need this so bad from you."

I think back to the last time we had sex; we didn't touch like this because I couldn't. I could barely get my shit together enough to grab her hips. The time with her and Ryder was the first time I was with someone in six years, and I couldn't even touch her like I wanted. But I can now.

"Here?" I ask.

This is the first place I ever noticed her; the moment I knew I needed this girl like I needed air. It seems fitting that the first time I can enjoy her touch, that would also be here on this swing, overlooking the city she rules over.

"Yes."

I slide my hands under her shirt, pulling it over her head, revealing a black lace bra cradling those perfect breasts. I lay her shirt on the swing, kiss each one, then her chest and neck. She sighs again, running her fingers through the hair on the back of my head. I feel a shudder wrack my body, but not because anything is creeping up; it feels so fucking good.

I reach behind her and unhook her bra, laying it with her shirt after carefully sliding it down her arms, letting my fingers brush against her skin. Her nipples pebble instantly, goosebumps popping up on her flesh, and it isn't because she's cold.

"I want to touch you too," she whispers. She slides her hands under the hem of my shirt, pausing to ensure I can handle it. I take a deep breath and nod. She slides it up and over my head, laying it with her discarded clothes. She runs her hands down my chest, and I shiver again; her hands pause below my pecs. "Is this okay?"

"God, yes," I rasp, jerking her lips back to mine.

It's a deep kiss, one I can feel in my soul. Slow and unhurried, we explore each other's mouths and exposed skin; neither of us can get enough.

I turn us so I can lay her back on the padded swing, stretching my body over hers. Kissing down her neck and chest, I run my hands up her sides before gently massaging both breasts, her back arches pushing them further into my hands. "Beautiful," I whisper before pulling her nipple into my mouth.

"Dex," she whispers my name like a prayer, needing this contact as much as I do.

I switch between both nipples before kissing down her sternum, down her stomach, then kissing a line across the skin directly above her shorts.

I stand up from the swing, kicking my boots off before shedding my jeans so my cock can breathe. It's begging to be inside her, but I want to take my time with her. Show her what I wanted to show her six years ago and the other day when I bent her over the bed. I pull her shorts and panties off before I climb back on the swing, getting my face situated between her thighs.

I take my tongue and swipe slowly from the entrance of her pussy to her clit, circling my tongue around it. Her taste explodes on my tongue, and I already know I'll be addicted to tasting her again. Her hips lift, and she lets go of one of those deep throaty moans, causing my cock to jerk in my boxer briefs. I follow the same path back and forth with my tongue several times, circling her clit each time. I lick beside her clit on each side before sucking it into my mouth.

"Ohhhh," she breathes, pushing her hips to meet my mouth,

shoving her hands into my hair. I sink two fingers into her pussy, twisting and rubbing until her hips jerk, sucking her clit into my mouth.

She tastes so fucking good, I want to stay here with my face buried between her thighs for the rest of the night, but I need to be inside her, my body sliding against hers. I just need to *feel* her.

I start working my fingers faster, sucking her clit harder until she's rubbing her pussy against my face, hips twisting. "Oh fuck, Dex," she moans, and I can feel her tighten on my fingers, pulling my face closer by her hold on my hair. When she finally lets go, I can feel her orgasm running down my fingers. Her back arches off the swing and her thighs try to close around my head. I lick her slowly to bring her down from her climax. When her body settles again, I kiss back up her body until I reach those pouty lips. She wraps her arms around my neck, pulling me closer. We get my boxers down between the two of us; I kick them off, not giving a fuck where they go.

I reach between us, and line my cock up with her wet pussy before slowly sliding in, letting her feel every inch of my fat cock stretching her.

"Fuck, Dex. You feel good," she groans when I'm all the way inside of her.

I pull back out slowly, sliding slowly back in. My chest is rubbing her tits every pass, the sweat coating our bodies, making it easy.

"I don't want this to end," I groan.

"Me either." She places her hands on my face, turning it so she can kiss me.

I move in and out, grinding my hips every time I sink in to put friction on her clit. I never speed up, and she never rushes me, just as content as me to make this last as long as possible.

I can't look away from her eyes, marveling at how beautiful this woman is, and she wants *me*. I pushed her away all those years ago because I thought she deserved someone better than me to have on her arm. Now I realize how much time I lost when I could have been with her and could have been able to move on from that horrible night a long time ago.

Her eyes are wide open, letting me peek at everything that's happening inside her mind, and right now, that's solely focused on me. Both of our breathing is harsh because of all the emotion surrounding this moment together.

We move in that sensual dance for what feels like forever and not long enough at the same time. I'm not ready to lose the contact of her skin against mine. My mind is blissfully empty of anything except her soft sighs, her chest sliding against mine, her hands rubbing up and down my back, and my cock sliding in and out of her.

"Alessa," I sigh her name and watch her pupils expand, her lips parting on a moan.

"Dex," she whispers, then her head tips back when I feel her tighten on my cock. I kiss a line down her exposed neck, sucking gently on her pulse point that's jumping in her neck. "Dex," she moans again, and I can feel her orgasm wash over her.

I don't need to make her scream to know I remember what I'm doing. This isn't about that. This is our bodies coming together again after a long time apart. I can finally hug her, touch her, kiss her, and cuddle her whenever I want. I don't have to worry about finding her upset and having to find one of the other guys to comfort her. She has me now too. Nothing will stand in the way of her and me ever again.

I make her come two more times before I even think about chasing my own release because I can't get enough of watching the emotion flit across her face. When I feel her third building, I place my arm under her head, anchor my hand on her shoulder, and hook my other hand on her hip. Her legs are wrapped around my waist, and her ankles are crossed at the base of my spine. I scoot up her body, changing the angle and pushing more pressure on her clit.

"Oh God," she breathes, running her hands down my sweaty back, rolling her hips with my thrusts. I know she's getting close when her pussy clamps down on my cock, and I know I can't fight off my release this time.

"Come on my cock again, Baby girl," I whisper, starting to move faster.

Her back arches, head thrown back, mouth parted in ecstasy. With the moonlight illuminating her body, she looks like the angel

Leo called her last night, with her black hair fanned out behind her. "Dex," she moans long, loud, her pussy milking my cock.

I lock my eyes with hers as I'm about to come, letting her see everything like she trusted me each time she came for me. I want to be vulnerable with her just like she is with me. With a groan, I finally come deep inside her, never looking away. I gently kiss her lips, my heart swelling ten sizes.

"I love you, Baby girl," I whisper.

Everything fucking stops. Her hands quit running up and down my back, her blue eyes snap wide, shock written all over her face. I didn't mean to let that slip out, but this moment with her cemented how I already know I feel, bringing it to the surface like a rush of endorphins. I refuse to take it back.

I love this girl with every part of my dark, damaged soul; I would do anything for her, be anything for her.

I pull my arm from behind her head and turn us so that we're lying on our sides facing each other, still buried inside her. I run my fingers down her cheek, refusing to move my body an inch from hers. "I love you." I run my thumb across her bottom lip. "You don't have to say anything until you're ready. But I need you to know that I love you. That I'm *in* love with you. I have been since the first moment I laid eyes on you." I smile at that because I know it's true. I see tears in her eyes; I reach up and catch one with my thumb before it can fall. "This moment was meant for you. The moment I finally let the walls down in my mind that kept me trapped."

When I found out about my aversion to touch the hard way six years ago, I made a promise to myself. When she was ready, I would claim this woman and give her all my firsts again. I made that promise come true tonight.

She crushes her lips to mine desperately, and I kiss her back just as desperately. She pulls back. "I love you too, Dexton. I have for a long time." She runs her hand over my face, across my scars, with a smile. "I was just waiting for you to come back to me."

I kiss her again, slower this time. The feeling I have at this moment, I can't even explain; all I know is I'm never letting this girl go. She is *mine*. I can't think of a better way to spend the rest of my life than cherishing this girl with guys I consider my brothers, even Leo.

A family can be found in many different capacities. Growing up, I didn't have a family; I found mine with Les, Ryder, and Gage. Holden is like a little brother I want to protect in every capacity. Watching him blossom with Les makes my heart swell even more.

I feel myself harden again, so I start moving my hips, sliding my cock back and forth inside her. She nudges my shoulder until I roll us, so she's on top. She breaks the kiss before sitting up, bracing her hands on my chest, doing something sinful with her hips that makes my spine tingle. Her head is thrown back, the tips of her long hair tickling my thighs. The moon backlights her making her hair shine, illuminating every square inch of her perfect body. I move my hands to her hips, helping her take her pleasure.

I don't know what will happen tomorrow, but I know I'm finally free at this moment.

CHAPTER 41
RYDER

Shit's heating up around here, and not for the right reasons.

Viktor Orlov is going to fucking die for taking a shot at Les. If I have to admit it to myself, it thawed every bit of ice around my heart when it came to Leo. I promised myself I would tolerate him for Les, but that was it. I wouldn't accept him like I did the others, but the moment I saw all that blood pouring from his wound, I knew that was bullshit. Was he automatically my best friend now? No. It just means there's a place for him when that time comes, and I'll take that step in trying to get to know him.

I know I was the hardest to come to terms with sharing her, but if anyone is worth trying for, it's Les. I will do anything in this world to keep that smile on her face. I know she's dealing with a lot, so we all need to band together and make at least one thing easier for her.

Telling Les, I love her last night was not part of the plan when I asked her to dance with me. There was just something floating in her eyes when I stared into them that I knew deep in my soul that I needed to tell her. Hearing those three words back is what I've dreamed about for years, but nothing compares to the reality of it. Les is mine now and forever; no one will take that from me.

I went to check on her last night after she had been gone a while, knowing she was on her swing thinking. What I saw was a shock, but not because I found her and Dex together.

She was riding him, her head thrown back in ecstasy, and he was touching her. Running his hands all over her like he couldn't get enough, that was the shock. Knowing Dex moved past his issues is another reason I'm determined to make this work. I heard them come in later, so I gave them space to reconnect. They didn't even realize I was there; they were so wrapped up in each other that I snuck back into the house.

And Dad said I couldn't share.

There's only one more thing I need to figure out after Gage brought it up...Holden. Last night after everyone else left the living room, Gage asked me what was going on with Holden and me. Ever since he mentioned it, it opened my eyes to what I already know. I feel more for Holden than friendship, and it took Gage's big ass mouth to make me realize that. Holden has a friendship with us; we're all equally protective of him, but he's always been closer to Les and me. We haven't had any close encounters since the gym, and I know he avoids it as much as I do. Neither of us wants to take that next step that can spell trouble if something goes wrong.

He developed a crush quickly on Les, not that I blame him. She pulled him out of that disgusting room and took care of him in any way he needed. The night we got him out, we couldn't believe what we found in that room, especially since we were on our way to kill the person hacking her.

I need to talk to Holden and get some things out in the open. I know Gage and Leo are still asleep because I just checked on Leo, and he's tucked safely against Gage. That whole thing still blows my mind but not the least bit surprising. I saw how Gage looked at Leo the first night we tied him up in the basement.

I heard Dex go into the gym about ten minutes ago, which means he probably left Les sleeping peacefully because there is no way, after what I witnessed, he would have let her out of sight last night.

I glance at the time on my phone; it's just after eight in the morning, so Holden's probably awake. My mind made up; I make my way to the corner office where he spends most of his time.

I walk in without knocking like I always do, and that's when I realize Les isn't sleeping peacefully upstairs.

She's currently straddling his lap on the little couch in the back with no shirt or bra on, hands buried in his curly hair while he ravishes her mouth.

I shut the door behind me, and they jerk apart. She looks over her shoulder with a smile, Holden peeking around her arm.

"Fancy meeting you here, *Il mio sole*."

"We were going over some files and got um...distracted."

"Distracted? That's what we call it now?" I ask, walking further into the room.

"It's a damn good distraction," Holden says, leaning forward. Her back arches, and I know that little shit just pulled her nipple into his mouth.

"Damn good," she agrees, letting her head fall back on her shoulders. "Are you joining?"

I walk over and brace my hands on the couch on either side of Holden's head, pressing my chest against her back. "What does Holden think about that?" I sweep her hair to the side, kissing a line up her neck but also watching his face.

His breathing speeds up, and he lets her nipple go with a wet pop. "Stay," he says, and it sounds like he's pushing the word out.

"You want us at the same time, *Il mio sole*?" I ask, laying more kisses on her neck.

"Yes," she moans, grinding her hips on Holden. "Lube. My room, in the bedside table."

This will be my first time inside of a girl with another guy. Dex and I shared her, but we were never in her at the same time.

I lay one more kiss on her neck before going to her room as quickly as possible. I jerk open the table drawer and rummage around until I find what I'm looking for before jogging back down the stairs. I open the office door, shutting it quickly behind me.

They made quick work of their clothes while I was gone, laying on the couch in sixty-nine. I almost choke on my fucking tongue when I see Holden's cock. Her hand can't wrap around the base, and her mouth only goes a little more than halfway. He has a tight grip on her thighs, eating her pussy like it's his last meal. Her mouth pops off his cock. "Fuck, Holden," she moans, still twisting her hand around him.

He doubles down on eating her out until she's riding his face, making his knuckles turn white from his grip on her. I would say he's a happy fucking man right now.

"Oh God," she breathes, pushing herself up on both hands on his abs. Her back arches. "Holden!" she screams, and I wince at the scream echoing off the walls. There's no way in hell they can't figure out what we're doing in here.

He slides her off his face and onto his chest with a huge grin, licking his lips. "Fuck, you taste good."

She laughs and nods her head for me to walk closer. Like a puppet on a string, I find myself planted right in front of her. She might be in control of everything else, but in the bedroom, I have a feeling Les likes it when we take control. When she took control of me in the hallway with her hand around my throat, I have to admit that I like her taking control too. Something I'm just now realizing about myself.

I wrap a hand around her slim throat because I saw how her eyes blazed when I did it last night. Her pupils immediately expand, so I tighten my grip. Her mouth pops open with a breathless moan. "On your feet, *Il mio sole*." I help her with my grip on her neck until she has both feet on the floor. "I think our girl here likes it when we take control," I say to Holden, who's transfixed on my hand around her throat. "If he touches your pussy right now, how wet will you be just from my hand around your throat?"

I apply more pressure stealing her air, and her face completely relaxes. *Fuck, that's sexy.*

"Slide your fingers inside of her," I tell Holden, placing a kiss on her lips. "Tell me how wet she is."

He sits on the couch behind her, her perfect ass in his face. He slides two fingers into her with a groan. "She's soaked."

I let my grip loosen so she can suck in air. "You like that?"

"Yes," she breathes, grinding her hips down on Holden's fingers still inside of her. I tighten my hold again, stopping her from moving.

"Hm," I hum, running my nose up her neck, making her shiver. "I need to fuck you," I whisper in her ear. "I want to feel my cock rub against Holden's." I can feel her moan vibrate against my hand. "You like that idea, *Il mio sole*? Knowing I'm going to like another man's cock inside of you?" She moans again, and I loosen my hold. "Answer me."

"Yes. God, Ryder," she moans, seeking the friction on his fingers again. She slides her hand down over my hard cock through my shorts and squeezes. She reaches up with her other hand and pulls my head back down. "You want him, Ryder?" she whispers.

I hiss air through my teeth. "Yes," I grit out. I'm painfully hard just from the thought of my cock rubbing against his through the thin skin that'll be separating us. There's no denying that I want him now. I slap her ass hard. "Ride his cock."

He helps her get turned around; she braces one knee beside his thigh and her foot beside the other. He grips his cock and lines himself up. I step back and watch his huge cock disappear inside her, his hands tightening on her hips. She puts the other knee down when he's all the way inside of her.

"Fuck, Bright eyes," Holden groans, his fingers flexing.

She braces her hands on his shoulders and rolls her hips, causing them both to groan.

I whip my shirt over my head and shed my boxers and shorts. I stroke my hand up and down my cock watching her ride him. I didn't think I would ever like this part, but there's something about watching your girl get pleasured by someone else; you can stand back and watch every second of it.

I walk back over and place my hands beside Holden's head again, except this time, she can feel my hard cock rubbing against her, and I have an unrestricted look at his eyes. I kiss up and down her neck, watching his eyes the whole time; they never leave my lips. There isn't any doubt left in my mind that he wants this too.

I uncap the bottle of lube, squirting it in my hand before closing the cap and tossing it on the couch. I rub it all over my cock, so I'm nice and slick when I slide inside her. It'll be a tight fit with Holden and me inside her.

She lays her chest against his to give me better access and a view of his cock stretching her pussy open. An idea pops into my head that I hope she doesn't beat the shit out of me for.

I notch my cock at her asshole, then slide down until it's beside Holden inside her. I keep a tight grip on the base, then push forward until the head pops into her pussy with him. Her head whips around; his eyes are wide and locked on mine. I want to feel them at the same time, not separated. "Can you take us both in your pussy, *Il mio sole*?" I grit out. It's fucking tight, and I just have the head of my cock inside of her.

She wiggles her hips back a little with a moan. "Yes."

I look at Holden, and he gives me a frantic nod. Still keeping the grip at the base of my cock, I push harder, feeling her pussy stretch to accommodate us both.

I get halfway in before Holden's hands fly out, landing on my hips. "Fuck. Your piercings," he groans, his eyes screwed shut.

I stop. "Does it hurt?"

"No. Fuck," he breathes, and his eyes fly open. "It feels good."

Her breathing is erratic, and her head is lying on Holden's shoulder. "Don't stop," she begs.

Placing my hands beside his head again, I start working my hips back and forth in short thrusts, feeling my piercings bump against the veins on the underside of his cock. I take a breath on the last short stroke and slam my hips forward, burying me inside her pussy with Holden.

Her head snaps up, and her hands slam down on Holden's shoulders. "Holy fuck," she pants. "Oh God."

"Are you okay, Bright eyes?" Holden asks in concern, taking one hand from my hips to rub her cheek.

She moans deep and low, causing our cocks to twitch inside her. "Fuck yes."

I lean against her, putting my face right in front of Holden's. If I lick my lips, I'll lick his too. Am I ready for that? Is he ready for that?

I feel his other hand go back to my hip, and it blazes a trail of fire down my leg just from his touch.

I start working my hips in short deep thrusts, my breathing already ragged from the overwhelming sensation of touching both of them at the same time.

I'm going to move in on his lips when he takes the decision out of my hands, slamming his lips against mine, surprising me just like he did in the gym. The shock wears off in less than a second, and I sink my tongue into his mouth with a groan.

I've never kissed a guy before Holden. When I thought about kissing him, I assumed it would be like kissing Les. I was wrong. Kissing Holden is consuming, like kissing her, but that's where the similarities end. His lips aren't as plump or soft as hers; they're rougher. And I fucking love it.

"Holy shit," Les whispers when she sees our lips locked together.

His hands slide up my sides the longer I kiss him, exploring my body. His hands are rough from working out, bigger than Les'. The only thing that rips through my mind is his hand wrapped around my cock. I groan again at that image, kissing him harder.

I finally pull away to suck in a breath, sweat rolling down my face. Laying my forehead against his beside hers. "Fuck, Holden."

"Yeah," he breathes. I know he's agreeing with everything that just went through my head.

I start moving my hips again, faster this time. A mix of moans and groans fills the room, the wet squelch of our cocks sliding against each other inside her.

"Oh God," Les moans, never lifting her head. Her legs start shaking uncontrollably, so I pick up the pace. She starts shaking harder, her moans never stopping. I feel the wet gush rush out of her, squirting all over our cocks. Her moans get louder, so I keep moving at the same pace. Holden hooks his hands under her ass to pull out and push back in at the same time as me. It's so tight inside her like this that we can't move much, but it's enough to shoot fire down my spine. Her back straightens up, and her legs shake again.

"Squirt for us again, *Il mio sole*," I pant into her ear. I can't get a real breath to save my life. If I die right now, I'll die a happy fucking man.

I feel that pressure against the head of my cock again, and then the wetness gushes out around our cocks, dripping all over the floor.

"I'm going to come," Holden groans, his short thrusts stuttering.

"One more time," I beg Les. "Give us one more."

She moans again, "I don't know if I can."

"You're almost there already. I can feel it." I'm addicted to the idea of her juices soaking our cocks, leaking all over the floor.

Holden and I start pumping harder; I wrap my hand around her throat again and squeeze.

"Fuck," Holden grits out when she squeezes us both.

I could feel my release rushing down my spine, drawing my balls up. She's so fucking close. One more thrust inside her, and Holden's head goes back on a groan coming hard, taking me along with him. I come with a shout; the release is so intense it's almost painful.

"Fuck fuck fuck," Les chants. "Fuck!" She starts bucking between us, so I pull out and lift her by the hips, so Holden's cock slides out.

Her body is shaking out of control, and a stream rushes out of her all over Holden's cock and legs, soaking the couch and floor, our come leaking out behind it. "Holden! Ryder!" She reaches between her and Holden, rubbing her clit back and forth, making more gush out.

"Holy fuck, that's hot, *Il mio sole*," I groan.

She collapses against Holden's chest; I collapse beside them. He's rubbing up and down her back, waiting for her breathing to return to normal. I slide my hand over the base of her spine while he rubs around her shoulders.

"Are you alive, Bright eyes?" Holden chuckles.

"No," she mumbles, her voice muffled where it's smooshed against Holden's chest.

I laugh. "You sound alive to me."

"My pussy is dead." She finally lifts her head with a blissed-out smile. "That was so good." She leans over, kisses me, then kisses Holden before laying her head on his chest.

"We definitely have to do that again," Holden remarks.

I chuckle, and it brings his attention to me. I lean in, slanting my mouth over his and sliding my hand from her back to his leg. “Yeah, we do,” I whisper against his lips.

I pull back and jerk Les’ lips to mine, giving her the same kiss. Les giggles and I pull back with a frown. “What’s so funny?”

“Nothing,” she laughs. “I’m just deliriously happy right now.”

“Me too,” Holden and I say at the same time, making Les laugh harder.

I will do anything to keep that smile on her face.

Starting with getting rid of Viktor Orlov.

CHAPTER 42
ALESSA

"I'll buy you a new couch," Ryder offers Holden once we showered and made it to the kitchen for breakfast. "There's no saving the other one."

Holden laughs. "It was worth it."

"Totally worth it," I agree from my seat on the counter in front of the island.

After my cry last night and initial freak out, I feel better, and I have Dex to thank for that. I never in a million years thought he would be the one to console me, but he dropped every wall he had... for me. We couldn't keep our hands off of each other after that. We made love twice more on the swing, then he carried me upstairs, where we made love again. All through the night, one of us was waking the other one to get more, and each time I fell asleep with my head on his chest, wrapped in his arms. I didn't think the day would ever come when he would let me back in.

When he told me he loved me, it was like everything was finally snapping into place; I didn't mean to freeze on him. I felt terrible he had to explain himself before I could form words, but he just shocked me.

Dex strides into the room, and when his eyes zero in on me, he's in front of me before I can blink. He slides his body between my thighs, buries his hands in my hair, and slants his mouth over mine, kissing me breathless.

He pulls back, laying a little peck on my lips. "Good morning, Gaby girl."

"Good morning, Dexton." I wrap my arms around his neck and marvel at the fact he doesn't even react.

He leans in beside my ear. "Sounded like you had a real good morning," he whispers.

"You heard that?"

"The whole house heard that," he chuckles. "What were they doing to you?"

I love that the guys ask me about my time with the others, it turns them on as much as me, and they want to ensure that I'm being taken care of.

"They fucked me at the same time," I whisper, rubbing my lips up his neck, making his whole-body shudder. "In the pussy."

He jerks his head back, grey eyes darkening. "They were in your pussy at the same time?" I nod, and he groans, "Fuck. Were you a good girl for them?"

"She made a mess of my office," Holden says proudly, tuning into our conversation.

Ryder snorts. "Understatement. We're going to have to buy him a new fucking couch."

Dex slants his mouth over mine again and jerks my hips forward so I grind against his hard cock. I shouldn't be able to get turned on after all night with Dex and the office with Holden and Ryder, but I could get Dex's cock out right now and let him fuck me without complaints.

Something is broken inside of me.

"For fuck's sake," Micah grouches, making Dex and me pull apart. "Not in the kitchen." He looks between me and Dex, his mouth dropping open at the fact that Dex is practically wrapped around me. His wide eyes turn to me, and I just smile.

"What about in the living room?" Gage quips, having followed him into the kitchen.

"I would prefer not to see my niece naked." Micah wrinkles his nose, and I can't help but laugh.

"Where are the Perez boys?" I ask, trying to change the subject. Dex turns around with his back to my chest with his arms folded; I wrap my arms around his chest, propping my chin on his massive shoulder.

Gage pops a kiss on my lips. "In the dining room." His eyes land on Dex, and he grins. "Does this mean I can hug you now without fear of death?"

"Hug me and find out," Dex offers, but I can hear the threatening undertone in his voice.

Gage moves in fast, wrapping his arms around Dex's waist, then dances out of his reach, laughing. "You know not to provoke me."

"Fucking children," Micah mutters under his breath.

Gage spins on his heel, facing Micah. "You want one?" he asks, holding his arms out. "Bring it in."

"Fuck off," Micah says, taking a step back when Gage advances on him. "Gage," he warns.

"Come on," Gage wiggles his fingers, arms still outstretched. "Just give in."

Gage takes several steps forward, causing Micah to take several steps back, running right into Evander, who's walking into the kitchen. Micah whirls around and ducks behind Evander, using him as a human shield.

"Come on, Micah," I remark. "He just wants a hug."

"I was deprived as a child," Gage pouts. "Just one."

"No. Get one from your boyfriend or Les." Micah waves his hand from behind Evander, making Evander laugh.

Gage turns his pout on Evander. "Just one?" he asks, and if I didn't know any better, I would think he's genuinely upset.

Evander raises an eyebrow but opens his arms for Gage. Gage whoops and wraps his arms around him, almost knocking Evander down. I'm laughing so hard that I have tears rolling down my face. This is a typical day with Gage in this house.

Mateo and Leo round the corner to find Evander wrapped in Gage's arms. Leo just shakes his head and walks around them. He looks much better this morning and isn't as pale or like he will pass out at the drop of a hat.

Leo leans back on the counter beside Dex and me. "Do I want to know?" he asks, nodding his head at Gage, stepping back from his hug.

"He was deprived as a child," Ryder repeats with a laugh. "He was trying to get Micah."

I kiss Leo's cheek. "How are you feeling?"

"Better, actually. Ryder changed the bandage this morning and said it was healing good."

I still can't wrap my head around Ryder being so attentive to Leo. He ensured he rested, took his pain meds, kept his bandages dry and clean, and checked on him every night and every morning. That part he doesn't think anyone knows about.

Gage walks over and cages Leo against the counter with his arms; Leo lays his hands on Gage's hips like it's the most natural thing. "I took care of something else this morning."

Leo's face heats up, but it's not from embarrassment. "You sure fucking did."

I punch Gage's arm. "Don't do anything to rip his stitches."

Dex laughs from his spot in front of me. "You aren't worried that one of your boyfriends got freaky with your other boyfriend. You're worried he could rip his stitches."

"Priorities," I laugh and peck Dex's cheek. "It's hot as fuck knowing they mess around."

Gage rubs his arm like I actually hurt him. "I just sucked his dick."

"Jesus Christ," Micah throws his hands up in the air, storming from the room. "I hate every single fucking one of you!" he yells.

"I don't see Evander and Mateo bothered by this conversation!" I yell back.

"Because they own a FUCKING SEX CLUB!" Micah yells back, getting louder with each word, then the backdoor slams.

"Fair point," Mateo laughs. "Why is he so high-strung this morning?"

"He walked in on Dex dry-humping Les," Holden says, stealing a strawberry from Ryder's plate and dropping it into his mouth. Ryder fake growls and Holden just grins.

"Little shit," Ryder chuckles affectionately. "Don't think I won't go in after it."

Gage's head whips around. "Please let me witness that."

Ryder shrugs, and hooks his hand on the back of Holden's neck, jerking Holden's mouth to his. He kisses him like he did in the office. Watching any of the guys give in to their desires with each other never fails to make me soak my panties. There's something about the almost brutal way they kiss each other but can be tender with one another too.

Everyone's mouth in the room is hanging open except for mine because I witnessed it first-hand. Ryder pulls back and licks his lips with a grin. Holden stares at him with a stunned expression, then leans forward, pecking Ryder on the lips.

"Holy shit," Leo whispers, "I never saw that shit coming."

"I did," Gage admits.

"Of course you did, Babe. You're nosey as fuck." Leo says.

Gage turns around slowly. "Did you just call me babe?"

"You have two nicknames for me," Leo points out.

Gage buries his nose against Leo's neck. "I do, Pretty boy."

"I fucking love this house," Mateo says, looking around the room.

"I'm quite fond of it myself," Evander agrees.

"Does that mean you're staying until all this clears?" I ask, hoping they say yes. I know it will make Leo feel better to have them here.

Evander and Mateo exchange a look, then Evander turns to me. "Temporarily, yes. I'd like to keep an eye on Leo."

Leo snorts. "I don't need a goddamn babysitter."

"I'm not staying as a babysitter," Evander says evenly. "I'm staying because your girl was kind enough to offer so we would all be safe."

Leo grimaces. "Sorry. I got off the phone with Mom earlier, and she was freaking out."

My head whips to him. "You told your mother that you got shot?!"

"No," he scoffs, "I told her I got hurt, but I didn't tell her exactly how."

I breathe a sigh of relief. I hate that he has to lie to her, but she doesn't need to know the truth. The truth in our lives can get you killed.

"I need to go to their house and get some stuff," Leo says, wrapping his arms tighter around Gage. "You two want to take me?"

"We have some stuff to do first," Gage responds, then looks at me. "Later?"

I nod. "Works for me." Then I level them both with a look. "But no freaky shit until his stitches are healed better."

Ryder laughs. "Sucks to be you."

I turn my look on him. "Keep talking shit, and I'll put you on that list too."

"Even after this morning?" he purrs, wrapping an arm around Holden's shoulders. "I think we could convince you, *Il mio sole*."

I snort. "You think I couldn't say no?" I say with false bravado. They don't need to know I will fold at the drop of a hat.

Dex chuckles and stands up with my arms still around his neck. "My money is on, Les." He hooks an arm under my ass, boosting me up, so I'm on his back and strides out of the room.

At least he has faith in me; I sure as hell don't.

THE DAY CONSISTED of checking the docks, meeting with Helena about the restaurant, and checking on Maximus and a few other venues. I haven't told Leo yet, but I'm giving him reins over the new place because he's expressed that he feels useless. Evander and Mateo gave him a few places to manage, but he isn't used to just sitting around.

It's after eight at night, and we're finally on our way to Evander and Mateo's house to get Leo some of his stuff. Gage is driving with his hand firmly on my thigh while I'm on the phone the whole time. I hate this part. Sometimes it's all quiet, but on days like today, I want to toss my phone out of the window again.

"Try harder," I tell Ghost.

"I swear to you I am," he sighs. "He's not taking the bait, and he knows something is up."

"Make him suspicious, then he has no choice but to show up, and when he does, you call me."

"Got it."

"Check back in later. I have to go," I tell him and hang up.

"Everything good, Baby?" Leo asks from the back.

"Yeah," I run my hand through my hair, "Except Ghost can't get that meeting with Spinner."

"He'll show, Pretty girl. Eventually, Viktor will wonder where Xander is," Gage says, swinging his car to a stop in front of the house.

"I hope so. Spinner is the lead I need on Viktor," I reply and climb out of the car.

We follow Leo up to the door, where he unlocks it letting us in. The house is eerily quiet since Evander sent his staff home since he's staying with me. The only person left behind is one of the housekeepers, Luna.

"Hello, Mr. Perez," Luna greets politely, "Ms. Poletti. Mr. Lawson."

Gage shivers. "Please call me Gage."

He hates being called Mr. Lawson because of his dad. Saying his dad is awful is an understatement. He was a mean drunk that did everything in his power to make Gage's life miserable after Gage's mom left when he was seven. I asked my dad once why he kept Gage's dad Conner around, and he told me it was because our house was the only good place Gage had. The first thing I did when I took over was run Conner off because Gage didn't need him there anymore.

Luna smiles. "Is there anything I can help with?"

"No," Leo smiles back, "I'm just packing some things up. Evander and Mateo will be by tomorrow to pick up a few things. Why don't you go on home?"

"I just have a few more things to do." She smiles again and disappears from the room.

Leo shakes his head, walking to the stairs. "That woman doesn't understand the word rest."

We walk into Leo's room, and I realize this is the first time I've been in here. It instantly smells like him, and the room is done in a mixture of blues and earth tones.

Gage swan dives into the middle of the bed.

"You're such a child," I laugh, walking around the room and looking at the pictures he has hanging on a bulletin board. Gage rolls off the bed, walks up behind me, and slides his arms around my waist. I lay my hand on his and glimpse Leo's life before me. There are pictures of him, Evander, and Mateo smiling at whoever is taking the picture, and that's when I finally see the slight similarities between them. All three have the same smile and crinkle around their eyes. I look further up. "Is this your mom?" I ask, pointing to one in the corner.

Leo pokes his head out of the closet. "Yeah," he answers before disappearing.

"Damn, he looks just like her," Gage comments.

"She's beautiful," I say with a slight pain in my chest for my own mom. Then I see one of the pictures we took together hanging there. I remember it like it was yesterday. It was our fourth date, and we wanted a cheesy kissing picture. So, we placed our lips together, and Leo snapped the picture with his phone. Because of how ridiculous it was, you could see us smiling around the kiss, but I never got to take the cheesy couple pictures. Now my camera roll is full of photos of the guys and me.

"You guys look so happy here," Gage says, running his finger down the picture.

I smile. "We were."

Gage hugs me tighter. "You ever feel like all this shit was meant to be?"

I frown. "Like fate?"

"I don't know if I believe in that," Gage replies. "I just mean, everything does happen for a reason, right?"

I want to believe that, but that doesn't explain all the bad stuff we have to go through to get here. Do I feel like everything is where it's supposed to be now? Yes. I just don't know if I can agree with something like fate.

"Do you have feelings for him, Gage?" I ask quietly, just for his ears.

He's silent for so long that I don't think he'll answer. "I'm getting there."

I turn in his arms, wrapping mine around his neck. "I want you to be as happy with him as I am."

"I'm happy as hell, Pretty girl," he says, kissing my forehead. "I have you in my life, and I'm hopefully building something with Leo. It couldn't be better."

I already know I love Gage, but something is always holding me back from telling him, even now. I never feel like he's ready, and this time is no different.

"I'm happy with you too," I say instead.

"I have to get some things from downstairs," Leo says, walking out of the closet and slinging a duffle on the bed, earning a glare from Gage.

"You aren't supposed to be carrying that," Gage says.

Leo rolls his eyes. "Then you carry it downstairs, he-man," he snarks and disappears out of the door.

Gage turns back to me. "I wouldn't change anything," he says, kissing me softly.

I feel like we're dancing around the same three little words, neither willing to put it out on the line yet. It was easy with Leo; we had been dating for four months. Ryder was obvious because I've been in love with him half my life if I'm honest with myself, and Dex made it easy to love him, even now. Gage and Holden are the unknowns.

"Let's go before he hurts his dumb ass self," Gage says, grabbing my hand and Leo's duffle and tugging my hand to go downstairs.

"He doesn't listen. Maybe he needs a spanking," I joke.

"Leo!" Gage yells. "Come here so Les can spank that ass!"

I laugh, rounding the corner, and stop dead in my tracks. Leo turns wide eyes on Gage and me, and my stomach drops to my feet.

I'm staring into the same blue-green eyes as Leo, just in woman form. The exact shade of brown hair except long.

It's none other than Leo's mother.

Fuck.

CHAPTER 43
LEO

I wanted Alessa to meet my mom, but not when Gage rounds the corner yelling about spanking my ass. All color has drained from Alessa's face, and she looks seconds from bolting, not that I fucking blame her.

"Mom," I say again, "What are you doing here?"

"You tell me you're hurt over the phone and don't expect me to come to check on you?" she says, then huffs. "Nice to see you too."

I instantly feel like shit and pull her in for a hug. "I always want to see you, but you shouldn't have come all the way here," I tell her, mainly because there's a psycho Russian out for blood.

"Nonsense," she says, patting my back. "Are you going to introduce me?" she whispers.

She knows about Alessa; I haven't shut up about her. She didn't know about Gage or my unconventional relationship with Alessa. How the hell do you bring that up to your mom?

I pull back from the hug and turn to a green-looking Alessa and an amused Gage. "Mom, this is Alessa and Gage. Guys, this is my mom, Katherine."

Gage reaches his hand out to shake Mom's, and Mom's eyes zero on Alessa's hand that Gage just dropped. "Nice to meet you," he says politely, kissing her hand when he shakes it. I roll my eyes, watching Mom fall for the charming shit.

Me too, Ma. Me too.

Alessa finally snaps out of her stupor and steps forward with her hand outstretched. "It's nice to meet you finally."

Mom waves Alessa's hand away and crushes her into a hug. "I've heard so much about you," Mom crows.

"Sorry," I mouth to Alessa when her eyes meet mine. Alessa glares, and I don't know if she's serious or not.

When Luna said I had a visitor and then walked around the corner with my mom, I almost fucking died on the spot. She must have jumped on a plane as soon as possible and come straight here; I should have kept my big mouth shut.

Mom pulls Alessa back to arm's length. "You're as gorgeous as Leo said."

Kill me right fucking now.

"Thanks," Alessa says shyly, and it's cute as hell.

"Where are your brothers?" Mom asks, looking around the living room. "This place is magnificent." I freeze because what the hell am I supposed to tell her?

Alessa levels me with a look that promises pain later and turns back to Mom. "They're staying with me while they have some renovations done."

"Oh, that's so sweet of you! Is Leo staying there too?" Mom asks.

"For now," Alessa says, making Gage choke on a laugh. Shit. I hope she doesn't think I set her up to meet Mom, and I haven't even broached the subject because she has so much going on. Alessa smiles sweetly at mom. "We were actually heading back there. Would you like to follow us?"

"Really?" Mom frowns. "I wouldn't want to impose."

"Not a problem," Alessa assures her. "Anything else you need?" she asks me between clenched teeth.

I beg with my eyes that I didn't set her up. "No. I'm good."

"That's great. You can ride with her. Ya know, catch up." Alessa smiles at Mom again before hauling ass out the front door.

Gage chuckles and scoops up the duffle bag, slinging it over his shoulder. "See you there," he grins and follows her out.

Fuck! FUCK!

I follow Mom out to her little rented sedan, sliding into the passenger seat with a sigh. Why the *fuck* did she come here?

"She's a little slip of a thing, isn't she?" Mom asks, shifting the car into drive, following Gage's taillights.

Alessa is tiny even compared to my mom, who's five-eight. But that doesn't make her any less intimidating, especially when she promises to cut your balls off with her eyes like she did me just now.

"And Gage seems like a nice boy," Mom continues, making me snort. I can describe him a hundred ways; nice never crossed my mind.

"Mom, why did you really come all the way here? I told you I was fine."

"I missed you, Leo," she says softly. "I haven't seen you in months."

Because I was with Les. "I know. I'm sorry."

"Do you want me to go back home?" she asks, pulling onto the main road behind Gage, who seems to be taking the back way to Alessa's.

"No," I sigh. "There's some stuff I wasn't ready to tell you yet."

Mom looks at me out of the corner of her eye. "Like what?"

I shake my head. "We will talk about it later. I promise."

My phone pings in my shorts pocket, and I pull it out, reading it with a wince.

ALESSA

You are so fucking dead.

I didn't do it on purpose. I didn't know she was coming!

ALESSA

'insert knife emoji' Dead.

"She didn't seem too happy to see me."

"Mom, because you just showed up out of nowhere. I don't think she's ready for this."

"You're my son, Leo," she says sternly. "I should be able to see you when I want."

I sigh and lay my head on the seat. It isn't because I don't want to see her; I missed her like crazy. But it isn't *safe* around me right now, and I can't tell her that.

We drive to Les' house in silence, and she gasps when we pull up to the gate. "I thought your brother's house was huge."

Their house is huge, but Alessa's house puts it to shame. It's everything you think a mansion is except bigger. I fell in love with this house the first time I saw it. It feels more like a castle on the outside and modern on the inside. The exterior is light and dark brick, with different size column-looking towers lining the front and big bay windows.

"What did you say she does again?" Mom asks, getting out of the car.

She's the leader of the Italian Mafia. "She owns several casinos, restaurants, and clubs."

"At twenty-five? That's impressive," Mom says, and I can't tell if she's buying my bullshit or not. She could always tell when I was lying.

I lead her up behind Gage and Les when Les opens the front door. I bet a thousand bucks she told Ryder, Dex, and Holden to make themselves scarce.

Gage takes Mom's hand and hooks it on his arm, leading her to the living room. I shake my head when I see her look at him like he's the biggest gentleman she's ever met. But it also makes my heart swell that he's trying to impress my mom.

"Would you like anything to drink?" Alessa asks when Mom sits on the couch beside Gage.

"No, dear, I'm fine," Mom answers, pulling me down on her other side.

"I'll be right back," Alessa says, hightailing it from the room.

"Go," Mom says with a smile when I turn to her, getting ready to tell her I need to fix this.

I pop off the couch and catch a flash of her black hair walking into the kitchen. I follow her in, and she rounds on me before I take a second step.

"Your mom?" she hisses. "We are in the middle of a war, Leo."

"I know! I didn't invite her here," I hiss back. "I'm just as surprised as you."

She punches my arm. "This is not how I wanted to meet your mother," she says, swiping her hand over her body. She's wearing a shirt that I'm pretty sure is mine and cotton shorts, but she looks beautiful to me.

"Wait," I say when it hits me, "You would have been okay with meeting her?"

She gives me a look like I'm stupid. "Yes, eventually, when it isn't turning into World War three around here." She runs her hand through her hair. "What does she know?"

"About?"

She gives me that look again. "About us, Leo. About the guys. About you and Gage. What does she know? I need to know what not to say."

"I'm going to tell her everything," I tell her, taking her hands. "I just didn't want to do it over the phone. I guess there's no time like the present."

"She's going to hate me," Alessa says sadly.

"She will never hate you, Baby. She'll love you as much as I do. She'll just have to get used to the idea."

She gives me a doubtful look but squeezes my hands. "Just give me a minute to get my heart out of my fucking stomach, and I'll be back out there."

I grab her face kissing those pouty lips. "I love you, Baby."

She scrunches her nose up. "I love you too."

"That wasn't very convincing," I chuckle.

She rolls her eyes. "Get out of my face before I stab you."

"Stab me or spank me?" I joke.

"Oh my God," she groans. "I forgot she heard that."

I laugh. "It's fine, baby. She'll just know we keep things spicy." I waggle my eyebrows, earning another sharp punch to the arm. Fuck, that hurt.

"Out of my face," she warns, pointing to the living room. I grin and start backing away. "Out, Leo," she says again.

I hold my hands up with a laugh. "Don't escape out of the backdoor," I say and make my way back to the living room before she can hit me again.

Mom is sitting there with Evander and Mateo when I walk into the living room. Evander turns to me with a raised brow, and I shrug before sitting back down. What else am I supposed to say?

"You look so much like your father," Mom says, causing Evander's eye to twitch.

"Yes, ma'am," Evander nods politely.

"Let's just hope you don't have his shitty personality," she mutters, causing Mateo to die of laughter.

"Not at all," Mateo promises.

Alessa comes back into the room, sitting in one of the chairs, and conversation thankfully starts flowing naturally. Mom gushes about the house, and Alessa effortlessly explains that her dad built the businesses and left them to her when he died. Minute by minute, it starts to feel less awkward, and I'm thankful to Gage and Alessa for keeping the conversation going.

After about an hour, Alessa stands up. "We'll give you and Leo some time together."

"I was just getting ready to head back to the hotel."

"Nonsense. You can stay here. There's plenty of room," Alessa says, and I can hear the hidden meaning. It isn't safe for Mom to be at a hotel alone. "I'll see you in the morning." Alessa smiles, and the guys follow her out of the room, saying their goodnights and leaving me to answer the questions I can see in Mom's eyes.

Mom sighs and turns to face me. "What aren't you telling me?"

"What do you mean?" I ask, trying to delay the inevitable.

She gives me the mom look. "Don't play dumb, Leo. You always were a horrible liar." She waves her hand to where Alessa left the room. "You said things were complicated the last time I asked about her; now you're staying with her?"

Fuck it. "Mom, what I'm about to tell you is a lot of information, but I need you to keep an open mind. Can you do that?" She nods, and I pinch the bridge of my nose, trying to figure out where to start. Mom is open-minded; she doesn't judge anyone and never met a stranger. But this is her own son. How will she react?

"I love her," I start, and she smiles.

"I know you do. I can see it all over your face." She takes my hands in hers. "Just tell me."

"I'm not the only one she's dating," I say, testing her reaction, and she frowns. "She's dating four other guys too."

"Is she not ready to settle down?"

"No, Mom, she is. I'm aware of the relationships. We are all in it... together." *I'm explaining this like shit.*

"I'm sorry, but I'm confused."

"All five of us are knowingly dating her. At the same time."

Her eyes widen, and I know she finally got it. "Oh." Oh? That's all she has to say?

"I'm also dating Gage." I might as well just drop the bombs right after the other.

"What?" she croaks. "You aren't gay."

"I'm bisexual, Mom," I tell her, and it's like a weight has been lifted off my shoulders. It's something I've needed to admit to myself since I was twelve when I realized that guys were attractive to me, but I lied to myself instead until Gage.

"Okay," she says, nodding her head. "Okay. I can handle this."

"Are you trying to convince yourself or me?" I say dryly.

She gives me the mom look again. "Don't be a smartass." She drops my hands and folds hers in her lap. "Are you happy?"

"Yes," I say without hesitation.

"So, this is like an open relationship?"

"No. We're loyal to each other."

Her eyes widen again. "She's not dating your brothers too, is she?"

I bark a surprised laugh. "No. It's me, Gage, Ryder, Dex, and Holden."

She lets out a shuddering sigh. "I don't know if I could have handled that."

"I know this is a lot to take in, and I didn't want to tell you this way," I retake her hands, "But just know I *am* happy with her and Gage. And with the other guys. They are like my family." Even Ryder, if I have to admit it. He's grown on me since he's been taking care of me; it's shown he isn't the gigantic dickhead I thought he was. Most of the time.

"Will I get to meet them?"

I shrug. "Honestly, I don't know. We all live here together, but that would be up to them."

She nods in understanding and leans back on the couch. I put my arm around her shoulders, hugging her close. I did miss the hell out of her. We sit there, lost in our thoughts, and I give her time to process.

"It was the dimples, wasn't it?" she asks about fifteen minutes later.

I laugh, knowing she's talking about Gage. "That was part of it."

"He's...bisexual then?" she asks hesitantly.

"He is openly bisexual. He has been for a long time."

"And Alessa is okay with you guys being together?" she asks softly.

"Alessa just wants us all happy. Two of the other guys are also maybe kind of dating." I have no idea how to explain what I saw with Holden and Ryder this morning. I know they had Alessa screaming down the house, and then they were making out in the kitchen.

"I just want you to be happy and...safe," she says, and I frown. Does she mean using protection? Because that ship sailed a long time ago. Alessa assured me they're all clean, and I assume she has the implant for birth control even though we haven't talked about it.

"What do you mean safe?"

Mom suddenly looks uncomfortable. "I know who Frankie was." She searches my face and still sees the confusion. "I know *who* he was."

Did Mom know Frankie was Mafia? Does that mean she figured out Evander and Mateo also are? And Alessa?

"I don't know what you're talking about," I say because I'm not confirming or denying that. The more she knows, the more danger she's in.

"I know there are some things you can't tell me, Leo." She sits up. "I just need you to promise me you will be safe."

"Hey, man. Have you seen..." Micah strolls into the room with his nose stuck in his phone. He looks up and stops mid-sentence when he sees Mom. "Who's this?"

"My mom, Katherine. Mom, this is Alessa's uncle, Micah."

"Oh," Micah opens the full force of his grin, "Nice to meet you."

"You too," Mom says. Is she fucking blushing?

"Are you looking for Alessa?" I ask between clenched teeth. Somehow, I know this is payback for this morning's conversation in the kitchen in front of him.

Micah looks at my face realizing he walked into a serious conversation. "Yeah. I'll find her."

"It was really nice to meet you," Mom speaks up.

"The pleasure was all mine," he smiles, and I grind my teeth. Shoving his hands into his pockets, he goes on his search for Alessa.

"Is it a rule to be gorgeous around here?"

"Mom!" I say, shocked.

She scoffs. "I'm old, not dead."

Is it rude to ask your mom when she's leaving?

"She knows," I tell Alessa and Gage the next morning. Mom hasn't made her way downstairs yet, so I take the time to let them know, especially since no one else is down here either.

"Everything?" Alessa asks from her perch on the counter in front of Gage and me at the island.

I nod. "Yeah. Well, most of it." I look between Alessa and Gage. "She said she knew who Frankie was."

Gage raises an eyebrow. "Like she knew he was Mafia?"

"That's what I got out of it. Which means she knows who Evander and Mateo are, and possibly you guys too."

Alessa frowns. "That's not safe information for her to know, Leo."

"I know. I didn't tell her one way or the other."

She tilts her head to the side. "She was cool with everything else?"

"She said she just needed to process everything before she went to bed." I shrug. "I think she's fine with it." I look at Gage. "I told her about us."

Both of his eyebrows shoot up. "What about us?"

"That we are," I wave my hand around, "dating."

"Is that what we're doing?"

Alessa throws a kitchen towel at him. "Stop being difficult."

Gage finally smiles. "Are we dating?"

"Do you want to be?" I say, frustrated.

"Are you asking me to be your boyfriend, Leo?"

"Gage," Alessa snaps, pointing her finger at him. "You're being a *testa di cazzo*."

"I don't know what that means, so I'm going to assume you called me sexy," Gage replies, and from the look on Alessa's face, that's not what she called him.

"You know what," I snarl, "forget I said anything." I slide off the stool, ready to walk away, when Gage grabs my arm.

"Leo," he says, tugging me back to look at him, "I was just messing with you."

"I just told my mom that I'm in a polyamorous relationship *and* that I'm bisexual." I jerk my arm away, ignoring the tug on my stitches. "I'm not in the fucking mood to be messed with."

Gage stands up, and it's the only time I've ever hated he is taller than me. "What do you want me to say, Leo?"

"I'm sorry would be a good start," Alessa says, looking between us.

"No," Gage says, all teasing gone from his face. "You want to date? We date. Do you want to fuck around? We fuck around. What do *you* want?"

I laugh without humor. "I was fucking stupid to think you would take this seriously. You think everything is a fucking joke."

I know it's the wrong thing to say when that cold look covers his eyes, the one he uses when he and Alessa are trying to scare people, and it fucking works.

"Fuck. You." Gage grits out before turning on his heel, barreling from the room, nearly running Ryder over on the way out.

"What the hell?" Ryder asks, jerking his thumb over his shoulder.

"What did I say?" I ask Alessa. Sure, I'm pissed, but I don't want to hurt him; I saw the hurt flash across his eyes before they turned cold.

She hops off the counter. "His piece of shit dad used to say shit like that to him because of his ADHD."

"I didn't know," I say miserably. I know something is different about Gage, but I never looked too much into it because I don't care. This little altercation showed me I don't know shit about any of them. Again.

"It's fine," she says, and it sounds anything but fine. "I'm going to go find him," she says, pecking Ryder on the lips on the way by.

I slide back onto the stool with a sigh.

"What did I miss?" Ryder asks, jerking the refrigerator door open.

"I told my mom that four other guys are dating Alessa at the same time as me. Oh. And I told her I'm bisexual." I laugh again. "And I told her I'm dating Gage when apparently I'm not."

Ryder stands up and slowly turns around. "Dude. That's a lot of info to drop on your mom in one night."

"I know," I agree. "But she deserved to know."

He shuts the door and leans back against it. "I can respect that." He shrugs. "Gage will be fine in like ten minutes."

"The more these conversations come around, the more I fucking realize I don't know shit. About any of you."

"Have you tried asking?"

"Where the hell do I even start?"

"You can start by not being a little bitch. Start by having a conversation with either of them. Alessa let you in; all you have to do is open the fucking door."

"Good morning," Mom says with impeccable timing while Ryder and I glare at each other.

"Morning," I say, turning to her and trying to plaster a smile on my face. "How did you sleep?"

"Wonderful! Those beds are like clouds," she crows, and her eyes widen when Ryder stands to his full height.

"Ryder, Mom. Mom, Ryder," I introduce and watch it dawn on Mom's face that this is one of the others.

"Oh," she says, sliding onto the stool beside me. "One of Alessa's guys?"

I jerk my head to her, and she seems...fine. Did she come to terms with it that fast, or is this for my benefit?

"Yes, ma'am," Ryder answers with a slight frown.

"Such manners," Mom sighs, and I roll my eyes so hard I can see behind me.

Ryder fights a smug grin. "My dad raised me right."

"What about your mom?"

Ryder's eyes turn sad. "She died when I was six."

I didn't know that either. Maybe he's right. Instead of waiting for them to spill everything, I need to ask questions.

"I'm sorry to hear that," Mom says sadly.

"Me too," I say genuinely.

Ryder acknowledges that with a nod and looks over my shoulder. Alessa walks around the corner with Gage in tow. He gives me a slight smile which I'll take at the moment with Mom sitting here. He slides onto the stool beside me. "Yes," he says, looking me in the eye. "We are."

It takes me a minute to get what he's saying. He's answering the unspoken question of whether we're dating or not. "That's what I want too." I squeeze his leg under the counter and know we still have a lot to work through, but deep down, I know we can.

I look over at Mom, and her eyes are glued in front of her. I follow her line of sight and almost laugh; she just caught sight of Dex.

"Mom," I chuckle, and she turns wide eyes at me. "That's Dex. Dex, this is my mom."

He nods. "Nice to meet you."

"You too," she replies, turning back to him.

"Don't worry. He has that effect on a lot of people," Alessa whispers between mine and Mom's shoulders.

Mom lets out a surprised laugh. "He's just so big," she whispers back.

Alessa shrugs. "He's harmless...mostly."

Mom laughs again, and I can tell she's starting to relax, which makes me happy. When I went to bed last night, I was afraid she would wake up this morning and not be okay with this. I know this isn't the life Mom dreamed for me, it isn't even one I dreamed for myself, but there is no other place I'd rather be than with these guys.

CHAPTER 44
ALESSA

Leo's mom showing up is not how I expected last night to go. I'm still in fucking shock that she's sitting in the living room laughing and joking with *all* the guys, including Micah, Evander, and Mateo. I wish I had a camera when she caught sight of Holden's innocent-looking face, but after what happened in the office yesterday, I know he's anything but innocent.

"I'm not your fucking errand boy," Micah gripes. I had him get food for all of us. We just finished eating and are sitting around the living room.

I roll my eyes. "I never said you were."

"You have a house full of guys." He waves his hand. "Why couldn't they go?"

"Are you really having a temper tantrum right now?" I laugh.

He smiles. "Fuck off, shithead."

I just shake my head and run through the list of things that need to be done, but I'm not sure when they're going to get done with Leo's mom here. She seems to take everything in stride, which is surprising as hell. The sad truth is, none of us had mothers or know what it's like to grow up with a good one, except for Leo. It's kind of nice to have her in the house.

We need to go to The Games tonight to meet up with Alexey and

Dmitri to get a plan in action for their mom. I need to check with Gerald and Boone about Lucas, Landon, and Playboy. I need to tell Leo that I'm giving him the reins to the new restaurant, and I have a surprise for Holden. I just don't know when any of that will get done.

My phone starts ringing, and I look at the screen before excusing myself. This isn't a conversation you can have in front of one of your boyfriends' moms.

"Hello?" I answer, closing the patio door behind me.

"I have a meeting set with Spinner," Ghost says. "Today."

I groan inwardly. "What time?"

"He's supposed to meet me at the garage around two. He said fucking Xander better be there."

"Xander won't be, but we will," I promise. I don't know how but business is business, no matter who's visiting. "I'll see you then."

"Alright," he answers and hangs up.

I start pacing, trying to figure out the easiest way to tell Leo we're leaving. I can't just sit around while everything else is going on.

My phone starts ringing again, and I almost don't answer when I see the name flash across the screen.

"Hello?"

"Hey, Beautiful," Zane greets. "How's your boy toy?"

"He's fine. Thank you again."

"Yeah," he replies, and he goes silent. I have to look at the phone to see if he hung up.

"Why are you calling, Zane?" I ask, trying to keep the impatience out of my voice.

"Can we meet?"

"Now isn't really a good time," I answer. It isn't the right time for so many different reasons.

"It's important, Alessa," he implores. "I need to see you."

I sigh. "I can, but it probably won't be today."

"The sooner, the better, Les."

"Yeah. Yeah. I get it," I agree. "I have to go. I'll let you know when." I hang up and drop into one of the patio chairs by the pool.

I lay my head back to stare at the sky. Now I can add two more things to the never-ending list of shit I need to do. I hear the patio door open and don't even look, thinking it's one of the guys until a floral scent hits my nose. I lift my head up when Leo's mom sits beside me.

"It's beautiful out here," she sighs. "I didn't realize California was this pretty."

I smile. "It has its moments." I look at her profile and can't get over how much Leo looks like her. He definitely got her lips with the same color hair, eyes, and the same proud nose. She's tall and thin and has one of the most relaxing personalities, just like Leo.

She turns to look at me. "I was wondering if we could talk."

I nod. "Of course."

She sighs and folds her hands in her lap. "It's a mom's duty to worry. I will always worry about my son, no matter how old he gets. I'm trying to be accepting of the life he's chosen for himself, and all I want is for him to be happy. He seems very happy here, and he loves you so much." She smiles at that. "I just need you to know woman to woman that I know who you are. I knew the name Poletti sounded familiar when Leo told me, but it didn't hit me until I saw this house." She grabs my hand. "I need to know you will keep him safe."

"I'll do everything in my power," I promise. "But Katherine, you *can't* know who I am," I tell her, hoping she gets the hidden meaning.

She waves her other hand. "You're Leo's girlfriend, and that's all I know." She squeezes my hand. "You have a house full of guys in there that adore you. I wanted to reject the idea last night when Leo told me until I saw you guys together. I'm glad he's found all of you."

"I'm glad I found him too," I reply honestly with a smile. "I love him."

She tucks her hand on my cheek; it is such a motherly thing that I want to cry. "You are a part of this family now. If you ever need someone, please don't hesitate to call."

I nod because my voice is all choked up. She pulls me into a soft hug before going back into the house.

Maybe her showing up isn't such a bad thing.

Leo, Gage, and Dex take Leo's mom to lunch and sightseeing, which leaves me two hours to get ready to ambush this meeting with Spinner. They're taking her to one of my restaurants which I deemed safe, and I don't think Viktor is dumb enough to wage an attack in broad daylight.

"He's supposed to be there at two," I tell Ryder. "We need him to get there, and then we can go in."

We're sitting in my office going over the plans for the day. Ryder has his feet propped on the desk on the other side. "We can stake it out, or we can go in hot." He shrugs. "It's up to you."

"What if this is a setup?" I ask the one question that has been plaguing my mind.

"You don't trust Ghost?"

"I don't know yet." I run my fingers through my hair, showing my agitation. "I don't know who I can trust."

He levels me with a look. "You can trust us."

I wave my hand."I don't mean you guys. A lot of people think I can't do this and that dad made a mistake putting me in this position." I sigh. "Maybe they're right."

Ryder's feet drop to the floor with a thud when he sits up. "They aren't fucking right," he says vehemently.

"Viktor never would have taken a stand against Dad," I point out.

"No. Probably not," he agrees. "But now you have to show Viktor he fucked with the wrong one. You were made for this, *Il mio sole*, never doubt that."

The problem is, I did doubt that, and I've never voiced it out loud except to Dex. I feel like I'm making all the wrong decisions and moves, and people think I'm weak. Since my grandfather, we don't run the Italians like his family before him. They hid behind their fancy gates and sent other people to do their dirty work. When my grandfather took the mantle, he didn't want to hide; he wanted people to see his face and fear that face. So, the tradition continued with dad and now with me. People like Viktor still live by the old ways that leaders lead from afar; they don't do it themselves. Since I took over, I've been on almost every assignment we've had, and it isn't because I don't trust my guys to get the job done; I want to be there.

My phone rings, interrupting me from my thoughts. The display reads Dex, and I slide to answer and flip it to the speakerphone.

"We have a problem," Dex rumbles as soon as the call connects.

"What kind of problem?" I ask, looking at Ryder.

"We have a tail. Been following us for the ten minutes Gage has spent trying to lose it."

"You're sure?" I need to ask because everyone is on high alert right now. The last thing we need to do is freak out Leo's mom because of it.

"One hundred percent," Dex replies.

"Where are you?" Ryder asks, already standing.

"Two twenty-two." Two twenty-two is one of the more rural back roads.

"Go to Dad's," Ryder says. "We're on our way."

Dex grunts in agreement, and the call disconnects.

Ryder already has his phone to his ear. "Dad. Special cargo is coming your way. We're on our way." Special cargo is our way of telling the other person we have an innocent with us. Ryder listens to whatever his dad says. "Yes, sir." He hangs up and looks at me. "Viktor?"

"I don't know," I answer, standing up and shooting off a text to Evander, Mateo, and Micah to meet us out front. We need all the manpower we can get if it's him. Dex and Gage were discreetly armed when they left, but there were just two of them. I saw the hell Viktor rained down on our limo, and I can almost bet that if there's one tail, there are more somewhere waiting. I shoot off another message to Holden to let him know we are leaving.

Ryder and I head out to the garage where some of our weapons are stored, so they're easy to grab in a hurry. We both slide our holsters on, loading each side with our favorite Glocks. I slide my leather jacket over it, and Ryder pulls on a button-up to cover his.

Evander, Mateo, and Micah stride into the garage dressed similarly, and I can see the flash of their weapons.

"They have a tail," I tell them. "They're going to Rocco's."

Ryder grabs the keys to the Chevrolet Yukon Denali we have for when we need more room. I pull open the passenger side door, and that's when I catch a glimpse of curly hair.

"Can I go?" Holden asks quietly, and the shock must register on my face. He holds up his laptop bag. "I have this in case we need it."

Ryder and I exchange a look over the hood before Ryder looks back at Holden. "Are you sure?" Holden nods, and my heart sinks. If we tell him no, he'll think we don't want him to go, but if we tell him yes, it's hard to tell what we're getting him into. Ryder and I exchange another look before Ryder jerks a nod. "Get in the back and keep your head down."

We all climb in with Ryder and me up front, Evander and Micah in the middle, and Mateo sliding in beside Holden.

Holden doesn't even have a fucking gun because he won't touch one. We've all tried several times to explain that he at least needs to know how to use one. He's adamant he was taught growing up, so if he ever needed to, as a last resort, he can shoot.

Ryder pulls the back way off the property, and it's about a fifteen-minute drive to his dad's. Five minutes in, my phone rings again.

I connect the call through Bluetooth in the SUV, and gunshots fill the car through the speakers.

"We got big fucking problems!" Gage yells over the noise.

Ryder floors the gas, and I know he'll get us there in record time.

"We're on our way, Gage," I promise him. "How close are you to Rocco's?"

"Almost there!" Gage yells back. Two bangs almost deafen me, and I know he fired off two shots. I hear Dex yell something, and the phone disconnects.

I look at Ryder in worry, and he presses his foot further down on the gas, the SUV swaying uneasily around the curves. Ryder's one of the best getaway drivers I've ever known, so if anyone is going to get us there in one piece, it's him.

Evander sits up between the seats. "Is this Viktor?"

There's no doubt in my mind now. "Yes. He must have people watching for us to leave."

"You think he could have flipped one of ours?" Micah asks, already looking pissed off at the notion.

"I don't know," I say miserably. Everything is spiraling out of control. I have three of my guys, with Leo's *mother* pinned down in a gunfight and a car full of people, including Holden driving into the unknown.

Ryder squeezes my thigh. "You got this, Boss." I can feel the warmth of his hand seep into my bones, relaxing me a little.

I finally see a glint of metal in the sun, and Gage's Range Rover is half on the road and half in the ditch, two SUVs sitting across from it while exchanging gunfire. Ryder slams on the brakes when we get close enough. "Stay in the car!" I yell at Holden before jumping out.

We jump out, take our spots around the SUV, and open fire. They pop off a few shots in our direction before realizing they're outnumbered and take off. Ryder takes two big strides forward before leveling his Glocks and emptying the clips at the SUV. The back glass shatters, and the SUV swerves before correcting. Good. Maybe he hit one of those assholes.

I jog over to the Range Rover when the other two SUVs disappear. I half-hug and half-tackle Gage when he steps out of where he was taking cover.

"Oof, Pretty girl," he grunts, wrapping his arms around me. "We're okay."

I step back and look him over to make sure he isn't lying to me. Besides the dirt on his shirt and jeans, he looks fine. Dex steps up on his other side, and I do the same thing to him.

Dex chuckles in my ear."Baby girl. We're fine."

I jerk a nod and pull open the backdoor to Gage's car. Leo is comforting a very inconsolable-looking Katherine. *Shit.*

"Katherine," I say gently, "are you hurt?" She shakes her head profusely and looks seconds away from having a panic attack. I squeeze Leo's arm in comfort before turning to Dex and Gage. "We need to get her to Rocco's."

Gage slaps Dex on the back. "Push me out, big fella."

Ryder barks a laugh. "Come on." He nods to Dex while Gage runs around to the driver's side.

We all return to the Denali with me in the driver's seat. Dex and Ryder heave at the back of the Range Rover while Gage hits the gas, trying to get it to gain traction so it will come out of the ditch. It finally finds purchase with a bark of tires, and Ryder jogs back to the Denali and jerks the door open.

I hit the gas, following Gage the two miles they had left to get to Rocco's. Ryder chuckles, and I look at him with a frown. How is this funny?

He nods his head at my lap. "You barely reach the gas pedal."

I frown harder. "It's not my fault all of you are freaks of nature." I didn't have time to adjust the seat when I jumped in, and Ryder is almost a foot taller than me. It makes him laugh loudly, causing the rest of my passengers to chuckle. "Fuck all of you," I mutter.

We finally swing around in front of Rocco's house, and he's already standing outside. "What's going on?" he asks when we're all standing in front of him with a silently weeping Katherine.

"That's Leo's mom," Ryder explains. "We need to take her inside."

Rocco nods, and we follow him in, where he leads us to the huge sitting room. Leo and I tuck Katherine on the couch between us. That's when I notice the blood on her eyebrow. "What happened?" I ask, concerned.

"I think she hit her head when those assholes hit the back of the fucking car," Leo seethes, and I've never seen him that pissed off.

I grab Katherine's hand, and she squeezes it as tight as she can. "I'm fine," she says with a shaky smile, trying to stop crying.

"I'll get a first aid kit," Ryder says, jogging out of the room.

Rocco looks at me with one of those looks demanding answers, and I just shake my head, letting him know not now. He raises an eyebrow and sinks onto the coffee table in front of Katherine. Ryder jogs back into the room and places the first aid kit into Rocco's outstretched hand. “I’m going to clean this wound,” he says softly, waiting for Katherine’s nod before he reaches for her head.

Rocco gently cleans her eyebrow, apologizing when she hisses at the sting from the antiseptic. He places a little band-aid over the top with such softness that it’s surprising for a guy his size. He’s about the same size as Ryder but hides it under fancy suits, which he isn’t wearing right now. I think it’s the first time I’ve ever seen Rocco in jeans and a polo shirt.

Katherine smiles softly. “Thank you”

“No thanks needed,” Rocco says, smiling just as softly. “Is everyone else okay?” We all nod, and he leans back from Katherine. “Someone going to explain what the hell happened?” he asks, and for a split second, I’m taken back to my childhood when Ryder, Gage, and I would get into trouble, and he would ask that same question.

I nod my head toward the other room, and he gets up from the coffee table, understanding I don’t want to talk in front of Katherine. I get up, and Gage takes my place, trying to comfort her. She stopped crying but is staring into space, lost in her mind.

Ryder and I follow Rocco to his office in the back of the house; he waves his hand in front of his desk for us to sit down. Ryder and I look at each other, grinning. We’ve been here before, also after getting into trouble.

“What happened?” he asks, folding himself into his office chair, steepling his fingers under his chin with his elbows on the desk.

I fight back a giggle. “Viktor Orlov.”

His eyebrows shoot up. “The Russian, Viktor Orlov?”

“One in the same,” Ryder answers, sitting back in the chair.

Rocco levels a look at Ryder. “Why wasn’t I aware there were any issues with Viktor?”

Ryder frowns. “I told you to be careful that we had problems. You didn’t need to know more.”

Rocco narrows his eyes on his son, and I want to hide under the desk. “What does that mean?”

“It means you wanted out,” Ryder says hotly. Once you’re out, you’re either dead or thrown out of the loop. Rocco is aware of that, but Ryder is still his son, and he worries.

Rocco folds his arms on the desk, leaning forward. "You watch your tone, boy," Rocco warns, and I have to fight a snort when Ryder sits back in the chair chastised. Rocco turns his eyes on me, and I try not to shrink back in my chair. "What about you, *Bellissima*? Do you have anything to add?"

My first instinct is to tell him nothing because Ryder is right. He wanted out, which means he isn't privy to any of this information, but he's the guy who ruled by my dad's side for as long as I can remember. "Viktor stepped on my trade, tried to take over the Vipers, shot at our limo leaving the gala on Saturday, and now this."

He levels his look back at Ryder. "You didn't think it was important to tell me you got fucking shot at?" he asks between clenched teeth.

Ryder gives him a dry look. "It was just a random Saturday for us, Dad," he replies, and he's right. We get shot at all the time, and I'm sure he doesn't tell his dad every time.

"You shouldn't have kept this from me," Rocco says.

"With all due respect, Rocco," I say in Ryder's defense. "This doesn't concern you anymore," I say softly. I don't want to disrespect him, but he still needs to remember who he's talking to.

Rocco chuckles and sits back in his chair. "I was wondering when that Poletti backbone would come out." He waves his hand toward the sitting room. "I would assume I'm now involved, though."

"Absolutely not," Ryder explodes. "We just needed a place to get them to, and then we're gone."

"He's right," I say, disagreeing with Ryder with a wince. "He's involved because I guarantee Viktor knew where they were going."

"He can't be involved! He doesn't even have full guards anymore," Ryder argues, and I'm already shaking my head. "*Il mio sole...*"

"Enough," I bark. I won't have this argument with his dad sitting there. Ryder's mouth snaps shut, and I can see that muscle in his jaw ticking. "He's involved." I turn back to Rocco, and he's hiding a smile with his hand. "Leo's mom can't go home now. Not since she was clocked with them today, but she can't stay with us."

"You want me to babysit one of your boyfriends' moms?" Rocco laughs, then sighs when he realizes I'm serious. "Do you trust him?" he asks.

"Leo can be trusted," Ryder grits out, and I jerk my head his way. "I would assume his mom can too."

"Does Leo or his mother know about this plan?"

"Not yet," I sigh. I don't know how either of them is going to take this. In the back of my mind, I'm hoping I can talk Leo into staying here with her so I don't have to worry when he's going to get shot again.

Rocco nods. "I'll do whatever I can to help."

"I'll be sending more guards here then." I raise my hand when Rocco opens his mouth to argue. "Non-negotiable." I stand up and squeeze Ryder's shoulder on the way by. "I need to spread the good news," I say sarcastically.

I make it back to the sitting room, and Katherine is nursing a bottle of water with color back on her face. I sit on the coffee table in front of her. "There is no easy way to put this, Katherine." She nods for me to continue. "What we're involved in is bad. Not just pretty bad, but really bad. You can't go back home alone now."

She frowns. "But they didn't see me; I don't see any reason why I can't go home."

"He has eyes somewhere," Gage says gently. I know Viktor did his homework because he knows he can't take me out, but he can hit me where it hurts. "He knows who you are."

Katherine raises a shaky hand to her mouth. "I'm in danger?"

"We all are, Mom," Leo says, gently squeezing her to his side. "What's the plan?" Leo asks me.

"She stays here with you and Rocco," I say, hoping Leo will automatically agree to be at his mom's side.

He frowns, and I know that's wishful thinking. "Not a chance in hell. I'm not hiding while you're in the crosshairs."

"Leo..."

"Save it, Baby. I'm going back home with you guys," Leo says with his jaw setting in that stubborn way that tells me I'm wasting my breath arguing with him.

"How long?" Katherine whispers.

"I don't know," I tell her honestly. "Things are starting to heat up, and it's going to get worse before it gets better." I grab her hands. "I need to know you're safe."

She nods, and it's an instant relief for Leo and me.

I hope I made the right choice by not sending her packing back to North Carolina.

CHAPTER 45
RYDER

After we got Leo's mom safely tucked away at my dad's, we had no time since we had to get to this meeting with Spinner. Les promises Katherine she'll have everything she needs while she's with my dad ordered and delivered as soon as we got back home. Les doesn't make any promises about when Katherine can return to North Carolina because we don't know when that would happen.

I don't like dad being involved, but I know I don't have a choice now. At least Les gave him babysitting duty.

We all pile back in the same way we got here with Gage, Leo, and Dex in Gage's smashed-up Range Rover. They're lucky the damn thing didn't roll when the other SUV pushed them off the road. I fucking hate seeing Leo's mom hurt and hate it even more that we didn't have time to take Holden home.

We pull over a block away, so he doesn't see us coming. I shove the car into park. "We can't leave Holden in here unprotected," I whisper to Les.

"I know," she says miserably, and I know she's worried about taking a stitched-up Leo in there too. She pushes her door open without another word, and we all follow her out, meeting the others at the hood of the Denali.

Les turns her eyes on Holden and pulls one of her Glocks from the holster. "I know you don't like these, but you need it on you anyway," she says in a way that doesn't leave any room for argument. This is Boss Les now, not his bright eyes. He takes it reluctantly and tucks it into the back of his jeans, pulling his shirt over it. "Shoot first. Ask questions later," she says and then turns to Leo. "Are you armed?" He pulls up his shirt, and I see the Glock tucked against his side.

"I didn't leave home without it," Leo says with a smile, pulling his shirt back down.

"How are the stitches holding up?" I ask, worried about the asshole too. He took a hit, getting knocked around in that SUV.

"Fine,"

"What's the play, Boss?" Dex asks, leaning back against Gage's damaged SUV.

She looks around at all of us gathered around, and I can see her resolve harden with none of the doubts I saw earlier. "We go in like we own the place. I want Ryder, Holden, Leo, and Mateo with me going in the front. Dex, Gage, Evander, and Micah go in through the back. Don't leave them any room to escape." She looks between Evander and Mateo. "I'm going to assume you can handle yourselves."

Mateo grins, and it looks just as crazy as Gage's does before we do this. "Fuck yeah, we can."

Evander rolls his eyes. "You don't have to worry about us."

Les looks at Holden again. "Stay close."

With that last warning, we make our way up the block, trying to stay as hidden as possible. We stop when the garage comes into view. I can see Les eyeing the situation along with Dex and me. Two guys guard the front, and I can almost bet the same is at the back. We don't have a clue how many are inside.

"We need a distraction," Les whispers to all of us. "We need them away from the front long enough to get in. Take out the ones in the back if you have to."

Gage grins. "A distraction?" He waggles his eyebrows. "Coming right up."

Les shakes her head with a quiet laugh. "Just get them away."

Gage rakes his fingers through his wavy hair, making it stick up every which way before he staggers off from us.

"Hey!" Gage yells to one of the guys, then staggers to the side. I hear someone snort a laugh behind me. "I need to talk to Xander."

"Get lost," one of them growls, and Gage frowns in exaggeration.

Gage starts scratching at his arms like a junkie looking for a fix. "He owes me some shit. Tell him to come the fuck outside."

"He's way too good at this," Leo whispers, and I snort.

"Gage is always a good distraction," I answer.

"We could tell you some stories about Gage and his distractions," Micah laughs.

"I told you to get lost, asshole." The other guy points a finger in the other direction.

"Who the fuck are you?" Gage snarls, trips, then giggles. I fight off a laugh. "I just need him for two minutes," he says, walking closer to the garage. We start moving slowly forward, knowing that Gage will make his move at any time.

"Fucking junkie," one of the guys scoffs. "Xander isn't here right now."

"Who are you calling a junkie?" Gage asks, bending down easily and hefting up a broken piece of the concrete sidewalk.

"Get ready," Les warns.

Gage pulls his arm back and launches it at the closest guy with such accuracy that it would make a baseball player fucking jealous. It smacks the guy right in the face. Gage takes off to the side of the building, his manic laughter following him with one hot on his heels. The other that's trying to soothe his broken nose follows more slowly.

We make a break for it and storm the garage, all eyes turning to us. The backdoor swings open, and the one without the bleeding face shoves Gage, causing him to trip. He immediately rights himself and turns to him with that crazy grin. "Have you met my friends?" Gage asks, nodding his head over the guy's shoulder where Micah has a Glock pressed to the guy's head.

"Move," Micah snarls.

They move forward, and Dex shoves the other guys, making

them sprawl on the floor. Evander steps in with the bleeding one's shirt wrapped in his fist, shutting the door behind him.

"Alessa Poletti," Spinner says, looking her up and down with his weird-as-hell green eyes. They're almost reptilian. "What gives me such an honor of your presence?"

Spinner is one of the youngest to work for Viktor and American, surprising everyone. He has slicked back brown hair and a scar that runs through his top lip, making it pull at odd angles when he talks.

"Well, you see, Jacob," she says, using his real name, knowing it will piss him off. "We got a tip that you were in the neighborhood, and we were just passing by; I thought I'd stop in and say hi."

Spinner's eyes automatically harden. "What would a princess like you be doing in gang territory?"

"Queen," Gage says, striding over and pulling himself to sit on the table beside Ghost.

Spinner's top lip pulls back in a sneer. "Why are you here?" he asks again.

"Oh," she pouts, "I was going to ask you the same thing."

I can see Dex, Evander, and Micah creeping closer, effectively blocking Spinner and his guys. I can tell which ones are Spinner's guys by how sharply they're dressed compared to Ghost's guys. Spinner has six guys in here, but that doesn't mean there aren't others lying in wait for a signal. It's what we would have done.

"I don't answer to you," Spinner spits, causing Les' head to cock to the side.

"But you do, though." She straightens up, and I can see her patience wearing out. "Something you and Viktor have forgotten."

"You don't run this place," Spinner bristles. "Not for much longer anyway." He grins, and I know he'll say something he will instantly regret. "How are you guys holding up? Heard there were a couple of shootings."

Les cocks an eyebrow. "I don't know what you're talking about." She pauses, then snaps her fingers like she remembered something. "You mean the limo? Shitty marksmanship, if you ask me. Today all I saw were your guy's running away scared."

He waves his hand, dismissing her. "You can go. We have guy things to discuss."

Les sighs, pulls her Glock and shoots the guy right over Spinner's shoulder, one of the ones from outside. The bullet whizzes past Spinner's head so close that he flinches. "Got time to talk now?"

"What the fuck?!" Spinner explodes, pulling his own weapon. He has all of ours pointed at him, including Leo and Holden. Holden's shoulders are set back, and a glare leveled on Spinner that I'm damn proud of. I knew he had it in him; he just needed to see it himself.

"You might want to rethink that decision," Gage laughs, sticking his Glock in Spinner's face.

"Tell me what I want to know, and no one else has to die." Les shrugs. "Or I take them all out and make you wish you were never fucking born."

My queen.

"I'm not fucking scared of a little girl playing gangster," Spinner says but tucks his gun away.

Gage aims in the other direction, effectively dropping another one of his guys.

"Two down. Four more to go," I say, stepping closer to Les. "What's it going to be?"

Ghost and none of his four guys have said a word since we came in, which is smart. For all Spinner knows, Ghost is against Les with Xander, and we need to keep it that way. Ghost is casually leaning back in his chair, watching it all play out. If Ghost wants to know how to run his crew, there is no better way than to watch Les in action.

"What do you want?" Spinner grits out.

"I want to know why Viktor is showing he has balls suddenly," Les says, tucking her Glock back in its holster. It's a power move to show him she isn't scared and that we have her back no matter what.

"How do you know Viktor is behind this? It could just be me."

Gage fires off another shot, dropping a third. "Wrong answer."

"Why is Viktor coming for me?" Les asks, getting tired of all this.

"He's not," Spinner grins, "Yet."

I fire off a shot, dropping a fourth, and the rest of the guys are starting to look even more nervous. None of them have pulled their weapons because Spinner hasn't given them a signal. That's how it works with them, and it's fucking stupid. "That's definitely the wrong fucking answer." I say.

Spinner slides his eyes over his almost dead crew like he couldn't give a shit. "You think I don't have more where that came from?"

"Oh, I'm hoping for it," Les says. "The more of you I can take out before I go after Viktor, the better."

"You think you're a bad bitch, don't you?" Spinner says casually, leaning back on the table. "This piss poor crew won't do anything against what I have waiting outside those doors."

Les raises a brow. "You think this is all I came with?" she asks. I know she's bluffing, but she says it with such confidence, even I believe her.

Dex fires off two more shots, taking the last two guys out. "I'm sick of hearing his voice," Dex rumbles, making Les laugh.

"Look what you did, Spinner." She shakes her head sadly. "You pissed off the giant." Les draws her Glock faster than I can blink, shooting Spinner in the thigh and making him scream in pain. "Shut him up!" she yells at Gage.

Before Gage can even move, Ghost lifts a big, booted foot, smashing it into Spinner's face and knocking him out cold. "Motherfucker," he growls before looking up at Les. "That was entertaining."

She shrugs, tucking her Glock away, and we do the same. "What can I say? All kinds of fun seem to follow us around." She walks over, pulls up the chair at the table, and sits down. "What did he say before we got here?" she asks, and even Ghost's guys are eyeing her warily.

"He kept asking where Xander and their shipment were."

"Did he message anybody while he was here?" Les asks.

"No," Ghost shakes his head. "He was about to before you guys barged in, though."

Les turns to Micah and Dex. "Make sure there isn't really anyone outside. I think he was bluffing as hard as me. If it's clear, bring the cars up." They nod, get the keys from Gage and me, and set off outside. She turns back to Ghost. "You need to lay low."

Ghost casts uninterested eyes over an unconscious Spinner. "What about him?"

Les grins. "He's coming with us."

TWENTY MINUTES LATER, we're finally back at the house. Dex, Gage, Micah, and Les are tying Spinner up downstairs with everyone else, all pretense of a civil conversation going out the window. Holden hightailed back to his office, and I don't have time to check on him no matter how much I want to; my first priority is Les. I pull open the door to the wine cellar that will take me to the hidden basement; they took Spinner in through the secret door in the garage. I catch Leo in my peripheral vision and turn around.

"Where are you going?" I ask, and he gives me a look that calls me stupid forty times.

"With you."

I shake my head. "You don't need to see this."

That sets his teeth on edge. "I'm going with you," he repeats.

I shut the door back and step into his space. "Do you know what's about to happen?" I ask, and he just looks at me without answering. "We're going to torture him for information."

"Okay," Leo says slowly.

"Some things you don't need to be involved in, Leo." This is one thing we might be able to save him from seeing.

"That asshole had something to do with what happened to my mom today," he grits out. "Quit trying to push me out."

"I'm not trying to fucking push you out!" I yell and take a deep breath to rein in my temper. "I'm trying to save you from shit you don't need to see."

"I don't need you to save me, Ryder. I'm in whether you want me to be or not."

I shake my head and pop the door back open. "It has nothing to do with whether I want you here or not."

I slide the panel to the side and place my thumb on the lock, waiting for it to read it and open the door. "So you admit you still don't fucking want me here?" he asks. "Fucking figures."

I stop dead, almost making him run into me. I slowly turn around. "I never said that."

"You didn't have to."

"You remember what I said about not being a little bitch? This is what I meant." I turn on my heel for the next door. It also opens with a click reading my thumbprint and the same with the next. I place my thumb on the next one that will let us into the basement. "Don't say I didn't warn you." It pops open, and I wave him to walk inside.

They already have Spinner hanging by his arms over his head, still out cold. Everyone is lining the walls except Les, Micah, and Gage, who are standing in front of Spinner. Leo is going to see Les and Gage in a whole new light. Asshole can't say I didn't give him plenty of warning. I take a spot beside Dex, propping a boot on the wall, crossing my arms over my chest. Leo walks over and stands between Evander and Mateo.

"Should he be down here?" Dex asks.

"I tried to tell him," I shrug, "Not my fucking problem now."

Les walks over to the table lined with all her knives, her heels clicking on the floor, and it hits me like a ton of bricks. We haven't grabbed someone for her to take out since she started seeing all of us. We were getting them once or twice a night, every night. I don't think she's done with her crusade, but something has quieted her mind enough to where she doesn't need to, and my only hope is that it's us.

Les picks up one of her ammonia capsules and glances at Leo. She sees the hard set of his jaw and shakes her head in resignation before walking back to Spinner. She cracks it open and waves it under his nose. "Wakey wakey," she singsongs, making Gage laugh.

Spinner groans in pain and slowly opens his eyes. He lost a lot of blood from the wound in his thigh, but she didn't hit anything vital, so he won't bleed out. "What the fuck?" he asks gruffly.

"It's time you answered some of my questions, Jacob." She pulls one of her favorite knives from the sheath on the back of her jeans. It's the wicked-looking curved one with her initials engraved on the blade, a gift from me. She runs the knife up his shirt from the hem, slicing it open and exposing his chest. "What's Viktor up to?"

Spinner grins with blood caked on his teeth, where Ghost kicked him in the face. "I don't have to tell you shit, you stupid bitch. You can threaten all you want; I won't say a word."

Les rolls her eyes. "Why do men have to resort to name calling when a woman is involved?" She steps closer and runs her knife up his thigh until it's nestled beside his cock. "I will cut this shriveled motherfucker off and choke you with it until you decide Viktor isn't worth it," she threatens, and I'm sure every man in the room winced; she's dead serious.

"Maybe if you let me choke you with it, you wouldn't be such a fucking bitch." Spinner laughs at his own joke, not expecting the next hit. Gage nails him right in the ribs so hard the chains swing.

"Don't you ever say that to her again," Gage says through clenched teeth.

Micah walks to the table and hefts a metal baseball bat off the hooks on the wall. He swings it around, making it whoosh through the air, drops it onto the toe of his boot, then grabs it out of the air when it bounces back up, the whole time still walking back to Spinner. *Show off.*

"What is Viktor up to?" Les asks again while Micah is walking behind him.

"Fuck you."

Micah swings the bat like he's going for a home run, cracking Spinner right in the ribs. You can hear the crunch, and Spinner locks his lips to keep from screaming.

"What is he up to?" Gage asks, stepping back.

"I'm not saying shit," Spinner replies, pain lacing his voice.

Micah swings at the other side with that sickening crunch; Spinner still doesn't scream.

He's going to be harder to crack than we thought.

"Tell me what I want to know, and this all stops," Les promises. I know she means she will just kill him.

"Fuck. You," he grits out and then spits blood on the floor at her boots.

"Well, that was uncalled for," she grumbles, looking down at the blood splatter. "That bullet wound looks kind of bad." She looks like she's inspecting it, then looks at Micah. "Exit wound?"

"Nope," Micah replies with a grin.

"Maybe I should get it out before infection sets in. We don't want you dying because of something as trivial as a fever. Am I right?" She hands Gage her knife while she pulls gloves on and then takes it back. "Hold still," she warns, knowing there is no way he can. She slices through his pant leg and looks at the bullet wound again. "That looks nasty," she comments before jabbing her knife in the hole.

I look at Leo with Evander and Mateo, the latter are standing stoically with their arms crossed over their chest; Leo looks seconds from puking.

"You stupid whore," Spinner seethes. "Wait until Viktor gets ahold of that perky ass." On that comment, she twists the knife, and he finally screams. It's so loud it echoes off the walls.

She jerks the knife out. "Viktor will never touch my ass," she says, pointing the knife at him. "Now, hold still so I can get this out."

She stabs the hole again and starts digging around, Spinner screaming the whole time. His screams finally turn to silence when he passes out. "Well, shit," Micah mutters under his breath.

"Give him a moment of peace because he won't get any when I wake him up again," Les says, wiping her bloody knife on his shirt. She turns to Leo. "You shouldn't be down here."

He bristles, immediately standing up from the wall. "Why not?" he challenges. "Ryder still doesn't want me here. Does that apply to you too?"

She levels him with a look that makes most men piss themselves. She isn't in the right mindset to be arguing with him. "I don't have time for your pity party, Leo," she says harshly. "I didn't say I didn't want you down here; I said you shouldn't be. There's a big fucking difference."

Leo steps forward to argue, and Evander clamps a hand on his shoulder, jerking him back. He whispers something to him harshly, and Leo slouches against the wall. Evander must be able to see the murderous look on Les' face that Leo hasn't recognized yet.

"Wake him up," she barks at Gage, and Gage doesn't even question her because he knows better. He jogs to the table and then back, waving the ammonia under Spinner's nose. Too many more times and that wouldn't wake him up anymore.

"Tell me about Viktor," she grits out as soon as his eyes open. Spinner shakes his head, and Les tucks her knife beside his cock again. That knife is sharp enough to cut through his clothes like butter. "Tell me about Viktor!" she yells, and Spinner flinches at the look on her face. Finally, realizing he's not going to win this.

"He's coming for you," Spinner laughs hoarsely. "I can't wait to see you fuckers in hell."

Les comes to the same conclusion as me; it's going to take a whole hell of a lot to get him to talk. We're wasting our time with this asshole and already know who's behind all this. She walks over to the table and exchanges the curved one for one with a straight blade before walking back. "*Marciume all'inferno,*" she mutters, then slices clean through his throat. His head falls back at an odd angle, blood pouring down him.

"Get rid of him," she orders. "Be ready for the games tonight."

She slams out of the room, and Dex and I exchange a look.

She'll be hell on wheels for the rest of the day if we don't do something.

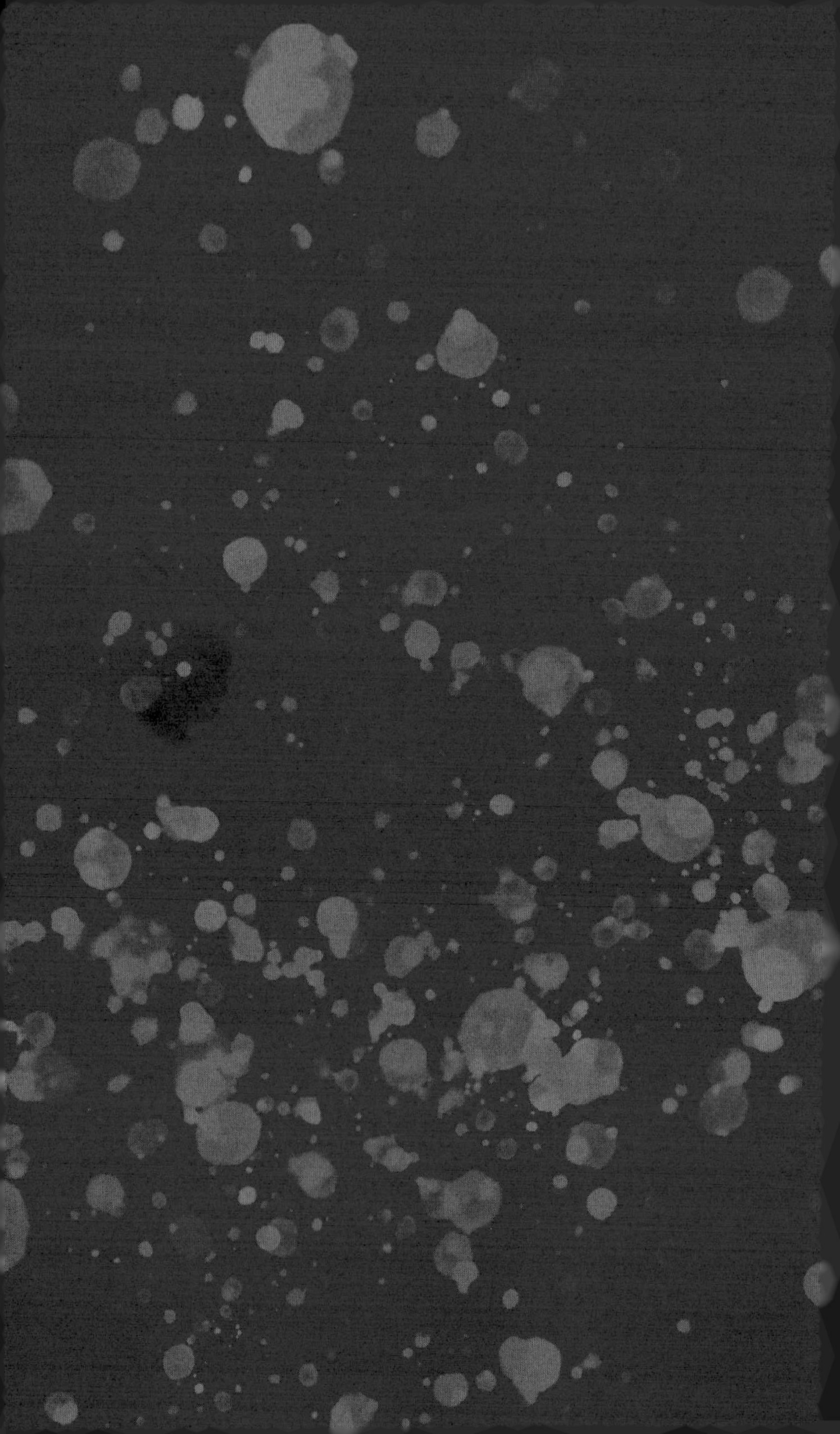

CHAPTER 46
GAGE

I watch Les leave the basement and make the executive decision to follow her. By the time I even make it to the kitchen, she's nowhere to be seen. I hear a door slam upstairs and figure she went to her room, so I jog up the steps and knock on her door.

"What?!" she barks.

"It's Gage," I say and twist the knob, thankful it's unlocked and hoping like hell she doesn't have a Glock aimed at my head.

She's pacing the room, running her hands through her hair in a way we don't see very often but happens when she gets overloaded. Today sure did the fucking trick.

"Pretty girl," I say softly, and it's like she doesn't even hear me. "Les," I say louder, and she still doesn't stop. I step in front of her and try not to cringe at the look she gives me. "Talk to me."

She steps around me to continue pacing. "I feel like it's all falling apart. I can't handle fucking Leo, much less Viktor Orlov *and* a stalker."

"Leo just hasn't learned yet," I assure her. "He will."

She whirls around. "His mom almost died today, Gage. *He* almost died Saturday. This is much bigger than me."

I frown. Where the hell is this coming from? "Pretty girl, we can handle this. You're being too hard on yourself."

She groans, and it sounds like she's in pain. "I don't think I can." Her breathing starts speeding up. "I'm losing control, Gage."

I grab her shoulders, forcing her to look at me. "No. You aren't."

"I feel like I am." She steps back and starts pacing again. "I just...I need...FUCK!" She jams her hands in her hair, and I grab her arm to stop her, risking getting punched in the face.

"What do you need?" I ask evenly.

"I don't know! I don't know," she says miserably, and she's seconds from losing it altogether. I run through options as fast as possible, coming to a decision.

I jerk her into my chest. "Let me help you." I slant my mouth over hers, hoping she just needs to let off steam in another way. One that I'm perfectly capable of helping her with.

She resists at first, then winds her arms around my neck. I kiss her hard, knowing she doesn't need soft right now; she needs someone to fuck her. Hard.

I jerk away from the kiss. "Get naked," I demand, and we both strip in record time, meeting back in the middle with a crash of lips. I pull her up with one arm around her waist, her legs wrapping around my waist; with my other hand, I position my cock to sink into her pussy. Once I feel the head of my cock slide inside her, I slam my hips forward hard, pulling her down at the same time.

"Fuck" she breathes. "Fuck me, Gage."

I walk us until I can lay her back on the bed. I wrap my hands around her hips and start pounding into her, pulling her onto my cock with my hold each time I bottom out.

She reaches down and grabs both nipples in her hands, pulling them and twisting them between her fingers. She's so keyed up that her body is still tight from the tension.

"What do you need?" I ask again because I feel it will be more than a hard fuck.

"Just fuck me," she replies, but I can tell she knows there's something else she needs.

I continue fucking her so hard the force of the thrusts is making the bed scratch against the floor, and she's right on the edge of her release, but she can't reach it. I can see her start to get frustrated, and

I refuse to give up. It has nothing to do with me; I know it's something in her head keeping her orgasm out of her reach.

I slow down and gently keep stroking my cock in and out of her pussy. "You need more, don't you, Pretty girl?"

She nods. "It's not you."

I smooth my hands down her stomach. "I know that," I assure her. I pull out, scoop my phone from my pants pocket and shoot off a message hoping they get it.

I climb up on the bed, laying on my back; she swings her leg over my waist, sinking back down on my cock. She moves her hips back and forth, grinding her clit on me. I just lay my hands on her waist and let her take what she needs.

I see the door open, watching Ryder walk in with Dex behind him. "What do we have here, *Il mio sole*?" He slides a hand up her back, and she shivers at the contact. Leo and Holden slide into the room behind them, answering the message I sent that simply said Les needs us. I sent it, hoping Leo can tuck away his hurt feelings from her yelling at him and Holden swallowing his discomfort of what happened at the garage. Them showing up shows me that all our focus is on one thing...our queen.

"Our girl here is a little tense," I explain, making Les breathe out a laugh. *Step in the right direction.* "I called in for backup."

Ryder steps behind her and hooks his hand around her throat, pulling her back against his chest. She's still firmly seated on my cock, so I get an unrestricted view of her chest heaving and feeling her pussy clamp down on me. "Are you tense, *Il mio sole*?" he asks in her ear, and I see his knuckles flex, tightening his hold. "You need us to help you?"

"Yes," she moans, and I know I made the right call. I'm man enough to admit that she needs more than me at this moment and an extra set of hands. Or four.

Ryder strips out of his clothes before climbing onto the bed, laying on his back, and patting his massive thighs. "Come here. I want that pussy."

She looks down at me in question, and I just grin. "This is your show. I'll take that ass." I slap said ass hard, making her clamp down on me again. She gives me a long lingering kiss before climbing over to Ryder. I get my first glimpse of his pierced cock, and my eyes almost bug out of my head. I twist around on my stomach. "Fucking hell, that looks like it could hurt."

Les throws a leg over him, he lines up with her pussy, and she sinks down slowly. I can see each barbell disappear inside of her. "It feels good, doesn't it, *Il mio sole*?"

"Yes," she groans, rotating her hips. Is it wrong I want to feel that shit disappear inside of me? I flash a guilty look at Leo for thinking that, and his face says he's thinking the same thing.

I hop off the bed and approach him. "Where was your mind just now, Pretty boy?" I ask, rubbing his hard cock through his jeans.

He hisses a breath. "Same place yours was."

I kiss him hard. "Lube is in that bedside drawer. Go show our girl a good time." He looks at Ryder and then back to me with a raised brow. "He's in the sweetest pussy ever. He's not going to care whose cock is rubbing against his."

Leo gives me one last doubtful look before jerking his shirt over his head; I help him out of his pants and boxers. He strides over to the table and pulls the bottle of lube out. Leo climbs onto the bed behind them, and Ryder doesn't even bat an eye. Leo rubs a thick amount of lube on his cock, making my cock jump from watching him. He truly has a magnificent cock. He smears the rest of the lube on her back hole before pushing her further onto Ryder. I step around the other side of the bed to get a better view. Leo notches his cock, still guiding it with one hand; he pushes forward. I know when he pops past the resistance because Ryder groans and Les lets out one of those low sultry moans.

"Fuck," Leo grits out, pushing forward. "I can feel your piercings."

"You should feel them inside of you," Les says, then moans when Leo fully plants himself in her ass.

"Fuck, this is tight," Ryder groans again, his fingers flexing on Les' hips.

Dex gets onto the bed on the other side on his knees, fully naked, and I have to take a second to appreciate it. Dex has one of those bodies you want to oil up and slide all over. He slides his cock between her waiting lips, sinking into her throat. I see her entire body relax, and I have to pat myself on the back.

I'm a fucking genius.

Holden is standing to the side, eyes glued to Les being fucked between three guys, his hand massaging his cock through his shorts. She looks like a fucking goddess.

"Get in there," I encourage before jumping back onto the bed on my knees behind a thrusting Leo. I kiss down his spine, grabbing the lube he tossed on the bed beside him. "You want my cock, Baby?" I purr.

"God, yes," he groans, stilling his thrusts.

"Wait," Les breathes, lips slipping off Dex's cock. "I want to watch."

Ryder chuckles. "Turn around and give me that ass then."

Leo pulls out of her with a hiss. As soon as he's free, I wrap my hand around him from behind, stroking in long hard strokes that I know he likes. "What about your stitches?" I ask because I don't want him to rip them open.

He shoves his hips forward fucking my fist. "They're fine."

Taking him at his word, I tighten my fist around him, watching Les turn herself around. I hand the bottle of lube to Ryder; he lubes up and urges her to sit on his cock. She looks at it and then back at me with wide eyes. I chuckle at her facial expression. "Problem, Pretty girl?"

She shakes her head with a smile, plants her feet on either side of his hips, and squats gracefully as hell over his waiting cock. He holds the base with one hand, lining himself up. She grabs Dex's and Holden's shoulders for balance since Holden decided to join the party. I continue to stroke Leo's cock, kissing his shoulder, watching Ryder feed his cock into Les' ass.

When he pops inside, and the first barbell stretches her, her head falls back, and her mouth parts in ecstasy. Ryder groans the whole slow slide inside of her tight ass, and Leo's cock jerks in my hand at the sound. When he's finally all the way inside her, they're both out of breath. Ryder reaches down and hooks his arms under Les' knees, spreading her wide for Leo.

I release my hold on his cock, and he sinks into her pussy, making them all groan again. I lube up my cock and scoot on my knees behind Leo. He feels me notch myself at his asshole and lays his head between Les' perfect tits.

I just so happen to look up into Holden's eyes, and the lust in them slams into me. He's looking between us, but his eyes keep straying to where I'm about to be buried in Leo. I push my hips forward so the head disappears, Leo's head comes up, and Holden grips his cock in his fist.

"Fuck," Leo breathes. "Stop fucking around, Gage."

"Impatient for my cock, Baby?" I tease, moving forward slightly. I hear Les and Ryder chuckle. "You think I should give him what he wants, Holden?" I ask, my eyes never leaving his. Holden nods his head, his breathing speeding up.

"Gage," Les laughs, then moans when it squeezes around Leo.

I start pushing forward into Leo's ass, watching Holden's pupils dilate.

"Fuck, Gage," Leo groans when I'm balls deep.

"Your ass feels good, Baby," I say, rubbing my hands up his back.

Dex is watching the whole time, then rakes a tattooed hand down his face. "Fuck," he grits out, turning Les' head so he can sink between her lips.

Does Dexy boy like what he sees too?

Les reaches out her other hand and wraps it around Holden's thick length, stroking him from base to tip, swirling her hand around the head.

I pull back and slam into Leo, pushing him inside of her.

"Goddamn," Ryder groans, pumping his hips up.

Every time Ryder or I move, it causes a chain reaction. Les lets Dex's cock go with a wet pop before turning her head to take Holden into her mouth, wrapping her fist around Dex.

I start moving faster inside Leo, making the most delicious groans leave his mouth.

"Yes, Gage," he groans, rocking his hips between Les and me, fucking her while he's fucking me.

Les lets Holden's cock go and moans so loud that I could come on the spot, "Are you going to come, *Il mio sole*?" Ryder pants into her ear. Then he looks up at Holden, and a look crosses his face I've never seen before. Uncertainty.

Ryder wraps an arm around Holden's back and jerks him closer so Holden's cock is hovering right at his lips. He licks around the head of Holden's cock, making Holden groan. I can see Ryder visibly steel himself, then close his mouth over Holden's cock.

Fuck.

"Ryder," Holden groans. "Fuck." Holden watches his cock disappear into Ryder's mouth, and I can see all the restraint he's using not to shove it all the way in.

"Holy shit," Les moans, then sucks Dex's cock back into her mouth.

Dex throws his head back, shoving his hips forward; I can see Les' throat bulge from taking him all the way in. Her nose brushes against him, and he looks back down at her. "Good girl," he rumbles.

"Fuck. She's getting tight," Leo half moans-half groans.

Dex reaches down between Les and Leo with the hand that isn't wrapped in her hair and starts rubbing her clit. I don't know where to fucking look. My cock sliding into Leo's ass, Dex's cock disappearing in Les' throat, or Ryder sucking cock like a fucking pro. It's stimulation overload. I start pounding harder, causing my skin to slap against Leo's.

"Harder," Leo encourages. I grip his hips and piston my hips as hard as I can. "Yes," he groans.

Les pulls back from Dex's cock "FUCK!" she screams, finally able to reach the climax she was looking for. "God, yes!"

Here's to hoping Evander, Mateo, and Micah went to the pool house.

I slam into Leo twice when I feel my balls start drawing up; knowing I can't hold off any longer, I hold myself as deep as I can, filling his ass up with my cum. I feel Leo tense below me and know he let himself go too.

"Alessa," he groans, pushing his hips back on my cock. "Gage."

I slowly slip out of him so he can slip from Alessa. He gives her a lingering kiss before collapsing back on the bed beside me. I pull his back to my chest, wrapping my arm around his waist. We have the perfect view at the end of the bed. Ryder is still buried deep in her ass, his hands holding her legs wide open, Leo's cum dripping out of her pussy.

"Fuck, that's hot," I comment.

Leo chuckles. "Yeah, it is."

Ryder lets Holden's cock drop from his lips. "Get in her pussy."

Holden slides around in front of Les, kissing her at the same time his huge cock disappears inside her. I can hear her moan into his mouth when he starts moving, not giving her a second to catch her breath, exactly how she likes it. Who knew Holden had it in him?

He starts moving faster, and I can see her legs start shaking in Ryder's grip, her moans getting longer and louder with each stroke.

"Fuck fuck fuck," she chants, pulling her mouth from Holden's. Her whole back bows and Holden pulls out with a gush of liquid. I fucking love it when she squirts.

"Shit," Ryder groans, and I know her ass squeezed his cock so fucking hard. "I'm going to come."

Holden shoves back into her, and Ryder lets go with a groan of his own, jerking Holden's mouth to his. I reach across Leo and massage one of Holden's ass cheeks because I can't help myself, making his whole-body shudder.

Leo chuckles under his breath. "You're going to make him come before he even starts."

Holden lifts Les off of Ryder so he can slip out, then gets situated with her on top, facing us with his head pillowed on Leo's thigh. Dex gets behind Les and smooths a hand up her back; I can see his other hand working lube on his cock. "Can you take me?" Dex asks.

"Yes," Les moans, arching her ass out in invitation.

"That's my good girl," Dex praises, lining himself up. From looking between Dex and Holden, I'm pretty sure they're the thickest, and they're about to stretch her out together.

Ryder collapses on the bed with his head at mine and Leo's,

watching Les' face crease with pain and then relax with pleasure. I love watching her face while she's getting fucked.

"Do they feel good, Pretty girl?"

She braces her hands on Holden's chest, rocking between him and Dex, nodding her head. "I feel so...full."

Dex cracks her on the ass with his hand. "Come for us again, Baby girl."

"Oh fuck," she moans when he does it again.

"You like my hand on your ass?" he pants out. She's working her hips so fast between them they aren't going to last much longer, and neither is she.

"Yes."

Ryder reaches out and wraps a hand around her throat, squeezing. Her face goes slack with pleasure. "Fuck her. Don't let her fuck you."

Leo peeks over his shoulder at me, and I can see he's getting turned on all over again. He could probably feel my cock growing behind him.

Dex and Holden find a rhythm, and you can hear the cracking of Dex's palm on her ass every once in a while. Ryder still has that grip on her throat, only letting up to let her suck in a couple of breaths before he squeezes again.

"Fuck. She's too tight," Holden groans.

"You going to come, Baby girl?"

She nods her head frantically the best she can with the hold Ryder has on her. I see her whole body tense, her short nails digging into Holden's chest. She starts bucking between them.

"Shit," Dex grunts, slamming his hips forward. "You take us so good."

Holden's head leans back on Leo's thigh, and he groans, emptying himself in her with the force of her orgasm. Dex's thrusts stutter, and he lets go with a half growl.

Ryder lets go of her throat, and she collapses onto Holden's chest. Dex slides out of her tight ass with a groan, and Holden picks her hips up so he can slide out because she's as limp as a ragdoll.

I run my fingers through her silky black hair. "Do you feel better, Pretty girl?"

"I do," she says with a sigh, sinking further onto Holden.

Ryder rolls off the bed and heads to the bathroom; I hear the water in the tub running. He comes out a few minutes later. "You need to get cleaned up, *Il mio sole*."

She shakes her head and latches onto Holden tighter, making us all laugh.

"Come on, Pretty girl. I'll help." I kiss Leo on the shoulder and slide off the bed. I walk over to the side of the bed and coax a boneless Les into my arms, carrying her to the bathroom. I carefully step into the tub, sinking into the water with her on my lap, both of us sighing at the warm water.

I gather her close to my chest, just needing this time alone with her. Someone closes the bathroom door, and I'm grateful.

I don't mind sharing her, but sometimes I just need her all to myself.

CHAPTER 47
ALESSA

After Gage gets me into the bathtub, he gathers me close to his chest; I wrap my arms around his neck and hold him tight.

"How did you know?" I whisper.

"Sometimes you need us, and you don't know how to say it," he shrugs. "I said it for you."

I feel terrible that he couldn't get me where I needed to be today. It's nothing against Gage's abilities in bed because he sure as hell isn't lacking in that department. I just had this crushing tension in my chest that I knew I needed to get rid of before it escalated to a point I couldn't bring myself back.

I feel a distinctive poke on my ass and raise my eyebrow at Gage. "Ignore him," he says casually, referring to his cock. I move my body to straddle his waist, taking him in my hand. "You don't have to, Pretty girl."

I know I don't have to, and I am deliciously sore, but I need this one-on-one time with Gage, something we haven't had. I place his cock at my entrance and slowly slide down his length, both of us sighing when I'm fully seated. I lay my forehead on his and start to move slowly. His crystal blue eyes lock with mine, and he doesn't look away. He's letting me see everything running through his head;

I let him see mine too. He places his arms around my back, pulling me closer but not speeding me up, letting everything build slowly. He kisses me, and it's the first time he's kissed me this sweet. Usually, Gage and I are like fire and gasoline when we are naked together, but something about this is...different. I feel my orgasm start building slowly from the tips of my toes, but we never change pace, happy to just spend this time locked onto each other. I pull back from the kiss, look back into his beautiful eyes, and it hits me why this is different. It's time.

"I love you, Gage Lawson," I whisper, staring into his eyes.

His arms tighten around my waist. "What?" he asks in amazement. Does he not know he holds an equal part of my heart?

I grab his face with both hands, never stopping the movement of my hips. "I love you so much, Gage. You're one of the few people who actually get me. If it weren't for you, I wouldn't have the life I have with everyone. I love you."

He crushes me to his chest. "I didn't think I would ever hear that come from your mouth. I've just been biding my time until you didn't need me anymore." He squeezes tighter. I don't get mad at him because I know how many people have walked out of Gage's life. I didn't know he felt that way, so I will spend the rest of my life proving to him that I won't ever leave him. "I love you, Pretty girl. Something in your dark soul calls to mine, and it quiets my mind. Around you, I can just...be."

I pull back from his chest so I can see his eyes again. "I will never leave you, Gage. You are mine, and you always have been."

"God, I love you," he breathes like he's been waiting to say it for a long time.

"I love you too."

We start moving slowly again, and my orgasm starts building again immediately, this time even sweeter. I latch my hands on his shoulders, keeping my eyes wide open so he can see what he does to me on a soul-deep level. He isn't wrong about something in our souls calling to each other. I felt that pull when his dad first brought him around. Now at this moment, it feels deeper. I tip over the edge, and it rolls through my body like a soft wave instead of the tsunami it usually feels like. Gage lets go right behind me, groaning out his release but letting me see his eyes the whole time. He gathers me back to his chest, almost squeezing me too tight but not enough at the same time.

We spend the rest of the bath gently washing each other off, and it's like we're exploring each other's bodies for the first time. When the water finally starts getting cold, he rinses us off before grabbing one of my big fluffy towels. He dries off quickly, wrapping the towel around his waist before grabbing another one for me. He helps me from the tub and dries me off, laying kisses on my shoulders before wrapping the towel around my breasts and tucking it in. I wrap my arms around his neck, his hands sliding onto my waist.

"I love you," I tell him again.

He closes his eyes with a sigh. When he opens them again, it takes my breath away. "I love you too."

He kisses me sweetly, then picks me up, swinging me around in a circle and making me laugh. He plants me down on my feet and lays kisses all over my face, saying I love you after each kiss.

Through all of my and Gage's faults, I know at this moment that he's mine, and I'm his.

After my bath with Gage, I know I need to find Leo and apologize. I know he was mad at me when I left the basement, but he came running as soon as Gage said I needed them. I don't even know how to describe what it felt like to have all of them with me together for the first time.

When I first went to my room, I felt like I was fracturing apart. Then Gage came and glued the first piece back together. Then they held me together one by one and brought me out of my mind. I don't like admitting that I'm at a loss most of the time leading this family. I feel like I'm making all the wrong decisions, no matter the outcome. I'm starting to second-guess everything, and I *hate* that feeling.

After Gage kissed me stupid one more time, he left me to get dressed, and it gave me a few minutes to reflect on the conversation with Leo downstairs. I didn't mean to snap at him, and I feel like shit for it. Gage told me how Leo felt out of place sometimes because I have a long history with the rest of them. It's not an excuse, but I wasn't in the right place to have that conversation then; I am now. After searching almost everywhere, I finally find him outside on the back patio where I should have looked in the first place. I quietly close the door and sit beside him on one of the loungers.

I had three messages from Zane insisting that we meet, and I can't risk meeting him in public, so I told him just to come here. I don't know what he's insistent about, but it sounds important.

Leo looks at me with a smile, but it seems strained.

"We need to talk," I tell him, swinging my legs over to face him. "I'm sorry about downstairs."

He shakes his head. "You shouldn't be." He turns his blue-green eyes on me. "Those were my insecurities talking; I know that wasn't a good time."

I grab his hand. "Leo, you have to talk to me about this stuff, or I don't know. I never want you to feel out of place here, or like you don't belong." Nothing breaks my heart more than him thinking I don't want him here with me as much as the others.

He takes a deep breath. "I just feel like sometimes they know you better than I do. They know how to help you in any way you need it. I don't think I add much to this."

I frown. "You're one piece of my heart, Leo. Yes, some have known me for a lifetime or almost a lifetime. But I chose *you* first."

"Ryder told me twice to stop being a little bitch." He laughs. "I didn't realize how much until in the basement. I was listening to you, but I didn't *hear* you or him. You just didn't want me to see what was going to happen." He looks at me again. "But I can handle it, Baby."

"I can't," I whisper. "There are parts of me you will see and don't understand. I never want that look in your eye that you had today."

"What look?"

"The one that said you were disgusted with me." My eyes fill with tears. "You looked at me like you didn't know me at all."

He swings his legs over to sit up, his knees bracketing mine. "Baby, I wasn't disgusted with you," he runs his fingers through his hair, "I was disgusted with myself because I wasn't disgusted with you. Does that make sense?" I shake my head, and he sighs, "When you turn into the Queen they all call you, it does something to me. I wasn't raised around this stuff like you guys were. I was raised by a meek schoolteacher in a rural country setting and shouldn't be this accepting. I should be questioning everything, including us." My eyes widen at that admission, afraid that he's going to tell me he can't do it anymore. "I'm just trying to come to terms with the fact that I don't care about any of it. The killing, the money, the status. I just care about you, and I will do everything to stay here, but you have to give me some credit too. Let me decide what I can and can't handle."

"I can try," I promise, knowing there are some truths that still need to be told. One I'm not sure he will be so accepting of. "That's all I can do."

He squeezes my hands. "I need to understand you better."

"What do you mean?"

"The more conversations that go on in that house, the less I feel like I know." He steels his spine. "I need to know what Frankie did to you." My first instinct is to pull away because opening that can of worms opens many more. "Please trust me with that."

"It's not about trust, Leo." I pull my hand away from his, ignoring the hurt look on his face. I wipe my sweaty palms on my shorts. "What Frankie did to me is something a thirteen-year-old should never have to go through." I pull my legs underneath me. "He ordered his men to take me. They called me the Poletti cunt while they raped me. There were four of them." I swallow back the bile, flashes of those days popping behind my eyes. "One of them would rape me with any object he could find; it didn't matter if it was sharp or not or which hole he was sticking it in."

"Alessa..." I hold up my hand, cutting him off. I started this, and I'm going to finish; I refuse to look at the pity all over his face. I can already hear it in his voice.

"My dad found me covered in blood from various wounds. He had to listen to the nurses and doctors detail everything that was done to me. I think that's the part that hurt the most. I know deep down he blamed himself, but it wasn't his fault." I finally dare to look at his face, and he has unshed tears in his eyes. "I found out at thirteen that I would never be able to bear children because of that sick fucker sodomizing me. Frankie took my childhood from me, so at twenty-two, I took his life from him." I scramble back off the lounger when he reaches for me. Every word just comes pouring out, and I can't stop it. "Micah and Ryder grabbed him one night and locked him in the basement. Micah told me I could finish what he started when I was ready. I went down to that fucking basement, and *everything* he had done to me, I did to him. Four days because that's how long he kept me. For four days, I tortured him the same way he had me tortured."

Dad never went after Frankie because I made him promise he wouldn't, telling him it would start a war, but in reality, even at thirteen, I *knew* Frankie was mine to kill.

"Baby, I didn't..." He rakes his hand through his hair. "Fuck I didn't know."

I shake my head because I'm not done. "Leo, I'm the Black Demon." He frowns for a second until I can see the lightbulb click on. "Frankie wasn't my first victim. I had my first kill at seventeen, and I've been doing it ever since."

"Baby, I don't understand."

"I'm the female serial killer who takes out the ones who were never convicted of doing horrible shit to innocent people."

That is how the cops have pieced it together that the Black Demon is responsible for all the disappearances; the motive. They won't ever find the bodies or the pieces they are hacked into after I'm done.

I can feel the tears falling down my cheeks, and in a way, it's like relief. Relief that he knows about Frankie and relief he finally knows about the Black Demon. "I can see the look on your face, Leo. Take that information and do whatever you want with it. But now you know the truth. The *full* truth." His face is a mixture of pity, sorrow, and revulsion. All of them aimed at me.

Everything slams into me at once, and I feel like I'm sucked back into that night, the night they grabbed me. A whimper escapes my mouth before I can stop it; I slap a hand over my mouth and take off toward the house.

"Alessa!" Leo yells, but I can't stop.

Visions of the four guys who took everything from me blind me one by one, making me stumble into the house. I told Holden this story; it hurt, but it didn't affect me like this. I feel like the walls of this house are closing in on me, and the only thing that keeps rolling through my mind is *run*. I haven't had a panic attack in years, but you never forget the feeling of one. I know that is what's happening, but I am powerless to stop it.

My lungs are starting to seize, and I can't get a full breath. My vision is beginning to black out around the edges. I stumble the rest of the way through the house and jerk the garage door open.

Run run run!

I smack the garage door button and fumble for my Ferrari keys. After I drop them for the third time, I can't stand up anymore. My knees hit the concrete in the garage so hard it jars my whole body; I slump down, trying to yell for help, but nothing will come out. Memories start assaulting me.

"Remember what your dad said," Garrett, one of my guards, says.

I roll my eyes. "Yeah yeah. Don't leave the bowling alley."

I am on my way to meet Ryder and Gage; we're notorious for sneaking away from where we're supposed to be.

"Seriously, Alessa, it's not safe," Garrett reminds me for the thousandth time.

I snort. "Nothing has happened before."

Henry, the driver, and the other guard stops at the red light and glances into the rearview mirror. "You need to start taking this seriously."

I shake my head because I know they're being overprotective. Henry accelerates through the green light, and something smacks into the side of the SUV so hard that it makes my head whip to the side and smack the window. What was that? I can see Henry's mouth moving, but my ears are ringing, and I can't hear.

"...get down!!!" Garrett's yell finally cuts through, and that's when I see four guys outside of our SUV with really big guns. They level them at the

front, and the glass shatters when they pull the trigger. I bury my head in my arms, but I can still hear the sickening thud of the bullets hitting Henry and Garrett's bodies.

"Henry! Garrett!" I cry, but it's useless.

Someone jerks open the driver's side back door that wasn't damaged, and I'm face to face with a guy with a mask on, his evil blue eyes glittering behind it. He reaches in, unsnaps my seatbelt, and then grabs me by the arm, dragging me across the seat. My dad's lectures about fighting finally register, and I start screaming, kicking, and trying to pull away. He's just too strong. He finally jerks me across the seat, clamping a hand over my mouth.

"Shut up, you stupid cunt," he hisses in my ear, half-carrying me to a waiting SUV. He slings me in the back between two other guys before jumping into the driver's seat.

"Daddy!" I yell, trying to fight, fight like Dad taught me.

The biggest one backhands me across the face. "Your daddy can't save you now."

They all laugh like he told the best joke, ripping their masks off. I clamp a hand to my face and let silent tears fall. Where are they taking me? Why did they take me?

The littlest one in the back rubs his hand up my naked thigh. I'm wearing my favorite pair of shorts, the ones Ryder picked out the last time we all went shopping. "I like when they fight."

I'm not completely naïve, so I know what he means. I feel the acid burn in my throat and know I'm going to vomit. It comes out all over the back floorboard until all I can do is dry heave.

"Motherfucker!" the big one yells. "You're going to pay for that, cunt."

He grabs a handful of my hair and yanks my head back, making me cry out. I try to claw his hands away, but it's like he doesn't even feel it. "I think we should get started now," the passenger says with a laugh.

"Bitch just puked in the fucking car, and you're turned on right now?" the driver asks. "You sick fucker."

"I like it nasty." The passenger laughs again, and I can see the unhinged look in his green eyes.

The two in the back roughly start pawing at the buttons on my shorts, and my fight increases tenfold. The little one has his hand ready to clamp over my mouth; I grab it and bite down as hard as possible.

He groans. "God, yes." He shoves his hand down the front of my unbuttoned shorts, and the big one tucks my legs between his, putting the weight of his elbow on my stomach so I can't move.

"No. No. No," I keep repeating, but they aren't listening. Why aren't they listening?!

"...Alessa!"

I frown because no one in this car calls me by my real name.

His hand starts moving in my underwear, and I can feel the acid bubble up again.

Hands tighten on my arms, and I know I need to fight. Fight them, Alessa!

".... goddamnit," one of them grunts, and I know I made contact. "Beautiful, you need to breathe."

Don't call me that!

"Alessa." Those same hands shake my shoulders, "Breathe, Beautiful. You're having a panic attack, and none of this is real."

It is real! Why can't I breathe?

"Open your eyes. This isn't real." I shake my head. "Yes. Please. Open those pretty blue eyes for me."

"What the fuck?!" someone yells, and I shrink back. Why do they sound so mad? Are they mad at me?

"Back off," the one holding my shoulders growls. "Breathe," he says much gentler to me. I take a small breath, my lungs still not fully expanding. "That's my girl. Now open your eyes."

I pry my eyes open, but everything is blurry. A whimper escapes me. What is wrong with my eyes?

Something rubs at my face, and I try to pull away. "Try again," they encourage, and I don't want to. I couldn't see anything! "Come on, Beautiful. Let me see those eyes."

I can't! I can feel the panic increasing all over again.

Strong hands grip my face. "Open them."

Something about the voice sounds familiar and safe. The guys from that night aren't here anymore. Just a light sandalwood scent and a cologne I've smelled before, but I can't place it.

Hands keep stroking my cheeks, wiping my tears away. "Breathe, Beautiful. In and out. Come on."

I focus on that voice. It's deep but smooth. A voice you want to whisper into your ear. I want to see the face attached to it. I finally pry my eyes open again and blink a few times to focus. His perfect face comes into focus. Strong jaw, dark stubble coating it. A slightly crooked nose. Dark slashed eyebrows over concerned whiskey-colored eyes. Full lips.

"Zane?"

CHAPTER 48
ZANE

"Zane?" Les' sweet voice whispers.

I rub shaky hands across her tear-stained cheeks again. "Yeah, Beautiful. It's me. I need you to take several deep breaths with me, okay?"

When I saw her drop to the floor of the garage, I almost forgot to put my car in park in my rush to get to her. I helped lean her back against the side of her Ferrari, yelling her name. Her mind was a million miles away, locked in memories I have seen so many times. I knew she was having a panic attack, but I couldn't get her to listen to me. Hearing her yell for her dad almost ripped my heart out.

She takes a shuddering breath; her eyes still locked on mine. Ryder is seething over my shoulder, but even he sees how important it is not to upset her after he first saw me kneeling over her in the garage.

"That's my girl," I praise. "A few more times." I imitate what I want her to do, taking exaggerated breaths. "One more time, Beautiful."

She takes a breath like someone that has been drowning and finally breached the surface; I see her eyes start to clear. I breathe with her until her breathing starts returning to normal.

I glance down at her poor knees tucked against her chest; they're cut and bleeding from where she hit the concrete. "I need a first aid kit and some water," I tell Ryder without turning around. He growls under his breath but surprisingly disappears into the house.

"What are you doing here?" she asks, voice hoarse from screaming. Her screams ripped through the garage, echoing all over the walls.

"You told me to come over," I remind her, and I can see the confusion all over her face. "I needed to talk to you."

She shakes her head, and I know she doesn't remember.

Ryder steps up beside me. "You can fucking go now."

Instead of arguing like I want to, I go to stand up because I don't want to upset her. She latches onto my arms before I can get to my feet. I glance at Ryder out of the corner of my eye. His eyes narrow, but he thrusts the things I asked for at me.

I crack open the water bottle and hand it to her. "Take a few sips." She stares at it like she doesn't know what to do with it. I tip it up to her pouty lips. "Open." She opens, and I tip it further. "Swallow."

When she had them before, it took her a little bit to become fully functional. The first time she had one in front of me, it was one of the nights she actually stayed the night at my apartment in the city. She woke up from a nightmare screaming, scaring the shit out of me.

"You drink. I'm going to clean up your knees," I tell her once she remembers how to take a drink. She nods, and I smile at her, stretching her legs out between mine. I gently take her water bottle and pour some over the cuts to wash them out before handing it back to her. I take a gauze pad and swipe around the cuts, wiping up the blood.

"Ryder?" I hear someone say quietly.

"She's okay, Holden," Ryder says so gently it surprises the shit out of me.

I start patching up her knees with her eyes locked on my face the whole time. I can feel her staring without even looking up. I know she'll be kicking my ass out once she's with it. And I'm just enough of an asshole to soak in whatever she'll give me.

I place the last piece of tape. "That should hold. They aren't too bad." I finally look up at her face, and some of her color is coming back.

"What happened?" Ryder asks, looking between Les and me. Les finally looks up at him, and you can see her mind struggling to catch up with the fact that she knows him. He squats beside her, realizing he looks intimidating as hell, standing over her. "Hey, *Il mio sole*," he says softly, and I have to keep from grinding my teeth.

"I don't know. When I got here, she was collapsing in the garage," I answer when I can tell she has no idea what happened.

"What the hell are you doing here?" Ryder asks between clenched teeth.

"She asked me to come," I tell him, taking great pleasure out of the shock all over his face. I look back at her. "We need to get you off of this hard floor. Can you stand?"

"I don't know," she says without an ounce of her usual bravado, so I know she still isn't entirely with me.

"Let's try it, okay?" I ask, grabbing her hands in mine. I stand and gently pull her to her feet in front of me. Her hands latch onto my arms when she wobbles, and I control the small shudder just from that slight touch. "You good, Beautiful?"

"Zane," Ryder growls, "I only have so much fucking patience for this shit. Don't fucking call her that."

Les shuts her eyes tight, and I can see her bottom lip quiver. *Fuck.* As much as I don't want to, we need to find that ice queen buried in there. It's better than this version that's making my heart bleed.

"Shit," Ryder cusses, "I'm sorry, *Il mio sole*."

She opens her eyes and smiles, but it's wobbly. "It's okay."

Her voice is so quiet, not the usual whipcrack I'm used to hearing. I don't like this at all. Even if the other version hates my ass.

"You know you're making it a habit for me to have to rescue you," I joke, and she frowns, some of her usual self showing in her eyes. She looks into my eyes for so long I start to get nervous, then she takes a step back, letting her arms drop.

"No one asked you to rescue me."

There she is.

"You need to go," Ryder says, pointing to my car.

Les frowns again and shakes her head. "No. He needed to talk to me."

Now is definitely not the time for me to drop the bomb I have. "It can wait," I tell her, but it can't. I can't risk upsetting her; this would, without a doubt, do just that.

"Obviously, it can't, or your messages wouldn't have been so urgent." She rakes her hand through her hair. "Ryder, take him to the office. Just give me a minute."

She walks toward the door, and Holden wraps his arms around her shoulders, kissing the top of her head. She slides an arm around his waist, leaning into his embrace.

"This better be fucking good," Ryder says.

"I wouldn't classify what I have to say as good," I say dryly, walking towards my car. I jerk open the door and pull out two folders, slamming the door shut.

Ryder eyes them suspiciously, then jerks his head for me to follow him into the house. He leads me to her office and points towards one of the chairs before leaning against the table behind her desk, crossing his arms over his chest.

After five minutes of Ryder and I glaring at each other, Les finally breezes into the room, looking slightly refreshed. She lowers herself into the chair and folds her arms on the desk in front of her. She looks so much like her dad when she does that.

"What's so important?" she asks, and I slide the two folders to her, knowing that when she opens those, our whole dynamic changes.

I lay my hand on it before she can grab it. "Just know I had nothing to do with this." I move my hand, and she slides it over, opening the top one first. I don't want to upset her after what I saw outside, but she needs to know this. She needs to be prepared for what is about to happen.

She flips through hundreds of pictures with Ryder looking over her shoulder. They're pictures of her anytime she went out with or without any of the guys. There are also pictures of her with me when we met at the docks. They all have two things in common. She's in all of them, and they were taken from a long-distance telescope camera lens. She flips to the last one, and I wait for her face to change, but it doesn't. It's two people dressed head to toe in black with a black mask concealing their features. The only thing you can tell about it is one of them is a female by the build and height, Alessa's size, and the other one is male, a very tall, well-built male.

She closes that one without comment and opens the next one. It's a case file on her, but it isn't the one the department is running; this one is personal. It's all her movements, the buildings she owns, and her known associates. Anything you want to know about her is in those files.

She looks up at me when she gets an idea of what she's looking at. "Where did these come from?"

"They were on the windshield of my truck."

Her eyebrows shoot up. "When?"

"The first day I told you I needed to meet you."

"You expect us to believe you just fucking stumbled on these files?" Ryder scoffs, and Les holds up a hand to cut him off before he says anything else. She starts massaging her temples, and I know that panic attack took everything out of her.

"Why give them to me?" she asks, looking back up. Anytime she even so much as looks into my eyes, my heart starts beating out of control. *I'm pathetic.*

Here's to hoping neither one of them is armed. "The department has been investigating you."

She raises an eyebrow. "They're always investigating"

I shake my head. "No. Serious investigation. They have evidence piling up. That," I say, pointing to the folder, "isn't a department investigation. That's personal." Ryder and Les share a look like they know something. "What am I missing?"

"Go get those other files, please," Les says to Ryder. You can tell he wants to argue, but whatever is on her face right now, he thinks better of it.

He gives me one last scathing look before storming from the room.

"What happened outside, Les?" I ask gently when we're alone.

"Nothing," she replies too fast, then sighs. "Look, I appreciate everything you've done with the shooting and now this, but this doesn't change anything, Zane."

"Why not?" I demand.

"Because," she says harshly, "you lied to me, and you became the enemy. I moved on."

"Did you?" I challenge, sitting up in my chair. "Why are you lying to yourself that what we had wasn't fucking real?"

"Because if it were real, you wouldn't have lied to me the whole fucking time we were together," she grits out. "You wouldn't have betrayed me. Or your dad."

"I was trying to get us out!" I half yell. "I was doing it for you." I stand up from my chair and take the risk of walking around her side of the desk. "Everything I did was for you," I say again, spinning her chair around so I can lean down on the arms, caging her in. "I loved you, Les, and I didn't want you to live this life." She sucks in a breath at my admission about loving her because we never exchanged those words, there were too many unknowns between us, and she was too fucking young. "Tell me you didn't love me too." I'm leaning so close to her face that I can see her pupils expand and feel her breath dusting across my lips. It would be easy to lean down and capture her lips with mine.

"I didn't," she whispers.

"Stop lying," I grit out. "Why can't you tell me the truth?"

"What difference would it make?" She shoves at my chest, and I don't budge. But I know if she wants me out of her space, she will make that happen.

"It will make all the difference in the world, Beautiful." I lean closer so my lips rub hers when I talk. "Tell me you feel this," I beg her.

"I don't feel anything."

"Your mouth is saying one thing, but your body is saying another," I tell her, watching goosebumps pop up on her arms, her nipples hardening behind that thin excuse for a tank top. I run my lips up her neck. "Tell me the truth."

"I can't," she half moans, her knuckles turning white from her grip on her chair, so she doesn't reach out to me.

"Because of them?" I ask. I don't wait for an answer; I already know. "They give you what you need?"

"Yes," she moans again when I rub my lips on her neck again. I forgot how fucking responsive she is; my cock is hard as a rock, throbbing behind my zipper.

"I could too," I whisper, and her body arches toward me.

"What?" she says, finally losing her battle and gripping my forearms. Just that little touch zaps through me like electricity.

"I could give you what you need too, Beautiful." I'm saying exactly what she thinks I'm saying. I'll share her with those assholes if means I can have her back in my life.

"You have to stop," she breathes when I kiss at her erratic pulse jumping in her throat. She shoves at my chest again, and I stand up this time, not even trying to hide what she does to me. I hear Ryder's boots stomping through the house and take several steps back, leaning against the bookshelf behind me.

He shoves the door open, narrowing his eyes on me again. Les' cheeks are still red from what I was doing to her, but she mostly collected herself. Ryder slaps the folders against my chest before walking to Les, putting his body between us.

I take the folders and return to my chair. I flip open the first one, and it's filled with the same kind of pictures I had. "Where did these come from?"

"Someone put some on Dex's truck a while back, then on Gage's a little bit after that. Now every time we go out, they appear," Les answers, watching my face.

I hold up one that has the word 'mine' scratched across it in red. "Mine?" I ask.

She shrugs. "They seem to think so."

I notice the guy's faces are scratched out on some of them except mine. "Why isn't my face scratched out?" I ask, looking at Les and me in a stare-off by the docks when she gave me the file on the shitty foster parents.

"That's what I want to know," Ryder says, leaning back against the table behind her again. "Seems pretty fucking suspicious, don't you think?"

"You think I did this?" I ask incredulously. "Why the hell would I bring you the same thing if I'm the one doing it?"

"To save your own ass," Les adds.

"You may not like me, Les." I point to the pictures. "But I wouldn't do something like this."

"There's more of them. More," she waves her hand around, "personal."

It takes me a second to catch up to what she's saying, and I can feel my blood boiling. "Someone has naked pictures of you?" I grind out. I'll kill this motherfucker for that alone.

"Yeah. Several," Les says. "Of me and some of the guys."

Someone not only has naked pictures of her, but they also have pictures of her in the middle of sexual acts. What the fuck?

"What are you going to do?" I ask, already knowing that answer. You won't live after doing something like this to her.

"That's none of your concern, Zane. Holden is on it, and we've been careful. That's all you need to know."

"It is my concern." I tap my finger on the folder on her desk. "Someone wants me involved."

She's already shaking her head before I finish that sentence. "That's beside the point. You know what we do isn't legal; you don't need to be involved."

"I can help you."

"I think it's time for you to go," Ryder says, standing up to his full height. Even I have to admit I know why Les uses him as her security; the fucker is huge.

I look at Les, and she won't even look me in the eye. I know she feels something for me; I just need to get her to admit it. I'll never force her into anything, but I can slowly push her into accepting it.

I stand up and lay her folders on top of the other ones. "If you need me, you know how to reach me."

"I won't," she replies. I feel like she's answering an entirely different question. Like she will never need me, and she will never admit what we had was real.

I jerk a nod. “The offer still stands.”

I return Ryder’s death glare one more time before letting myself out of her office. I hear him whisper something to her and the telltale sign of them kissing.

This isn’t over, Alessa Poletti.

CHAPTER 49
LEO

Alessa avoided me all damn day after what she told me on the patio. I tried to chase her down, but she disappeared from sight. Hearing her story fucking gutted me; I didn't even give a shit about her being the Black Demon. It isn't what I expected to come out of her mouth, but I just need to know she's okay.

We're on our way to The Games, and I'm riding with Dex, just like the first time. The only difference this time is Holden is with us. Alessa, Ryder, and Gage took off on their bikes before us, making me think about the first time I came to The Games. Everything started that night.

"Where's your head at?" Dex rumbles, and I realize that's different too. He actually talks to me now.

"Alessa," I answer honestly.

"What happened today?" Holden asks quietly from the backseat.

"She told me the truth." I run my fingers through my hair. "About everything."

Dex glances quickly at me before looking back at the road. "Everything as in?"

"What Frankie did and that she's the Black Demon."

Dex whistles. "That's some heavy shit."

"I don't care about any of that," I say harshly. "I just need to know Alessa is okay."

Ryder told me she had a panic attack in the garage when he was raving about Zane being at the house. He said after we talked to Alexey and Dmitri, she has more bombs to drop on us.

Holden squeezes my arm. "She's okay. She just needs a minute."

I pat his hand, thankful for the comfort. "Thanks, man."

"That explains the panic attack," Dex mutters. "Bringing that up couldn't have been easy."

"I had no fucking clue it was that dark," I say defensively.

Dex shakes his head. "I'm not blaming you. I'm just saying it makes sense." He rubs his scarred cheek. "Some things you can't forget."

"Yeah," Holden agrees from the backseat. "Sometimes memories sneak up before you can stop them."

"How do you guys get past it?"

"Les," they both answer at the same time.

Dex chuckles at that. "Now she needs us to get past it."

"I didn't say the right thing today, Dex. I didn't say anything at all," I admit.

"That's a lot to process, bro," Dex soothes. "She will realize that too. Let her get through this meeting with the Orlov assholes and make her talk to you."

I smile. "You don't like Alexey and Dmitri either?"

"Fuck no," Dex says grumpily. "I hate how they look at her."

"Can you blame them, though?" Holden says dreamily, making Dex chuckle again. "I don't like it either. Or Zane."

Dex grunts. "Zane is a bigger fucking problem," he snarls, his hand tightening on the steering wheel.

He's right about Zane. He and Les have a history together, which I'm starting to piece together from what the guys talk about.

Dex turns into the abandoned airstrip where they hold The Games and stops beside their bikes. I can see Alessa standing between Alexey and Dmitri with Ryder's arms wrapped around her waist.

"I see we aren't the only ones," I say, nodding to Ryder marking his territory.

Gage runs over and jumps on the brush guard on the front of Dex's truck, moving up and down so the truck rocks.

"Crazy fucker," Dex mutters, then jerks the door open. "Get off my fucking truck!" Gage just grins and flips him off.

I shake my head and follow them out of the truck. I walk to the front where Gage is standing, admiring his ass in those riding leathers.

"You like what you see?" he asks, and I'm taken back to the first time he asked me that.

"Yep," I agree without hesitation.

He slings his arm around my shoulders, guiding me toward the rest of the group. He leans against the side of Alexey's Lambo and pulls me to stand in front of him with my back to his chest, tucking his fingers into my pockets. "Is this okay?" he asks. I know he means the PDA with him.

"It is."

"Good," he breathes. "I like people knowing you're mine."

Something about that possessive comment makes me shudder.

"You're mine too, Gage."

"Absofuckinglutely, Baby," he agrees, kissing the side of my neck.

Holden shuffles up beside Ryder with his head down. Ryder leans down and says something, causing Holden to hold his head higher. Ryder slings an arm around his shoulders, pulling him closer to him and Les.

"Isn't this cozy?" Dmitri comments, looking at all of us when Dex leans beside Gage and me.

Alexey looks at the seriousness on Alessa's face and runs everyone else off, leaving just us. "What's going on, *Moya sokrovishche*?"

"I told you to stop calling me that," Alessa warns. "Your dad took a shot at me after the gala."

"You wouldn't know anything about that, would you?" Ryder adds.

The shock on both their faces lets me know they didn't know.

"That was you? We heard someone's limo got shot up, but no one said whose." Alexey says.

"It was mine," Alessa growls, getting pissed off all over again. "He almost took out one of *my* guys."

"Motherfucker," Dmitri explodes.

"We're going through with our plan for your mom," Alessa says, ignoring his outburst. "And it goes down tomorrow night."

"No. We can't ask you to do that," Alexey says. "We'll find another way."

"This gives her a clear shot at the guards and your dad," Dex points out. "Les will make sure your mother gets out safely."

Dmitri waves that away. "We aren't worried about that. We know Alessa will, or we wouldn't have asked her." He looks at Alessa. "Are you sure?"

She nods. "I am. If you have anyone in that house you want out, you better figure out a way because everyone fucking dies."

"You guys need to make a big show of not being home," Ryder says. "You fuckers will be his first suspects."

"We got that covered," Alexey says and then sighs. "Tomorrow?"

"Tomorrow night, we get her out," Alessa says. "And your dad has to die."

"We understand," Dmitri says.

We lapse into silence, everyone lost in their thoughts, watching all the action around us. I can't get over how they put all this together right under the cop's nose, but as they told me last time, they couldn't bust it up anyway. Too afraid of who's just casually standing around.

Gage pulls me close, running his nose up and down my neck, which he loves to do.

"Look at these fucking queers," some drunk says and then obnoxiously laughs, walking by our group with his buddies.

Holden turns before anyone can react, nailing the guy right in the nose with a mean jab, sending him sprawling on his back. Blood spurts out everywhere. "You broke my fucking nose!"

"Who are you calling a queer?" he growls out. "That's not very fucking nice."

All of us are in stunned silence that *Holden* is the first one to react. Quiet, respectful hacker Holden. Gage is the first to shake off the shock and starts howling like a wolf. "That's my fucking boy!"

Holden turns his eyes to us, and I realize he's just as shocked as us. I don't think Holden has ever hit anyone out of anger in his life.

Alessa gives Holden a look that makes him blush, then walks forward, laying the toe of her boot on the guy's balls. She pulls a knife from the sheath on the back of her leathers, twirling it between her fingers. She adds pressure to her foot, squashing his balls and leaning forward. "Who are you talking to?"

Something in the look on her face makes his eyes widen comically behind his hand, holding his nose. "I... I...I didn't mean anything by it."

Alessa points her knife at the three guys with him. "You think he meant anything by it?"

The taller one snorts, shoving his hands in his pockets. "He's a dick." He nods his head, and the others follow him, leaving Alessa with their bleeding friend.

"It looks like your buddies didn't share your thoughts," Gage comments, pulling me closer. I've never had anything derogatory or nasty thrown at me, but I can imagine Gage has. I don't like the idea anyone would ever say anything that might hurt him. Gage nods his head at Dex. "This guy beat the shit out of my dad for calling me that once."

I jerk my head around to look at Gage, and he's dead serious. His own dad? I know they have a testy relationship, but what kind of piece of shit puts their own son down like that? It makes me think of how accepting my mom was, and when I called today, she asked about all the guys.

"I didn't mean it!" the guy says, panicking, then groans when Alessa applies more pressure.

She twirls her knife again and then presses it to his throat. "Apologize," she grits out.

"I'm so...sorry," he stutters.

"I don't think he means it," I say. "What about you guys?"

Gage breathes a laugh in my ear. "I don't think he did. What about you, Ryder?"

"Nah," Ryder says, pulling Holden to him again. "What about you, Holden?"

"Not at all," Holden agrees, wrapping his arm around Ryder's waist.

"Verdicts in," Alessa laughs. "You're fucked."

She steps to the side when Dex starts walking up, cracking his knuckles menacingly. The guy scrambles back so fast to get away he slips several times before he finally gets his feet underneath him, taking off as fast as he can. Our laughter follows him the whole way.

"You guys are fucking crazy," Alexey laughs.

Alessa finally looks over at me and gives me a slight smile realizing I'm not running away from her. We still need to talk, but I'll take this over her silence for now.

A familiar BMW Alpina pulls up with Evander, Mateo, and Micah piling out of it. Alessa looks at me with a raised eyebrow before looking back at her uncle and my brothers. "Did we miss curfew or something?" she snarks.

"Ha. Ha. Shithead," Micah says, leading them over. "I told you we'd be here."

"Yeah, and I didn't believe you. This place is not high-class enough for the great Micah Poletti," she remarks, bowing at the waist to him.

Micah glares. "I've been to The Games before."

"You should have brought your bike, so I could have dusted you on the track," Alessa challenges with a grin.

"This should be good," Ryder laughs.

"You think you can take me, little girl?" Micah taunts when Ryder thrusts his helmet and keys into Micah's hand.

"Let's do this," Alessa laughs.

Alessa and Micah get on the bikes, jamming their helmets on, so the rest of us pile into the back of Dex's truck to watch this go down, Gage following behind on his motorcycle. I take a look at my brothers' and realize they're actually dressed down for once in faded blue jeans and regular t-shirts. They look uncomfortable as hell to be here. Alessa told them they need to start making more of a showing at events, so people know they aren't hiding, and Micah is helping with that.

We all line the fence as Alessa and Micah line up doing their burnouts. Alessa blows him a kiss and opens the throttle up. It's so fucking close you can't tell who won until the sign lights up over Alessa's lane, signaling her the winner, and we go fucking nuts cheering for her. They get to the end of the track and slowly make their way toward us, the revving of the bikes reminding me of being pressed against Gage on his and watching Alessa's ass in front of us.

Gage presses up close behind me. "What were you just thinking about?"

"Being on your bike," I tell him honestly. I don't hide anything from him anymore.

"You like being pressed against my ass, Pretty boy?" he says, running his hand down my cock, not giving a fuck that we're standing around a load of people.

"Yes."

"I want you to fuck me," he whispers, and I jerk to look over my shoulder.

"What? You said you don't bottom."

"I said I don't bottom for just anyone. You aren't just anyone, Leo."

"What does that mean?"

"I only bottom for people I care about, which has only been one other person," he explains, his hand still massaging me against my jeans. Ryder glances back, raises an eyebrow, then moves his big body to block Evander and Mateo's view of us if they turn around. *Thanks, man.*

"You care about me, Gage?"

"I do, Baby," he says adamantly. "I told you that you're mine. I fucking meant it." He removes his hand from my cock and turns my head, kissing me fiercely. "Mine," he growls against my lips.

"Mine," I echo.

I have to admit hearing him say it is a weight off my shoulders. I thought he was only doing this because I was willing, and when he got bored, he would move on. I realize I didn't give him much credit for his intentions, unfairly judging him because of his I don't care attitude. But he feels deeply underneath the jokes, laughs, and just Gage's craziness. He fiercely protects everyone in his life, loves with his whole heart, and never holds a part of himself back.

Micah and Alessa walk into the crowd, playfully shoving each other. "It was the bike," Micah grouches, handing the helmet and key back to Ryder.

Ryder scoffs. "Trust me; it wasn't the bike."

"Aw," Alessa pouts, "Are you being a sore loser?"

"I think he is," Evander laughs, and I feel the look Micah lights him up with. *What the fuck is that?*

I look back at Gage and realize he's paying attention this time. He's looking rapidly between Evander and Micah before breathing out a laugh.

"Care to share?" I whisper.

"Oh. They're so going to fuck," Gage whispers back before laughing out loud.

"Shhh," I laugh back, and all heads turn to us.

Evander raises an eyebrow. "Do the lovebirds have something to say?" he comments, looking at me being pressed against Gage.

That sets us off in another round of laughter, causing Gage to snort. Alessa walks over to stand in front of me, and I slide my hands around her waist. It feels right being pressed between them. She lifts up on her tiptoes to whisper in my ear, "You guys look fucking hot together." I slide my hands down to her ass, jerking her closer.

"Hands off my nieces' ass!" Micah yells. "At least in front of me. Jesus Christ," he gripes.

Alessa giggles, giving me a quick kiss on the cheek.

"Can we talk later?" I ask her.

She nods. "I'd like that."

"Come on, *Il mio sole*. Let's go stunt on these assholes," Ryder calls out, walking away, his arm snuggly around Holden's shoulders. I know he's doing it because Holden's not used to these crowds, but it's almost like he can't keep his hands off him.

Alessa claps excitedly before running and jumping on Ryder's back. She slides her legs around his waist, and he tucks one arm under her ass, holding her up.

Gage kisses my neck one more time before leading me forward. He swings his legs over his bike, grinning and shoving his helmet on.

I saw Alessa do the stunts the last time, but Ryder was too pissy with me being here to actually enjoy himself. Some sort of calm has settled over him now.

The rest of us move to the fence where the stunt area is, Dex and I putting Holden protectively between us.

"Have you ever seen them do this?" I ask Holden.

He shakes his head with a smile. "No."

"It's badass," Micah comments, leaning up on the fence. It still surprises me my brothers actually showed up, and I can see the weird looks they're getting. "What the fuck are you looking at?" Micah barks at the guy glaring at my brothers.

The guy turns with a sneer until he realizes who he's looking at. "Nothing," he mumbles and walks away. I don't miss Micah's shit-eating grin.

They start stunting, and I realize I didn't see anything the last time. They're doing wheelies, leaning them so far back sparks are flying off the back, stopping and popping them up on the front tires. They can maneuver those bikes in a dance, twisting their bodies to sit in different positions while riding, commanding the machines to do what they want. It's sensual, or all the sex is frying my brain.

"Wow," Holden comments, walking closer to the fence. "They're fucking awesome."

"Fuck yeah, they are," Dex agrees, slapping Holden on the back.

I don't feel like they're showing off. They look free while on the bikes like nothing else exists except this moment. I want to learn how to ride, I want the feeling I can feel pulsing from them, and I know two people who will be more than willing to teach me.

Alessa rides beside the fence, parking her bike. She runs over to Gage and climbs on his so she's straddling his waist facing him. She wraps her arms around his neck when he takes off, he pops the bike into a wheelie with her plastered to the front of his body, and I can't get over the immense trust she has in him not to hurt them.

"That's hot," Holden says with a laugh.

I think about all of us with her this afternoon, coming together after Gage sent out that group text. I had no idea what to expect when I walked into that room. What happened exceeded my expectations when I thought about what would happen when we all finally had her at the same time. It was like an unspoken bargain between us that we would put everything behind us and help her find the pleasure her body desperately needed. Her body responded to us in the most beautiful way, and she handled five demanding guys easily, like she was built just for us.

"Where's your head at?" Dex asks, leaning on the fence in front of us, watching Alessa, Gage, and Ryder talk to Alexey off to the side. I didn't even realize the noises of the bikes had stopped.

"In Alessa's room this afternoon," I admit with a laugh. Do my thoughts really play all over my face?

Dex chuckles. "That's a damn good place for your head to be."

I remember Dex's reaction to Gage sinking into me, and I want to ask him about it, but we aren't that close yet. He looked turned on by it, but it could have been Alessa making him feel that way. I have to admit it makes me think about what it would feel like to be dominated by Dex. I can see that dominant side lurking below the surface of his carefully constructed control.

Gage and I discussed what would happen if one of the other guys wanted to touch us and agreed, like Alessa did, that if it occurred within this group, we're okay with it. Being with Gage opened up something inside of me that I'd been avoiding for years. He's so open about who he is that it makes me appreciate him helping me do the same. What that guy called us earlier slammed me with shame at first and made me want to pull away from Gage because I wasn't used to that sort of thing. His arms had tightened around me, which let me know I was never alone in this.

"Has Ryder's ass always looked that good in those pants?" Holden asks, making us chuckle.

"Ryder's ass looks good in all pants," I agree. The man has the nicest ass next to Gage, but I'm biased.

Dex shrugs. "I can't even argue that."

Holden and I exchange a look; he's thinking the same thing I am. I have a feeling things are about to get even crazier.

After they ride around a few more times, Holden and I pile back into Dex's truck, following behind Alessa, Ryder, and Gage on the bikes. Dex pushes several buttons on his dash display, and their voices filter through the truck. He must be able to pick them up through their helmets; it's cool as hell.

Alessa's laugh filters through, and I can't help but smile. Music filters through right after, and I realize that her music is linked in their helmets because I hear Gage and Ryder chuckle. I can't place the song at first until Ryder starts to sing along; it's Church by Chase Atlantic.

"Is that Ryder?" Holden asks, sitting up between the seats.

Dex nods. "Yeah."

"He can sing?" Holden asks in amazement. I listen closer and realize that he can sing damn good.

"I'm about to take you back to church," Ryder croons.

"Well, tell me your confessions, baby; what's the worst? Yeah."

"Baptize in your thighs till it hurts. 'Cause I'm about to take you back to church."

"I'm not going to lie," Alessa says after the song finishes. "I'm fucking wet right now."

"Goddamn it, pretty girl," Gage groans. "Remember what happened the last time you started talking dirty through the helmets."

"What happened?" Alessa says innocently.

"Leo and I rocked your fucking world. That's what happened."

"Maybe you should refresh my memory," Alessa teases, and I hear Ryder growl.

"Unless you want me to spank you both, I suggest you shut up," Ryder threatens.

Gage's laugh filters through. "Do you think that's a threat, big boy? As long as you let me feel your piercings after I'm game."

Dex chokes on a laugh, pushing a button on his steering wheel. "I'm going to spank all of you," he says.

Alessa moans loudly. "Please, Daddy Dex."

"Fucking hell," Dex mutters before pushing the button again. "Watch it." All of us laugh at that.

"He acts like he hates it, but you secretly love it, don't you, Daddy Dex?" Alessa purrs.

Dex shifts in his seat. "No. I don't. But hearing that tone in your voice makes my cock rock hard."

We spend the rest of the drive back to the house bantering back and forth, laughing the whole way. In times like this, you can forget that we have a war breathing down our necks because they know once they make a move on Orlov's wife, that's exactly what we're doing. Viktor has already made moves against Alessa, and this is going to be her fuck you.

We pull into the garage, the bikes filing in behind us. Evander, Mateo, and Micah make their way to the pool house, saying goodnight. I hang back, waiting until Alessa swings her leg over the bike and puts her helmet in the cabinet. I need to ensure she understands that what she told me today changes nothing. I ask her if we can talk, and the other guys make their way into the house, leaving us in the garage.

The first thing I do is wrap her in a hug. "I need you to know that I'm not going anywhere, and I don't care about anything but you."

"That's the thing, Leo. You should care." She pulls back so I can see her face. "You're too good for me, for this life. You got hurt because of *me*." She sighs. "But I'm too fucking selfish to let you go, and I promised I'd try to let you make your own decisions, so that's what I'm going to do."

I'm relieved she isn't pushing me away. "I hate that I caused what happened today."

She shakes her head. "That wasn't your fault. I let the memories rise to the surface and ran away before I could hear what you had to say, and I had already convinced myself that you couldn't handle it."

"Baby, when will you realize I'm stronger than you think?"

"I know you are, Leo." She winds her arms around my neck. "You've accepted this better than anyone would have ever imagined."

"That should bother me, but it doesn't," I admit. "I should be scared that I'm not bothered by it. But I feel like maybe this was meant to be. I was meant to be in this life."

"I don't know about you being in *this* life, but I think you were meant to be in *my* life. Our life."

I grab her face and kiss her, pushing all of my feelings into the kiss. I meant for the kiss to be sweet, but it turns heated like any other time with Alessa. When she sucks my tongue into her mouth, I want nothing more than to bury my cock balls deep in her. I pull my lips from hers and start kissing down her neck. "I want to fuck you over your bike."

She moans and tilts her head to the side, giving me better access. "Please."

I roughly palm her ass through those leather pants. "Pull them down and put your hands on the seat."

Alessa smiles seductively before walking toward her bike, popping one button open at a time. She parts the sides, and I see the dark purple lace peeking over the top. "I was feeling nostalgic," she says with a laugh. They're the same ones she had on the first night with her and Gage. She turns around and shimmies her pants down with her panties until they drop to her ankles. She places both hands on the seat and tilts her ass toward me.

I quickly pull my pants and boxers down to free my aching cock, palming it as I walk up behind her. "This is going to be fast and hard, Baby."

She wiggles her ass and looks over her shoulder. "Fuck me, Leo."

I line up and sink in with one firm thrust, watching her head fall forward on a moan. I wrap my hands around her hips and slowly pull out before slamming back in again. God, she feels so good. I grip harder on her hips and start to move. I widen my stance and start using her hips to fuck her pussy back onto my cock. I shove my pants, so they drop down at my ankles, out of the way. My skin is slapping against hers, her ass jiggling with each thrust. Her little breathy moans are about to drive me over the edge. I don't let up, just giving it to her like I promised. I can feel sweat gathering at my hairline from the force of the thrusts.

"Fuck, you feel good," I groan.

"Fuck, Leo," she moans, shoving her hips back, encouraging me to go harder.

I start slamming my hips forward at the same time that I pull her back. Her head tilts back with one of those low deep moans. "You like my cock, Baby?"

"Yes," she says breathlessly.

"Who's fucking you?" I ask. I just need to hear my name out of those pouty pink lips.

"Leo," she moans then I feel her tighten up on me.

"Yes," I hiss. "Come for me."

It's like a detonator for her. Her back bows. "LEO!"

I keep fucking her through her release, her tight pussy pulling me back each time I pull out. I feel another release rip through her right on the heels on the first, and it pulls me over the edge.

I pull her hips back, burying my cock as far in her as I can. "Alessa," I groan like a prayer.

With great effort, I release my grip on her hips, slide my hands down her ass cheeks, and spread her wide, watching my cock slide in and out of her.

"You're still hard," Alessa giggles breathlessly.

"I am," I agree, still sliding in and out of her, watching in amazement as her greedy pussy sucks me back in. I don't know how I'm still hard after I had just come so hard. It has been too long since I had her all to myself, so I'm going to take advantage of the situation for as long as she'll let me. I keep moving slowly, and her breathy little moans start up again, and I know she's game too.

"Get the rest of your clothes off." I pull out slowly, watching my come leak down her thighs. I don't give a fuck that we're in the garage.

When we're fully naked, I jerk her to me, slanting my mouth over hers. Reaching down, I hook my hands under her thighs, lifting her. She wraps her legs around my waist, kissing me just as hard as I'm kissing her. I walk forward, blindly pressing her against the first solid surface I can find, sinking back into her pussy.

She breaks the kiss, her head falling back on a moan. "Fuck," she breathes. Her head hits the car I have her pressed against, and she breathes a laugh.

Confused, I take in which car it is. "Seems fitting it's Ryder's."

She giggles again, then moans when I shove my hips forward. "You feel so good inside me, Leo."

I wrap both arms around her waist, using it as leverage to pull her down on my cock. "You are everything to me, Baby," I grunt. "I don't know what I would do without you."

Her hands run up the back of my head, pulling my forehead to rest against hers. "I don't know what I'd do without you either. You allowed me to open my heart back up."

"I love you, Alessa," I breathe, staring into her blue eyes. "I want you in my life for the rest of our days."

"I love you too," she moans again, and I know she's getting close. "I'm yours."

I let her words wash over me with a sigh. This girl is my whole life, and *nothing* is going to take her from me. I continue to stroke my cock in and out of her, watching all the emotions play over her face.

Her breathing starts to pick up, and her pussy clamps down on me. "Leo," she moans, and it's one of the sweetest orgasms I've ever seen run through her. I empty into her seconds later with a groan, slanting my mouth over hers in a sweet kiss I meant to do when this first started.

I kiss her like that until I feel her shiver, the cold air from the garage blowing against our overheated skin. I let her legs, so her feet hit the floor.

"Get your clothes," she says with a laugh, scooping hers up. I pick mine up, and she grabs my hand, pulling me to the garage door. She peeks through and takes off in a dead sprint pulling me with her, both of us running butt naked through the house. We hit the stairs, laughing under our breaths, trying not to get caught.

She pulls me into her room, shutting the door behind us.

She pushes me back against the door, and she's on me again, not wanting this to end.

I will spend the rest of the night showing this girl how much I love her.

CHAPTER 50
HOLDEN

"I got it!" I yell from my office, jumping from my chair and running into the kitchen, where everyone is just waking up. I smell the food as soon as I enter and know Micah has already been in here. None of us could cook for shit.

Ryder looks up from his spot at the island, coffee cup midway to his mouth. "Got what?"

"I got into Viktor's security feed at his house," I say excitedly, slapping the printout from one of the cameras in front of him before sliding onto the stool beside him.

"No shit," Ryder breathes, looking at the paper, then he looking at me with that signature grin. "That's my boy."

Does he know what that does to me when he calls me that?

Ryder slides the paper across the island where Les is standing. Her smile lights up her face. "I knew you could do it."

I'd been working on this for *days,* running every program I could think of, and I still couldn't get past his security system. I was starting to doubt myself because I couldn't find the stalker either, so I got up early this morning and started again. When his live feed popped up, I almost fell out of my chair trying to get in here.

"It's live," I tell them. "I can see everything in real-time."

"We never had any doubt you would get in," Ryder says, squeezing my thigh under the island.

It still surprises me when he openly touches me, and how he kept me protectively tucked against him last night made me fall even harder for him. I knew from the first day I loved Les, and last night cemented my feelings for Ryder. I know he's taking things slow with me, and I appreciate it, but I'm ready to take it to the next step. I just don't know how to tell him.

"That is why you're the office-dwelling mad genius," Gage jokes, placing his hands on either side of Les' hips, leaning in to look at the paper.

Les elbows him in the stomach, making him grunt. "I told you to quit calling him the office dweller." It's something he always calls me as a joke. "Besides, he's not quite the office dweller anymore."

Gage rubs his stomach with a frown. "No, he's playing with the big dogs now," Gage grins. "That fucking jab yesterday," he says, mimicking my punch to that guy's face. "World-class, baby."

Dex slides onto the stool on my other side, slapping me on the back. "Perfect form, and that dude's nose was definitely broken."

I almost felt bad about that until I remembered the look on Leo's face when he said it. He looked like he was on top of the world right before that, leaning against Gage, then his face fell, and I reacted. Besides sparring with the guys, I've never hit another person in my life. I've been doing a lot of things I never had before, like holding a gun to a person in a threatening way. That slimeball from the garage pulled a gun on Les, though. I know she can handle herself, but that doesn't mean we can't help her. I want to be more involved in everything they do, but I know she doesn't want me to be. I need to grow some balls at some point, and now feels like the right time.

Leo walks towards Les, and Gage growls, caging her back into his arms. "Back off. You hogged her all night."

Les laughs. "Yes, he did," she says suggestively, looking at Leo around Gage's arm.

Gage clamps a hand over her eyes. "No sexy eyes."

Les laughs again. "What the hell is sexy eyes?"

"Those eyes you get when you want one of us to rip your clothes off and fuck you on the closest surface," Ryder remarks.

That's what I want from him. I can feel my face blush at that thought.

"I don't do that," she says, pulling Gage's hand from her face with a grin. She knows she damn well does.

Dex snorts. "You're doing it now."

"I am not," she argues, trying not to laugh.

"You're a dirty, dirty girl," Gage says, kissing the side of her neck.

"Would you want me any other way?" she taunts.

"Naked. Preferably very naked," Gage jokes, stepping back from her next elbow jab.

Leo swoops in, laying his lips on hers in a kiss that heats up the kitchen.

"Fucking hell. Not in the kitchen!" Micah yells, causing them to break apart, grinning at each other.

"This isn't your house, Micah," Les reminds him. "I can do whatever or whoever I want in the kitchen."

His mouth pops open. "Why would you scar me like that?"

"Like you haven't ever done something like that," Ryder says with a laugh, laying his arm on the back of my stool.

"Of course I have, but I don't tell my niece about it," Micah argues with a shudder.

"I didn't tell you anything just now. I just simply pointed out that if I wanted to fuc...."

"Shut up," he growls, causing the rest of us to laugh.

She grins sweetly at him. "You're too easy."

We all make a plate from the breakfast Micah cooked, eat, and joke around. I didn't realize how much I wouldn't miss sitting in my office until I actually started coming around. I thought I felt better and safer there, but now I realize it's not the place I was in; it's the people I'm around.

Les slides her plate to the side when she's done. "I got news yesterday. Where are Evander and Mateo? They need to hear this too."

"Pool house," Micah answers, pulling out his phone and shooting off a text. "They're on their way in."

Ryder came into my office yesterday getting the folders, grumbling under his breath, but he wouldn't tell me what it was, just said Les would tell us.

Once everyone is in the kitchen, Micah cleans up, and Gage retrieves the folders she asked for. I can see the seriousness written all over Ryder and Les.

"We have problems," Les says, flips open a folder full of pictures, and spreads them out over the island.

Micah picks up one, looking closer. "Where did these come from?"

"Zane," Ryder grits out.

"How did he get them?" Micah comments, and I can see he doesn't like Zane either.

"I would have thought that it was him," Les says, shuffling through the pictures and pulling several out. "Except these were in there." She shoves them across to us, and they're all of her and Zane when they meet.

"Is this because he has ties to you?" Evander says, putting the pieces together.

Ryder jerks a nod in answer, folding his arms on the island. "I still don't fucking trust Zane, *Il mio sole*."

"I don't either," she says, but I can see something like guilt flash across her face before she covers it up. "But he handed us these files for a reason."

What is she feeling guilty about?

"To get back in your pants," Gage remarks from sitting on the counter. "What other motive could he have?"

She rolls her eyes heavenward. "I'm not going to keep having this same conversation concerning Zane," she says in exasperation. "We have bigger issues than that."

"He's right, though," Micah agrees. "He's been after you since he had no fucking business being after you."

She angrily points to the folders. "Bigger issues," she says between clenched teeth. She pulls the other folder out, slapping it in front of him. "Everything about us. Our businesses. Known associates. *Everything* is cataloged in those papers. They even have all our information. Birthdays, ages, and social security numbers. Every fucking thing, and you're worried about Zane?"

"He's saving our ass. Again," I say quietly, almost shrinking when every head turns toward me. I push my shoulders back like Ryder taught me. "He saved Les from the middle of a shootout, and he got Leo out before he died. Who cares what his motives are?"

Ryder squeezes my shoulder in support. "As much as I don't want to admit it because I fucking hate that dick, Holden's right."

"This is some serious stalker shit," Mateo says, ruffling through the pictures. "All these pictures have Alessa in them, but it always looks like she's looking right at the camera. Like you are looking at the person taking them." He picks up one with who I assume is Ryder and Les from the heights in their gear when they go out for the Black Demon. "Except this one."

"If he has that, what else has he seen?" Micah asks.

"I don't think he took that one," I comment, putting my hand out for Mateo to hand it to me. I look closer. "It looks like it was pulled from security cameras."

"How can you tell?" Ryder says, leaning closer to look. I try to ignore his scent wafting past my nose.

I pull another one over for comparison. "See how grainy this one is?" I ask, pointing to the one with the masks, and he nods. "All the other ones are crystal clear; they are taken with state-of-the-art equipment."

"Why would he have it, though?" Leo asks.

"That's a good fucking question," Les says, running her fingers through her hair. She looks at Evander and Mateo. "Might as well get this out now. I'm the Black Demon."

That truth hits the island in front of us, and all heads turn to them for their reaction. She's risking a lot by telling them, but I don't think they'll ever say anything. I don't know why, but I immediately trusted them.

"As in the serial killer, the Black Demon?" Mateo asks with a tilt of his head.

"One in the same," Gage says, jumping down from the counter. He stabs his finger at the mask picture. "That's what's going on here."

Evander leans back in his chair. "You trust us with that information?"

"The way I see it, you will find out one way or the other. It's better coming from me," she shrugs. "Call me crazy, but I trust you."

Evander nods. "That means a lot given our past. If we didn't trust you, we wouldn't be here. You've been more than generous with your protection, and we'll help in any way we can."

"So, back to the original question," Ryder says, "Why does he have it? There is no way he put it together that this is you."

"He knows something about those masks," I say, pulling the folder toward me, and rifling through it, an idea forming in my head. I pull out what I had a feeling was in there, sliding it to her. "Those are the transactions when Micah got them. All he would have to do is run the prototype through a recognition program until he got a hit."

"This had to have been before Holden started covering your tracks," Dex throws in. "He's been following you for a while. I bet good fucking money there are more pictures and a lot of them."

"Who the hell stalks the head of the Italian mafia?" Gage asks in confusion.

"Someone who has nothing left to lose," I say, coming to the realization. "I'll keep digging." Something is telling me this guy has nothing left. There is no other reason you would risk going after someone like Les.

"Thank you, Holden," Les says with a smile. "I have something else."

She walks from the kitchen before returning with another folder and handing it to Leo. He opens it with confusion before his eyes widen in surprise. "You're giving me creative rights to the new restaurant?"

She shakes her head with a smile. "I'm giving you *the* restaurant."

The rest of us knew about this; she wanted to make sure we were cool with it. She said Leo had expressed that he felt useless because the rest of us had duties.

"I can't take this," Leo says, shoving the folder back at her.

"You will be doing me a favor." She takes the folder from him and lays it on the island, wrapping her arms around his neck. "I have enough on my plate. I've had Holden look up your work, and I trust you to make this place a success. It's yours, Leo."

"My name is the only one on that, though."

"I know. I don't need it. I want you to feel like you have a place here."

He finally wraps his arms around her waist. "Are you sure, Baby?"

"I am." She pecks his lips. "Surer than I've ever been." I feel she's talking about more than the restaurant.

He sinks into another kiss, making Micah groan like he's going to puke. Leo flips him off behind Les' back but doesn't stop.

"Finally, some balls," Ryder chuckles, earning a glare from Micah.

She pulls back with a smile. "I have something for you too," she says, looking at me. Ryder grins at that, sliding off his stool before striding toward the garage door.

I frown. "For me?" What could she have for me? She gave me everything by getting me out of that hellhole.

She walks over, grabs my hand, and pulls me off mine. "Yep," she replies, pulling me to the front of the house, everyone else following closely behind us. She opens the front door and steps out on the porch, waiting for something.

An identical to Les' BMW M8 pulls in front of the house, except this one's a convertible. Ryder gets out of the driver's seat and tosses the keys at me, and I catch them one-handed, even more confused. This is my dream car.

"It's yours, Holden," Les explains, pulling me down the steps.

"I don't know how to drive," I say miserably. I know the basics from when I had my learner's permit and my dad taught me, but that was years ago.

Ryder walks up to my other side. "We're going to teach you."

Les snorts. "Ryder is. I'm a shit driver."

"You are not," Ryder laughs. "You just tend to drive really fucking fast."

She grins at that. "I love it."

Their joking is pulling some of the tension from my shoulders. They have enough to worry about besides teaching me how to fucking drive.

I kiss her lips softly. "Thank you."

"You're welcome," she replies, wrapping her arms around my waist and hugging me tightly.

God, I love this girl. Every time I see her, it bubbles up, ready to spill out, but I don't have the courage to tell her.

She pulls back with a smile. "Go on."

"Now?" I say, furrowing my brows. "You don't have to do this."

"No," Ryder agrees, "I want to. We're already set with Viktor. Everything else can wait."

I look at Les again. "You aren't going?"

She pulls my ear down to her mouth. "Take this time with Ryder," she whispers.

I have been alone with Ryder thousands of times. Why the hell am I so nervous now?

"These cars have sensitive gas pedals," Ryder explains. "Just go easy on it."

He drove us to one of Les' many worksites around the city. It's now abandoned, just an empty parking lot and a trailer sitting at the end that would be used as an office. Before too long, it'll be a huge hotel. It has been sitting empty for a while due to other projects getting pushed ahead of it.

I take a deep breath and shift the car into drive. I barely lay my foot on the gas, making it lurch forward. I slam on the brake, causing Ryder to catch himself on the dash.

"Just a little lighter," he says calmly.

"I can't do this," I say for the twentieth time.

"Yes, you can," Ryder says in that same calm voice he's been using. "You're just learning, Holden. All of us sucked the first time we tried."

I snort. "I find that hard to believe." Any of them could jump into any car and easily drive it. I can't even drive this one.

"I almost took out a building," Ryder says with a laugh. "Les almost flipped the car. It took mine and Les' dads four months to teach Gage how to drive."

"What? No way," I say with a laugh.

"I think I shaved ten years off Dad's life."

"But you're the best driver." He really is. He could handle any car to get them out of any situation.

"That's because I practiced," Ryder says, turning to me. "Which is what you will do. Now go."

I steel myself and switch my foot from the brake to the gas, thanking my lucky stars they didn't put me in something that I had to fucking switch gears. The car lurches again, but not as bad, so I hold pressure on the pedal.

"See," Ryder comments, leaning back in his seat. "Take us around the lot."

I slowly take us around the lot, getting the feel of the car. Everything is sensitive about it, the steering, the gas, and the brake. Ryder has me start and stop several times until I can pull out smoothly. Feeling my confidence build, I start going a little faster.

Ryder is relaxed the whole time, letting me take as long as I need to drive him in circles, calmly offering advice. He has me park in an actual spot, drive in reverse, and parallel park. I start relaxing in the seat and finally appreciate that I'm driving my dream car, from my dream girl, with my dream guy sitting beside me. I don't know what the hell I did to get so lucky, but I'm never going to question it.

"Pull up in front of the trailer," Ryder says, pointing at the far end of the parking lot. I smoothly pull in front of it, putting the car into park. "There you go," he praises.

Now that we aren't moving, my sole focus is on him, and I'm nervous again. Hyper-aware of everything about him. The way his jeans stretch across his thighs, his hand braced on the side of my seat, his other hand laying casually on his leg, and his smell. He shifts in the seat, and my heart starts beating double time.

"You keep looking at me like that, and this trip will end a whole different way," Ryder says, causing my eyes to jerk up to his. He's pulled his sunglasses off so I can see his dark eyes.

"Like what?" I croak, giving away how nervous I am.

"Like this." He moves before I can register what he's doing, slanting his mouth over mine. The first contact of his tongue with mine, I groan into his mouth. Kissing Les feels like this, that all-consuming feeling of their mouth on yours, but Ryder is rougher. I love kissing them, the feel of their lips pressed to mine, their tongue sliding against mine.

"Fuck," Ryder breathes, sitting back in his seat, adjusting his cock through his jeans, unashamed that I did that to him. "What are you doing to me?"

Feeling bold from the kiss, I tentatively reach over and run my hand across the crotch of his jeans, feeling how hard he is. "The same thing you're doing to me."

Ryder's head hits the headrest with a groan. "You have two choices, Holden. Move your hand, sit back in your seat, and I'll drive us back home." He levels me with a look. "Or get out of the car and follow me inside." I don't need him to explain what will happen if I follow him inside. I don't even think about it before I pop my door open and get out.

Ryder slides out right behind me, pulling keys out of his pocket. He unlocks the door, opening it for me to pass. I walk in, swallowing my nerves, knowing this thing between us is about to explode. He roughly grabs me by the arm, pushing me against the closed door. He steps up and slants his mouth back over mine with his hand wrapped around the nape of my neck.

His whole body is pressed against mine, and I can't breathe; I don't want to. I've dreamed about this day, the day Ryder would be pressed against me, his lips on mine, and I'm not backing down now.

I run my hands down his back, feeling his muscles shift under my fingers. He moves closer and grinds his hips forward, rubbing his hard cock against mine through our jeans.

Ryder pulls his mouth away from mine, laying his forehead against mine. "Tell me you want this, Holden."

"I want this," I pant.

He groans again, rubbing harder against me. "You don't like something; we stop. This goes as far as you want it to go. No questions asked. Got it?" I nod in understanding, and he steps back.

He walks over to the desk behind us, pulling open the drawers. "Thank you, Gage," he mutters, pulling out what he was looking for. He shoves it into his back pocket before I can see, but I have a feeling about what it is. Gage used to hang out here when the construction guys were tearing the old building down, and I'm pretty sure he hooked up with one of them.

Ryder leads me to an oversized couch, and I'm attacked by nerves again. He wraps his arms around me from behind. "Are you sure about this?"

"Yes. I'm just nervous," I admit.

"I am too," he says, shocking me. Ryder nervous? He kisses the side of my neck. "We go as slow as you want."

"Why are you nervous?" I ask, leaning into his arms.

"Because I don't want to do anything that might hurt you. I've never been with a guy before, Holden." I figured that but hearing him admit it makes some of the nerves settle, knowing we would be each other's first. What if he doesn't like it? What if it's just curiosity, and once it's settled, he changes his mind? What if he doesn't want me after this?

"Talk to me," he encourages, his arms still wrapped around me.

"What if you don't like it? What if I'm not good enough?"

He presses his hard cock against my ass. "Holden, I'm so fucking turned on right now that my cock is throbbing. *You* did that to me with a kiss. There is no way in hell I won't like whatever happens between us," he says adamantly, turning me to face him. "You're important to me. Let me prove to you that you're enough."

He pulled out the one thing I didn't want to say. That I'm not enough. For him. For Les. For this family. I had it beaten into my head for years when I was locked up, and it's a hard habit to break. I still have moments when I'm with Les that I can't figure out why she wants me. It's time to let that go.

"Okay," I whisper.

Ryder slants his mouth over mine, walking me backward until the back of my knees hit the couch. I sit down with him following me, urging me to lie down. He stretches his body over mine, never letting my lips go. The longer we kiss, the more comfortable I feel. He's rubbing against me again, and I need more.

I pull my mouth away. "I want to feel your skin on mine."

He helps my shirt over my head before sitting back on his knees, fisting the back of his shirt and jerking it over his head. *Fuck.* I have admired Ryder's body from a distance, but now I'm going to feel it on mine.

He lays back down so we are pressed chest to chest, and I feel like I'm going to self-combust. Ryder is covered in muscles and tattoos. He works hard on his body every morning, and every morning he trains me. He taught me how to lift, box, do yoga, and do any other thing he knew. He, Dex, and Gage helped me build the muscle I so desperately needed.

I run my hands down his bare back and hear him suck in a breath. Knowing he's just as affected as I am somehow makes it better. I remember the feeling of my cock sliding between his lips when we were with Les. I want that again, except, "I want to taste you," I tell him, hoping he gets my meaning without me having to explain.

His breath rushes over my neck. "Fuck, Holden. You sure?"

"Yes."

He stands up from the couch, kicking his boots off. He strips out of his jeans, boxers, and socks before roughly palming his cock. Ryder is standing completely naked in front of me, ready to do whatever I want. I stand up and follow suit, stripping out of my own clothes. Ryder pulls me close again, wrapping a big fist around both of our cocks. Our hips are moving, fucking our cocks into his fist, the barbells from his piercing rubbing against the underside of my cock.

I remember what they feel like when we were both inside Les' pussy, but this is different.

He kisses me again before letting my cock go and sitting on the couch. He sits down with one arm on the back of the couch, the other still stroking his thick cock, his legs spread wide. He looks so confident sitting there that it's hard to believe he's nervous. The only thing that gives him away is the rapid rising and falling of his chest. I lay down on my side on the couch with Ryder's cock right in my face. My cock is so hard I couldn't have laid on my stomach if I had tried.

I wrap a tentative hand around the base of his cock after he moves his hand before stroking it. The piercings look like they hurt really fucking bad, but it looks sexy as hell on Ryder's thick cock. It also makes me scared of how that will feel sliding inside me. Les says they feel amazing, so I'm going to keep that in mind so I don't freak the hell out.

I lean forward and lick around the head of his cock. The first taste of the salty precum hits my tongue, and I already know I'll be addicted to this taste. I make a few passes with my tongue before sucking the head into my mouth, still fisting the base.

"Goddamn," Ryder groans, and I feel his thighs stiffen underneath my arm.

I start slowly sucking his cock into my mouth, learning what he likes and doesn't, just like I did with Les. When his hips begin moving fucking my mouth, I know I got it right. One hand of his hands is fisted at his side, and the other is still propped on the back of the couch. I know he's trying not to scare me, so I reach up and pull his arm down, placing his hand on the back of my head, letting him know it's okay. I want him to take control of my mouth.

He groans before putting pressure on the back of my head, pushing down on it while pushing his hips up. I moan against his cock and wrap a hand around my own. I'm so turned on I could come right now. He pushes a few times, testing my limits before he starts pushing to the back of my throat. I can't take him like Les can yet, but I'm going to make this good for him either way. He suddenly pulls my mouth off of him.

I look up, worried. "Did I do something wrong?"

He barks a laugh. "Fuck no. I was about to come."

Relieved by that answer, I relax. "Isn't that the point?" I quip.

"If you didn't get it before, I don't plan on coming down your throat, Holden," he says, and the look on his face almost knocks the wind out of me. There is color high in his cheekbones, his eyes are entirely black, and he's looking at me like I'm his last meal.

He reaches down and grabs his jeans, pulling what he hid before out of the pocket and tossing them back on the floor. It's exactly what I thought it was...lube. He brandishes it in front of me. "Are you still sure?" I nod. "Words, Holden. I need your words for this."

"Yes, I'm sure."

He jerks me up to kiss him again. "Lay back."

I lay back on the couch with him back between my thighs. "I'm going to get you ready," he says softly, and I can't get over how delicate he's being. He always is with me, but he's making sure he doesn't do anything before he tells me.

The couch is huge, easily accommodating both of us even with my legs spread wide open with him between them, but somehow it feels too small. I can feel Ryder everywhere, and he isn't even touching me yet. He squirts the lube on his fingers, then recaps it, setting it on the floor beside us. He leans back down to kiss me slowly. When he feels me start to relax, I feel his hand slide between my ass cheeks. I feel his slippery fingers slide across my hole and tense up again. He pulls back from the kiss and kisses down my neck. "Relax," he encourages, still just rubbing his fingers in a circle. I have to unlock each muscle physically, but the longer he rubs, the more I realize it feels good. The moment he feels me relax, the first finger slides inside.

"Holy shit," I whisper, grabbing onto his broad shoulders. He starts slowly working his finger in and out. I can't describe the sensation at first, except it feels weird, and I feel hot, his fingers lighting up every nerve ending. If this is just his finger, what would his cock do? I groan at that thought, giving in to the sensations.

"That's my boy." Ryder kisses my neck again. "Let me make you feel good."

I nod, ready for what he's willing to give. He kisses down my chest, his finger still moving inside me. He sucks my cock into his mouth at the same time that he adds a second finger. I tense up again at the burning sensation of being stretched, and he moves them slowly, letting me adjust while torturing my cock with his hot mouth.

"Oh God," I pant when he rubs against something inside of me that I can feel in my fucking toes. My legs fall open further, giving him full access. He starts sucking harder on my cock, and I have to pull his head away. "I'm going to come."

He grins. "We can't have that yet now, can we?"

Ryder fucking Venchelli is grinning from between my legs, his mouth was just on my cock, and his fingers are buried in my ass. Is this a dream? Did I die and go to heaven?

He kisses back up my chest, laying his forehead on mine again. He starts fucking me harder with his fingers, and I almost lose it. I feel my hips start moving with his hand more than ready.

"Are you ready for my cock?" he asks, kissing my neck again. His breath washing over the wet skin makes me shiver.

"Yes," I groan, almost ready to start begging.

"I'm bigger than my fingers."

"I trust you," I tell him honestly. He pulls back to look into my eyes.

"God, what are you doing to me?" he asks again before taking my mouth in a searing kiss. He pulls back before reaching down with his other hand, grabbing the bottle of lube, and handing it to me. "Lube my cock up," he says, scooting up on his knees, still finger fucking my ass. I squirt a generous amount on my hand before wrapping it around him. His head falls between his shoulders with a groan when I stroke from base to tip. "What position do you want this in?" he asks.

"I want to see your face," I tell him. After what happened to me, I need to see his face as a reminder that this is Ryder. Plus, I need to look into his eyes to make sure he likes what he's about to do.

"I was hoping you would say that," he groans again.

I let him go when his cock is easily slipping through my fist. He slowly pulls his fingers from my ass and lines himself up with my asshole; still gripping the base, he pushes his hips forward, and I feel the head of his cock slide in. I can't help from tensing up, and he stops. "Fuck, I don't want to hurt you," he grits out.

"Please, Ryder." I'm not above begging at this point. I need to feel him inside me.

He puts his big hand on my thigh and pushes it so my pelvis is pointed up. Then he starts to push again, and I feel him pop past the resistance.

"Please don't stop," I tell him breathlessly. It hurts like a motherfucker, but I don't want him to pull back.

He pushes his knees under my ass, lifting me more so he has more room to slide in. He braces his hands on the arm of the couch over my head and shoves his hips forward. His cock slides all the way, and I can feel every drag of his barbells scratching my nerve endings.

"Are you okay?" he asks when his thighs are firmly pressed against my ass.

I take several steadying breaths, breathing through the pain before I answer. "Yes." I feel so fucking full, and it's burning, then I feel a rush of pleasure. "You can move."

He places both arms crossed under my head, then slowly drags back out. "Shit. You feel good," he groans before sliding back in.

It still burns a little, but it's mixed with such intense pleasure I don't even care. He rubs my prostate with every slow drag in and out, making my whole body tingle. "Faster," I groan, and he starts moving faster, causing my back to bow. "Holy fuck."

My hands fly to his shoulders, and I take advantage of having full access to his body, running my hands everywhere. I want him to lose control and to fuck me like I've seen him fuck Les.

"Ryder," I groan.

"Yeah, *Bello?*" he groans in my ear.

"Fuck me," I beg. He feels amazing like this, but I need him to really move.

He shudders against me, and I can feel his carefully constructed control; I want to obliterate it.

He kisses me hard before levering up on his knees, jerking my hips to meet his thrust, giving me exactly what I want.

"I love your cock inside me," I groan, and Ryder slams into me again.

"Fuck, Holden. I don't know if I can hold back." I can see the tendons standing out on his huge shoulders and his fingers flexing on my hips.

"I can take it," I assure him.

His fingers tighten at the same time that a determined look crosses his face. He starts moving faster and harder, ramming his cock into my ass, and all I can do is hold on. His thighs are slapping against mine, our grunts and groans filling the room. Besides being in Les' pussy, I've never felt this much pleasure in my life.

Ryder wraps one hand around my cock, the other still braced on my hip. He starts stroking me in time with his thrusts, and I know I won't last much longer.

"Damn, *Bello*," he grunts, "I'll never get tired of this ass."

I can only groan in response with him hammering into my ass with his fist wrapped around my cock. I can feel my release building from my fucking toes; it's the most intense thing I've ever felt.

"I'm going to come," Ryder pants out. "Where do you want it?"

"Inside me." I don't even hesitate.

"Fuck," he says, stroking me faster, trying to get me there at the same time.

I feel my spine start to tingle then my balls draw up. "Ryder!" I yell, busting all over my chest and his hand.

He hooks his hand back to my other hip, pounding three more times. He holds himself deep inside me when I feel him swelling; my cock twitches at the feeling, so I wrap my hand around it, stroking it hard. More cum pours onto my chest. "Holden," Ryder groans, and it's the most delicious sound in the world.

He collapses forward, catching himself on his hands beside my head. "Was that okay?"

I can't help but laugh. "That was more than okay, Ryder."

"Good," he smiles, kissing me again. "It's your turn next."

I jerk back in surprise. "You're going to let me fuck you?"

“Hell yeah,” he replies, and I can’t hide the shock. Ryder doesn’t seem like the guy to give up control like that. “I want to feel whatever had that pure blissed-out look on your face.” He looks down at my softening cock. “On second thought,” he jokes, talking about the size.

“Shut the fuck up,” I laugh.

He laughs, then pulls out with a groan, and I can feel his cum leaking out. “Let’s go get cleaned up.”

He stands up and then pulls me to stand from the couch, smacking my ass when I stand up, waggling his eyebrows.

And just like that, we’re Ryder and Holden again.

Just a little closer.

CHAPTER 51
ALESSA

After Holden and Ryder left, Dex practically dragged me upstairs. He had me naked and was inside me before we hit the bed. I'm now curled up on his chest, still trying to regain my ability to breathe with him drawing patterns on my back.

"What are you drawing?" I ask when I can breathe.

"I." He draws the I. "Love." He draws a heart. "You." He draws a U.

I look into his grey eyes, the sincerity shining through. "I love you too."

He tucks me closer to his side, and I can tell something else is on his mind. I lay there and wait for him to tell me what he's thinking.

"I'm worried about tonight," he admits. "This is big, Baby girl."

"I know." I snuggle closer. "We're the best, though. We got this."

"Is Leo going?"

I sigh. "Yeah. I promised I would let him make his own decisions. He doesn't want to be put on the sidelines."

I listened to Doc rave yesterday about how good Leo was healing and how good Ryder was taking care of the wound. He's allowed to remove the gauze during the day so it can breathe, and it's hard to believe that he was shot three days ago.

"Leo is tougher than we gave him credit for," Dex rumbles.

I laugh at that. "I know. He made sure I was aware that I've been underestimating him."

"What happened yesterday, Baby girl?" he asks, and I don't need him to elaborate.

"I don't know," I say honestly. "I told Leo the truth about what happened with Frankie and who I was. My head had already concluded that he wouldn't stay, and suddenly, I couldn't get away fast enough. I felt like I needed to claw my skin off, and the only thing running through my head was I needed to run. Memories kept popping up from that day, and the panic attack hit. It all played out in my head like I was watching from someone else's eyes."

"That's what used to happen to me when someone touched me. It was like someone was playing my biggest failure on a big screen," Dex admits, and I freeze. He never talks about this. "I convinced myself all those years ago that you wouldn't want me after that, so I pushed you away instead of running. Every one of those panic attacks or doubts you have; is triggered by something." I feel my eyes fill with tears and try to stop them before it drops onto his chest. He pulls my face up to look at him. "You helped me through mine. Let us help you." The fact I am practically lying on top of Dex proves that I did help him.

"I don't know how," I admit quietly. "I don't know how to admit I have a weakness. I'm not supposed to be weak."

"You aren't weak, Les," he says, pulling me up so my arms are crossed on his chest so I can look into his eyes. "You're human with human feelings and emotions. You just need to learn to lean into your human part, not shut it out."

"I'm afraid too. I'm afraid I'll fall apart if I let the human side all the way in."

He puts his big hands on my face. "We're here to put you back together. You have five guys more than willing to lay down their lives for you. Let us be who you need us to be. I see the human Les in there. I see her with every I love you, every sigh, every laugh, every kiss. Let her be free."

"I'll try," I promise, tears running freely down my face. They always joked for a long time that I was the ice queen, but one by one, these guys melted the ice surrounding my heart, allowing me to *feel* again, and it scares the shit out of me. I'm afraid once I let her out, I won't be able to lock her up again when I need to make split-second decisions about whether someone lives or dies. What if I make the wrong decision, and one of mine dies because of it? I look at Dex through tears and take a leap of faith. "If I jump, you guys have to catch me."

"Always, Baby girl." He crushes me to his chest.

My biggest shame is letting Zane through that carefully constructed wall. He slid right through every defense I have, and my body reacted to him just like it used to.

"I almost let Zane kiss me yesterday," I admit with my cheek buried against Dex's chest. If any of them can stay levelheaded, I hope it's him. I feel his muscles tense under me and brace myself.

"Explain that," he simply says.

I explain the meeting in the office, what happened after Ryder left, and everything Zane said and admitted to. I had no idea he became a cop for the reasons he told me; I never gave him a chance. The hatred for police runs deep, and it's not something I could cope with.

Dex is quiet for so long that I take a chance and peek at his face. He doesn't look mad, exactly. He looks like he's contemplating murder, but not mine, at least.

"Do you still have feelings for him?" he finally asks.

"I don't know," I answer. "What Zane and I had was forbidden then. Ya know? It was hot, secretive, and fun."

"Baby girl," Dex says sternly, making me look at him again. "If that's all it was, it wouldn't have hurt that bad when you realized he lied to you."

He hit the nail right on the head. The one thing I've been trying to avoid this whole time is admitting I ever cared about Zane. Dex knew about my relationship with Zane; he was always my confidant. He just doesn't know one thing.

"The night I found out he was a cop, I was going to tell him how I felt. I was going to tell him I was ready to tell my dad about us like he had been begging me to."

"Fuck," Dex grumbles. "Does he know that?"

I shake my head. "No."

"I don't trust him, Les. He might have implied he was willing to share, but there is no way that motherfucker would or could."

I don't want to point out I didn't think Ryder could either, not that I am considering letting Zane in. He sighs, pulling me up on his chest, watching everything play across my face. "You know we will give you whatever you want. Is Zane something you want?"

I shake my head automatically. "I have all I need, Dex." My body might have reacted to him yesterday, but I'm not going to let it happen again. I won't risk what the guys and I are building with each other.

I snuggle back into his chest when he starts drawing patterns again, knowing I have a thousand things to do but not wanting to leave his arms.

Taking the time to reconnect with Leo on a singular level last night made me realize I need to spend more one-on-one time with my guys. I'm glad Dex dragged me upstairs; I need this time with him too. I love my time with all the guys, but they need to know they're as special to me as I am to them.

Even though the aftermath of telling Leo the truth resulted in a massive breakdown, I feel like a weight has been lifted off my shoulders. He knows everything now, including that I can't have children, something I was okay with until I met these guys. They deserve someone that could give them kids that they can raise. All the guys would make amazing fathers, and it hurts me that I can't give them that. I'm sure it's a conversation we will have later on down the road but now isn't the time. Even though I know deep down in my soul I love every one of them, we're still in the beginnings of a relationship.

After another hour of lying around, Dex and I finally climb out of bed and take a shower together. He washes my hair and cleans me off, all with no intention of trying to have sex with me again. Most of the time, when we are close to each other in some sort of undress, we end up fucking. Dex says he wants to take care of me, and I let him because I'm going to try to let that part of my guard down.

Admitting to him that I feel like my human side is my weakness comes with the realization that hiding her is my trigger. I won't let her in, so when I do, it bombards me with emotions.

We slowly make our way downstairs in search of much-needed food. When I walk into the kitchen, I immediately step back out, peeking around the corner.

"What is it?" Dex whispers.

"You look," I whisper and clamp a hand over my mouth to stop the laugh threatening to bubble out.

Dex peeks around and steps back. "What the fuck?"

I look around to make sure my eyes aren't deceiving me, and sure enough, I see what I thought I saw.

Evander is standing at the counter with Micah close behind him, whispering something so low I can't hear, but Evander's face tells me all I need to know. What is going on in that pool house?

"What are you..." Gage says, popping around the other corner.

Dex clamps a hand over his mouth, and we drag him to Holden's office, shutting the door.

"What the fuck?" Dex says again, letting Gage go.

Gage looks between us. "What the hell is wrong with you two?"

"I'm pretty sure my uncle was just talking dirty to Evander in the kitchen," I say, the laugh finally bubbling over.

"I knew it," Gage hisses, pumping his fist in the air. "I'm going to investigate." He slips from the room before we can grab him.

He's gone for five minutes before we walk out to see what's going on. Gage comes sliding out of the kitchen laughing, Micah hot on his heels. "Abort mission! Abort mission!" Gage yells, running toward the front door; it shuts with a bang behind them.

Evander walks out and looks at me with a look I can't decipher. "So, what's up?" I say as casually as I can, making Dex cover a laugh with a cough.

Micah stomps back into the hallway from outside. "Go get your boyfriend," he growls, pointing to the front door. I notice the grass stains on Micah's jeans and lose it laughing, knowing he and Gage were wrestling in the front yard. It wouldn't be the first time, either. "Cut it out, shithead."

That just makes it worse, causing Dex to double over too. Micah makes a grab for me, and I run with a screeching laugh. Ryder pops through the garage door with Holden right when I'm in front of it. I jump into his arms and slide behind him, clinging to his neck.

"What the hell?" Ryder asks with a laugh, tucking his arms under my ass.

Micah comes to a dead stop in front of us. "What did you see?"

I lock my lips and shake my head. I didn't see much, but the way he's acting, more happened in that kitchen than dirty talk. Evander walks in and casually leans against the wall in front of us, not at all bothered by current events. *Interesting.*

"Alessa," Micah warns like I'm a child.

"I thought you said not in the kitchen," I say and start laughing again.

"Someone care to explain," Ryder says, looking between us all. I lean down and whisper in his ear what I saw but tell him to make it seem like it's more. "Holy fucking shit," he exclaims, playing into it easily.

Micah bares his teeth, then stomps toward the backdoor to the pool house. I look at Evander. "You and my uncle, huh?" I ask, still perched on Ryder's back.

Evander looks down the hall and back at me, shaking his head. "No."

There's a lot of weight with that one word, making me wonder what I *really* stumbled into.

"What's going on?" I ask, dropping all teasing.

Evander smiles, and it's kind of sad. "Nothing."

Ryder lets me slide down his back onto my feet. I step closer to Evander. "If you ever need someone to talk to, I'm here." Something about his eyes breaks my heart. He doesn't usually show his emotions, but they're written all over his face. Whatever happened or didn't happen with Micah is hurting him.

"I appreciate that," Evander says, reaching out and squeezing my hand. He tucks his hands in his pockets and makes his way down the hallway.

"Why do I feel like we stepped into some deep shit?" Dex asks, watching Evander disappear from view.

"Because we did." I don't know how I know, but I do. Something major is brewing in that poolhouse.

I need to let Leo know he needs to check on his brother. Maybe he can talk to him.

"It's crawling with guards," Holden says, pointing at the monitors running Viktor's feed. We are t-minus one hour before leaving; this is not what I need to hear.

I lean back in my chair beside Holden. "The more, the merrier, I guess."

He grabs my hand and tugs my chair closer to his before kissing my knuckles. He folds my hand in his, laying it on his lap. "I don't like this, Bright eyes," he says quietly.

Truth be told, I don't either, but I can't tell Holden that; the worry is already written all over his face. "It'll be fine. We've done this before."

"I know you're more than capable," he says with a little more steam. "That's not the point. The people I love are going into that house." He realizes what he said the same time I do, and his eyes flash to my face. I can see him withdrawing from insecurity, and then something amazing happens. I watch the resolve settle over him; he stands up, jerking me to my feet with him. He drops my hand to grab both sides of my face so I have to look into those beautiful chocolate eyes. "I love you, Alessa." He shakes his head. "I'm in love with you. You're my everything. My brightness in the darkness. My savior. My soul. My heart. My *life*. And I'm done fucking hiding. I love you."

I can feel the tears flash down my cheeks, and I don't even try to stop them. I wrap my arms around his neck and hold him as tightly as possible. "You are *my* brightness, Holden. I knew who you were the moment you came home with us. I've always been so fucking proud of everything you did to get out of that hellhole. I love *you*. I'm in love with you." I pull back to look back into his eyes. "It's okay to love Ryder too."

His cheeks darken, and it's always my favorite thing. "That is why I love you so much, Bright eyes. You don't see it, but you're perfect. Perfect for me. Perfect for us. You gave me my life back."

I haven't, not yet. Not until his shit uncle is dead, but that's for another time. "Please never lose who you are, Holden, not in this mess."

He shakes his head. "I won't."

He pulls me close again, but this time his lips are on mine. I wasn't joking when I said Holden is a fast learner. The man can turn me into a puddle at his feet with a simple kiss. I want to show him how much I love him with my body, but we're already pressed for time. I pull back from the kiss. "Later," I promise. He nods but continues kissing my neck. "Holden," I say, and it's supposed to be a warning, but it comes out more like a breathy moan. *Distraction time.* "What happened with Ryder today?" He yanks me closer, rubbing his hard cock against my stomach, then slides his hand down my ass. Okay. Wrong thing to ask, apparently.

He walks me backward until my legs hit the couch; he presses his advantage by following me down, stretching his body over mine. Fuck it. "Make it quick."

His head jerks up. "What?"

"Fuck me. Hard and fast."

He groans and jerks me back to my feet. He starts unsnapping and unzipping his jeans, then yanks them down, freeing his huge cock. He kicks them the rest of the way off when my shorts and panties hit the floor. "I want to try something," he says while blushing.

"Okay," I say slowly, praying he's not wanting to stick that baseball bat he calls a dick up my ass right now.

He rubs the back of his neck. "I want you to bend over."

"Doggy?" I ask, and he nods. That I can do. I smile at him before turning around and placing my hands on the couch cushions, pushing my ass out. "Like this?"

"Yeah," he croaks, rubbing his hand over my ass to sink two fingers into my pussy. "You're always so wet for me."

All the guys talk dirty, but it's always so much dirtier coming from Holden's innocent mouth. "Cock inside me. Now."

He laughs, pulling his fingers free. He notches his cock at my entrance. "Yes, Boss," he quips, grabbing my hips before slamming his hips forward, burying himself in my pussy in one firm thrust.

My back bows with a moan. It's always such a delicious burn taking Holden.

"Fuuuuuck," he groans, his fingers flexing on my hips.

"Fuck me, Holden," I beg, wiggling my ass. "Please."

He doesn't have to be told twice. His grip on my hips turns bruising, then he pulls out and slams back in. He's so deep this way I swear I feel him in my stomach, but I fucking love it.

He starts at a fast pace, fucking me so hard he grunts each time his thighs make contact with my ass. He has noises coming out of my mouth I'm sure I've never made. Mewls, whimpers and I'm begging him to fuck me harder.

"Fuck, Les," he breathes, never slowing his strokes. "Your pussy feels so good."

He raises one leg, planting a foot on the couch beside my knee, then leans forward, bracing one hand on the back and the other wrapped around my waist, changing the whole fucking angle.

"Holy shit," I moan when he starts fucking me like that.

I have nowhere to go because he's holding my waist against him. His thrusts never stop the fast pace, but he stays so deep inside me that his cock is constantly rubbing my g-spot.

"Is this okay?" he pants out beside my ear.

"Fuck, don't stop," I beg. I can feel my orgasm building really fast.

"Ryder fucked me today," he whispers.

"Oh God. Was it good?"

His thrusts get harder. "I'm addicted to it just like I'm addicted to this sweet pussy."

Where the hell is my Holden? This isn't my Holden, but I sure as fuck am not complaining.

"Holden," I moan, "Fuck."

He tightens his arm on my waist, his hips still hammering forward. "You going to come for me, Bright eyes? I can feel your pussy strangling my cock."

"Yes. Yes. Fuck yes," I pant with each hard thrust.

"Where are you going to come?"

"All over your cock," I moan loudly. My release is hovering on the edge, just building bigger and bigger.

He reaches down and pinches my clit; it's all I need. I feel that normal pressure building from deep down, and I know what will happen. He pulls out, still pinching my clit, causing me to squirt everywhere. He starts rubbing my clit in tight circles, making more liquid gush.

"Fuck! Holden!"

He slams back inside, grabbing my hips again, fucking me harder than he was before. My head falls forward, my arms barely holding me up. His thrusts start to stutter, and then I feel him start swelling.

"Alessa!" he comes with a shout. Feeling him fill me up with his cum makes a short sharp orgasm rip through me, surprising us both.

"Shit," he grunts when I squeeze down on his sensitive cock. I can't help the laugh that bubbles out, making me squeeze him again. "Oh. Shit," he groans, pulling his cock out.

His cum is leaking down my thighs, and he seems transfixed by the sight. "Whatcha looking at?" I tease.

He drops to his knees behind me, running his fingers through the mess he made. "Your leaking pussy."

"Stop," I groan. I could already feel myself getting turned on again.

"So, this is gathering intel?" Both our heads snap around to Leo's dry tone. He's leaning against the closed door with a smirk. How long has he been there?

"It's not my fault. Les can't keep her hands off of me," Holden jokes.

My mouth drops open. "You lying little shit," I say, standing up and whirling around. He's still on his knees in front of me with a shit-eating grin. "You're already ruined."

He shrugs. "We can blame Gage."

Leo laughs. "I like that idea."

"I should make you clean up your mess," I say, gesturing to my thighs. Holden looks up at me with heated eyes before shoving my hips back, making me land on the couch on my ass with a bounce. He puts his hands on the back of my knees and spreads me wide. "Holden, I was joking," I say breathlessly.

"I'm not," he says gruffly before his tongue swipes up my thigh, where our releases are mixed together. "We taste amazing together."

"Fuck," I hear Leo groan, and my eyes flash to his. He's just as turned on as us, and we're definitely out of time.

Holden licks up my other thigh, cleaning it up before burying his face in my pussy. "Shit," I moan, my hand flying to his hair. I feel his tongue swirl around my entrance before he starts fucking me with his tongue. "Holden."

He hums before licking up to my clit, his eyes on me the whole time. It's the hottest fucking thing anyone has ever done. He doesn't care that he is tasting his own cum; he's enjoying it as much as me. He sucks my clit into his mouth, and a surprising orgasm rushes through me with such force that I can't even scream. He slides his tongue back down, lapping up my orgasm before sitting back on his heels, smiling.

"What am I going to do with you?" I ask with a breathless laugh. I guess he wasn't joking when he said he was done hiding.

"Keep me," he replies.

"Forever," I promise, running my hand through his hair.

I look up at Leo. "Both of you."

Leo smiles and walks forward, laying a kiss on my lips. "Forever and ever." Then looks down at Holden. "You're a dirty fucker."

Holden laughs. "You're just mad you didn't get to taste it."

"Fair point," Leo agrees.

Holden hops to his feet and jerks Leo's lips to his by his shirt, sinking his tongue into his mouth. Leo is shocked still for two seconds before kissing Holden back.

Holden pulls back with a grin. "Now you tasted it."

Leo's eyes are wide, and the look on his face is hilarious. I can't help but bust out laughing.

I don't know what happened with Holden today, but I love this open side of him.

Even if he is randomly kissing *another* one of my boyfriends.

CHAPTER 52
RYDER

"What the hell is wrong with you three?" I finally ask after the tenth time Holden, Les, and Leo looked at each other and started snickering.

Holden's cheeks bloom with color. "Nothing."

That makes Les lose it, and she doubles over with laughter; Leo won't even look me in the eye.

Gage comes in with a handful of bulletproof vests, throwing them on top of all the other gear we've been carrying in. He looks at them, then looks at me. "Who broke Les?"

She laughs even harder. "Holden," she gasps out.

"Out with it," I demand, looking at Holden. He takes a step back, shaking his head. "Holden," I warn.

Les draws in a breath, trying to get her laughing under control. "Leave him alone."

I don't even look at her; I just continue staring at Holden. That's when I realize he seems nervous. He shifts his eyes between Les and Leo, then finally looks back at me. I can see him physically steeling his spine. "I kissed Leo."

Gage grabs his chest dramatically. "You kissed my man?"

The first thing I feel is jealousy, and I swallow it down—no way I'm making him feel bad for going for what he wants.

"After he licked his cum from her pussy," Leo mutters.

My eyes flash to his. "What?" I croak. I'm no longer jealous of him kissing Leo. I'm jealous as fuck Leo got to taste that.

Holden shrugs, embarrassed. "I wanted to see what it tasted like."

Gage scrubs a hand down his face. "I didn't need that visual before this mission."

"You're not mad?" Holden asks, looking like he's about to run the other way.

I step closer to him. "No, *Bello,* I'm not mad at you." I look at Leo. "Him, on the other hand."

"Hey!" Leo says. "I'm an innocent victim."

"Baby, you're anything but innocent," Gage laughs.

"Okay. Okay," Les says, waving her hands around. "We need to focus."

We all snap to attention because she's right. We have pulled off some big things before but never at this magnitude. We're about to storm a literal fortress filled to the teeth with armed guards. Les has everyone on the payroll ready to roll out, which means we have forty extra armed men with us, but it doesn't make it any less dangerous.

Once everyone is in the living room, Les steps to the center of the room. "This is a shoot first; ask questions later. Everyone that they wanted out of the house should be out. The *only* person who remains safe is Nina." She passed a picture around earlier so everyone could familiarize themselves with her. "You all have a syringe with a sedative that will keep her out for about two hours. Use it. We don't need to draw attention to us with her screams." That's the part that we all hated. Nina knows it's happening; she just doesn't know when. We need the element of surprise, and her fear will sell it. "You all have your assignments. Get going."

The rest of the guards file out of the room, leaving us in the room with Les, Evander, Mateo, and Micah. "I hate to say it, but if it gets too thick, we have to leave her. I can't risk you guys for that." She runs her fingers through her hair. "We get in a situation we don't think we can get out of; we bail." We all nod, letting her know we're on the same page.

We all wore black cargo pants for extra clips, black shirts, and black combat boots, including Holden. He would be monitoring the cameras from the van, talking to us through our communication earpieces. Something we've done before, but he usually stays home. He begged Les earlier to let him watch from the van, and she agreed reluctantly.

She slides a bulletproof vest over Leo's head, helping him strap it on. We ran him through the paces on the shooting range earlier, and he's a dead shot. He can't afford to freeze, and sadly that happens sometimes. I can see the strain with him going all over Les and Gage's faces, but they both agreed he needs to make his own decisions. He just chose to go on this mission when he should be staying home.

I grab a vest and help Holden. Even if he's in the van, he needs to be protected. I make sure it's on good before handing him a black hoodie. He slips it over his head. "I'll be fine," he says when his head pops through.

"I know," I say because he has to be. I kiss him once before stepping back and grabbing my own vest.

The rest slide our vests and hoodies on. Les picks up four black masks and hands them to Holden, Leo, Evander, and Mateo. "Micah had these fitted just like ours. No one can tell what you look like in them, not even your eye color. The eyes are completely black, but they have night vision." She flips it to the side to show them the little switch to change it.

She twists her hair into a bun on the back of her head before sliding the mask over her face and flipping her hoodie up. It always looks creepy as hell, especially in the dark, because it looks like you don't have a face.

"That's scary as fuck, Baby," Leo comments.

Les laughs, making it even creepier coming out muffled behind the mask. She slides it to the top of her head. "That's the point." She turns to Evander and Mateo. "Now's the time if you want to bow out. I won't hold it against you."

Evander shakes his head. "We're in."

Mateo grins. "Let's get this motherfucker"

We have to park a little ways away because this asshole lives on a dead-end road, and a bunch of blacked-out vans flying toward your house draws too much attention. All the other guards are already spread out around the fence, out of sight of the cameras and guards. I have the Russian AK-74M strapped to my back. Les had a good laugh about going after the Russians with a Russian weapon. We actually all got a good kick out of that one. I have my holster on with my trusty Glocks and a pocket full of ammo. The rest of us are carrying the same thing, but if I have to guess, Les has a knife or two strapped to her somewhere.

We step out of the van, pulling our masks on and flipping the hoods up. We already knew we would have to go in guns blazing, even going in behind the guards. They'll take out whoever they can as soon as Les gives the signal. Les looks back in the van at Holden before she slides her mask on. "You see anyone coming toward you, you fucking run."

They already had this argument on the way over, so he nods. "Yes, Boss."

She shuts the door and pulls her mask down, concealing that beautiful face. She flips her hood up and motions with her hand that we need to move. *It's go time.*

We do a comms check with Holden when we're far enough away to get the all-clear from him. I can feel my heart thumping against my ribcage and the nervous energy radiating off of everyone. All the guys form a circle around Les, not because she can't protect herself, but because we need to conceal her as long as possible. Her height gives her away easily. Plus, she doesn't know it, but we all agreed we will protect her whether she wants us to or not.

The gate looms in the distance, and Dex gives the signal to stop. It's cloudy as hell tonight, so it works to our advantage to sneak up undetected until we can't anymore.

"Heads up," Les says into the comm, and I know she's about to give the signal. "GO!"

It's quiet for a second, then the cracking of the guns echoes, signaling it's time. We take off at a dead run; there's no turning back now.

On the last count, sixty fucking guards lurk around this place, and Les knows some of hers will probably be lost. That's the part she always struggles with the most.

I punch in the gate code Alexey gave us, and the gate swings open. There are already bodies lying around and a gunfight in front of us. We had the element of surprise when we sent the first set of guards in. Still, our advantage dropped drastically when Viktor's guards figured out what was happening.

We all spread out in a single file walking as one, weapons at the ready, popping off shots when we need to. We need to get into that house fast while our guards have Viktor's tied up.

"Shit," I hear Gage grunt before firing a shot to his right. "It got the vest."

The hoodies are also fitted with Kevlar, making them bulky and heavy but protected as much as possible.

Three guards charge us, causing us to have to jump behind the ugly as fuck statues Viktor has on either side of the driveway, splitting up the group.

Les counts down to three on her fingers to whoever is closest on the other side; I can't tell anyone apart in this shit except Dex and Les because of the heights. They pop out at the same time, leveling two of the guards before dropping back behind the statue. The third guard fires rapidly at the statue, causing chunks of concrete to fall on us.

Someone rolls out onto the driveway from the other side, and I instantly know it's Gage. He pops off three shots before motioning for us to come out.

"Fancy footwork, Gage," Dex comments quietly.

"All in a day's work, big fella," Gage responds and Les snorts a laugh.

We fall into single file again, finally making it to the door. Dex raises a big, booted foot kicking it open; we spill in and are met with way too many guards to count, semi-automatics aimed right at us.

Fuck.

We dive on either side of the doors and start exchanging rounds, not even knowing if we're hitting anyone. When he heard the commotion outside, Viktor must have pulled more inside to protect his punk ass.

Les peeks around the door and leans back with a hiss. "Fuck."

"What is it?" Micah asks harshly.

"I got hit. I'm fine," she replies through gritted teeth. She levels her weapon in front of her before taking several deep breaths. She pops it around the corner, keeping her head hidden, and sprays the inside with bullets. You can hear the distinct sound of bodies hitting the floor, and I know she's at least done some damage.

She nods to the other side, and they do the same as she just did.

"What's the play, Boss?" I yell over the shots still ringing out.

She lets her head hit the wall. "We have to go in. Viktor's in there."

"They're all mostly downstairs," Holden crackles through the comms. "Only two upstairs guarding a door. Two downstairs through the right corridor guarding another door. None anywhere else. He has them all stationed there and outside."

"We've got it under control out here," Mani's voice comes through. "Take that dick out."

"How many in this front room?"

"Twenty to twenty-five." Holden answers.

"Alright," Les says, and I can hear the ice queen in her voice. She checks her clip before tossing it to the side, digging in her pocket for another one. "Reload. Go in hot." We all switch out, the snapping of the clips ringing across the porch. "On my count."

"Wait," Dex rumbles. "Let one of us go in first."

"Dex..."

"No fuck that," Dex says harshly. "You hired us to fucking protect you; now let us."

Her head twists his way, and it's eerie as hell, but I can imagine the narrowed-eyed look she's giving him right now. To my surprise, she slowly nods before stepping around Dex so he takes point.

"Don't ever fucking talk to me like that again," she says. "Now go."

Dex chuckles, not at all threatened. "On my count."

"Got it," Micah says, throwing up a salute.

"One. Two. Three." Dex counts, then they both pop out, spraying bullets all over the front room.

They take two steps forward before I see Micah's body jerk and slam onto the porch onto his back. Whoever is next jumps in beside Dex.

"Micah!" Les screams.

"Go," he groans.

"I'll stay," Evander says, and I see a black figure kneel beside Micah. "I've got this, Alessa; go," he says when she hesitates.

Micah's wearing a vest, but it still hurts like a motherfucker to take a bullet like that at close range, and I'm hoping it hit fully on the vest. We're mostly protected, but there are still ways for the bullets to slip through and do some damage.

I hear Les growl and know she's really pissed now. I try to grab the back of her hoodie to pull her back, but she slips right through my fingers, charging right into the house.

None of us take a second to think; we just follow her.

We open fire on what's left in the front room and then look at the carnage. There is blood and bodies everywhere you look.

"Check-in," Holden says.

"How many?" Les asks, sweeping her gun around.

"Two to your right." I can hear him clicking keys. "Three to your left."

Les nods, and we split again, walking around the side of the large spiral staircase in the middle of the room.

"Boo," I hear Gage say before he and Mateo start cackling like maniacs. I can hear them through the comm, even over the gunfire.

I roll my eyes and creep around the corner. The first guy jumps up and tackles me so hard that we both slam to the floor, knocking the breath from my lungs.

Fuck, that hurt.

I open my eyes in time to see Les jerk the guy's head back and slit his throat. I give him a shove off of me and heave in a breath. I hear shots pop off behind Les and know the other guard is down. Les reaches down and pulls me back to my feet. "You good?" she asks softly.

"Yeah. Nice save, Boss."

She shakes her head and tucks her knife into the sheath, pulling her gun back up. I knew she wouldn't go without at least one of them.

"Have you seen Nina?" I ask Holden.

"No. But she must be in one of the two guarded rooms."

"We have to split up," Les says quietly so only we can hear. "Ryder and Leo with me. Dex, Gage, and Mateo take the upstairs. Micah?"

"He's good. We're taking cover," Evander answers.

"Leo?" she asks softly.

"I'm good," Leo answers and turns his head so she can pick him out.

She nods. "Let's go."

Guns at the ready, we step around the right of the staircase toward the back corridor. We don't see anyone standing around, so we know they're hiding, but we can't risk asking Holden and giving away our positions. I don't like splitting up, but we need to get out of here.

We get one door from the last one on the right, and one of the guys jumps out straight at Les. His fist pulls back and lets it fly right at her face. Her head snaps back, and his body jerks before falling to the ground. I look up to watch Leo lower his gun slightly.

Nice fucking shot.

I grab her to steady her, my blood boiling. This asshole picked what he thought was the easiest target. Les jerks her arm away before signaling for us to move.

I want to take her home and tuck her back into safety. We did this all the time, but nothing compares to watching the girl you love walk right into danger and not give a fuck.

I push Les behind me, risking getting stabbed before stepping further up the hallway. We all exchange looks when the other one is nowhere to be seen.

"Where are they?" I whisper into the comms.

"That room to your right," Holden answers about the time shots are fired upstairs.

I take a deep breath before jerking the door open and sweeping the room. It looks like a fucking jungle in here with trees and flowers everywhere. It's a huge greenhouse built on the inside of the house.

Sweat starts trickling down my spine from the humidity. We search every square inch with no sign of anyone. Why are they guarding this door?

"Holden, there's no one in here!" Les says after the second sweep.

"That's the room they were guarding, I swear."

"Guys," Leo hisses, pulling back some branches on one of the tall trees and revealing a hidden door.

"There's no handle," Leo comments, running his hand down the smooth surface.

"It's a safe room," Les replies, walking forward. "Holden, can you get us in?"

"I'm already on it." I can hear him rapidly clicking keys.

"Dex. Check-in," Les says into the comms. No answer. "Gage?" Her head swings to me when he doesn't answer, either. "Anyone?"

"Still here," Evander answers.

"All clear outside," Mani says.

"Dex," she says again, and I can hear the panic start to rise in her voice. "Gage! Mateo!"

"They might be hiding and can't answer, Baby," Leo tries to soothe.

"I can't hack the door, but I can shut the power off. When it goes out, open it."

"Do it," Les says urgently, flipping her night vision back on.

The power goes out on cue, and Leo jerks open the door. I hear a high-pitched squealing sound and realize he just triggered an explosion. This room was a setup. I jerk him away from the door before diving on top of him and Les right before it detonates.

CHAPTER 53
ALESSA

"Alessa!"

I barely hear someone yelling my name, but I can't focus from all the ringing in my ears. I don't know what hurts worse, the sound from the explosion or getting football tackled by Ryder.

"Alessa!" I hear it again and realize it's coming from my comm.

"Move," I grunt at Ryder, shoving at his huge chest.

He lifts his head and sits back on his knees. I take a big breath and start hacking from the smoke from that room.

"Shit," Leo grunts. "You're a huge fucker."

"Goddamnit! Alessa!" I finally register the voice and realize it's Dex. Holy shit!

"Dex," I cough out.

"Thank fuck," he breathes. "The door is locked."

All of our heads snap to the door we walked through. How the hell did it get locked?

The explosion seems to be contained in that one room, so what is he hiding there, or did he just sacrifice his wife to save his own ass?

Ryder gets up and creeps to the door sweeping the room as he walks. Leo jumps up and pulls me to my feet, both of us ready for anything.

My whole body hurts from getting knocked down, my face hurts from that fucker punching me, my ears are still ringing, and I have a splitting headache. And still no sign of Nina. Or Viktor.

I run through every possible scenario and come back to one. Did Alexey and Dmitri set me up? My heart immediately says no, they're friends. But my brain is yelling at my heart, telling it not to be stupid. They're the sons of my biggest enemy.

Ryder jerks the door, jamming his gun in the closet guy's face. Dex scoffs and knocks it away. "It's just us."

They all come strolling in, all in one piece and also empty-handed.

"Anything?" I ask.

"Nope," Gage answers, looking around. "Like what you did with the place," he says, gesturing to the now-fried room.

"Why the fuck were they guarding these rooms then?" Ryder asks

"To hide what they're really hiding," Leo says, and all heads turn to him. "What?"

"You're fucking brilliant, Baby," Gage says. "We need to search this whole house. She's here somewhere."

"Let's just hope she wasn't in there," I say, swallowing the bile threatening to rise. Is Viktor really that dirty?

The answer to that is yes. Yes, he is.

"We need every room searched. Every square inch of this property," I command. "Holden?"

"Yes, Boss," he answers automatically.

I smile behind my mask. "Any company?"

"All clear."

"No more splitting up," I say, rolling my shoulders to relieve some tension. I'm wound up so damn tight. This went in no way like we planned.

We start sweeping downstairs, hearing all clear from the guys outside searching. Where the fuck is she? And did they really set me up? Those two things keep running through my head after every room we search, and it's clear. Is Viktor even here? There is no way he would let me ransack his house without his presence being known; his ego is too big for that.

We clear the downstairs and head upstairs, stepping over bodies everywhere. This house is huge, with at least twenty rooms to search. Ryder reaches for a door handle, and I grab his wrist to stop him. I hear a whimper coming from the room across the hall and listen closer.

"Is that what I think it is?" Gage whispers. So, I'm not going crazy if he hears it too.

I walk closer to the door, with them following closely behind me. I press my ear against the door and almost give up before it sounds again. It's feminine, and they sound scared.

"Nina?" Ryder whispers, and I shrug. One way to find out; I reach for the handle only to be jerked back behind Dex.

"Stop fucking doing that," I growl, getting pissed that they keep pushing me to the side.

"Remember what we talked about, Boss?" Dex reminds me of our conversation about letting them take care of me sometimes.

I wave my hand impatiently for one of them to open the door. Ryder reaches for the door, slowly twisting the knob and shoving the door open. He walks in with Dex at his back, guns at the ready. An ear-splitting scream echoes off the walls, making me cringe.

I rush in between them, pulling the syringe from my pocket. Nina is tucked beside the bed and wall, trying to scramble back from me, but she's as far as she can go. Sending a silent apology, I jam the needle into her leg and push the plunger, cutting her off mid-scream.

"Let's go," I tell the guys. Ryder walks over and scoops Nina up in his arms after I step back.

"Holden, bring the van to the house," Ryder says, walking for the door.

"What?" Holden croaks.

"You can do it, *Bello,*" Ryder soothes. "Now move."

I hear rustling, and then a door shutting. We make our way downstairs, and I survey the damage as I go by, kicking one of Viktor's guards' guns. The asshole couldn't even equip his guys with the best; they are cheap semi-automatics, and why they resorted to tackling and punching people when they jammed.

We hit the porch, and my eyes immediately search out Micah. That hit he took scared the shit out of me. I can't lose him, and in an instant, I almost did. Evander has him leaning against the side of the porch, crouched protectively in front of Micah, gun at the ready. He swings it our way when he hears our boots scuff and immediately lowers it when he sees it's us.

The van's headlights flash across us before it comes to a screeching halt in front of the porch. Holden jumps out and opens the back doors for us. I climb in, and Ryder gently lays Nina down on the floor with her head cradled in my lap. The rest of them pile in with Ryder and Dex up front. Everyone pushes their hoods back, pulling off their masks. I've never been so grateful than this very moment to see everyone's face.

"Damn, Pretty girl," Gage says from his spot in front of me. "Who got your face?"

I gently touch my nose. "Some asshole downstairs." Evander is stripping Micah's hoodie off and then loosening his vest, Micah groaning the whole time. "Micah?"

"I'm okay, shithead," he says, then groans again when Evander pulls the vest over his head.

"Sorry, man," Evander apologizes. "I need to see how bad it is."

"It got the vest. It will just bruise like a motherfucker. I'm fine," Micah says harshly, trying to push Evander's hands away.

"Or you can quit being a dick and let me look," Evander says evenly.

The rest of us exchange a look that witnessed what happened earlier in the kitchen before our eyes are pulled back to them. I'm more than intrigued at this point.

Micah drops his hands and huffs. Evander takes that as his cue, pulling Micah's t-shirt up and hissing between his teeth. The bullet hit Micah right in the middle of the chest, and the bruising is spreading rapidly. "Fuck, man," Evander says hoarsely, raising his hand like he's going to touch Micah before dropping it to his side.

"How long to Marcella's?" Micah asks, groaning again when Ryder hits a bump in the road wide open.

"Twenty minutes. Giovanni can look at it," I tell him, pulling out my phone and shooting a message to Marcella that we are on our way, then calling Mani. "Status report," I say when he answers.

"Five," he responds.

"Go home and get some rest. We'll be there later."

"Yes, Boss"

The call disconnects, and my heart sinks. I lost five guys, five guys that probably have families, and I need to find out who so I can pay for everything and help the families. Not as if that matters to them, but I never know what else to do.

"Leo?" I say softly when I look up at him. He's sitting beside Gage, just staring at the gun in his lap. His eyes lift to mine. "Are you okay?"

"I don't know," he answers honestly. "I killed more people tonight."

This is what I was afraid of. "Bad people," I remind him. Anyone who protected Viktor Orlov is a piece of shit in my book.

He shakes his head. "That's not what I mean."

"Baby, you aren't making any sense," Gage says, removing the gun from his lap and laying it gently on the floorboard.

"I don't care," Leo says and looks up at me. "Shouldn't I care? I just killed in cold blood, and I can't find it in me to care."

Gage squeezes his shoulder. "You're just in shock."

"You took out the one that did this to my face," I joke, pointing to the face in question.

"He fucking touched you." Leo frowns.

Mateo slaps him on the back from Leo's other side. "Dude. I didn't think you had it in you."

"This isn't funny," Leo grouches, jerking his arm away from Mateo. "I killed people," Leo enunciates it slowly like we don't understand.

"We all have," Gage says. "Not a person in this van hasn't taken a life. And I want to tell you it gets easier, but that won't fucking help. All you can do now is either accept it and move on or don't accept it and let it eat at you. But Baby, that last option is not what we want for you."

"He's right," I say softly. "You know I never wanted you to take this path, Leo, not because I don't want you there but because I want better for you."

"Not one of us will judge you for bowing out," Gage adds. "Just because you don't come in the field with us doesn't mean you still don't have a place in our lives."

Leo squeezes Gage's thigh with a nod and then falls back into silence, which we all need after what happened. Every so often, I check Nina to make sure she's still breathing, relieved when I see the soft rise and fall of her chest. I have questions I need answers to, and none of that can be done over the phone. I need to call Alexey and Dmitri and see what they know. Like, where the hell was Viktor? Why did that room explode? Why were his guards there with no protection and shitty weapons? Sure, we had the element of surprise, and my team is damn good, but I lost five men, and he lost all of his that didn't run.

Ryder finally takes the last turn into Marcella's driveway, and I'm more than ready to get the hell out of this van. Ryder pulls to a stop, and I hear the front doors open and close before Ryder and Dex open the back doors up. Marcella, Giovanni, and Vincenzo are all waiting outside the doors. Ryder helps Evander get Micah out before everyone piles out behind them. Ryder steps into the van, gently lifting Nina from my lap before handing her off to Vincenzo outside the door. He turns back, sticking out his hand for me to grab, then hauls me to my feet. His lips are on mine before I can blink. I fall into the kiss, ignoring my throbbing face, and feel grateful that none of my guys got hurt.

He places both hands on my face before pulling back from the kiss and gently kissing my nose. "I love you, *Il mio sole.*"

"I love you too," I whisper back.

He leads me to the back of the van before hopping out and grabbing my hand to help me down. Marcella comes rushing over, her shaking hands bracketing my face. "What happened?"

"Some guy got a lucky hit. I'm fine," I answer with a smile. How bad is my face? "I need Giovanni to look at Micah."

Marcella waves her hand around. "He's already taking care of it.

Let me take care of you." She grabs my hand and starts dragging me toward the house, muttering in Italian.

"You do remember I speak fluent Italian, right?" I say with a laugh when I catch her saying something about dumbass kids.

She huffs. "Trying to give an old woman a heart attack. You said you would be here at one a.m. It's three! You show up with a bruised face. Micah can barely breathe." She opens the door, still pulling me behind her, still muttering, and I just let her go.

She pulls me into a little room just off the living room, sitting me in a chair in front of a vanity mirror. I grimace after getting the first look at my face. I'm going to have one hell of a black eye and some bruising over the bridge of my nose. Luckily the mask took most of the damage; I can only imagine if I wasn't wearing it. Marcella comes bustling back into the room with an ice pack wrapped in a towel, shoving it against my face. She starts looking me over and sees the hole ripped through my hoodie. I completely forgot I got grazed outside the house. She huffs again, motioning for me to take my hoodie off. I lay the ice pack down and pull it over my head. "And a bullet wound!"

"It's a graze, Marcella."

She gives me the most motherly look I've ever gotten. "From a bullet," she says evenly and then shakes her head. "Let me clean this." She rummages around in the set of drawers beside the vanity table, pulling out a first aid kit. She swipes it with antiseptic, and I hold back the hiss from the sting. She applies antibiotic ointment and then tapes a little gauze pad over it. She pulls me into a hug, surprising me with her ferocity. "You need to be more careful."

I'm not about to tell her that isn't in the cards right now. "Yes, Marcella." She squeezes me tighter before letting go and pulling back. "I need to check on Micah."

She nods. "This way."

She leads me back through the living room and through the kitchen before taking a right where there are several doors. She knocks on the closest one before opening it. Micah is sitting on the edge of the bed, and Giovanni is wrapping his upper torso tightly in a huge ace bandage. Micah is pale as a ghost and sweating bullets.

"You look like shit," I say, walking into the room.

"You don't look any better, shithead," he replies.

Marcella throws her hands in the air and disappears from the room. Evander is leaning against the wall in front of the bed, his arms crossed, staring at Micah.

"Nothing seems broken. This will help with movement, and he can take it off when he feels ready," Giovanni says. "He's lucky." He finishes securing the bandage. "I'll leave you guys to it." He walks by and ruffles my hair like I'm still a kid, shutting the door behind him.

"You can go," Micah says to Evander, tugging his shirt back over his head.

"Are you fucking serious right now?" Evander says, pushing off the wall, fire blazing from his eyes.

"Yes," Micah says between clenched teeth.

I look between them. "Maybe I should go." I turn on my heel and reach for the doorknob.

"No," Evander says, walking toward me, "I'll go." He slides by me, jerking the door open and striding out.

I shut the door back and turn to Micah. "What the hell, Micah?"

"What?"

"Why are you being such an asshole to him?" I ask, crossing my arms.

"I'm not," Micah scoffs, standing slowly from the bed.

"You are," I reply, getting angry.

"I don't get involved in your relationship, so stay the fuck out of mine."

I lift an eyebrow. "So, there is a relationship?"

"What? No!" Micah sighs. "Can we drop this?"

"Oh hell no. Start talking."

He shakes his head. "There's nothing to talk about."

I tilt my head to the side. "Something's going on that you aren't telling me."

"Because I don't have to tell you everything!" he yells, making me jerk back. Micah has never yelled at me.

"Wow. Okay." I drop my arms. "Fuck you then," I reply hotly, pulling the door open.

"Alessa."

I don't even turn around. I know he is okay, and that's all I need to know. I take a left out of the room toward the backdoor. I know this house like I know the back of my hand, and this door leads right out to the fence by the field. I just need some fresh air to get my thoughts straight and figure out what to do next.

Micah yelling at me hurt. Sure, we argued and had disagreements, but we never fought, and we sure as hell never yelled at each other in anger. Whatever is going on with him, he can figure it out on his own now.

Marcella's is the only place I know where I can hide Nina until we can figure out what to do with her. I slide onto the swing that overlooks the field and pull my phone out of my pocket. I dial Alexey, and he answers on the first ring.

"You have her?"

I try to listen to any clues in his voice that he thought there might be a chance I wouldn't get her. Perhaps because he knew I walked into a suicide mission. "Yes."

I hear him relay the message. "Where?"

I can't bring them here until I know the truth. "I can't tell you that."

"What?" Alexey asks, his voice dropping several octaves to that tone his dad uses. If I were anyone else, it would have scared me.

"Some shit didn't sit right with me tonight, Alexey. Meet me at six at the docks."

"Where is my mother?"

"Alive. That's all you need to know. Six o'clock," I remind him and hang up.

Call me paranoid, but I feel like they set me up to walk into a death trap. Yeah, we got Nina out, which was the main goal, but something still doesn't feel right. Was Nina in on it too? We have another hour before the sedative wears off, and she wakes up. She was just in a nightgown, so she didn't have her phone, and Vincenzo knows the drill, so he would have taken any jewelry off her that may have a tracker in it. We may have gotten out of that house, but Viktor's still alive. That's a big fucking problem.

"Can I sit?" My head jerks up, startled from my thoughts. I didn't even hear him walk up.

"Sure," I answer, scooting over so Evander can sit on the swing.

He takes a deep breath. "It's nice out here."

I pull my legs up to my chest, getting comfortable. "It's my favorite place to be when I need a break from real life."

"I can see why."

It's on the tip of my tongue to ask him about Micah, but he looked hurt walking out of that room. Plus, it's none of my business. Both of us stare out into the distance listening to the animals in the barn. I need to check on Nina and my guys, but I can't pull myself off the swing. I'm so damn tired, and my day is still going with no end in sight.

"You have my full respect, Alessa," Evander says, pulling my eyes toward him. "In the short time I've been around you, I've seen the way things are done in your family." He looks over at me. "That is how I wish to run my own."

"I appreciate that," I say lamely, too stunned to say anything else.

"I was skeptical about you with my brother," he chuckles. "About the relationship he's entered into. But I've watched him come alive since being with you. And Gage. I fully trust him with you."

I frown. "Why does it sound like you're saying goodbye, Evander?"

"Because I am," he answers, looking back into the distance. "I need time away from Abbs Valley."

"Does Leo know?"

"Not yet, but I'll tell him."

"What about Mateo?"

"He knows and may go with me for a few weeks. I don't know when I'll be back."

"Does this have to do with Micah?" I ask gently.

"Not entirely," he answers honestly, turning to me with a smile. "You're smart, so I know you've figured out something, but he's your uncle. I won't break that trust between you guys. He can tell you when he's ready." He reaches over and squeezes my hand. "Take care of Leo."

He gets up and walks back toward the house. Why is he talking like he isn't coming back at all? How will Leo handle this? Why did he tell me first?

So many more questions are piling up with no answers in sight.

Nina woke up almost an hour after I dosed her, screaming her head off until she saw me. She looked confused at first, then relieved, showing me she had no idea who was in that house to take her. Could I be wrong about the twins, or was she just in the dark? I asked her where Viktor was, and she said he left yesterday to go out of town on business, and that made me suspicious all over again that he left the day before all of this went down.

Dex, Ryder, and I decided we needed to meet them and leave the other guys to look after Nina and Marcella's house. We ran home, changed, grabbed Ryder's SUV, and now we're sitting here waiting for them to show.

"I don't know how I feel about this," Ryder says for the tenth time.

Dex leans up between the seats. "Me either, Baby girl."

"What else am I supposed to do? Make their mom disappear without finding out if they fucked me over? You know that's not my style."

Alexey's familiar blue Lambo comes into view, stopping beside us before both of them step out. We climb out and meet at the hood. "Where's Mama?" Alexey growls, and it's the second time he's used that tone with me.

"I just risked my ass to get your mom out of that house. I suggest you. Back. The. Fuck. Up." I grit out. I'm in no mood for this bullshit; I just want to sleep for days.

Dex leans casually against the hood, crossing his arms over his chest. "What I want to know is why the fuck there were all those guards, and your dad was nowhere to be seen?"

"How the hell should I know?" Alexey says. "We weren't there. Just like you fucking told us not to be."

"Seems suspicious to me to have that much manpower guarding a woman you say your dad is abusing," Ryder comments, mirroring Dex's pose.

"You think we set you up?" Dmitri asks incredulously. "Why the fuck would we do that?"

"Maybe you're closer to your father than I thought." I shrug. "Like father like son and all that."

Alexey steps into my space. "We are *nothing* like our father."

"You have exactly two seconds to step the fuck back, or I will rip your intestines through your asshole and feed them to your brother," Ryder threatens, standing to his full height.

Dmitri jerks Alexey back by his shoulder. "Sorry, Alessa. We're just worried."

Alexey shrugs off Dmitri's hand. "I apologize, Les. We would never do anything to betray your trust."

I look between them, trying to find the lie, and don't see one. They honestly had no clue all those guys were at his dad's.

"One more thing," I say. "Why the hell would your dad rig a room to explode in the conservatory?"

They both frown at that. "What room?" Alexey asks.

"It was a safe room off to the back. It blew the second the door was pulled open," Ryder explains. "Almost blew three of us to shit."

Dmitri shakes his head. "We've never heard anything about it."

Ryder, Dex, and I exchange a look before I look back at the twins. "I'll text you the address and let Gage know you're on your way. You better hope you aren't betraying me because his threat," I point at Ryder, "will look like fucking child's play compared to what I'll do to you."

"You aren't coming?" Alexey asks while pulling his car door open.

"We have something to take care of. We'll meet you down there,"

I tell him, climbing into Ryder's SUV with the guys following behind me.

Ryder watches the twins drive off before turning to me. "We don't have anything to take care of."

I shrug, trying to hide a smile. "Take the long way back to Marcella's," I answer, firing off the address to them and a text to Gage.

He frowns but jerks the SUV into drive and pulls through the docks parking lot. I slide across the console and into the backseat with Dex.

"What are you doing, Baby girl?" Dex asks with a chuckle.

In answer, I kick off my shoes and then undo my jeans, sliding them off my legs with my panties. I catch Ryder's eyes in the rearview mirror and finally grin.

"What the fuck, *Il mio sole*?" he growls, glancing at the road and back at me in the mirror.

I throw one leg over Dex's and brace the other on the back of the passenger side seat, giving Ryder an unrestricted view in the mirror. It's dangerous as hell to distract him like this, but I need him; I need *them.*

Dex slides his hand between my thighs, rubbing my clit. "Is this what you want, Baby girl?"

"Yes," I moan, knowing it won't take much to get me off. I'm wound up so tight that I need to find release and fast.

He starts rubbing my clit in smooth circles, causing my hips to roll with the movement chasing what Dex is giving me. I can already feel my breathing speed up, and Dex increases the pressure. He angles his body to face me and slips two fingers from his other hand inside my pussy, pumping them in and out in time with his circles on my clit.

"Fuck," Ryder cusses before I feel the car swerve toward an exit.

"You going to come for me?" Dex rasps in my ear.

"Yes," I moan long and loud.

He takes my lips in a searing kiss, and I explode all over his fingers. He works me slowly back down before slowly removing his hands. "Good girl," he whispers after pulling back from the kiss.

I sit back up in the seat and go for Dex's jeans. I get them undone, and he lifts his hips so I can slide them and his boxers down. His fat cock springs free, and I wrap my hand around it, making it jerk in my hand. "You want my cock, Baby girl?"

I stroke from base to tip in a rough grip, just like I know he likes it. "I always want your cock, Dex."

I scoot my ass back on the seat, leaning over and licking the precum already leaking from the tip. I swirl my tongue over the head several times before sucking him into my mouth. He doesn't let me keep control long before he closes a fist in my hair, shoving my head down. I open my throat to take his whole cock in my mouth. "Fuck, this mouth," Dex groans, using his grip on my hair to work my mouth up and down on his cock. "Suck hard," he commands. I hollow my cheeks increasing suction. "Good girl," he groans.

I love when they take control of my body, and I love being Dex's good girl. I never thought it was something I would like, but hearing it come from that deep raspy tone when Dex is turned on would ruin my panties. If I was wearing any.

I feel the car take a sharp left, then drive for a minute before jerking to a stop. "Get out," Ryder demands before getting out of the car.

I pull my mouth from Dex's cock with a wet pop and look out his window. Ryder drove us to the beach house and is already walking in, leaving the front door wide open.

Dex chuckles. "You're in trouble now," he comments, tucking himself back in his pants but not bothering to zip up. I'm on a secluded part of the beach, so it doesn't really matter.

I smile, jerking my shirt over my head and then unhooking my bra. "Are you going to punish me, Dexy?" I let the bra fall and slide out of the car completely naked.

He's behind me in two steps before spinning me around and throwing me over his shoulder. He lays a sound slap on my ass, making me moan. "Something tells me a punishment wouldn't be a punishment to you."

He strides up the steps and into the front door, kicking it shut behind him. He flips me back over and onto my feet. He kicks his boots off and makes quick work of the rest of his clothes before stalking toward me with purpose. Having someone the size of Dex coming after you with a raging hard-on should be alarming, but to me, I'm turned the fuck on.

He crowds into my space, making me crane my neck to look up at him. "I think she needs to be punished for that stunt. What do you think, Ryder?"

"Hm," Ryder hums from behind me, "I think so. That was dangerous as hell, *Il mio sole*, fucking with me while I was driving." I feel him step in behind me. "And you know how we feel about your safety."

"I think we need to teach you a lesson," Dex adds before stepping back. "Go to the bedroom, get on the bed, ass in the air."

I feel the crack of the authority in his voice and instantly obey, walking to the bedroom. I climb onto the bed on my hands and knees like he told me to. I can hear them rummaging around in the house, and the anticipation is killing me. I finally cracked Dex's dominant side, and something tells me it would fuel Ryder's. I hear them walking toward the bedroom and shiver.

"She can follow directions," Ryder comments, and I turn my head toward him. Somewhere between the living room and now, he's blissfully naked. It might not have been wise to fuck with two of my biggest guys.

"Put your arms in front of you, chest on the bed," Dex commands. I stretch my arms out toward the headboard so my chest and head are on the bed, but my ass is still in the air. "Spread your legs wider." I slide my knees out. "Good girl."

He knows what that does to me. It makes me want to do anything he wants me to do without question so I can please him.

I feel something slide across my ankle. "You don't like any of this; it stops," Ryder says, and I peek at him. He's holding a roll of silky-looking rope.

"Okay," I reply instantly.

He wraps the rope around each ankle and then ties it to the bedpost at the footboard, making it impossible to close my legs. I feel Dex at my arms; he wraps the ropes several times around my wrists, locking them together. He wraps another piece of rope through them before tying it to the headboard, tossing the other side to Ryder to do the same.

I hear them both step back and peek between my legs to see them both standing at the end of the bed, looking at me, completely exposed to them.

"You have such a pretty pussy, *Il mio sole*. Pink, pouty, and always so fucking wet for us."

"Look at you all tied up for us," Dex says, rubbing a hand over my ass cheek. "I want to turn this ass red," he says, then bites one of the cheeks. "Then fuck it." I can't help the needy moan that slips out, and he chuckles deep and low. "You like that idea, don't you, Baby girl?"

"Yes."

He slides his hand over my ass and then hauls back, slapping it with an open palm without warning, much harder than he ever has before.

It hurts like hell until he smooths his palm over it, and warmth spreads from it straight to my clit. He waits for my moan before he smacks the other side, smoothing his hand over it directly after.

"What do you think, Ryder? You think she's ready?" Dex asks like I'm not even in the room.

"Fuck yeah. Look at how wet she is," Ryder replies, and I can't even be embarrassed that I'm soaking wet.

Nothing happens, so I start to relax, realizing that's what Dex is waiting for. He starts raining blows with his palm onto my ass, one right after the other, even on the back of my thighs. I lose count; all I can do is tense and jerk against my bonds. He doesn't let up until I whimper, and they immediately stop, his big hands smoothing all over my backside and thighs. It takes longer for that warm feeling to spread, but it's even more intense when it does. I don't even recognize the noise that leaves my mouth. My nipples are rock hard, my breath is coming in short gasps, my clit is throbbing, and my pussy is clenching around nothing.

"Oh my god," I moan when Dex's mouth attacks my pussy. I

don't even need to look to know who it is because all the guys have different techniques, and I know them.

He licks, nips, and sucks at my clit, driving me fucking crazy, before sliding his tongue into my pussy, stroking his tongue in and out. I can feel sweat start to build on my skin and know it will be huge when I'm finally allowed to come.

He licks around the entrance of my pussy before I feel his tongue slide to my asshole. I jerk against my bonds. "Dex, what are you...." My words are cut off when he spreads my ass cheeks, licking me around my back hole, a moan taking its place. No one has ever had their mouth there, and I'm not complaining.

He kisses each cheek before I hear the telltale sign of a lube bottle being uncapped. He spreads it all around my asshole before slipping two fingers inside, plunging them in and out. His fingers slip free, and I feel the bed dip with him climbing on. "I'm not going to go easy," he warns before he notches his cock at my back entrance and pushes in. I stretch to accommodate him, and he waits until the burn turns into pleasure and starts to move.

He grabs my hips in a bruising grip and starts ramming into my ass, his thighs slapping my already sore ass, causing aftershocks of warmth to spark through my body.

"Fuck," I moan. Tears start leaking down my face but not from pain, from pleasure.

The bed dips at my head, and I open my eyes to Ryder's pierced cock at my mouth. "Open," he demands. I open my lips for him to slide inside. He has one knee at my head and the other at my chin; he places his hands on the other side of my head and starts fucking my mouth like he would my pussy. They have complete control of my body, and I'm in heaven.

Ryder is going in deep hard strokes into my mouth, and Dex is doing the same to my ass. My orgasm is built up so high that it's starting to hurt. My whole body is tight as a bowstring, and they are doing just enough to not send me over the edge.

"Fuck, Baby girl," Dex groans. "You look beautiful swallowing his cock."

I moan around the head of Ryder's cock, causing him to groan. "You like this, don't you, *Il mio sole*?" he breathes out, never stopping fucking my mouth. "You like when we take what we want from you?" I moan again, and he slips his cock out so I can breathe. I know there's drool all over my chin from him using my mouth like that, but I don't care.

"I love it," I answer breathlessly.

Dex slows his strokes. I can't stop the whimper from escaping when he pulls out. "Shhh, baby girl. We got you."

I feel the ties fall away from my ankles and arms, freeing me. Dex pulls me up to my knees and molds his chest to my back. He turns my head to the side and slants his mouth over mine. He devours my mouth, sliding his hands all over my tits and stomach but never going any further. I roll my hips, and he pulls my mouth away. "When you come again, it will be on our cocks."

"Please," I beg, rubbing my ass on Dex's hard cock.

Ryder stretches out on his back in front of me, fisting his cock. "Climb on, *Il mio sole*."

I crawl on my knees over his thighs, lining myself up before sliding my pussy over his cock, and slamming my hips down.

"Fuck," he grunts, grabbing my hips. He starts hammering into me from the bottom, and I brace my hands on his chest and welcome it.

"Lean forward," Dex commands, so I do. Ryder's thrusts slow, allowing Dex to slide into my ass. He notches his cock and slides forward, filling me up again. "Damn, that's tight."

"You feel amazing, filled with our cocks," Ryder praises.

"You feel amazing like this," I moan.

They immediately find a rhythm to drive me up to the edge again. I'm writhing between them, so Ryder latches a hand around my throat and squeezes. "Stop moving."

I nod, and they start moving again, Ryder's hand resting on my throat. I'm so close that if they don't let me come soon, I'll go crazy. "Please," I beg.

"Please, what?" Ryder asks.

"Please let me come."

"You think she deserves to come?" Ryder asks Dex, their thrusts never slowing.

"She took her punishment like a good girl. She's going to feel that for a while," Dex comments casually. "You think she learned her lesson?"

"Hm. Probably not," Ryder chuckles, then groans. "But that means we can do this again."

Their strokes intensify, and I almost groan in frustration. Dex slips a hand between Ryder and me and pinches my clit at the same time Ryder squeezes my throat hard enough to steal my breath. I go off like a shot, feeling it from the tips of my toes to the top of my head. My mouth opens in a silent scream, and I come so hard I almost pass out. Stars pop off behind my eyelids, and I hear them both shout their releases, filling me up from both ends.

I feel hands smoothing down my arms and realize I did pass out for a second. They have me on the bed between them, facing Ryder, and I don't even remember getting here. "You okay, *Il mio sole*?" Ryder asks, kissing my tears away.

"Yes," I say happily, "I love you guys."

"And I love you, Baby girl," Dex says, kissing between my shoulder blades.

"I love you so much, *Il mio sole*," Ryder says, kissing me sweetly before tucking me against his chest.

I'd love nothing more than to snuggle up and pass out between these two, but so many things still need to be done.

Duty calls.

CHAPTER 54
GAGE

"Where have you three been?" I ask, storming out the front door when I hear them pull up.

Ryder grins. "Beach house."

"What the hell would you be doing..." I say, then stop when I realize. "You dirty fuckers."

Les laughs. "That they were," she says before smacking me on the ass and walking inside.

I glare at Dex and Ryder fist bumping each other before following that delectable ass inside. Leo's still passed out on the couch where I left him.

"What is this?" Ryder asks, walking in behind me.

Holden is laid out on the chaise; Leo's head is pillowed right on his crotch, with Holden's hand resting on Leo's shoulder. They look cute as fuck; then I look at Ryder. "Are you pissed?" I never can tell Ryder's normal voice from his pissed-off one; they sound the same.

"That they're cuddled together, no. I'm pissed they actually get to sleep," Ryder replies, shaking his head.

"Yeah, but you guys got to fuck off your post-mission adrenaline. I call that a win," I reply, pissed as hell at that.

Dex shrugs. "Fair point."

"I hate you both," I say before storming into the kitchen, making them both chuckle.

"Where is Nina?" Les asks, sliding into a chair at the table very carefully.

What the fuck is that?

We slide around the table with her. "Back porch with Alexey and Dmitri. Giovanni is keeping an ear out," I answer.

She readjusts in the seat. "We need to figure out what to do next."

"You want me to get them?"

"Not yet. I need coffee first," she replies, going to stand up.

"I got it, *Il mio sole*," Ryder says, jumping up. "You rest," he says, kissing the top of her head on the way.

She gives him a grateful smile before fidgeting again. "What the hell is wrong with you?" I ask, and Dex chokes on a laugh.

She glares at him, then smiles sweetly at me. "Nothing."

Dex shoots her a look that could melt my boxers off, and she blushes. Fucking blushes! Les doesn't blush unless it's from being turned on.

I definitely need to know now. "Tell me, Pretty girl." Leo walks in right when she opens her mouth, stretching and yawning. "Have a nice nap, princess?" I ask him.

"Sure did," Leo responds, grinning. "Hey, Baby," he greets Les, giving her a kiss.

"What am I, chopped fucking liver?" I gripe. She gets hot sex and a kiss from Leo.

"Hey, babe," he laughs, kissing me before walking to the other side of the table and sitting down.

"Les was just about to tell us what she, Ryder, and Dex got up to," I say, looking expectantly at Les.

"No, she wasn't," she replies, taking the cup of coffee from Ryder.

Leo raises an eyebrow. "Why are you sitting funny?"

She huffs. "I'm not."

"You are," Ryder laughs, fist bumping Dex again.

Holden walks in and gives her a kiss, distracting her again. "Sit the fuck down," I say, making Holden jerk away from her.

Les punches me in the arm hard. "Don't talk to him like that."

Holden slides into a chair. "What crawled up your ass?" he asks me.

Dex starts laughing. "That's the problem. Nothing has crawled up his ass."

Les chokes on a sip of coffee, and Holden reaches over, patting her back. I cross my arms and huff. "I just want to know what happened."

"Fine," Les says, setting her coffee cup down. "Ryder and Dex... taught me a lesson."

"She thought it would be a good idea to get naked in the backseat," Ryder adds, leaning his folded arms on the table.

I jerk my head to Les. "You did what?"

She shrugs. "I was horny."

"We took her to the beach house and taught her a lesson for putting herself in danger for distracting Ryder while he was driving," Dex says, giving her that look again.

Now I'm intrigued. "Then what?" All ears at the table are tuned in now since we are talking in hushed tones.

"We tied her up," Ryder continues.

"I turned that ass red," Dex adds. "Then I fucked it."

"You spanked her?" Holden says, all innocence with his eyes wide.

"Hard. Didn't I, Baby girl?"

"Uh huh," Les says, her face blooming with color. "Then they both fucked me."

"Now I have a boner," I say, looking down at my lap.

Leo laughs. "You wanted to know."

I did, but dammit, why couldn't I have been there instead of babysitting the terror twins and their mom? I can't be pissed at Les, though. She's under a lot of pressure, and she always goes after what she wants, and it just happened to be Ryder and Dex.

Les finishes her coffee and looks around again. "Where's Micah?"

I shrug. "Asleep last time I checked. Giovanni gave him something for pain, and he passed the hell out."

An uneasy look crosses her face, and she darts a glance at Leo. "What about Evander and Mateo?"

"They went to help with chores, I think." Leo shrugs. "Do you need them?"

She shakes her head. "No. Let's get this over with."

I jump up and get Alexey, Dmitri, and Nina. Marcella gave her some clothes to wear since she was in her nightgown when we grabbed her. They follow me inside, and I motion for them to take a seat. Nina bundles Les in a hug before she sits down. "I never thanked you properly," she says before she sits down.

"I'm sorry it had to happen that way, but I didn't know Viktor wouldn't be there," Les says, casting an accusing look at Alexey and Dmitri.

"As I said," Alexey says evenly, "we didn't know he wouldn't be there."

"Honestly, Alessa," Nina says, grabbing Les' hand. "He left quickly for some business."

Les acknowledges that with a nod. "We need to know your plan now."

Nina looks down at the table. "I don't know. He will kill me if he finds me."

"Has it always been this bad?" Les asks, gently squeezing her hand.

Nina smiles sadly. "No. He was a good man once. I don't know what happened," Nina says, wiping a tear from her eye. "One day, everything was good, and the next, he was taking his anger out on me."

Dmitri sits up in his chair. "How long?"

"Years," Nina whispers.

"Mama," Alexey says, anguished. "Why didn't you tell us?"

"I didn't want to put my troubles on my boys," Nina says, straightening her spine. "It doesn't matter now anyway. Alessa got me out." Nina looks at Les. "I'm sorry I don't have more of a plan, but I want to return to Russia for a while."

Les shakes her head sadly. "You can't. Not yet, anyway."

"She's right," Ryder adds. "That's the first place he'll look."

"I have people all over," Les says, running her hand through her hair. "People I trust that you can stay with until Viktor is taken care of."

"Taken care of?" Nina asks wide-eyed.

"You have to know he has to die, Mama," Alexey says harshly with no remorse. "For laying hands on you, for starters, but he also took a shot at Les and her guys."

Nina's head whips around the table, taking everyone in. "He did?"

"The night of the gala, he shot up our limo, and I took a bullet in the process," Leo says absently, rubbing where his stitches still are.

"He's gone too far," Les says. "He's been trying to take over my business; he's sent guys after us twice, and now this. I have to do what needs to be done."

"I understand." Nina nods. She's been in this life for a long time and knows you can't let this slide.

"You can stay in New York with Aldo," Les says, then smiles. "He's my most trusted besides the guys here. As soon as we take care of Viktor, I'll get you to Russia."

"I can't impose on someone like that! I don't have any money or clothes..." Nina says anxiously, and Dmitri squeezes her shoulder.

"We took care of that, Mama, and it's just short-term. Right, Les?" Dmitri soothes, looking expectantly at Les.

"If I have anything to do with it, the sooner he's dead, the better. I'll contact Aldo and set everything up. You need out of here." Les pulls her phone out. "Today."

"I'll get the jet ready," Ryder says, pulling his own phone out and leaving the room.

"You have a jet?" Leo says incredulously.

"Uh. Yeah," I reply like it should be obvious.

"You never know when you need to escape the country," Dex says seriously.

"Can it be tracked?" Alexey asks, sitting up in his chair.

Holden shakes his head "Nope. I buried it in a dummy corporation so far that it never leads back to Les."

"If anyone can make something disappear," Les points at Holden, "It's him."

"You're sure your friend won't mind me being there?" Nina wonders, looking nervous again.

I laugh at that. "If anything, he'll be happy you're there."

"Aldo is," Les waves her hand around, "different." She takes in Nina's alarmed look. "He's a great guy. Just think of your basic idea of an Italian mobster, and that's Aldo."

"I don't know if I like this idea," Alexey worries.

"It's your only choice." Les shrugs. "Take it or leave it."

"Is that how it's going to be between us now, *Moye sokrovishche*?"

"Call her that again, and you won't be alive to find out," Holden threatens, causing all eyes to turn to him.

Les laughs. "I warned you," she says to Alexey.

Ryder strides back into the room. "He can have it ready in two hours."

"You need to say your goodbyes here," Les says, motioning between Nina and her boys. "I can't risk anyone seeing you at the airstrip." She looks at us. "This is the part you guys aren't going to like."

"What is it?" I asked, dreading the answer.

"I'm going to have Zane take her."

"Absofuckinglutely not," Ryder explodes. "We don't need him."

"He's the only one no one will expect Nina to be with," Les says evenly. "Viktor will think this was me with or without proof."

"I can wipe the cameras, and one of you can take her," Holden reasons.

"That's even more suspicious," Les explains. "Zane can take her openly, and no one will ask questions."

"One of us could, too," I add. "We have burner cars for a reason."

Les stands up so fast that her chair almost tips over, causing Nina to jump. "I didn't ask," she grits out. "I'm telling you that Zane is taking her to the fucking airport, and that's that." She storms off, phone already to her ear.

Alexey chuckles. "I think you pissed off your girl."

Nina looks around the room again, and you can see when she

puts the connection together. "Your girl?" she asks anyway, even though she knows the answer.

"Yeah. Our girl," I answer when no one else does.

Nina smiles, looking proud. "I knew she was a smart girl."

"Mama!" Dmitri says, looking at his mom in disbelief.

"Oh, honey," she says, patting his hand, "It's not uncommon in Italian families to take more than one lover."

"I could have gone my whole life without hearing you say lover," Alexey mutters.

"And we're sending her to an Italian family," I say, waggling my eyebrows just to get a rise out of them.

Alexey slams his fist down on the table. "She's not fucking going now."

"Language," Nina says sternly, and I can't help but laugh when Alexey shrinks back in his chair.

"My mom is with an Italian man," Leo says, then grimaces. "Why the hell did you have to say that?"

"My dad's nothing if not traditional," Ryder says with a straight face. "He's got a lot of brothers."

Leo's face goes pale, and he stands up. "I'm calling Mom."

"He's just messing with you, Baby!" I yell at his retreating back; he flips me off and keeps walking.

Dex chuckles. "He will have his mom on the first plane back home."

"Baby?" Nina squeaks after hearing what I called Leo.

"Yeah. They're together too," Dmitri says with a laugh and motions between Ryder and Holden. "They are too."

Holden blushes, and Ryder chuckles, "What's the matter, *Bello*?"

Holden's blush deepens, but he smiles. "Nothing."

I shake my head with a laugh. "I'm going to go check on Les."

I stand up and follow the path she took. I find her on a swing that overlooks the property and flop beside her. She's having an animated conversation in full Italian, and I can only pick up on a few keywords. Les tried to teach me Italian, but it was too damn complicated. She says her goodbyes and turns to me. "If you're here to argue, you can go right back in the house."

"I wasn't arguing, Pretty girl. I get what you're saying," I soothe.

She snorts. "No, you don't. You just don't want me pissed at you."

"That too." I smile.

She rolls her eyes. "You and those damn dimples," she mutters, pulling up Zane's contact. She flips it to the speakerphone, and I feel my teeth gritting.

"Well, hello, Beautiful," he answers, and I barely resist cussing his punk ass out.

"I need a favor," Les says without preamble. "This goes above anything I've asked you to do before."

"Does it involve a dead body?" Zane deadpans. I feel my lips twitch and fight the smile. I refuse to find him amusing.

"No," Les huffs. "I can take care of those myself."

"Beautiful. Do I need to remind you who you're talking to?"

"Trust me; I remember you're a traitor."

"Hm," Zane hums, ignoring that dig. "What do you need?"

"I have a friend on the run from an abusive husband. I need you to take her to the jet."

Zane's quiet for a minute. "You said this is bigger. What aren't you telling me?"

I have to give it to him; he's fucking smart. This isn't a simple drop-off at the airstrip with a random abused woman.

Les looks at me. "It's Viktor Orlov's wife."

"What the fuck, Les?" Zane growls. "You kidnapped the man's fucking *wife*?"

"He beats the shit out of her, Zane," Les says quietly. "I wasn't lying about that."

"Fucking hell," he mutters, then takes a deep breath. "When do you need me?"

Just like that, he agrees. Les doesn't know the power she still holds over that man. He risked his life for her, and now he's risking his job. That's one of the reasons I want her to stay the fuck away from him. I see how she still looks at him, whether she wants to admit it or not. Les still has deeply buried hurt feelings about Zane, and one of these days, they're going to bubble over. I just don't know how it'll end. My choice would be to fucking kill him and get him out of the picture. But something tells me that will hurt Les no matter how much she threatens him to do it herself.

"Two hours," Les says. "I can't have you come to where we are. I need to throw him off this trail."

"Are we talking police escort or what?"

"I can't have you risk picking her up in the station's car," Les says, laying her head back on the swing. "I shouldn't be asking you to do this anyway."

Zane chuckles. "I'm already in it, Beautiful. Now tell me the plan."

"We'll be in a burner car. I'll text you what kind and where to meet us when we figure it out."

"You need to send one of your guys. You don't need to be involved anymore," Zane says, and I feel myself agreeing with him. *Mark it down because it will never fucking happen again.*

"What is it with all you assholes thinking you can tell me what to do?" Les rages, getting pissed all over again.

"I'm not going to ask what other assholes," Zane says. "But if they're worried about your safety, they have my fucking respect. You're getting in too deep, Les."

"It's my fucking job!"

"No," he says evenly. "Your fucking job is to run that family and let the ones you trust protect you."

"You're telling me you think I should hide behind them?" she scoffs.

"I'm telling you, I want you to live to breathe another fucking day. Because a life without you in it isn't one to live."

I agree with him again and want to punch myself in the face. He just told my girl that he can't live without her, and I'm nodding my head like a dumbass. *What the hell is wrong with me?*

He isn't wrong, though. I can't imagine living without Les in my life I will follow her into the afterlife, no questions asked.

"Please don't do this right now, Zane," Les pleads, and I can see the guilt creeping onto her face. The same look she gets every time something about Zane is brought up. That tells me all I need to know. Les still has feelings for Zane.

"One day, Beautiful, you will listen to me," Zane threatens. "Text me the details," he says, and then the line goes dead.

She drops the phone onto the swing and pulls her knees to her chest, wrapping her arms around them.

"Talk to me, Pretty girl," I say and silently promise I'll listen to whatever she says.

She lays her head on her knees to look at me. "He tried to kiss me the other day."

I swallow down the expletives. "And?"

"I was going to let him," she whispers, her eyes filling with tears. "I have five of the best guys, and I was going to let him."

I thumb a tear away before rubbing a hand up and down her back. "You aren't over him," I say simply, shaking my head when she goes to argue. "You need to stop denying it, Pretty girl."

"It's been six years," she says miserably.

"And you guys never worked through any of that bullshit."

"Are you telling me to talk to him?" she asks, surprised, and then shakes her head. "I don't need to."

"Yes, you do," I say, harsher than I meant. I take a breath and try again. "Yes, you do. I don't know why the fuck I'm telling you to, but you need to. For you."

"I'd rather just hate him," she sniffs, turning her head away.

"You don't hate him. If you hated him, you wouldn't find ways to keep him in your life," I tell her honestly, causing her head to flip back to me. "Quit lying to yourself."

"I can't do that," she says, tears flashing down her cheeks. "The moment I admit what I already know, I can't ignore how I feel anymore."

"As much as I don't want to say this," I sigh. "We would do anything for you, Pretty girl. That includes whatever happens with Zane."

She laughs, but it's watery. "I think Ryder may feel different."

"You would be surprised what Ryder would handle for you."

She looks over the property and doesn't say anything for a long time. I rub her back and give her time to get her thoughts together.

Do I want her with Zane? No. But will I deny her if she wants him with her too? Also no. I just want Les in my life, and the truth is, Zane isn't a bad guy. Yeah, he lied to her and made her feel like their whole relationship was a lie, but Zane would lay his life down for her just like the rest of us would.

"This is going to have to be a problem for another day," she says, finally standing up from the swing. "We have too much going on."

She walks away, and I watch her until she disappears into the house. That's going to be her excuse until the end of time. We always have something going on; it's the way of this life.

I might just have to push her a little.

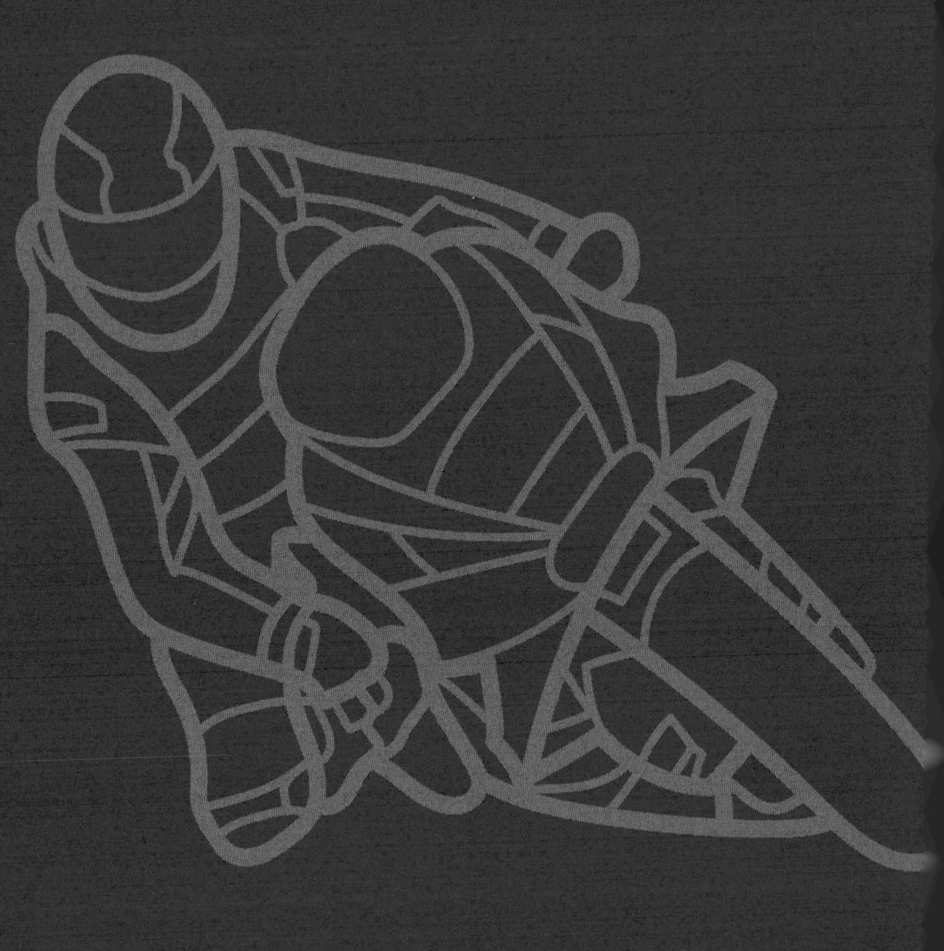

CHAPTER 55
RYDER

"I don't like this," Dex says, leaning back in the passenger seat.

"Which part?" I grunt. "Watching Les and Gage boost a car or them meeting Zane?"

"I don't give a shit about Zane. I meant this whole thing with Nina. Viktor is going to hit back tenfold."

I've already thought about that and know she's more than ready for whatever Viktor throws at her now. Something hits me, and I look at Dex. "What do you mean you don't give a shit about Zane?" He should because this man is hot on Les' ass and has been for years. If she didn't get so fucking mad about him becoming a cop, I have no doubt they would still be together. And where would that leave all of us?

"I mean, Zane is the least of our worries," he sighs, and I can tell whatever is about to come out of his mouth I'm not going to like. "He tried to kiss her at the house."

"What?" I explode, slapping my hand on the steering wheel. "I fucking *knew* something was off when I walked back into that room."

"He implied he was okay with sharing her. With us." Dex finally looks at me. "She still loves him, man."

Gage and Les get the car they're taking fired up, and I drop my

Explorer into drive. "I know," I reply, pulling out behind them. It's something I've always known, and she would never admit it. She buried her feelings in anger. Now that he's making his intentions known, it's getting harder for her to hide how she feels.

"What do we do?" Dex asks.

"What can we do?" I ask harshly. "If we do anything to fucking hurt him, Les will have our asses."

"I don't mean that," Dex replies evenly. "I mean about her feelings for him. She can't keep that shit buried too much longer."

"Are you telling me you want her to tell him how she feels?"

"No. I'm saying she needs to. It doesn't matter what we want."

"Have you lost your fucking mind?" I ask him because I'm pretty sure he has.

"I'm the only one who hasn't lost their fucking mind," he argues, fully facing me in the seat. "We agreed that Les gets whatever makes her happy because she deserves that. What if that's Zane?"

Gage takes an exit off the highway, and I keep going straight. We agreed this is as far as Dex and I can go for the risk of being seen. We just needed to watch their backs in Concrete Row when they stole a car in broad fucking daylight. We're going to meet them after they drop Nina off so they can ditch the car, and we can go the hell home and finally sleep. We dropped Holden and Leo off at the house, and Giovanni brought Micah, Evander, and Mateo over later. I'm so damn tired, and all this talk about Zane makes me crazy.

"I don't know if that's something I can give her," I answer honestly. Sharing her with these guys was hard enough at first. Bringing in the man that betrayed her isn't something I think I can do.

"She's going to eventually go after what she wants, and that's Zane," Dex says impatiently. "You might want to wrap your thick head around it now."

"Why are you suddenly okay with this?"

"Since I talked to her about it. I would do anything to keep that girl."

"Are you saying I won't?" I ask angrily.

"Will you quit putting words in my fucking mouth? I'm just

warning you now that if Les ever came to me and said she wanted to try with him. I wouldn't tell her no."

"I can't, man," I say gruffly. "I saw what he did to her."

"And something tells me he regrets that decision." He shrugs. "We've all done shit we regret. His is hurting Les."

I pull into a vacant lot, throwing the car in park to wait for Les' call. Laying my head back on the seat, I think back to her finding out.

She was hurt, but she was covering it up with anger. She didn't know I could hear her crying at night when I would stay over, and I never brought it up. She cut him entirely out of her life and never would give him the chance to explain, and something tells me that's her regret. I watched the girl I loved for a fucking year sneak around with that asshole, and there wasn't a damn thing I could do about it; I was too big of a coward then to tell her how I felt.

I'm not that boy anymore, and I'll be goddamned if he gets in between us again.

"It's been too long," I tell Dex after we haven't heard from Les and Gage in over two hours. It should have taken them an hour to drop Nina off with Zane and call us. I texted them both over thirty minutes ago, and still no answer. I probably wouldn't have been as worried, but we got a call from Mani that said a creepy doll was dropped off at the front gate earlier. The doll was tied inside a box and looked eerily like Les. There was also a folder filled with pictures that reminded us her stalker is still watching her every move.

"You think they snuck off somewhere?" Dex asks with a chuckle.

Gage was pissed as hell when he found out about the beach house, so I shrug. "Could have, but I think she would message one of us with everything going on."

"We didn't," he reminds me.

I jerk the car into drive and turn toward the direction they were meeting Zane. "I can't shake this feeling, man. Somethings wrong."

Dex nods. "Should we call Holden?"

I shake my head because there's no use in worrying anyone else; they're probably sleeping. "Nah. Let's check the meeting spot and figure it out from there."

We drive quietly to the meeting spot less than ten minutes away, with no sign of them or foul play.

"I'm telling you, Gage is balls deep in her somewhere," Dex jokes.

I want to agree and chalk it up to being away from Les, but something is gnawing at my stomach. I got a text from the pilot earlier that he had Nina, so I know that part is taken care of. If Gage snuck her away and didn't tell me, I'll kick his ass.

We drive up and down the road they may have taken, seeing nothing. She's supposed to call to tell us where to meet her, so everything is kept a surprise, so I have no fucking clue where they would have been going.

"I don't fucking like this," I finally say, dialing Holden.

"Hello," he answers groggily, and I feel like shit for waking him up. He isn't used to these missions that sometimes keep us up for over forty-eight hours.

"Hey, *Bello*, I need you to track Gage and Les."

"What's wrong?" he asks, instantly alert.

"Maybe nothing," I assure him. "I might be being a paranoid dick, but we haven't heard from them in over two hours."

I hear rustling and then a door opening. "I'm going downstairs," he says, and I can tell he's jogging. I listen to him open his office door and keys clicking. I try to stay patient while he taps away, but I can feel the edge of panic creeping up. "Ryder," he says quietly. "They aren't together."

I jerk the car to a stop on the side of the road and look at Dex. "What do you mean?"

"They're firing up in two different spots. Hold on," he says, and I can hear the tapping intensify. "Gage's phone is like two miles from you." I stomp the gas and ignore the beeping of the horn from the car I just pulled out in front of. He rattles off the streets to turn down. "Right there!"

I stomp the brake. “I don’t see anything, Holden.”

“It’s right there,” he says desperately.

I connect the call to my phone and step out of the SUV. We’re in a shitty neighborhood, and people are eyeing us warily.

“What can I do for you, fellas?” An older black gentleman asks, leaning against a brick wall.

“We’re looking for someone,” Dex says. “Six-two. Dark wavy hair might be with a pretty girl with black hair.”

“You lose your girl?” the guy chuckles, and I try to keep my temper in check. He shakes his head. “Haven’t seen him.” This is the type of neighborhood where they never see anything.

“We aren’t fucking cops,” I say impatiently, tired of the games.

“I know who you are,” he says, narrowing his eyes. “I don’t like your kind around here.”

“My kind?” I ask incredulously.

“Mafioso. Boys with egos too fucking big, thinking they run the place.”

“Come on. We don’t have time for this shit,” I tell Dex, and we start to walk away. More guys step out from behind the building, blocking our path, and I’m done with this shit. I pull my Glocks at the same time Dex does. “If you know who the fuck I am, then you know I’m not playing games. Move,” I threaten.

“Ryder!” I hear Holden yell from my phone and put it back to my ear. “The phone is flashing two buildings down; I narrowed the search.”

“We seem to be in disagreement with the neighborhood friendlies,” I tell Holden.

“Look, man,” Dex says, never lowering his weapons, “The girl we’re looking for is the girl I love, so I suggest you tell your boys to move, or we will level this fucking neighborhood.”

The guy tilts his head and flicks his cigarette toward us. It lands right at my boot. “Go on then,” he finally says and jerks his head for the others to follow. They all slink back into the building the guy was leaning against. We tuck our guns away and take off at a dead sprint. We round the corner of the building Holden indicated and come skidding to a stop.

The car they stole is full of bullet holes, and Gage is slumped over the steering wheel. We run at the same time. I jerk open the driver's side door, and Dex pulls open the passenger side.

I put my phone on speakerphone and lay it on the dash. "Gage," I say softly. His eyes are shut, blood pouring from his head and out of his mouth. I'm afraid to move or touch him, so my hands flutter around him. "Gage!" He doesn't stir, and I meet Dex's eyes from the passenger side.

"There's no sign of Les, and there is blood in the seat," Dex says, closing his eyes. They burn with panic, worry, and anger when he opens them again.

"What's going on?" Holden asks, and I can hear the quiver in his voice.

"Where's Leo?" I ask, checking Gage for a pulse. It is weak, but it's there. I try not to slump in relief. He needs an ambulance. Now. "Dex, call nine-one-one, then call Doc. We can't take care of this at home." Dex nods and whips out his phone.

"Asleep."

"Wake him up. Now." Holden doesn't answer, but I can hear him run from the room. "Gage. Goddamnit, don't die on me."

There is too much blood, and he's so damn pale; his usually smiling face is slack.

"Fifteen minutes," Dex says, sticking his head back in. "We can't be here."

"We can't fucking leave him!"

"Ryder," Dex says harshly. "Doc will meet them there. We'll wait until we hear sirens, then we can follow them to the hospital, then find Les."

I don't even want to think about that. If Gage is this bad and Les is missing, they were ambushed. Could Viktor have organized that fast?

"What's going on?" Leo's voice filters through, and I fill him in as fast as possible. "I'll meet him at the hospital." I hear him gulp. "Is he going to die, Ryder?"

"No. He's not," I say adamantly. Mainly to soothe him but also to soothe myself. "He's not, Leo, and we will find Les."

Fifteen minutes is too damn long, so between Dex and me, we lay Gage back in the seat, and his eyelids don't even flutter. The front of his white shirt is drenched in blood, and I can't even begin to look for a wound. Dex pulls out a knife, flips it open, and slits Gage's shirt. What I see makes me want to fucking fall apart.

"Fuck," Dex whispers, and I can see him fighting it too.

"What is it?" Leo demands, and I can hear him moving through the house.

Gage has a hole in his chest that's pouring blood. I whip my shirt off and jam it against the wound, trying to stop the bleeding. There are two more bullet wounds, one on his shoulder and one in his stomach.

"Ryder!" Leo yells when I don't answer. I close my eyes because I don't know what to tell him. "It's bad, isn't it?"

I meet Dex's anguished eyes again. "It's bad, Leo," I tell him honestly.

"Fuck," Leo whispers. "What about Les? You have to find her."

"We will, Leo," Dex promises, and I can see murder in his eyes.

"Was this Viktor?" Micah's voice cuts in. Holden must have grabbed him too.

"I don't know!" I say miserably, pushing more pressure against the wound. "I don't fucking know."

"We need to move," Dex says, listening to the sirens wailing in the distance. He levels me with a look when I don't move. "Now!"

"Don't die on me, Gage," I say again, kissing his forehead. "You can't fucking die."

We take off toward my car, skidding to stop beside it and diving in. I pull it into drive and hit the gas before Dex's door is even shut. We drive down to the next and pull into a parking lot, so I can still see everything going on. I hate this. We never call the fucking ambulance because cops come with them. But we can't do this ourselves, Gage needs serious help, and we can't provide that.

We watch as the paramedics hop into action. Before long, Gage is being loaded up in the ambulance, and they're pulling away. I can feel my heart being pulled with it.

"They're on their way," I tell them on the phone. "We will meet you there."

"Go find my niece," Micah growls. "We will take care of Gage. Holden's staying at the house, trying to narrow his search on her phone. Bring her home."

Dex and I share a look. "On it."

"Take care of yourself," Micah says softly. "I'll let you know as soon as I know something."

I agree and hang up. I take a second to collect my thoughts before calling Holden back. I know Micah can handle this, but I feel torn. I need to find Les, but I need to make sure Gage is okay.

"Micah's got this," Dex assures me.

"I can't do this, Dex."

He grabs my arm and squeezes. "We need to keep it together for Les and Gage. Micah is Gage's contact on everything, and he'll take care of that. We'll take care of Les."

I can feel my whole world crumbling. "There was so much fucking blood in her seat."

"Man, don't freak out on me," Dex says harshly. "I'm barely holding it together. Put the fucking car in drive and call Holden. NOW!"

Something about that whip crack in his voice has me pulling myself together. I angrily swipe the tears from my eyes and do what he says. As soon as I speed out onto the road, I call Holden.

"Take the next left," he says as soon as he answers. I take a sharp left, cut a car off, and stomp on the gas. "Go straight three miles," he says, tapping at the keys on his keyboard.

"*Bello*," I say softly.

"No," he barks, "Don't do that right now. Keep driving. She's fine. I don't need you to baby me; I need you to fucking find Les."

I slam my foot on the gas and wait for his next instructions. We take three more lefts and a right and drive ten miles before he yells for us to stop. It's an abandoned lot with nothing in sight. We jump out of the car and take off running. "It's right there! To your right!"

Dex and I desperately search; I feel myself growing impatient when Dex stands up with Les' phone in his hand. "Someone dumped it."

I spin around in a circle, trying to glimpse that silken black hair. If someone dumped the phone, they knew we can track it. And if they dumped it and then took her, she's in serious trouble. "I need to call Zane."

"I'll try to crack into his. All police departments have tracking on those phones," Holden replies and hangs up.

I dial Zane's, and it goes straight to voicemail. I dial it repeatedly while Dex and I search every square inch of the lot. We keep getting weird looks when people ride by, seeing a giant and a guy with no shirt. My phone pings with a text message, and I have to swallow the disappointment.

MICAH

They took him straight back to surgery. Anything?

They dumped her phone. I can't get ahold of Zane. Holden is trying to track him.

MICAH

Let me know. We have to find her.

I know, and we will.

I can't imagine what Micah is going through right now. She might be the girl we love, but this is his niece; they're the only family they have left.

My phone rings, and I jerk it back to my ear without looking. "Hello?"

"His phone is there too," Holden says. "Why would his phone be there?"

That's a damn good question. Gage and Les were going to meet him to drop off Nina, and then Zane would have been going the opposite way. What the fuck is going on?

We follow Holden's directions and find his phone about twenty feet from where Les' was, buried under some rubble, which is why we didn't find it in our search. I scoop it up and try to power it back on. The phone looks scratched but otherwise unharmed. We run back to the car, and I jam a charger back into it, waiting for the logo to pop up that it's loading.

"It has a fucking password," I bark at Holden.

"I can get in it," he assures me. "I'm searching for all the security and street cams they would have passed. We will find her."

Whoever took her better hope we find her without a hair harmed on her head. Because if they hurt her?

This whole fucking world will burn until they pay for it.

Three hours, twenty-two minutes, and twelve seconds.

That's how long it's been since my world crashed around me. There's no sign of Les, and Gage is still in surgery. I've paced this waiting room for so long that my feet hurt, but I can't sit down. Every time I try, I pop back up and started pacing again.

When they told us they were taking Gage straight to surgery in the emergency room and rushed him off, all the faces of the nurses and doctors were grim. I almost didn't keep it together when I saw Gage covered in blood, eyes closed, and blood running from between his lips. When he comes out of this, and he will, I'll kiss him stupid and tell him how much I love him.

I can't imagine who's dumb enough to take Les, but all I can hope is she's fighting like hell to get away because my girl is a fucking fighter. My heart is being pulled in two different directions. One to stay here and one to jump into the search for Les. We have to find her; I can't live without her. None of us can.

Micah told me earlier that Dex and Ryder are on their way here with Holden to regroup because, right now, they're just driving around aimlessly.

Dex, Holden, and Ryder round the corner, looking as miserable as the rest of us. Holden goes straight to a chair, pulling his laptop from his bag, probably still running searches on anything and everything.

Ryder strides straight up to me and jerks me into a bear hug. My shock lasts a second before I wrap my arms around him. "She's going to be fine. Gage is going to be fine," he says adamantly in my ear.

I nod against his shoulder. "They have to be."

He pulls back, grabbing both shoulders, and I can tell by the look in his eyes he knows what I mean. Life without Les and Gage would be awful, and none of us wanted to live with that. "Any word?" Ryder asks, pulling me towards a chair. He pushes me in it before sitting in between Holden and me.

"No," Micah replies, running his hand through his hair. "They said it was bad, and surgery could take a while."

Micah has been to the nurses' station every ten minutes for an update, and everyone's too scared to tell him to sit the hell down. The hospital has Micah listed as Gage's brother, so he can always get information on him, and with the blue eyes, they can pull it off.

I close my eyes at the thought of seeing Gage's and Les' beautiful blue eyes. Gage's are a couple of shades darker, but they can see straight through your soul. I would give anything to hear either one of their laughs right now. I feel a hand squeeze mine and look down at Ryder's hand in mine. I don't know when we made it here, but I'm not passing up his comfort. Evander and Mateo are here, but all they can offer are platitudes I don't want to hear.

I squeeze back. "They have to be fine, Ryder." I hear my voice break on that last word and know I'm about to lose my shit.

"I know," he whispers back, and I know he's hanging on by a thread too. I open my eyes and look at Dex and Holden. Dex is sitting ramrod straight, hands balled into fists, staring into space. Holden is hunched over his computer, tapping away, but I can see the strain and worry lining his eyes.

Ryder starts sending text messages to anyone he can think of to keep an eye out for Les or Zane because we assume they're together or he knows something. We need everyone she's ever done a favor for to help us, or I know there will be plenty of threats being thrown around.

"Would Zane take her?" I ask because it's been running through my mind since I found out their phones were together.

Ryder shakes his head. "I want to say yes just so I have someone to blame, but he would never do that to her."

"Then explain the phones," Micah demands. "He didn't give a fuck when he was taking advantage of an eighteen-year-old girl. What makes you fucking think he gives a fuck about taking her?"

Ryder levels those dark eyes on Micah. "If I could fucking explain it, jackass, I wouldn't be sitting here with my thumb up my ass."

"You guys promised to protect her! You let her go off during a fucking *war* with one of you. Now, look! Les is gone, and Gage could die!" Micah rages, exploding from his chair.

"You're blaming us?" Ryder growls, standing up. "Les is the boss. What do you want us to do? Tie her up somewhere?"

"I don't think this is the time to have this conversation," Evander says, trying to keep the peace. "You're blaming the wrong people."

"Shut the fuck up," Micah grits out. "Why are you even here?"

Evander's eyes narrow. "My brother needs us, and I care about Les and Gage."

"All you motherfuckers can leave for all I care. You obviously can't do shit anyway, so there's no point in you being here," Micah says.

Dex moves so fast that no one has a chance to react. He grabs the front of Micah's shirt in a tattooed fist, slamming him back against the wall. "You have one more thing to say, and I will rip you limb from limb," he growls in Micah's face. "You can blame us all you want, but it's not doing shit. Get your head on straight."

Ryder walks up and places a hand on Dex's shoulder. "Let him go, man." I can hear the wheezing breaths from Micah from the hit he took last night. Having someone the size of Dex slam you into the wall doesn't help. Dex peels his fingers away one by one but doesn't step back. "Come on," Ryder urges, trying to get Dex to back off. Dex gives Micah one last withering look before falling back into the chair. Ryder looks at Micah. "Are you done?"

Micah jerks a nod, and Ryder walks back to his seat.

"I found something!" Holden says excitedly, tapping keys like crazy. "There's Les and Gage pulling in."

We crowd around the computer and see the car they stole pull into the lot, Zane's truck right behind them.

"What the hell?" Ryder mutters, pointing at the truck. "What the fuck is he doing?"

No sooner than they park, two SUVs come into view, four guys jumping out and firing at the car. You can see Zane duck behind his door and pull his Glock, firing back at the SUVs. That answers that question. He wouldn't be firing at them if he were involved. Gage and Les don't even have time to react before they have the car surrounded. One of the guys fires several shots at Zane, and you can see him slump against the side of his truck.

You can't see any details about the guys. They're in non-descript SUVs with masks on, and no one questioned gunfire in that type of neighborhood.

One guy jerks open the passenger side door, dragging Les out by the hair of her head, and she's fighting like hell. He backhands her across the face, and everyone watching tenses.

"Motherfucker," Ryder growls.

The guy in front of the SUV fires at the windshield, and I know the moment Gage takes the hits. His body jerks several times before slumping onto the wheel. You can see Les screaming and up her fighting. Kicking, punching, anything to get away.

I clamp a hand over my mouth, and Ryder pulls me in again. I can feel his whole body vibrating with rage and know that they will raise hell on earth to bring her back.

The guy holding Les jams something in her neck, and she drops to the ground; he doesn't even try to catch her. He scoops her up and dumps her in the backseat of Zane's truck. Someone else comes around and grabs Zane hauling him inside too; then they jump inside. They all peel out of the lot and disappear from sight.

No one says anything for the longest time, just staring at the screen at Gage's body slumped against the wheel.

"Can you track them?" Ryder asks Holden.

Holden nods, picking up his laptop back up from the table."I can," he answers, bent back over the computer.

I feel fucking helpless, and I know they're feeling it too. We have no idea if this is Viktor or not.

"Why would they take Zane and not Gage too?" I ask. That question is plaguing me because they could have left Zane there to die, also.

"I don't know, man. But we will find out," Dex answers.

With that promise, we lapse into silence; the only noise is Micah arguing with the nurses.

We need answers. And we need them now.

CHAPTER 57
ALESSA

Everything fucking hurts.

My head hurts from whatever they dosed me with, my arms from being strung up over my head with my toes barely touching the ground, and the bullet wound that they roughly came in and patched up earlier. They wore masks, so I can't tell who they are, and they never spoke. I repeatedly asked about Gage and Zane, but none of them would fucking answer me.

I saw the hits Gage took and felt my soul leave my body. Is he dead?

A sob escapes my throat before I can stop it. I can't break down now. I have to believe they're both still alive, or I won't make it through this. I need to figure a way out.

I test the chains on my wrists, which are attached to solid chains wrapped around a steel beam. Someone's making sure I don't escape, so it's someone that knows what I'm capable of. I go over my options. I can dislocate one of my thumbs to slip out of a cuff, but I can't get the other one out without dislocating them both. They're cinched so tight they're pinching the skin.

I look up at the chain, thinking I can pull myself up and over that beam that will get the chain to fall, hopefully giving me more options.

"Fuck," I whisper desperately. I have no idea what to do. I hear coughing, and my head snaps to my left. "Who's there?"

"Hey, Beautiful," Zane answers before coughing again. He's on the other side of a raggedy curtain. What the hell is he doing here?

"Are you okay?" I ask.

"Yeah," he answers, coughing again. "I think they broke my fucking ribs."

"You got shot," I point out dumbly. Of course, he knows that.

"I had a vest on," he answers, and I can hear him shift and groan. "Why the fuck didn't you?"

I close my eyes, feeling stupid as hell that we didn't think about it. "I don't know."

I hear him shifting again, stopping when he starts coughing again. The cough sounds wet, like he has a punctured lung. I hear him groan in pain then the curtain is pulled back with a jerk.

He wrapped his leg around it because his arms are tied behind his back. I feel tears prick my eyes at the sight of him. His lip is split, his nose has been bleeding, and you can see the pain in his whiskey-colored eyes. "*Tesoro*," the old nickname falls from my lips easily.

He closes his eyes and leans his head back against the pole. "I didn't think you would ever call me that again." He opens them, and I can see him checking me for injuries. "They hit you," he grits out when he sees my own bleeding lip. He almost knocked me out from the pain of hitting me almost directly over top of my black eye. Zane almost had a mental breakdown when he saw it when we first dropped Nina off. The only damn reason he followed us was that Gage convinced me I needed to talk to him. Gage would cover for us until we worked through whatever this is. I pulled Zane into whatever shit I got myself into. This doesn't feel like a Viktor attack, but I don't know what else it can be. And why the hell would he take Zane? A fucking cop and not Gage? The thought of Gage brings the panic rushing back. I can't lose him no matter what happens to me; Gage deserves a place on this earth.

I can't stop the near hysteric laugh from coming out. "That's the least of our problems," I say, jerking against my chains.

Zane tests the bindings on his wrist and grimaces. "They're

tight." He jerks against them again and starts coughing all over again.

"Please stop moving," I beg.

He spits blood from his mouth. "I have to get us out of here," he says, jerking harder on his wrists. I can see the muscles in his arms bulge and flex. He coughs the whole time and never stops. I know he has a punctured lung, and if he doesn't stop, he'll drown in his own blood.

"Zane," I say quietly. "Zane!" I whisper shout. I don't want to bring any attention to the fact we're awake yet. "*Tesoro,*" I say desperately, and he freezes. "Please stop," I cry because I can't stop it now.

"They have you tied up, Beautiful," he says, lifting sad eyes to mine. "I have to get you out."

I smile the best I can. "*We* will get out." I don't know how true that is at this point or if we do get out if it's going to be in a body bag.

I look up at the chains again and decide the only way out is to see how these chains are attached. I have a little wiggle room with my wrists, so I hook my hands on the chain and pull myself up.

"What are you doing?" Zane asks in a desperate tone.

"Shut up," I grit out, pulling myself up further. Putting one hand as far as it will reach in front of the other, thanking Ryder and Dex for every grueling upper body strength training they put me through, the ones that I used to cuss them for.

Zane laughs, then coughs. "There's the Les I know and love."

I pause. "Don't say that."

"Say what? That I love you? It looks like this might be the only chance I get, Beautiful."

"Tell me when we get out," I grunt, moving again.

He snorts, then groans. "Fuck, that hurts."

I get closer to the top and look at the rings holding the chains to the beam, they're at least four inches thick and soldered together. "Shit."

"What is it?" Zane asks, and I finally look down at him. I'm about twenty feet off the ground, and he looks tiny from up here.

"I'm not going to be able to get out of these chains or break them."

"Get down from there then," Zane demands, and I shake my head.

"Yes, Daddy," I mutter.

"What did you say?" he asks darkly.

"Nothing," I say quickly, lowering myself as slowly as possible.

I get about halfway and lose my grip, sliding down the rest of the way. I grab ahold before the chain can straighten back out so it doesn't break my wrists.

I can feel the fire burn over my shoulder and down my arm. I know I tore something in my shoulder from grabbing the chains and jerking my body to a stop. I breathe through the pain to stop the scream.

"Fuck Les. Are you okay?"

I breathe in through my nose. "Yeah," I answer raggedly.

"Look at me, Beautiful." I turn my eyes to him, and I see the hopelessness in them. "I love you."

I shake my head because he's saying it like he knows we'll likely die here. "Please, Zane." To be honest, I think we will too.

"I love you," he says more forcefully. "I love you so fucking much, Les. I hate myself for doing that to you. If we get out of here, I will spend the rest of my life making it up to you."

I swallow the tears and guilt. "I love you too." Finally, admitting it brings a sense of relief, and I hate myself for not saying it sooner. We're facing the unknown, and I don't know if we'll ever get a chance to tell each other that again. "I always have."

The door swings open, smacking the wall with a bang. "Well, isn't that fucking sweet." A man drawls from behind a white skull mask. I look to my right, where he walked in, trying to place that voice. It's muffled with the mask, but I've heard it somewhere.

"Who the fuck are you?" I ask, drawing up as much bravado as I could.

"You don't remember me? What a shame. I sure as hell remember you," he comments, ambling closer. I listen closely as he talks and still can't pick up from where I've heard him. I've been around too many people, and I've pissed off most of them.

He signals behind him, and three guys spill in wearing the same masks, heading straight toward Zane. "Can't have you drowning in your own blood. I need you alive for the show."

They roughly untie Zane and jerk him to his feet. Zane moves before his feet ever find purchase, head-butting the guy in front of him, then swings a mean right hook toward the other. The third guy punches Zane in the face, making his head snap back before they all grab him. "Get him the fuck out of here. Make sure he doesn't die." The guy, who I'm assuming is the leader barks, and they hustle Zane out, still struggling between them.

"Goddamnit! Let me go," Zane growls, throwing his body forward and fighting their hold. He throws an elbow back, catching the guy in the face and making him grunt. The guy loosens his hold, and Zane swings the other way, hitting that guy with his elbow and then landing a solid boot on the last guy's chest. He makes a beeline to me and slants his mouth over mine before they can grab him again, ignoring the blood on our faces. His kiss fills me with butterflies just like it used to, and I pray to whoever listens to me anymore that we can share many more.

They grab him again, and he lets them this time. A fire is burning in his eyes now, and I know Zane hasn't given up. "I love you, Beautiful."

"I love you too, *Tesoro*."

They shove Zane out of the room, and the guy that first walked in turns back to me. "You aren't the only one with resources," he says and reaches up and slowly pulls his mask off.

I can't help the gasp of shock. Of all the people, I never thought it would be him.

"Jay?"

AFTERWORD

Sorry, that cliffhanger was fucking brutal. Have no fear, part two is out!

Want to stay up to date?

Join Ames Mills on TikTok, Instagram, and Facebook!

TikTok - author.ames.mills
Instagram - author.ames.mills
Facebook reader's group - Ames Mills' Black Demons

Sign up for my newsletter for announcements, signed paperbacks, merchandise, giveaways, and bonus content at amesmills.com

Comments, questions, or concerns? Email Ames at hello@ amesmills.com

ACKNOWLEDGMENTS

Wow. I'm not sure what to say here. Riches to Riches was my debut novel, and I never thought I would make it to this point. First, I would like to thank my mom for listening to me rave about this book when it was just a vision in my head and for giving me the courage to write it. I want to thank my two daughters for giving me up for hours at a time so that I could put this book into words.

To my readers, thank you for taking a chance on a first-time author! Riches to Riches is just the beginning, and there will be much more from Abbs Valley. I hope you are excited for more to come.

P.S. My editor has invoked all rights to Gage 'insert grinning emoji'

Also by Ames Mills

Abbs Valley series

Riches to Riches

(Reverse Harem/polyamorous Mafia Romance)

Part one

Part two

All I Have

(Reverse Harem/polyamorous Mafia Romance)

Part one

Part two

A Very Merry Mafia Christmas Novella

(Reverse Harem/polyamorous Mafia Romance)

The Heart of Psychos

(Reverse Harem/polyamorous Mafia Romance)

Part one

Part two (releasing April, 24th 2023)

ABOUT THE AUTHOR

Ames Mills is an indie author who lives in rural West Virginia with her two beautiful teenage girls. She writes reverse harem/polyamorous romance. She has a soft spot for damaged heroes and heroines that she loves to piece back together, bi-awakenings, and anything in between.

Go stalk her on social media and join her reader's group. She'd love to have you!

Made in the USA
Columbia, SC
30 September 2023

23671525R00386